Andrew Klavan has won two Edgar Awards from the Mystery Writers of America, and the Thumping Good Read Award from WH Smith. Born in New York City, he was a newspaper and radio journalist before turning to writing full time. He lived in London for seven years but has now returned to America where he lives with his wife and two children.

Praise for Andrew Klavan

HUNTING DOWN AMANDA

'Powerful and dark . . . A plot-twisting, nail-biting novel noir that defines edge-of-the-chair suspense' *Faye Kellerman*

'Absorbing and hugely enjoyable' *Publishing News*

TRUE CRIME

'Andrew Klavan's new novel is impressive. The narration is cooly detached, immensely detailed and totally convincing. Every character is brought to life' *Sunday Telegraph*

'In Andrew Klavan's deft hands, we get a brilliant, nail-biting, rollercoaster of a novel that grips tight as the restraints on an electric chair'
Val McDermid, *Manchester Evening News*

THE UNCANNY

'Klavan, cackling all the while, demonstrates again that his ability to make a genre his own is simply . . . uncanny'
Publishers Weekly

AN ANDREW KLAVAN OMNIBUS

MARS

The Uncanny

and

Hunting Down Amanda

Two novels in one volume

WARNER BOOKS

A *Warner* Book

First published in this omnibus edition in 2001
by Warner Books

An Andrew Clavan Omnibus Copyright © Andrew Klavan 2001
The Uncanny © Amalgamated Metaphor, Inc. 1998
'You Do Something To Me' by Cole Porter © 1929 (renewed) Warner Bros Inc.
All rights reserved. Used by permission.
Hunting Down Amanda © Andrew Klavan, 1999
'Shine, Perishing Republic' from *The Selected Poems of Robinson Jeffers* by Robinson Jeffers.
Copyright © 1925 and copyright renewed 1953 by Robinson Jeffers.
Reprinted by permission of Vintage Books, a division of Random House, Inc.
'*Stardust*' by Hoagy Carmichael and Mitchell Parish © 1929 (renewed)
EMI Mills Music, Inc. and Hoagy Publishing Company in the USA
All rights reserved. Used by permission Warner Bros. Publications Inc. Miami, FL 33014

The moral right of the author has been asserted.

A CIP catalogue record for this book
is available from the British Library.

ISBN 0 7515 3176 6

Printed and bound in Great Britain by
Clays Ltd, St Ives plc

Warner Books
A Division of
Little, Brown and Company (UK)
Brettenham House
Lancaster Place
London WC2E 7EN

www.littlebrown.co.uk

The Uncanny

This book is for my mother and father.

ACKNOWLEDGMENTS

This is a work of fiction, and fiction of the most fantastical kind at that. Any mention of real names or places—John Wayne, Jack Nicholson, Sotheby's etc.—is strictly for the purposes of verisimilitude. I've borrowed them as archetypes; neither they, nor anyone else alive or dead, has ever been involved in these events.

And as this is fiction, I won't waste the reader's time with a long list of living or printed sources of research information. But I must express special thanks to Dr. Jennifer Ellis and Dr. Richard Scofield for their medical expertise; to James Cohan for introducing me to the people and places of the art world; to Paul Sieveking of the wonderful *Fortean Times* for the lowdown on magazine work; and to Simon Brett for vetting my British culture and vocabulary.

Some authors also deserve special mention. Jennifer Westwood's *Albion: A Guide to Legendary Britain* is possibly the only encyclopedia I've ever read cover to cover with intense pleasure. Lynn H. Nicholas's *The Rape of Europa* provided a complete picture of the Nazi pillage of European art—which I then blithely changed to suit my purposes. And the books of Charles Walker provided a useful compendium of every possible paranormal conspiracy theory on the planet. I took the story of the Nazi witches from *The Demonic Connection* by Walker, Toyne Newton and Alan Brown. I adapted Mormo's prayer from Francis King's *Sexuality, Magic and Perversion*, quoted in Walker.

Finally, my personal thanks to my agents, Barney Karpfinger—who provided immensely helpful suggestions for the book's third draft—and Frank Wuliger and his crew at Innovative Artists; to Ann Patty for her brilliant edit and advice; and, as always, to my wife, Ellen, for aid, comfort, support, patience, criticism and dinner.

"Stay, Illusion!"

—HAMLET

I

PROLOGUE:

BLACK ANNIE

HIS EYES! His eyes were full of fear. And, though I had seen him in London only six months before, he seemed since then to have aged as many decades. A man like myself in his early thirties, he peered at me through the half-open door of Ravenswood Grange with all the tremulous hostility, the white-eyed apprehension, of some ancient anchorite disturbed at his grimmest meditations.

I had already dismissed my trap. I could hear the horse's hoofbeats fading behind me on the Grange's long drive. The autumn darkling was closing around me, the windswept clouds of a lowering sky pressed down on me from above. The house itself, the whole great stone edifice, loomed menacingly before me as with an *adsum* to my *conjuro te*. All this—and the horrid ravens peering blackly at me from the gutters and gables of the place—served to magnify the thrill of dread I felt as I stood on the threshold and stared into the ravaged features of my old schoolmate.

"My God, Quentin!" I managed to expostulate at last. "My God, man, where are the servants?" For he had come to the door himself and, save for the taper guttering in his trembling hand, the hall behind him, the house around him, were all in darkness.

At the sound of my voice, Quentin glanced about, distracted, as if he only now realized he had been forsaken. Slowly, his frightened gaze returned to me—and yet, I felt, it passed right through me. I might have been a spectre, invisible, and he seeing only the empty drive where it stretched into the twilight overhung by gloomy rows of copper beech.

"Gone," he said then, in a high, cracked whisper, an old man's whisper. "All gone. They would not stay. Not one of them would stay with me. No, not one."

The wind rose. The dead leaves swirled and chattered at my feet. From a gable peak came the hoarse cry of a raven, weirdly triumphant, horrible. I shivered. Then, bestirring myself at last from the first shock of seeing my friend in his shattered state, I stepped forward, extending my hand. Quentin merely licked his lips furtively, and faded away from me into the tenebrous front hall.

I followed him, entered. The heavy wooden door swung shut behind me with a melancholy reverberation. I forced myself to ignore it as I ignored the ominous penumbra that quickly gathered round the edges of his solitary flame. Again, and with a soothing word, I came towards him. This time, I was allowed to approach. Taking the poor man by the elbow, I led him gently inside.

I lit a fire in the sitting room, but it could do little to dispel the aura of dejection that had descended over the place. It was a house abandoned. Dust gathered by the wainscoting, cobwebs hung from the rafters. Papers and notebooks were strewn carelessly over the furniture and the floor. Whatever heat and cheer the hearthglow afforded was soon lost, swallowed by the lofty ceilings or transformed into a threatening phantasmagoria by the sombre tapestries hanging on the wall and the thick drapes around the narrow, arched windows.

When I stood from the grate, I found Quentin had sunk into an armchair. Open-mouthed and silent, he sat as if transfixed by the shadows now darting and receding across the complex patterns of the oriental rug. The light from the grate, the light from the candle he still gripped loosely in his hand, dragged at his sallow cheeks like red fingers, like a premonition of hellfire. I removed the taper from his slack grasp and used it to light a lamp on the table beside his chair. Standing over him, I contemplated his macabre transformation with bafflement and with sorrow.

Sorrowful indeed it was and more sorrowful yet for my memories of what he'd been not half a year before. Then, in my rooms in town, we had sat, like the schoolfellows we lately were, casually flung over chair and settee, debating long into the night with all the gay ferocity of old. A churchman with a lucrative Sussex living, Quentin was, as he had ever been, a fervent defender of the faith, an apologist for Newman, a supporter of Pusey, an ardent advocate of the high ritual and the deep *mysterium.* I, a physician with a small but growing practice in Harley Street, was equally determined to ride out upon the lists for science, to preach Reason and Experiment as the keys to comprehending the internal mechanisms of this clockwork life. How well I remembered the passion with which Quentin opposed me, the brightness of his eyes, the vibrancy of his voice as he proclaimed the miraculous and supernatural as our surest guides to the truth.

Now—not a fortnight since he had returned to Ravenswood to settle the affairs appending to the sudden death of his elder brother and sister-in-law—his strong, open face was lined and sunken, his lean, manly frame as much a ruin as the fragments of the old abbey that stood without the Grange's walls. For all my physic, I could think to offer him nothing better than a dash of brandy. This, my hand supporting his wrist, he raised unsteadily to his lips.

The medicine had its effect. Coughing slightly, he set the empty glass beside the lamp, blinked and looked up at me as if for the first time.

"Neville," he said. "Thank Heaven, you've come."

"Of course I've come, old fellow," I responded, as bluffly as I could. "As soon as I got your letter. But what the devil's the matter? You look as if you've been through Hell."

At this, some memory seemed to rekindle the terror in his eyes. He turned from me and stared into the now-blazing fire. "You were wrong, you know, Neville."

"Wrong? In what respect?"

"All of it. All of it," said he, his tone mournful. "There *is* a world beyond the world we know. There is a world beyond, and it's . . . it's . . ." But he did not—could not—finish. Rather, lifting his face once more, he showed to me an expression of such pitiable horror that no further utterance was necessary. "Neville," he whispered then, galvanized suddenly, leaning towards me urgently. "Neville, I have seen it. I have seen *her.*"

"Her? Who?" I said sharply. I was moved to irritation by the chill that had begun to edge up my spine. "What the devil are you talking about? Whom have you seen?"

With that, the energy seemed to drain out of him. The poor fellow subsided weakly in his chair, his chin sunk on his chest, his features limp. His voice, when it came again, was as solemn as the echo from an empty tomb.

"Black Annie!" was all he said.

I did not know whether to laugh at this or to recoil at the further evidence of his disturbed senses. In the end, averting my face to hide my reactions from him, I said merely, "I say, do you think there's anything to eat in this mausoleum?"

Fortunately, there was. For it now transpired that not all the servants had entirely deserted the place. One girl, at least—in very pity for her young master, as I suspected—remained. She had agreed to attend to my friend's needs by daylight on the stipulation that she might be well away from the house before the onset of dusk. Thus, on investigation, I found a cold repast had already been laid out in the dining room. No more than a modest portion of mutton, a half loaf of bread and a rather unfortunate claret, still it sufficed. I brought the provisions into the sitting room, where we made a rude feast of them before the hearth.

We ate in silence. To be honest, we drank a good deal more than we ate. Quentin, at my urging, did manage to pick desultorily at his chop. For my own part, however, I mostly sat brooding over my wine, reflecting on what I had so far heard.

Black Annie. The name—uttered in such awful tones by my companion—was not entirely unknown to me. There was, I remembered, a legend attached to the old Grange concerning such a figure. Quentin himself had related the tale to me on one of those evenings at school after lights-out when we attempted to disturb each other's sleep by whispering scare stories across the space between our beds.

I rose from my chair and went to stand before one of the windows on the far wall. Looking out between the dented leaden cames, I saw that night had now drawn down around the place completely. A gibbous moon, sporadically visible in the gaps between the racing clouds, cast a pall of faltering and sickly light over the sere expanse of grassland to the east. In that field, now visible, now vanishing as the moon went once again behind its shifting cover, there stood an ominous and melancholy apparition: the ruins of Ravenswood Abbey—the broken wedge of a chapel wall, the slanting monuments of its ancient churchyard.

In the days before the old religion fell prey to the depredations of our eighth

Henry, the ground where the Grange now stood had been within the abbey confines. It was with this ancient institution that the story of Black Annie was associated. It was hardly an original tale. I don't think there is a ruin such as this in all of England that does not have some deceased monk or other gallivanting about it of a midnight. In this case, so the legend ran, the cowled spectre of a nun—Black Annie—had taken up residence among the decrepit stones. In life, she had been seduced by a canon of the Augustinians—one of the black canons, so called for the colour of their robes. There followed the necessary sequel: the poor woman was soon with child. But before her sin could become evident, she mysteriously vanished. In fact, with the conspiratorial aid of her sister nuns, she had contrived to hide herself within a secret chamber in the nunnery's dorter. There, the sisters brought her food and drink—and kept watch during the frequent visits of her paramour. As her time approached, however, it became clear that the deception could not be continued indefinitely. What was more, the abbey was now under heavy pressure from the minions of the vicar-general, who were then touring the countryside on the king's behalf in search of useful evidence of corruption among the clergy. Terrified of discovery, the canon persuaded his lover to give their child into his charge. He promised her he would remove the infant to some safe and secret place, where it would be well cared for by a local nurse of his acquaintance. But, having taken the babe away, the perfidious canon, hoping to set his crime permanently beyond the investigators' ken, slit the helpless creature's throat and hid its little body somewhere on the abbey grounds. Inevitably, word of this horrible deed found its way to the distracted mother in her hiding hole. When the royal ministers arrived to make their inspection, they were led at once to the secret chamber where—no doubt to their considerable satisfaction—they found the unfortunate woman hanging dead at the end of a stout rope she had secured to the rafters.

This was the gruesome story Quentin had whispered to me one night in our boyhood dormitory. And he added, with appropriately spooky inflections, that the black-cowled spectre of that much-injured sister was said to walk the ruins of the abbey to this very day.

I'm afraid I must have made a soft noise of derision at the recollection of this melodramatic yarn, for Quentin, as if reading my thoughts, said from behind me, "You remember, don't you?"

I gestured from the window. "I remember some nonsense you told me back in school, but . . ."

"True, Neville, all true!" he exclaimed. In a fresh bout of agitation, he leapt from his chair, paced to the centre of the room. He stood there beneath the tapestry of Susanna, whose time-faded flesh the firelight made to seem roseate and alive under the leering gaze of the elders. Quentin's pale, tormented features were also scored by flame and shadow, also given a tortuous life of their own as he lifted a shaking hand to point at the window. "I've *seen* her, I tell you. Out there. By the abbey. And what's more . . ." But his arm dropped to his side and he shook his head.

"What's more?" I prompted.

"Oh!" It was a sound of such hopelessness that all my impatient scepticism was swept away by a tide of compassion. "I knew you would not believe me, Neville. You with your Science and your Reason—your new religion so eager to replace the old. But I tell you, I have seen her and what's more . . . what's more, I have *heard* her." He turned such a sidelong, knowing look then at the chamber's oaken door that, for the first time, I began to suspect he was truly mad. "In the house," he muttered. "She has been in this house."

Shaken—by his expression, by his tone—I tried once more to strike a hearty note of unconcern. "Well, then! It hardly matters whether I believe you or not. If she will appear to you, I hope she will not scruple to appear to me as well. Then I shall have 'the sensible and true avouch of my own eyes,' and I have no doubt," I added in an undertone, "that we can begin to get to the bottom of this whole affair."

Quentin, nodding, only turned and walked heavily back to the blazing hearth. "Be careful what you say, Neville," he remarked. Then he sagged once more into his chair.

"I am not afraid," I told him.

But that was a lie. I was very much afraid, though not for the reasons he might have imagined. It was my friend's sanity I feared for. Whatever vision had appeared to him, it was clear to my physician's understanding that it was no "extravagant and erring spirit," but rather the product of his disordered faculties. What I could not yet discern was whether those faculties were still within reach of treatment or whether Quentin was—and I have seen such cases—spiralling irretrievably into lunacy. I expected—not to say dreaded—that that very night would tell me all.

So we kept vigil, he and I. The fire waned and the oil in the lamp burned away. The shadows wafted slowly down from the rafters and came to enshroud us. The figures on the tapestries blended with the darkness until only a glancing eye, an enigmatic smile, a grasping hand flared into view from time to time with the cracking of an ember.

I had opportunity, in those hours, to think more or less deeply on my friend's situation. My own beliefs notwithstanding, I am, I hope, no enemy to honest faith. Yet I could not help but wonder if it was perhaps Quentin's spiritual studies that had so unnerved him. The civilized religion which we practice in this modern day has still its links to antique creeds and half-forgotten superstitions. Was it these, I asked myself, that haunted the abbey ruins, moulded by my friend's fevered brain into the likeness of Black Annie?

As I meditated thus, the lamp went out. The embers in the grate continued to settle and hiss and a deeper blackness yet enclosed us. I studied my friend surreptitiously, growing even more concerned as the enervated condition in which he had begun our watch slowly gave way to a nervous attitude of growing tension and suspense. Somewhere beyond the room, a clock chimed. It was midnight.

Suddenly, Quentin was on his feet. "This is the hour!" he exclaimed. "She is here!"

Before I could respond, he had rushed across the room to the window, had pressed himself close to the glass. I was fairly at his heels, was peering over his shoulder an instant later.

His breath misted the pane as he cried hoarsely, "Out there!"

"I can't see a thing!" I answered. Beyond a yard away, I could make out nothing but thick, sable night.

And then the wind rose. I heard it in the chimney. I saw it a moment later in

9

the movement of an elm as its naked branches bent and shivered. For as the wind rose, the clouds raced—and the moon appeared behind their wisps and traces. Its eldritch silver glow drew the landscape out of the darkness. Out there, beyond the sinuous silhouette of the elm, stood the abbey ruin, sullen, black and grim. The faltering illumination, laced as it was with the running cloud shadows, gave to the entire scene a floating quality, weird and dreamlike. We seemed to stare through the glass as through a torn curtain at another world revealed.

And as we stared, I saw her. A cloaked and hooded figure—raven-black, so black she seemed less a being than an absence of existence—was moving with slow and awful majesty among the churchyard headstones.

I cannot describe the suffocating horror that swept over me at that uncanny sight. I was unmanned, paralysed, my marrow ice, my sinew water. For long seconds, as the thing glided steadily towards the fragment of the chapel wall, I could not move or speak—I could not breathe—but only gaped unblinking as if I had been petrified on the spot. Death itself would not have seemed as forbidding to me as that ebon wraith who appeared the herald of a realm beyond death, a realm beyond reason, a realm, most terrible of all, beyond the reach of mercy or forgetfulness.

The silent, mournful phantasm proceeded with its lifeless grace to the end of the churchyard, to all that remained of the chapel. There, beside that ruined wall; there—though I write it who can hardly credit his own eyes; there, as I stood watching, frozen and amazed, the jet absence of her seemed to sink at the same stately pace, sink lower and lower into the hard earth, until only the cowled head remained above the surface. And then that too—all, all of her—had vanished.

At almost the same instant, a mass of clouds, propelled before the wailing wind, surged towards us above the ruin. In seconds, it had swept over the moon. The torn curtain closed. Utter darkness pressed once more against the window.

Still, as second after second passed, I could not move, but gazed upon the viewless night as if the extraordinary scene were still before me. It was Quentin's stifled cry that broke the trance. When I turned, I saw that he had fallen into a paroxysm of trembling. Dry, strangled sobs were forcing their way out between his clenched teeth. I feared the onset of an apoplexy. Willing myself to action, I clutched his arm roughly.

"It's all right," I said—shouted, more loudly than I had intended. "It's all right, man, pull yourself together. It's over. She's gone."

"Gone?" The voice that broke from him did nothing to ease my qualms. It sounded choked and high, hollowed by an undertone of barely suppressed hysterical laughter. "Not gone," he said, eyeing me brightly. "You fool. She is not gone. There are tunnels, you see. Out there. Under the abbey. Drains, passages for supplies. Covered over now, yes. They're all covered over. But there's a whole network of drains and tunnels. And one of them . . . one of them leads . . ."

Before he could finish, there came a noise—a noise *from within the house!* Soft, but definite, insistent, it seemed to rise up from below us, to spread through the walls until it filled the darkened sitting room.

Tick-tick. Tick-tick. Tick-tick.

I have heard people say that their hairs stood on end, but I had never before experienced it myself. The sound was like that of a clock's pendulum and yet more resonant; softer, thinner than a knock at the door, and yet as chillingly deliberate. There was a pause as my gaze travelled slowly over the umbral forms and faces on the hanging tapestries. And then again:

Tick-tick. Tick-tick.

I returned my attention to Quentin. He smiled at me, but a smile of such wild misery that I despaired of his reclamation. He leaned forward, whispered almost gleefully:

"One of them leads to the priest's hole."

Tick-tick. Tick-tick. Tick-tick.

There were often, I knew, in abbeys and the neighbouring houses, secret chambers and hideaways built to protect imperilled priests during the Tudor persecutions. It would not have been surprising if these "priest's holes" were connected to the rest of the abbey by the underground passages which King Henry always claimed were employed in the canons' secret amours.

"A priest's hole," I said, as the soft ticking sound repeated yet again, as the febrile gleam in my poor friend's eyes grew brighter. "Where is it? Can we get inside? Come on, out with it, man."

For the second time that night, Quentin cast a queerly knowing look at the door.

Tick-tick. Tick-tick. That infernal noise again. What was it?

"In the study," Quentin said.

I did not hesitate; the slightest hesitation would have done for my resolve. I marched, with more boldness than I felt, across the room to the fireplace. I seized a candle from the mantelpiece, bent to touch the wick to an ember. When the taper ignited, I carried the flame back to where Quentin stood. His face in the wavering glow was stretched and taut with apprehension as he began to understand my intent.

"Neville," he gasped, "we can't, we mustn't . . ."

"We will," I said sternly. "Follow me."

I pulled him from the window, fairly dragged him after me to the door. It was harsh therapy, but effective. As Quentin was torn from his passive terror and offered the prospect of an enterprise, a measure of his former vigor seemed to return to him. His trembling ceased, and by the time we broke from the chamber into the corridor, he was following after me of his own volition.

With every step we took, the sound grew louder, nearer. Yet always, always, it surrounded us, vibrating behind the portraits, beneath the flooring, above the beams.

Tick-tick. Tick-tick.

At my shoulder, Quentin began to protest again, his expression urgent in the trailing candlelight, his words tumbling over one another.

"Neville. Neville, listen . . . For God's sake . . . You don't know what you're dealing with . . . You don't understand . . . Listen to me . . . Listen, before it's too late . . ."

I raced on, ignoring his admonitions, closing my mind to them lest they dissuade me from my purpose. The persistent, rhythmic tapping all around us grew yet louder, nearer. I felt as if it had entered my brain, was rapping at me from within.

Tick-tick. Tick-tick.

"Neville!" Quentin cried again.

"Is this the door?" I said, as we reached the study. Raising my candle high, I grasped the iron handle. At a nod from Quentin, I pushed it down. The door swung slowly inward.

We entered the small room, the candlelight breathing over the veiled windows, the shelves of books, a desk littered, like the sitting room, with documents heaped and strewn about. The flame's unsteady respiration seemed to plunge the place into an element like water. The objects seemed to undulate and swim in and out of view before us.

Tick-tick. Tick-tick.

I stepped forward cautiously, Quentin at my back. It was here, whatever it was—here, or just nearby. The sound seemed to vibrate up out of the very heart of the chamber. I could not help but tense, the flame flickering as my grip on the candle tightened, as the sound came again.

Tick-tick.

"Where is it?" I whispered hoarsely.

"Neville . . ."

"Where is it?"

He inclined his head towards the books on the wall to my left. "That case there," he said reluctantly.

In two strides, I was at the bookcase he indicated, a tall case of some dark wood, its shelves lined with musty leather volumes. Uncertainly, my hand went out to touch the bindings. Quentin continued to protest behind me.

"Neville, let us turn back, let us consider, there is more to say, much more you do not know . . ."

A book—a heavy black book with no lettering on its ribbed spine—shifted inward beneath my fingers. There was the sound of a latch giving way. The entire case seemed to snap free of the wall. With a whining screak, it swung towards me on a hidden hinge.

I pulled the case open as if it were a door to reveal the narrow staircase winding into the blackness below.

Tick-tick. Tick-tick.

Now, at last, as if drawn from the house's timbers, drawn from the air around us, from my own brain, the sound resolved itself upon a single centre, a single source. It ascended in its unceasing, funereal tempo from the dark at the base of the stairs.

Tick-tick.

I started down to meet it.

"No, Neville!"

As I descended, step by slow step, the damp wooden boards groaning thickly beneath my soles, Quentin's gibbered warnings spiralled into a frantic skirl.

"You do not know, you have not understood, you must believe me, I have thought on these things for weeks, I have tried to comprehend . . ."

My own shadow dodged and capered in bizarre shapes on the dripping stone walls around me. My heart was thudding in my chest and there was a thickness in my throat that nearly made me gag.

As my foot touched the bottom step, I felt a clammy draught twine round my legs. The candle flame swelled and, in the broadening glow, I saw before me a door of rotted wood hung in hammered iron bands.

Tick-tick. Tick-tick.

The sound was coming from behind the door. Nervously gnawing my lips, I willed my hand to reach out for the ring that secured it.

"Neville. For the love of God!" Quentin cried. "There were weeks before she died. Weeks when she left her hiding hole, when she wandered the abbey grounds by night. Nights when she used a spade, don't you see! In her distraction, a garden spade, trying to dig through the stone! She was searching . . ."

The door opened heavily, grinding against the floor.

Tick-tick. Tick-tick. Tick . . .

And there was silence. The tapping stopped short. The candlelight faltered, recovered, bathed the priest's hole in its bleak, liquid candescence.

But the place was empty.

Together on the threshold, Quentin and I found ourselves peering into a cramped dungeon with low beams above walls of uneven stone blocks. Nothing moved within and the quiet was so complete it seemed almost unnatural. Not even a rat scrabbled for cover as we two stood baffled, gawking.

Then Quentin blurted, "There! Look!"

I lifted the taper. The light spread over the entire chamber. My gaze, following Quentin's gesture, fell on a small white mound of flakes and powder that had collected on the floor at the base of the wall. It was immediately apparent that the debris had fallen from one of the stones above. I could see where the stone had been chiseled, its edges frayed and chalky as if—just as if someone had been digging at it with the point of a spade.

Before I had time to think, I was moving forward, one hand holding the candle high, the other stretching towards the stone. Quentin shouted my name again, but my fingers were already digging at the jagged edge where the blade had bit into the rock. I gripped it, pulled. The stone shifted easily, wobbled, rolled from its position. It slipped from my grasp and there was a loud crash as it dropped to the floor at my feet. In the same instant, the air seemed to shake. Quentin shouted wildly. I gasped. But these noises were washed away by an indescribably hideous shriek. It flew up around us from everywhere and nowhere at once: a ragged howl full of hellish rage and a grief beyond the soothings of eternity. The entire house seemed to quake and shiver to its foundations as the anguished wail went on and on and on.

For there, in the niche revealed by the displacement of the stone, preserved in that airless cell so that its skin had grown leathery and tight, its mouth had been yanked wide and its eyeless sockets had a stare of endless agony—there, its neck slashed open, lay the body of an infant, which decayed and crumbled to dust even as we gazed upon it.

II

STORM, LIFTING HIS
TRAGICAL EYES

1 A glass shattered across the room and Storm, lifting his tragical eyes, saw, though too late, a woman worth dying for.

The book of ghost stories was still open in his hands. His lips were still parted on the final phrase—*crumbled to dust even as we gazed upon it*. But the phrase, the whole story, had been blown right out of his mind. By the woman, by her beauty. Just the sight of her had brought him from his chair to his feet.

Which was pretty ridiculous when he came to think of it. What was he going to do next? Leap into the air like a cartoon character—his tongue out—his eyes hanging from their sockets on springs—the Valentine shape of his heart boinging through his shirtfront? He was a modern guy, after all, an American guy, a Hollywood guy. A real person with nose hairs and psychiatric problems and an anus. This was life, not the movies. It wasn't possible—was it?—that he had just fallen in love at first sight?

Maybe not, but he went on gawping at her. She was standing in the drawing-room archway, one of the guests who had drifted in when Storm had begun to read aloud. In the sitting room behind her, the great Scotch pine with its colored Christmas lights seemed to him to frame her, to set her in relief. A girl of, say, twenty and some. Not the sort of anorexic starlet he was used to, not one of his usual airheads inflated with silicon and ambition. Hers was a real figure in low-cut black velvet. A waist and hips of substance, womanly in the extreme. A bosom from the days when bosoms were bosoms. A swanlike neck, damask cheeks, skin of ivory, hair of jet. Brown eyes, the palest brown eyes imaginable, bright and snappy and quick. *Woof,* he thought; *Jesus.*

The others around her—all of Bolt's London sophisticates—had begun to laugh now and applaud her. She was still frozen with the hand that had held the glass extended, with her startled gaze on the fragments where they lay. Fragments and glistening slivers on the tan carpet. A spreading, colorless stain. The glass had just slipped from her fingers apparently, must've hit the edge of the butler's tray on the way down.

"Oh," she said finally, "how stupid of me."

Storm reeled inwardly, mentally clutched his chest. What an accent, too, he thought. That real English stuff. Like Julie Andrews in *Mary Poppins.* He could still remember some of his boyhood fantasies about Mary Poppins. The things she would croon to him with that accent. *Oh, Richard. Oh, young master!*

I'm sorry, he was about to say aloud, *sorry if I frightened you. It was just a stupid old ghost story.* But he was already coming to his senses. And Bolt, anyway, was out of his armchair, was going to her, and Bolt was the host.

"Oh, Frederick, let me clean it up, I'm an idiot," she said to him.

"No, no." He took her arm. "I've already dispatched my minions." The two women who had knelt to retrieve the shards glared up at him: a man plummeting into middle age like a bomb, shaped like a bomb, squat-bottomed, potbellied in his green suit and waistcoat. A serpentine, cynical face deeply scored by Bell's and Rothmans. Shaggy gray hair dropping dandruff. Cigarette dropping ash. "And anyway, I rent the place," he said. And he led her gently from the room.

Storm watched—bleakly—as the two of them turned out of sight down the front hall. He could hear their voices receding.

"I am sorry, Frederick, I shouldn't have come, I'm just knackered. I was in Ohio yesterday, and Berlin last week . . ."

"Don't be ridiculous. I live for your visits. I'll save the pieces as a relic. I'll build a shrine on the spot . . ."

Someone clapped Storm on the shoulder. Someone else said, "Well read. Spooky stuff. You put the wind up her anyway."

"Who is she?" Storm murmured, staring at the place where she had stood.

And someone answered: "Oh, that—that's Sophia Endering. Her father owns the Endering Gallery in New Bond Street. Not half bad, eh?"

Storm nodded. Remained on his feet a few moments more, his gaze now wandering aimlessly over the room. A cozy alcove, chairs clustered together, run-of-the-mill pseudo-Victorian prints hung above low shelves of frazzled paperbacks. A wide archway into the long sitting room where the Christmas tree sparkled and the gas fire burbled and recessed lights beamed on bottles of white wine. And where the group that had gathered to hear him read was now dispersing. And the party conversation was resuming.

Above the rising chatter, he heard the front door shut. He could feel it: she was gone. He sank slowly back into his chair.

Sophia Endering, he thought. He sat there with the book held slack on his thigh, his thumb holding the place for no good reason. *Sophia Endering.*

But what difference did it make? It didn't matter now. He was not in love with her. He could not be in love with her. He could not be in love with anyone.

He sat there, silent, slumped, withdrawn again into his unhappy depths.

2 But why? thought Harper Albright. Why should he be so sad?

From her perch among the embroidered cushions of the window seat to Storm's far left, she had seen everything. She had seen Storm rise to his feet with his first look at Sophia. She had seen the ache of passion animate his features, had watched as it drained away again, as his eyes became hollow again, and his expression once more grew distant with despair. It made her think of certain mud crabs who can "throw" their claws, actually detach their claws to break the grip of an enemy. It seemed to her that Storm—she supposed she had to call him by that ridiculous name if only out of respect for the American miracle of self-invention—it seemed to her that Storm had similarly "thrown" his heart, detached his heart to break the grip of life.

And she pondered on this, sitting there, her withered hands clasped over the carved wooden dragon's head that topped her walking stick. She was a grim, peculiar-looking person, this Harper. Not an old woman particularly, sixty perhaps, but dilapidated nonetheless. With lifeless gray hair bobbed on a furrowed brow. Slack, sagging cheeks under deep, gray pouches. And spectacles thick as goggles, through which she blinked intently. A pipe with a meerschaum skull for a bowl was clamped between her yellowing teeth, yellowish smoke trailing out of it. She rested her round chin on the back of her hands. And she wondered:

Why *shouldn't* Richard Storm love Sophia Endering? He was older than she was, certainly—forty at least. But he was youthful and handsome. Rangy, muscular. With a full head of short, sandy hair, and features as rugged as the great western land from which he came. More rugged, probably, seeing as he came from Los Angeles. And Harper knew him to be unmarried; that is, divorced. Humorous and easygoing, and gentle in a lady's presence. She herself was aware of having developed some sentimental feelings for him since he had come to her. Possibly. Some. So why should he disengage himself? From Sophia. From everyone, really. Harper Albright turned the question over and over.

He was, she thought, for all his American amiability, a man of mystery to some extent, of hidden depths at least. A producer, a highly successful producer of Hollywood films, some good ones, some she'd seen, many that were in her line, having to do with horror and the supernatural, ghosts, werewolves, the occasional latex demon or two. And yet, a month ago, he had apparently left this lucrative career behind. He had turned up all unknown in London. He had arrived at her door without introduction and volunteered to serve as an unpaid intern on her little magazine, *Bizarre!* He was tired of making movies about the paranormal, he told her. He wanted to work with her, to get at "the real thing." And that was pretty much all he told her. But uncomplaining—and, again, unpaid—he took to bounding after her like some great red setter, joining her journalistic investigations into claims of haunting, witchcraft, vampirism, alien abductions, and the like. And the question of what he was really after—and why it was he remained, in some way, set apart—had begun to worry at her.

Her reverie was interrupted, however, as Bolt reentered through the archway.

"Well," he growled nastily at Storm. "It was well read anyway, I'll give you that."

This was what had started the incident. The ghost story. About half an hour before. Bolt had been holding forth, pronouncing upon ghost stories in general: Christmas and December gatherings and ghost stories and so on. Storm had said that he had always loved the English variety. *Loved* them, he'd said—that's what had done it—all that Yankee enthusiasm. It wasn't that Bolt disliked Storm in particular, or Americans in general. But there was some vivacious something about both of them that was an insult to his cherished pessimism. Suddenly, anyway, after that, Bolt had felt that he had to play the expert. He'd shifted up a notch from pronouncing to pontificating. And when Storm had said that he thought the Oxford collection was sensational— *Absolutely sensational!* he'd said—it had just been too much for poor Bolt.

"Well, I suppose," the journalist had said. "If you don't mind the fact that they left out 'Thurnley Abbey.' I mean, I don't expect it to be complete, but, after all, it is *The Oxford Book of English Ghost Stories,* which I think entails certain responsibilities. I mean, they left out 'Thurnley Abbey'!"

"Yeah, 'Thurnley Abbey,' that was a good one," said Storm. "I think they put that in the Victorian collection."

"Pff!" said Frederick Bolt.

And Storm, mildly, changed the subject. "Hey, have you ever read 'Black Annie,' by Robert Hughes?"

It was a soft answer, Harper Albright thought, meant to turn away wrath. But it had only made things worse. Because it rapidly became clear that Bolt *hadn't* read "Black Annie," that he'd never even heard of it. Which meant it couldn't possibly be worth considering. And he said so.

"Oh no, no, you're wrong!" cried Storm. Rising from his chair, he went to the shelves. Strolled over, too familiarly, as if it were his flat instead of Bolt's. He plucked out *The Fourteenth Fontana Book of Great Ghost Stories*. "It's in here. You oughta read it, it really is good."

He held the book out to Bolt. Bolt scowled at it. "Fourteenth! They must've been pretty thin on the ground by then." But Storm continued to proffer it. And Bolt's lips curled wickedly. "Why don't *you* read it?" he sneered. "Go on—Christmas by the fireside—a gathering—a ghost story—give us a reading, Storm."

"Oh, for pity's sake," Harper Albright had muttered. Bolt could be intolerable.

Later, though, she wondered whether he hadn't perhaps fallen into the American's trap. Storm took the book back to his chair and began to read "Black Annie" aloud—and Harper was immediately reminded that his father had been an actor; he *had* told her that. He proceeded to deliver a witty and yet genuinely spooky rendition of the piece. And by the time Quentin and Neville were making their candlelit way down the ominous, sombre and melancholy corridors of Ravenswood Grange, most of Bolt's party guests were here in the drawing room and most of them were spellbound. At the last sentence, there were one or two people who actually gasped.

And the lovely Sophia Endering had dropped her glass.

"It was well read, certainly," Bolt conceded now again. "And not without interest. Without originality, or irony or invention—or literate prose. But no one could say it was without interest."

Storm only spread his hands and spoke with such sincerity that Harper Albright thought it would kill Bolt on the spot. "Ah, well, you know. I first read it when I was maybe ten years old. And it just hit me, like: Pow! The English Ghost Story. It got me started in a way. The first film I ever made, twenty years ago, I was, I don't know, twenty-two. *Spectre*, it was called. I'd never even been to England. I wrote it, directed it, shot the whole thing in California. But I set it here, you know, in this total 'Black Annie' world I made up from the story. It just—I don't know—it always stuck with me in this . . ."

His voice trailed off. He shook his head. Well, he was American, Harper reminded herself, and had evolved beyond the need for complete sentences. But what he said— what he was trying to say—did set her thinking again. Chomping on her skull pipe, leaning on her dragon-headed cane, blinking through her goggly spectacles. He certainly *did* love the English Ghost Story, did young Storm, she thought.

And perhaps, she thought, that would ultimately explain everything.

3   Outside, meanwhile, in the bleak city of midwinter, Sophia Endering hurried up the slope of the narrow mews, her heels rapping the cobblestones. The

bosom that Storm had so admired was thrumming with agitation. That story, Sophia thought. That idiotic American and that idiotic story.

She held her handbag pinned to her overcoat with one elbow. Her other arm was swinging freely, march-style. Her face was set resolutely forward. She felt the wind brush her cheeks; flecks of a faint, cool rain.

Tick-tick. Tick-tick.

It was an absurd coincidence, of course. That story, that repeated noise, that race down the corridor of the haunted house. *Tick-tick.* The way it echoed her memories almost perfectly. Her earliest memories. Her worst memories . . .

At the top of the mews, at the brink of the junction, she pulled up, had to breathe in the night chill to calm herself. Above her, a burly sea of clouds, backlit by the full moon, billowed swiftly overhead. It rolled over the impending tree wall, into the cryptic reaches of Holland Park.

Tick-tick. Tick-tick.

Irritated—more upset than she admitted—Sophia scanned the road for a cab. It was unusually quiet here. No cars at all. No people, no sound of footsteps, no sound but her own breathing. It must be late, she thought, after midnight. She checked her watch: in fact, it was after one. She could feel the deserted mews behind her. To her right, there was the unbroken hush, unnerving. She glanced to her left, down the street, down the hill, to the corner. A dreadlocked Jamaican kissed a poxy blonde in the glare of a streetlamp. Some cars rushed by. A group of boys swaggered past, jostling each other. Their laughter reached her and then they were gone and it faded away. She would go down there, to the avenue, she thought. Hail a taxi. She would be sure to find one. She was a woman cabs stopped for.

Tick-tick.

Sophia went rigid. It had almost sounded real that time. Had it been real? A ticking noise on the cobbles behind her? She braced herself. Looked over her shoulder. Brought her body half around and faced the mews.

The passage sloped away from her between old brick walls hung with dead ivy. No. It was empty. Most of the small houses were dark. Even the lighted windows here and there were heavily curtained. Sophia swallowed. This was becoming absurd. The story, her agitation. Dropping that stupid glass in front of everyone. The American with his dramatics . . .

She gave the mews one last look, then turned again. And cried out: "Oh!"

A man was standing directly before her. Close, standing too close, standing over her, his face pressing down on her out of the dark.

Her first instinct was to try to charge past him. Don't talk. Don't engage him. She lowered her head, stepped forward. The man put out his hand. Which made her heart catch. Which made her seriously consider screaming for help.

"Wait," he said. "Miss Endering. Sophia. Don't be afraid."

That stopped her. The fact that he knew her name. His tone of voice. The perfect English, a German accent faint, refined. She pulled up. Examined him. An earnest young man, bundled in a pea jacket, the collar turned up around his cheeks. Very handsome, very young. Incredibly earnest. With wavy blond hair and a warm gaze she could see even in the dark. But a stranger, she was sure of it.

He smiled. "No, no, you don't know me. I am the Resurrection."

The first jolt of surprise was gone. Sophia was in

command of herself again. Still nervous—with him so close, and the shadows so close around them, with him a head taller than she, towering over her, and so close that she felt the heat of him in the cool air. Two minutes ago she had been in the warmth and the light and the crowd of Bolt's party. Surrounded by chattering, laughing people, the taste of wine on her lips. She missed all that pretty badly just now, alone with this man in the cold. The Resurrection.

But she knew she could trust her voice to sound collected, firm. "You're standing too near. It's threatening," she said. "Step back if you want to speak to me."

He did at once, but he didn't seem glad of it. Seemed uncomfortable in the brighter light of the street. He looked in both directions quickly. When a taxi raced down past them towards the avenue, Sophia saw him tuck his chin into his collar to keep his face out of the beams of the headlamps.

"All right," she said then. "Go on. What is it?"

The taxi was gone. The street behind him was quiet again. The moon was hidden in the clouds. The young man lifted his earnest gaze to her. Licked his lips nervously. A lock of his yellow hair stirred on his brow, a brow boyishly smooth. There was something just then so naked in his expression that Sophia felt herself soften, touched.

"I'm going to be murdered tonight," the young man said to her all at once. He gave the breath of a laugh, as if embarrassed by the melodrama. "It is the man who buys *The Magi* who will kill me."

Sophia's mouth opened, but she only nodded, nodded cautiously. She pressed her hands awkwardly into her overcoat pockets, pressed her arms to her sides against the cold. Looked away from the young man, looked at nothing, trying to think.

"Miss Endering, you must—" the young man began.

"Let's walk down to the avenue," Sophia said. "We'll find a coffee shop where we can have a civilized conversation."

The German made a gesture of apology. "I'm sorry. I mustn't be seen. *You* mustn't be seen with me. It would be very dangerous. I am sorry—but I want to be out of the light." He had edged over her again, out of the gray glow of the street. "I do not threaten you, so help me. I only want for you to understand quickly what I say so I can go."

Sophia sighed, looked up at him, her heart beating rapidly, her expression composed. "All right," she said. "Go on. What is it?"

"My name is Jon Bremer. You will remember that?"

"Jon Bremer. Yes?"

"And he will buy *The Magi.*"

"You really are serious, aren't you?"

The young man put his hand on her arm. She could feel the urgency of his touch even through the woolen sleeve of her coat. "He is the Devil from Hell," he blurted, lips trembling, like a child's. "All the Resurrection Men are dead. The man who verified the panel: tortured—mutilated—murdered. The couple who found the shop in the east, the same. Tortured, killed. Even the shop owner—his body was pulled out of the Elbe three days after the panel was recovered. His eyes . . . horrible . . . That's five people now—five people have had *The Magi* in their hands, Miss Endering. Four are dead. I am the last."

Sophia murmured, "Good God." She knew that it was true—and yet it made the conversation seem unreal to her, nightmarish. The two of them huddled together like this at the edge of the mews. The words smuggled between them, hurried, secretive, menaced. It was all too ridiculous. The Devil from Hell . . .

"Well, then, you must go to the police," she said decisively.

"No!" The young man's head went back, his eyes went wide, frightened. "His people are there as well. They are everywhere. You are the only one we can trust." His grip on her tightened. She felt his thumb digging into her upper arm. It was painful, but it made her aware of his fear. It made her pity him. She pitied all of them. "It has to be you, Sophia," he said. "It's *The Magi*. You know all the players. You can be there, ask questions, without anyone suspecting. When you see who buys it, when you know—then—carefully—you can approach . . . the authorities . . . your friends in the press . . . someone . . ."

After a moment, she nodded again and he released her. His voice grew softer, the words came faster. "I have arranged for the piece to be auctioned on behalf of a charitable organization—an anonymous donation with good title, all arranged. It will be in Sotheby's mid-January. I've arranged for it to remain in transit until then, so I think it will be safe. That is what I will tell them when . . ." She saw his Adam's apple work between the collars of the jacket. "When they find me," he finished. He went on more slowly. "He will buy it, he will pay anything for it. Do you see? At the auction, he will finally show himself. Do you see?"

The wind whirled. The clouds barreled by. An arc of the full moon shone above their ruffled fringes. The fingery branches of winter trees waved sable against the sky.

"No," Sophia said, staring blankly up at them, frowning. "No, I don't see. Why should he pay anything? Why should he kill for it? The thing isn't worth more than twenty-five thousand pounds, fifty thousand possibly, if you find the other two panels. How can you be so sure this is what he'll do? Your people—"

"Are all dead," said the young man. The naked, urgent earnestness had come into his expression again. "They are all dead. And I am sure. I have come to know him, in a way. He is afraid of nothing; he will let no one else do it for him. He will be there."

Now, at last, he stepped back from her. Sophia felt as if she had been released from a smothering embrace. The young man glanced up and down the street again. Peered at her from what already seemed a great distance. "I don't know why he kills for it, or why he will pay," he said. "But he has killed, and he will pay. He will pay anything, more than anyone. So the one who buys the painting, he is the man. The Devil from Hell. That is what you must remember. Whoever buys the painting . . ."

He seemed to be slipping from her, slipping away into the current of the night. She wanted to stop him, to stop the whole thing. "Look," she said. "You really must go to the police. I can't—"

"Remember," he said—it came out hoarsely, but the word carried to her even as he moved across the street. "Whoever buys the painting has murdered me, has murdered all of us. Whoever buys *The Magi* . . ."

Sophia stood and watched him: stepping up onto the opposite pavement; moving into the shadows of the park wall; grasped by the shadows of branches and drawn into them.

"Whoever buys *The Magi* . . ."

But she could not have heard him whisper it again. He was already gone.

✦

That night—it was a rotten night, if ever there was one. Some of the worst dreams she'd ever had, and she was given to bad dreams. Everything became all jumbled together in her sleeping mind. The cowled figure of Black Annie became the three cowled kings of the Rhinehart *Magi*. The haunted corridor of Ravenswood Grange became an endless labyrinth through Belham. She was wandering, feeling her way. *Tick-tick. Tick-tick. Remember, Sophia. Whoever buys* The Magi . . . She kept waking up, afraid—really terrified—and then sinking back helplessly. *Tick-tick, tick-tick.* The dreams like quicksand, seizing her. The dread seizing her. Corridor after corridor, searching in the dark, and every picture on the walls was the *Magi* panel. *Remember, Sophia . . .*

Finally, with a noise as much of anger as of fear, she wrenched herself out of it. Lay dumbly sullen in her bed, rubbing her arms to keep warm. A blank moment. No memories, a vague hazardous ambience. The familiar shapes of her bedroom congealing: tall frames of exhibition posters, oversized art books on a low case, the curve of her rolltop desk, the friendly bulk of the computer beside it, the towers of books on the floor . . .

The alarm went off. The radio. "This is BBC Radio Four. It's seven o'clock . . ." And the time tones: bing, bing, bing . . .

The Resurrection, Sophia remembered suddenly. Her heart dropped like a hanged man. *I am going to be murdered tonight . . .*

And then the newsreader started speaking: "The body of German antiques dealer Jon Bremer was found floating in the Thames this morning. Police say his murder may have been the work of Satanists. A rising and respected figure in the European antiques world, Bremer was the victim, before he died, of what a police spokesman called 'diabolical torture.' The spokesman said Bremer's eyes were punctured . . ."

Sophia sat up in bed.

". . . and strange symbols carved into his chest."

"Oh," she whispered.

The newsreader moved on to other stories. And Sophia covered her mouth with her hand. She stared into the rising light. Stared at where her desk had been, her books, her computer. At where now she saw only the image of Jon Bremer's youthful, warm and handsome face—his living face. Staring back at her with the gory, running sockets that had been his earnest eyes.

"Who is this Sophia Endering?" said Richard Storm suddenly.

"Shh!" said Harper Albright.

Storm forced a stage whisper: "I was just wondering. Do you know her at all?"

Harper didn't answer, didn't even look at him. So he was still thinking about her, she reflected—and it was almost two weeks since Bolt's party; it was practically the end of December now.

The two of them were standing alone together in a Devon churchyard. At midnight, of course, because that was when the beast was said to prowl. A stabbing, slushy snow had already covered the bracken to the base of the headstones. Worse, it had made a shapeless white mass of the venison sirloin they had placed on top of the churchyard wall: their bait.

Harper herself, this odd little woman, had collected a fair half-inch of ice on both the brim of her Borsalino and the shoulders of her cloak. Leaning staunchly on her stick, she could feel the cloak's gray wool growing heavy as the melt soaked through. She could feel her old flesh growing clammy as the chill began to reach it. And there was no lull in the bitterly thick wind either. It rode to her continuous over hedge and hill. It reached her with a straining, dying note that made her recollect the pixies of the Dart. They were said to have lured a farmboy to his death in the river by crying his name: *Jan Coo! Jan Coo!* She could almost hear them now in the crying of the wind.

Comes the hour, she thought irritably, but not the *thing*.

And yet, cold as she was, cranky as she was, she was still able to stand through the long surveillance stock-still, so still she might have been one of the graveyard's more eccentric monuments—had it not been for her eyes, ferociously quick behind her spectacles' thick lenses.

Storm, on the other hand, was bouncing around like a bottle on the ocean waves. Like a neon-orange bottle: he was dressed in some fantastic downy concoction, some bloated anorak from Ski-Meisters Of Hollywood or someplace, with triangles of bright green and purple scattered chaotically across the front of it. What he really looked like, Harper thought, was a deflated weather balloon. But he had the cameras ready, one hanging in each armpit, both wrapped in blue plastic bags, and their black straps crisscrossing his chest like gun belts. With any luck, the next issue of *Bizarre!* would feature the monster on its cover.

Storm whapped his shoulders with his hands, puffed his scarlet cheeks under his woolly watch cap, kept hopping up and down, up and down to stay warm in the driving snow.

"For pity's sake," Harper muttered. Even her lips were motionless when she spoke.

"Wh-wh-what?" said Storm.

Harper gave another grumpy huff or two. But then she relented. "All right. All right. I know her. I know about her, at any rate," she said softly.

"Sophia? This Endering girl, I mean?"

"I know quite a lot about her, in fact. Does she interest you, young Richard?"

"Me? Nah. She just popped into my mind." He managed to chop the words out between his chattering teeth. "While we were standing here. I was thinking. That's all. Really."

Harper let the lie pass. Her eyes made a slow half-circuit of the scene before her. The toppled steles, the ice-fringed tombs, the castellated tower of the church itself, lopped and moldering at the fringes of the visible. Beyond the graveyard's low stone wall, the snow obliterated her view of the surrounding moor.

"Her grandfather was in trade, as I understand," she said in her gravelly rasp.

"Her grandfather?"

"You wanted to know about her."

"Right, right. Her grandfather. So he was in trade, huh?"

"An antiques dealer. In Surrey, I believe. In a way, it's quite a romantic story. When his son, Michael Endering, fell in love with an archdeacon's daughter, her parents thought him not quite the thing. They forbade the match, and the girl—Ann—was sent off to school in Switzerland. Five years later, however, Michael applied for her hand again. And by then he had become a millionaire many times over."

"What, in five years?" said Storm, chattering, bouncing.

"Yes, and the money did the trick, apparently. He got the girl, her ancestral manse—Belham Grange—a knighthood eventually, plus the blessing and acceptance of an all-forgiving aristocracy. So far as I know, the rumors concerning the Nazis were never even mentioned."

That stopped Storm bopping about, at any rate. He stood flat-footed, panting. Dragged a neon-orange cuff across his dripping nose. "The Nazis? You mean, like, the Nazi Nazis? The evil German guys from World War II?"

"The very ones." She turned her head, faced him—and she'd stood so rigid till then under her gray mantle that it really did give the impression of a statue coming to life. "They had plundered much of the art of Europe, you'll remember, slaughtering many of its rightful owners along the way. Sometime after the war, the stolen masterpieces flooded the black market. England's strict laws concerning ownership made the trade dangerous and difficult here . . ."

"So you're saying Sophia's father was a fence for Nazi loot."

"I'm saying there were rumors to that effect—largely discounted then, and long forgotten now. He married Ann, set up his art gallery in New Bond Street, moved into Belham Grange, and had three children, Sophia being the youngest. His life after that was without any tinge of public scandal. That is, until nineteen years ago, when Ann hanged herself."

Storm's mouth opened. White balls of mist spilled from his lips, whipped away on the howling wind. "She hanged herself?"

"Fortunately, all the children were in London with their grandparents when it happened. Sophia was five at the time."

"Jeez. Nazis and suicide," Storm said.

"Precisely," said Harper.

A long moment passed. The old woman examined her

companion closely. "Young Richard," she said. "If you are planning to approach Miss Endering—"

"No, no, I'm not," he answered at once.

"But if you are, you should know—"

"I'm telling you, it's nothing like that, Harper. I'm not approaching her. I'm not going anywhere near her. Not anywhere. Believe me." He met her gaze almost fiercely, his expression uncharacteristically hard and taut. "I didn't come here for that," he told her.

Behind the dripping lenses of her spectacles, Harper's quick eyes narrowed. She held him then with such a slow, gimlet scrutiny that Storm at last averted his face from her. He frowned miserably into the blizzard.

But when Harper spoke again, her tone had softened. She had long since satisfied herself that there was nothing malevolent in the man. Indeed—she was forced to admit it now—she was developing a definite fondness for him. "All right," she said, more gently. "Why *did* you come here, then?"

Fighting down a violent shiver, he made a clipped gesture before hugging himself tightly again: he was trying to indicate the vista of crumbling stones, the blizzard-whipped church, even the invisible moor around them. The usual—puzzling—melancholy of his eyes was plain to see. And his tone too, Harper thought, had become wistful. "I told you—it's England. I've been making movies about this place my whole life. Places like this. I mean, look at it, the whole country, it's a movie set, I swear."

"Mm. Yes." She followed his gesture with a thin smile. "Some of us rather prefer to think of it as a fortress built by Nature for herself against infection and the hand of war— but yes, a movie set, all right. And so?"

Storm still gazed visionary at the place, with those sad eyes of his. Gazed at a spot where a small elm bent and swayed in what seemed like mourning over the cornice of a decaying crypt. "So, to me, this is where the ghosts live." He murmured it, almost to himself. The snow streaking his face with wet, his watch cap sodden, his anorak sodden, flattened, the puff gone out of it.

Even Harper now, statue that she was, had begun to feel the shivers rising from her depths. And still she stood, her wrinkled hand frozen to the dragon head of her stick, the stick planted in the gathering snow, the snow eating through her boots, through her cape, through her Borsalino. And still she stood motionless, watching the graveyard wall through her streaked lenses, watching the snowy mound that was the venison bait.

"I came here," Storm said, "because I wanted to see—"

"*Shh!*"

He stopped. Harper had gone electric, tensed. The two of them listened, their faces tilted into the blizzard's teeth. There seemed to be something . . . They listened, vying with the storm.

Yes. Suddenly, there it was. Borne to them on the wind, almost a part of the wind's wail. Soft but piercing, a preternatural squall. More than one voice, it seemed. A chorus of voices. A chorus of tormented voices, of subterranean laments breaking free into the swirling air. Now, as they cocked their ears, it strengthened, became one high, screeching yowl, a single, tortured stridor. Rising, blooming, peaking. Then bursting, splintering again into that pitiful choir. It went on and on.

Now am I come where many a plaining voice smites on mine ear, thought Harper Albright, every muscle tight. *There shrieks are heard, there lamentations, moans, and blasphemies . . .*

And even Storm whispered, "Jeepers. It sounds like the damned."

"Yes," she replied aloud. "A very encouraging vocalization."

And then it stopped. It faded into the wind until they couldn't tell it from the wind. Until the wind cried alone, all around them, forlorn. Harper narrowed her eyes behind her streaming glasses, peered intently past crypt and statue, peered and peered at that lump of snow, that hunk of venison, on the wall.

"Do you think . . . ?" Storm began to say.

And the creature took both of them completely by surprise.

There was no warning. A silent enormity of movement—a fluid leap, as of the night itself—and it was on the wall. Not where the venison was, not where they'd expected it. It was crouching, poised, to their left, not five yards away, just above their heads. Its carnivore eyes glittered down at them.

Storm threw himself in front of Harper, his arms spread to defend her. It was a lovely gesture. It warmed the cockles of her heart. But this was no time for warm cockles. She'd lifted her stick. Her right hand gripped the dragon head. Her left was wrapped round its shaft. She drew the two apart to reveal a flashing length of stainless blade.

"Never mind me," she growled. "Take pictures!"

She rejoiced to see him go at it. All courage, steely as her sword. Moving at her command on the instant. Snapping the plastic bag from one camera, snapping open its case even as he pulled the strap loose over his shoulder.

Harper felt a moment's anxiety. The cameras—all things mechanical—were as mysterious to her as the White Horse of Uffington. But Storm raised the device expertly, his hand shielding the lens.

There was a flash. It caught the creature. And the creature snarled, glared lightning strokes of white death across the corner of the snowy graveyard, into the camera's single eye.

Harper let fly with her double bark of a laugh: "Ha-ha! Oh, that's our cover art, I think. Well done, well done. 'So one tracks love, whose breath is deadlier . . .'" She had a weakness for quotation.

The beast shifted its panting bulk their way.

"Hoo, boy," Storm breathed. But to Harper's delight, he never wavered, never stopped clicking the shutter, setting off the flash. "What the hell is it?"

"*Felis concolor*, my boy," she cheered, unrestrained. "*Oregonensis*, judging by its size and Bergmann's Rule. The puma, the panther, the cougar—the catamount, I think you call it in your part of the world—which is its natural element, by the way, from Vancouver to Patagonia."

"Swell," said Storm. The thing growled down at him as the flash went off again. "So what's it doing here?"

"I really couldn't say. Probably trying to decide whether to devour the venison—or us."

At which—as the camera flashed once more—the monstrous brown cat reared and snarled, fangs bared to the weather, one claw raised as if to swipe both humans from the face of the earth. It could do it too, they could see that. Even coiled as it was for a muscular spring, it was clearly a long and ponderous thing, and knew its business. It could cut them from the planet like cookies from dough. It would leave nothing but Harper- and Storm-shaped holes in the material of existence.

"Foof," said Storm. "Any wisdom in running away here?"

"I shouldn't think so. Of course, it does prefer a leap of ambush to the running chase."

"Well, there you go . . ."

"But it can leap twelve meters."

"Foof."

"The question is," Harper said, "can it scent the bait in all this weather?"

It could; it did. But it took its own sweet time about it. It stretched the moments to the breaking point. Feinting at the two of them with its claw again. Rearing, looking gigantically down. Only then, finally, leisurely, insolently, did it lengthen itself and arch, did it stride, with one baleful backward glance over one shimmering shoulder, along the top of the wall toward the venison. Storm followed its surefooted progress with his camera, Harper with her bright eyes and throaty chuckle. There was another second of enormous, flowing movement, another huge shift in the snow-lanced dark. As swiftly as that, the white mound on the far wall was ravaged, the venison was plundered—and the creature had leapt away into nothingness.

The camera dropped from Storm's trembling fingers, fell to the limit of the strap around his neck and dangled down around his belly. Harper, her limbs loosening at last, pushed her dragon head and shaft together, sliding the tapered blade back into its oaken sheath. The call of the wind, the patter of the falling slush returned to them—it was as if the volume of the surrounding world had been shut off for the length of the confrontation.

Storm and Harper turned to each other, dazed.

"So," said Harper after a long moment. "You were saying?"

"Huh?"

"You were saying you came to England because you wanted to see . . . To see what?"

Storm stared at her. Then he laughed, a wild, high laugh. "To see if the dead can walk, babe," he told her. "I want to see if the dead can walk."

5   The editorial office of *Bizarre!* was on the second floor of Harper's mansion in World's End. The mansion was, for the most part, a pleasant Edwardian town house of white stone, with elegant, high-ceilinged rooms. But in the office, the character of the place was lost, buried under the magazine's paraphernalia. The yellow-striped walls were almost totally obscured by old covers hung all around. And these were adorned with photographs of outlandish beings never before seen. Alien babies corkscrewed from insectile wombs, human reptiles breasted the banks of Brazilian rivers, translucent wraiths floated in ancestral halls, Momo, Morag, Mokele-Mbembe—even Mothman, in one fuzzy shot—were seen gaping, seething, prancing, escaping into the crannies and caches and swamps of their various habitats.

These grimacing visages presided over a broad square of a room cluttered with memorabilia equally odd. A fishbowl holding a pickled claw. A planter from which some stuffed thing stared. A vase in which a cactus unknown to botany now and then opened, drooling, at the approach of a fly. More prosaic furniture took up the spaces in between. A striped chaise longue by the wall of high sash windows. A computer workstation against a windowless wall. An antique draftsman's table, a few tatty armchairs. Plus, finally, an immense fireplace, its marble mantel supported by a pair of grotesque telamons with hairy faces contorted into expressions of hellish torment. Which Harper found charming.

The magazine had gained in popularity of late—there was always a living to be made in the paranormal, as Harper had sometime remarked, if one could just hold on till the millennium. As a result, anyway, the journal had recently gained a publisher, full color on covers and some pages inside, a more regular monthly schedule, and a circulation soon predicted to rise to over a hundred thousand worldwide. In spite of this, the staff remained what it long had been: two people, Harper and her young factotum, Bernard. There were also several handfuls of eager stringers stationed everywhere around the world. And the occasional unpaid intern—currently Richard Storm.

Storm was brooding by the fireplace this rainy afternoon early in the new year. Harper was lolling on the chaise longue, chomping on her pipe, observing him.

Bernard, as always, was at his computer, his willowy torso curving up out of the strange, backless rocker he used, his shaven head glimmering in the dull light. He tapped away at the keyboard. He studied the screen. He had forced the computer on the business when he'd first started work here five years earlier. It had since become, in spite of Harper's Luddite resistance, the Brain of the operation. To her, it remained inscrutable, vaguely threatening. Yet Bernard seemed able to command the device as easily as a sorceror making dead objects dance. A few runes stroked onto the keys and it would edit like a magic pencil, cut like a razor, paste like a wax mangler—and then fly off like Puck to put a girdle round the earth in search of potential copy from the international press.

Bernard raised his lovely, aesthetic face from the perplexing mechanism now. "A dowager in Lincolnshire is seeking to sell her alien rectal probe," he remarked languidly.

"Is she, by God?" said Harper, round the stem of her pipe.

" 'I need the money for my poor cats,' says Mrs. Huddlestone of Theddlethorpe-St.-Helen," Bernard went on. " 'Though I hate to part with it, as it's a souvenir of a very memorable experience.' "

"Ha-ha. I daresay," said Harper. "Yes, I think so. 'Notes from All Over.' I think we really must."

Resting a shoulder against one misshapen telamon, staring down morosely into the bluish gas fire, Storm snorted and shook his head.

And Harper watched him. She smoothed her gray schoolgirl skirt down over her swollen knees. Removed a matchstick from the pocket of her white schoolgirl blouse. She struck fire on her blackened thumbnail with what she hoped was regal negligence and held the flame to the crown of the meerschaum skull, drawing smoke. And she watched him.

How could she help but be reminded of the whirligig beetle? With its divided eye, half in the air, half in the water. It sees above and below the surface at the same time—and so she felt she was seeing now. But what was she seeing? Storm's rugged western face, set and withdrawn. His lean figure in jeans and work shirt, relaxed and mopey. And under the surface of those images—what? Some great, roiling tempest of emotion? she wondered. Grief? Loss? Terror? She wasn't sure.

"Did you really come here to hunt for ghosts?" she asked him from the midst of a pearly cloud. "Do you really expect to find one?"

He lifted a broad shoulder, still staring into the flames. "I don't know," he said. "A ghost. A voice from beyond. Something uncanny, you know. Anything. One lousy uncanny thing. You wouldn't think it was so much to ask for."

"Exclusive recent photographs of JFK and Lee Harvey Oswald show them laughing over the hoax that allowed them to consummate their love in secret," drawled Bernard.

"I think not. No," said Harper, waving the smoke away.

Storm pushed off the telamon. It watched him, bellowing in anguish, as he stuffed his hands in his jeans pockets, strolled over the delicate rose pattern of the rug. He paused before the fishbowl, absently considered the pickled claw. "I mean, nowadays, you try to believe in something— in anything—people think you're some kind of idiot. You know? Everything's got to have an explanation, nothing's allowed to be spiritual or mysterious anymore. The scientists— they want to take everything away from you. That DNA guy, Crick. Carl Sagan. Richard Dawkins. All these scientists. They tell you you're just some kind of machine, your body's some kind of machine, even your mind . . . And love is just some kind of pheromone or something. And God turns out to be some kind of mathematical formula. Even if you have a near-death experience—nope, sorry, that's just some mental defense mechanism or a hallucination or . . . I don't know . . ."

Harper shifted her elbow thoughtfully on the chaise's cylindrical pillow. The gray light pouring down on her through the fringes of the silken curtains seemed to age her even more, to burn the last luster from her lifeless cap of hair, deepen the black semicircles under her spectacles, etch the slack flesh of her sagging cheeks with lines. Yet she pointed her pipestem at Storm vigorously. "There is nothing so powerful as an idea whose time has come, Richard—

regardless of whether that idea is true or not. The notion that a scientific explanation somehow negates the mysterious core of a phenomenon—this is a prejudice of the age—no educated person can be free of it. To borrow a page from Lecky, if we believed in ghosts, a hundredth part of the evidence we possess would be enough to convince us. But since we do not believe, a hundred times the evidence would not suffice."

"A gang of Argentinian cannibals were arrested after they sent out for a pizza delivery boy," Bernard remarked. "Authorities discovered a large mushroom and anchovy pizza and a pair of running shoes at the scene."

"Oh, all right, phone the Argies to confirm it," said Harper. "Or E-mail them, or whatever it is you do."

"Lecky," Storm muttered sullenly. "Lecky-shmecky. You're the same way." He flashed a hand at her, at all the monsterly covers on the wall. "I mean, no offense or anything, but I've been here two months now. And everything we do, it turns out to be a phony. We go hunting for the Beast of Dartmoor, it's just an old mountain lion from some shut-down nature park. We get a video of an alien autopsy, you prove it's a guy slicing up a Ken doll with tinfoil on its head. Christ, three independent experts confirmed psychic activity in that basement in Chipping Norton, you go down there with a shovel and dig up a couple of humping badgers. You're as bad as anyone."

"Me? Never. *Alieni nil a me humanum puto*. Ha-ha." But somehow the pun seemed to be lost on him.

"I mean, look at all these covers here," he said. "All these pictures, all these articles you publish. Is it all nonsense? Haven't you ever seen anything really mysterious? Don't you believe in anything?"

"I have seen a great deal, and I believe nothing," said Harper Albright gravely. "Nothing at all, you understand. It's almost a lost art, but I'm a mistress of it."

"Well, then, what do you do it for?"

"History, Richard. History," she announced grandly. "My life has led me to it." The meerschaum skull glowed red as she drew in two puffed cheeks' worth of smoke. Then the smoke flooded out in a coiling rush as she said, "Your trouble, young Richard, is that you confuse these fictional ghost stories you so admire with the genuine article. The English ghost story of fiction had its heyday between 1850 and 1930, a period very much like this one, in that the prodigious leaps made by scientists such as Darwin and Freud promoted materialism and naturalism and shook the foundations of religious belief. The Sea of Faith was receding with its melancholy, long, withdrawing roar, and so spirits rose up in the popular magazines specifically to ask the question, 'Man of the worldly mind, do you believe in me or not?' Ah, but history, Richard, history—that is the province of your true phantom. You've heard of history even in Hollywood, surely. People writing with quill pens, wearing bodices and so on . . ."

"Two Gloucestershire boys were hospitalized for shock last week after they mistook a local constable for a ghost," said Bernard.

"Ha-ha," said Harper. "Cute."

Storm threw up his hands and turned back to the fire.

"The boys had entered the grounds of Belham Abbey on a dare to look for the Grey Lady, who is said to haunt the abbey's ruins, carrying a murdered child in her arms. The boys were terrified when the specter of PC Tim Bayliss rose up to chase them off instead. The none-too-ghostly plod had been summoned by Sir Michael Endering, the owner of the neighboring house, who requested—"

"No, no, no," said Harper quickly. "Forget that one, leave it—"

But it was too late. Storm had swiveled back from the mantelpiece, one hand outstretched. "Wait a minute!" he said.

"Storm, Storm . . ." said Harper.

"Let me see that. Michael Endering. That's him. That's Sophia's father, that girl's father."

He strode across the carpet, barely flinching from his course as the cactus snapped at him. In a moment, he was peering over Bernard's shoulder, reading the screen. He was muttering, "Sir Michael Endering. Sure. And that ghost. In an abbey. With a murdered child . . ."

"It's a White Lady, Richard," Harper cried, overly expansive, waving her pipe about in the air. "A Gray Lady, a Black Lady, whatever you want to call it. We have them all over the country. In my *Island Notions* I link her with the Teutonic goddess Berchta, who was charged with receiving the souls of dead children." Storm did not look up. She continued, louder, "The Christians, you see, demoted her to a witch, used her as a sort of bedtime story bogeyman. It was a natural progression from there to ghost. It's all in my book. Perhaps you should hire someone to read it . . ."

He ignored her completely. "It's Black Annie," he said. "I'll be damned. *That's* why she dropped her glass. That's why she looked so pale that night. I read that story, and right out at her father's house, there's a ghost just like Black Annie . . ."

"Now as for Black Annie, she was no doubt her author's reformulation of the legend of Black Annis," Harper ploughed on desperately, "who was a child-devouring witch of the Dane Hills, more closely tied to the Celtic Anu than to Berchta but perhaps also a folk memory of the anchoress Agnes Scott. History, you see, Richard, hist—"

"I'll bet she's seen it," said Storm, addressing her as if she hadn't spoken at all. "I'll bet anything. You saw the way she acted, Harper. The story really shook her up. She dropped her glass. She went all pale . . ."

It was hopeless. Storm studied the screen again, his expression intent, his face almost level with Bernard's. From Harper's perspective, their profiles overlapped: a cinema cowboy and a Renaissance angel, both in the monitor's white glow. She could only gaze upon them with anxiety—sadly— even grimly. They were all that was left to her in these latter days—all she would ever allow herself—of the cherished company of men.

"Belham Abbey," said Storm. "Belham Grange—that's what you said her house was called, right?"

Heaving a weary sigh, Harper Albright worked her feet to the floor, worked her way up off the chaise longue.

"Richard," she pronounced gently, coming to stand beside him. Her tone made him look at her, look into her thick glasses for a moment. But he couldn't hold her sharp gaze. He turned away. "There is no need to approach her in this fashion, to question her about this." Storm didn't answer. "You could simply ask her for a date."

"It's not about that," he muttered, without any conviction at all. "It's just good journalism, Harper. There might be a connection here. It's a legitimate story . . ." His voice trailed into silence.

Harper sighed again. Placed the pipe in her mouth. "As you like," she said then. She took a brief pace, away from him, back. "But in that case," she said, "in any case, there is something you should know."

Storm bridled, seemed about to object. Harper pushed on regardless.

"Sophia Endering is the product and the proof of her father's ascension to the upper classes," she said. "I know—you may not think that counts for much nowadays, but it counts with him. It counts a good deal. Sophia's education, her social standing, even her appearance—these are the old man's *bona fides*. She has been raised, in a sense, to maintain and protect his position. And she is very, very good at it. The woman is cool, smart, close-mouthed. She has a glance, I'm told, that can turn an intruder to sand. There are no men in her life, despite her beauty. There is no one to whom she entrusts her secrets."

Storm lifted his chin at her. "Yeah. Okay," he said. "So what?"

"So, given her history, it is safe to assume that, if she has a heart at all, it is held in check with considerable force. And if ever she is deprived of her monumental defenses, my guess is you will find her to be as fragile as bliss—and every bit as precious."

✦

"Historeeee, Richard, historrreeee," Bernard mimicked her when Storm had gone. "A historreee cloaked in mistorrreeee."

"Oh, be quiet," Harper grumbled.

She was standing at the window now. Leaning on her dragon stick. Touching her pipe to her lip meditatively. Frowning deeply at the misted panes.

Behind her, Bernard had tilted back from his keyboard,

had folded his arms over his thick woolen jumper. He was regarding her with infuriating drollness, she knew, tongue in his seraphic cheek, one eyebrow cocked.

"You didn't tell him all of it, did you?" he said.

Harper humphed. "I told him what he needed to know."

"Oh, for God's sake, darling," Bernard said.

She humphed again. Stared at the window pane resolutely. Darts of rain on a sheet of condensation. A blurry swatch of the outdoors through one broad runnel. The narrow street below, the brick houses homily lit across the way. The corner entrance to The Sign of the Crane smokily enticing.

Bernard wouldn't stop. "Have you ever seen that first picture of his? *Spectre*? Have you ever watched it?" he asked.

"A long time ago," Harper murmured.

"Well, then, come on. He *just happens* to come five thousand miles to work with you. He *just happens* to read that story on the night she *just happens* to be there. It *just happens* to be her . . ."

"Coincidences do happen, lad."

"Yes, I know," he said, stretching one long leg out before him, rocking one trainer back and forth on its heel. "But they happen more frequently, more profoundly, whenever we get close, whenever the trail gets warm again. Recurring numbers, accidental meetings, unlikely chains of events. They're the spoor of our quarry." Bernard leaned forward, towards her. "There's no way out of it, darling. He's the one we've been waiting for. He has set the thing into motion. And you know it."

"Even if that were true, it wouldn't matter. I don't want him to be hurt. It's not his hunt. It's mine."

"It's ours," said Bernard shirtily. "And you would think,

after more than a quarter of a century, you would be a little bit more eager to see it on again. We can't protect poor Richard from his own destiny."

"Don't talk nonsense," Harper said. "Destiny!" She brought the pipe away from her mouth. Stretched out a hand to the window, stretched out a finger to the glass. Droplets rolled from her fingertip as she slowly sketched a figure in the mist.

"You didn't tell him," her assistant went on behind her, "that before Sophia's mother hanged herself, she opened a vein—"

"Mere rumor. A confused constable's testimony."

"She opened a vein—"

"Never confirmed. The family will not speak of it. We've had a hundred leads far better than that, a thousand—"

"She opened a vein," Bernard insisted, "and made, in blood, upon the wall . . ."

Harper lowered her hand to her side. On the window now, already dissolving in fresh mist and running water, was a symbol something like a horseshoe surrounding something like a figure eight.

"Exactly," said Bernard, lazily triumphant. "She made the mark of Iago."

6 Sometimes the world seemed to come with subtitles, like a foreign film. So help her, sometimes people's hidden motives, their lies, their rationalizations, were so pitifully apparent that Sophia felt she could just sit and read them. Every word they spoke, every gesture they made, revealed them as clearly as words spelled out beneath the scene.

She was at Belham Grange for the weekend. She was having coffee in the morning room with her older brother and sister. It was a small, rich, soft, well-lit room. Windows floor to ceiling which let in the fleeting hour of winter sun. A warm sheen on satinwood dish cupboard and side tables. Paintings of Arcadian dancers amidst Roman ruins on the cream walls.

The seats were in a sort of broad, erratic circle on the rug. She, Sophia, was perched on the lyre-backed Adam chair. In white blouse, tan slacks; her legs crossed at the knee. She was facing the other two. Laura on the cushioned settee to her left. Peter draped over the French armchair to her right. Her father's chair—his enormous Chippendale throne—was empty between them in the falling wedge of sunshine.

Little Simon, Laura's five-year-old, Sophia's nephew, was crawling around under the table. Running his Christmas Batmobile over the rug, battling his Batman figure against the tea table's fierce-looking claw-and-ball leg.

Sophia stirred sugar into her second coffee and observed them. Feeling weary, jaded. Too much work, she thought, too little sleep. *Tick–tick, tick–tick.* Too many worries. Too many bad dreams. The auction was a fortnight away now. *Whoever buys the painting, Sophia . . .* The voice of that poor Resurrection Man was hardly ever out of her hearing. *He is the Devil from Hell.* And then his body in the Thames. *Tick-tick.* His earnest face staring with those gore-drenched sockets—an awful image for her to wake from, alone in bed.

Never exactly the cheeriest soul even at the best of times, Sophia was afraid she was entering one of her really black patches. Which probably accounted for this cynical sense that she was reading life between the lines.

"Darling, do come away from the tea table," said Laura,

for about the third time. A sweet-faced woman with still-silky, still-blond hair. But frantic eyes, and her mouth pinched. "It's Grandpa's antique. You'll scratch the finish. You'll upset the pot. Come away before you break something. Why don't you play over by the window?"

The subtitle: *It kills me that you're enjoying the Batman car Aunt Sophia gave you, when Mummy bought you a perfectly good pirate ship and enough connector sticks to build the Taj Ma Bloody Hal.*

"Oh, for Christ's sake, would you leave the poor boy alone, Laura." This came from Peter. From behind his *Guardian*. Which he was reading with his leg—in jeans—swinging over the arm of his chair so that the antique walnut creaked. The subtitle being: *I'm not afraid of Father.* Which, of course, he was. Sophia, tasting her coffee, thought: And he must've driven five miles before breakfast to buy that paper too. As if having a few opinions and voting Labour made him Danton.

Laura, who could not stand disapproval of any kind, immediately left off Simon—who was ignoring her anyway—and went on the direct attack. "You're looking absolutely beautiful this morning, Sophia. Although how anyone can look beautiful at eight-thirty in the morning, I really don't know. I always tell Spencer that if he wanted me to be spectacular round the clock, he shouldn't have asked for a son and heir."

I have a husband and have produced an offspring—our father's grandson—and you're a frigid, sterile bitch.

Peter lowered his paper, showing a face too old for his haircut. Puffy cheeks and tired eyes under ridiculous curls. "What's keeping the Great Man anyway? It's a small country—how long can it take to suppress every trace of artistic originality?"

And not only are you frigid, but your life's work is absolute crap.

Sophia tucked her silver spoon between cup and saucer. She smiled thinly, her pale eyes lidded, her smooth features serene. Because that was her role in the scenario: to look lofty, to be unassailable, to be the elegant, living proof of her father's ascension to the gentry. Her own subtitle, she supposed, might read: *No matter how many grandchildren you produce, Laura—no matter how bold and independent you pretend to be, Peter—I run the gallery; I'm the one.*

Because for all of them, it was always about Daddy. Novelists make such a mystery of these things, Sophia thought, psychiatrists make a living out of them. But it was amazing to her, as she sat there, how obvious it was, how stupidly plain and inescapable. That chair of his—a Gothic cathedra, practically, carved beechwood with crocketed pinnacles flanking a traceried arch: it stood in the dying sunshine at the center of their circle, and he stood at the center of their lives, and that was that. Why not just come out and say it, she thought, print it plain beneath the picture? Here they are, they revolve around him. They cover the same old traces yearly. Laura cowers and offers the fruit of her womb and knows she's pathetic but can't change. Peter proclaims his leftist politics more and more bitterly, a moral sop to his self-esteem as one after another of his professional ventures fail. And Sophia guards her place at the right hand of power by the simple expedient of being ceaselessly perfect, and frequently depressed. And that's this week's episode of *The Enderings.* Come back next week, and it'll be exactly the same.

"Watch out, Clawface!" said little Simon, under the tea table. "Here comes Batman!"

And then, all at once, he was among them. Sir Michael himself. Charging into the wedge of light, striding from the doorway to his chair. Six-foot-two, ruddy-faced, big-featured, barrel-chested, broad-shouldered in his green country gentleman's tweed jacket and waistcoat. Silver hair in a knife-sharp widow's peak, pointing like an arrow. Chin like a prow. Sophia smiled to see him. The size and power of him made her smile. Sixty-four years old, with the vigor of a bull, with the headway of a ship at sea.

"Morning, all."

Peter had managed to keep his leg draped over the chair all this time. Sophia wondered that it hadn't fallen asleep. Or fallen off. He snapped his paper in half loudly, making sure the *Guardian* logo remained visible. "The day's work all finished?" he asked. "Servants all bullied? Monies gouged? Tendencies to modernism eradicated?"

"And the peasants trod under my horse's hooves, Peter," said Sir Michael, settling into his chair. "It's been a very satisfactory morning."

✦

"Is it me, or has Peter become rather a sad figure?" Sir Michael asked a short while later. He was walking with Sophia in the garden. The two of them treading slowly in step down the flagstone path between scarlet dogwood and robinia. Column fragments, and statues weathered to near-shapeless hulks, stood at intervals in the wild grass, lining the way: the garden had been the abbey cloisters some five hundred years before. "All that moral superiority and outrage," he went on in an undertone. "I suppose it's what one clings to in lieu of success, but still . . ."

"He only does it to provoke you," said Sophia. She took

his arm. Being wifely, on purpose. Because it soothed him. Because it relaxed them both.

"All that talk about the *people*," he said, in his favorite harrumphing lord-of-the-manor style. "Sounds like an American. We the *people*. I mean, it's incredibly sentimental, isn't it? He should be better than that."

Sophia lifted her face to the bracing northern wind. Watched the huge cumulus clouds crossing like a ghostly fleet in the broad blue sky. The red dogwood swayed around her, the robinia swayed. She felt her father's thick bicep under her fingers, under the tweed, and she leaned against him. Life always seemed more tolerable to her out in the garden.

"The *people* have had this century pretty much all their own way, as far as I can see," Sir Michael was going on. "And what have we got for it? More mass slaughter than all the crowned heads of history combined could ever have dreamed of. Gas chambers and cultural revolutions, that's the work of the people. Then, when a Churchill or a Roosevelt sorts things out for them, they start wailing, 'Oh, it was our leaders who did it, our leaders misled us.' Well, who were their leaders? Cobblers and peasants and house painters. What did they expect? The people. Anything they can't murder, they degrade. Television, fast-food restaurants . . ."

Modern art, thought Sophia dreamily.

"Modern art," Sir Michael said. "'The people are turbulent and changing; they seldom judge or determine right.' You know who said that?"

She stroked his sleeve affectionately, thinking, *Alexander Hamilton*.

"Alexander Hamilton," Sir Michael declared. "And he was in the we-the-people business long before Mao Tse-Peter in there."

By the garden's far wall, she drew him up a moment before one piece she found particularly pleasing. It was a small stone Madonna, set under the rose bushes. At least that's what she thought it was. Time and rain had eroded nearly all its features. Only the sweet sweep of the mantle remained around the head, and the graceful gothic S-curve of the figure. Daughter and father stood looking down at it, hand in arm.

"He really must've got under your skin this morning," said Sophia, "if we're going to blame him for both the Chinese and the Americans in one sentence."

The Great Man gravely pressed his great chin against his great chest to suppress a smile. "You probably think I'm an old fart," he said. "Well, I am an old fart. I'm in the very prime of my old fartdom. I've earned it. I won't let it be taken away from me."

Sophia laughed once, laid her head against him. What she thought was: There was more blood and spirit in him than in half a dozen Peters. She thought he was *worth* revolving around.

"You know, I remember standing in London on a bomb site once," he said, and Sophia was glad because she always liked this story. "I couldn't have been more than twenty or so. And there was a real, old-fashioned pea-soup fog on, covering everything. Everywhere, all you could see were just jagged shapes jutting out of the fumes. Hollowed window frames staring like eyes. Skewed doorways opening up onto nothing. Rubble. A moonscape. This acid smell. And this unnatural silence all around, as if the world had simply disappeared."

They turned and began walking slowly back up the path towards the house.

"And I had a vision standing there," Sir Michael said. "And I realized that the world I knew was over, that the best of civilization was done. Europe was sick of itself and done. Its will to greatness was spent. And I thought to myself: There will be no more Raphaels, not ever. No paintings worthy of him, ever again. There'll be no more great operas written or symphonies composed. No odes like Keats's odes, no plays like Shakespeare's. Never. People will forget how to love them, I thought. They're already forgetting. They're learning to love smaller things, baser things, and they're becoming smaller, baser things themselves. One day they'll squat in circles on the ground and hold the relics of the old treasures in their hands and they'll grunt to one another and say, 'What was this? Who thought that this was good?' Like apes gawking at a broken lyre."

The Grange was visible up ahead, beyond the garden wall. Not a stately mansion by any means, but a venerable old manor, set against the Cotswold hills. Long, two-storied. Some of the original fifteenth-century limestone still in place. Those grand, tall windows on the ground floor, two beautiful gabled oriels flanking the pitched roof above. It had been her mother's house, built on what had once been Belham abbey's granary. A double row of copper beeches led away from the broadly arched front door. Through the branches, Sophia could see the ruins of the abbey's chapel. The right triangle of the shattered wall. The churchyard headstones bowing towards the grass.

"I became very depressed and started to walk," Sir Michael continued. "Away from the site, into the City. All through the fog, lost. No idea where I was heading. And then—just like some fairy tale—I heard voices, singing. A choir, singing 'Jerusalem,' the sound coming to me through the fog. I followed it and, sure enough, I came on a church. St. James it was called, I'll always remember. Anyway, I went in and, except for the choir, the place was empty. They were rehearsing—for some big occasion, as I recall, something at St. Paul's. But the place was completely deserted otherwise, and yet there was this choir, still singing to the rafters. A sort of hopeful symbol, I thought. You know—the congregation has departed but the song goes on. By that time, they were singing something else. Something with a lot of hallelujahs. 'Seek thee first the kingdom of God . . .' And one girl stepped forward to do a solo. This lovely creature. With this raven hair, this reverent face. Completely absorbed in the music. Beautiful voice, beautiful. Mezzo-soprano. Timbre like a pearl. 'And all these things shall be given unto you . . .'" He stopped in the path. He patted the back of his daughter's hand. "That was the first time I ever saw your mother."

Sophia tried to smile, but today, somehow, the story turned her heart to lead. She averted her face, looked away, looked off towards the garden shed, just visible through dripping clematis. She was vaguely aware that the caretaker was sitting there. Harry. Straddling the roof. Plucking tacks from between his lips. Tapping them into the side of the rain gutter. *Tick-tick, tick-tick.*

This *was* going to be one of her black patches, she thought. One of the worst of them ever. She didn't know if she was going to be able to endure it.

"By the way, while I'm thinking of it," Sir Michael said. "You know *The Magi* is coming up at Sotheby's in a fortnight. I think we should buy it."

"What?" She turned back to him at once, but she did have time to realize that this was completely normal. Just what he would say, what he should. *The Magi* was German Romantic, right in their period, exactly their kind of thing. They'd be expected to bid on it.

"Yes," she said carefully. "Absolutely. If the price is right. Thirty? Forty, maybe?"

"No." Sir Michael tilted back that impressive head, hoisted that powerful countenance to the heavens. "I don't care if it's twice that. Three times. I don't care. I want it. Buy *The Magi*," he said. "Buy it—no matter what."

✦

Her mother's portrait hung on the wall across from her bed. Her old bed, upstairs at the Grange, her childhood four-poster. As she lay beneath her duvet that night, she could see the painting below the fringe of the canopy.

It had been done shortly after her parents' marriage. Ann must have been almost exactly Sophia's age. In an evening dress of ivory satin. Looking gloriously over one shoulder, her throat bare above the drape neckline. A ludicrous pose nowadays. And the picture was flattering to the point of sycophancy, every individual quirk glossed away. But the likeness to her younger daughter was plain: the same black hair, the same high cheeks, the same brown eyes and pearl complexion. Only in her mother, Sophia thought, it was all warmer somehow, kinder, sweeter. The gaze more gentle, the smile more forgiving and amused. The whole posture seemed to be one of offering . . .

Looking at her, Sophia found the ache of loneliness almost insupportable.

Now, all of a sudden, she was drawing the duvet back. Slipping out of bed. No idea what she was doing or why she was crying. She stepped from the room into the dark of the second-floor corridor. There was a grandfather clock at the far end. *Tick-tick, tick-tick.* The noise was maddening. It clouded her brain. As she went towards the stairway, the worn runner gritty under her bare feet, the landing's perspective seemed to skew. The walls seemed to angle inward overhead. The portraits on them seemed to glare down at her from a great height, as if she were a child. She was afraid. Her heart was beating fast. Her nightgown, so white it seemed to glow, seemed to heave and flow around her; she seemed to be swimming in it as she headed down the stairs.

Tick-tick, tick-tick. Yes, this was exactly how it had happened. She remembered everything now. That's why she felt so small, so frightened. Like a child. She had been a child. Four or five years old. She had gone down the stairs. Like this. *Tick-tick.* Calling for her mother. Following that sound. The house was silent except for that, silent and sleeping as it was now. And she had reached the front hall and turned. Left? Yes. She turned left and kept on walking, swiping her wet cheeks with the heel of her palm, tugging at her running nose.

Another long corridor, a corridor of doors. Paintings and side tables in between; clocks, candlesticks, empty chairs. An arras at the end with a many-headed dragon rampant, its tail up among the stars. *Tick-tick.* She had come calling for her mother. To the last doorway. Her father's study. On her left.

She pushed inside. Closed the door behind her. Turned on the lights. Two dim, yellowish bulbs in shaded wall lamps: they only served to make the place more shadowy, forbidding, gloomy. Shelves of hulking volumes were to her left and right. Before her was her father's desk, stern and mammoth. Its carved mahogany ram's heads brooded at her from the tops of their pilasters. Behind it, the tall leather chair, framed by green velvet drapery, was tilted back slightly from long use. It seemed to regard her suspiciously, as from under lowered lids.

She knew it was stupid, but she really did feel afraid. She wished the curtains had been drawn. She knew the ruined chapel was out there in the darkness. The old graveyard. She stared at her own reflection on the pane, and was half fearful something would drift out of the night, press itself through her own image to the other side of the glass. Black Annie . . .

Tick-tick, tick-tick. It was coming from her right, from behind one of the shelves. That's what had happened. She had heard it. She had called for her mother. She had reached for the secret door. She felt the books beneath her fingers now. The ribbed bindings. Leather, fleshly. There was a click, and the shelves were coming to life beneath her hand. Pivoting from the wall. Swinging outward. *Tick-tick.*

Suddenly, the shelves flew open on a hidden room and there stood her father, covered in blood.

Sophia cried out, "Are you a murderer, Daddy?"

"Yes," he panted hoarsely. "I'm rather afraid I am."

It was only another of her dreams, of course. But it was terrifying, and when she awoke, there was still the sickening memory of her father in the garden. *Buy* The Magi. *Buy it— no matter what.*

She sat up under her mother's tender gaze, trying to blot out the memory, the dream, the whole thing. Lifting her knees beneath the duvet, resting her elbows on them, screwing her palms against her brow.

Whoever buys The Magi, *he is the one who killed me.* The bloody holes that had been Jon Bremer's eyes gaped at her. *Four are dead already. He is the Devil from Hell. He will pay anything, more than anyone. Whoever buys* The Magi, *Sophia . . .*

Sophia's jaw hurt. She was grinding her teeth together.

Buy The Magi *no matter what.*

She only wished she had been more surprised.

7 On the eve of his approach to Sophia, Richard Storm prepared himself with a meditation on John Wayne.

He had a framed, autographed picture of the cowboy star still enveloped in bubble wrap in a suitcase in the closet. He got it out, unwrapped it, and laid it on the flimsy folding table in his cramped service flat. He sat beside it, in a creaky chair, surrounded by the marbleized yellow wallpaper, the falsely gilded mirror, the matted flower prints that decorated the overpriced motel of a place. He was drinking from a mug of decaf, nibbling at a tasteless Shapers diet sandwich from one of those Boots drugstores: prawn and peach with dill mustard, or some other revolting British concoction. Between bites, he practiced the *prana-patistha*—a sacred form of breathing that this blond babe had taught him at Big Sur. She said it was supposed to infuse an image of your guardian ancestor with life. He also used it to cool his coffee while he sat and studied the photograph.

The picture showed the Duke full-length, striding towards the camera. Squinting from beneath his hat brim, Winchester hanging from his hand. It was a publicity still from *Hondo*, Wayne's favorite of his own films and one of Storm's. All about a rugged rambler who rides out of the horizon to rescue a woman and her boy. Storm had had the photo since he was nine years old, but it was in mint condition. He had always taken extremely good care of it.

Because Wayne *was* a guardian ancestor of sorts. He had given Storm his family name. Storm's father had been Jack Morgenstern when he'd left his old man's Brooklyn haberdashery in the late forties and set out for the West Coast. Shortly after he reached Hollywood, he and his craggy good looks had been rechristened Jack Stern. He had been billed as Jack Stern in his first few walk-ons, as a gangster, a Spanish waiter, and the popcorn vendor who shouts "This way!" in *Strangers on a Train*. But then came his big break. And he traveled down to hell-and-gone Mexico somewhere to play the role of Cade in *Hondo*.

It was James Arness, the co-star of the film, who introduced the newcomer to the Duke. Out there on location amidst dust and scrub, surrounded by mouse-eared cameras and canvas chairs. Wayne—who was in the middle of a wild, hot-blooded divorce at the time—was standing in his fringed Indian scout outfit with a bunch of sweating men in suits. When Arness called him over, Wayne approached Storm's father with that patented swagger, thunderous and balletic at the same time. He sent a truly Duke-like gaze off towards the far horizon, then threw himself side-armed into a big handshake, which the newcomer eagerly joined.

"Duke," said Arness, "this here is Jack Stern."

Wayne's gunfighter squint went up and down the younger man. He spoke—and the voice, the twang, the drop-dead Midwestern syncopation all turned out to be genuine.

"Storm," he drawled slowly, "is the name you want."

And so he had been Jack Storm in *Hondo*, in *Rio Bravo*, and forever after.

And there were many other things—gestures, expressions, phrases—that Storm had inherited from Wayne, through his father, who had imitated them all in developing his persona both onscreen and off. And there was this too, this photograph, that the Duke had presented to Storm personally on his ninth birthday.

Dear Rick, the inscription read, *Live right, shoot straight, walk tall—and have a happy birthday. Your friend, John Wayne.*

All right, *shoot straight*—it was a little hard to know exactly what that meant in a modern context. But the other instructions were clear enough, and tonight Storm felt the burden of them. He was pretty sure he had neither lived right nor walked particularly tall in these last few years since his divorce. There had been some drugs, and some women he'd treated shabbily. And a couple of deals that had cost him more than a couple of friends. He had boasted during that time, "I not only swim with the sharks, I sleep with the piranha." Big man. He wasn't so proud of that anymore.

Because there had come a Reckoning—that awful September morn. A few nights before, he had been coked, tussling in bed with a femme director who thought he would give her work. He had rolled over, fallen, and cracked his head open on the edge of the VCR. There had followed the short, dreadful stay at Cedars-Sinai. And then he had been released, bandaged, gray and visionary, everything changed. He had driven over to Mann's National Theater in Westwood. Gotten out of his Jag and stood beneath the titanic marquee of his latest film. *Hellfire.* With a cutout of Jack Nicholson that must have been two stories tall. A rising billboard of flames. And the words *Produced by Richard Storm* running maybe six feet across, his name as big as his body. And, for the first time, Storm realized that it would all go away. Not just the poster, the credit, the success. But him, Nicholson, the audience—the theater, Westwood—the whole city, Los Angeles, plunked, rootless, in its smoky basin. The far-flung skyline, the Escher-esque coils of freeway, the villas and the slums: the earthquakes would take them, and the ocean waves. In time, America itself would fall, the millennia would make a ruin of it, like Rome. He saw these things: cockroach archaeologists trying to make sense of the rubble of Disneyland—green cows descended from aphids grazing amid the tattered remnants of the St. Louis arch—Charlton Heston pounding the sand next to the fallen Statue of Liberty—he could imagine it all.

And what then would be left of him? Big man. His mother was gone, his father was gone, his graspy bitch of a wife was gone and his house was gone with her. He had no children, no real friends, no relations whom he'd met. He did not even know a line of poetry by heart. He was utterly alone.

Storm set his coffee mug down. Blinked back tears so as not to shame himself before the Duke. Live right, shoot straight, walk tall, he thought. The time had come. Tomorrow, when he met Sophia Endering, he would remember the words with which Harper Albright had described her to him:

If she has a heart at all, it is held in check with considerable force. And if ever she is deprived of her monumental defenses, my guess is you will find her to be as fragile as bliss—and every bit as precious.

Which only underscored what Storm already knew: that love was off-limits to him. Sex, flirtation, even an excess of tenderness were all off-limits, because he would not be able to shield her from the terrible consequences. He wanted to find out if Sophia had seen the ghost of Belham Abbey? Fine. It was to be a purely metaphysical inquiry, that was it, that was all. It might be hard to restrain himself. He might be tempted. It didn't matter.

He rose from his chair, his eyes narrowed to a gunfighter squint. He felt good. He felt strong. He felt prepared for his meeting with Sophia. His meditation had been a success, and he dwelt now within the truth he had been seeking:

A man's got to do what a man's got to do.

8 Oh, but then she was so beautiful. The moment he saw her again in the scrumptious flesh, he felt all his resolutions weakening. This was the very next afternoon. He'd been hanging around outside the Endering Gallery for more than an hour. Pretending to study the shirts in a recessed storefront across the street. He didn't know what store it was; he didn't care which shirts. He was just trying and trying to figure out the best way to approach her.

The logistical problems seemed insurmountable. Should he be direct with her? Casual? Sneaky? With her glance that turned men to sand and her heart packed away under pressure, it sure sounded like she had an impressive arsenal against unwanted intrusions. He didn't want to make a mistake.

It was already four o'clock. The winter daylight was already failing. The weather was chill and gray, and Storm was cold, his hands clenched in the pockets of his trench coat, holding it closed. And still, he couldn't make his move.

Then he saw her—her reflection first, in the darkened storefront. Then he turned and saw her in the life, charging through the gallery doors into the deepening indigo of the afternoon. A thrillingly competent stride she had. Swift, unaffected, self-possessed. Marching without hesitation under the bright banners and bay windows of New Bond Street. Despite the cloudy sky, despite the moist wind, she wore only a light cardigan over a blouse unbuttoned at the throat. Her legs were sleek in nylon below the knee and covered with a pleated skirt above that Storm found girlish and adorable. He watched her, thinking, *Oh, oh, oh.* He had forgotten, until that moment, just how crazy he was about her.

He waited until she'd passed, then broke from his cover and followed. Moving quickly to keep up. Dodging between pairs of sharp-suited shoppers. Squeezing past elephantine American tourists. Struggling all the while to belt his flapping trench coat against the steady breeze. He had never tailed anyone before. It turned out to be kind of a strain on the nerves. Out of the corner of his eye, he could see his own image racing over jewelery store windows and he suddenly wondered: What the hell was he doing? What if she saw him, recognized him? What the hell would he say?

Fortunately, the whole thing didn't last that long. The green and gold flag of Sotheby's was just ahead. Sophia was already under it. And then, without breaking step, she had straight-armed the door and disappeared inside.

Storm pulled up a moment. Another new experience: he'd never been in an auction house before. The façade of the place looked pretty daunting. A commissaire dressed like a U.S. Marine patrolled before rose marble entry columns. An obstacle course of reception desks was visible through the glass doors. Past that, there was a formidable pair of sphinxes preening on baize mats, guarding the grand staircase in the front hall. All in all, it seemed very formal and forbidding. Storm wished he'd worn a suit and tie instead of his black jeans and pearl-buttoned hoedown shirt.

But he went in. Tried to look comfortable, confident. Tiptoed clumsily over the Persian rugs spread out before the stairs. Passed between the sphinxes, started up the steps. Now, where had Sophia gotten to?

He reached the landing. He moved off into the viewing galleries. Now he was in a labyrinth of off-white partitions all hung with paintings. Fine paintings, it looked like, though he only caught glimpses of them. Waxy flesh. Golden halos. Feathery wings. Eyes turned heavenward in supplication. He could feel the ecclesiastical chill of old art as he moved down one brief corridor after another, rounded one corner after another.

He scanned the people, searching for the girl. There sure was a lot of money in the place, he could tell that right away. Husky, aggressive Americans with metallic eyes. Dark continentals, with big lips and big lapels. Silver-haired Englishmen in pinstripes that seemed to run down through the core of the earth. They all milled quietly around the maze, gliding slowly before the paintings, studying them with a faintly predatory air. Salespeople danced attendance on some of them—crisp young gentlemen or cardiganed sylphs—but no Sophia.

Storm stepped out into a central aisle and came to a stop with a rosy-toned crucifixion on the wall above him. He cursed silently, looking this way and that. He seemed to have lost her.

And then, there she was. All alone in the farthest corner. Motionless before a single painting there. Perfectly placed . . .

Storm moved up behind her, his hands dangling gawkily at his sides. She'd worn her hair up, and now he saw the downy nape of her neck. And saw that the track lights meant for the paintings brought out a streak of auburn in her black twist. And now he was right up close to her and caught the scent of her and it was like—he didn't know what—like a garden. Heartbreaking. Forbidden. He wanted to turn before she saw him and get the hell out of there.

But now, as his eyes traveled over her, he noticed something else. The painting she was looking at, the lone painting on the off-white wall. His focus shifted, and he saw it clearly.

"Wow!" he whispered aloud.

Sophia whipped around, looked up at him. Let out a quick breath, surprised.

But Storm kept staring over her shoulder at the picture.

It was the very image of Black Annie.

✦

The resemblance seemed incredible to him. The painting showed night falling over blasted trees, the tortured branches drooping over broken stones, the trunks sinking into a deep brown gloom which seemed to rise from the rough earth to swallow them. And there, in that haunted setting, was the ruined chapel. A wedge of wall. A splintered reticulation of a window gaping on a barren sky. And under it, the cowled figure, profoundly somber, moving over the blighted winter ground. Black Annie.

True, there were two other figures in the background, two other cowled phantoms moving in tandem with the first. Maybe it wasn't like the story exactly. Still, thought Storm, what were the odds against the two of them meeting over just such a scene?

"It isn't incredible at all," Sophia said to him curtly, as they walked back along New Bond Street together. It was full dark now. The bays and storefronts were lighted. Glittering jewels and mellow paintings showed behind the glass, warm against the night. Above them, the shop banners, sinking into shadow, made the street seem narrower, more homely than it was. And still, the pavement was crowded with shoppers and tourists, who jostled the two of them on either side. "German Romantic and English Gothic drank pretty freely from the same well, as it were. It was all a sort of reaction to the Enlightenment, all that logic and science and classicism. The German Romantics wanted to bring back a bit of the mystery and religion of the Middle Ages. That's where the ruined abbeys and cathedrals come in: a nostalgia for the days of faith. Your ghost story—'Black Annie,' was it?—that came later, a sort of cheap, commercial version of the idea in which the spirit world is accepted as real, yah? What Rhinehart was trying to show was that the world as we see it is never a thing-in-itself but is always infused, à la Kant, with our own spiritual consciousness."

"Uh-huh," said Storm, whose own spiritual consciousness was infused with the V of creamy flesh beneath the hollow of her throat, and the scent of her on the cold air, and that brittle accent, which absolutely slew him. All the same, he couldn't help noticing that this lecture of hers was rather brisk and distant, dismissive almost. As if she were waving him away. He wanted to ask her, *What about the ghost of Belham Abbey, out by your father's house? What about the fact you dropped your glass when I read the story?* But he sensed that if he did, she would shut him out completely. So he only said, "I don't know. That painting—it sure looked like Black Annie to me."

She brushed this aside, offhanded and yet insistent. "'Fraid not. It's Rhinehart's romantic version of the Magi, that's all. It's supposed to be the Three Kings bringing their gifts to the infant Christ. We know that because it was part of a Nativity triptych. One of the other panels shows a very folkloric sort of Madonna in the woods, the other's just the babe in the manger. I'm afraid it hasn't anything to do with murdered nuns and that sort of thing."

"Still, isn't it kind of a coincidence? Me coming over, you standing there . . ."

"Not really," she answered at once, very coolly now. "We're considering making a bid at the auction next week. I don't see any sort of coincidence about it." And with that settled, she busied herself straightening the golden brooch pinned to the breast of her cardigan: a design something like a horseshoe enclosing something like a figure eight.

Storm was afraid to press the point. "That's nice," he said, for want of something better. "Nice brooch."

"Oh, thank you. It was my mother's." She went on fussing with it, not even glancing up. "I haven't worn it since I was a child."

They reached the front of her gallery. Stood between two little spruces in cast-iron planters, under the wine-red awning with *Endering Gallery* written in gold letters, and beside the window in which was displayed a landscape of rocky hills and misty distances in a heavy frame. Sophia paused here with her hand on the door, her face turned up to him, her brown eyes remote. He stood over her with his shoulders low, his own hands pressed deep into his trench coat, his own eyes flooded with longing and sadness.

"Would you like to come in?" she said finally—reluctantly, he thought. "We have plenty of works from the period."

She held the door open. Storm went into the gallery.

The place was darkly paneled, dimly lit, a long room hung with paintings all the way down the line. A balcony ran along the wall to his left, with another long gallery of paintings above.

There was a pretty blonde seated at a desk just in front. She was only a bit younger than Sophia, but she smiled up at her deferentially. When she held out a few pink message slips, Sophia took them from her with hardly a glance.

"You see? It's really just the style you're reacting to," Sophia said to Storm. "Look around. You'll find half a dozen paintings in here that remind you of your ghost story."

Then she turned away from him, leaned on the desk, and the two women conferred in low voices as Storm moved deeper into the room. He pretended to look at the paintings on the wall. The tortuous rocks piercing turbulent skies. The crucifixes shooting up among stark, towering pines. Cathedrals draped with ominous gloamings. And moons dying into misty seas. He took in only a sense of their haze and fervor, image fragments and the seething ambience. He was seething himself meanwhile. Struggling with an agony of regret. All this time wasted. All this blather about paintings and theories and whatnot. And now he was going to walk out of here and never see her again.

"That one hung in Carinhall." Sophia was standing behind him suddenly. He found her looking past him at the painting before which he'd stopped: a silhouetted castle on a silhouetted hill.

Storm gazed at her blankly. "Carinhall?"

"It belonged to Hermann Goering during the war," she said. "The Nazis loved this sort of thing. The medieval imagery, all the links to folklore, all the hearkening back to the Holy Roman Empire, it was right up their street. Some people say German Romanticism—the *malaise allemand*—was responsible for the Third Reich. They say the work is tainted with evil . . ."

Storm gave a slow shrug. He remembered what Harper had said about the Nazis and her father. He thought maybe he should say something to reassure her. "Well. Those guys are all dead anyway," he said after a while.

Sophia shifted her attention to him, smiled wryly. "The past is past, you mean."

"Hey. If the past isn't past, what is? Right?"

She seemed about to answer, but said nothing, only shook her head, her lips parted. Then, as if confused, she looked away, fussed with her brooch again. "I think nothing ever dies," she murmured. "It all gets chiseled into the skin of things."

And then, when she lifted her eyes to his again, to Storm's astonishment, everything was different. They had a "moment." That's what they called it in the movie business: a "moment." "We need a moment between the hero and the girl here," Storm would say about a script that wasn't working. "When they first meet, there's gotta be a moment." A "moment" was an exchanged glance, a gesture, a frisson, *something* where emotion or information passed between two people without words. When Sophia lifted her eyes to his, their distance, their flatness, their coolness had fallen away. Her gaze was wide and deep and desperate and there was a "moment" between them, in which Storm thought, *Oh man, she's in trouble. She's afraid.*

But a moment was all it was. It ended so quickly he wasn't even sure it had happened. She sniffed disdainfully, brusquely turned her head. Storm didn't know what to say. He gave a nervous laugh, a nervous gesture.

"Well, I gotta admit, all these paintings all together like this, it does make the place look pretty ghosty," he said. "Don't you ever get nervous when you're here by yourself?"

"Never," she answered at once, facing him again. And the vehemence of what she said next—all in those crystal tones—astonished him.

"I love it here," she told him. "This is where I want to die."

9   A strange feeling came over him now as he wandered home, a thundercloud of foreboding. Nothing felt right to him. Nothing felt good or clear. The sensation rose from the center of him and seeped out into his surroundings. Everything began to seem dead to him and strange.

He traveled back on foot, along the thoroughfares. Piccadilly. Knightsbridge. The wide streets were rushing and rumbling with black cabs and double-decker buses. The sky was roiling, grandiose, over the Wellington arch, over the statue of the Iron Duke mounted, watchful. The dome of Harrod's was lit by little white lights like Christmas, and the sidewalks underneath were bustling and wintry. And yet it all looked flat and dead to him, dead and strange.

On the Fulham Road there was an old hospital, a looming brick Victorian monster, ponderous with history. There was a brick wall beside it, overhung with robinia branches. As Storm passed it, hands in his pockets, shoulders hunched, a black mongrel barked at him. The owner, an old woman, tried to rein the dog in, but it strained against its leash and snarled, backing Storm to the wall. Slowly, the old woman managed to drag the hound away. She called apologies to Storm over her shoulder. He walked on. But the incident upset him. Hounded, that's how he felt.

What was he doing here? he asked himself. In this foreign city, with all these foreign people around him. What had he come here to find? Ghosts? Really? A smart guy like him? Was he really looking for ghosts? Well, it had seemed a reasonable idea at the time. After all those movies he'd made. It had seemed like a logical step. Sort of like what Sophia had said about the Enlightenment and the Romantics: this was his own private quest on behalf of faith and the human spirit, his answer to the relentlessly rational, the implacable scientists, the doctors with their bland, pitiless expressions. It really had struck him as a sensible thing to do.

Now it seemed ridiculous. Ludicrous, useless, stupid. Here he was, five thousand miles from home, hanging around with an eccentric old crazy woman, breaking his heart over a girl half his age, running away, wasting his precious days . . .

He reached his building, a huge block of concrete squatting on the corner like a white toad. He moved, brooding, through its wide automatic doors, past the sleepy woman at reception, past the elevators to the stairs. As he climbed slowly, he felt himself pursued, still. As if something terrible were coming up behind him, its footsteps muffled on the thick green carpet. His legs felt shaky, weak, as he climbed.

He reached the third floor. A long, long hallway. He had to push through heavy fire doors, one pair and then another and then another. His arms began to feel shaky now too. His whole body began to feel heavy and thick.

Midway down the hall, he reached his door. Fumbled with the key. Let himself into the small flat, and punched the lights on with the side of his fist. He slipped out of his trench coat, made to hang it on the edge of the closet door. It fell to the floor instead.

The light on his answering machine was blinking. He ignored it. Trembling, he moved into the kitchen. Ran himself a glass of water. Carried it back into the sitting room, to the sofa. Sank down into the cushions wearily. Only then did he reach out and weakly hit the machine's playback button.

"Hello? Hello? Is it recording now? Damn these things."

Harper. Her voice sounded far away. Hollow. Echoing.

"Richard? I've come across something I think you should see . . . see . . . see . . ."

The words seemed to him to reverberate foggily. He looked around him at the yellow walls and matted flower prints and the falsely gilded mirror. At the colorless chairs and the orange blocky thing on which he sat. All foreign to him. All dead and strange. What was he doing here anyway?

"It's a little something . . . something . . . something . . . called 'The Alchemist's Castle' . . ."

He raised the glass to his mouth and the water jerked from it, spilled over his pearl-buttoned shirt, but he still didn't realize what was happening. His hand was shaking violently, but it too seemed foreign, far away, dead, strange. And then the glass slipped from his fingers. Struck the leg of the sofa. Shattered. Fragments and glistening slivers on the carpet. A spreading colorless stain. *Sophia*, he thought. And he looked down blankly and saw another stain spread over the thigh of his jeans. A single razor of pain sliced through his forehead. And, finally, he understood. He clutched his temples with his two hands. He raged—raged—against the relentlessly rational: the implacable scientists, the doctors at

Cedars-Sinai with their bland, pitiless expressions.

"The Alchemist's Castle . . . The Alchemist's Castle . . ."

Six months, you bastards! he cried out in his heart. *You told me I still had six months!*

Then the convulsions struck and he fell to the floor, unconscious.

III

THE ALCHEMIST'S CASTLE

OR

THE VIRGIN'S FATE

1 ANNA HAD LAIN in the moldering family vault this long year past, and her bereaved husband Conrad would not be consoled. Indeed, the villagers had begun to murmur that the hereditary madness which had destroyed Conrad's father had now claimed the son and heir, the last of that illustrious line. Night after night, the young man could be seen sitting at the window of his melancholy, isolated chateau. His ghastly, grief-stricken features made him seem a spectral presence to whatever rude woodsman or peasant passed within sight of the gloomy Gothic manse. Hectic and wild of countenance, he would stare through long hours over the blasted landscape towards the tangled and forbidding recesses of the Black Forest; or betimes would raise a febrile eye towards the crumbling ruin of a nearby tower, which was all that was left of the once-magnificent Castle of Blaustein.

There had been some hope among the local population that Conrad would recover the blithe aspect of former days, especially after the arrival of his cousin Theresa. The child had been given into Conrad's charge after first one, then the other of her parents had succumbed to that plague which had scourged the countryside the year before, sparing neither the great nor the humble.

But alas, the hopes for Conrad's recovery proved as unavailing as they had been fervent. Theresa was a cheerful and lovely child, golden of hair and white of limb. Often, she could be seen playing solitary within the shadows of the chateau battlements, dancing and singing a sweet air to herself even in that tenebrous gloom, or picking whatever flowers had the audacity to grow out of the barren, rocky terrain. And yet, despite the girl's vivacious presence, Conrad, so it was said, continued to appear night after night at the window, gazing in savage despondency at the dismal forest and the tower which stood black and decaying against the turbulent sky.

2 ONE NIGHT, SOON after Theresa had reached her twelfth year, just as her girlish beauty was softening into the more tender loveliness of blossoming womanhood, she awoke suddenly to discover Conrad standing over her bed. It was a night of tempest, thunder resounding through the vaults and corridors of the glowering old mansion, lightning chasing fantastic shapes over the archaic tapestries that draped the mossy walls. It was precisely such an atmospheric clamor that brought the maiden's eyes flying open, whereupon she recoiled at the sight of Conrad's pallid visage hovering above her. A blush swiftly replacing the wonted ivory of her cheeks, Theresa clutched her counterpane to her breast in the first untutored promptings of virginal modesty.

"What is this, cousin," said she, "that you disturb my rest at so unholy an hour, and on so tumultuous a night that my heart nearly fails me for fear?"

Conrad, in a mournful voice fit only for the anguished soliloquies of the sepulcher, would answer only, "You must rise now, child, and come with me."

Accustomed to obeying her guardian in all matters, Theresa asked no further questions for the moment. When Conrad had withdrawn from her chamber, she arose, shying and trembling at the periodic ragings of the storm without. She dressed by the light of a single candle and performed what ablutions she could posthaste; and when she had done, she joined her elder cousin where he paced, brooding, beneath the sinister arches and macabre statuary that decorated the chateau's massive front hall.

To her astonishment, Conrad, himself already wrapped in a greatcoat, now extended to her her own warmest cloak.

"Surely, dearest cousin," Theresa cried, thinking her guardian meant to have some bizarre amusement at her expense, "surely you cannot intend for us to make an excursion in this uproar, for it is as if the heavens themselves were to be swallowed by some terminal maelstrom!"

He replied nothing, but with a second, more insistent gesture, urged the mantle on her so that she had no choice but to receive it from him and clothe herself withal. Then, with an inarticulate groan that sent a tremor of premonitory terror over Theresa's delicate limbs, Conrad hurled open the mansion's ponderous door, and drew her out with him into the storm.

Their heads bowed against the raging gusts, Conrad and Theresa crossed the sere wasteland in a moonless blackness illuminated only by the forked daggers of lightning which at intervals cleft the sky in twain. The furious din of thunder which followed each such incendiary eruption only served to deepen the tremulous foreboding which step by step rose in Theresa's heart, filling her innocent bosom with dread imaginings she knew not how to name.

"Whither go we, my dearest, most trusted guardian?" she ejaculated passionately from time to time. "Oh, in the name of that wife you sometime loved before a good and merciful God found fit to call her to his everlasting peace, ease my foolish virginal fears and tell me whither we go!"

But Conrad, staring into the distance with a disordered mien that did nothing to console his pavid charge, only tightened the grip he held upon her arm and hurried her through the night.

At length, Theresa raised her eyes to find they were approaching the solitary ruined tower of Castle Blaustein. A little gasp, lost in the commotion of the tempest, escaped her full lips as her eye fell on the disintegrating stones, which seemed to be made animate by the violent oscillation of the surrounding trees.

But now the frightened maiden turns her gaze aloft; now for the first time she spies a wavering glow of red light in the highest window of the tower, which was always heretofore plunged in the umbrageous obscurity of abandonment.

"Cousin, oh cousin, what is this?" she cries. "Who is it who can have come to live in this so desolate abode?"

And finally, her guardian directs his burning glance upon her upturned face, and shouts his answer at her above the ferment.

"It is the alchemist!" he shrieks with an intonation of insane joy. "It is the alchemist come at last!"

3   WHAT A PASSION of horror thrilled Theresa's maiden breast as the rotting gate of the tower closed behind her with a reverberant crash.

Her cousin's mysterious and yet strangely appalling words still echoed in her ears as an even more complete darkness than before now enshrouded them; and that sable cerement was made only the more suffocating to Theresa by the weird, flickering tongues of scarlet luminescence which, falling from some unknown chamber above, brought the shape of a stone spiral staircase faintly into view before her. Towards this, Conrad drew her now. And—hark!—as they began to mount the crumbling steps, a faint noise drifted down to them, becoming audible as the howling storm without was muted by the impenetrable thickness of the tower's walls:

Tink-tink, tink-tink.

"Sweet merciful heavens," gasped Theresa, clinging to her cousin in the blackness. "What is that, guardian?"

"It is only the alchemist at work, my child," answered Conrad.

Slowly, he continued to mount the steps, pulling his reluctant ward in his train. The lambent glow above grew brighter; the enigmatic noise grew louder as they climbed.

Tink-tink, tink-tink.

"But what is it, what is it?" Theresa cried out. "What is it, cousin, that makes that sound, for at each repetition of it my heart misgives me?"

"He only hammers the iron rings into the wall," Conrad muttered. "Be still, my child."

Cobwebs brushed against Theresa's soft cheeks, tangled in her silken hair as her cousin continued to drag her up and up and up the spiral staircase. And the flickering light grew brighter above, and the hammering louder.

Tink-tink, tink-tink.

"Oh, what now, what now, my cousin, my trusted guardian?" Theresa babbled in a paroxysm of fear.

"He makes the chains, he only makes the chains," said Conrad, his eyes fixed on the turning path above him. "Have no fear, my child."

On and on, he drew her, up and up. The glimmer of the flames—for such is what they were—now appeared to rise ubiquitous on the walls around her; the noises of the unseen workshop were magnified in Theresa's frenzied imagination until she nearly swooned with affright at each reiteration.

Tink-tink, tink-tink.

"Oh, by the mercy of sweet heaven, what is it?" she whimpered, clutching her guardian's arm with fresh force.

"The fetters now," said he in an eldritch, distant tone. "He forges the fetters, I think. Be of good cheer, my child."

At this intelligence—and at a renewed occurrence of the chilling sound—Theresa fell to her knees on the damp stone of the stairs, clasping at her cousin's hand with quivering fingers, lifting up her beauteous and tear-stained face in blind beseeching. "Oh, my cousin, my guardian, to whom my parents trusted me in their hour of death, in the name of all that you hold dear, take me no farther, do not make me go before this alchemist, for I swear by heaven the thought of him terrifies me exceedingly."

Her fear charged her tender limbs with peculiar strength and for several moments she held Conrad immobile so that he peered down at her through the darkness, confused.

"Not go? Not go?" said he. "When I have sent for him, waited for him all this time? When he has traveled to me all the way from Rome? Not go?"

He knelt before his cousin, took her soft shoulders in his strong hands so that, for an instant, she fancied he might be about to show some familial compassion to assuage her torment of suspense. But Conrad, by a brutal exertion, only lifted her once more to her feet, compelled her once more to rise towards the flames and the hammering.

Tink-tink, tink-tink.

"Not go?" Conrad whispered in Theresa's ear as he carried her all but limp form up another step and another until they neared the top. "When he is known to possess the greatest knowledge of the ancient mysteries of any man alive? Not go to him, my child? When for my sake—nay! for the sake of my beloved Anna, who this bleak, desolate, seemingly endless year past has lain mercilessly imprisoned in her tomb, that flesh which once gave to me my greatest pleasure unpreserved by the tears which I have lavished upon it night after night—when for her sake, I say, he has composed a potion which will restore her to my arms, to my desire—to my love which is so great that it transcends the fear of earthly decay and merely waits for the opportunity to enfold her as in our happy days of yore? Not go? How can you say such a thing, my dear little Theresa? The work is almost complete! The potion of resurrection is freshly prepared!"

And so saying, Conrad brought the girl to the top of the spiral staircase and came before a great door of solid iron, which stood ajar so that the dancing scarlet light of the flame and the repeated metallic percussions seeped out onto the landing where the cousins stood. With a mighty effort of one hand, Conrad oped the door wide, while with the other he dragged the all but insensible Theresa into the room beyond.

And there stands the work table, littered with every macabre, unnameable instrument and beaker of the alchemist's art. There are the chains and manacles bolted into the thick stone of the walls. There the flames soaring and dying in the tower grate and the jet-black pot which holds the unholy potion churning, frothing.

And there, before the poor girl's streaming eyes, stands the alchemist himself, his stare bright beneath his black cowl, his features crimson in the infernal radiance of the fire,—and in his hand—oh, in his hand—one final, most terrible implement of all, its thin, curving blade red and glittering.

"Oh, cousin, cousin!" Theresa shrieked. "Why have you brought me to this dreadful place?"

"Because we need just one ingredient more!" Conrad cried.

And he slammed the door behind her.

4

THE CHATEAU ON the borders of the Black Forest has stood empty of life now, lo, these many years; and the tower of Castle Blaustein has long since fallen to dust. Neither Conrad nor his young cousin Theresa was ever seen after that one tempestuous winter night; and there are some who say they removed themselves to a family villa in the south, while others tell far grimmer tales of what befell them. Whatever the truth of the matter, the villagers rarely go near the old manse, fearing, in their unsophisticated way, that even the sight of its decomposing battlements can portend no good. And yet, there are those informants who report with an air of complete authority that one chamber in the chateau's uppermost story remains occupied, if not peopled; and that anyone temerarious enough to brave the rats and spiders, cobwebs and spectres of the place may see for themselves the antique marriage bed on whose tattered and putrefying sheets lies the skeleton of Conrad—forever entwined with the crumbling bones of Anna, his cherished bride.

IV

SOPHIA,
THE NOOSE AROUND
HER NECK

1 "Something is terribly wrong," said Harper, tapping the kraken's eyeball.

"What is it?" asked Storm.

"I. Just. Don't. Know," she said, each word a sentence, each sentence punctuated by another tap of her fingernail against the glass. The jar stood on a stone pedestal between them. In the jar—in a clear preservative that filled the jar—lay the carcass of an enormous serpent, its flat, white, gelatinous body rolled into a coil the size of a firehose. Harper Albright leaned in close to the glass and peered through it at Storm. The curve of the jar magnified and distorted her features. The orange torchlight hopped on the lenses of her spectacles. "Every word Sophia said to you, every gesture she made, conveys to me a message of distress."

"No, I mean, what is it?" Storm repeated. "This. In the jar."

He circled around it until he stood beside her. Hands behind his back, he leaned in too. He examined the leviathan's horned proboscis.

Harper, in turn, cocked her head to study him. "The first sighting of such a creature was, I believe, recorded in 1555 by Olaus Magnus, the archbishop-in-exile of Uppsala, Sweden," she murmured thoughtfully. "The occasional reappearance of its kind in northern waters over the next two centuries has led some modern commentators to speculate that they were the prototype of Iormungand, the serpent of Midgard, who encircles the world, and whom Thor might have landed with an oxhead for bait were it not for the cowardice of the giant Hymir."

"Don't tell me, let me guess: it's really, like, a big roll of toilet paper or something." And with a derisive snort, he moved away towards the giant pig of Chalfont St. Giles.

Harper frowned sternly. "A ribbon worm," she said, screwing the point of her stick into the earthen floor. "Phylum *Nemetinea*. And quite rare at this size, actually. Smuggled in from Osaka, where it washed ashore on New Year's Day, 1995. Many Japanese believe that their appearances serve as predictors of earthquake . . . The spike secretes poisonous mucus," she called, in an attempt to hold his interest, but he had already rambled off under the flambeau.

They were in the Secret Museum, a network of medieval vaults beneath a street of warehouses in Southwark. Forgotten, presumed destroyed, the catacombs had been appropriated by a small group of connoisseurs for the display of their bizarreries. Beneath the low stone arches of the underground corridors, jars, aquaria, display cases and picture frames stood on top of pedestals, rested on tables, leaned against derelict sarcophagi, or hung upon the walls. They were lit only by fire—by torches guttering here and there in iron cressets, filling the place with oily smoke. This was an admittedly melodramatic touch, but some of the less scholarly visitors seemed to enjoy it.

As Storm continued away down the corridor, Jorge Swade, the museum's curator and sole cicerone, found himself caught uncomfortably between his most cherished patron and the man he presumed to be her beau. His bloodshot eyes blinked furiously, his buck teeth chattered like a dentist's toy, but he didn't know what to say to ease the tension. He settled for making ridiculous and servile bows in both their directions. Which made his lank hair brush the shoulders of his red sports jacket, leaving an oily stain.

As for Harper, she went on frowning at the retreating Storm for a few moments more. Of all the curios in the place, she really found him the most curious of all. Clearly, he was besotted with the girl—clearly enough to pinch her own antique heart with a twinge or two of jealousy. Why the pretense of indifference then? Why did he insist on it?

With a determined tug at the brim of her Borsalino, with a firmer grip on the dragon head of her stick, she waddled after him now, under the torch, down the corridor, brushing past the cringing Swade.

"A woman like Sophia Endering doesn't just cry out for help," she growled. "Not to a perfect stranger. Not to anyone, I suspect."

Storm had already abandoned the pig. He skirted the pickled rat ring. Passed the mermaid skeleton with only a quick glance. She caught up with him as he headed down a short cul-de-sac lined with framed photographs and lit by a single torch.

"What crying for help?" he muttered, pretending to give his full attention to a picture of Popobawa, the winged cyclopean homosexual dwarf of Zanzibar. "Who says she's crying for help?"

"You know she is." Harper wagged a wrinkled finger at him. "Why else would she adjust her brooch?"

"What?"

"You have a Hollywood producer's eye for detail, Storm. You miss absolutely everything of importance." She shook her head reproachfully. "When you expressed your touchingly ludicrous American belief in the evanescence of history, she adjusted her mother's brooch—which she had never worn before—and disagreed. Which was as much as to say that the issues surrounding her mother's death had arisen in some fresh way to disturb her."

"Harps. Sweetheart. Gimme a break here. I mean, she adjusted her brooch." And barely looking at her, Storm moved on.

"Er . . . the book," whispered Jorge Swade, "the manuscript." He had come scurrying along after them, anxiously grinding his palms together. His nerves simply couldn't stand this dissension. "I've set it out for you. It's all prepared." He gestured hopefully towards a nearby alcove.

"In a moment, my dear," Harper said with a dismissive wave. "Young Richard . . ." He was at the cul-de-sac's far wall now, shaking his head at the latest portrait of Nessie. "You described the conversation to me yourself . . ."

"Described it? You pumped me with questions about it for two hours."

"Sophia adjusted the brooch that belonged to her mother—her mother who committed suicide—and then she told you she wanted to die."

"She didn't tell me she wanted to die, Harper!" he said over his shoulder. "She told me she wanted to die in the gallery."

"Why should she want to die anywhere?"

"Oh, for crying . . ." He lifted his eyes to heaven. "Please!"

Harper rapped the point of her stick impatiently against the earth. It made Jorge jump about a foot behind her, but seemed to have no effect whatsoever on Storm. "What is the matter with you, young Richard? You admitted you sensed it yourself. The woman is asking for your help, crying for your help."

And here, to Harper's surprise—to her dismay—he rounded on her almost ferociously.

"Not my help, Harper," he said between his teeth. "Someone's help maybe—maybe you're right—but not mine."

Harper Albright cocked a gray brow at him. This was decidedly out of character, not at all like the easygoing man she knew. She could see he regretted the outburst immediately. The way he looked down at his shoes, the way he snuffled, annoyed with himself. The way he turned away, averted his face. And yet suddenly Harper wondered whether there might not be an awful logic to it too. An intuition struck her, and she wondered whether all his behavior might not make a terrible kind of sense. Behind her glasses, under her broad-brimmed hat, her eyes narrowed. She frowned again, more deeply.

"Anyway," said Storm in a low, embarrassed tone, "like I told you, we mostly talked about art. She's real smart, she knows a lot about art, and that's what we mostly talked about."

He was now moving back towards her, along the row of photos on the wall to Harper's right. Harper studied his profile, noble brow to heroic nose to cleft chin. She saw for the first time—admitted for the first time that she saw—the new sallowness of his cheeks, the new weariness in his eyes. The way he massaged his left arm from time to time and nursed it. But she pushed her instinct down. She wasn't ready to accept it yet. She drew a breath and launched into him again as if nothing had occurred to her.

"What about the coincidence then? You approached her

just as she was standing before that painting . . ."

"What coincidence?" He was still irritated. "I followed her. There's no coincidence."

"Yes, so she went to great lengths to convince you. There's no coincidence, she said—and that was the other time she touched the brooch. Suggesting that the reason she dropped her glass when you read 'Black Annie,' and the reason she was upset by that painting, and the reason she is contemplating suicide . . ."

"She's not contemplating suicide, Harper. For Christ's sake."

". . . are all connected with the circumstances of her mother's death."

"You're driving me crazy," he said, jutting his face at one photograph after another as he came back towards her. "The whole thing was just a mistake. She just happened to drop her glass. The picture just happened to look like the story. There's no coincidence. There's probably no such thing as coincidence. I read that once. It's just some sort of mathematical deal where stuff sort of falls together and everyone thinks it's this big synchronicity thing and the whole business just doesn't exist. Hey, who the hell is Iago?"

"Ah," Harper Albright said.

He had stopped—he had pulled up short—in front of the photograph just beside the torch. Its glazing was alive with shadows in the flutter and flare of the flames. His face caught the reflected glow as he stared.

Harper's squat form hobbled through the light and shade until she was at his elbow. Little Jorge lagged, fussing, gesturing helplessly at the lectern in the alcove beside him.

Storm and Harper looked at the picture together. "This is one of the reasons I brought you here," she said.

It was an old black-and-white photo, much enlarged, much distorted and blurred by the enlargement. The grain—plus the haze and smoke in the scene itself—gave the setting a poetic, dreamlike quality. So Harper, anyway, had always felt. The photo depicted a compound of wooden barracks in the process of burning to the ground. In the moment at which the shutter had snapped, the flames of the individual buildings were being swept together into a single surging inferno. The smoke was thick. The sky was black with it. The barracks were no more than spectral suggestions at the core of the thing. Only one human figure was visible, there in the forefront: a smallish form charging through the blaze, charging through the tall wooden gate of the compound's entryway, charging, it seemed, to safety, cradling a bundle in the shelter of its arms.

Jorge had written the legend:

THE END OF IAGO

A female follower of "Saint Iago" carries a baby through the fire that destroyed the cult leader's compound in northeast Argentina. One hundred thirty-three of Iago's followers are thought to have died in the blaze. At least forty-four of the dead were children, many of them believed to have been fathered by the cult leader himself. Aside from this disputed photograph, there is no other evidence that the event took place. The fate of the escaping woman, therefore, remains a mystery. (Cat. 44)

"This . . ." said Storm.

"Yes," said Harper.

He was pressing his finger to the glazing, pointing at the high crossbar of the gate above the escaping figure. Burnt into the crossbar's wood, just visible through the grain and haze, was a symbol: something like a horseshoe enclosing something like a figure eight.

"It's the same as her brooch," said Storm.

"Exactly," said Harper.

She heard him curse under his breath. "What're you trying to tell me? This picture has something to do with Sophia and her mother and everything?"

"I'm telling you it might."

He glowered down at her. "All right," he said. "So who the hell is Iago?"

Harper's gravelly voice, her brusque, marble-mouthed accent, seemed somehow far more suited to the form of narrative than conversation. She never began a long story without a certain hint of relish in the set of her pale lips, a certain glint of it in her eyes.

"His name—or so he pretended—was Jacob Hope," she said up at Storm. "And it is remarkably difficult to discover anything else specific about him. He was probably British, though he seems to have traveled extensively not only through Europe but in Africa, America and the Middle East as well. He appeared on the scene some thirty years ago. A drifter, traveling with other drifters, the new breed of young vagabonds—there were a lot of them at the time." She paced away from Storm, her chin lowered pensively. Her stick bobbed up and down in the air in front of her as her wrist rose and lowered. "Hope claimed to have mystical powers. The power of prophecy, healing. The secret of eternal life as well. He promised eternal life to those who would believe in him, follow him. And many young people did believe him and did follow. Men and women both, but women especially; he had enormous sexual appeal. Women—girls—who had run away from home, who were lost and alone, on drugs some of them, some of them simply confused, gave themselves to him in great numbers, even eventually bearing his children, gladly." She paused, turned, faced Storm again, the lenses of her spectacles awash in reflected flames. "His claims for himself, and his offers to his followers, became more and more inflated, more grandiose. He said he was an oracle. He said he was a son of God. Ultimately, a little over twenty-five years ago, Saint Iago—that's what he was calling himself by then—led his people out of England, on a long pilgrimage. Some of the followers believed the exodus was to climax in the world's final cataclysm. After which, I suppose, their boy was to be crowned king of heaven, his apostles at his right hand. In any case, they followed him. And the great journey took the cult through Spain and Western Africa and finally to South America. There, in the jungles of the Paraná Plateau, Saint Iago made camp, presumably to await the end." She paced back towards Storm again.

He glanced at her, then went on studying the photo. "So how'd it come to this?" he asked her.

"There was one," she said. "In the jungle, in the compound—there was one disciple of this madman who finally—finally—began to guess the truth. Even in the depths of her enslavement to Iago's charisma, there came the glimmer of understanding. She began to suspect that her master's miracles and prophecies, his promised apocalypse, were not simply deceptions—but were deceptions intended to conceal another, more terrible agenda. Children of the camp—Iago's children—had begun to disappear. Their mothers sometimes too. And one woman had gone raving mad and killed herself before anyone could stop her.

"At last, one night, when most of the camp lay sleeping, the Suspicious Disciple noticed certain of the cult's inner circle leaving the compound. She slipped from her bed and followed them into the surrounding jungle."

Now Storm kept his eyes on Harper only, as she drew breath, braced herself, went on. "Trembling with fear, the Suspicious Disciple threaded a narrow path beneath trees so thick they blocked the moonlight and plunged her into a shadowy darkness pierced by terrible animal cries and ominous scrabblings. Finally, the low murmur of voices up ahead led her to the edge of a steamy clearing. Pushing aside the leaves, she peeked through. And there, by the light of a single torch, she saw all her half-formed suspicions confirmed. And worse."

Harper squared her shoulders, blinked through the flame-light on her spectacles. "Iago was standing before a stone altar," she said. "And lying on the altar was a child. One of his own children—a mere toddler—looking up at his father with sleepy, trusting eyes. Around them, a few of the inner circle stood watching, mumbling some arcane chant. And at the clearing's far edge, a young woman was struggling wildly in the grip of two hulking apostles. It was the child's mother, and her wild stare was white above the gag that stifled her screams.

"And then, as the Suspicious Disciple looked on in helpless horror, Iago raised a curved dagger into the air above the child's naked chest. And with a dreamy grin, he—"

"Jesus," said Storm. "Jesus Christ. Don't tell me, all right? Jesus."

Harper went on more quietly. "The scales of a years-long madness fell from the Suspicious Disciple's eyes. She turned to rush back to the compound, to raise the alarm. Unfortunately, in her panic, she fell, gave herself away. She only just managed to evade capture, dashing into the surrounding jungle, working her way back to the camp, where her own infant lay sleeping, as the others hunted for her.

"It was then that Iago—realizing the game was up—set fire to the compound, burning his own followers in their beds, shooting even those of the inner circle who tried to escape."

Storm grimaced. "Like Waco. Like Jonestown."

"But years earlier than both. In fact, one strain of scholarship holds that the Reverend Jones was much inspired by his predecessor."

"Swell. A boy's gotta have someone to look up to."

"No doubt. In any case, no one escaped from Fort Iago alive."

"What about this one?" Storm gestured at the photo with his chin. "The lady with the kid. Is she the—whatchamacallit—the suspicious one?"

"Perhaps. In any case, no one knows what happened to her."

"Well, why not? I mean, all these people dying, someone's gotta know something."

"People disappear all the time, Richard. Especially drifters, runaways."

"Yeah, but I mean, like, how come I've never heard of this? How come it wasn't in the papers or anything? What about this picture—who took the picture?"

"It's said to have been taken by a *Daily Telegraph* photographer named Elton Yarwood. Who subsequently went missing without ever filing a story. In fact, no one ever filed a story. Whatever research has been done on the subject has appeared in such journals as *The Fortean Times, Journal X* in America. And, of course, *Bizarre!* But as far as the mainstream press—as far as any official source—is concerned, Iago never existed and the entire incident never took place."

"So how'd the picture get here?"

"Ah." Harper shrugged, smiled. "One does not inquire too deeply into the acquisitional methods of the Secret Museum, young Richard. Our friend Jorge here is, you will find, a very resourceful man."

Jorge—who respected Harper to the point of idolatry—preened.

Storm, meanwhile, was intent on the photograph again. He had his head up close to it, tilted like a bird's head to bring one eye nearer. "So wait a minute, wait a minute," he said. "This was twenty-five years ago?"

"Approximately, yes."

"And you said Sophia's mother killed herself when Sophia was four or five. Which can't be more than twenty years ago."

"Nineteen," Harper said.

"So how could she have known this Iago guy unless he. . . ?" His mouth still open on the word, he turned to cast an appraising glance at Harper. She had drifted away now to the edge of the torchlight. He studied her there, turned to the photo again, to her again. Then to the photo again, so close now his nose was almost pressed to the glass.

"You know, it's funny," he murmured, "this woman here, this one trying to get out—she looks kind of like you, Harper. Harper. . . ?"

To his surprise, when he looked again, she had vanished.

Only Jorge Swade was there, jogging his oily hair as he bounced up and down inside his red sports jacket.

"If you would ... Over here, if you could ... this way ..." he said, gesturing fitfully towards the recess in the stone wall.

Squinting against the firelight, shielding his face from the heat of the torch with an upraised hand, Storm moved in that direction. And there was his queer old friend. Leaning on her stick in the alcove, in its deep shadow. Waiting for him by the lectern there. With a ceremonial flourish, she motioned to the lectern's slanted surface. There lay a large, thin volume with a brown leather cover. Storm drew nearer. Harper flipped the cover open so that it fell against the lectern with a *whap*.

"This is the other reason I brought you here," she said. "*Tolle, lege,* young Richard." And when he gawped at her clueless, she translated: "Take up, dear boy, and read."

She and Jorge stepped away to murmur together. Storm approached the book, stood over it. Gripped the lectern by its edges like a preacher. Bowed his head over the open page. He traced the illegible script through the darkness, made out that it was in some foreign language. Found the translation printed more neatly beside it. And read:

Anna had lain in the moldering family vault this long year past, and her bereaved husband Conrad would not be consoled . . .

2 There was a man standing on the corner outside The Sign of the Crane, and Harper didn't like the look of him one bit. Big he was, and hunch-shouldered. With piggy eyes under a brutally cut forelock of tawny hair. Plus he had a scar on one side of his mouth that gave him a permanent sneer. He hung back, out of the glare of the streetlight. Nursed his cigarette in his cupped hand to hide the glow. It was almost nine-thirty now, so he'd been standing there like that for more than twenty minutes. Ever since Harper and Storm had entered the pub, in fact.

Harper remained at the window, eyed him. Gnawed on her pipestem. Stroked the jaw of the meerschaum skull with her tobacco-blackened thumb. She would not have thought so jaded, so scarred a heart as hers still capable of such flutterings, such mixed emotions. But there they were. Fear. Weariness: she felt much older than she was. And excitement too. She had to confess it. Adrenaline tuning her nerves, making her pulse tympanic. Was it possible, after all the blind alleyways, after a quarter-century of faint clues and faded trails—could it really be possible that the hunt was finally beginning in earnest, that she had smoked her adversary out at last?

If so, then Bernard was right—it was Storm who somehow had made it happen. His coming here. Reading that ghost story. Somehow that was what set the whole thing into motion. And this also was a burden to her, a weight of dread and sadness.

She adjusted her vision. The man outside on the streetcorner blurred. Storm, his image reflected on the window, came into focus.

He was sitting at a small, round table behind her. Chin down. His left hand wrapped round a glass of Diet Coke. His right hand massaging his left shoulder. He didn't know she was looking at him and was staring into the fizzy brown surface of his drink with all the grief in his grief-stricken eyes plain to see. Around him, the dark wood tones of the tavern faded into obscurity. Only the brass rail of the bar was gleaming. A couple of older fellows stood propped against it, pints in hand. Talking at times, but mostly staring into the gas fire, which burned high, blue and orange, in the large grate. Except for a video slot machine—sparkling with blithe idiocy in a corner, unused—the place was dim, the yellow lanterns on the wall kept low. The atmosphere was mellow, as usual, quiet.

After a while, Storm stirred where he sat. "All right," he said slowly. "Run this by me again."

Harper had to dredge herself out of her brown study. She answered with a sigh. Not turning. Keeping watch on the scarred man outside as he smoked in the shadows. " 'The Alchemist's Castle,' " she said. "It was published anonymously, in German, sometime around 1798, about a hundred years before the English story 'Black Annie.' When I raised the issue of a possible link between 'Black Annie' and the Belham Abbey ghost, Jorge was reminded of the German work. He located the 'Alchemist' manuscript in a private collection in Dresden. In Dresden, mind. The collector attributed the work to one Hans Baumgarten, who was a member of the artistic circle that included Rhinehart. Baumgarten wrote the story in Dresden, shortly after the turn of the nineteenth century. At the same time and place, in other words, at which Rhinehart painted the triptych of which *The Magi* is the first panel."

"Right. Okay." Storm went on kneading his arm, working his way down from shoulder to elbow. "And all this is stupendously incredible and fantastic because 'The Alchemist's Castle' and *The Magi* have absolutely nothing to do with each other."

"Precisely," said Harper Albright. "*The Magi*—with its cowled figures before a wedge of wall—is reminiscent of

'Black Annie.' But 'Black Annie'—with its foully murdered child and its reiterated sound—reminds us of 'The Alchemist's Castle.' A possible inference is that all three works had a common, earlier source."

"You mean the painting I saw at the auction house with Sophia and the story of Black Annie might actually be based on the same thing."

"So a reading of 'The Alchemist's Castle' would suggest."

Storm thought this over, massaging his arm. "So then I was right—when I saw the painting and said it looked like Black Annie, I was right. And all that stuff Sophia was saying about German Romantics and English ghost stories was—"

"Interesting," said Harper, "but not to the immediate point."

"I'll be damned," Storm said softly. "So what you're saying, you think maybe Sophia was trying to throw me off the trail? But why would she do that?" And then he answered his own question at once: "Because maybe 'Black Annie' and the painting *and* 'The Alchemist's Castle' are all somehow related to the ghost out at Sophia's house. And maybe that's why Sophia dropped her glass when I read the story."

"Ah," said Harper.

"All of which is supposed to have something to do with this cult guy, this Saint Iago."

"I must say your grasp of the implications is admirable."

"My grasp of the . . . Hey, listen, I love it when you talk like that," said Storm with a forlorn laugh. "Only what I'm grasping here is that you think Sophia's in trouble with a dead cult leader who may never have existed and somebody in a cowl going tick-tick who's over two hundred years old."

"Well, it's a ghost you were after," Harper Albright said grimly. "It was a ghost you came here to find." And now she did turn, she did face him. Left the thug on the corner to fend for himself, left her fear and excitement in abeyance, and faced him squarely.

Storm had dropped back against his seat, had stopped nursing his arm. He had started to spread his hands in a comical gesture of confusion. But when their eyes met, when he saw what Harper was thinking, his hands sank down again, and he dropped the comedy.

"Hey," he said.

"You're dying, aren't you, young Richard?" asked Harper Albright.

She felt her spirit grow heavy, felt it fall heavily inside her, as the air rushed out of him, as his hands came to rest on the tabletop and he sagged towards them. "Yeah, pilgrim, yeah," he told her. "It sure looks thataway."

Harper had left her dragon stick leaning in a corner by the fireplace. So she had to hold on to the back of a nearby chair. The old, weary weight of pity again. She had felt it often in her life.

"And this is, I presume, a certainty?" she asked gruffly.

"Yup." Storm winked at her. "It's that old devil brain. Being eaten away apparently. Listen, in my business, it isn't even a liability."

"There's nothing they can do."

He snorted into his Diet Coke. Flicked his wrist and tossed the drink down. Then he set the glass on the table with a bang. "Yeah, well, see, that's the whole thing. That's the whole thing right there. There isn't—but that wasn't gonna stop them. At first, when they found it, they sort of blurted the whole thing out. The tumor's too deep, they said.

Too involved with vital functions. Blah, blah, blah, this and that. Then—you could see it—their fingers started itching for the scalpel. 'Well, we *could* do an exploratory. We *have* got a new technique. We *might* just run a tube into your head and pump the radioactive stuff right on in there.' It wasn't gonna stop me dying, see. They just wanted to make sure I'd be as miserable as possible before I went."

Harper did not want to trouble him with her tears. But the smile at the side of his mouth, the hard glint of humor in his eyes, the courage . . . She turned away from him, back to the window. She glared at the scarred thug on the corner. She felt only a simmering anger for him now.

"So I ran away," Storm said. "They wouldn't stop, you know. They were like Satan or something. Tempting me. A small chance of remission. Good results in a test in Baltimore. I was afraid I would lose my nerve, seize the chance—and then they'd have me, they'd butcher me for no reason, ruin the rest of my life. So I ran away. Came here. I figured, what the hell. I wouldn't have even known I had it if I hadn't cracked my head one night. Had to have a CAT scan, and that showed something. Then they did this magnetic image thing. I wouldn't even have known, if it wasn't for that. Doctors said I might go another six months to a year without even having any symptoms . . ."

Here his voice trailed off in a manner that squeezed Harper's heart. He touched his arm once more, lightly, and she understood that the symptoms were already upon him. Before she could say anything, though, she heard his chair scrape, saw his reflection on the window as he stood up.

"Anyway, now you see the problem. With Sophia, I mean."

Quickly, Harper rounded on him again. Frowned at him.

"I do not. If I'm right, and she needs help . . . if I'm right and she's shown a certain unconscious inclination to confide in you as she's never been known to confide in anyone . . . then I refuse to see the problem. A man and woman should be able to help one another without its becoming . . . overly complicated."

He laughed, working his trench coat off the back of his chair. "They should be, sweetheart, no question," he said. "But they're not. And even if they were, I wouldn't be, not with her. I'm like a tinderbox around her. It's not just her looks, either. I don't know what it is. Every time I see her. I want to kill a rhinoceros for her, or build a castle or something—and then make love to her till the universe turns to clay." Shaking his head, he slid the coat on. Made an ironical expression. Standing there, hands in his pockets. Tall, fit, youthful, lively. It was hard for Harper to tolerate the sight. "Great timing, huh?" he said.

He walked towards the double doors, towards her. Stopped to stand beside her, with his hand resting lightly on one door's brass push-plate.

"Hey—don't look at me like that," he told her. "What can I do?"

"That's not for me to say," Harper answered slowly. "I can only tell you that the young woman seems to me to be in trouble. Judging by the fervor with which she denied it, I would guess it does have something to do with *The Magi.* Perhaps the auction represents some sort of crisis point—"

"Don't, don't, don't," he said. He closed his eyes a moment, held a hand up at her. "Don't. I mean, if you're right, and she took to me for some reason, and she wants my help—and if, like you say, she's fragile, you know, in the emotions department—then it's even worse, Harper. Best-case scenario:

I break her heart. So please. All right? I haven't been a saint. I want to go out clean."

And then he did go out—fled from her, practically, out into the winter's night. And she watched him from the window, sad and afraid.

A terrible moment followed. As Harper looked on. As Storm stepped into the middle of the narrow street, glancing this way and that for a cab. The thug on the corner tossed his latest cigarette into the gutter. Straightened. Two other hulking figures detached themselves from the surrounding darkness and began to close in on Storm. Harper's entire body went rigid. Storm, finding the street empty, had begun to move away to the corner. The scarred thug gave a look to his two massive henchmen, a signal with his eyes.

And they withdrew. As Storm strolled casually past them, they dropped back into the shadows.

Harper relaxed. Nodded to herself. That was as she thought it would be, as she thought it should be too. No matter what mystic role Storm's arrival had played—no matter what role he himself would play—in the events to come, this was not his hunt, not his battle. It was hers.

And she was the one they were after.

| 3 | The siege wore on. |

The scarred thug left the corner for a while, but was replaced by one of his mates. A real Frankenstein's monster, this one—cinderblock head and gorilla arms and all. Harper sensed there were still others, standing by, out of sight. She was going to need reinforcements.

She phoned Bernard—twice—from the pay phone at the far end of the bar. He wasn't in, of course. She could hardly have expected him. He lived above the office, in her house right across the street, but he seldom returned there before dawn. His nights, she understood, were spent in the sort of prowling debaucheries she only wished were beyond her wildest imagination. Just in case he should call in, as he sometimes did, she tried to leave a message on his private machine. It being a machine, however, and she being herself, she wasn't quite sure she had succeeded.

So she retired to the fireplace. Sat at a table. Nursed a warm pint of Guinness. Fitfully smoked her pipe, relit it nervously, lay it steaming on the tabletop beside her Borsalino. And prayed that help would somehow arrive.

Shortly before eleven, the two old gentlemen at the bar packed it in and headed for home. Harper was left alone with the barkeep. Robert. A likely lad, sinewy in his paisley shirt, with stand-up hair the color of wheat and a pendulous jade earring in one lobe. But she could no more put him at risk than she could Storm. She was out of options. She finally accepted the fact that she had to call the police.

"Phone's out," Robert told her. She had already picked it up, had already tasted the acid gout of fear at the sound of silence down the line. "Went down about twenty minutes ago."

"You have a house phone," she said.

"That one's out too. Bizarre, isn't it?" He shrugged one shoulder, flipped through the pages of a magazine. "There's another pay phone down on the next corner, you could try that."

"No," said Harper. "That's all right."

"Last call, by the way," said Robert. "We close in ten minutes."

"I'll just finish my pint," she said.

She waddled back to the window. Glanced out. The scarred man had taken up his post again. Was raising his overturned hand to his lips, drawing smoke from the hidden cigarette. He'd grown bold now. He was staring directly at her. His sneer widened when he saw her there.

She showed him her back and hobbled once more to her place by the fire.

The last minutes before closing ticked away. She sat over her stout and brooded. Perhaps it had been a mistake to let Storm leave her here. He would have gladly stayed if she had asked him. He would have wanted to. And he had the courage for it, she had seen that.

But no. This was not his business, not this part. Despite all his talk about ghosts and the paranormal, he was a child of the century. Its prejudices were his, more than he knew. Psychology. Science. Materialism. He could understand only with the understanding of his age. No. It would have been wrong—it would have been sinful under the circumstances of his illness—for her to enlist him against an enemy he could not possibly comprehend. The burden of the Uncanny was hers.

There are few who work the work of wonder. She was one. For others, there could be skepticism or belief; there could be credos, sciences, religions; theories or philosophies; politics; a point of view. For her, there was only ever this slow, steady tramp into the dark, and the narrative trail it left behind. If this should be the end for her—if help did not arrive, if the barkeep should call time and send her out into the street alone—then she would go in the fullness of unknowing. And so she would go whenever time was called. Because unknowing was her nature, the first rule of her game. The burden of the Uncanny was hers.

In the event, however, just as the clock struck eleven, Bernard wafted in. Heavy-lidded, foggy-eyed, he stepped, as if by magic, out of the gent's lavatory. Robert the barkeep started. But Bernard only waggled his fingers at him as his willowy form drifted past like smoke.

He settled into the seat across from Harper. Harper sniffed at him.

"Hmph," she said, so that her Guinness rippled. "You reek of your perversities." She really had been frightened, and her heart was hammering now. "Also you're drunk—or whatever it is you get."

He made a listless gesture of indifference. Sat slumped in his black windbreaker and jeans with his legs splayed under the table, his trainers towards the flames. His shaven head shone in the firelight. "Also, I'm here—which you should be bloody thankful for," he said. "How many of them are there outside—twenty-seven?"

"Three that I've seen so far."

"I had to slither through the toilet window like a snake. No offense, darling, but in your case, I don't think so. What were you planning to do, handbag your way home?"

"All right, all right, I'm glad to see you." Her heartbeat was slowing down again. "If nothing else, I'm gratified by this evidence of our mystic nexus. You seem somehow to have sensed my troubles telepathically . . ."

"Yes, they came to me as in a dream," he said. "I had just called in for my messages, when suddenly I heard a strangled muttering followed by a curse with two old geezers talking football in the background. A mental image formed—I saw before me an idiosyncratic Luddite incompetently attempting to communicate with my answering machine from a local pub. I thought it might be you."

"Ah."

"Time!" called the barman.

Harper tilted her Guinness high, polished off the bottom foam. Set the glass down decisively. "Time," she said. Bernard nodded. They both stood.

The young man fetched her cape from the stand in the corner, helped her shrug into it. He smoothed it down her back as she buttoned the front. Harper then slipped her pipe in her satchel and pulled the strap over her shoulder. Clapped her Borsalino onto her head; adjusted her glasses. Bernard retrieved her stick from the chimney corner and handed it to her. Completely recovered now, she patted his high cheek.

"Thank you for coming, lad. I should not have liked to've been bundled off like washing."

He squeezed her hand. "We'll go as we lived, darling— flailing about."

"Ha-ha."

She lifted the dragon's head to the barman. Walked with Bernard to the double doors. They both paused there, peering through the etching of the crane on the glass. The thug was no longer at his post on the corner. No one else was visible either. The street was empty. It seemed empty, anyway.

"Well," said Bernard under his breath. "It's only thirty steps home."

But they got no more than ten.

She pushed her door open. He shouldered through his. They stepped out onto the corner, under a streetlight. Began to cross the street. Bernard stayed close to Harper's left shoulder. They looked to either side of them. Bernard glanced behind. No one was visible in any direction.

They went across the road diagonally, moving from the streetlight towards their own portico. About midway, they stepped out of the streetlight's glory, into darkness.

And the scarred man came at them as if from nowhere.

He approached them swiftly, without breaking stride. He pointed to his wrist. He smiled, but his scar distorted it into a toothy smirk.

"Have you got the time, darling?" he said.

But he never stopped coming at them, charging at them. And there were other footsteps now, running footsteps, all around them, closing in.

"The time," Harper growled, "is not yet." Her stick was in her left hand, her right was pulling the dragon, pulling the sword's blade free of its sheath. She brought the sharp steel arcing over her head, brought it slicing straight so that the point halted in the air just as the scarred man reached it. He had to brake—hard—on the balls of his feet, and even so, the sword pressed nastily into the hollow of his throat at the place where his overcoat opened.

Bernard, meanwhile, curled around behind her. He set his back to hers—and not a moment too soon. There were four others and they were rushing at him from every side.

Bernard gave a raw, steamy hiss as he pressed out his *ibuki* breath with a tightened abdomen. His right hand described a smooth *shuto-uchi*—the knife-hand stroke—in the air. With that, he slipped into his fighting posture.

"Oi-ya!" he added for effect.

It seemed to work: the four men stopped short. They hovered in a semicircle around him. Each glanced at the others, waiting for someone else to break the ring of fear.

The scarred man put his hands up humorously. With the

blade at his throat, he grinned even wider. There was murderous rage in his small, damp eyes.

"There's no need for all this," he said. "Just a word in your ear, darling. That's all I want."

But the other four were edging, dodging around, seeking a chink in Bernard's defenses. Bernard kept his arms in motion before him, kept his head and eyes swinging from this side to that.

"Go on, then!" said Harper—she barked it, too loudly, she was that scared. She cursed herself for a craven old crone. "Go on and say what you have to!"

The Frankenstein monster to Bernard's left faked a lunge. Bernard shouted. This time, his *shuto-uchi* sliced the air so quickly it seemed to whistle. The monster dropped back.

"You're outnumbered, you see," said the scarred man in a shaky voice.

"The first one to reach me wins a wheelchair," Bernard sang back at him over Harper's shoulder.

The four thugs kept dancing, shuffling, feinting. One waggled a box-cutter. One swished a black, mean, flexible cosh. The Frankenstein just balled his fists. Bernard kept shifting, his back to Harper's.

"The game's not worth the candle," said the scarred man. Tilting his head away from the pressing sword that held him at bay, he still managed to fix Harper with his furious, piggy eyes. "I wouldn't kid you, it isn't, I mean it. It's just a small thread you've got hold of, darling. I'm just here to tell you to let it be. Let it be and we all go home happy."

"A small thread," she said to him. "But perhaps I'll pull it and see what unravels."

At which point, the four other thugs attacked.

The box-cutter flashed out, slashed past Bernard's

windbreaker as he drew back. Bernard trapped the attacker's wrist, twisted it. *Snap.* The attacker howled, his cutter clattered to the blacktop; so did he. Now Bernard's body slanted as he drove a *kansetsu* kick into the space just over Frankenstein's shin. The enormous monster staggered, toppled onto his side while, at the same time, Bernard gave a lightning flick of his inverted fist—*uraken*—in the other direction. It drove a third attacker's nose into his face with a splash of cartilage and blood.

But the fourth man's cosh got through. An upward backhand which Bernard only half blocked with his free arm. The weapon glanced off his brow. Bernard saw the sky swim and was suddenly down on one knee. The thug with the cosh moved to stand over him, planted himself just above him. With a grunt of effort, the thug lifted the blackjack high in the air, ready to slam it down with all his might into Bernard's exposed skull.

Still kneeling, still dazed, Bernard drove his open hand up between the man's legs and made a fist.

"Oof," said the man.

He curled up like burning paper and went down to the pavement.

Bernard swayed unsteadily up Harper's back. Regained his feet, leaning against her. Frankenstein and the thug with the splattered nose were already up as well, weaving around in front of him, but not quite ready to attack again. The other two were rolling in the street, clutching wrist and crotch, groaning.

The man with the scarred lip made a move in anger. Harper jabbed—hoisted him onto his tiptoes at the point of her blade.

"You know, I'm just crotchety enough to kill you," she said.

"You stupid old slag," the scarred man spat back. Pinned high at the end of her sword, he let his pink eyes flame down at her. "You know who you're mucking with. He's being good to you, isn't he? For old time's sake. You think he can't finish this whenever he likes? *Whenever* he likes? No fear, bitch."

Terror and fury and excitement all went through Harper in a bolt and she cut him. Jerked him off the point of her sword with a flick that nicked his chin.

The scarred man cried out, staggered backwards, grabbed at the wound with both hands. He looked down at the blood on his fingers. Cursed and stared black death at her.

"Since I am a bitch," she said, "beware my fangs." She had a weakness for paraphrase too.

The scarred man was speechless. Bleeding. All he could do was point at her. Point a threatening finger at her once, twice, three times—but all the while, withdrawing, fading away from her down the street, into the night. The others, seeing him go, were also starting to pull back. The two on the ground, clambering up shakily, joined the retreat. All sent dark warning glances at Bernard where he crouched, panting, with his hands up weakly before him.

And so the circle of men dissolved backwards into the shadows. They grew dimmer and dimmer, the scarred man still pointing his finger at Harper, pointing again and again.

Harper let her sword droop slowly to the blacktop. Tired. She was very tired suddenly. Her eyes, her arm, her whole body. Heavy, tired. And frightened, truly terrified. Trembling violently as the reaction set in. She could hear Bernard gasping for breath behind her. She could feel his narrow back leaning against hers. She had to lean against him as well to stay upright.

For an endless moment more, she could still make out the scarred man, retreating. She could see his pink, piggy glare, his pointing finger. An endless moment more.

Then the two of them, she and Bernard, were alone in the darkness.

4 The evening of the auction arrived and—just as Harper had feared—Sophia hanged herself. For her, it was the end of a long, dreamy day.

First thing in the morning, she had burned all her snapshots of her mother. Sitting at home, very businesslike at her escritoire. Dressed in one of the usual uniforms: blue cardigan over white blouse, pleated gray skirt. She glanced sometimes through the balcony doors, out at the gabled roofscape of South Kensington: chimneys and attic windows, a stone church spire against the solid gray sky, sedate and lovely. One after another, in the ashtray at her fingertips, the photos burned. The char closed in a rough circle over those features so like her own.

Sophia felt cool as she watched this happen. Remote and clear in her mind. Having decided what she would do, there seemed to her a very straight line of perfect clarity between her and the doing of it, an open corridor that proceeded through precise, logical and predictable steps towards the image of her own body, dangling. It was the world surrounding this corridor that appeared hazy, veiled, uncertain. It was that misty periphery which gave the day its dreamlike quality.

When she had done with the pictures, she opened the balcony doors and cleared the air, waved the smoke out over the Little Boltons with the back of her hand. Then she walked down the corridor to the bathroom. Emptied the last load of laundry from the dryer. Folded these clothes in her bedroom, on her bed. Packed them in the suitcase that lay open there. As if she were going on a journey. She felt this would be easier for everyone and would leave less of a mess behind.

She had decided for some reason upon eight o'clock— 8:00 P.M. She thought that was about when the auctioneer would reach *The Magi*. After that, of course, the whole situation would become impossible for her. Her father would acquire the panel, and she would be forced to choose between him and her promise to the murdered Resurrection Man. Which really was no choice at all. Either option was intolerable. How could she betray her own father? And how could she keep the secret that he was involved in something monstrous? *Whoever buys* The Magi . . . *He is the Devil from Hell* . . . Sophia was all for fortitude, but there came a time when to suffer a situation was absurd. That was the time: 8:00 P.M., when they sold *The Magi*, when her father bought it. So she had decided.

She finished with her clothing. Next she packed her CDs into cushioned envelopes, addressed these in her scrupulous hand. Her classical pieces—oceans of Bach mostly and some Mozart—she would send to her sister Laura. The American popular music she sometimes enjoyed—Sinatra, Louis Armstrong, Ella Fitzgerald—would go to her friend Tony; her brother Peter despised it. She would send him her few rock albums instead, plus the Lucian Freud poster she knew he liked.

She tidied her flat, then carried the packages to the post office on Fulham Road. It was farther away than the branch on Earl's Court, but she found the drug dealers and fast-food restaurants near the tube stop depressing. This walk was far nicer. Past whitewashed mansions, under garden walls, through the hanging branches of cherry and chestnut trees. Forsythia that would bloom so yellow come spring. The air was cold and damp and invigorating, refreshing on her cheeks, in her hair.

As she walked, she thought some more about the face in those photographs she had burned. It had been even clearer in these than in the portrait on her wall at the Grange: while her mother's features *had* been very like her own, her manner, her expression had really been quite different. They had been warmer. They had been better, Sophia thought as she walked. That sweet way she would tilt her head to one side. And the way her eyes always looked faintly worried, as if there were some service or kindness she might have neglected. Her smile was so eagerly agreeable too. Even in the Kodachrome square of past time, her generosity made itself known to her daughter. Sophia felt it with a pang. One did wonder sometimes how things might have been different . . .

After she had posted her packages, she took a cab to the gallery.

"Would you be a darling and go to the auction for me tonight?" she said to her assistant, Jessica. "I really don't feel up to it."

"You're not ill or anything?" Jessica asked her. Blinked up at her with her limpid fawn eyes.

"I'll be all right. You're a brick." Sophia squeezed the other girl's shoulder through the soft cashmere cardigan. Very odd—but her mind was so clear now that she felt she could actually look right into Jessica's soul, understand her down to the ground, even see into her future. Blond and cherub-cheeked, vulnerable, deferential and not terribly bright, Jessica would have her pick of the gallery's most opulent clients. She would marry one, would enjoy his luxuries, would suffer his adulteries and would learn to live for her children and her comforts, resigned and only slightly frantic. It really was very odd; Sophia looked into Jessica's big eyes and saw the whole thing right away. She squeezed the girl's shoulder again, with compassion this time. "Sir Michael wants *The Magi*," she went on, and then wittily imitated her father's huffy baritone, "at all costs!" Jessica smiled uncertainly. Gently, Sophia said, "It won't go much past fifty, I'm sure, but he said he would go to three times that, so we have the wherewithal. Just be firm, you know, top the bids quickly, and you'll scare the rest off."

"Yes . . . yes, all right," said Jessica, not very firmly at all. "If you really need me to."

Sophia gave her an encouraging smile. It would be a big moment for her, she thought. Something to remember in her later days. On an impulse, she unclasped the brooch from her own cardigan and pinned it onto Jessica's. "Now listen, if Antonio's there, I want you to flirt with him a little, yah? Especially when the Antwerp lots come up, distract him. Tell him I've got a perfectly good Reubens *Pan* for him and I don't want him spending all his money before I get my hands on some of it. Tell him I was very severe about it. He likes that; it excites him, makes him feel English or something. All right?"

"Isn't this your mother's brooch?"

"It just suits you. The little lapis pieces set off those flecks in your eyes."

"Oh, but I couldn't possibly—"

"No, I want you to wear it," Sophia said. "It looks much

better on you than it ever did on me. I'll consider it yours until I see you again. All right?"

At that, Jessica looked so confused and grateful and admiring that Sophia's heart welled with pity for her and her humiliating future. But she only smiled back, wryly. In her clarity, she understood that what would be, must be. And she continued down her lucid corridor, through her dreamy day.

So she came that night to sit alone in her upstairs office. The gallery closed, dark, quiet below. She swiveling idly in her black chair, only the lamp on her rolltop burning. The electric clock at the corner of the blotter told off the last quarter hour before eight. And, having decided on eight, Sophia waited, nervous now, impatient for the time to pass. She tapped her fingernail twice on the blotter's leatherette border. Twice quickly, then twice again. *Tick-tick, tick-tick.*

She glanced out through the open door, out to where the lamplight died, to where the upper balcony curved along the wall into dusky nothing. She imagined her body hanging there. Hanging, turning. The paintings hanging on the wall above it: the moonstruck mountains, the cryptic glades, the seductive ruins in the grass. The body turned and turned and turned towards her and she imagined its face. The same face that had smiled up at her from the ashtray that morning, that had curled and blackened and crumbled away.

"Your mother cared very deeply about the suffering of others," her father had told her once. "Too deeply, I sometimes thought. She wanted the world to be better than it is. She took on too much of the guilt of things: injustice, poverty and so on. We can only go by our own lights, after all, cover our own patch, you know. We can't solve the troubles of the universe, can we?"

And no, Sophia had answered, we can't. And yet, one did just wonder. If things might have been different. She tapped the blotter with one hand. The other moved slowly across her middle. That face, her mother's face, was so charitable and concerned and responsive and yet so like her own, that one did just think that she, Sophia, might have been more like that herself. Had her mother lived, that is. Had she been around to teach Sophia the trick of it.

This thought only deepened her depression and lone-liness, the black well of them inside her. And anyway, it was minutes to eight. She rose, switched off the lamp. Her navy overcoat hung on a stand by the door. She drew the belt from its loops even as she stepped out onto the balcony.

She walked along the balcony slowly. Now one hand slid over the rail and the other held the belt, the belt trailing. The muffled whisk of Bond Street traffic reached her. The glow of headlights rode up over the far wall. Over the paintings, over a desolation of rocks, a sunset, a figure gazing into the vanishing point. Then it was gone. The gallery was dim around her, quiet. Quiet, except for her own footsteps on the hard floor. *Tick-tick, tick-tick.* She thought of how she had heard that sound in her bed, how she had gone downstairs, calling for her mother. Moving to the door at the end of the corridor, the last door . . . After that, she couldn't remember.

She stopped in the middle of the balcony. It seemed a likely place. She tied the belt to the rail, tested it. Made a simple slipknot in the other end and brought the loop down over her black hair. This business and the business of hopping up on the rail, of bringing her legs around to the other side, sitting on the edge of the balcony—this was the worst of the thing, the most depressing bit. It all seemed so shabby finally and miserable. And sitting there, gripping the rail, looking down, she thought unhappily: One should have been taught to love, so that help would come.

Then she looked at her watch. It was just eight, just exactly. They must be auctioning *The Magi* right this minute.

That was the last thought she had before she pushed off the railing.

5 But as it happened, *The Magi* had come up for sale some fourteen minutes earlier. And it was just then—just as the panel was being lifted onto the display easel—that Richard Storm walked into the Sotheby's auction room.

His entrance, in fact, made a lot more of a stir than the display of the panel. The broad, well-lighted room was packed when he came in. The rows of folding chairs were all occupied. Buyers lined up along the white walls, two deep in some places, the aisles blocked. More buyers clustered at the back. There were even some standing behind the phone tables, behind the neat, wealthy-looking young ladies who sat shoulder to shoulder there, waiting for call-in bids. And everywhere, as Storm entered through the double doors at the rear of the room, attention was paid. A subtle effect, but definitely there. The crowd that was gathered before the doors parted slightly to let him through. Heads turned, briefly. Women's eyes went up him in appraisal; men's eyes went down him in critique. All over the room, fine ladies touched the tips of their hair. One egotistical French industrialist unconsciously straightened his posture; an Arab oilman smirked; a Silicon Valley whiz kid snorted derisively and then had to wipe the snot off his lapel. The girls at the phone tables turned like a row of cranes in unison to get a glimpse. The auctioneer himself glanced down from his podium on high, sensing a change in the relative gelt humidity, feeling out the weather.

All because of Storm. And he knew it too. Hey, the man was in battle gear this time, babe. Broad shoulders squared by the slashing planes of an Armani suit. A blinding spit shine on his black Guccis. An elegant splash of gold glinting at his cuffs, and on his tie. Silk at his throat, at his pockets. A hundred and fifty pounds of style on his sandy hair—and we're talking pounds sterling, sweetheart, not the scale kind. There were people in that room who were like computers in judging these things, in assessing potential lovers, customers, rivals. But even to an untutored eye, even to a casual glance, the guy looked like a major tycoon, like an American multi-millionaire at ease with power and glamour and fame. Which, of course, is exactly what he was.

He stepped across the threshold, engine gunning. On a mission, clearly. For Storm felt good again, felt new even, reinvented. The reaction to his seizure had dwindled away. The physical weakness, the gape-faced shock, had dwindled. And his moral strength had returned to him in their wake—a reaction to the reaction. Thus, in the days since his last meeting with Harper—since he had fled from The Sign of the Crane, from the judgment he thought he saw in the old woman's eyes—he had been locked alone in his measly room. He had been warring there with the inner demons of his death. A cast of thousands. An epic, bleak and bloody spectacle, forty years in the making. Day after day, he had flailed in the ravening clutches of his mortality. Night after night, he had scorched his cheeks with tears. Tailor-legged on the carpet. Streaming eyes lifted to the ceiling. Life, oh life, he had cried out to the gods.

And then it had ended. Only hours ago really. As he slumped exhausted just that morning. The answer he sought had suddenly come to him, had suddenly risen before his eyes like a thunderous dawn. And the answer was: Irv Philbin. Or, that is, the immortal words of Irv Philbin, who just happened to be the best goddamned movie publicist between the Canyon and the Coast. It was Irv, seven years ago, who had rescued Storm's worst film, *Castle Misery*, who had slam-dunked the brain-dead spook show down the public's throat with one of the great ad campaigns of all time. And it was the words of that campaign that dawned before Storm at this critical hour, the very words that were once emblazoned across the *Castle* one-sheet in every multiplex lobby in America. These words shone in Storm's mind through the forest of doubt; at the exit of the valley of shadows they shone:

In the battle between Love and Death, there can be only one Survivor!

Storm was here to find Sophia.

Now, at the front of the room, a man in blue overalls was adjusting the easel canvas holders. Now he was stepping back. There was the panel, displayed: the ruined abbey, the broken window, the winter trees, the shadows, the cowled, ghostly figures gliding by the base of the chapel. Hanging from the ceiling above it, an enormous electric toteboard reset itself to zero. Pounds, dollars, deutschmarks, yen—all zero, straight down the column. The glimmer of it caught Storm's eye. He heard the riffle in the seats as the buyers resettled. They crossed their wrists in their laps, focused their blasé regard on the Rhinehart.

"The Magi," announced the auctioneer, up on his platform, behind the wide wooden podium with *Sotheby's* written across it in gold. He was young, tailored, arrow-straight. Prim, thin-lipped, arrogant. A boy whom his colleagues called promising. "Lot ninety-four, a panel of Rhinehart's Nativity triptych, recently rediscovered in the former East Germany and offered as an anonymous donation to the Children's Resource Fund."

It was now thirteen minutes before eight.

Storm scanned the crowd. Still standing amidst the people clustered at the doors, he slowly moved his eyes over the buyers leaning against the white wall to his left. Next he passed his gaze over the audience in their seats, checking off one coiffure after another. Finally he examined the girls at the phone table one by one. No Sophia.

"I'll take an opening bid of twenty-five thousand pounds." The auctioneer went into his practiced drone. Nasal, hypnotic, seemingly slurred, deceptively precise, the words flowed from his thin lips. "Opening at twenty-five thousand, twenty-five, I have twenty-five thousand, do I have thirty? Thirty, thirty thousand from the phone. Thirty-five. I have thirty-five thousand."

It started happening that fast. Storm tried to see where the bids were coming from. He remembered Sophia had said that her gallery might buy the panel. He tried to follow the auctioneer's eyes, but the auctioneer barely moved his eyes. And yet the guy seemed to see everything, everywhere in the room.

"Forty, I have forty thousand from the phone," he said.

From the phone. Storm looked to his right just in time to catch the slightest gesture from the table. A noble swan of a young woman in the regulation cardigan was looking up from her handset to raise one eyebrow, one finger.

"Forty-five thousand," the auctioneer went on. "I have forty-five, forty-five thousand, forty-five, I have fifty . . ."

The green lights of the electric toteboard winked all down the column. Fifty thousand pounds, seventy-five thousand dollars, one hundred ten thousand deutschmarks, incalcuable yen, eight million something. The price of the Rhinehart panel had doubled in just two minutes. It was eleven now before eight o'clock.

The auctioneer massaged his gavel—a heavy disc of wood—as he hummed right along. Now a barely perceptible jut of his chin made Storm turn his attention to the left-hand wall. Yes: another signal. The flutter of a slender white hand, the glint of a gold bracelet, as the price of the panel went up again. Storm nudged his way through the crowd of people around him. He edged along to the right behind the last row of seats. Trying to get a better look at the standing bidder.

Now he could see her in profile. No, it was not Sophia. Some cuddly blonde, hardly twenty. Pouting with effort, her forehead shining too much in the overhead lights.

Storm was about to turn away from her when he remembered who she was. The girl in Sophia's gallery, the receptionist.

"Fifty thousand, do I have sixty, do I have sixty thousand, sixty, sixty . . ." The auctioneer—with that skill for which his friends detested him—had sussed the action, upped the bids. "Sixty, I have sixty from the rear, sixty thousand."

Automatically, Storm glanced back to the rear of the room. Caught the brief wave of a numbered paddle. Another bidder—a man, this one. A tall, slim figure in a white suit. Wearing green gloves, weirdly enough. With black hair flowing to his shoulders. A thin, angular face, almost diamond-shaped, somehow feline, somehow feral. He was standing relaxed as the action popped, his eyes amused, witty. Standing back, out of the glare of the overheads. But even so, Storm took that one look at him and knew he was going to win the auction. He was that type. Storm had been around enough of them to know. Storm had been in auctions for books, for screenplays that had gone into the stratosphere; he understood the psychology. This guy was scorched earth, he was take-no-prisoners. Unless that was the U.S. Treasury on the phone, *The Magi* was as good as his. Sophia's blond friend wasn't even in it.

"Seventy, seventy, eighty thousand, eighty thousand, ninety . . ."

Whoa, thought Storm, getting interested now. The lights on the toteboard couldn't keep up. Even in Hollywood, things didn't move this fast.

By the clock on the wall just behind the board, it was nine minutes to eight.

Storm looked back at the girl against the wall, the blonde from the Endering Gallery. Yeah, as he'd figured, she was beginning to crack. The corners of her lush red lips were turning down, her eyes were frenzied. Every time her bid was trumped, Storm could see her blink, recoil, dismayed.

She fluttered her hand again.

"A hundred thousand pounds," said the auctioneer. And immediately, "One hundred twenty-five thousand from the gentleman in the rear."

That sent a stir through the audience, not quite silence, not quite sound. Several faces surreptitiously came round to get a look at this "gentleman in the rear." And Sophia's assistant—Storm saw her—whipped a stricken look over her shoulder so fast it made her hair fly.

Storm smiled at that. Then he stopped smiling. When she turned that way, he could see the front of her for a moment. He could see she was wearing Sophia's brooch.

The bidding went around the triangle again. The phone table, the blonde, the man in the rear. The auctioneer, with a feel for the atmosphere almost tactile, had sped the bids once more. He was leaning back from his podium with his eyelids lowered as if with passion.

"One-fifty, one-fifty, one-fifty, one-seventy-five, one hundred seventy-five thousand, two hundred. Two hundred thousand . . ."

Wait a minute, thought Storm. This isn't right.

It was seven minutes to eight.

What's she got Sophia's brooch for? he thought. What, were they all part of this evil cult Harper had told him about? That was crazy. It didn't make sense. Her mother's brooch. Which she'd never worn before the other day. She wouldn't have loaned it to this other girl, would she? A cold sweat broke out on the back of his neck. He heard Harper speak to him as if she were standing at his shoulder: *Something is terribly wrong.*

"Two hundred, two hundred, I have two hundred from the rear, do I have two hundred and fifty, do I have two hundred and fifty thousand pounds, two-fifty, two-fifty . . ."

Now the murmur of the crowd was clearly audible. The swanny dame at the phone bank, Storm saw, gave a short, level chop of her hand in the air. The buyer on the line had withdrawn from the fray. It was between the blonde and the weird guy in the white suit now. The blonde's small hand trembled upward like a leaf on the wind.

"I have two hundred fifty thousand—three hundred," the auctioneer said instantly. "Three hundred thousand from the gentleman in the rear."

As the excited murmur of the crowd grew louder, Storm began to move, to edge through the standing buyers, to feel his way behind the backs of the last seats towards the left-hand aisle.

The lights of the toteboard fluttered up front. Three hundred thousand pounds. Four hundred fifty thousand dollars. Nearly seven hundred thousand deutschmarks. Yen beyond imagining. Storm could see the blonde against the wall practically spastic with terrified indecision. Her lips trembling, her eyes filling, her hands hovering before her, unsure.

Then he lost sight of her in the crowd as he moved closer. He heard the auctioneer say, "Three hundred, three hundred, three hundred, three hundred and fif— Four hundred thousand. The bid is four hundred thousand pounds from the gentleman in the rear."

Jesus, thought Storm, as he started pushing down the aisle. This white-suit guy is a killer. He looked over his shoulder and saw him again. Got a closer look at him now. A killer, no question. Something in the brutally cut facets of his face—something in the weirdly smoky depths of his eyes—made Storm shudder, made his collar go clammy. He turned away, glanced up blindly at the toteboard. Noticed the clock instead: five minutes to eight. *Something is terribly wrong.*

Making terse excuses, Storm wedged himself between two people blocking the aisle. Squeezed between two more. Pushed out to see the blonde at the wall just ahead of him. He was near enough now to see her nostrils flare in panic as her hand jerked up again like a marionette's.

"Four hundred fifty thous— Five hundred thousand pounds from the gentleman in the rear."

Storm put his hand on the blond girl's arm. She spun on him with eyes the size of saucers, her lips parted, her skin slick.

"Where's Sophia?" he asked her.

"I . . . I . . . I . . ." she said. And then she seemed to recognize him and whispered harshly, desperately, "She said fifty. I don't know what I'm supposed to do!"

"Five hundred, the bid is five hundred thousand, the bid is at half a million pounds . . ."

Storm nodded, squeezed her arm. "Drop it, honey. You're licked. The guy'd go to a zillion. Where's Sophia?"

"Five hundred, five hundred, five hundred . . ." The auctioneer lifted his gavel. The blonde turned to stare at him with her hand lifted as if to bid again.

"Trust me on this, kid. Drop the potato," said Storm. "Where's Sophia?"

Her face rolled back towards him, she gawped up at him as if from a nightmare. His eyes went to the brooch on her sweater. To the dim-witted terror in her perky, cherubic face.

"I don't know," she said. "She told me to come here instead . . ."

"She told you . . ." said Storm. *The woman is asking for your help*, said Harper Albright in his mind, *crying for your help*.

"*Sold!* For five hundred thousand pounds!" said the auctioneer.

His forearm fell. The gavel hit the podium. *Whack.* Storm felt the blond girl jump in his hand.

Perhaps the auction represents some sort of crisis point . . .

The audience burst into loud applause, loud laughter and conversation. Storm's gaze arced over the room wildly.

Caught a glimpse of the man in the white suit. Holding up his paddle—number 313—in his green-gloved fingers. Grinning, his teeth predatory. And the others in the seats with their hands moving, coming together. The toteboard caught at five hundred thousand.

Sophia saying: *This is where I want to die.*

"Oh my God," said Richard Storm.

It was one minute before eight.

There were some people in the audience who figured he had stolen a purse or a necklace. It was their best guess when they saw him drive back recklessly up the aisle. Wielding his broad shoulders left and right. Shoving people aside without mercy.

But then he was gone, dashing through the rear doorway, and no one was screaming "Thief! Thief!" so it must've been all right. The Rhinehart panel was already being removed from the easel. Another painting was already being lifted into place. The audience turned away and forgot Richard Storm. The business of the auction went on.

Out on New Bond Street, Storm fired through the doors of Sotheby's like a missile. He didn't believe what he was thinking. He didn't dare to. He just ran—the way they'd taught him in high school track: legs stretching, body straight, elbows pistoning. The storefronts whipped by on either side of him, the store banners whipped over his head. People dodged out of his way, looked after him: in his fine suit, in his fine shoes, running as if the devil were on his tail. He didn't think about it. He didn't dare to think anything. He just ran.

He was at the Endering Gallery's door in thirty seconds. Under the port awning, between the two spruces. Plastered to the glass like a bug on the windshield. He probed the dark interior over the fog his breath made on the door. The fog expanded, shrank as he panted. The gallery beyond was still. The front desk empty. The paintings undisturbed on the wall. Everything appropriate, right. He thought it was okay.

Then he lifted his eyes and saw her, seated on the balcony rail. He could make out the line of the belt around her neck.

Storm felt as if gasoline had been thrown on the smoldering coals inside him. Doubt, suspicion, anxiety all flared into a sudden blaze of fear. He grabbed the door handle, yanked. It was locked. He shook it.

"Damn!"

He let the handle go. Once, twice, he slapped the glass with both palms. He felt as if it were he up there with the noose around his neck.

"Sophia! Sophia!"

She didn't hear him, didn't react.

"Sophia!"

Storm clung to the smooth surface, powerless. She sat there another moment. He spun, his mind desperately empty, his eyes looking anywhere, for anything.

The spruce in the cast-iron planter. He bent down, seized the planter, lifted it into the air. It flew up too easily— for a moment he thought it would be too light to break the door's thick glass. But that was the adrenaline: he was so jazzed, he could've lifted the building. He stepped back. Raised the tree, the planter, over his head. Dirt and cigarette butts poured down into his expensive haircut. He hurled the planter into the door and the door shattered.

The black cascade of soil and the white cascade of glass went blue as the gallery's alarm light started flashing, as the siren started shrieking to the sky. Storm charged through the jagged opening. The shards of the door crackled under his feet. The planter was still tumbling to a stop as he leapt over it. He dashed for the stairway, shouting.

"Sophia!"

But she had already dropped off the railing. While he was lifting the planter into the air, she had done it. Her body hung jerking at the end of the belt.

Storm roared and grabbed the curling bannister. He could see her struggling, clawing the rope. His senses burned in electric connection to her as if it were he choking, dying. He vaulted three steps, another three. She was still fighting it, still there. He made the landing. Saw only the flashing blue light, felt only the siren screaming in his head where his thoughts should've been.

"Sophia!"

And he launched himself at her. Up onto the railing, his body stretching out. One hand grabbing hold of the rail, one reaching down. The belt was short. He could reach her. He had her, by the arm. He shouted again wildly. Muscled her up. Tumbled back off the rail under the weight of her.

He fell to the floor, bringing her down with him. Instantly, he scrambled to his knees. Grabbed her. She was gagging. He seized the loop around her neck. Wrenched it over her hair, roughly, with a furious curse. Sophia sank back, coughing, choking.

Storm knelt over her, seething, crazy with rage at what she'd tried to do. He wanted to slap her. His hand flew up over her head. It hung there, trembling. He clenched it, clenched both his hands and shook them at her.

"Oh!" he shouted in his outrage. "Oh!"

Sophia drew a rasping breath. And then another. And then she gave a hoarse, forlorn, animal cry and punched him.

Her fist hit him weakly on the chest. Her hair flew across her face and she punched again, blindly, catching the side of his head. He gave another curse. Snatched at her wrist.

But she was finished. She sagged to the floor, making raw, hacking noises, her hair spilling forward, her beaten figure pulsating with the blue light. As the shriek of the siren rose and fell, Storm heard her sobbing miserably. He reached out with a shaking hand and touched her as gently as he could. But she swept her arm around, knocked him away.

Now people were rushing into the gallery below. There were voices calling. There were figures running to the foot of the stairs. The siren screamed. The blue light flashed and flashed.

Panting, Storm knelt on the floor with his palms braced against his thighs, his head hanging.

Sophia sat there beside him and cried and cried.

V

YOUNG WILLIAM,

A BALLAD

"Who is it who comes knocking there?"
     the widow Annie said.
"And who would come this late round my door
     on a night so dreary?"

Tap-tap. " 'Tis I, your son, Young Will,
     who once around thee played.
Oh, open, mother, and let me in,
     for I'm cold and weary."

"Is it thee, long lost this many a day?
     Is it thee, my darling boy,
who knocks at my door in the dead of night,
     so I feel I fear thee?"

"It is I, it is I, your long-lost child,
     Young William, your pride and joy."
Tap-tap. "Open, mother, and let me in,
     for I'm cold and weary."

"And where have you been this many a day?
     I sought and mourned thee so,
and thought you had left your mother behind
     for some winsome dearie."

"I have been round the old Jew's castle,
　　　where you warned me never to go."
Tap-tap. "Open, mother, and let me in,
　　　for I'm cold and weary."

"And what did you do there, my only child,
　　　my son, my joy, my pride?
And how return after so long a time
　　　with the night so dreary?"

"Oh, I spoke to the old Jew's daughter,
　　　and she bid me come inside
with a voice so sweet that I had to obey.
　　　Oh, I'm cold and weary."

"And what did she do there, my only child,
　　　long gone this many a day?
For my heart misgives me to hear the tale,
　　　and my eyes grow teary."

"Oh, she drove her jeweled knife into my heart
　　　so my dear life bled away
and I lay as cold as a stone in the road,
　　　so cold and dead and dreary.

"And she used my blood to make her wine,
　　　and my flesh to make her bread."
Tap-tap. "Open, mother, and let me in
　　　for I'm cold and weary."

And the widow Annie cried out to hear,
    and leapt from her lonesome bed.
And she opened the door but saw nothing there
    save the night so cold and dreary.

And she wandered the village streets alone,
    till at Prime she heard the sound:
Tap-tap, from the earth neath the abbey walls:
    Tap-tap, so lorn and weary.

And they dug at that very spot until
    Young William's bones were found.
And were laid in a grave in the chapel yard
    on a day so sad and dreary.

VI

HARPER ALBRIGHT
AND
THE CLOCKWORK OF
HISTORY

1 Circle of standing stones. Murmur of incantation. Dead of night.

This was the crossroad of the Sussex leys, the dowser's crossroad. Subterranean rivers intersected here. Power swirled and vibrated in the very air. Seven spirals of chthonic force were known to snake up from the earth into the tall grass, to coil round the seven mysterious boulders that stood in their ancient ring brimming with intensity.

It was Candlemas Eve, a witch's sabbath, and the old man had brought a sacrifice.

The grass swished, the fallen leaves snickered as he came. Silver light and black shadow raced across the ground in turn. The man traveled with them quickly. He was alone. He was completely naked. His face was puffy, his white breasts pendulous, his belly domed. His phallus was shrunken by the cold.

He murmured to himself as he came:

"Arise, infernal. Hel, Hecate, Goddess of the Crossroad, Gorgo, Mormo, Moon . . ."

The canvas bag hanging from his right fist was writhing. A frightened whimpering could be heard coming from within. The old man's lips were dry, his eyes were glassy. In his left hand he gripped the athame, the sacrificial knife.

Now he arrived at the prehistoric circle, the seven man-sized stones rising beneath the turbulent sky. They were said to be seven maidens who'd been cursed for dancing on a Sunday. Their shapes were undulant. The tortuous rock was animated by the running light from the unbroken passage of clouds over the full moon.

The old man stepped into the circle's center. He could feel the cadence of occult energy, the broadcast of the waters converging underground. He could almost hear the throb of the maidens' music. He knelt before the kindling he had piled up in a small pyramid. He felt pebbles and grit under his bare knee.

The air grew hushed. Leaves, trapped beneath the kindling, chattered softly. The wind haunted the perimeter of the place, seeking ingress, moaning.

"Thou who goest to and fro at night, torch in hand, enemy of the day, friend and lover of darkness. Thou who dost rejoice when the bitches are howling and warm blood is spilled . . ."

He set the bag on the hard earth before him, set the athame on the hard earth, beside the lighter he had left waiting there. He clasped the scruff of the wriggling mass inside the canvas sack. He spread the neck of the sack. Puffing, he worked the shivering animal out into the cold.

The puppy looked up at the old man hopefully. It lapped at his thumb—the thumb that held it fast.

The old man kept the puppy pinned with his left hand, took up the lighter in his right. He worked the strike-wheel, made the flame. Squinted at it, pupils zooming.

The puppy yipped, begging to be set free, to play. The old man leaned across it, held the lighter to the leaves.

"Thou who art walking amidst the phantoms in the place of tombs . . . Come on, come on, flame."

A leaf took, burned. There was a low snigger as the fire spread. A red glow slowly leaked out of the pyramid, spread over the ground.

"Good. Good," the old man said.

The puppy squeaked at him, thumped its tail against the earth.

The old man lifted the athame.

"Now." He hoisted the knife up to the level of his thin, silvery hair. His voice grew louder.

"Thou whose thirst is blood, thou who dost strike chill fear into mortal hearts. Hel, Hecate, Gorgo, Mormo. Cast a propitious eye upon our sacrifice."

With that, he made a heave of effort, his breasts jiggling. The knife went high, went up against the clouds, against the moon.

There was a sudden suction of fumy air. The pyramid of sticks exploded in a mushroom of sparks and fire. Amidst the stone maidens, behind the burgeoning flame, out of the frozen night, there arose a black figure.

The old man cried out in terror.

The figure spoke. It boomed: "Lay not thy hand upon the dog! Neither do thou anything unto it!"

The blade of the athame sang a single note as it slipped from the old man's fingers and hit the stony dirt.

"Harper?" he said.

"Oh, let the poor creature go, Jervis, you stupid old goat." She came humping round the bonfire on her stick. Lowered a demanding hand. "Now."

The old man made a deep frown, mopey, his fun spoiled. But he handed the puppy over to her. Harper held it against the shoulder of her cape. It licked her jowls happily, skewing her specs and Borsalino.

"And snap on a pair of shorts, there's a good fellow," she said. "My virgin heart is all aflutter."

She retreated back behind the fire. She averted her eyes from his nakedness, communing muzzle to muzzle with the little dog.

Jervis, grumbling, towed his wobbly buttocks out of the stone circle, back into the grass to find his clothes.

"Ha-ha!" Harper barked, pleased with the puppy's enthusiasm. It was climbing right up her shoulder to lave the side of her head. "What is it?" she called. "Part retriever?"

Jervis reentered the circle, carrying a bundle of clothes. He held on to the Y-fronts, tossed the rest to the ground. Grumpily, he pulled the shorts on, cracked the elastic band into their groove beneath his overhanging flesh. "How should I know?" In a gruff croak. He unfolded a woolly jumper next. "It was some child's, some girl's." He yanked the jumper over him, popped his head out. "The little idiot left it to wait for her when she went into the news agent. So I borrowed it."

"Oh, Jervis, Jervis," Harper intoned, "you make insult superfluous." But she could only harpoon the old sinner with one eye: her other lens was foaming with puppy spittle. She was busy holding her hat on with her stick hand too. But she went on. "And what's this? Alone on so high a holiday? Where's Granny and Uncle Bob and all the kids? Shouldn't they be gathered round the Black Sabbath tree, singing Black Sabbath carols? Or something."

The fire snapped between them, sinking down. Jervis hawked and shot a gob of phlegm into it. Arched a shrewd eyebrow at her. "Bastards deserted me. All of 'em. I couldn't figure why till now." He plucked his trousers from the foot of a stone. Holding them, he laid a finger against the side of his nose. "You scared them off, didn't you? You warned them you were coming."

"I thought we should have a chat alone. And you can be difficult to find."

He made an animal growl, deep in his throat. Even the puppy paused and glanced at him. "Arrogant, aren't you? Sure of yourself. Aren't you?" He smiled nastily. "Well, what I hear, your days are numbered. You've crossed the line, Harper. Got above yourself. You only walk the earth on his sufferance."

"And you walk free on mine," she said. The dog was growing sleepy, was making a bed of her cape collar, settling in with its chin. Readjusting her Borsalino, blinking behind her smeared spectacles, Harper paced thoughtfully from the fireside towards one of the standing stones. The old man, meanwhile, was jamming his spindly gray legs into the baggy pants. "Imagine my surprise, Jervis, when a charming boy at the Art Loss Register mentioned the name of a mysterious Dr. Mormo, who had been a major figure in the smuggling of wartime plunder. Until then, I had always thought you a harmless conjurer of evil spirits and murderer of children's pets. By the same token, the ladies and gentlemen at Scotland Yard's Bureau of Arts and Antiques have not got my interest in the arcane, and so they have thus far failed to connect you with your alias. But I have done so, haven't I?"

He buckled his belt, battled with his zipper. "Haven't you had enough, you old cow? How many warnings do you think you're going to get?"

Harper moved out of the stone's shadow into the dying firelight. One hand holding the pup at her shoulder, the other the dragon on her stick, her hat half crushed, her glasses lopsided, she was still formidable.

"Why did he want *The Magi*, Jervis?"

"Do you think I'm barmy? You'll get nothing from me."

But Harper smiled thinly. She knew her man. He was half mad, but he was all coward. "Look around you, Jervis," she said. "Your coven's blown. Gone without warning, without even a whispered word. How fast they forsook you when they knew I was coming. Why? I'll hazard a guess. Perhaps it's because daring the powers of Hell is one thing, but facing the inside of Her Majesty's prisons is another and worse. You are old, father Jervis. A word from me, and you'll die on the inside. Let us, therefore, hold high converse with one another. Why did he want *The Magi*?"

She waited, tense. The thrill of the hunt was in her. She had no doubt of it anymore: she was onto her beast. At last. She had him by only a tentacle perhaps, only the tip of a tentacle held between her fingernails, but after all this time it was a true beginning, and she wasn't going to let it go. "It was him, wasn't it?" she couldn't help asking. "At the auction. It was him."

He made no direct answer, but her breath hitched at his reaction. A fearful glance around him; the sign of the cross, the transverse down around his navel, the vertical up to about his chest.

"Come on, then," she said hoarsely. "Out with it, you old fool. For twenty-five years, he lies low. Nothing but little black flashes of him: the body of a child beneath the bogs of northern Finland, another washing up out of the bay in Port-au-Prince; a suicide here and there, a symbol scrawled in blood. Then, suddenly, into the limelight, he steps full-blown before all the world. To buy a painting? Clearly, this was too important a matter to delegate."

The warlock gave her a sullen, sidelong glare. "There are

worse things than to die in prison, Harper." But he was already folding, she could tell. Petulant, with his hands in his pockets, his shoulders up around his hairy ears. "Anyway, it isn't just *The Magi*, is it," he grumbled. "He wants all of it. Of course he does. It's no good without the whole Nativity triptych. *The Magi, The Madonna, The Christ Child*. He wants them all."

He had slunk away from her to the far side of the fire. The puppy stirred and shifted on her shoulder as she stepped after him.

"All right," she said. "Why does he want the triptych, then?"

This brought some of the gleam of nastiness back into his eye. He managed a damp, spiteful smile at her.

"You really don't know, do you? Eh? You're just stumbling in the dark, aren't you? You're walking the same trail he discovered twenty years ago, and you don't even know that it's under your feet."

"Perhaps you could enlighten me," Harper drawled.

"There, that was always your problem," he muttered back at her. "If you ask me, it's the whole flaw in your worldview. You get mired in details. A dead child pops up here, a suicide there, a symbol, a cult in Argentina. You think each thing's just another thing. But they're all one thing, Harper. They were all always one thing."

Harper kept silent, waited. Those who deal in the occult were forever spewing out these grandiose maunderings. She wasn't interested. Little minds think great thoughts, but great minds proceed in the smallest stages. Harper wanted something specific, something she could go forward on.

Her imperturbability seemed to inflame the warlock. He grew insistent.

"Are you blind or just stupid?" he cried. "Do you think he would come out into the open for nothing? *He's onto it, Harper!* He followed the trail and he's onto it."

"Onto what, for heaven's sake?"

"Ach!" He tried again to escape her unbroken gaze. Turned his back on her, waved a hand over his shoulder, walked away. Then whirled on her, cried out angrily, *"The secret, woman! The secret!* Would he show himself at Sotheby's for his health? It's the very secret of the Templars, the secret of the Grail!"

"Oh, come now, Jervis. Really. What's that supposed to mean?"

"Well . . . as for that . . ." he answered darkly. "I know only as much as I'm told."

"And you're told that an eighteenth-century religious triptych contains the secret of the Holy Grail? Really," Harper said again.

"All right. All right. Don't believe me, then. But if you only used your head for two minutes you'd see the sense of it. Do you think Sotheby's puts stolen pictures up on auction? You talked to the Register. They must've run a check on the thing."

Harper gave one of her Zeus-like nods. "They did. The painting had no listed owner. It vanished long before the war."

The warlock clenched his hoary fists at her. "Not vanished, Harper. The coven had it. The Nazi coven."

"Haushofer, you mean? That lot?"

"Yes, yes. Haushofer, of course. But witchcraft ran deep in the Third Reich. High and deep. Right to the top. Don't forget that Haushofer taught Hess. And Hess was imprisoned with Hitler. And Haushofer visited the two men in Lansberg every day they were there." He announced all this proudly. "Haushofer—he knew about the triptych, all right. They all knew there was power in it, anyway. But what? That was the thing. What power? They couldn't crack the code because they didn't know what they were looking for. And then, when the war ended, when the bombers came and the Allied armies and it all came tumbling down around them, Haushofer committed hara-kiri . . ." He opened his hands, spread them. "The triptych was lost."

They were on opposite sides of the fire now. On opposite sides of the stone circle, the light and shadow falling on them from above, racing over them. Harper stood still, frowning, prodigious, the eighth maiden, a boulder of disdain as hushed and hard as the others.

"And you're saying that Iago knows what the Nazis didn't," she said. "He knows what the secret of the triptych is."

"Has done for twenty years," growled Dr. Mormo.

"Then why now? Why has he only come after them now?"

He rolled his eyes at her obtuseness. "Well, he came after them then, of course!" he cried. "He came to me even then. But they were lost behind the Iron Curtain, you see. If any of it had come over on the black market, who would have known it if not me? No, try as he might, he couldn't find them then. It wasn't until the Curtain came down that *The Magi* finally came to light."

"*The Magi*," Harper echoed him. "And the others?"

"The others," said the old man with a shrug. "That's the whole thing, isn't it? That's why he was at the auction, out in the open like that. Whoever has the others, he wanted them to see. To see who they were dealing with. A man who would pay enormous prices for their panels—or who would come and take them by other means." He gave a particularly unpleasant little giggle. "And it's worked, hasn't it," he said. "They're already beginning to nose their way out of the woodwork. Oh yes, they are. They'll all come to Dr. Mormo in the long run, you'll see."

Harper answered nothing, mulling this over. The puppy continued to fidget on her shoulder, started whimpering. It would mess on her cape soon, she thought distantly. And the little girl who'd lost it was probably still awake, still sobbing. No doubt the police would know who she was . . .

"And you say it's all one thing," she said. "Even the cult in Argentina was part of it. Are you suggesting that Iago was searching for these paintings even then?"

"No, no, no," said the warlock sharply. "But it was all part of it, just the same. Part of the secret. Part of the Grail."

The fire clicked and cackled. Jervis, unexpectedly, cackled too. Brought his knuckle to his forehead and rattled it against his skull. "Oh, if you could see your face, Harper. If you could only see your face. You don't think. You don't know. You don't understand what you're dealing with, still. It's not the triptych, or Argentina, or this murder or that. It's not even the Nazis or the war or the Iron Curtain. It's none of it. It's *all* of it." He leaned towards her. The orange flame-glow washed up over his puffy features, his crazy eyes.

"It's the whole clockwork of history," he told her, whispered to her under the moaning of the wind. "That's what you're missing, you blind old woman. The clockwork of history. Tick-tick. Tick-tick!"

2 | From time to time, Sophia woke to find life muted, slow, subaqueous. Whatever the doctors were giving her, it had sent her to Atlantis, submerged her in a world beneath the waves. Through this element, reality passed like a dream and dreams like reality. She traced her own footsteps down corridors of Belham Grange, corridors extending into an ominous infinity. She passed her father's portrait on the wall—the eyes followed her—and she passed another portrait, and that was her father too, as was the next and the next . . .

She went on and on. Passages ran off to the left and right of her, ran off to nowhere. On and on. From one such passage a nurse emerged, a pink phantom, silent and deliberate. Then, suddenly, Sophia was in her bed again, her high hospital bed. Looking down the enormous wavering length of her own sheeted form to the figure gliding by beyond the gleaming steel rail.

"Sister?" Her own voice was like a slow recording. Her lips were parched, her throat was terribly sore.

"You're all right. Just try and get some sleep."

"Where am I?"

Beyond the steel rail was the door—not the orange door of the hospital room but the hidden door at the end of the corridor.

"Mother?"

She was drifting towards it, drifting without volition as if she were floating ghostly above the ground. She did not want to go. She cried out against the irresistible tide.

"It's all right, Sophia, it's all right."

Some cool hand was in hers, comforting. She looked up to see her sister. Laura, her real sister. Her small, sweet, worried face made big and blurry with her tears. Her blond hair tied back in a prim style . . . Perfect for a hospital visit, Sophia noted dimly.

"It's all right," Laura whispered again. "No one knows anything. It's all been kept quiet. Daddy's taken care of the whole stupid business for you."

Sophia moved her lips. "There was so much blood."

"Shh, it's all in the past now, darling. No one knows anything."

Sophia tried to smile and nod. Tried to martial her forces, cut through the sea. She wanted to be clear, to be Sophia again. But the warm undertow dragged her down.

"This is a nightmare," she tried to whisper.

Because it was. The dreaded figure waiting for her, cowled, faceless in the dark at the end of the corridor, black, lifting its cloaked arms to receive her, looming larger and larger—she knew that specter—she did not want to see what she knew—she knew she was dreaming and did not want to dream—but she was drawn on and on by the overpowering tide, on and on down the corridor, past tapestries and portraits obscurely perceived, towards the cowled shape, waiting for her, lifting its arms, coming closer and closer until it slowly, slowly raised its face to her, its gory, empty sockets . . .

He will buy The Magi, *Sophia. At any price.*

The shock woke her up with her heart thundering, her eyes wide. There was gray daylight at the windows. Rain dripping from the branches of the plane trees. The cough and grumble of heavy traffic stopped at a light somewhere below. She rolled her head on the pillow as her pulse slowed. The blank screen of the television stared at her moronically from the bureau. And there beside it—to her vague surprise—was her brother Peter. Slouched in a low-slung armchair, his legs crossed at the knee. Brutally flipping through a copy of *Time Out*.

He caught her movement and saw she was awake. Immediately, he slipped into an attitude as if off the rim of a pool. He became insouciant, droll. He tossed the magazine aside.

"You should take it easy with this suicide business, Sophia," he said. "You might hurt yourself."

She licked her lips. Swallowed painfully. The room gave a nauseating roll. She saw the transparent bag above her, the transparent fluid in it, the tube running down to her wrist. She saw the smeary punters in the print of Cambridge on the blue wall. Everything tilting over. And then her brother again. Wearing the bulky white pullover she had brought him back from Dublin. Looking pale and old beneath his curly black hair. Raw and sore.

"Tell them to stop drugging me, Peter," she mumbled.

"Ah . . ."

"I won't throw myself out the window or anything. Promise."

"Yes, well, the worth of your assurances is a bit low on the exchange just at the moment."

"It's making me ill."

"I'll do what I can, darling. The Great Man, as ever, guides these matters with a more or less inflexible will." He smirked, but his smirk looked painful. He pushed from the chair to stand nonchalantly. Strolled nonchalantly to the window. One hand in the pocket of his jeans, the other tossing about at his belt line. He glanced nonchalantly at the traffic below. He was very nonchalant. "You've led him quite a merry chase these last two days, you know. It hasn't been easy on him. Lying to the media, tranquilizing Mr. Plod.

He's been a busy little knight of the realm indeed." A casual look back at her, a raised eyebrow. "You've developed asthma, by the way. That's how we're explaining things. I thought you should know. We're all running around like mad, telling everyone about poor Sophia's asthma. They send their condolences."

"Poor Sophia," she whispered, trying to help him out, trying to catch his ironical tone. But she was getting woozy again, sleepy, sinking. The waves were rising over her as she went down. She made a noise of exasperation, shook her head in an effort to get her chin up above water.

"It's of great importance to the *gallery*," Peter went on. He had his backside propped on the windowsill now. The slate sky, the fingery branches were behind him. His face was eclipsed. He saluted an imaginary general. "Scandal to be avoided at all costs. The good name to be preserved. As if anyone gave a *shit* about us or the gallery or our good name. Though I suppose it would have made an image for the tabloids, you hanging there."

"Yes," she said. The word stretched out like elastic. Her own voice breathed it back to her from somewhere far away.

"Oh, and we're a bit concerned about your American."

"American . . . ?" She closed her eyes for a second. Yes. That stupid, stupid man. That Richard Storm. She was falling into the image of him. She sucked air in sharply through her nose, forced her eyes open. ". . . oh . . ." she said.

"He *says* he'll be quiet, but he won't take our *money*, thank you very much," said Peter. "I told Father, 'Don't be silly. He's an American. Taking money is what they do, for Christ's sake.' I mean, maybe he doesn't understand English. Perhaps we should wave the notes in front of him and shout, 'Lookee, lookee, money, money.' What sort of name is Storm anyhow?"

It was no good. She was losing her grip, going down. "Don't know . . . Don't know him . . . really . . ."

"Well, he saved the old man's arse at the auction, that's certain."

Her eyes shot open one last time. ". . . auction . . . ?"

But she was irresistibly swept under now. She wanted to call out, but she was just too tired and he was too far away. For a while she thought he was pressing his hand to her cheek. She thought she was smiling. And somewhere above her, she thought she heard his voice again, distant, suddenly bitter.

"Don't worry, Sophe. I'll make the bastards stop poisoning you. They're all a lot of bastards anyway. Bastards."

Then it was Richard Storm who had her, his hand in hers. He was pulling her along over a Rhinehart terrain: ground mist and half-discerned crags against an anemic sky, leaning gravestones, looming ruins. Storm drew her towards the moldering fragment of a wall. She didn't want to go with him. She was supposed to be angry with him, she knew. But she found somehow she trusted him, trusted him completely. And he was laughing, urging her to come along, calling back to her gaily over his shoulder, "Tick-tick! Tick-tick!" Cowled figures in the mist moved, like the mist, around them. One raised its head to watch as they passed. Sophia caught a glimpse of eye sockets drooling blood onto decaying flesh. Then Storm pulled her on. She dug in her heels, but lightly, girlishly, laughing too, unable to resist him. "I was never happy like this in real life," she said. He grinned and nodded and tugged at her. "Tick-tick," he called. They were in vaults—a dream transition. They were in an underground passage. There was dazzling brilliance at the exit to her left, but in here there was only the dark. There were effigies of the dead in niches, crawling with spiders, hung with webs. One effigy was Sophia herself—no, her mother; it must have been her mother because she herself was standing there with Storm beside her, with his arm strong and warm around her shoulders, his body so hot it nearly melted into hers. And they went forward together, approaching the hidden cavity behind the stone. "Do we have to do this?" she asked him. "Won't it be dead?" "Tick-tick," he said. It scared her but she trusted him. Then the climax came in a rushed jumble. They removed the stone. A fanged cobra sprung at her, filled her vision.

She gasped, woke, breathless. Looked. And almost gasped again.

There was Richard Storm. In the flesh. Sitting in the armchair where Peter had sat, hunched forward, his elbows on his knees. A cowboy in faded denim and jeans. His face blunt, rocky, handsome.

Sophia shut her eyes tight and opened them again but, no, unfortunately, he was still there.

He lifted his chin to her. "Hiya, kid. How you feeling?"

For another second or two she could tell herself that she was still confused, still caught between sleep and waking. But she noticed that the drip was gone. And time had passed, night had come; the window was dark, the plane tree branches a black latticework against a perse sky. And her mind was getting sharper every second. The drugs had all but worn off.

And she could no longer delay her rising awareness of a richly excruciating sense of embarrassment.

Storm gave her a lopsided smile. "I came for a rematch,"

he said. He pointed to his nose. "Go on. Throw that right again. I bet I could block that right if I was ready for it."

Sophia burst into tears. Which made things even worse. It was all so humiliating. Mortifying. The thought of herself twirling around in the air, gagging, strangling—in front of a near-total stranger. And now crying like this. She felt like an utter fool—which made her hate him—which only confirmed her vague first impression of him as an irksome American jackass.

"Here," he said. He was beside her, holding out a tissue.

She snatched it from him. Blew her nose. But she wouldn't look at him. She didn't like him looming over her like this, his belt buckle at eye level. She was wearing only a nightgown under the sheet.

"Stop . . . looming," she managed to say, waving her hand at him. She went on crying. The man was an idiot.

"Oh. Sorry. Was I looming? I'll go over here." He thumped over to the window. Thumped down on the sill, crossed his arms on his chest. Bigly. That stupid half-smile was still plastered on his enormous face.

"And don't . . ." She had to blow her nose again, blew it angrily.

"What," he said. "What am I doing now?"

"Don't expect me to thank you," Sophia said. "I didn't want you to help me and I'm not glad you did."

"Yeah, well, tough luck."

"It wasn't any of your business. Why couldn't you just leave me alone?"

"Hey. Guess what. I don't need a reason. You do."

She was ferociously wiping her cheeks, her nostrils, trying to stem the flow, but the tears kept on. She hadn't done this in front of anyone since she was ten years old. She detested him.

"A pretty girl like you," said Storm. "Young. Successful. Smart as hell, anyone can see that. Hanging yourself? Hey, I mean, gimme a break. You got some kind of glitch in your inner life, I mean, Jesus Christ, lady, fix it. Don't go . . ." He didn't finish this, just shook his head, glancing out the window as if seeking moral support from the benighted city.

Sophia could only look at him in disbelief. That he would talk to her like that. As if he even knew her. She felt bitterly conscious just then of the fact that her feet were bare, because she would have taken enormous satisfaction in breaking his head open with the heel of her shoe. As it was, she just lay rigid under the sheets, clenching her soggy tissue in her fist, vibrating with rage at his arrogance and his intrusiveness. Snorting and sniffling, trying with all her will to stop.

Finally, when she felt she could work a sufficient amount of venom into her voice, she said, "Is that what you do with your inner lives in America—fix them?"

"Well, yeah," he said with a shrug. "Why, what's the matter? You don't have psychiatrists in this country? Is that, like, in violation of the Stiff-Upper-Lip Laws or something?"

"No, no, I love it, really, it's a charming idea," she said acidly. "Something wrong with your past, just haul it into the shop and have it fixed. Better yet, get rid of your past altogether. I suppose that's how someone like you ends up with a name like Storm."

Which made him throw back his head and whoop like a spotted hyena. Which almost made her despair. Was there no way to hurt the man's feelings?

"All right," he said, chuckling away like a clown. "All right. You can't fix the past. But you don't kill yourself over it either. Like I said, if the past isn't past, what is? I mean, jeez."

She could only roll her eyes. It really was beyond

frustrating now. Her head was getting all stuffy with crying, and her throat hurt and her temples throbbed and he was sitting there with that gigantic self of his, saying, "If the past isn't past, what is?" and at this point even she wasn't sure whether this was pure American cobblers or a nugget of Buddha-like wisdom.

"Well, you tell me," he went on. "What are you supposed to do with your problems if you don't fix them? Put them in a museum, make them a holiday? What am I missing here?" He was off the window again, his voice rising, his hand wagging at her. "I mean, how could you do a stupid thing like that, a girl like you? What're you, nuts or something?"

"Who on *earth* do you think you're talking to?" she finally blustered, appalled. She now saw clearly that she had attempted to hang entirely the wrong person. "Stop . . . doing that with your hand."

He stopped doing that with his hand. He looked at his hand as if he hadn't noticed it was there before. Then he threw it up in the air. "Man!" he said.

"I mean, who on *earth* do you think you are? I'm sure you're not even supposed to be in here."

He nodded. "You're telling me." Turning back to the window, muttering, "You oughta see the security out there. I felt like Obi-wan Kenobi sneaking around the Death Star."

The man was such an idiot, she almost laughed. He glanced over his shoulder at her.

"What was that? Were you just laughing?"

"No, of course not."

"Are you sure? I thought you were laughing."

"Well, I'm not."

"Well, all right."

For a while then, he stood planted there, his back to her.

His back in the denim jacket, hulking, solid, thick. Like his brain.

Sophia had now stopped crying finally. In fact, she was beginning to feel better all around, more like herself. Cool and ferocious.

So she said, "Well, thank you *so* much for coming to see me, Mr. Storm."

And he had the gall to whoop again, to turn to her, grinning. "Yeah, yeah, yeah. I get it. 'Thank you so much for coming to see me.' That's good. That's Brit-speak for 'Get the hell out,' right?"

"I think it's lovely you're learning to speak the language."

And he laughed again. "That's great. I love that. I wish I could say things like that. 'Thank you *so* much . . .' No, that's great, really, I mean it. It's, like, Rex Harrison or something." He swaggered back to her bedside. "All right, I'm going," he said. "But listen up." And he pointed a finger so close to her face that only her impeccable manners kept her from tearing it off with her teeth. "I like you. A lot. Which is Yank-speak for 'I like you. A lot.' Okay? So don't hang yourself anymore. Okay? It really, really bothers me. You hear what I'm—"

"Oh, for God's sake, would you just leave!" she burst out. And she lashed her face away from him. It was the only way she could keep him from seeing her laugh again. *Don't hang yourself anymore.* Christ, he was ridiculous. She heard his footsteps fading across the floor.

Then something occurred to her. Reluctantly, she looked back. He had just reached the door.

"Wait."

He waited. Still with that ludicrous smirk.

"What happened?" she asked him. "At the auction.

About *The Magi*. Peter said . . . What happened?"

"Don't worry," said Richard Storm. "Like I told your father. I got your girl out of it. They were at half a mil with no sign of stopping."

"Half a . . . half a million pounds?"

"You got it, kid, and it would have gone on forever, too. So I called your lady off."

Once more, Sophia's mind began to cloud, to cloud and roll and throb. "Wait . . . You mean, my father . . . the gallery . . . we didn't buy the painting?"

"That's right. But hey, don't bother to thank me again— I'm already leaving."

"Yes, but who . . . ?" she managed to say after a moment. But he had already gone.

3   "The trouble with Americans is that they're so grotesquely forthright about everything, it's impossible to tell what they're really after."

It was her father, Sir Michael, at the window now, framed by the night-dark panes. Bristling and huge in his black suit. With his red silk handkerchief, red silk tie. Clasping his hands behind his back. Frowning a great frown on his great face.

Sophia, propped up on pillows, leaned over the swing-table pushed up before her. She moved a fork around the chunky white mess on her plate. Still thinking about Richard Storm.

She was becoming depressed again, even more painfully than before. The hospital room was getting her down. It was beginning to hang on her like a leaden shawl. It was a private institution, luxurious as a decent hotel. She had cheery blue walls here. Prints of boaters, skaters. A bright pattern of swallows, crowfoot and water lilies on the curtains. Her own bureau, her own TV. But it was drab, really, she thought, just under the surface. The furniture spat out by some machine somewhere, browned with a cursory coat of factory shellac—it filled her with distaste. And she felt hemmed in by the icy metal of the bed rails. And made nervous by the brisk padding of the nurse's soft shoes out in the hall.

But more than anything, she found the place oppressive with the image of her own suicide. The memory—almost the vision—of her own body dangling from the gallery balcony. That picture inhabited the air around her. Her body turning and struggling there. Seconds from dying—dying by mistake—by a terrible mistake. And then Storm had come.

Storm had come. And shattered the door. And run to her. And hauled her up. She still had the bruise on her upper arm from where he'd gripped her.

"What's he think he's up to?" Sir Michael said. Bouncing on his toes. Popping, simmering. "Hanging about. Sneaking into your room like that. We've offered him money. What does he want?"

She went on toying with her food. Funny, but she knew it would never occur to the Great Man that Storm simply liked her. A lot.

Sir Michael began to pace thoughtfully back and forth across the foot of her bed. Chin down, eyebrows gathered like rain clouds. Musing: "Something American. What do they do over there? Sue each other. Go on chat shows. He can't be thinking of suing us—not in a British court. And I've *offered him money*."

Sophia smiled, thinking of the ridiculous Storm. *Don't*

hang yourself anymore, okay? "He isn't going to sue us."

Sir Michael pulled up right before her. "Good God, you don't think he'd go on a chat show?"

She gave him a look. "No, Daddy."

"I mean, you haven't . . . bared your soul to him or anything."

"Hardly."

"Hm. Good. Still, I don't trust him." He paced back to the window. Stood there, rocking on his heels. Grandly surveying the scene beyond—whatever it was—Sophia didn't know, she hadn't looked. After a moment he said, "He didn't happen to mention the auction by any chance, did he?"

Sophia laid her fork down slowly. She sat back against the pillows. Rolled a tired glance in her father's direction. She saw his face reflected in the pane, a dim, dark, patchy picture of him, the eyes unreadable. And she realized wearily: This was the way they were going to talk about it. This half-spoken, elliptical way. The way they talked about everything. As if the truth were understood between them and need not be spoken aloud. As if the silent subtext were common knowledge. Her whole life she had assumed that this was how people in families did communicate with one another. Yet just now, she found it terribly frustrating. Because she *didn't* know the truth. She didn't understand it at all. She had almost killed herself because she didn't understand it. And she was so tired now. She was tired of subtlety and Endering machinations. She kept thinking about Richard Storm.

"Not really," she answered him thickly. "He said he pulled Jessica off at half a million."

"Yes," he murmured, as if to himself. "Funny he would do that. Impertinent. Funny."

"You didn't want to pay that much for it, did you?"

He only shrugged in answer.

Then there was a long pause. Sophia was so tired of this, so depressed. She did not want to start the whole business again. But it seemed inevitable somehow too. Speaking carefully, she said, "Who finally got it?"

Sir Michael once more lifted his broad shoulders. "Some mystery to it apparently. Fellow delivered a check in the name of some foundation. Children of Hope, I think it was called. The check was perfectly good. But the foundation doesn't seem to exist. No one knows who the man was. No one's ever seen him before."

She looked at him standing there, looked at him a long while. Children of Hope? she thought. And that turned out to be the Devil from Hell? She had almost hanged herself, thinking it was her father, and it was some nonexistent organization? Children of Hope? But then why had Sir Michael wanted *The Magi* so badly? Did he know, had he heard about the murdered Resurrection Men? Why hadn't he spoken to her directly, saved her from what she'd tried to do to herself? Storm had saved her, a stranger. Why hadn't her own father?

"Daddy . . ." she said.

"Anyway, it was just a whim," said Sir Michael. Coming around to face her, cutting her off. "Always liked Rhinehart, thought it would be worth having. Just a whim."

She fell silent, hurt by the lie. He moved to her bedside. Took her hand in his large, spotted paw.

"The important thing is for you to get better. Put all this nonsense out of your mind." He hung over her awkwardly. Touchingly concerned, clumsy, helpless before what he doubtless viewed as her mysteriously feminine inner troubles. "Look," he went on gently, "I don't mean to sound like a thoroughgoing egotist. It's the timing more than anything that suggested it. What I mean is: this ridiculous business at the gallery the other night. It didn't have anything to do with us, did it? With me, I mean?"

Sophia's lips parted and closed several times before she could answer. "You are a thoroughgoing egotist," she said softly then. "No. Don't be ridiculous. It was just one of my bad patches, that's all. It's over now and I feel very silly."

"Ah," he said, straightening at once. Smiling; pleased. "Good. Well. Onward and upward, then." He let her go, clapped his palms together with a hollow report. "Perhaps we'll get the next one."

Called from her own thoughts, she looked up at him distantly. "The next one?"

"Yes. Since the auction, there've been all sorts of rumors that *The Magi* wasn't the only panel of the Rhinehart triptych to turn up in the East. The word is the *Madonna* may be on the market soon."

"The *Madonna*?"

"Yes," said Sir Michael, rubbing his hands. "The rumor is the third bidder—the bidder on the telephone at the auction—has got it, and is looking for a buyer."

"Oh," Sophia said, closing her eyes.

✦

She really was terribly weary of this. And depressed. And alone. *And afraid*—especially as the night wore on towards dawn. It went round and round in her mind. *The Magi*—the *Madonna*—the Resurrection Men—Jon Bremer's butchered eyes . . . She should go to the police—and yet what if that meant her father's arrest—or his ruin? Either one would almost certainly kill him. And she couldn't trust the police anyway. Whoever this Devil from Hell was, Jon Bremer had said he might have contacts on the police. Well, he might have contacts anywhere. She couldn't trust anyone, really, couldn't talk to anyone. Which was nothing new. She never had been able to trust or talk to anyone. She had never confided in a single person her age-old suspicions about Sir Michael, or her childhood memory of that night at Belham Grange. And so it would all just go on and on like this if she didn't stop it. She would be right back in the same nightmare she'd been in for weeks. For years, really. Really, if it came to that, for all her life.

So, as the sky was slowly infused with a tired gray, she rose from her hospital bed. Moved to the window. Divided the curtains with her wrists, reached in between them and lifted the sash. The cold morning air washed in over her, penetrating the thin cotton of her nightgown. She heard tires hissing in rainwater below her. The sough of wind through the plane trees. She raised her eyes to look off down the street.

She was in the old Victorian building's corner turret, the fourth floor. Across the broad intersection, through the branches, over the traffic lights, she could see the Thames glinting dully, seething sluggishly beneath the Chelsea Bridge with an incoming tide. A cormorant flew black over the bridge's white cables, heading towards where the clouds were parting on a feeble dawn.

And she thought: *Yes. The fall from here would do it. That would finish it off for good and all.*

Then there was a *boom* and a *thwack* behind her. The door had flown open, hit the wall. She looked over her shoulder to see Richard Storm amble in, his idiotic smirk screened by a bouquet of roses and freesias, which he held splayed as if he'd just yanked them from a magician's hat.

"Morning, glory," he said. "I'm back—and better than ever. How you feeling?"

"I'm glad you're here, Mr. Storm," said Sophia quietly. "I need your help."

4

Thump-thump. Thump-thump. Thump-thump.

Between the demon Asmodeus and a portrait of Ogopogo, the zeuglodon of Lake Okanagan, Storm had found an empty slice of yellow-striped wall against which to bang his forehead repeatedly. He'd been doing it, with pauses to moan Sophia's name, for more than half an hour now, and it was driving Bernard absolutely around the bend. *Bizarre!*'s factotum was on a sort of dream quest through the Internet, following reports of a pixie who had apparently crossed Hudson Bay from Baffin Island and was now said to be traveling downcountry towards Saskatoon. Rocking on his backless workstation chair, dabbling at his keyboard with one hand, Bernard was currently in electronic communication with a copper miner's daughter named Gwen. She, in turn, was feverishly gathering and transmitting reports that a four-inch-high green glow wearing a forester's cap was busily baking oatcakes in a fallow wheatfield somewhere to the south of her. The whole business required concentration. And to have Storm doing that on the other side of the office—*thump-thump, thump-thump, Sophia, Sophia*—it was crazy-making.

Finally, lifting his angelic features to whatever gods may be, Bernard gave in, logged off. He swiveled around to face the other. Storm was standing with his back to him, hands in the pockets of his jeans, head down, rocking gently to bring his brow into contact with the wall.

"I sense somehow that you're distressed," Bernard said.

Storm glanced over as if he'd only just noticed the factotum was there. "Anguished," he said. "This is how I do anguished."

But, to Bernard's infinite relief, he left off. He wandered gloomily over to the planter in the corner, the one from which some stuffed something stared with goggly eyes. He stood over it, stared back.

Bernard waited, studied him, wistfully. He had already deduced that his American co-worker was ill. Now, seeing him with his sad eyes ringed and his craggy features somehow blurry, overly pale, he was beginning to feel the situation was even worse than he'd imagined. He didn't like this, not a bit. On top of which, he was given to occasional bouts of hypochondria, and hated to think about such things.

"You know what it's like," said Storm, "when you want to—just—pour a woman into a glass and—just—drink her—just drink her down, one gulp, body and soul?"

Bernard made a bemused frown. "Not really. I'm appalling."

"No, hell," said Storm. "Different strokes . . ."

"No, I mean, I'm a *Pauline:* all things to all people. I have died from time to time, I suppose, and worms have certainly eaten me—but not for love."

Storm, who clearly had no idea what Baldy was talking about, merely shrugged. "Well, you're not missing anything, believe me. I swear to God, I don't understand her."

"I've heard that's part of it."

"No, I mean Harper. I don't understand why she told me

to get involved with this. What did she think would happen?"

The factotum didn't answer. One long leg stretched out, he used the heel of his trainer to shift his chair around. He had his own doubts about Harper's motives, but he thought it best for now to keep his opinions to himself.

Storm lifted his eyes suddenly. Looked over the office as if for the first time: over the magazine covers with their photos of strange creatures, over the strange creatures in the aquaria here and there, over the shrieking telamons supporting the fireplace mantelpiece, and the carnivorous cactus panting against the high windows, against the darkling winter sky above World's End.

"What does she, own this place?" he said. "This whole building? Where does she get the money for this?"

Bernard smiled. That was better. He loved gossip. And this was exactly the sort of pertinent question that the man from Hollywood so frequently neglected to ask.

"Ah," he said, settling in, lifting an exquisite hand, "I see she hasn't told you about her father. Her Magwitch . . ."

"Magwitch? What kind of name is that? How can her father be named Magwitch?"

Bernard sighed. "No, no, her father isn't *named* Magwitch . . ."

But just then there was a noise below. Locks and latches rattled. The ground floor door could be heard to crack open. Bernard placed a finger to his lips.

"Do you think it possible that in the reticula of medieval architecture we are seeing the subconscious reconstruction of shell patterns found in the earliest protista?" Harper shouted up to them from the foyer.

The two men shook their heads at one another. By

following the assorted bangs, creaks, rattles and glubs—not to mention her continued shouting—they could clearly follow Harper's progress into the house. She was hanging up her cape in the foyer. She was thudding to the fireside, where she invariably relit her pipe. She was at the butler's tray, pouring herself a glass of water from the pitcher beside the mounted Tatzelwurm.

"Some claim that one planarian which ingests another can then imitate, without instruction, the behavior learned by the victim during its life," she continued—then paused to swallow. Storm pressed the heels of his palms against his temples. Bernard merely rolled his eyes. Harper's labored footsteps now sounded on the stairs, her voice growing louder as she ascended. "We admit the inheritance of instinct," she called, "but could the substance of a more complex memory have been transmitted by more and more complex means until the smithy of a soul contains not just the conscience of its race . . ." She appeared in the doorway, breathless, propped on her stick, her free hand thoughtfully twisting the mouthpiece of her pipe into her chin. ". . . but of all creation?"

"I shouldn't think so," said Bernard.

"Ah," said Harper. "Well, then perhaps we'll go with the cover story on giant leeches."

Crossing the threshold, she let her stick fall against one screaming telamon. Fished a manila envelope from her satchel and humped across the room to stuff it in a pigeonhole on Bernard's workstation. Humped back to the chaise longue in front of the high windows. And, with an enormous groan, sank down onto it.

Through all this, Storm watched her. Bernard watched her. She took her shoes off, massaged her feet, and they watched her do that. She stretched out on the chaise.

Smoothed down the viny print of her dress—a vomitous mess of green leaves and purple grapes. Storm stood with his hands in his pockets and watched her. Bernard sat. Watched her.

"What?" she cried finally. "What? What?"

Storm shook his head, lifted a hand. "How could you do this to her, Harper?"

"Ah." Her pipe had already gone out. She wagged the dead stem at him. "I take it Miss Endering has turned to you for help."

Still shaking his head, he stepped over to the window beside her. Leaned against the wall with one shoulder, staring out into the dusk. "When I was walking to the hospital this morning, I looked up and saw her standing in this, I don't know, this big brick turret-like part of the building. She looked like a fairy princess up there, captured in a tower."

"Ha-ha," said Harper Albright.

"Then, the minute I walked into the room, she said she wanted to meet with me. Tonight. Secretly. She said she didn't want her father to find out." For a moment he squeezed his eyes shut painfully.

But Harper only said, "Good. She has an important story to relate. She's probably been living with it for ages and needs to get it out. I have no doubt she will tell you everything."

"She hardly knows me, Harper."

"Don't be ridiculous. You saved her life. You were absolutely cinematic about it. If she's a princess in a tower, you're a knight in shining armor. Besides which, I strongly suspect she has no one else to trust."

His hand went up again. His tone was one of fierce complaint. "That's what I'm afraid of."

The last light of day flashed on Harper's spectacles, obscured her eyes. But Bernard could see her lined face soften as she looked up at the man. "She's a big girl, young Richard. A grown woman. Tell her the truth, and she can make her own decisions."

Storm rolled over until his back was against the wall. For a second or two his expression was naked, lost, almost childlike. It was precisely moments like this that made Bernard hanker after debauchery—to take the edge off.

"I don't know if I can tell her," said Storm. "I don't know if I can tell her."

They were all silent after that, and it was sad in the room. Storm gazed up at the pendant toplight. Bernard studied his trainer tips, Harper the skull of her pipe. None of them looked at either of the others.

Then Storm pushed off the wall. He moved to the threshold without a word. Stopped there, hands in pockets. Frowned down at the back of Harper's head.

"How could you do this to me then?" he said quietly. "I mean, I was out of it. You know? I was home, babe, I was gone. The cord was cut. I was, like, sailing away and it was all right. You know? Now . . ."

Bernard waited for Harper's answer, but she made none. She went on studying her pipe. And after another moment, Storm walked out.

✦

Then, though—then, when Storm had gone—Harper was on her feet. Padding back and forth in her stockings over the rose pattern of the rug. Tapping her pipestem to her chin again. Murmuring with grim excitement.

"Getting there, Bernard. We're getting there. Tonight,

one night, with what Richard discovers, with what I might find, who knows, we may understand everything. Everything."

Bernard stood abruptly. Paused to recover his accustomed grace. Then wafted off into a connecting storeroom, just out of Harper's sight. He was agitated, and didn't want her to see it.

The storeroom was small, windowless. There were old copies of the magazine stacked up here. Folders of newspaper clippings. Boxes of pencils, razors, layout sheets; a broken wax mangler. Mostly things that Bernard's computer had rendered obsolete, but that Harper nonetheless insisted on keeping. There was also a basin and a small refrigerator with an electric kettle set on top. And bags and boxes of makings for tea, coffee and hot chocolate. A tin of stale digestive biscuits—Bernard munched on one of these as he filled and started the kettle.

He could still hear Harper pacing in the office proper, muttering to herself. "Arrogant, arrogant, yes. He traipsed after his own ego into the limelight. After all these years. A mistake. Finally. Tonight, we'll get at the truth."

Bernard dropped a teabag into each of two black mugs. He regarded the hissing kettle with hooded eyes.

"How long do you think Richard's got to live?" he called in to her after a while.

He heard her footsteps cease. Steam rose around his face as the kettle's switch clicked off.

"I don't know," she answered gruffly then. "My suspicion is he'll need a doctor's care within a year."

Bernard nodded, his stomach souring. Poured the water into the mugs. "And you don't think there's something just a teeny, tiny bit, oh, say—unforgiveable—in using him in this fashion? To gather information from La Endering, I mean, when he's obviously in love with her?"

As the mugs were filled, images formed on their black sides: the white-domed, hollow-eyed faces of aliens. They were etched there in sensitive ink, and the heat made them visible. The mugs were silly toys that *Bizarre!*'s new publisher gave away to subscribers. For some reason, the trick always delighted Harper.

"Ha-ha!" she said when Bernard carried them in to her, presented her with one. She was sitting on the edge of the chaise longue now, had slipped her feet into her shoes again. As Bernard drifted back to his chair, she held the mug to her lips with both hands, huddled over it, blew softly on the steam as it misted her glasses.

"If he is being used, it is not by me," she said finally, when he had seated himself, when he had swiveled around to her. "You said it yourself. It is Storm's coming here that has set things into motion. He is tied intimately to events, and probably has been from the beginning. That story he read at the party, his connection with the girl, even his nonsensical ghost-hunting—all of it has played a part. A hero is led by destiny, Bernard; everyone else is simply dragged along by it. The only question left for Richard Storm is whether or not he is to be the hero of his own life."

"And Endering?"

Harper wagged her head. "If I were she, I would fall in love with him."

"And have her heart broken."

"Have it broken open, yes."

Bernard could no longer contain himself. "God!" he said, setting his mug down by his keyboard with a careless thud. "Talk about arrogant. You're as arrogant as Iago."

Harper nodded slowly. "He works his work, I mine."

The factotum swung away from her, swung round to his computer. Laid a hand here and there aimlessly about the workstation, looking for something to occupy his attention, to keep him from showing his feelings—which he generally hated to do. That was how he came to hit upon the manila folder that Harper had placed in one of his pigeonholes. He drew it out. Opened the clasp. Pulled a page from within.

"So what's this?"

"Ah. Yes. That is what I meant about tonight." Harper set her mug down on an endtable, rose to her feet. She stretched, gathered her pipe, her satchel. "That is a fourteenth-century ballad called 'Young William,' which I recovered from an anthology in the London Library. I translated it from the Middle English for you, in light of your progressive education."

"Cheers."

"I take it to be evidence that my suspicions were correct and that 'Black Annie,' 'The Alchemist's Castle,' and the *Magi* panel were all inspired by a single earlier source, probably English, and probably predating the thirteenth century. The similarities are too obvious to ignore."

"And this strikes you as interesting somehow?"

She had recovered her stick, had paused beside the mantelpiece. Was regarding him sternly from there, her squat figure not much taller than the grotesque telamon howling beside her. "Bernard," she said, drawing out the syllables reprovingly. "Bernard, Bernard. It strikes me as everything. Reason it out. Iago is after the Rhinehart triptych and he doesn't seem to care who knows it. He *wants* people to know it so that the owners of the other two panels will come forward. What does worry him is that someone might find out *exactly what it is* about the triptych that interests him."

"And the answer is buried in all these stories?"

"Exactly. They are the trail, at least—the trail our warlock friend Dr. Mormo kept raving about—a trail of ghost stories, which I suspect led Iago to the triptych in the first place, and which now may lead us to the answer as well."

Bernard examined the ballad, frowned at it.

"That must be it," Harper continued. "You'll notice: Iago did not become concerned with us until I had Jorge unearth 'The Alchemist's Castle'—the one story that forms an essential bridge connecting the tales to the paintings. When I discovered that, he sent his thugs to attack us. Now, if I can continue to follow the story trail to the common source of all these works . . ."

"Then perhaps he'll send his thugs to kill us."

"Hm, well . . . That is what I'm going to find out right now. An oblique note in the anthology said the ballad was connected with a work by none other than the greatest of ghost story writers, M. R. James. So I am going to see Mrs. Ponsonby. And if she can supply me with another link in the chain, and if young Richard can work his way through Miss Endering's defenses . . . who can say?"

With some effort, Bernard had recovered his best languorous manner and was tilted back, stretched out in his chair again, his long lashes veiling his eyes.

"So what do you suppose it is, this secret?" he drawled as Harper turned to go. "This thing that Iago wants, is it some sort of weapony business, you reckon? The key to world domination and suchlike? Has he got some political agenda or something? One of those blueprints for the greater good that are bound in actual practice to make the world a living hell? Because, I mean, if that's all he wants, he may as well break out the champagne: we're already there."

Harper paused long enough on her way to the door to cock an eyebrow at him. "You are too young to be so cynical," she said. "And I am too old and wise. No, I'm certain we're beyond politics now. There are only two things Iago and I have in common. And one is a richly sustaining indifference to the question of personal philosophy. It is completely irrelevant to either of us whether one tortures and kills in the name of racism or brotherhood, oppression or liberty, the devil or God. History is not written by the hand of intent. It's the deeds alone that matter."

"Do you really believe that?"

"I believe nothing."

"Oh."

"Well, then. I'm off."

"A trifle peculiar, perhaps."

"Ha-ha."

"What's the other thing you and Iago have in common?" Bernard murmured wryly—but by the time he murmured it wryly, he had already heard the front door shut, and her stick rapping away over the pavement into the night.

5 Shortly thereafter, Harper grew terribly afraid.

She was in a cab. Squeezing up Drayton Gardens from Fulham Road. Lost in thought. Rubbing her wrinkled chin with a wrinkled hand. Gazing vacantly out past the driver's head through the windscreen, at the headlamps coming towards her through the dark.

Gradually, a phenomenon began to work its way into her consciousness. The taxi was stopping and stitching along the narrow strip of road between parked cars, dodging in slow motion through the oncoming traffic. And it occurred to Harper that a disproportionate amount of that traffic bore weirdly similar license plates. Some combination of the numerals one, three and three kept recurring: 133, 313, 331—two digits, three permutations, over and over.

She knit her brows, sat up, took notice. Her cab was just now reaching Priory Walk. A sprawling brick and stucco building was to her left, an automobile dealership to her right. There were arc lights over the dealership, and streetlamps all along the pavement; the scene was quite well lit. It was perhaps two hundred yards from here to the junction with Old Brompton Road. Not that far. Harper started counting.

Nine cars went by in the time it took her to reach the traffic light on the corner. Of those, four—a Rover, a Volks, a BMW and a Volvo—had the numbers on their plates: 133, 313, 331 and 133 again.

Harper told herself it was only a mild case of synchronicity. Happens all the time, to everyone. And yet, an intuition brought the goosebumps out in force on her arms.

Coincidences happen more frequently, more profoundly, whenever we get close, whenever the trail gets warm again. That was how Bernard had put it. *Recurring numbers, accidental meetings, unlikely chains of events. They're like the spoor of our quarry.*

Now she was watching for it—which complicated matters. Were the number combinations actually appearing more often, or was her attention picking them out, excluding others?

In either case, as the cab wove through the backroads of South Kensington, the phenomenon abated for a while. Harper began to relax, began to shrug it off.

Then the taxi broke out onto Kensington High Street. A

newsie near Marks and Spencers hawked the late edition of the *Standard:* "1:33 to Nottingham Derails." The taxi climbed up Kensington Church Street, and the price tag of a brass curfew seemed to stand out from the window of an antique shop: £313. The cab began traveling faster now, traveling farther north into Notting Hill. Harper looked up at the spotlit charity thermometer under the steeple of St. Peter's . . .

She found herself shuddering, found herself thinking against her will: *Near. He is very near.*

A few moments later, the cab slid over to the curb. Stopped.

"Here we are," said the driver, smiling round at her. "One-three-three Portobello Road."

✦

Rose Ponsonby lowered her ninety-year-old frame into the purple pillows on the settee, and her cats swarmed over her. They mewed and nuzzled her, flexed and purred. Rose had to hold her cup and saucer well above their heads as she took a dainty nibble of her biscuit.

"I myself believe the severing of the jugular to be decidedly orgasmic," she said sweetly. Her voice was high and tremulous and creaky. "But the other ladies fell out over the use of teeth, you see. Margaret was very disagreeable and insisted they were entirely phallic, while Joan—who is getting on and can no longer hear quite as well as she used to—was shouting terribly loudly that their phallic qualities were a mere screen to protect the vulgar mind from the obviously vaginal threat of the fanged mouth." She chuckled happily. "I do so love discussing *theories,* don't you? Pointless hostility is such a wonderful stimulant, I find."

"Yes, yes, charming, charming," Harper muttered—but her mind was elsewhere. The tea in her blue willow cup was untouched, the biscuit on her plate untasted. She had been alternately tamping and lighting the tobacco in her meerschaum skull for the last ten minutes, but she hadn't actually smoked the pipe at all. She was perched on the edge of an ancient pink sewing chair, a black Manx glued around one of her veiny ankles. Her eyes were darting nervously, continuously about the small parlor.

It was a room filled with books, shelves of books, stacks of books, clogging the fireplace, overflowing from the mantelpiece. And with the bay window covered by heavy green drapes, and the round tea table and its mismatched cushioned chairs virtually filling whatever floor space was left, Harper was beginning to feel closed in, clammy, claustrophobic. Because she kept hitting on little occurrences, dangerous little events. The miniature mantelpiece clock, for instance, was stopped at 3:31. A disordered pile of library books among the tea things were all from the section on the supernatural, all bearing the index numbers 133. A little bust of Constantine stood in one corner of the floor beside a sleeping Persian. And why on earth Constantine? Harper couldn't help wondering. And she couldn't help noticing that its inscription read, *In Hoc Signo Vinces*, part of the vision that the emperor saw in 312 A.D., and that caused him to take the cross a year later.

"But you wanted to talk about Monty," said Rose Ponsonby. "Get off there, you naughty things," she added, as a tiger and a tortoiseshell leapt up on the table and butted heads over the teapot. "He's upstairs, you know—Monty—but I doubt he'll come down. He hasn't, I'm afraid, since Julia Fitzroy-Leeman-St. John insulted him last autumn.

She asked him why he hasn't been more malevolent since he died—because the revenants in his own stories were always such horrid pills, you know. As if dear Monty could be malevolent if he tried." She cooed this, stroking a Maltese curled up in her lap. "The truth is Julia has always been jealous of his fondness for me."

"Yes, hm, ha-ha," Harper murmured, lifting her teacup, touching the cold tea to her lips. A newspaper wedged between two books in a tall stack displayed its browning folio line: *Friday, March 13, 1992*. Harper felt a cool sheen of sweat at her temples. She half expected Iago's minions to burst right through the door, to kidnap her where she sat.

Rose Ponsonby loosed an elaborate sigh. Pensively touched the silver bun at the back of her head. A long tabby stretched up the shapeless front of her, blinked a greeting into her face. "We were just reminiscing about the old days, Monty and I, the days before the Great War, before the Great War swept the world away. I was barely born, of course, but Monty remembers. He was Dean of Kings College Cambridge, as you know, and I was getting him to talk about the Christmases there, the famous Christmas Eves."

Harper frowned and grumbled impatiently as the old woman went off into a fugue state: smiling to herself, rocking slightly in her chair, stroking the cats that all but covered her. Harper, meanwhile, noticed an apparent phone number scrawled on a piece of paper atop a lamp stand: 313- . . . and the rest covered over with flotsam.

"There would be services first in the beautiful chapel," Rose Ponsonby said. "Then dinner and hot spiced beer and a game of cards. And then a select group would retire to Monty's rooms. And there, finally, finally," she went on, leaning forward over the cats in her lap with brightening eyes, "Monty would go into his bedroom and come out with his latest manuscript. And he would blow out all the candles except for one. And he would sit in his great wing chair with that one candle beside him and his manuscript in his hand— and he would begin to read. Oh, imagine, Harper, imagine—to be the first to hear those great stories. 'The Ash Tree' or 'Abbot Thomas.' Or 'Whistle and I'll Come to You, My Lad.' Those great ghost stories. The greatest ever written, I believe. And now to be a ghost himself, poor dear . . ." She shook her head, sighed again, another elaborate sigh.

Harper's cup rattled against her saucer as she set them down on the table. She seized her pipe and began once more to tamp it furiously. But she knew her friend could not be rushed.

Rose Ponsonby poured herself just another splash of tea. Gave it a speculative taste. Said: "Ah!" Then: "Robert Hughes was at several of those readings, you know."

Harper stopped tamping her pipe. Stopped casting anxious glances here and there. She gave all her attention to the other woman, to the slack, sagging face in the yellow light of the fringed lantern above them.

"Robert Hughes," Harper said slowly. "The author of 'Black Annie'?"

"Well, yes, dear, you wanted to know about the 'Young William' ballad, didn't you? It was Hughes who brought Monty the illuminated manuscript on which the ballad was based. A very nice young chap he was too, Monty says. And even at the time, of course, not without literary ambitions of his own. Anyway, this illuminated manuscript. It was done by one of the monks at Belham Abbey in Buckinghamshire apparently, and had somehow found its way to Germany after the Dissolution of the monasteries. A friend of Hughes's had only recently rediscovered it there and brought it back to England and so Hughes showed it to Monty, who was, of course, one of the great medieval scholars of his age. Oh, Monty can still be very cross on the subject of the Dissolution, let me tell you. Especially in regards to the frightful carelessness about the books, you see. Aside from the most cursory listing by Leland, King Henry took absolutely no care whatsoever to preserve the monastery books! Isn't that awful? All those lovely illustrated manuscripts that the dear monks took such pains over—lost, just lost. It upsets Monty quite terribly; I don't even like to mention it in front of him."

"No doubt," Harper murmured, chewing her pipestem with great vigor. "And so you say Hughes somehow came into possession of this illuminated manuscript. And gave it to James. And James based a ghost story on it?"

"Oh, no, no, no, no!" cried Rose Ponsonby in her high screak. "*Mr. Hughes* based his dear little ghost story on it. That one you mentioned: 'Black Annie.' That was inspired by the medieval manuscript. All Monty did was translate the manuscript itself. From the Latin, you know. He had thought to publish his translation in the *Cambridge Antiquary Society Publication*, but doubts about its provenance prevented him. And, of course, he considered it far too shocking for his Western Railway guide to the abbeys. So it was never published at all."

Harper had now leaned so far to the edge of her sewing chair that she was in danger of slipping off. She peered eagerly through her glasses at Rose Ponsonby. "Rose. My love. What happened to this manuscript? The one written by the dear monk and so forth. The one from Belham Abbey."

"Yes," said Rose, wistfully lifting her chin. "It was put in the British Museum."

"Ah."

"And destroyed, I'm afraid, on the tenth of May, 1941. German bombs, you know. It was burned along with two hundred and fifty thousand other books. A terrible loss."

Harper felt her throat going dry. "Yes. No doubt. And what about James's translation?"

"Oh, that was in the library at Kings."

"But . . ."

"But it was stolen, apparently, some twenty years ago."

"I see." Harper swallowed—which was getting to be hard work. She reached under her spectacles, rubbed her eyes. "So—as I understand it—this manuscript from Belham Abbey no longer exists. There is now no copy of either the original or of James's translation."

"Well, except for this one, of course," said Rose Ponsonby. And she leaned forward—three cats falling from her to plop onto the carpet. She tugged a manila envelope out from under a stack of books by her feet. Lifted it. And presented it to Harper across the tea table.

Harper seized it with a trembling hand. "This is a copy of James's translation?"

"Well, no, not exactly," said Rose. "Monty was kind enough to dictate this to me some time ago when I expressed an interest in it during one of our conversations. But you can be sure I wrote it all down quite faithfully."

Harper closed one eye, examined her friend. "The ghost of M. R. James dictated this to you."

"Oh, it's all right," said Rose Ponsonby. "His memory is quite, quite prodigious, you know. And anyway," she added with a naughty little hoist of her shoulders, "I checked it against the original, many years ago at Kings, before the manuscript was stolen. And what do you think? It was exactly right. Why, it was absolutely word for word."

✦

Had Harper been less excited, she would probably have been more alert to the danger she already knew was pressing in around her. But as tense as she'd been, as wary, every other thought was now pushed aside by the realization of what she had in her possession: the source; the last ghost story. Secreted in a hidden pouch within her cape was the translation of the document she believed had inspired 'Black Annie,' 'The Alchemist's Castle,' the ballad of 'Young William,' and the Rhinehart triptych itself. This, she believed, was what Iago had discovered twenty years ago, what had started him on the triptych's trail. And now, all at once, it had simply been placed into her hands. She could think of nothing else but getting home to read it.

Hunched against the night chill, she trundled down the short path in front of Rose Ponsonby's dainty little house. A cortege of cats danced attendance on her as far as the picket gate. Rose waved from the doorway. Then the cats disbanded and Rose Ponsonby withdrew. The door closed and Harper was alone on the Portobello Road.

Her head bent in contemplation, her hat pulled low across her brows, her stick rapping the pavement, she walked beside the empty, narrow street. A grim brick housing estate hulked in the shadows to one side of her, a row of modest houses stood on the other. A streetlamp passed over her head. She passed through its glow—and then out of it into darkness.

And a cab pulled up slowly behind her.

If she had been less excited, if she had been more alert, she would have noticed. That it had been following her, moving along with her. That it sidled up to her now only as she stepped into an all-but-deserted stretch of shuttered antique shops and abandoned stores.

As it was, she was brought out of her meditation when the beams of the taxi's headlamps entered her peripheral vision. Turning to discover the cab, she smiled at her luck and raised her hand to hail it.

The cab moved to the curb alongside her and stopped. The front window came down. Harper leaned into it. The driver, on the other side of the car, tilted back so that his face was obscured by the night.

"World's End," Harper said.

"Absolutely right, darling," said the driver.

She climbed into the back, settled into the seat. Set the tip of her stick against the floor between her feet, rested both her hands atop the carved dragon's head, rested her chin upon her knuckles. And she sank deep into thought again as the cab pulled away.

Her thought was so deep, in fact, that it was many minutes before she realized what was happening. By that time the taxi had strayed from any possible route into her neighborhood. Instead, through a series of sharp jolts and turns, it had veered off into the backstreets of Kensington. And Harper, furiously discussing with herself the long and complex history of Anglo-German cultural exchanges— from the Celtic migrations to the dropping of bombs on the British Museum—glanced up in complete astonishment to find herself passing eastward under the Royal Albert Hall.

She straightened. Her eyes went quickly to the plaque fastened on the seat in front of her: *The number of this cab is*

331. Suddenly more frightened than she had been since she could well remember, she lifted her gaze directly to the rearview mirror.

And she saw the burning malice of the driver's reflected stare. Saw his scarred mouth twisted into a grin of jeering bitterness and cruelty.

Harper could only gape another long moment at that face—the face of the man who had attacked her outside The Sign of the Crane.

The taxi's doors and windows—as she discovered a moment later—were all securely locked.

6 Not far away, on Waterloo Bridge, went Richard Storm, his heart leaden. The city; the city—the Big Smoke, the gray lady, London—so beautiful all around him: it was tearing him apart. *Look, look at it!* he thought. The dome of St. Paul's blossoming into a haze of spotlight to the east. A flock of birds wheeling and diving in perfect harmony around it, brushing their balletic patterns on the dew of night. The Houses of Parliament at his other shoulder—the clock tower, finials, spires and fletch spearing and doodling on the dark. And the bridges launching themselves over the river. And the lights hung like bunting above the riverside walk. The ships, towers, domes, theaters and temples—all this crushed him as he barged south across the water, his hands in his trench-coat pockets, his soul racked with longing.

Because he wanted to be here a lifetime and he didn't have a lifetime left. Because he wanted to be here with Sophia, wanted the churches and the bridges and the spires to be the backdrop for their kisses and intimate conversations.

And he couldn't even run the movie of it in his mind because it was so impossible, because the impossibility hurt too much. He kicked the pavement as he went, butted the cold, damp air. He had been free! he kept telling himself. He had been out of it. He had cut himself loose from life and desire. He'd been Buddha. He'd been Humphrey Bogart in *Casablanca*. The Goodbye Guy. He had been ready to go. Now this.

Trolls, he thought. That's what it was. Religious people believed God ran the world. Atheists figured it was indifferent nature. But it was trolls. Sadistic little homunculi in leather jackets with lots of zippers. Hiding behind the scrim of being. Working the machinery to maximize human suffering for their own amusement. Thumbing their noses, wagging their puds. He could almost hear them laughing at him.

Yeah, and they were good, sweetheart. They were real good at their jobs. When he'd crossed the bridge, when he reached the southern embankment, when he saw Sophia there—the exquisite arrow of pain that went through him: it was a masterpiece of natural cruelty. Fucking trolls.

She was leaning against the stone balustrade, under a string of lights. Looking quietly down at the muddy banks of the Thames. She straightened and turned as he approached her. Her cheeks were pink with cold above the lifted collar of her navy coat. A kiss-me curl was blowing from beneath the silken kerchief on her hair. She was as he'd seen her first, cool and superior. Her stance relaxed but straight. The line of her mouth firm, faintly ironic, faintly smiling. A ball of white vapor broke from his lips as the full effect struck him.

He reached her. They stood at a loss for words. Then she extended a small, delicate hand and shook his briskly.

"Thank you for coming, Mr. Storm," she said.

They walked in silence together above the Thames. The gulls crying, sailing, landing. The efficient, imperial skyline of Whitehall across the way. The jagged concrete wedges of the theater complex hanging over them. Storm's mind raced, searching for something to say. But he had only one thing to say and he couldn't bring himself to say it. He could no more speak of his illness to her than a married man, feeling as he did, could have mentioned his wife; it would have killed the illusion of possibility.

So they strolled and he stole glances at her, watching her organize her thoughts. Then, finally, she stopped. He stopped. She looked up at him.

"I'm afraid . . ." she said. And all at once, she started laughing.

Bewildered, Storm smiled, waited.

She tried again. "I'm afraid I . . ." She covered her mouth with her hand. Her shoulders shook. She fought the laughter off. "I'm afraid I . . ." But it broke out again, high, musical peals. She waved quickly at the air as if to erase them. "I'm afraid . . ." She was overcome with laughter. She veered away from him, staggered towards the balustrade. Storm, still puzzled, still smiling dopily, scratched his head. Sophia hugged herself, giggling. Glanced her apologies at him but was laughing too hard to speak. She hid her face behind her arms, struggled to compose herself again. Lowered her arms. Said, "I'm afraid I've made rather a bad first impression . . ." But that was as far as she got. The laughter crippled her. She fell back against the balustrade, slapped the top of it. Her whole body quaked as she laughed.

Storm went on grinning blankly, went on waiting. Watched her laughing, his hands in his trench-coat pockets.

Life, sex, money, springtime, his own skin—he had never loved anything so much. He had never really even understood that it could happen. Like this, like a song. Like a really bad, clichéd song. One of those songs that went: *I never kneeeeew—that love could be so truuuuue—until I met yoooooou . . .* That kind of thing. And what was worse—what was potentially disastrous—was that if she went on leaning there, against the balustrade, against the background of the city, went on leaning there, laughing, red-cheeked, he was actually going to start singing that song, or one very much like it, right there, right then, out loud. Oh, that would be a bad, bad thing, he knew. But the urge was strong upon him, almost irresistible. And he suddenly realized: here he was, Richard Storm, of Hollywood, of America, of the twentieth century's end, of the planet Earth—and there was poverty and race hatred and terrorism and those horrible nose rings girls were wearing and Western culture was probably in free fall and people said words like *fart* on network television— and here he was, standing in his own sad body—his own rapidly decaying body—*and there was a song in his heart!*

Good Christ, if he didn't kiss this woman soon, he was going to explode.

"Oh!" said Sophia Endering finally—finally exhausted, finally tapped out. Holding her cheeks between her palms, rocking her head wearily. "Oh. I don't know why every time I'm around you I'm reduced to such absolute *imbecility*!" She wiped her eyes. She stared at her feet, at the concrete under her feet. She shivered. The laughter had all blown out of her. "The very first time I saw you I spilled my wine all over the place. And the next thing you know I'm jumping off a balcony with a belt around my neck. And then I punch you, and then I'm in hospital, crying like a baby. And now I'm laughing like a complete idiot. A bad impression! You must think I'm stark, staring mad."

She raised her face to his for an answer, but he said nothing; he could think of no verbal equivalent to lifting her in his arms and carrying her away to a castle in the clouds.

"But you see, the thing of it is," she went on helplessly, "that that's exactly why . . ." She narrowed her eyes, trying to catch the idea, phrase it. "That's exactly why I wanted to talk to you, I think. To see you. So badly. Really. Because everyone else—yah?—well, I don't know how to put it without sounding terribly egotistical, but everyone else thinks . . . I don't *do* those sorts of things. Everyone else thinks I've got everything under complete control. All the time. And when I lose control, when I do do something irrational, everyone just ignores it. So it's as if I hadn't done it at all. And now here you are, and you must think at this point that I never do anything else. You must think: Oh yes, Sophia Endering, she's that absolutely insane girl who's always throwing herself off balconies and so forth. Crazy old Sophia, you must think—I don't know what you must think of me, actually. But here you are, you know? And there you were in hospital. And you said . . . you liked me . . ." She averted her eyes, embarrassed. "I know it's absurd—it sounds absurd even to me as I say it—but you said you liked me and it just seems rather remarkable to me at this point that you should. That anyone should." She drew a long breath of the damp air, held it; braced herself. "And so I wanted to see you. To talk to you. It's all got so confusing that I wanted to explain things to somebody who won't . . . hate me for them afterwards. Is that . . . is that all right? Do you mind?"

Storm started singing.

"Yooooou dooooo something to meeeee," he sang,

"something that simply mystifiiiies meee."

Sophia's jaw dropped. She stared at him.

"Tell meeee why should it beeeee," sang Storm. "You have the power to hypnotiiiiize meeeee. Let meeeeee live 'neath your spell. Do do that voodoo that you do so well. 'Cause yoooou. Doooo. Something to meeee—that noooobody else can dooo. 'Cept you," he added as a jazzy little flourish of his own and then brought it on home with, "That noooobody else can doooo."

"I . . . Well . . . I . . ." said Sophia. And then she smiled at him.

Storm stepped forward, took her by the shoulders, and kissed her.

He hadn't been in the movie business for nothing.

+

"Look, I'm no good at sex," Sophia said. "I suppose that's very important to you, being a man and everything."

Sex? Storm thought. Sex? Here they were. Here they actually were, walking back across Waterloo Bridge. With St. Paul's behind her, and the wheeling birds and the backdrop of London. And her eyes were hectic with his kisses, and he could feel her body tense and then yield every time he took her to him, and her face was turned up to his, confused and appealing.

"Couldn't I just look at you for now?" he said. "Like that, against the dome, with those birds?"

She glanced over at them vaguely. "Dome?" Which presented her cheek to him, so he brushed it with his lips. "It's just . . ." She turned back, bringing her lips to his. She held him off gently, her fingertips on his face. So he kissed her fingertips. "It's just that people think . . . Men are always . . . There are just all these *things* I have to tell someone. About me. I have to . . ."

He gathered her up again, felt her tense again, yield again, and kissed her a long time, deeply. He was having an insight. An erection and an insight, both profound. No, no, his insight was saying, no, no. Not *trolls*. You idiot. How could you ever have thought it was trolls? This incredible, this resplendent city; this cathedral in the mists of night; this bracing winter breeze, those stars; this flesh, this flesh—this vehicle for bringing two souls together at the mouth, at the loins: it's the work of fucking Santa Claus, Jackson! Even Death; even Death was sweet in that it made a moment out of this, which was too fabulous to last for more. That Claus, what a man, you could count on him to get the whole thing perfect.

"Then tell me," he said, breaking away, coming up for air. She was hankering after him now, following after his lips with hers. "Tell me everything. Tell me why you tried to kill yourself. How could you? How could you do it, Sophie? I was so mad, I was so crazy. I wanted to slug you. I *would've* slugged you if you hadn't slugged me first."

She laughed at him, patted his cheek. They let each other go. She moved to the bridge railing, looked down into the streak of glimmering light on the black water. She shuddered once, so that he wanted to hold her again, but he restrained himself, waited.

"I have these black patches," she said. She made a face. "That's what we call them. In my family. Sophia's black patches. It's the oddest feeling. Everything gets very heavy and sort of brown and I feel thoroughly detached from it all and superior and miserable at the same time. I know everything's the same as it was before, but it's all just—*blah* somehow suddenly, yah? I feel funny telling you this. We never talk about it."

Storm sniffed. His nose was beginning to run with the cold. "Who never talks about it?"

"We . . . you know, my family. They'd be horrified if they knew I was telling you. An outsider." She smiled, as if at a fond memory. "Once I even ran my father's car off the hard shoulder of the M4 at about ninety miles an hour. There was a dreadful row. The police came . . . Daddy was browned off something chronic. We *never* talk about that!"

Distracted, Storm took a quick, secret swipe at his nostril. He didn't want her to see him streaming. He wanted to be perfect in her sight. "Is that all it was? You got depressed?"

"No," she said, after a moment. "There was something else." She studied the water again and he studied her, surprised at how hard it was for her simply to speak to him, to tell, wondering at it. "There are these people. They call themselves resurrectionists. Most of them are just professors and dealers and so on. But some of them operate more like . . . like spies and suchlike, in secret. Basically, they try to find the artworks that were plundered during the war. They try to recover them, get them back to their rightful owners. There are still thousands of them, masterpieces, missing, lost. It can be dangerous getting at them, you know, because the people who deal in them tend to be . . . unsavory, of course. Fascists, neo-Nazis. Or just thieves." She looked at him directly, forcefully. As if it were an effort for her to do that too. And Storm kept wondering at it, thinking about it, how hard it was for her. "That night, after the party where you read that . . . that ghost story. One of them approached me. Outside. A man named Jon Bremer. He said that people had been killed because someone was trying to get *The Magi*— the Rhinehart panel, the one—"

"Yeah, yeah."

"And that he had arranged to have it auctioned, here, in

England, with the idea that it might draw the murderer out into the open."

Jacob Hope, Storm thought. The Iago guy. The resurrectionist had obviously been right. But he waited to hear what she would say.

"And then he was killed, Bremer, that same night. They found his body in the river." She inclined her head towards the water below. "And then my father told me we should buy the painting and I was in one of my black patches and I thought maybe he was responsible . . . for Bremer . . . for something. I don't know what I thought now."

Storm, pressing his arms close to himself against the cold, dug his hands deep in his pockets. Found, to his great relief, a crumpled Kleenex. Wiped his nose.

"Poor thing, you're freezing," said Sophia.

Shivering, he waved this off. "But did you know this guy, this Bremer?"

"No. I'd never met him before."

"And he just came to you? Out of nowhere like that? Because you're, like, a Rhinehart expert? What."

He knew at once it was the right question—he almost began to understand. He saw how she looked down, began to walk off, along the bridge, so that he had to follow behind her.

"No," she said. "No, the thing is . . ." She stopped. They stood in the wind face to face, hands in pockets, both shivering now. "The thing is, I've done a few favors for the resurrectionists before. They're so awfully . . . decent, you know. Germans mostly. Very earnest, idealistic. Trying to set things right about it all. They like to bring works into England, because the laws on ownership here are much more stringent. Most countries, if you buy something in good faith, it's more or less yours, but here, if the work is stolen, the original owner has the stronger claim. So sometimes, when things were difficult for them, I've offered to help because . . . well, because . . ."

And Storm finally got it. Spoke it without thinking, "Because you're trying to make up for your father," he said.

She made a noise. Looked up with her lips parted in surprise and her head faintly shaking. Made a whispery "Oh," of such relief and gratitude that it went right through him. He reached for her. Drew her to him, drew her head against his chest.

"You're right," he said. "I am freezing."

✦

"There's been nothing for years," she told him. "Nothing definite. But I've always known."

They were in the American Bar now, at the Savoy Hotel. Shoulder to shoulder in a corner banquette. He aching towards her, muzzy with her scent, with the light in her hair. In a confusion of guilt and desire: He had to tell her, to tell her the truth before it went too far. But he was still listening, thinking, trying to work it out, his Diet Coke undrunk before him.

The piano man was hammering out "If Love Were All" as if it were a march. But the piano was on the other side of the large room. It was quiet in their little section. The lights were soft. The waiters, the other diners were far away among the neat laquered tables and the huge stuffed chairs.

Sophia was gazing at nothing. Rolling a G&T between her palms, the ice melting. She seemed almost dazed, resigned to the flow of her story.

"I don't even know when I first heard them—the rumors," she said. "I can't remember anyone ever saying a word to me.

Not directly. It was just always in the air somehow. That Daddy had got rich off black-market art from the war. That everything we had was somehow . . . tainted, you know." She looked at him, added quickly: "There's never been anything dodgy on my watch. Not ever." Storm didn't let his gaze waver or darken. So she went on: "It's just . . . now and then . . . I don't know. I'd find an entry in some account I don't control and I'd start to wonder. Or . . ." He saw her mouth twist with distaste. "Once or twice, someone's approached me. At the gallery. Someone not quite . . . savory. Sometimes someone like that would speak to me . . . *familiarly*, if you see what I mean. As if they expected me to do something for them, as if it were understood." She pulled into herself as if a spider had walked across her hand. "No one's ever done it twice, though. No one." She glanced at him. He breathed her in. He loved her eyes: besieged, alone, unyielding. He thought he saw almost everything now. "You probably think I should have done something, said something. But one doesn't. In my family. And anyway . . ." It hurt him to see her face pull down, her mouth pull down convulsively. "It would've killed him. Any hint of scandal. Even just to know for certain that I knew . . . it would've killed him. I couldn't have stood it." She closed her eyes a moment. "I always took care of him, you see. After my mother died. My sister got married and my brother . . . well, of course, he wasn't interested. And Daddy was always so helpless about the little things. 'Where have I left my diary, Sophia?' 'Where is my dinner jacket?' I think it was the one area in which we could communicate, really. And then at the gallery . . ." She let her drink go, drummed the surface of the table softly with her fist. "It's all so long ago. The war. What does it matter now? I mean, at the end of the day—at the end of the day, it's only *art,* isn't it? It's only paintings he's dealing in. It isn't as if he ever killed anyone."

"Then why were you so ready to believe he was the guy the resurrectionists were looking for?" said Storm at once.

"I . . . Well, it was just . . ." She looked at him, pleading.

"Tell me what happened to your mom," he said.

Sophia covered her face with her hands.

✦

" 'My heart swims in blood because my legion of sins has made a monster of me in God's holy eyes,' " she said wistfully. "How did you know it was my favorite?"

"Hey, with catchy lyrics like that, how could I go wrong?" he said.

He had put the CD of Bach cantatas on her stereo. Had selected it from between the oversized art books on the tall shelves. Sophia sat on the sofa and watched him, her smile ironical, her eyes defenseless. Now, as the soprano sang the lilting recitative—*Mein herze schwimmt im blut weil mich der sunden brut in Gottes heilgen augen zum ungeheuer macht*—he was moving from window to window, drawing the curtains closed. Despite her smile, he understood that she was in his hands now, had given herself over to him. He moved around her flat as if he owned it. Crossing the airy room to the fireplace. Kneeling to work the cock, to touch a match to the gas nozzle, bringing a low flame up between the panels of William Morris tiles. And she sat still, watched. Defenseless.

"It's just like Laura—my sister—it's just like her to have put them all back," she said dryly, only a faint quaver of suppressed hysteria in her voice. "The CDs. I posted them to her before I . . . before I went to the gallery that night. She couldn't just return them, you know. Everything had to be just as it was, so we wouldn't have to talk about it."

"You want a drink, you want another gin?"

He was at the little cherrywood cabinet in the corner now. Trying to figure out the latchwork hidden in the Asian-style carvings.

"No. No, I've had enough," she said.

"Good. I can't figure out how to open this thing anyway."

The cushioned armchair was by the fire, across from the sofa, facing it. He went to it, sat there, to put some distance between them, to keep his mind as clear as he could. Still, she suddenly seemed awfully small and forlorn, all alone there on the sofa. Under the wide white wall between the windows. There was a large framed exhibition poster over her head. Two men looking off towards the moon, from a Berlin show of Caspar Friedrich. He thought of her picking the poster out, framing it, hanging it carefully. It made him sad for her, for her lonely life.

He leaned forward uncomfortably, working his hands together between his knees. "So . . ." he said.

"So she killed herself," said Sophia, and laughed. "Which was a bit of a bore."

"Ah, come on!" He went off so loudly, sat back so roughly in his chair that she winced. " 'A bit of a bore about dear Mother.' Gimme a break here, Sophie-girl. Christ."

"I'm sorry." She tried to regroup, re-present herself, but only managed to look so lost to him that he wanted to fling himself at her feet. "It's just we don't . . . I've never really spoken to anyone about it."

"Well, speak to me," he said, more gently. "Just tell me. Okay?"

Apparently it was—okay—because Sophie-girl did. Drifting into that dazy passivity again. Speaking as from a dream, the long-dammed current of the tale flowing out of her, seeming more alive than she.

"I hardly remember her. Except her smiling. Sitting in a chair, watching me play with Nanny in the garden. I know she loved the Grange, our house. Her family, her family history. It was very important to her. Fulfilling her responsibilities, you know. To our tenants, the community and so on. Everyone says she was just wonderful. Very warm, very charitable, kind. And fun—she liked shows and music. Oh, and the cinema—she adored Hollywood films. She had a wonderful sense of humor . . . You get left with that, traits like that, words . . . They don't really tell one very much, do they? But I have . . . I used to have photographs. And she seemed . . . There was something lovely there, generous. People say she balanced my father. I can imagine that. He's so definite about everything. Very old guard, very conservative. Peter—my brother—says Mother used to tease him about it, bring him out of it. I've tried to do that sometimes, but . . ." She shook her head, shook this off, still gazing away. She tried again to adopt a more businesslike tone, her usual tone. "Apparently people say she got very depressed after each of the children was born. What we would call post-natal depression nowadays. But back then . . . I don't know. I don't know why she did it, really. Killed herself. Sometimes I feel quite cross with her about it. I suppose that's awful of me."

She betrayed herself with a quick glance at him—a glance to see if he thought it was awful too.

"It's just natural, kid," he said. "It's just one of those things people feel."

The blood rushed to her cheeks. *Auf diese schmerzensreu fallt mir alsdenn dies trostwort bei,* the soprano sang on the stereo.

"As I say, no one will ever talk about it," Sophia went on. "Certainly not my father, and he's the only one who might know."

Storm rested his head on his hand, between thumb and forefinger, his elbow on the arm of his chair. He was growing careful now. He composed his expression carefully. He knew—he sensed at least—how exposed to him she was, how delicate. *If ever she is deprived of her monumental defenses, you will find her to be as fragile as bliss—and every bit as precious.* Storm even breathed carefully, tense. "But—what?" he said. "You think your mother's suicide might have had something to do with your father's . . . with his business dealings."

"No," she said quickly. Then, vaguely, she waved her hand. "I don't know. I really don't."

"But something made you think your father might be involved in the murder of the resurrection guy. Something about your mother's death. Is that right?"

She made a show of pulling herself together, straightening where she sat, straightening even her long neck, folding her hands calmly in her skirt. In a precise, clipped voice, she announced to him as from a height: "Well, I do have this memory. It sometimes gives me bad dreams."

He waited. Listened.

"When I was four or five," Sophia said. "Sometime before my mother died. I woke up one night in bed. Something woke me. I heard a noise. A ticking sound in the walls. *Tick-tick. Tick-tick.* Like that."

Storm's hand fell slowly away from his face, his arm sank slowly to the armrest.

"I called to my mother, but she didn't come," Sophia went on. "So I got up and went to find her. My parents' bedroom must have been empty. I don't remember. I just know I went downstairs, down a corridor, calling my mother, following that sound in the walls."

"Jesus," said Storm.

"Yes," she said. "It's just like the story you read, isn't it?" She continued in the same steady tone. "I'm rather confused about what happened next. I seem to remember I came to the last door, which is my father's study. When you read the story, I could almost see the book-lined room. But in my memory—I'm not sure—I also seem to remember furniture all around, old boxes, chairs, a big something-or-other in the middle of the room—just like a storeroom or something. And that ticking sound, getting louder. And as I came down the hall, the door to this storeroom opened, and there . . ." Her voice hitched. It seemed to annoy her—her eyes flashed. She pushed on. "And there—it's all very confusing. Sometimes I think it's not a memory at all, but just a dream. Or maybe I read the story once and remember that. But I think I saw my father, crouching over my mother, struggling with her. He was struggling with her—and then he stood up. And there he was, standing up over my mother, holding something in his hand, some kind of weapon. A knife, I think. And my mother . . . she was lying there, curled up on the floor. And they were both . . . covered . . . covered in blood."

She looked into his eyes so coolly then that he almost bought it, almost believed she was that far above things, that tough, that hard.

He shook his head. "But she hanged herself, didn't she?"

"That's what I'm told, that's what everyone says. But I don't remember anything after that night. My father saw me right away, sent me back to bed. I only had a glimpse and I'm not even sure of that. Nanny came and sat with me, I think.

I suppose it was all explained away somehow. I suppose I went back to sleep. I don't remember."

They sat silently. The music went on. *Ich, dein betrubtes kind, werf alle mein sund . . . in deinetiefe wunden . . .* Sophia sat as she had, erect, gazing at him, almost looking a challenge at him now that her story was finished. The gas fire bubbled. The windows bucked and rattled with the wind outside and the curtains stirred. To Storm, the room felt isolated, floating: they were in space, they were the last two people left anywhere.

He remained quiet. Instinct told him he couldn't take her too much farther. Even if he could, he didn't think he could stand that look she was giving him. Everything marbelized on the outside, everything immolated within.

But there was something wrong with her story, he knew. Something off, something missing.

"Have you ever heard of a man named Jacob Hope?" he asked after a while. "Or Iago? Or Saint Iago? Or anything like that?"

She thought, shook her head curtly. "No. What a strange name. No, never."

"That brooch, your mother's brooch. You know where she got it?"

A shrug. "I always assumed it was an heirloom. It's supposed to be some Norse symbol, I think. As I say, the family history was very important to her, and the Abingdons like to believe they have Viking blood. I think the symbol is meant to represent the secret word of hope that Odin whispered in the dead Baldr's ear."

"Yeah. Yeah, that was my first guess."

She smiled only faintly.

Storm slapped his hands down on his knees. "Well," he

said. "I guess now I know why you dropped that glass of wine, huh?"

"Yes, I suppose so," said Sophia. And she began to cry. "I'm sorry, I'm sorry," she said, trying to brush it away.

But he was over her, had her by the shoulders. Lifted her to her feet, held her. She squeezed her eyes shut, pressing her face to his shirt. "I remember thinking, just before I jumped off the railing in the gallery, I remember thinking how shabby it all seemed. My life, me. Everything. Just so shabby and miserable."

Und mir nach reu und leid nicht mehr die seligkeit noch auch sein herz verschliefst.

"Nothing about you is shabby and miserable," said Richard Storm. "Not to me."

✦

She was right: she was no good at sex. Stiff as a board, dry as a bone. And frantic and apologetic and distrustful of him all at the same time, which tended to make things worse and worse.

But by the happiest coincidence, this precise situation seemed to bring out two of Richard Storm's most appealing character traits. For one thing, he was capable of displaying almost boundless patience and good nature with people he truly liked, women especially. He'd been born like that probably, but formative years of dealing with a fractious, theatrical and yet adorable mother had honed this feature of his personality to a skill. Of course, even for him, patience wasn't particularly easy just then. Sophia was even better looking with her clothes off. Lying on her bed on her back, with her breasts spilling wide. Her face turned up to him, her eyes panicky and entreating. Her skin may have felt frosty to her, but it was burning under his hand, burning. And she had one white knee bent, parting her legs to him, a sight that made him so hard he was afraid he might go off like a rocket and end up three blocks away. He had been dreaming of taking her—against a wall, on the floor, over a chair—a little knockabout passion, a little ripping of clothes, a little Brando action from *Last Tango in Paris*. He wanted to send her richocheting off the stars like a pinball. *It's never been like that for me before, Richard!* He'd had the whole thing pretty well worked out in his mind.

But that was the other thing about him: his nature, his business, a not altogether inattentive eye on the world, had combined long ago to convince him of the important fact that things almost never shake out the way they do in the movies. He scoped the real lie of the land pretty quickly. He held her, stroked her, kissed her. He cooed to her long after the inner powers were shrieking for him to morph into a human jackhammer. And in the end, with jazzman fingers and a serpent's tongue—and with a little bit of the gunk from a diaphragm that looked like it hadn't been used since 1947—he was delighted just to slip inside her with a semblance of sweetness and ease. Which is where he wanted to be when he told her he loved her. Which he did, kissing her panicky eyes till they softened, letting great handfuls of that raven black hair cascade from his grip onto her valentine cheeks. Drawing from her, finally, some small signs, at least, of spontaneous pleasure. Which would serve for now. Which was enough.

✦

Spent, of course, he was almost instantly appalled. He was still in her, still on her. She was clinging to him. He was caressing her face. There was light in her brown eyes and she was smiling as if she thought she had done something exceptionally clever. She was even glancing coyly at him. Mata Hari suddenly. Marilyn Monroe. The femme fatale of the universe. He adored her.

And he was appalled that he had let things come this far without confessing to her, without telling her how short, how terrible their time was bound to be.

Storm buried his face in Sophia's hair, sick with himself and sick with love. He closed his eyes and breathed in her scent and wanted this to be what the world was like forever. Maybe it would turn out all right somehow, he thought. Maybe the doctors had been wrong. It could've been one of those farcical mistakes. Like *Send Me No Flowers*, with Rock Hudson and Doris Day. He felt fine. He felt good, in fact. Since that one night all those weeks ago. There'd been nothing. Some headaches. Which anyone could have. A little weakness in his left arm—but only sometimes, only off and on. And other than that, he was terrific. Great. Excellente, Clemente. Life wouldn't make sense otherwise. God wasn't going to teach him to feel like this for someone, make someone so dear to him, and then just snuff him out. Was He? Come on. Not a swell guy like God.

Sophia let her arms fall to the mattress on either side of him. "Gosh, I'm so *hungry*," she said. She clasped him again. Hummed. "Was that all right? Was it all right for you? Gosh, I've never felt so *hungry*."

His heart swam in blood because his legion of sins had made him a monster in God's holy eyes.

Or, as he put it to himself, *Oh, Magoo, you are such a shmuck.*

7   Now at about the same time Storm and Sophia were starting back across Waterloo Bridge, as they were heading for their drink in the Savoy Hotel bar, the taxi numbered 331 was driving down the Strand past the hotel's entrance. With the scarred man squinting his piggy eyes at the windscreen, the cab chugged along in the thick traffic without stopping. Just ahead, teeth bared, the city's griffin loomed rampant on its pedestal. Harper Albright looked out at it from the cab's backseat.

She clutched her dragon stick tighter with both hands. Pressed her lips against her knuckles, her lips trembling, her knuckles white. Here, where the West End became the City, where the flash and flicker of theaters gave way to the dimmer, narrower canyons of Fleet Street, she had her last notion of escape. She might rap on the cab's windows, she thought. She might gesticulate at the thinning crowds of passersby, or at the other drivers edging along the clogged thoroughfare. It would be a long shot, given the noise of traffic, given the nature of cities. And it would be a risky business, given the death-rays of vengeance beaming out of the eyes that now and then glanced at her in the cab's rearview mirror. She had no doubt the driver remembered that notch she had made upon his chin with her sword. He was just looking for an excuse to even the score.

But once they left the crowds behind, once they entered the deserted City streets, her last chance would be over. She would be at the mercy of her enemies. She knew it was now or never.

And she just sat there. Hunched over her stick. Lip-gnawing her knuckles. Afraid—melting inside with fear—but silent, unresisting.

The cab went on, towards the canyons.

What a stubborn old woman she was. She could've kicked herself for it. But the fact was she had to satisfy her curiosity. It was that more than anything that held her there. She had to know what was going to happen next.

Of all the questions left unanswered about Iago—of all the thousand questions—the greatest was this: Why hadn't he killed her yet? Out of pique if nothing else. Or in his determination to keep her from finding the very manuscript she now had hidden inside her cape. Why the warnings, why the threats? Why not just snuff her out? Her own uncomfortable suspicions on the matter tantalized her. The desire to confirm or disprove them—the desire to discover any answer at all—the desire simply to know more—were such powerful drives in her that she felt there was no overcoming them. This imprisonment in a London cab, this drive to nowhere, to somewhere: it felt to her almost like fate.

An aggravating business. It angered her. Here she was, being sucked into a vortex, being carried down and down into certain danger, and her most powerful emotion—aside from this liquifying fear—her most powerful emotion was *anticipation.* Which was confused in her mind with that other, hateful anticipation: the anticipation she had felt in the old days at the prospect of seeing him again.

What a foolish old woman. She really could have kicked herself. She clutched her stick, gnawed her knuckles, angry. Afraid. Excited.

Then, to her surprise, the cab pulled over. Stopped. Just on the far side of the griffin, still within sight of the West End crowds behind it. The movement wrenched her from so deep a study that for a moment she didn't recognize the place. She saw the scarred driver give a glance to the heavyset newsie standing just outside on the pavement. The newsie, in turn, glanced at two ancient and enormous iron doors set in the wall behind him, shut tight.

The driver turned in his seat. Leered at her.

"Here you go, darling. Just what you asked for. The end of the world."

The newsie darted forward. Yanked the door open. Stuck his horny hand in at her. "Right this way, love." He was leering too, leering down at her.

"And none of that Smith and Sons nonsense," said the driver with a rueful nod at her stick. "It won't help you anyway. It's too late for all that now."

"I should've pinned you like a bug when I had the chance," Harper grumbled. But she slid across the seat towards the open door.

She'd be damned if she'd take the newsie's hand. She worked her way out herself. And when he touched her shoulder, she sloughed him off with a vehement shrug. Out in the open air, she smoothed and straightened herself. The newsie hovered near her. Tried to take her elbow. She glowered him back. "I'll break those sausagy fingers if they touch me again."

He scowled, but kept away. Contented himself with a rough gesture at the iron doors.

"All right, all right," she groused.

Hoisting her satchel strap over her shoulder, she waddled, muttering, towards the wall. Slowly, as if magically, the doors opened inward at her approach.

Harper's teeth clamped, her breath caught as the corridor beyond was revealed to her. She saw a downward slope through a constricted close. She had a glimpse through windblown sycamore branches of the west porch entry to the church of the Knights Templar. She knew where she was now. The entrance to the Inner Temple Court.

The newsie dropped back behind her. She passed under the entryway. The great doors swung shut.

She was alone in the dark alley with the damp night wind.

She halted. Harrumphed. Looked around her. Sneered angrily at the descending passage. But this was all bravado, in case anyone was watching. If she'd been melting with fear in the cab, she was practically a puddle now. It was another long moment before she could bring herself to head down the slope to whatever lay below.

The wind rose higher, a hoarse moan of warning between the walls on either side of her. Just what she needed, just what the scene required to feel really terrifying. But she moved on, regardless, her squat figure pulled into itself, her stick stabbing the pavement as if she would drive it right through the stone, her Borsalino bowed against the cold.

When she glanced up, she saw the Temple Church slowly moving into view from behind the alley's corner, through the trees.

The Knights Templar—guardians of Jerusalem after the Crusaders took it, after they slaughtered its paynims and established the rule of the armies of the Prince of Peace; protectors, in legend, of the Holy Grail; pattern of the Teutonic Knights of Germany and rival of the Knights Hospitalers; soldiers, bankers, politicians; and finally, outcasts accused of Satanism and infanticide; disbanded, tortured, burned at the stake: they had built this church in 1185, some sixty-five years after their inception. Its round tower—one of only five round church towers in England— was modeled on Jerusalem's Church of the Holy Sepulchre.

Its castellated crown lowered blackly against the dull sky as Harper moved under it.

And there was more of the eerie wind business—the tree branches whispering and chattering all around her. And there were the ancient coffins oddly shimmering at the tower's base. And there was the western porch of the church right before her, its obscure entryway: a chiseled Norman tympanum receding to the shut door. That recessive shape seemed to her to give a tide to the darkness, a tide that was dragging her in. She had again that irritating sense that she had come to this place helplessly, in answer to an over-powering summons. She had an awful feeling that everything to come was expected, had been expected for a long time, forever.

She felt sickened—but not surprised—when she heard a muffled thud as of a body dropping, and the heavy church door began to swing open.

She stopped before the archway. Steeled herself, squared her shoulders. The door continued to swing back until the interior of the church—or, that is, the utterly lightless murk of its interior—was displayed before her.

"You always did love an effect," she muttered to no one between her teeth.

Then, her stick clicking on the stone, she stepped under the arch. Staring blankly ahead, she hobbled under the tympanum. She entered the church.

At once, the door swung to behind her, shut with an echoing boom. She'd been expecting that, but it didn't matter, she couldn't help herself: her whole body went so tense it thrummed. Now the dark was complete. It surrounded her. She could see absolutely nothing. Could only feel the church's dank and stony atmosphere. Could only smell—

what was it?—something fetid and hot, something panting, dangerous, close. He was there. With her. She knew it. Circling her, predatory. She was so frightened she began to shiver. She wanted to shout out in fury: *This is unworthy of you!* But she didn't. She wouldn't give him the satisfaction. And anyway, it was nonsense: this was right in his line.

"You know, you remind me, in some ways, of the Pacific salmon," he said from directly behind her.

Again, she couldn't help it—she gasped, startled. She spun towards his voice.

"I think I must've taught you about the Pacific salmon. I always took great pains over your education, as I'm sure you remember." He was already moving on, moving along the circular walls. Harper turned where she stood, trying to follow the sound of his voice. "Really, it's an amazing creature. The salmon. It smells its way out of the ocean, upriver. Smells its way hundreds of miles, against the tide, against all obstacles. Finally comes back to its home waters, its headwaters, the place where it was spawned. And there it mates—and then it dies."

His voice ceased. Harper was still turning in her place to follow him. But he was playing with her. When he spoke again, he was once more behind her.

"What I mean is, it's an awfully long way to travel for love—and then death. Isn't it? But then the salmon can't help itself. I think an instinct for self-destruction must be built into the nature of its desire. That's what I'm getting at: some people are like that too. Maybe most people. You, for instance, come after me and after me because you can't resist me, can you? Even knowing that I'm going to kill you. Is that a labored metaphor? It just popped into my mind."

"A little. It's a little labored." Harper had to moisten her lips before she could say any more. "But since we're in it, I do seem to recall that the salmon, just before it dies, grows fangs to fight with."

He laughed happily. "You do remember." And he lit a match.

An explosion of red blindness. Her hand flew up. Then, shadowy vision came seeping in from the edges . . . Grotesque stone heads sculpted on the encircling arcade. A demon, a satyr, a dead-eyed king. Staring at her from between the arches' columns. A tortured soul with a beast's jaws clamped to him. A twisted nose-picker, a grieving peasant. Head after Gothic head. And now, the light dwindling, Harper, lowering her eyes against the glare, saw the effigies of dead crusaders at her feet.

And then she looked up at Iago.

He was holding the match to a candle wick now, looking from the flame to her, smiling wryly. And the moment she saw his face in the yellow glow, she remembered what it was about him.

He was not only a handsome man, with his slim, straight figure in the white suit, his long black hair, his sharply faceted face and those smoky, hypnotic eyes. There was something else. A certain unbridled, animal vitality, a pent energy in every movement he made; a kind of ease and confidence; a fluid comfort in his own skin. He was all alive, and the world sat so lightly on him.

It was an attractive quality. Standing there in the respiring flame light, Harper had to fight to remember what he'd looked like when she'd seen him last. That night after she'd crept from her bed in the cult's compound. After she'd pushed the branches aside and peered into the clearing.

There he'd stood. In the mists of the Argentine jungle, in the flare of the bonfire. His acolytes chanting. The mother shrieking through her gag. His own face mad, exalted, as he lifted the curved blade. And the child lying trustingly on the altar before him. His own child.

Twenty-five years she had hunted him for that. She had to remember it now.

The candle caught. He held it up. He held it out to her with one green-gloved hand, drawing his long hair clear of his cheek with the other. He moved the flame to and fro slowly in front of her, examining her minutely, as if she were some statue he had discovered in a cave. She stood like a statue, clutching her stick—so tightly that the ears of the dragon bit into her hand. But she shrank inwardly, wishing to hide herself under her hat, behind her glasses. She knew what he was seeing—every sag, every wrinkle, every premature, flaccid pouch of flesh.

"Oh, Harper," he said at last. "You've grown so old."

And it stung her. In spite of everything. Still, she managed to answer him with a frown like granite thunder. "It's been twenty-five years."

"Oh yes, I know, but really." He pursed his lips. "You've gotten all . . . grim and wrinkly."

"Ah. Well."

"That wasn't necessary."

"I'm afraid it was."

He laughed. "Because of me, you mean."

"Yes."

"Poor baby. All because I showed you who you are."

"You showed me who I could be, Jacob, who I might be," Harper said. "You showed me who *you* are."

He laughed again. And stretched, spreading his arms like

Christ. The candle in his hand lifted a dim, yellow dome of light over the church's round: the gaping sculpted heads; the effigies in their tormented postures on the floor.

Stretched like that, he resumed pacing gracefully around her, looking her up and down, his tongue in his cheek.

"Who I am," he repeated slowly. "But really, darling—you always knew who I was."

"No," she tried to say, but the word caught in her throat.

"You did," he said. "You knew. And yet I seem to recall I was your lover."

Harper forced herself to stand still as he circled. The glow of the candle passed and faded from before her. He was behind her now, out of sight. It made the skin prickle on the back of her neck. She had to fight to keep her exterior steady and stern as her insides churned, molten.

"I—was—your—lover," he insisted.

"If that's what you call love," she shot back.

He stopped at last, beside her. Just beside her. She felt his breath on her cheek. Hot, wet, rank. A panther's breath. He went on in the same easy, ironical tone.

"You're right," he said. "Let's not mince words. I was your master. Wasn't I?"

Harper's lips worked as she tried to swallow her distaste.

"I mastered you, Harper," he continued softly. "I mastered you, and then you begged me to master you again. I remember the sound of your voice as you begged me."

The words burst from her. "I was young."

"Not that young."

"And half insane."

"Only half."

"It was a long time ago, Jacob."

"Not that long, really. You remember it too. I can see you

do. You remember it in your flesh. Don't you?"

She barely turned her head towards him. Barely lifted one corner of her mouth. She was afraid she would start to quake. "I remember. Yes."

"And that's why you can't stay away from me. Even if it's only to feel my hands on your throat."

"You know why I've come after you," she said.

He rolled his eyes. "Oh yeah. I forgot. The children. The dear, dead little children. Tell yourself that's the reason."

"That is the reason."

"For this obsession? For this compulsion to irritate me?"

"To destroy you, Jacob, actually. Yes."

He let out a breath, threw up a hand. She flinched away from it. But it was only a gesture of mild frustration, the gesture of a teacher with a dense student. "You know, dear, I really did teach you to be more honest with yourself than that. I showed you how to plumb the ugly depths, didn't I?"

"Yes."

"But you're going to stand there looking like my maiden aunt and tell me that you gave your life, you wasted your prime, you wore away your beauty, trailing after me—all because you cared so very, very deeply for a few armloads of dead babies?"

"Yes."

"Oh, I don't think so, sweetie."

She couldn't hold it down any longer: a painful shudder went through her, head to toe. She had forgotten the weakness—the limp, physical weakness—that invaded her whenever he came this close.

No, she had not forgotten. She had fought to believe it was a thing of the past.

"Look at you," he whispered. "Harper. Trembling. Look at you."

She made a gulping noise. Rapped her stick convulsively upon the stone. "I . . ." she said. She took a breath. "I am not the woman I was, Jacob."

"Oh no? Really? Then why are you here?"

He came swinging around in front of her. She could see him in the candlelight with his head tilted to one side, his smile gleeful, his black eyes smoky and seductive. He looked so vital to her, so relaxed, that she began to feel like a fusty old crone just standing there, frowning at him like this.

But she stood there. Frowned at him. And swallowed hard. "What do you want me to say?" she asked hoarsely. "You're the philosopher, Jacob, not me. I only know . . ." She shook her head.

"What?" he said, smiling. "What do you know?"

"I know my spirit opposes you."

"Your spirit! Oh my!"

"And not just my spirit."

"Dear, dear. What more?"

"All of it," she barked. "All of it opposes you. The . . ." She groped for words. "Oh, all right. The Everlasting Thing."

Jacob Hope guffawed at her. Threw back his head, one hand on his belly, the other—the one holding the candle— held to his brow. Laughed and laughed, staggering where he stood, his feet among the dead crusaders. Then he shook his head. He daubed the corner of his eye. He wound down to a low chuckle.

And then—suddenly—he roared at her: *"For Christ's sake, woman—look!"*

The curtain of his black hair crackled and fizzed as he

held the candle up to his own face. The flame seemed to rise along his skin in a caress. The murky depths of his eyes seemed to turn like slow Catherine wheels. Her own image in them seemed to turn like Catherine.

She looked. And she saw that what she feared was true. What she had suspected since Storm had described him to her. It was impossible to deny it now.

He was a man of thirty—of thirty-five at most. As he had always been. As he had been the day she met him.

In all these years, he had not aged a single hour.

"I *am* the Everlasting Thing," he said. "I feed on the marrow of time. I was here before the oceans turned black with life, and when the deserts are white with death I will remain. And you're really starting to get up my nose, Harper," he went on in his normal tone. "So maybe you ought to reconsider your position."

Whoosh—he blew out the candle. Harper hissed, recoiling, as the inky air clamped over her. There was only his voice again now; that harsh breath; that feral smell. The dark.

"Oh, Harper, Harper, Harper. You really can piss me off at times. I swear, after Argentina, I wanted to kill you. Oh . . ."

In that blackness, he made a noise, a low growly hum, a sound of such sensual hunger that she felt certain he was going to kill her right now.

But he went on: "That's just the sort of debilitating woman you are, you know. You made me doubt my own destiny. Almost. But—but, but—I still had the Grail. The blue flower, the blue stone. I still had more than enough of it, and that's what brought me to my senses. I mean, when a fellow just buys something like that—just picks it up wandering through a Moroccan bazaar—that's not just chance, that can't just be chance. Whatever you say. 'There will arise one who will become the eternal creature.' That was the prophecy. So, in spite of what you managed to do to me, I knew I'd been chosen. I *knew* that. And I lay low." A tone of self-congratulation had entered his voice. He was bragging to her, Harper realized. "I lay low. Patience, patience. And sure enough, just five years later, in a little place off the Edgware Road—on the road to Damascus, Harper—like a flash: a spilled soda, and the next stage was given to me. The trail of stories. Oh, I know you know. Well, let me tell you, darling, it's been twenty years. I had to wait twenty years before I could follow that trail to its end. Patience, patience, though my time ran short. And just when things were getting desperate, just at the brink of disaster, the wall came tumbling down and my destiny was all before me again. All before me. And now—again—*you . . . !*"

She was scorched by the word. He must've leaned within inches of her. Even in darkness so complete, she thought she could make out the glint of his stare. "I can see how far you've come on the same slender thread. And well, why not? I taught you everything you know, didn't I? I'm proud of you, old girl. I admire you for it. In fact, I admire you so much that if I thought for a second one chance remained, that even one copy of the final text was still in existence, so help me, so help me, I would give myself the pleasure: I would grind your bones to make my bread."

Again, his breath burned her. Her hand spasmed, jerked, her stick tip ticking twice on the stone. *Why didn't he? Why didn't he just do it?* In spite of everything, her curiosity almost made her ask aloud. But she mustn't. It might tempt him. It might give him ideas. For the sake of her life, she must force herself to keep silent.

It seemed to provoke him. He snarled: "You think I can't?"

"Why don't you?" she blurted out. What a foolish, foolish old woman. "Why don't you just do it? Why don't you just kill me?"

He drew away. The heat of his breath diminished, at least. But no, he had retreated from her, she could feel it. She stood where she was, staring after him, seeing nothing. She tried to swallow, but her throat was dry as dust.

"It's the boy, isn't it?" she said softly. "You want the boy. Our boy. You need him somehow. Not just his life. You need him with you, you need him on your side. That's it, isn't it? Isn't it, Jacob?" He made no answer. Where was he? She couldn't tell. She took an unsteady step forward, called after him in the darkness. "If you killed me, he would know. He would know it was you. If I were hit by a car, by lightning, drowned in the Thames—if I died in my sleep— he would still know who was to blame. And it's the one thing he would never forgive you for. It's the one thing that would keep him away from you forever. You don't want to make me a martyr to him. You need him on your side. Isn't that it? Isn't it?"

But aside from her own frightened wheezing, there was no noise in the round, in the church anywhere.

"Jacob?"

Nothing. Nothing she could hear or see. And yet . . . And yet, the silence had a quality of motion. The emptiness, the blackness had a life. She could feel it, in the prickpoints of her skin, in the warp of her nerves. He was still there. He was stalking, circling around her. Closing in on her. There were shuffling footfalls on the stone—she could hear them. Coming towards her. He was closer with every moment.

Gripping that curved knife she had seen in the jungle. Lifting it. She could hear the swishing upswing of the blade.

"Jacob!" she cried again, in terror this time, her voice trembling. The dragon stick fell from her slack fingers. It clattered on the stones. She grabbed her satchel, yanked it open. Drove her hand in, fumbling around. What a mess. She felt her glasses case. Her compact. A lipstick. Some tissues. Some receipts. Her keys. Half a Twix bar. Then her matches—she found them—she seized the box. Drew it out, the satchel dropping free on its strap. She heard herself panting as she fumbled for a stick. She struck it on her thumb. Again, there was the blinding flame. The shadows scrambling like rats. The round of the church. The staring heads on every side. The stone bodies of the knights at her feet. The long nave. The far altar, the faint glow of stained glass above . . .

But empty, all of it, otherwise. The entire place. Utterly empty. Except for her.

"Crikey," she whispered.

And she grabbed her stick and got the hell out of there.

8
   Weary, weary, weary, she reached home. Hung up her hat, her cape. Climbed the stairs. She had to rest halfway, her hand upon the banister, her head against the wall. Then she climbed on.

She reached the third floor landing. Paused again. Peeked in through Bernard's half-opened door. She watched the factotum sleeping for a moment. She allowed an unwonted expression of tenderness to cross her face.

Bernard had placed a bottle of Gilbey's by his bed. He

had filled his room with marijuana smoke and left a pile of snuffed-out roaches in the ashtray. It was childish of him; he confessed as much to himself. But it was such a rare thing for him to sleep in his own bed that he feared it would betray how worried he had been for her, how frightened he had been.

So he had set the scene. Too much alcohol, too much dope. The television on at the foot of the bed, the sound off, the images glimmering. And he positioned himself like Chatterton in the painting: lying atop the covers fully dressed, one arm dangling decadently over the side. His mouth was open, his eyes were closed, his faint snore was almost convincing. Through slightly parted lids, he watched Harper as she paused, as she watched him. He saw the uncharacteristic emotion in her expression. Saw the heaviness too, the savage work of gravity on her exhausted features. Without stirring from where he lay, but with an undeniable little thrill of terror and excitement, he thought, *She's seen him!*

Then Harper passed on, out of his view.

She went up the stairs again, to her own room. An attic cell. A cupboard, stacked with books, littered with loose papers, pictures. A bed, a rocking chair. One small window on the night sky. Divested of her stick, her satchel, she stooped, grunting, to light the gas fire. Sighing, she sank into her rocker before the feeble blue flame.

She set the chair into motion. She had had some vague idea of sobbing her heart out once she'd reached the privacy of her home. Sobbing for her sins, for her weakness, for her misspent life. But she found she couldn't be bothered. She was too tired. The grief was too deep for tears. And anyway, she had work to do before she could get to sleep.

She bent to drag her satchel to her. Brought out her pipe,

her baccy. Brought out the envelope that she had transferred from the pocket of her cape. Brought out the manuscript and placed it on her skirted lap.

Well, at least he wasn't infallible, she thought with some small satisfaction. He had reckoned every copy was destroyed. He hadn't counted on the ghost of M. R. James.

She adjusted her glasses. She chomped her pipe. Torched the skulltop. Primed the flame. Rocked and smoked awhile, Iago's words reverberating in her mind. *I was here before the oceans turned black with life, and when the deserts are white with death I will remain.* Strange words. Overwrought. Silly. And yet eerily familiar somehow.

The room was quiet but for the rhythmic shifting of the rocker's joins: *tick-tick, tick-tick.*

The clockwork of history, Harper thought.

And she began to read.

VII

THE MONK'S
CONFESSION

I AM DYING. There can be no mistake. The same lines of discoloration that heralded the demise of the others have now appeared on me, running from my knuckles to my wrist on my right side, from my knuckles all the way to my elbow on my left. On both sides, they are creeping slowly up my arms. Having witnessed the end of my two companions in this undertaking, I can have little doubt of what is waiting for me: the torment, the living decay, the insanity of remorse. For William and Anselm, the terrible process overtook them within five years of the beginning of our venture. Simple arithmetic killed them, as a little consideration might have told us that it would. I only am escaped alone to tell this because of a talent for deceit and a practiced way with women, and through the complicity of one who shall remain nameless lest his body be exhumed and cast out of holy ground.

It is all one now, however. What I had thought was deliverance has only been delay. It will not be long before the thing is fully upon me. There is no time left to satisfy the hunger of the stone. There would be no time, even if I had the spirit for it, which I no longer have.

Nor can I pray. I cannot unburden myself before the Lord. So great is the love of Christ that I fear He might forgive me. I could not abide that: it will take an eternity of damnation to cleanse my soul of these sins.

Instead, I make this addendum to my chronicle of Belham Abbey. I record what I cannot confess.

+

It is now almost forty years since the people of Belham burned the town's Jews. It was done in the time of the first King Henry. The Jews had taken refuge in the abbey's infirmary chapel as they had once before in past troubles. This time, however, the people were so enraged against them that even the law of sanctuary could not restrain them. Leaders of the mob bolted the chapel's doors and hurled brands in through the windows, setting the building on fire.

Though most of the monks were at supper on the far side of the grounds, we were well aware of the disturbance. As the flames rose, I myself could hear the shouts of the men trapped within, the shrieking of the women, the children crying. It was, however, a long time before Anselm sent a novice to beat the board and summon us to help.

By then, the fire was raging so fiercely that the infirmary's iron doors glowed red at the edges. Many of us ran to fetch water from the rain tank and even from the clock. But when the cold water hit the burning building, the very stones cracked and collapsed so that, in the end, no more was left of the structure than a single scorched and crumbling wedge of wall. The bodies within had been reduced to charred flesh and bones; skulls that seemed frozen in their death cries.

And all this occurred because I had told a story, a tale I invented in my desperation to save my own life. I had spread it among the people that it was the Jews who had murdered the infant, that it was they who were responsible for the little body that had recently been discovered near the abbey grounds. I said the Jews had sacrificed the babe. I concocted an arcane rite, invented enough details to make it sound convincing. I said the Jews had stabbed the child and used his blood to make their Paschal bread: an abominably distorted version of the mass. I made it all very believable.

And the story slowly spread until the people rose up in a mob and took their vengeance in the chapel.

By then, of course, poor Annie was too far gone in madness to convince anyone of the truth.

✦

For weeks before the child was found, Annie had wandered the streets, babbling about the murder. She said she heard the baby tapping at the earth above his secret grave, tapping and tapping night and day. She would roam the village in her rags, her hair hanging down around her face in filthy tangles. Her eyes had a wide, white, almost mystical aspect. She would seize the arm of any passerby who would stop for her.

"Listen!" she would whisper. "Tick-tick. Tick-tick. Hear him? Hear him? He is trying to get out. He is trying to come back to me."

Anselm, William and I suffered agonies of suspense for fear that someone might actually pay heed to her.

In the end, as it will, disaster came like a thief in the night. We monks departed mass one morning shortly after Easter, to find a large crowd had gathered just beyond the cemetery garth, where the walls had been undergoing repair. I was sent to investigate—in what state of guilty tension I cannot describe—and there found many of the local farmhands clustered in a murmuring circle. I pushed my way through and what I saw brought my heart into my mouth.

There was Annie, lying on the ground half naked. She had torn her rags from her body with her clawed hands. Her long nails were black with dirt. Her fingertips were bleeding.

She had dug up the infant's body.

Because the builders had been mixing mortar there, the earth was rich with lime. The child was thus in an advanced state of decay. And yet, Annie clutched the rotting thing to her bare bosom as if it still lived and might take nourishment.

"You see? You see?" she cried up at the horrified farmers. "He was trying to get out. Tick-tick, tick-tick. I heard him. He was trying to come back to me all along."

As I looked from her wild face to the faces staring down at her, I knew I must act at once. Thus I began to spread my story about the plot of the Jews.

✦

It was some months prior to this that the murder of the child was first proposed to me. Anselm himself summoned me from my bed in the hour after Lauds and led me without a word across the silent cloisters to his lodging. There, seated at a table in one corner, was a man I had never seen before. He was outfitted as a brother of the

Knights Templar, of whom I had then only heard reports from the pilgrims returning from outremer. But I recognized the red mantle and the gules cross blazoned on his robe.

Before him, on the abbot's table, was a small brazier with a cauldron set upon it. The steam from the boiling liquid within wreathed the templar's face in mist, the glow of the coals gave a fiery cast to his long, melancholy features. This was my first view of William, who had but lately returned from Jerusalem.

As I make no confession, I make no excuses either. The moment the three of us were seated at the table, I knew it was a dark business. The fact was revealed by our lowered voices and huddled postures, our faces leaning together over the steaming cauldron. The mist with its thick, sour smell and the unholy glow rising around us seemed to me even then the visible token—the aura—of a bloody conspiracy.

The blacks of William's eyes were gleaming as he pressed in towards me. "Tell me," he murmured in his low, oily tone. "Why did you become a monk?"

I explained briefly that I had been brought to the abbey in my eighth year, had been raised and schooled there and had known little else.

"And yet you received the tonsure as a man," he said. "You freely took the vows of poverty and of obedience."

"I did," I said.

"And of chastity," said he.

I averted my eyes from him. "Of chastity too."

"A life dedicated to labor and prayer. In the hope surely of an eternal life of joy hereafter."

"It is written that whosoever believeth in Him should not perish but have everlasting life," I replied cautiously.

At this, William only nodded.

Using a pair of tongs, the Templar now lifted the cauldron from the brazier and set it aside on the table to cool. For the first time, I noticed that a length of twine had been dipped into the cauldron, one end submerged in the bubbling liquid, the other hanging over the lip of the pot. From time to time, William pinched one end of the string in his fingers and tugged on it gently, as if bobbing a line to tempt a fish.

"You dedicate your life on earth to Christ because he offers you an endless life hereafter," he said. "That is the chief reason, is it not?" He toyed with the twine as the cauldron cooled. He smiled at me. "But what if I myself could promise you as much—not on faith but in truth, not hereafter but here and now?"

I glanced from William to Anselm, who watched us eagerly. "Promise me . . . ?" I asked.

"That you should not perish, but have life everlasting," the crusader said softly. "If I should offer you the power of Christ's Sangreal and, as I believe, the secret of his resurrection, for your own use. If there were no prayers required, no sacrifice, if you need not wake to Matins and toil to Vespers and Compline. If I offered you an eternal joy not of hosannas but of the rich, round women of the earth, its wine, its powers, its free fresh air. Whom then would you serve, brother?"

I looked again from him to the abbot, from Anselm back to him. I was about to recite on the subject of the Last Judgement, which is to all men no matter how long their earthly lives.

But it was clear that this was no place for such hypocrisy. I said nothing. Indeed, my tongue felt as if it had turned to sand as I realized for a fact what I had until then only suspected: that my own corruption was but a dram of the poison that had eaten into the abbey's very heart.

When he saw that I would make no answer, William smiled again. Again, he lifted the twine that ran into the cauldron. He lifted it this time until it came clear of the boiling mixture. He held it up before my eyes and I saw, through the mist, that a chain of bluish crystal had formed around it, and clung to it. Its facets grew out on every side like the petals of a blossom.

"This is the 'blue flower,'" he said. "The blue stone: the sangreal. The formula for the making of it was given to me by a paynim magician in the Holy City. It was the ransom for his life. First, the ingredients are heated together, and then allowed to cool and crystallize. Then, a bit of the crystal is dissolved again in water—just the littlest bit. And this creates a medicinal fluid. Immersion in that fluid once every six months so restores the natural substances of the flesh that it forestalls the process of ageing. The body—this body—your body—can be made essentially . . . deathless."

I stood up with such violence that the bench I had been sitting on overbalanced and fell to the floor behind me. Even in the cold of night, I felt the sweat break out all over my skin. I felt my heart beating powerfully against my ribs.

"This is the devil's work," I said. "Why have you brought this to me?" My mind raced in search of an answer, found none. "Why have you brought this to me?"

"Sit down, sit down," Anselm muttered. He leaned over, righted the bench that had fallen.

Slowly I sank into my seat again.

The red light of the coals seemed to grow brighter on William's features as he smiled. His eyes shifted to Anselm once and Anselm nodded.

"The stone is only part of the elixir," William said, so softly I had to lean closer to hear him. "In order for us to test its efficacy—we require one ingredient more."

✦

One ingredient more.

I will not attempt to mitigate my crime by detailing the struggle with my conscience that followed that conversation. The truth is, no matter what pangs I suffered, no matter what qualms arose, one thought from the beginning burned uppermost in my mind. Life! Eternal life! Eternal youth! With such a gift on offer, what did conscience matter? What was conscience in any event but the fear of punishment after death? The threat of death removed, the threat of Hell postponed forever, what power had conscience? What power had God? With life and youth guaranteed, I would be as a God myself, able to shrug off the petty fears and limitations of humanity. I would be free to indulge whatever desires, seize whatever prizes appealed to me, without terror or remorse.

All this—an eternity of pleasure—in exchange for just one ingredient more.

And so I went to see mad Annie.

It was painfully easy to bring her in on the scheme. Even then the woman was so simple and deranged that she was really little better than an animal. Often, in the days of my passion for her, she would present herself to me exactly as an animal would: dropping to all fours the moment I approached her, hiking her shift to her waist, grunting, drooling. On her, I had satisfied the cravings so long denied, content that she was too debased to feel an ordinary woman's affection or shame, assured that she would never be believed if she decided to reveal the truth. It seemed a perfect arrangement.

Until, one day, I realized she was with child.

Fearing that her condition would betray me, that her chants and babblings would reveal what it was becoming impossible to deny, I decided to take precautions. I had arranged for her to be secreted in the forest, in the home of a cunning woman with whom I had had some previous dealings. It was there I went to see her now.

By this time, Annie was very near being brought to bed, yet I suspect she still only half understood what was happening to her. When I explained what was to be done, she agreed to it instantly—distantly, as one speaking from a dream.

It was a distasteful meeting, but necessary. This is why Anselm and William had come to me in the first place. Because the stone needed to be tested. Because they were childless and Annie was close to term.

Because they needed this one ingredient more.

✦

And so we conspirators met again soon after, met again in the night, in the woods this time, beyond the farmland. The elements of the crystal were once more mixed together, placed in a small cauldron over burning coals and finally cooled and allowed to crystallize. The formula had by then been made known to me. I record it here for him who has eyes to see with, and no fear of damnation or no soul to save.

The crystal was carried to an iron tub. A bath was drawn from the river. A small piece of the crystal was broken off and dissolved again in the water. It bubbled furiously as it dissolved.

Then, at the appointed hour, Annie arrived. She was carrying our newborn infant in her arms.

That scene will be before me when I die. It is before me now, has been before me ever since. I have no doubt it will be before me always and will add the torture of conscience to the torture of the everlasting flames.

We three stood cowled and waiting. The trees around us seemed to bow together as if to screen us from the eyes of the angels. In what little I could see of the sky above, there was no moon, no stars. Only the low scarlet glow of the coals illuminated the overhanging branches, and that with so hellish an illumination that there could be little question into whose care we had commended our spirits. The red branches stretched down towards us like grasping hands.

A damp, cold breeze was blowing. The woods groaned with it. The trees seemed to whisper one to another. No birds sang, and the chatter of night creatures was so low and consistent that it was only another kind of silence.

Annie stepped forth from the darkness of the forest. I felt my breath catch, and a fever spread through my blood like a stain. It was clear from the way she supported her burden, from the wordless tune she murmured to it, that even in her befuddled state an animal tenderness had been excited in her by the birth of her cub. On reflection, I do not think she truly understood what we were about to do.

She handed the baby to me. I did not have the courage to look down at it. I looked only at Annie as William took the bundle from my arms. The poor raggedy creature stood unprotesting while William spoke the portentous paynim incantations. The slackness of her face, the deadness of her eyes reflected, I felt, the slackness, the deadness that seemed now to have invaded my entire soul. I felt as if I were floating in a sea of space, with every sensation muffled, every thought as still as the woods around.

Chanting, William laid the infant down on the flat rock that was to be our altar.

The chanting went on—a long time. It rose slowly until it reached a climax, filled the quiet wood. Even as I averted my face, I saw in the corner of my eyes the gleam of the gold-handled knife as William lifted it above his head, as the blade caught the red light of the coals.

There was a single, inquiring syllable from the babe. A single noise from Annie—a dumb, despairing moan—as the knife came plunging down.

Then, Anselm was stepping forward with a silver chalice to catch the gushing blood.

I let my robes fall to the ground and stood naked in the night air. I stepped forward and submerged myself into the chilly bath.

There was silence. There was the wind. Anselm came towards me, bearing the chalice.

Something in me even now, degraded as I am, hardened as I am, damned as I surely am, cries out at the memory, wails, weeps. But I will resist. It would be foul of me to argue a case for mercy now, to make a pretense of humanity now, to make a pretense of repentance. The will of man is free and the love of Christ is boundless. And I in that wood, on that night, made my decision.

And in despair of Heaven, and in the sight of those present, I was washed in the blood of the lamb.

✦

So I have written it here that it may be known. I have put it down so that it shall not die with me. I have lived for almost forty years since that day. I have seen one and then the other of my companions perish, as some accident or failure left them short of the blood they needed, that precious ingredient more without which the stone is useless. I have seen the flesh curdle and rot then on their living frames, have heard them shrieking with the pain of it. I have seen the light of a terrible realization enter into their helpless eyes, too late, too late. I have seen that light finally, mercifully extinguished.

And yet I hear them shrieking still in the pit of their eternal master.

But I have gone on. I have been a wanderer on the face of the earth. I have crept among my fellow men and hidden. I have seduced their women and slaughtered each of my own offspring even as it drew breath. I have libeled and condemned the innocent in order to protect myself. I have lived as the fox lives, hunted. Men cross themselves when they mutter my name. Children cry when their mothers invoke me. Priests deny my existence, and the bravest knights fear my presence in the woods. I have made myself their nightmares.

This is the life everlasting that was promised to me.

And yet—and yet I must say it—the promise has held good. I am dying now, but I have lived these forty years. I have lived—and I have not grown old. My body is the same today as it was those decades hence. Others have aged and crumbled, others have died, but I am as I was. I am unchanged.

This is what I feel compelled to declare. I feel compelled to proclaim it, knowing not even now whether I write the words in horror or in joy: the grail is real! The legend of the stone is true! I am the living testament to its powers, the dying testament. He who has eyes to see, let him see.

I conclude with a prophecy, and a warning. This is what I believe.

I believe that, in the days to come, there will arise one stronger in courage than I, more replete with cunning, one who will realize all the potential of this thing which has been heretofore hidden from us, and become the eternal creature that I sought to be.

But two things he must remember, two things he must keep in mind always.

The first thing: the blood must be found; every six months, the blood must be made available or all is lost. It was a failure to accomplish this which has killed first my companions and now me.

But there is a second thing as well: the stone dissolves. Only a little bit is needed each time, but once it is dissolved it cannot be reconstituted. The exact formula for its creation must therefore be always remembered, always preserved. For this reason, as I say, I have recorded that formula here.

Always remember: If he is deprived of either the blood or the stone—either one—his death, the most horrible death imaginable, is a certainty.

And contrariwise, if he—this future man—if he can find the blood, if he can maintain his supply of the blue flower—then it is all before him as it was once before me. Then—ah, then—what power will accrue to him, what endless power. If men worship Christ for the mere promise of immortality, what will they give to him who possesses it in living truth? If Kings kneel before the cross, what will they not lay at the feet of an actual presence? In him, I have my hope that the coming death, this awful death, will not be in vain. To him, I leave this document, this formula, these words.

And from the depths of Hell, where I soon shall surely be, I salute him across time.

VIII

THE NIGHT
OF IAGO

1 The day's light faded. Rain swept against the high windows of the mansion in World's End. Blasts of wind plastered the panes with water. An observer looking up from the street would have seen only a blur of yellow lampglow within, the suggestion of a fire in the grate, a dancing orange shimmer. Even in the moments when the storm subsided, when the rain on the glass drew into streaks and droplets, the editorial office of *Bizarre!* was hidden from the world by clouds of roiling smoke, an interior fog that also obscured the squat figure standing in there, made of it no more than a dim, dark outline.

Harper Albright puffed another gout from the meerschaum skull and watched night fall. The others were behind her, no one speaking. Bernard was playing solitaire on his computer, the repeated click of the mouse sounding curt, violent, agitated. Storm was brooding on the high stool, drumming his fingers atop the draftsman's table or sometimes, absently, massaging his left arm. Sophia, by the fire, hugged herself, rubbed her shoulders, nervously eyed the grotesqueries staring from the covers on the wall, from the jars and aquaria around the office.

And Harper stood, smoking without surcease. She could see the others, all of them, in wavery reflections on the rain-washed glass. For the most part, however, she let them fade from her consciousness, melt from her focus.

She was thinking about the trail of stories. About what it had revealed to her. About how it had led her to this dangerous night.

It had been ten days now since her meeting with Iago. It had been enough time to work out her understanding of the thing. The chronology, anyway, was more or less clear to her.

Some thirty or forty years ago, before Harper had met him, Jacob Hope had chanced to purchase a supply of a blue crystalline stone at a bazaar in Morocco. That much he had revealed to her himself. The merchant who had sold him the stone must have told him some version of the Belham monk's confession—some legend, anyway, of the stone's power to grant eternal life. Obviously, either Iago had believed the tale at once, or he had tried out the powers of the stone for himself and found the story to be true. In any case, Harper had no doubt that the pleasure of killing an infant would have been motive enough for him to proceed.

After that, he had returned to Europe. There, he had begun to collect his followers. At a time when cults were springing up everywhere, he had invented a cult of his own. But the cult, of course—as the warlock Dr. Mormo had suggested—the cult was merely an excuse. What Iago was really after were the women. The women, and the children he could sire off them. The children—and their blood. The cult was a perfect system for creating a steady supply of that "precious ingredient more without which the stone is useless."

And so, in the compound in Argentina, he had carried out his experiments in the jungle. Dissolving bits of the blue stone in water, completing the elixir by murdering his children for their blood. In this mixture, he had bathed himself every six months. Indeed, judging by the looks of him, he had somehow continued to feed the hungry stone, even after Harper had discovered him and he had burned the compound—and his children—to the ground. Using charisma and cunning, Iago had somehow kept the children's blood flowing for the last twenty-five years.

But finding the blood he needed—that was only half his problem, wasn't it? There was still the difficulty of the stone itself, the crystal. As the monk had warned, the stone would not last forever. Each application required a bit of it to be dissolved. Iago knew he would eventually use up his Moroccan supply. And so far, apparently, he had been unable to analyze the components of the thing or reproduce the process by which it was made. Ultimately he was going to have to figure out how to create the stone for himself. And he would have to do it before the lines of discoloration began to appear on the backs of his own hands, before he, like William and Anselm and the monk of Belham Abbey, suffered the agonies of living decay.

And that's where the trail of ghost stories had come in. Twenty years ago. After the destruction of the compound in Argentina. After five years in exile. "In a little place off the Edgware Road," as he had told her. Somehow, something had led Iago to "Black Annie." Something had led him to connect that story with "The Alchemist's Castle," which linked it to the Rhinehart triptych, and with "Young William," which linked all the others to the monk's confession.

And it was the confession, it was surely that, which had begun his twenty-year search for the triptych itself.

Because when he read the monk's confession, he had

noticed—as Harper had noticed—the monk's claim that he had recorded the formula for the stone in his document. But if that was true, then where had he recorded it? It was not in the words. It appeared nowhere in M. R. James's translation. Therefore the scribe must have encoded the formula into the illuminations, the pictures. Which were destroyed when the British Library was bombed in 1941.

But which—possibly, even probably—had served as the inspiration for the Rhinehart triptych.

This was the ultimate message of the story trail, of its convoluted chain connecting the Belham monk's confession to the Rhinehart work. Because if the Rhinehart work was based on the confession, then the triptych was not—as Iago clearly believed it was not—a depiction of the three magi visiting the Madonna and child. No. It showed instead the three conspirators meeting Annie in the woods to perform their sacrifice.

And if Rhinehart had copied the pictures from the Belham manuscript, he might also, knowingly or unknowingly, have copied the coded instructions for the making of the crystal.

He who has eyes to see, let him see.

For years, anyway, an oral legend of some kind had surrounded the triptych with an aura of mystery. The Nazi magicians—those mad black artists who hung around with all the other madmen of the Third Reich—had clearly known there was some sort of power in the paintings, some valuable secret that needed to be brought out. They had been unable to find it, unable to crack the code, because no one had known what to look for.

Until Iago. Until now.

What had led him to it? she wondered, as the darkness drew in before her. What had happened in his "little place off the Edgware Road," that had led him to "Black Annie" and the other tales? The connections weren't obvious, they weren't easy to make. How had he found them, how had he even known to look? They were important questions because—from the moment Storm had read the story at the party—she had become aware of the uncanny aura of coincidence and destiny that hung over the whole affair. And if she could figure out how it had got started, she might be able to deduce the shape of it. She might be able to seize control of events, or at least outrace Iago to their conclusion.

Already, some possible answers were beginning to form in her mind. But for now . . .

For now, she had a plan to draw Iago into the open once again. A plan she had formulated when she was out by the standing stones with Dr. Mormo. She knew there was only one way to do it. There was only one piece of bait that was certain to work. And this time, if he rose to that bait, she would be ready for him. She would bring her quarter-century hunt to a close right away.

She continued to stand there, continued to send up plumes and tendrils of smoke from her skull pipe. Bernard went on clicking away at his computer solitaire. Storm went on drumming his fingers on the draftsman's table. Sophia went on fidgeting nervously by the fire.

And then the phone rang.

Harper turned around. The others froze. The double chirp of the phone sounded again as Harper hobbled across the carpet to the stand beside Bernard's desk.

She lifted the receiver.

"Yes?"

"Harper." She recognized the harsh croak at once, the warlock's voice. "It's Mormo."

"Jervis," she said dryly. "How good of you to ring."

"Never mind that. I've got it."

Harper felt her heart hitch. She swallowed, said nothing.

"It wasn't easy either, let me tell you. The competition's stiff."

"But you've got it in your possession now?" said Harper.

"Come after full dark," the warlock went on. "And make bloody well sure you're not followed."

There was a click, and he was gone.

Harper laid the receiver down slowly. She raised her eyes to the steady gazes of the others.

"He's got it," she said.

She heard Storm and Bernard and Sophia all let their breath out at once. She tipped the stem of her pipe at them.

"Tonight, after full dark, Bernard and I will go to Lonsdale Square."

Storm curled his fingers into a fist, thumped it softly on the tabletop. "What about me?" he said.

Harper turned her head to look first at him, then at Sophia.

"You have another job," she said. She sighed. "Before we can get to the end of this business, it's necessary for us to get to the beginning of it. And I have reason to believe that that involves the suicide of Ann Endering."

"My mother?" Sophia said. "What has she got to do with it?"

"That's what I don't know," Harper told her. "But it's possible your father does."

Sophia drew back, drew erect, stared at her.

"My friends," said Harper slowly, "I'm afraid I must ask you to go out to Belham Grange."

2   Dr. Mormo hung up the phone. He sat there on the floor, disgruntled. His round, bloated face was pale. His round, bloated belly, under a sweat-stained shirt of shiny gold, was gurgling ominously. The trouble with working for the devil, he reflected bitterly, is that you get paid the wages of sin.

He sat cross-legged. His black pentagram banner was spread out on the carpet before him. His black candles were lit, the low flames wavery. A stuffed goat's head sat to one side of him, its glass eyes flickering with the light.

And between them, in the center of the pentagram, sat the *Madonna*.

The panel was in a box, the box was standing open. The candlelight played over the features of the virgin, spread into Rhinehart's tangled brown background and breathed it to tenebrous life. The tubby warlock brooded over the picture gloomily.

Mary was in the winter woods. She was down on one knee, clasping her hands together. She was clothed in drapery of royal blue, which set her off from the stark snarl of lifeless branchwork all around her, and from the great, twisted dead oak that hung over her, like threatening doom. Her face was round, fleshy, Bavarian, a peasant's face, but with pale eyes mystic and tender. She had a lovely, distant smile.

Looked more like a fairy-tale princess than the Queen of Heaven, Mormo thought. Looked more like Snow White in the Disney movie than anything.

He could hardly wait to get the holy bitch out of here.

He reached up, grabbed hold of the bedstead. Grunting, he hoisted himself off the floor. "Too old for this," he grumbled miserably. His bare feet white beneath the cuffs of his dirty corduroys, he padded to the bedroom door and out into the hall.

The house was dark around him, all the windows shuttered against the rain and the fading light. But Mormo knew the place, one of his more familiar hideaways. He trudged surely through the shadows to the top of the stairs. The floorboards creaking in the surrounding silence. The old man grumbling. All this intrigue. All this danger, he thought. He was way too old. It was way past time to get out of the business, retire, settle down. Get himself a place in Cornwall by the sea. Gather a cozy little coven about him. Spend his declining years in quiet contemplation and blood sacrifice, appeasing the dark powers in hope of the life to come.

He started heavily down the stairs. Well, he thought, tonight should pave the way, provide him with a nice little nest egg. Assuming it didn't kill him first.

He came slowly down into the foyer. Caught an obscure glimpse of himself in the mirror there. Poor old bloke with not a true friend left to him, he thought. Hard done by. Everyone on him and on him. Difficult to know who to be most afraid of at this point, really. The old Nazi who'd passed him the panel, there was a right spooky loon if ever there was one. Going on and on about death and culture. "It takes a mountain of corpses to make a Madonna," he'd said. His eyes all shiny. Mormo could hardly wait to get the hell away from the lunatic.

But the Nazi had been more terrified even than he was. He knew he'd put his tit in the wringer when he'd phoned Sotheby's to bid on *The Magi*. He knew Iago would cotton onto him, come after him double quick and no mistake. And now poor old Dr. M had that to worry about too, didn't he? Iago. He shivered.

He continued his trek, through the darkened sitting room towards the kitchen. No noise anywhere besides his footsteps and his sighs.

He didn't want to think about what Iago would do to him if he caught him at this. He didn't want to think about it for a minute. But the truth was: Iago—he would do for him sooner or later anyway, wouldn't he? At the end of the day, there was no percentage at all in dealing with a man like that.

Which left him with Harper, the devil forgive him. Fancy him making arrangements with that sanctimonious old cow after all these years. It was against his religion, no question. But there he was at the end of the day. When he'd balanced all, she was his safest bet. He could evade Iago if he had to. Been doing it on and off for years, hadn't he? Master of shrouding himself in darkness, that's what he was. Enough safe houses to become an estate agent and all the powers of Hell on his side.

But Harper. Now she had connections. She seemed to be able to find him wherever he was. Turn up right in front of him like Hecate herself, she did. And she'd set the Yard on him too. She'd said so. At the kitchen doorway, he shivered again, grumbled again: "Too old." Too old for prison, that was for bloody sure.

He switched on the kitchen light. The fluorescents crackled, flickered on. The old warlock blinked against the sudden brightness. The linoleum tiles felt cold against his bare soles.

This was why he'd always favored this house: the kitchen. A nice big one. Nice big larder behind the door to his left. Nice big fridge, lots of worktop space round the basin. Dr. Mormo liked to cook. It relaxed him. And he could do with a bit of relaxation just now.

He opened the fridge and stuck his head in. American-made—you could practically walk right into it if you had a mind. It was comforting just to hear the hum of it. The place was too quiet, almost creepy here all by himself.

He gathered up the onions, tomatoes, scallions, prosciutto. Brought the whole armload to the worktop and laid it out beside the cutting board.

He rummaged through the cutlery drawer, removed a formidable cook's knife. Lifted it, held it expertly to the light to make sure it was clean. It was plenty clean. The stainless steel was gleaming.

Iago's grinning face was reflected on the blade.

Mormo saw it, let out a weak mewl of terror. The knife fell from his slack fingers as he spun to face the open larder door. He felt his legs turning to water, his bowels turning to water. He felt the front of his corduroys going hot and damp.

The shiny knife fell down and down to the floor, turning and turning in the air as it fell. The reflected wedge of that cruel, leering countenance flashed on the blade, disappeared, and flashed again as the knife spun.

The thud of the steel on the linoleum was very loud in the silent house.

3

"I won't do it!"

Sophia had, when she meant to, a voice that slashed like a saber. She had seen men, at the sound of it, look down appalled as if to find themselves cut off at the knees. It was that voice she used now on Richard Storm, who was crouching in her kitchen, rummaging through her small refrigerator.

"I've never heard of anything so ridiculous. It's unnecessary. It's cruel and stupid. And, in any case, it isn't going to happen. I won't go."

"Let me ask you something," Storm said, not looking up. "Is there, like, some big warehouse or something in this country where you guys keep the other halves of all your refrigerators?"

Sophia felt the flush of anger in her cheeks. "Don't do that. Don't just dismiss what I say to you."

"I'm not dismissing you," Storm answered mildly, reaching in deep. "I'm ignoring you. Which is hard because you're so beautiful and I love you like music. And I only want to do things that make you sing tra-la and dance around in the fields throwing daisies everywhere. But you asked me to help you, and I think you ought to reconsider."

"Well, I won't," she said. She crossed her arms on her chest.

"Can I eat this?" He had found a plate of cold chicken, brought it out.

She had swung away, and barely glanced at him. "Go ahead."

Storm stood up, flinching, working out the kinks in his knees. He came out through the open doorway into the dining room, out to the long table. She was standing on the other side of it, against the curtained doors to the balcony. Seething, flashing her anger at him.

"I mean it," she said. "I won't."

"Hey, what do you expect me to do?" he said. "Throw you over my shoulder and carry you out there? It'd be fun, but I don't need the hernia." He set the plate down, started to undo the plastic wrap that covered it.

"I think your friend Harper is a nutter," said Sophia.

Storm laughed.

"I think she's playing some sort of ridiculous game.

Whatever conspiracy theory she's come up with, I'm sure my mother could have had nothing to do with it."

"Yeah, Harper's a kook all right, no question. Except everything she says always turns out to be true. You don't have any Coke or anything . . . ?"

The question broke her chain of thought. She massaged her forehead. "I don't know. No. There's some sparkling water in the cabinet left of the basin."

But Storm remained where he was another second or two, rubbing his arm, puffing his cheeks. Tired. She noticed now he looked terribly tired. The rings deep under his melancholy eyes. The rugged face puffy and slack. She felt herself softening towards him—which was irritating, because she found that kept on happening: whatever he said, she was always feeling herself soften towards him sooner or later. It was all that naked affection he threw at her. The goofy American earnestness. Even the fact that he did not react to her wrath in the manner to which she was accustomed was bizarrely endearing.

"Are you feeling all right?" she found herself asking as he wandered back into the kitchen. "You look tired."

He didn't answer her. He was opening the cabinet.

"You mustn't let that old woman run you ragged with her nonsense."

"At my advanced age, you mean." He was reaching up for the water bottle now. "Hey, maybe you're just embarrassed to have your dad see you're dating an old man."

"Don't be stupid. You're not an old man. I like how old you are."

"Or that I have no culture."

"Well. Never mind," said Sophia. "You have many other lovely qualities."

Storm laughed again, shaking his head. Looked at her like . . . like she didn't know what. The man had absolutely no rein on his warmth at all. "I really do love you," he told her. "I think you're the greatest."

She forced herself not to smile. "Well, you do. And I'd be proud to introduce you to anyone."

"Gah."

"Well, I would. You know perfectly well it isn't that."

"I need an opener for this."

"It's in the—"

"Oh, wait, I got it," he said, pulling a drawer open. "Somebody ought to break the good news to these jokers about the twist-off cap."

She watched him as he ambled back towards her, swigging from the bottle. Watched him with the first, faint, frightening realization of what he meant to her, of the power she had somehow given him. At first she had thought him just silly—a shallow American. And, well, he was. But she had come to understand that that American shallowness ran very deep. He knew how to overlook things. Like her history. Like her problems in bed. Like all her terrible character flaws. And she saw now that she had come to rely on that.

She was thoroughly dismayed to hear the tone of appeal in her voice when she spoke again.

"My mother didn't do anything wrong, Richard," she said.

Storm only shrugged, which made her go sour inside. He sat down at the table. Pulled the plate to him. Didn't look at her. Pulled the salt shaker to him.

"Oh, you can't eat that with your fingers," she muttered. She came around the table to the tall sideboard, pulled a knife and fork from one drawer, a linen napkin from another.

Storm was already tearing into a slice of breast, wrestling

the meat off with tooth and claw. But he took the silverware from her without a word. Silently put the napkin on his lap. Salted the chicken again and attacked it this time with the fork and knife.

Sophia stood behind him, looking down into his sandy hair.

"Stop doing that," she said finally.

"What?" he said. "I'm eating. This is the way we do it."

"I mean stop thinking that. What you're thinking."

He set the knife and fork down. Scratched his head.

"My mother was a . . . sweet, liberal, charitable woman. Everyone says so. Everyone. I'm sure she didn't have anything to do with any of your friend's imaginary villains, or with anything. And to go out to Belham Grange and interrogate my father over a twenty-year-old tragedy . . . Maybe he hasn't been perfect. Maybe he was once involved in some dubious business. I don't even know that for sure . . ."

"Yeah, well, that's the thing," said Storm. He shifted in his seat to look up at her—to gaze up at her. Chewing his food, choosing his words. "You don't know. You see?"

Sophia was turning away from him when he caught her hand. He held it, stroked the back of it.

"You don't know, and it's eating you all up," he said. "You can't think about it and you can't think about anything else, so you can't think about anything. You don't know, so you can't forget about it—you can't forget about what you don't know. See? That's why I think you ought to do it. Because it's got you all . . . bunged up and frozen."

She drew her hand away, hugged herself with it. "That's just . . . You're just . . . talking about sex. It's just not that important to me."

He balled his napkin in his fist, set it on the table. Stood up, stood beside her, stood close. "I'm talking about you being depressed all the time. And having black patches. And being crazy, doing crazy things."

She faced him and his power occurred to her again, more clearly, more frightening this time.

"I don't want to do it, Richard." She could not believe it: she was pleading with him now. "Asking my father about this, confronting him. It would be . . . too painful."

"Painful?" He touched her hair gently. "Excuse me, but aren't you the girl I saw throwing herself off a balcony? How painful was that?"

"I meant painful for my father," she said up into his eyes. "He's an old man. He's not as strong as he looks, as he thinks he is. He's not as independent. He lives . . ." *In my good opinion,* she was about to say. But she stopped when the thought came to her that she now lived in Storm's, that she had allowed herself to live in Storm's. And she was scared of what was going to happen, what he was going to make her do. "Stirring things up," was what she said when she went on. "Making trouble over all this old business. What's the point?"

He had his fingers deep in her hair now, combing them through, holding her arm with his other hand.

"The point is for you to have a life," he said.

"I have a life."

"Have a big life. Have a real life, Sophie. With, like, musical numbers and chariot races. Even just inside, even just a Fred and Ginger dancing around in your head. It's important. Trust me on this, kid. I know about this." He seemed about to say something else, something more. His eyes had grown deep and hot—and mournful; they were so sad. " 'Cause it's short," he said after a moment. "It really is.

We don't stay long. You gotta do it big-time."

She lifted her chin curtly. "I haven't the faintest idea what you're talking about."

His lips pulled back, his teeth bared, as he seemed to look about the room for the words he wanted. His glance rested finally on the table.

"Look . . ." he said. He let her go, picked up the salt shaker. Unscrewed the metal top. He licked the tip of his index finger and dipped it in, brought it out with a circle of white crystals clinging to the tip. He set the shaker down and returned to her. "Here," he said. He moved his finger towards her lips.

Sophia blinked, recoiled. "What . . . ?"

"Shh," he said. He took her elbow. "Here."

He brought his finger closer. Closer until it touched her lips. He moved it gently through, gently into her mouth until her lips encircled it, until the salt was on her tongue. Instinctively, Sophia sucked on his finger, unable to break the hold of his gaze. Frightened by the sudden intensity of it.

Then his finger drew away. She licked her lips, the flavor still spreading over her palate. Storm's face stayed close to hers. His eyes stayed on her eyes.

"What," she said helplessly. "It's salt."

"It's *salt*!" he told her softly, urgently. "Salt! See? It's like . . . *Close Encounters*, you know? When the mother ship comes down out of the sky and it's the size of, like, a city? Like *Die Hard*, when the whole building just goes *bang*, just explodes and the fountain's all going. It's *salt*."

Sophia shook her head, afraid. Tears swam into her eyes.

"Here. Here," he said. "Let me taste."

He took her face in his two hands, drew her to him.

Pressed his lips to hers and then slid his tongue into her mouth, over her tongue.

Sophia tasted the salt and the chicken he'd eaten and the warmth and the size of his tongue. She was confused, her thoughts hectic. And, as his tongue went on moving over hers, she realized—realized with a sinking weight of fear and depression—that she was going to do whatever he wanted. They were going to talk about it, on and on, into the night. And then she was going to go out with him to Belham Grange.

Storm drew back, drew his tongue out of her. But he went on holding her face, holding her close to him. His eyes, she saw, were swimming too.

"Salt," he whispered hoarsely. "Live. Live, Sophia. It's the only thing I'll ever ask you to do for me."

4 Bernard's Morris Minor, meanwhile, was gunning wildly round the corners of Chelsea's backstreets. The rain walloped the windscreen, covered it, spit, slippery, out from under the tires on either side. The night was now so dark, the streets so sparsely lit, that it was all but impossible for Bernard to see much ahead. Still, the car darted through the tempest like a minnow as he worked the stick and wheel in the same languid, offhanded way in which he noodled his computer. He checked the rearview mirror frequently. He was trying to make certain there was no one on his trail.

The automobile, like all machines, was a complete mystery to Harper Albright. But she was so used to her factotum's mastery of such things that she was thoroughly unconcerned.

Slicing dodges between other cars, rugby-player dives under amber traffic lights, explosions of speed over abbreviated straightaways rendered invisible by the rain: she took no notice of any of them. Her stick propped on the car's damp floor, her hands crossed over the stick's dragon head, her chin resting on the backs of her hands, she cogitated quietly.

"I think," she murmured after a while, "that we had better discuss arithmetic."

The Morris skidded out onto the embankment, sped along the river, spangled bridges whipping by.

"It was simple arithmetic," Harper went on, "which, according to the Belham scribe, led to the death of his two partners in the enterprise of the stone, whereas he himself was saved by the complicity—that was his word—the complicity of one who remained nameless. Do you understand what I'm getting at?"

"Would anyone?" Bernard asked, casting a glance in the rearview as he swept in and out of oncoming traffic to overtake a van.

"It's the underpinning of the whole business," Harper insisted. "The very reason the scribe was brought into the conspiracy in the first place was that he had already impregnated the town's madwoman; she was close to term. You see, in order for the crystal's properties to be effective, one must apparently dissolve them in a bath of blood and water and then be baptized in the mixture once every six months. Without the constant repetition of the treatment, the fatal reaction sets in, beginning with the lines of discoloration which the Belham monk described. In the case of William and Anselm, such a reaction did set in within five years of the first experiment. Because of arithmetic. You see?"

The Morris flashed under the raised sword of King

Alfred, past the twin towers of Westminster Abbey. Shot like a cannonball into the enormous roundabout of Parliament Square. The place was ablaze with racing headlights, loud with horns, streaked and foggy with the angling rain. The car plunged into the melee. The cannonball became a sewing needle: the Morris stitched its way neatly through the chaos, Bernard rapidly steering, rapidly shifting gears. They were through—and speeding away into the broad canyons between the granite monoliths of Whitehall.

"There is a clear inference—so clear that the monk didn't even think to spell it out: in order for the stone to work, the blood must come from one's own child," Harper continued calmly. "That was the mathematical problem Iago was trying to solve when he gathered his cult around him. It takes, as you may have heard, nine months to produce a baby. The amount of blood required for the bath is clearly enough to kill the infant. Given the time of gestation—not to mention the occasional female resistance to any of various stages in the proceeding—how does one produce enough of the priceless stuff to bathe in it every six months?"

"You know, I think I had that problem on my last maths exam."

Harper, with rigid dignity, ignored this. Went on, "But what if mad Annie's child was not the scribe's first? What if he also had a child already grown? It might be possible to take the necessary amount of blood from an adult without killing him—often enough, at least, to fill in the gap between new births."

Bernard pondered these matters in silence as two huge double-decker buses converged on either side of him, threatening to crush the Morris to cinders. He downshifted nimbly, causing his car to spurt forward. The buses lumbered after him like two elephants in the slipstream of a jet.

"Which brings us back to that word—*complicity*," Harper said. "It would require complicity on the part of the adult offspring. No reasonable scenario can be imagined in which the blood is continually taken by force. Even if you locked your victim away, you would be hard pressed to keep him alive for very long. And in Iago's case, for all his powers, his own nature would work against him. Because any offspring of his would likely inherit at least a measure of his strength of will. Such a captive would almost certainly commit suicide rather than be a toad and live upon the vapor of a dungeon."

"Iago has obviously managed to produce all the offspring he needed this last quarter-century," Bernard said.

"Perhaps," said Harper. "But perhaps only just. Who knows how many times he's come close to the limit? And all the while leaving no child behind who could grow to adulthood, who could offer him a steady supply of what he needs."

Bernard gave a slight shake of his head. "Well, why didn't he think of that before?"

"I believe he has been thinking about it these last twenty-five years."

"Tell me something, darling," said Bernard suddenly—and speaking suddenly with peculiar sincerity. "We enjoy our little subtleties, you and I, but—"

"Stop the car!"

They had reached Lonsdale Square.

They had reached Lonsdale Square—and Harper had noticed something peculiar about the house on the corner. This was in spite of the fact that Bernard, at her command, had hit the brakes so hard that the Morris had gone into an hellacious skid. They were corkscrewing insanely through the narrow strip between parked cars. Bernard was wrestling desperately with the steering wheel. Harper was craning her neck to keep the house in sight.

"Interesting," she said.

There was a gap at the curb beside the garden. The Morris slid into it, bumped up onto the pavement, headed for the garden's iron gate—then stopped, as Bernard, downshifting, braking, used the concussion to bring the machine under control. It came to rest with two tires up on the curb, two in the street. He gave his companion a glance of mild exasperation.

"Look," she said to him. "Turn off the headlamps and look."

Bernard sighed. Killed the lights. Bent his head to peer up through the windscreen at the narrow, gabled building in front of them.

The square was quiet, dark. A claustrophobic crunch of buildings round a tangled winter garden. The narrow façades of the townhouses lanced the sky, irregular, looming, Gothic. The sharp points of their gables seemed to close like teeth on the purple clouds above.

The rain was softening again, a thin fog drifting in over the garden's branches. A streetlamp threw a halo of pink light into the weather, but the façade of the corner house seemed to shrink back from it into the folds of night. Every window was shuttered. No light shone through the gaps, no sign of light or life at all.

"What . . . ?"

"Wait for it," said Harper.

Then there it was. As the two watched through the windscreen, through the broad, clear arcs left by the ticking wipers. A white spot appeared through the slats of an upstairs shutter. It lengthened to a white line, angled off. It was gone. Then it appeared again, moving. Glaring for an instant at the point where the shutters joined. Then it vanished.

"A torch," said Bernard.

"Yes," Harper said.

A few moments later, it went on again—on and off at a window lower down. Whoever held the flashlight was descending through the house.

"Why would he be using a torch?" said Bernard.

"Exactly my point," said Harper Albright.

She had her Borsalino resting on her lap. She lifted it now, put it on, pulled it low on her brow. She clutched her stick, her eyes alive behind her spectacles. She watched, her nerves electric. She did not stir.

The light flickered again; the outer edge of its nimbus touched the slats of a shutter on the ground floor.

"He's coming out," Bernard said softly.

Thirty seconds went by like an hour. They watched. The wipers ticked.

Then the door to the corner house came open, closed. There was an obscure movement in the recessed entryway. Harper could hear her pulse in her ears, could hear Bernard breathing beside her.

A hunched, stocky figure emerged from the recess, stepped out onto the pavement. He stood. Looked left and right along the deserted street. The rain dampened the slash of his tawny hair. The lamplight glinted in his pink, piggy eyes; it drew his features out of the shadows.

It was the scarred man.

"Turn off the wipers," Harper hissed. "Quickly."

Bernard did, and the windscreen misted over. The Morris's engine popped and hummed.

The scarred man stepped to a hulking black car parked at

the curb. He pulled the door open, ducked inside.

"He'll see us if he comes this way," Bernard said.

"Shh. No. Maybe not. He's in a hurry."

The black car started up, moved out into the street, came towards them. Harper heard Bernard's breathing stop. Her own breathing stopped. They sat absolutely still.

The black car roared, accelerated swiftly. Swiftly, it was past them. Out of the square.

Harper threw open her door. She was in the street in a second, heading for the house.

"I'll go after him," Bernard shouted, and he threw the car into gear.

Harper took another step before she realized what he'd said. She stopped dead, turned in the fog and rain, her eyes widening with fear.

"No, no!" she shouted.

But it was too late. The Morris was already twisting off the pavement, spinning in the road. Its headlamps flashed on as it swiped by her, caught her with one hand outstretched, her mouth open on her cry.

But Bernard either didn't see this or ignored it. The Morris kept spinning. The engine gave a hoarse rumble. The Morris darted forward—and then was gone after the black car. A moment later, and the noise of both their motors faded away, leaving the square humming softly with city noises, pattering with rain.

Harper's hand sank back to her side. She stood, gazing at the place where the cars had gone out of sight, her heart thumping heavily.

Then a wrenching, tormented scream sounded above her.

Startled—frightened—she lifted her eyes just in time to see an enormous black shape launch itself from the corner house's gable top. A raven—its wingspan enormous—soared off above her head. A vast, outreaching blot against the sky. Then it was past her, over the dead garden trees. Out of sight. Another shriek, fading into the distance. And the street was quiet around her once again.

Harper let out a breath, raised a hand to her thundering chest. She looked at the dark door of the house, from the house back to the corner where the cars had gone. She knew an evil omen when she saw one, and she felt dread in her belly like a weight of stone.

Her shoulders slumped, her steps weary, she headed towards the house.

5   She did not ring. She pushed the door. It came open—she expected that—but it made her swallow hard just the same.

She stepped across the threshold. The foyer was dark, but there was a light on somewhere in the back of the house. In the misty fluorescent glow of it, she could make out the objects strewn about her feet. An overturned umbrella stand. A flimsy lowboy under a mirror to her right, pulled open, emptied. Umbrellas, drawers, papers scattered everywhere. She stepped gingerly through the mess into the sitting room.

The light was brighter here, filtering in directly through an open doorway. Harper could see the upended sofa. A standing lamp lying lengthwise. The peaks of books that had been cast from their shelves to the carpet. The carpet was slashed into strips. The entire place had been ransacked.

Her breath came out unsteadily. She shifted her grip on her stick. She hobbled forward, kicking the books aside. She reached the lighted door. Her eyes, behind the thick spectacles, peered into the kitchen.

In the purplish glare of the fluorescents, she saw at once the cook's knife gleaming on the kitchen tiles. There was a small puddle beside it. Harper moved to the puddle. Her knees cracked as she knelt down over it. She sniffed. Wrinkled her nose. Urine. The weight of dread inside her grew heavier still. Poor old Jervis, she thought. He must have been very scared when they came for him. And no doubt, he had good reason.

She went back—through the ransacked sitting room, to the foyer, to the foot of the stairs. She looked up grimly where they rose before her into blackness.

She moved to the foot of them. Started up.

She climbed slowly, step by hesitant step, almost blind, her stick probing before her. She could not help but picture the scene as if she were watching it from the front row of a cinema. Richard Storm himself might have filmed something exactly like it. The apparently deserted house, throbbing with danger. The old woman climbing the steps into a threatening gloom. *You idiot,* she would be thinking to herself as she munched her popcorn. *Don't go. Get out. Run to a phone. Call the police.*

Which was pretty much exactly what she *was* thinking to herself.

She reached the top, stepped up onto the landing. Shadows and darkness. Blackness, down the hallway to her right. To her left, a low, orange, wavering glow: candlelight. She forced herself to head towards it.

She shuffled unsteadily over the runner, one hand reaching out to guide herself along the wall. She expected the sudden onslaught of Iago's minions any moment.

But the onslaught didn't come. She reached the glowing doorway and looked in.

The candle was on the floor at the foot of a four-poster bed. A single black candle, burned nearly down. Its orange glow danced, reflected, in the glass eyes of a stuffed goat's head. The thing was staring up at her from atop a black silk banner with a silver pentagram in its center.

A box sat on the pentagram. Its lid was open. Harper had to step closer before she could see what was inside.

She stepped closer. She saw. And her whole body went acid with fear.

There was a photograph in the box. A black-and-white snapshot of a woman holding a baby in her arms. Harper could not remember whether she had ever seen the photograph before. But she knew the woman's face well enough. She recalled the desperate eagerness of her eyes, the tremulous misery of her smile. She recognized the beauty of her youth though she had watched it decay and crumble in the mirror with unnatural speed, almost overnight.

The photograph was scarred and partly covered by a mark drawn over it in black ink. Something like a horseshoe enclosing something like a figure eight.

The mark of Iago.

Harper gripped her stick, trembling. The acid of fear within her turned to the acid of anger. She cursed herself. He was still smarter than she was. Still. Smarter and quicker and more cunning by half. She had meant to acquire the *Madonna* and set a trap for him. Well, he had got there first. And now he had set a trap for her.

No, not for her. He had set a trap for Bernard.

And Bernard was headed straight into it.

6 As it will in England, the rain ceased suddenly. The clouds blew out of London to the northeast, and Bernard trailed his quarry through clear weather.

The scarred man's black car—a Mercedes, Bernard determined—tooled smoothly over the glistening roads ahead of him. Down the back ways and closes to avoid the traffic, over switchbacks to anticipate the complex system of one-way streets. Slithering like a silverfish through caulk, seeming sometimes to meander. But south ultimately, Bernard noticed, always south. And faster, probably, than by the main roads.

It was a cabbie's route, he thought, a Knowledge run. The scarred man definitely knew his way through town.

It made it difficult for Bernard to keep out of sight. To lose track of the Mercedes' red taillights even for a moment on those twists and turns might be to lose track of the car entirely. But to stay on it, to stay after it on the short spurs, round corner after corner, Bernard had to stay close behind. Sometimes the Morris's front end was no more than a few meters behind the Mercedes' boot. Sometimes the two cars were alone together on an empty stretch of road. And twice—once in Finsbury and once as they descended together through Clerkenwell—Bernard thought he saw the scarred driver lift his pink eyes to the rearview and stare directly back at him with piercing intensity. Bernard braked and slipped back into the night then. But it didn't reassure him much. His heart was beginning to rap against his ribs like a fist. He had to tighten his abdomen, practice his *nogare* breathing by force of will to keep himself steady at the wheel. Had he been spotted? He wasn't sure.

The Mercedes went on—and the Morris followed—into the dense and suffocating alleyways beneath the Barbican.

Moment by moment now, Bernard had very little idea where he was. Modern offices, warehouses crowded close on either side of him, moldering homes and faceless blocks of stone replaced them and hemmed him in. Boarded pubs, empty bakeries and restaurants, an open construction site, all dark, all deserted, were before him, then past. The Mercedes kept winding round, turning, avoiding the thoroughfares, hiding from the traffic.

And Bernard trailed along. His angelic face was tense, his eyes ached with staring at the red taillights before him. Despite the smooth movements of his hands upon the stick and the wheel, his body felt brittle, his muscles throbbed. Ahead, the Mercedes' pace remained even, unhurried.

Was it possible, he wondered after a while, was it possible that he was being drawn in?

Oh, Harper, he thought. You old witch. He had seen her back in the square. With her hand outstretched, with her mouth open. She had been trying to stop him, hadn't she? And he had ignored her. Because he was always tailing after her and she was always telling him what was what and she was always right about everything and, well, it rankled from time to time. So he had ignored her, and driven on as he thought best.

Was it possible, he wondered now, licking his dry lips, was it possible that she had been trying to save him from exactly this?

The Mercedes turned again, headed now along a curving street so narrow that the crumbling Tudor bays to the left and right seemed to hang directly over them. Then, all at once, with a harsh splash through a gutter puddle, the black car dashed out of sight, down an alley.

This was too much. In so tight a space, Bernard would be

a fool to follow. He let the Morris glide past the corner. Glanced over as he went by, just in time to see the black car's taillights wink out.

The Morris rolled on another short distance. Then Bernard pulled it to the curb beside an overflowing skip.

He switched off the engine. Flumped against the seat, his head falling back wearily. He shut his eyes.

He'd had a glimpse of the street in which the Mercedes had parked: a dead end, a walled close with barely a hand's breadth of space on either side of the car. Trail the scarred man into that and he would come out with his head under his arm. And here he had been so looking forward to a ripe old age of moral degeneracy and exquisite perversion.

He cursed aloud, and then shouldered the Morris's door open.

His long figure unfolded from the car. He was all in black. Only the shaven dome of his head shone under the single streetlight. He moved swiftly, with his willowy lope, back along the housefronts to the alley entrance. He pressed himself to the corner wall—feeling like a right idiot, feeling like a cinema spy—and peeked around the edge.

It was a forbidding prospect, worse than he'd expected. The alley was thick with night. The oppressive walls seemed to angle towards each other as they went in. The hulking form of the Mercedes rose between them. And beyond that rose another shape, big, dark: a rearing hump of stone, a silhouetted spire. A church, sinister, against all that was visible of the sky. With this, the alley abruptly ended.

Bernard hesitated. There was, he saw, a weird blue glow coming from the place, and a vertical line of yellow light—as would appear at the edge of a shrouded window. He licked his lips again. His heartbeat was fierce and loud. His palms, pressed to the wall behind him, were clammy.

He peeled off the building and started into the alley.

Crouched, his hands lifted, held before him, he moved with predatory grace. He was now, he decided, absolutely terrified. His eyes darted here and there. To crannies of blackness. Clutters of bins and boxes. To the hump of the Mercedes, which seemed to him ready to rear up at any moment and spring. The alleyway closed over him, the dark closed over him. Yes, *absolutely terrified*—that was the phrase he wanted.

He came up behind the waiting car. Peered, as well as he could, through the rear window into the unlit interior. It was quiet in there. There was no movement. But he couldn't make out the floor in back, and beyond the front seats he could see nothing at all.

Yet he began to squeeze around it. A tight squeeze. The brick wall scraped the back of his black windbreaker. The door handles plucked at the buckle of his belt. He could be fairly certain now that the car was empty. He edged past it, around to the front, under the rising church.

He crept on, towards the end of the alley. The church's spire pierced the blowing clouds above him. The small domed hexagon of an apse grew huskier and more imposing as he neared. His senses were all electrified, his nerve ends naked and snaking like live wires. He could smell things— not just ordinary things, but everything. Not just the rotting garbage and the grainy sting of old exhaust, but the dirt of shoe soles and cigarettes ground into the pavement over time, the edge of seawater in the southwestern breeze—and something else, some citrusy smell, which was mighty like the aroma of his own fear. And he could hear—the sussurus of the city, a burst of laughter from far away, a baby crying—

but also, he was almost certain of it, a portentous undertone of voices through the heavy stones of the church walls, the burr of a conversation within. And the weird blue glow—he could see now: it was light filtering out through a stained-glass window. He could even make out the figures on it and guessed they were Christ with Lazarus rising. And he could see that the thin line of yellow light did not come through a shrouded window but through a fissure in the apse. Its narrow panes were clear and, though the light was faint, his eyes were so wide, so receptive, that the glare of it seemed to scorch his pupils. And to draw him on.

He was stopped. He had reached an iron railing close against the church wall. He grimaced, intensely aware that the wisest course was to turn and run for it. Instead, he grasped the heads of two spikes and vaulted his long legs over the rail with a single, swinging motion. He landed on the opposite strip of pavement without a sound.

Now the spire stretched up out of sight above his head. One angle—two sides—of the apse pushed in towards him. He reached out and his fingertips touched the damp stone, glided over it as he stepped around the angle's point to the lit fissure. Slowly, he stretched his body up to peer through the window's bottom half.

The murmur of conversation still reached him, not much louder than before, no clearer. But he couldn't find the source of it at first. He was looking slantwise across a vault in the end of a stunted transept. Whatever the source of the light was, it was out of sight. All he saw was the dim yellow glow of it, spreading from somewhere up the aisles, dying within his field of vision. By pressing far to one side, he could take in some of the front pews running up to the altar. But the scene was mostly in shadow.

After another moment or two, he began to make things out. The spiral staircase leading up to a simple pulpit. An enormous crucifix sunk back into the dark behind it. The gnarled shape of the figure hanging on the cross. He saw the muted colors, the faint glimmer of a stained-glass window on the wall above. But, beyond that, there were only half-delineated forms hunkered before invisible recesses. The hollow reaches of the church seemed to drift with a sort of smoke of gray darkness. Then a movement caught his eye . . .

And he saw three men. The featureless figures of three men. They were gathered together on the far side of the chancel rail. They were standing in a tight cluster. They were talking almost in whispers. One of them laughed, a deep chuckle. Another nodded, the black shape of his head bobbing.

Bernard strained to hear, strained to see. Raised now on tiptoe. His neck hurting as he craned it to keep the men in view.

And, as he looked, he heard another noise—a dreadful noise—a faint, low, agonized sob from somewhere in the shadows.

Bernard's eyes moved to the sound. His mouth opened. The air came out of him in a long, unbroken gasp.

The body on the crucifix was moving.

It shifted weakly. It moaned again. "Don't know. Don't know." Bernard saw the dark liquid lines trailing down from the palms. Saw the arms straining against the ropes that held them. Feebly, the crucified figure lifted its head.

Bernard gaped. The man's eyes were gone. Pools of gore were spilling out of his sockets, running down his cheeks. His head dropped forward.

Shocked, Bernard lost his grip on the fissure. He fell away, took a step away from the church. He whispered harshly, "Jesus Christ!"

And at once, he heard another laugh, another deep chuckle. Only this time, it came from directly beside him.

"Not exactly, mate," the scarred man said.

Bernard was fast. Jumped back even as he spun to face his attacker. But he was still so staggered by what he'd seen, so fazed by the first jolt of it—and much too surprised by the ambush to fend it off. Even as he leapt, even as he dropped into a semblance of a fighting stance, even as he lifted his hands in an attempt at self-protection, the small, burning eyes, the disfigured mouth of the scarred man completely filled his field of vision, completely overwhelmed him.

The sap was falling before he knew it. It struck him on the side of the head full force.

Bernard saw the sky, saw the spire, spinning, wheeling. And then he pitched over, onto the railing, clung to it, hung from it—and finally slid senseless to the ground.

7   Sir Michael Endering sat erect behind his huge mahogany desk. Sat pressed into his high-backed leather chair like the statue of a man enthroned. The lights in the study were off, all of them. The green velvet curtains were drawn. The walls of bookshelves were only faintly visible.

Belham Grange was silent all around him, silent everywhere.

The great man sat stalwart. The prow-like chin was raised, the mighty head upheld. He seemed unaware that his features had collapsed over the last several hours, had thinned amazingly and grown old. His lips were parted and flecked with white drops of spittle. His cheeks were suddenly hollowed and pale, the ruddiness gone from them. His silver hair was in frantic disarray.

His eyes, glinting in the dark, were shifting, quick, afraid.

This was how they were going to get at him, he thought. In the cruelest way. Through his daughter.

Long minutes passed. Sir Michael stirred. He reached into his waistcoat pocket and brought out a ring of keys. He gazed down at them lying in his big hand as if he was not sure what they were. He murmured wordlessly. Swiveled slightly. And bent down to unlock the desk's bottom drawer.

He brought out an elegant box topped with studded green leather. He set it on the blotter before him. Unlocked it, opened it.

On a tray in the box lay a line of Havana cigars and a sterling silver lighter. The tray lifted out to reveal a swatch of velvet underneath.

Underneath the swatch of velvet was an ugly and brutal-looking revolver.

It was a snub-nosed .38, American, Smith & Wesson. So compact he could nearly swallow it in his enormous palm. A cardboard box of bullets lay beside it.

Sir Michael lifted the pistol out, cracked the cylinder. Spun the chambers once to assure himself the gun was oiled. His long fingers were unsteady on the bullet box, but he got it open, removed a bullet, two. He sniffed once, as if disdainfully, but then his whole body shuddered.

His daughter was coming to the house tomorrow. His daughter—and Richard Storm.

It seemed to Sir Michael now that he had been dreading this day for twenty years, that he had been watching for it, ever since his wife died. But the fact was, for much of that time, he hadn't believed the warnings were real. He had thought they were all a figment of Ann's final madness. He hadn't known enough. He hadn't got sufficient information. All he'd had to go on were his wife's ravings, the things she had said to him that terrible night when she lay on the floor, the blood gushing from her. *Get the Rhinehart triptych. Don't let him have it, no matter what. Iago. He'll kill you for it. He'll kill everyone.* And on and on in the same vein. *Don't speak to anyone. Don't trust anyone. Everything depends on it. He'll kill you. He'll kill anyone.* Well, what on earth was he supposed to have understood from that?

All the same, he had done what he could. Then and now, out of loyalty to her, he had done what he could. But he was stumbling blind; he had never been certain what it was he was dealing with. When *The Magi* came up for auction—out of loyalty to his wife—he had sent Sophia to make a strong offer for it, more than strong enough, he thought, to secure the thing. It was only when poor Jessica was outbid, when the price skyrocketed as high as it did, that he began to believe—to believe truly—that Ann's hysterical gibberish might have been grounded in fact.

And now, tonight, there came the rumors from the street. That the *Madonna* was in play. That that crazy old bastard Jervis Ramsbottom had vanished, might even be dead. And now, tonight, the real fear, the terror, had struck him like a blow. And he had begun to think: Yes. Yes, it's all happening, just as she said it would. *Iago. He'll kill everyone.* And Sir Michael had finally thought, *Good God. I'm next. They're going to come for me next.*

Then—even as he'd thought it—Sophia phoned. She was coming here to the Grange tomorrow, she said. She was coming with Richard Storm.

And everything fell into place. He had been suspicious of Storm from the very beginning. Calling Jessica off at the auction like that. Weaseling his way into Sophia's life like that. Now he was certain: if Storm was not this Iago fellow himself, he was surely working as his agent. This was how they were going to get at him. Through the American. Through Sophia. By corrupting the daughter he loved more than anything in life. By stealing the one thing he loved best—just as they had before.

His broad shoulders straightened. His weary features set. Well, if they thought he was going to lie down and take it this time, they had another think coming. Another think entirely.

Richard Storm, is it? Sir Michael thought angrily, sitting there. *Richard Storm indeed.*

And then, slowly, he began to load the revolver.

IX

SPECTRE

130   INT. THE CRYPT OF ST. JAMES

The repeated CLANG-CLANG continues and DR. PRENDERGAST, with the faithful HEDLEY trailing after, rushes in, following the sound.

They stand for a moment at a loss. Then, again: CLANG-CLANG.

> DR. PRENDERGAST
> This way, Hedley!

> HEDLEY
> But there's nothing here . . .

Ignoring him, PRENDERGAST rushes to a large sarcophagus in the center of the crypt. He seizes the stone lid.

> DR. PRENDERGAST
> Lend a hand, Hedley!

Baffled, HEDLEY joins the doctor. With a massive effort, the two men manage to push the lid off. It falls to the floor, breaking into pieces.

> HEDLEY
> By Jove, Prendergast: a stairway!

The CLANG-CLANG sounds again from beneath the crypt, much louder now.

> DR. PRENDERGAST
> Follow me!

First DR. PRENDERGAST, then HEDLEY, climb into the sarcophagus.

131   INT. HIDDEN STAIRWAY

DR. PRENDERGAST and HEDLEY descend into utter darkness.

Again: CLANG-CLANG.

> DR. PRENDERGAST
> Quick, Hedley, a torch!

HEDLEY produces a flashlight and the beam plays eerily over the mossy walls, suddenly illuminating . . .

The flayed body of SERGEANT ANDERSON, hanging in chains.

They examine the corpse grimly.

> DR. PRENDERGAST
> (continuing)
> Poor devil.

CLANG-CLANG.

> DR. PRENDERGAST
> (continuing)
> Come on, Hedley, there's no time to waste!

DR. PRENDERGAST continues his descent. After another moment confronting the body, HEDLEY follows.

132   INT. UNDERGROUND PASSAGE

DR. PRENDERGAST and HEDLEY reach the bottom of the stairs and enter an underground passage. An ominous RED GLOW is visible at the far end.

DR. PRENDERGAST touches HEDLEY's arm and nods at the flashlight. HEDLEY turns it off.

They move slowly, cautiously, down the passage as the CLANG-CLANG sounds again.

The RED GLOW grows brighter as they near the end of the passage. Their faces tense, they round the bend into . . .

133   INT. THE GREAT VAULT

The whole scene lies before them. JACOBUS, in the full evil splendor of his miter and pentagram robe, stands triumphant before an altar on which lies a purple blanket.

ANNIE, her clothes torn, is chained to the wall, writhing in her bonds.

As the CLANG-CLANG sounds again, we see . . .

The hunchbacked GORGE hammering out the blade of the jeweled SWORD OF THE SEIRIZZIM.

JACOBUS looks up at DR. PRENDERGAST with a calm smile, as if he had been expecting him.

> JACOBUS
> Why, Dr. Prendergast, I'm so glad you could make it. I left Sergeant Anderson to show you the way.

HEDLEY starts forward angrily, but DR. PRENDERGAST restrains him.

> JACOBUS
> (continuing)
> You're just in time to bear witness to my final apotheosis.

GORGE, his work finished, now shuffles forward, bearing the SWORD to his master.

ANNIE struggles on the wall, crying out through her gag.

JACOBUS handles the SWORD lovingly, then lifts it into the air.

> JACOBUS
> (continuing)
> Poor Prendergast. That you ever thought to defeat me. Could you not see that I am the agent of an immortal power? In such incarnations as this, I travel through the centuries. I feed on the marrow of time. I was here before the oceans turned black with life, and when the deserts are white with death I will remain. The petty hindrances you have put in my way have only served to amuse me. But that's all over now.

He raises the SWORD higher. And then . . .

Then, with bright eyes and an eager grin, GORGE steps to the altar. With a swift movement, he pulls the purple blanket away to reveal . . .

ANNIE'S BABY, lying naked on the altar!

ANNIE shrieks behind her gag, struggling on the wall.

JACOBUS raises the SWORD above his head, ready to drive it into the infant's breast.

But DR. PRENDERGAST only smiles with grim calm.

> DR. PRENDERGAST
> Not so fast, Jacobus . . .

X

BLACK ANNIE II:
THIS TIME,
IT'S PERSONAL

1 *His eyes! His eyes were full of fear. And, though we had seen him in London only two weeks before, he seemed since then to have aged as many decades. A man in his middle sixties, he peered at us through the half-open door of Belham Grange with all the tremulous hostility, the white-eyed apprehension, of some ancient anchorite disturbed at his grimmest meditations.*

No shit, thought Richard Storm, as the withered, hostile, white-eyed face of Sir Michael peered out at them.

We had already dismissed our cab. We could hear the car's engine fading behind us on the Grange's long drive. The winter afternoon was closing around us, the windswept clouds of a lowering sky pressed down on us from above. The house itself, the whole great stone edifice, loomed menacingly before us as with an adsum *to our* conjuro te.

Well, all right, the house didn't loom exactly. It was a neat, pretty old mansion, a long stone structure with lots of windows, light and airy. And there were no "horrid ravens peering blackly from the gutters and gables of the place" either. But Storm did feel a "thrill of dread" sure enough at the sight of Sir Michael's "ravaged features"—his pale, sunken cheeks, his watchful eyes glaring out through the crack in the door. He felt a thrill of dread and a whirling, dreamy, febrile sense of swimming distances and unreality. He had a faint headache too, which had been bothering him all morning.

Sophia stepped from beside him to kiss her father's sagging cheek.

Storm took a last glance over his shoulder. Back up the empty drive, "where it stretched into the distance overhung by gloomy rows of copper beech." The clouds barreling in over the hills were thunderheads, great and threatening. The February wind was wet and chill, and the day was darkening to a false twilight.

And through that dark, through the dead, dangling branches intermingling above the drive, he could just make out the ruin of the abbey in the distance: "the broken wedge of a chapel wall, the slanting monuments of its ancient churchyard."

Storm straightened and took a breath, trying to clear his head. He turned to the house again.

Sophia had crossed the threshold. Sir Michael was holding the door open for him.

Well, he thought, he had come to England to find a ghost story, hadn't he?

And, forcing a smile, he walked into Belham Grange.

2

Detective Inspector William Pullod stood in the church round and watched the old woman. She was moving slowly among the stone effigies of dead crusaders. Prodding them with that freaky dragon stick of hers as if she half expected them to come to life. Frowning and muttering under her wide-brimmed hat, darting glances here and there from behind her goggly spectacles.

DI Pullod sluiced the air from one cheek to another, rolled his eyes.

He was a small, quick, sinewy man, a balding weightlifter with shoulders that seemed ready to burst the seams of his raincoat. He hated wasting time and he hated dead ends. And he hated churches too, if it came to that. He found them creepy, lonesome and yet weirdly alive—like a house where all the clocks have suddenly stopped ticking.

This one, the Temple Church, was bright enough with its big doors open to the noonday sunlight. Busy enough with a group of Japanese tourists chattering as they examined the stained-glass windows down at the other end. Here in the round, though, there were disturbing, distorted faces sculpted on the columns of the arches. They stared down from every side at the stone knights lying twisted on the floor. And it was creepy. Like the old darling herself.

Still, Pullod thought, there was definitely something about her. Nutter that she was. With her Saint Iago who never lived, and her Argentinian cult that never existed. Supernatural conspiracy theories. Little gray men and such. She ought to work for ITV, he thought. Still. Her eyes were sharp as a needle, smart. And she looked like she'd been alive forever. Sounded like it too with her gruff, grave voice. Not to mention the fact that she'd identified Lester Benbow from his photofit, and Pullod would've given his teeth to catch up with that scar-lipped assassin.

He strolled over to the woman now, his hands in his overcoat pockets.

"Everything look in order, love?" he asked her. He kept his voice low. Churches had that effect on him.

"Yes," murmured Harper Albright after a moment. "Yes." She went on prodding the dead crusaders with her stick.

Pullod ran his eyes over the gibbering faces on the walls. He could not restrain a weary sigh. "You're sure this is where you saw him last, this Iago fellow?"

Harper only nodded. "I didn't expect him to return, but it seemed worth trying. It was something he said about being chosen. I have a sense, you see, that he is not only following this trail of stories, but attempting somehow to inhabit them. As if he thought they were all about him in some way, as if he thought he were their ongoing protagonist. It makes one think he might seek out locations that bore some relation to them. That he might use them as the base for his operations."

"Aha," said Pullod. He put his tongue in his cheek to keep from smiling.

Harper Albright looked up at him sharply. "I don't expect you to believe me, Inspector. All I ask of you and your people is that you let me know the moment you locate Bernard's car."

Pullod, caught out, lost the smile and nodded briskly. "Morris Minor. We're keeping our eyes peeled."

She studied him through those goggles of hers for a long, uncomfortable moment. Then she sniffed.

"Please do," she said. "Because whether you believe me or not, the truth of the matter is: We haven't got very much time."

3   Then a church bell tolled some unknown hour and Bernard began to come around. He had no idea where he'd been, where he was, no notion of what had happened to him. For a long time the only thing he knew for certain was that the business of living had turned dimly dreadful.

Then, after a while, his eyes came open. Slowly. Breaking

the dried crust that had held them shut. He looked.

Nothing. Blackness. Darkness more complete, more empty than any he had ever known. He became aware now too that he was deeply uncomfortable. Lying on his back, inert, twisted. Knees to one side, one hand flung up by his face. The reek of the air was foul. There was a stench of vomit that made him want to vomit. He could feel the stuff soaking his shoulder through his shirt, viscid, lumpy. There was the smell of urine as well: his crotch and thighs were stinging with the drying damp.

A steady throb in his forehead was fast becoming intolerable. The taste in his mouth defied description.

Well, he'd woken up in a similar condition any number of times. But no, this wasn't an ordinary hangover. He was remembering now. The church. The crucifix. That moan; that man. His head lifting. His eyes . . .

Bernard made a weak, shuddering noise, a sound he'd never heard himself make before. The blackness seemed to be growing heavier, thicker. Closing in around him. Smothering him. Entombing him.

Entombing him. The thought started a stain of panic spreading up towards his chest from his loins. He could feel now the rough stone beneath his shaven pate. He moved his hand—felt a wall of the same rough stone to the right of him, another to his left. Rough stone was at his feet when he tried to extend his legs. And then, slowly, fearfully— *prayerfully*—he upstretched his fingers.

There was a slab of rough stone right above him, not six inches above his nose.

Buried alive. The panic swarmed up over him like rats. A chill sweat bathed him from head to toe. His breath grew short, shallow, his pulsebeat quick. A whispery voice spoke over and over in his head: *buried alive they've buried me alive I'm buried alive* . . .

He had to get the hell out of here.

With a choked cry, he thrust both hands up through the blackness. Instantly, the pain in his skull became excruciating, the veins bulging against his temples like spiked balloons. He pushed against the slab that covered him—pushed and pushed—struggling with all his sinewy might against that unyielding weight.

It was still unyielding. The breath stuttered from him in intermittent grunts. Then he gasped out the rest of it, and his arms collapsed on top of him.

"Help!" he shouted wildly. "Help!"

Then he retched, turning onto his side as best he could to keep the acid spittle off him. Then he plumped onto his back again, staring into the blackness.

Then he began to weep.

Buried alive. Christ, Christ, he didn't want to die like this.

"Christ," he whispered, sobbing. "Christ."

He worked his arm around in the cramped space, reached his trembling hand to his cheek to swipe away the hot tears.

And his heart seized in him like a dry engine.

There was something lying beside him in the blackness.

He had touched it with his knuckles. He could feel it there, an inch from his face. He could feel the smooth, yielding surface of moldering bone. The empty eye sockets. The image formed in his head as if he could see it: a human skull. Gaping at him, grinning at him. He was in a stone coffin—a sarcophagus—with a rotted corpse.

His body bucking with wild terror, he drove his hands against the coffin lid again. The pain was even worse this time. White pinpoints danced before his eyes. He almost lost consciousness. But he poured his strength into his arms, his soul into his arms, a high screek tearing from his throat as he fought to move the slab even a millimeter, even the width of an eyelash.

It was no good. The stone wouldn't budge. Bernard lay gasping, sobbing, trembling. *Buried alive I'm in the earth in a grave I'm buried alive . . .* He could feel his mind trying to tear free of its tether, trying to career out of his control. He was about to start shrieking . . .

No. He set his teeth. No, no. He pressed his fists against his mouth, gnawed at the skin on his knuckles to force the scream down into his throat. Once he started that, there would be no end of it. He had to hold on. Hold on—by main force—there was no other way.

He summoned his will. He shoved the whispery voice of panic down, down. His breath. He focused all his concentration on his abdomen, on his breath.

He lay still. There was the dark, and the inner frenzy of his helplessness, the smell, the damp, the terrible pain. And yet he lay still, focusing on his breath.

He came down from the panic in notches, bit by bit. After a time—he didn't know how long—he became aware that he was whimpering, and forced himself to stop. His muscles began to relax. His fists sank down from his mouth, sank slowly over the length of him. He kept his hands directly above him, kept his elbows pressed close to his side to avoid touching that horror just next to him, that gaping horror.

"Help! Help me! Help!" Bernard shouted, not wildly this time, but as loudly as he could.

Then he lay very still, trying to control his breath so he

could hear. Lay with his eyes wide against the impenetrable blackness. Listening, listening.

"Help!"

Each time his voice ceased, the silence that followed seemed deeper than the silence before. It seemed to flutter down over him like a shroud and swaddle him round. A man could suffocate in such a silence. He could almost hear the worms crawling in it. He could almost hear the skull beside him speaking, whispering, *buried alive buried alive buried alive* . . .

"Help! Help!"

A high note of hysteria entered his voice and he clamped his mouth shut, clamped his eyes shut. Clamped his hands together over his belly, clamped his elbows to his sides. Hearing his breath, hearing his heartbeat, hearing the whispering skull beside him: *buried alive* . . .

And then—possibly—he heard something else. A noise. Possibly. Outside.

Bernard's eyes sprang open. His body, taut as it was, went tauter still. He stopped breathing altogether, and there was only the throb of his pulse, the throb of his head.

And, yes, something else. Definitely now. Rattle, crank, creak, thud. The sound of a door, he thought. A heavy door with a metal latch. Opening, then swinging shut again.

"Oh!" he said. Fresh tears surged from his eyes, tears of relief and gratitude. He wasn't under the earth, not buried, not yet.

"Help me!" he shouted.

Painfully rigid, he listened, yearning upward towards the coffin lid, beyond it.

And there were footsteps. Footsteps on stone. Steady, echoic. Coming nearer.

They stopped.

Bernard, crying, hardly dared to speak again. He stared upward, ached and prayed upward into the darkness. Someone was standing there, just over him, just on the other side of the stone, just on the other side of the blackness. He could feel the presence. Standing there. In the light, in the open air. Looking down at him.

Bernard licked the mucus from his upper lip. Swallowed it. Sniffled. Spoke through his tears in a tremulous whisper.

"Help me. Would you please."

There was another moment's silence. And then the presence spoke. A voice distinct and mellifluous. Casual, gentle, even kind. Strange and yet strangely familiar.

At the sound of it, some warm, potent emotion he couldn't name bubbled out of Bernard like blood from a wound, ran like blood all over him.

"I'm here, son," the presence said. "I'm here."

4   The silence was oppressive. The chink of cutlery on china. The slow crunching of cold food. Sir Michael sat at the head of the long table, swirling the wine in his crystal. Staring before him. Not speaking. Storm found the old man's sunken features, his disheveled hair, his wild glare painful to look upon. He kept his own head down, picking at the roast beef and carrots on his plate.

The dining room was narrow, but trim and pleasant enough. The lunch was laid out in gleaming plates and servers, blue and white. The crystal chandelier sent dancing rainbows over them and onto the flocked paisley on the long walls. Low sideboards and a serving table ran along one of those walls. And above these, there hung a gilt-framed painting of shepherds on sunlit hills. The landscape was almost a reflection of the landscape visible through the tall windows on the wall opposite, the wall Storm was facing. Out there, though, through the port-red curtains tied back with golden cords, he could see the hills stretching away under gathering clouds, a roiling black mass of them. A hem of thunder sounded from time to time, distant at first, but growing closer.

Sophia sat with her back to the scene. Her black hair, her pale valentine face were etched sharply against the sallow, murky light of the afternoon. Storm glanced up at her. Her figure was softened by a fuzzy tannish sweater with snow-flakes all over it. But she held herself very straight and he could feel the tension in her. He tried to catch her eye, to telegraph his question: When would she speak out? When would they begin?

She seemed not to look at him. Her head moved almost imperceptibly. A little forbidding shake of it: not now, not yet.

He went on eating, impatient, nervous. His head aching; thick; foggy. He did not feel well.

More thunder sounded, a longer grumble this time, and closer. Storm thought he caught a bland silver flash over the far horizon. The yellow light outside grew thicker, dimmer. He could see isolated trees bending here and there before the wind. He could feel the heat of Sir Michael's feverish eyes.

Let's cut to the damned chase, he thought. But he glanced at Sophia again, got that look again, that shake of the head.

"I'll make coffee, shall I?" she said softly.

And before either of the men could answer, she had risen and left the room.

Storm and Sir Michael sat in silence and listened to her footsteps fading down the corridor.

"I'm going to kill you, Mr. Storm," Sir Michael said then.

Storm was spearing his last piece of beef. He heard another roll of thunder. He took this in a full second before he comprehended Sir Michael's words. Then he raised his eyes to the other man. His lips parted, but he couldn't think of a thing to say.

Sir Michael had placed his glass down on the table now. He sat relaxed in his chair, with his hands folded over the belly of his vest. The great head seemed almost to have caved in upon itself. It reminded Storm of corpses he had seen in museums, half preserved, the skin clinging to the skull. Except for those eyes. Those eyes were alive enough, boiling, almost bulging out at him. Storm felt his stomach curdle, felt a point of pain stab at his temple.

"What?" he said.

"I'm going to kill you," Sir Michael repeated quietly, hoarsely. "Do you think I care what happens to me? Do you think I'm going to sit back and let you or your people do this to me again? Good Christ, whom do you think you're dealing with?"

"Whoa!" said Storm.

"You should be more careful, Mr. Storm. You should learn to leave a man something worth living for. I only have Sophia, and I won't let you use her to get at me, to get what you want."

"Hey, hold on a minute . . ." said Storm.

But Sir Michael plowed on irresistibly. "I've made inquiries. Do you understand? I'm not without contacts, here or in the States. I should hear back at any time, perhaps even today, perhaps within the hour. And the moment I'm certain you're who I think you are, I'm going to put a bullet in your head."

"Hey, listen up here a minute . . ." said Storm.

"No, you listen up. I'm going to blow your brains out,

boy, with pleasure. In my wife's memory and for Sophia's sake, and the consequences be damned." With a short, sharp motion, he snapped up his wine again. "I strongly suggest you run for your life."

Storm opened his hands, opened his mouth. He found himself utterly at a loss for words. His heart was racing. His mind was racing. Was Sir Michael making some kind of mistake? Or did he know why Storm was here and mean exactly what he said? Storm didn't know where to begin to answer him.

"Lookit . . ."

Hurried footsteps in the corridor stopped him, stopped them both. Sophia came back in. Pale, her lips working, she moved at once to Storm's chair, put her hands firmly on his shoulders. Even in his confusion, he heard the pitiful urgency in her voice.

"Come on, Richard," she said quickly. "While the coffee's brewing. I'll show you around the place before it rains."

"Sophia . . ." he said.

"Come *on*!"

5   The open-air market on the Edgware Road was in full swing. Harper Albright threaded slowly through the crowd. The pavements were still wet with rain but the London skies were clearer. The people were out in force, filling the spaces between stalls and bazaars, paging through racks of tie-dyed and heavy-metal T-shirts, milling past open boxes of vegetables, tables of pottery, jewelery, antiques, junk. Loud, tuneless music blasted from speakers under the canvas that covered some of the stalls. The shouts of hawkers

blasted back from their uncovered stands. "Cabbages! Lettuce! Tomatoes five a quid!" The tide of the crowd came on against her, but Harper pressed into it steadily. Her shoulders hunched, her stick jabbing at the concrete, her head uplifted grumpily and her quick eyes peering out from under her hatbrim, taking in the scene.

She took in everything. A young man pierced and bedizened at the ears and nose and eyebrows. A young woman holding a baby under one arm, examining a Grateful Dead shirt with the other. A John Bull toby mug on a table. A Chelsea football strip fluttering from a hook in the wind . . .

She took in everything. But what exactly she was looking for she did not know. She didn't even know exactly why she had come. She supposed it was enough at this point that a nagging instinct summoned her. She supposed it had to be enough; it was all there was.

And Bernard was out there—still alive. Captive, but still alive, she was certain of it. She could feel that much, she could feel him living. Feel it in the termites of anxiety gnawing steadily at her innards. Iago had no reason to kill the lad yet. Not yet. It wasn't his life he wanted. He wanted his blood. An endless supply of it. And for that, he would need to win over the factotum's will. He would have to poison his mind, gain his complicity. In other words, he would have to steal his soul.

And that would take some time. Bernard's soul was strong. It would take some time, but it would not take forever. She had to find him—soon.

And she had to find him on her own.

She had seen the look on the inspector's face. She had seen that look before in her dealings with the police. She had seen even worse looks than that sometimes; she knew Iago had his minions on the force. She could not trust the police to help her. She could not trust anyone. She had no clue to go on, no direction to follow, no spot to search in the wide world that seemed more likely to her than any other. Her enemies were legion, and she was only three. She had nowhere to turn, no one to turn to.

The time had come for her to catch the current of the Uncanny.

That was why she was here, really, she supposed. Shopping in the open market for inspiration. Peering down the aisles between the clothing racks. Running her eyes over the heads of lettuce. Watching the faces of the shoppers, the bopping rhythms of their youthful strides. She was seeking for coincidence, the pawprint of her adversary.

A little place off the Edgware Road. That's what Iago had said to her. *On the road to Damascus,* he'd said. That was where he had had his own inspiration twenty years ago. Whatever had happened then, somewhere near here, it had started him down the trail of stories. From "Black Annie" to the Belham Chronicle. Everything that had followed radiated from that one instant. Ann Endering's suicide. The hunt for the Rhinehart triptych. Even, perhaps, Richard Storm's arrival. From Iago's instant of revelation off the Edgware Road had come everything that had led them to this hour.

So she pushed through the crowds in the Edgware market. Her eyes moving. The anxiety gnawing away. Searching, she supposed, for the mystic spark that would put her inside Iago's mind. That would lead her to Bernard.

Her chance of making such a connection, in ordinary terms, was almost nil. And in one sense, ordinary terms were all she had. There is no life but life, she knew. There is no world but this one. If the Uncanny operates at all, it does not operate above the laws of nature but through them. The unseen moves forever in the manifest, the spirit speaks in the language of material; the soul lives in the interplay of neurons; and God, if He is anywhere, is in the details. Even coincidence—the spoor she was seeking—could be shown to exist within the rules of probability. But it did exist, the hidden tides and patterns of it. The trick was to find them when you needed them most.

And the trick to that—as always—was to believe nothing. To believe nothing lest the pattern of your beliefs be imposed upon the pattern of events. To believe nothing, and keep your eyes open. In wise passivity, to strive, to seek . . . and not to yield . . .

She reached the corner. The light was with her, but she paused, uncertain. Across the street, the market ended. The crowd thinned. Litter blew along the pavement, between whitewashed walls, past lampposts, under traffic signals, off down the avenue into the piebald sky. To her left, a man was selling sports caps. To her right, an Englishwoman dressed like a gypsy fortuneteller sat sullenly behind a table of used books. A tinker with a baby carriage held her hand out to the passersby.

Harper, for comfort, worked her fingers over the ears of the dragon head. The anxiety was seething now all through her. She felt like an empty sack full of racketing nerves.

And a voice spoke in her ear: "Oh, hey, look here. Look at this."

Without thinking, she glanced over, towards the speaker, to her right. There was just a boy there, in his late teens. A pale, pimply face pocked with red spots under a wisp of beard. A dull-eyed girl beside him, her arm in his, her nose and eyes and lips so full of studs and rings she seemed to be held together by them.

The boy had lifted a book from the table. Was holding it up to her.

"Look at this. Do we have this one?"

Harper did look. And as the lad rotated the book in his hand to study it, she saw the cover of *The Fourteenth Fontana Book of Great Ghost Stories.* The book Storm had read from at Bolt's Christmas party.

Harper stood and gazed at it. She felt a slow change begin to take place inside her. Her nerves continued racketing around, but now, instead of eating at her, they began to fuel her, to energize her. Anxiety was changing to excitement. She had found what she was looking for.

A little place off the Edgware Road, she thought.

The hunt was on.

6

"Do you know who I am?"

The voice came down into the sarcophagus like a tendril of smoke. It mingled like a smell with the smell of vomit and urine and sweat and fear. It coiled around Bernard's body where he lay with the tears still streaming down his cheeks, with his nose still running, with the agonizing pulse still beating in his head. He was aware now that there was blood at the pulsing spot, a stain half-dried, half-sticky where the sap had caught him. He was feeling woozy again and weak and sick. And the voice in the utter blackness came to him as with the cool of the open air, with the light of day. That first passion he had felt at the sound of it still coursed through him.

"Yes," he said, his own voice trembling. He cleared his throat. "Yes. I know who you are."

"Good. It's about time we became acquainted with one another."

Bernard could feel the coffin's stone lid pressing down on him, the rancid air growing more rancid yet. He could feel that skull beside him, not inches from his face, staring, grinning.

"I've never stopped keeping watch over you," said the voice. "You might know that."

Bernard closed his eyes, opened them. It made no difference; there was only the dark.

"Yes," he whispered.

"Some of the people you've met on your night excursions. Some of the people you've . . . played with, been intimate with . . ."

"Yes."

"You've known that."

Bernard cried quietly.

"In fact, I feel I already know you fairly well," said the voice. "In fact, I feel you already know me, but . . . But the truth is, I don't feel that you know you know me. If that makes any sense. I don't feel that you admit to yourself that you know me as well as you actually do."

"Let me out." The plea broke from Bernard before he could stop it. He screwed up his face, furious with himself for his weakness. But when he tried to slow his crying, he only produced a loud and humiliating sob.

"That's why I'm here," the cool voice went on, went on like smoke, filling the sarcophagus like smoke. And the worst thing about it, Bernard thought, was that it was so much better than nothing. He could feel how desperately he was holding on to the sound of it, holding on to the power of the presence above him, the power to set him free. He had to hang on to it. Where there was life . . . he thought. "I want to let you out," the speaker went on. "That's all I want. It's as much to my benefit as it is to yours. Maybe more. But I have to make sure you hear first what I have to say. So the bargain is: you promise to listen, I promise to set you free. Is that fair enough?"

Bernard shuddered, trying to control his breathing, to fight his panic. He didn't want to answer. It was degrading to agree where he had no choice.

But the voice insisted: "Isn't that fair enough?"

"Yes, yes," he said angrily, his own voice full of tears.

"Because everything you know about me, every single thing, has been told to you by one person, one person only. And that one person—I tell you this in all honesty—that one person has every reason to hate me. Isn't that true? Even from what you already know, wouldn't you agree that she's not an objective observer? Wouldn't you agree with that?"

Bernard hugged himself. "I don't know," he said wearily. "I don't know."

"Well, if you don't know," said the voice, "then it's because she hasn't told you everything. It's because she hasn't been as honest with you as I'm being right now."

Christ, thought Bernard. *Christ, Christ.* Hugging his shoulders more tightly, arms crossed like a corpse. He didn't know how to answer this, even within himself. He had always thought that it didn't matter, that he never minded. That he even enjoyed the unspoken knowledge, the tacit understanding between himself and Harper. He had been raised by a sturdy innkeeping family up in the lakes. Educated at a boarding school outside London. But Harper's visits to him had been frequent even in his childhood. Her conversations with him had always been intimate and pointed. She had explained her mission to him so thoroughly, so steadily, with such maternal assurance, that he had understood, from the earliest age, that it was his mission too, by birth, by right. Was it dishonesty for her not to speak aloud the fact he already knew?

"I can't breathe!" he screamed. His hands flew up, scrabbled at the rough slab. The flesh at his fingers tore and the blood ran down over them. Then his hands fell back again. He lay there, crying. "I can't breathe."

"When I first found her," the voice went on, unmoved. Cool, smoky. "When I first found her, she was in ruins. Her mother gone, her father in prison. Her own life a round of the worst kind of self-abuse: your life, believe me, is a poor imitation. It was she who attached herself to me, Bernard, not the other way around."

"I know that," Bernard said, under his breath so it wouldn't be heard.

"Good," said the voice. "I'm glad she told you that, at least. Because the rest was the same. If I degraded her, if I hurt her, it was because she wanted me to. Begged me to. Crawled to me on her knees, Bernard, and demanded it. On her knees, Bernard."

Bernard felt he was going to be sick again, sick unto death this time. He felt he was going to vomit up everything inside him, blood and guts, the very tinkerbell-flicker of life itself. The smell and the worsening air had all been displaced by the miasma of that voice. It seeped into his skin, cool and vital and refreshing. His own weird passion met it, and he felt sick and poisoned unto death.

"And now," the voice went on. "Now the memory of that

disturbs her, and she puts it all onto me. Her own desires are off the hook and I become the villain of the piece. And that's . . . distorted. It isn't the truth. It not only deprives me of the right to defend myself—but it deprives you too. It deprives you of that part of yourself that is just like me. Because you are like me, Bernard. And that makes you afraid. You suppress it. It becomes anathema to you. You indulge in petty, humiliating perversions to—how can I put it?—to *stave off* the real urges, the real *impetus* of your nature. She's made you like that. She taught you to despise yourself, that part of yourself that's like me. And why? Because she's peddling a worldview in which she has no responsibility, in which I work like some sort of . . . grand puppeteer on the world stage and she just dances. All I'm asking you to accept, Bernard, is the possibility—just the possibility—that there's another worldview. A worldview in which you can live freely as what you really are."

Bernard covered his face with his bleeding hands. Felt the damp, sticky surface of his flesh beneath his fingers. He was experiencing a remarkable floating sensation now, as if he were detaching from his own body. As if some part of him were being drawn up out through his pores and into the smoke, becoming part and parcel of the smoke. He could feel himself striving to float with it, float on, float up through the coffin's stone, float up into the freedom of the presence above him.

"I'm sorry, Bernard," the voice said calmly. "But there comes a time—it comes for all of us—when you have to consider the possibility that everything you've been taught is a lie; when you have to entertain the idea that the people you love best have in fact deceived you."

Bernard floated in the smoke. The smoke caressed him.

"I am who you want to be, Bernard. And you contain me within you," said the voice. "We are, both of us, Saint Iago."

7 The sky above Belham Grange churned with black rainclouds. The wind that carried them in from the south rattled the naked branches of the trees overhanging the front drive. It made mysterious trails in the grass, swift, swirling strips of lighter green as the blades bent over before it. These swaths appeared in front of Storm and curled around him and vanished. They appeared again as the wind picked up, moving off into the hills like ghostly footprints.

Sophia was marching quickly into the darkening day, charging angrily away from the house, away from the drive and off into the field. Storm had to take long strides to keep up with her, hurriedly belting his trench coat against the cold.

There was thunder above, and Sophia's eyes were flashing. Her own overcoat was open. It blew back around her. The wind swept over her hair and sent wisps of it across her face, into her mouth. She snatched at them, pulled them back.

"We can't go through with it," she said. "We can't. He's sick. You can see that. He's ill, Richard, something's wrong with him."

"You're telling me," said Storm. He rubbed his aching brow. "He just threatened to kill me in there."

"What?" She barely broke stride, barely glanced at him. "Don't be ridiculous."

"He did, honey! He said he was going to blow my head off. Really."

She snorted. "I'm sure he was making some kind of joke."

"Hey, ha, ha, ha," said Storm. "The guy's a comic genius."

She stopped. Faced him fiercely with the swaying beeches behind her and one stone wing of the house with the gathering clouds on its dark windows. She crossed her arms beneath her breasts. Oh boy, he thought, pulling up short. He'd seen *that* look before. He'd had to have a couple of them surgically removed from his neck. Jesus, there were moments with women when it seemed a man was born two apologies behind.

"I cannot believe I let you talk me into coming here," Sophia said. "I can't *believe* you expect me to interrogate and . . . and torment that man about a . . . a tragic, tragic thing in his life that happened twenty years ago. Especially now, especially when he looks like this. He's sick, Richard."

It was a tragic, tragic thing in your life too, Storm wanted to say. But he was a mite too experienced for that. Go head to head with a girl in this state and you wound up explaining to the judge why you should be allowed to keep the clothes on your back. This called for a little Relationship Judo.

Sophia kept glaring at him. The first jagged fork of lightning fired off clear of the horizon. Storm flinched, but not because of the lightning. The cold wind carried the thunder to them, long and low.

"So why don't you ask him what's wrong with him?" Storm said finally.

"What?"

"You come home, your dad looks like the cat dragged him in, how come you don't say, 'What's the matter, Pops? Should I call the doctor?' How come you don't ask him that, okay?"

The glare faltered. Thank God. "Well, I . . . I don't know, I . . ."

"I mean, like you said, Sophie—look at him."

She shifted from foot to foot. Glanced away. "Well, if he doesn't want to talk about it . . . I mean, if he's . . . reluctant . . ."

"He wants to talk about something, that's for sure. The man threatened to shoot me."

"Oh, he did not."

Pain raked through the fog in his head. He said, "Yes, the hell he did." It came out rougher than he'd meant, and he was sorry at once. But he saw too that it made her believe him. Suddenly uncertain, she ran her hand up through her hair. Her eyes grew frantic. Her lips trembled. Which was worse than the glare. "Something really is wrong here, Sophia," he said more gently. "I think you have to find out what it is."

"Oh, I don't know what's what anymore," she whispered. "You've got me all confused."

"Look." He stepped closer to her. "Harper didn't send us out here for nothing."

"Oh, I don't give a *tinker's damn* . . ."

"Awright, awright. But . . ." He lifted his hand to calm her. "She thinks that finding out about your mother might help her figure where Iago is headed."

"Oh, *Iago*!"

"Awright. But these guys . . . these bad guys who killed your friends . . ."

"They *weren't* my friends . . ."

"Awright, awright. But the thing is . . . I think they're closing in somehow. That must be what your father's afraid of, see. That's my guess. He must think that I'm the one they've sent."

The way she frowned at him then—it burned into his chest like a brand. "Well, maybe you are," she said. "I mean, how do I know?"

It was so dark now, the clouds so heavy, that the air seemed thick between them. There were no birds singing. And though Storm could see a small highway off in the hills by a distant church steeple, there was no sound of traffic, no noise louder than the wind.

"You don't believe that," he told her. "You'd just rather say something like that than find out about your mother's death, than come right out and talk with your father about how she died and what you remember. And it's no good, Sophia." He let out a breath, lifting his face. The answering wind was damp on his skin. Cooled his forehead, cleared his mind. "Everything with you and him depends on these secrets," he said. "It's all what you don't tell each other, what you don't ask. I don't think you have time to go on like this anymore, to keep doing this."

Sophia brought both hands up to her hair now, clutched it. And Storm, watching her, just felt terribly lonely. It only took an instant of her anger to remind him that her affection was his only comfort just now, might be his last comfort forever. It only took an instant of her confusion and simmering panic to remind him of how much stood between him and what he needed from her. How much dead life would have to be cleared away before they could really be together.

These were not the sort of ghosts he had wanted to find.

"Why are you doing this to me?" she said softly, in a voice that was not like hers at all. "If I can't handle this, well, then I can't. Why do you keep pushing and pushing me? Why does it matter so much to you? Why is it so important to you, Richard?"

As if she had spoken into his thoughts. And Storm knew that his misery showed in his eyes for an answer. His failure.

His hypocrisy. All this talk about honesty, about airing secrets. And he had never even found the courage to tell her that most basic truth. To say to her: I'm dying. My love is as selfish as anyone's. I need you to be free in your mind so you can give yourself to me and I won't be alone for this. I need you to break out of your past so I can feel I've done something for you, so I can feel I've left a life I love behind.

He reached out and put his hand against her cheek. And she—to his surprise—closed her eyes and leaned into it, took hold of it with her own. It just about broke his heart.

"All right," he said, swallowing hard. "Listen. Listen. There's something I have to tell you . . ."

"Sophia!"

In the rising wind, the call seemed to come from a great distance. But, looking back across the field, Storm could see movement through the screen of beeches. Sir Michael was standing at the door of the house.

"Sophia!"

Calling her.

She glanced up at Storm. Their eyes met quickly. He tried to speak again, but couldn't. She patted his hand and drew away without a word.

Storm stood alone under the low clouds with the wind trails appearing in the grass all around him. He stood with his hands in his trench-coat pockets. He watched as Sophia ran off towards the house.

Then, with a sigh, he turned away. Turned away, and confronted, for the first time, what had been behind him all this while.

There, beyond the sinuous silhouette of an elm, stood the abbey ruin, sullen, black and grim. An ominous and melancholy apparition: the broken wedge of a chapel wall, the slanting monuments of its ancient churchyard. The faltering illumination, laced as it was with the running cloud shadows, gave to the entire scene a floating quality, weird and dreamlike.

Eesh, thought Storm, his heart like a stone.

And, as if compelled, as if driven by the wind, he began to move across the field.

Towards the abbey. Towards its ancient graves.

---

8   A ghost story. "A Little Place off the Edgware Road" was the name of a ghost story. A fine one, in fact, by Graham Greene. It was included, with "Black Annie," in the collection from which Storm had read. It was this, no doubt, that had brought the particular phrase into Iago's mind when he was speaking of his inspiration.

Harper spent the next several hours in the basement of the London Library. Paging slowly through the bound volumes of newspapers twenty years old. She knew now what she was looking for. She suspected, at least, what she was going to find. But she couldn't afford to rely *too* much on coincidence. To make a mistake now would be to lose what little time she had. She had to make certain she was right before she proceeded. So she went on, page after slow page.

Outside, the short winter's day edged on towards evening. Within, the fluorescents shone their misty bluish light down on the tall shelves, the long wooden tables. It shone down on Harper's bowed head, on her short, dull gray hair. On the stick propped against her chair, and on the hat set beside the open volume.

Her eyes scanned the newspaper columns slowly. And when, finally, she came upon the advertisement she wanted, she had a feeling inside her like a long, slow sigh. She wasn't yet sure how this was going to help her. But the confirmation of her suspicions was encouraging. It indicated, at least, that Iago was like everyone else in one respect: whenever he spoke, he gave away much more than he intended.

The phrase that formed the ghost story's title had no doubt come into his head unbidden as he thought back on the revelatory event. There was no reason it should have stuck with Harper, no reason she should have worried at it. But now, as she sat alone in the windowless basement under the fluorescents' grainy glare, she understood why she had.

Because the little place off the Edgware Road was, in the Greene story, a cinema. Iago had been in a cinema twenty years ago when he'd had the revelation that started him down the story trail. And the newspaper advert before her was for the Odeon Cinema, on Church Street, just off the Edgware Road. The advert told her what, all this time, she had really known. That the inspiration that had led Iago to "Black Annie"—and the other stories and the monk's confession at last—had been a film.

One day, twenty years ago, Jacob Hope had gone to see *Spectre*. Written, produced and directed by Richard Storm.

9 From time to time, Bernard still sobbed weakly, but there were no tears anymore. They seemed to have all dried up. Everything inside him seemed to have dried up so that it felt as if even his sweat had stopped flowing, even his blood had stopped flowing. Even his swarming panic had become a motionless thing, a weight of dread, squatting on his chest like a gargoyle.

Only his mind . . . Only his mind kept drifting, floating, losing itself within the fumy substance of that voice. Iago's voice.

"Let me ask you something, Bernard. Have I ever hurt you? Before this, I mean, when my hand has been forced by circumstance? Have I ever done you personally any harm?"

"That man . . ." Bernard could barely move his lips to speak. "You . . . crucified that man."

"Ach," Iago said. He laughed pleasantly. "I've killed hundreds of people. Tortured lots of them. And laughed? Let me tell you, for comic relief? There is nothing quite so hilarious as other people's suffering. When they're bouncing around like pachinko balls, screaming, begging . . . Oh. Well. One day, you'll see what I mean. No, no, no, that's not what I'm asking. You have to listen, Bernard."

It seemed now that he leaned in close, that he must have pressed his lips right to the sarcophagus lid. The cool voice seemed to pour down over Bernard's face, queerly refreshing with its tincture of power and freedom. A memory came into the prisoner's drifting mind of a lover who smoked cigarettes, who kissed him with a lungful of smoke, and released it into his mouth so that he breathed it in while they kissed. Sickening, exhilarating, beautiful.

"I'm just talking about you," said that voice. "All right? Have I ever done anything personally harmful or painful to you? Or to Harper, for that matter? Or to any of your friends?"

Bernard lay silent under the weight of dread and stone and smoke and pain.

"Nothing of you or yours has been harmed by me in any way," Iago continued casually. "Not a thing. And if that's true—if that's true, Bernard—then all your objections to me, all your fear of me, all your loathing even, is purely abstract, purely philosophical. You hate and fear me because you have an idea—an abstract idea—that the things I do are somehow wrong. That they're nasty. That one is not *supposed* to do them. And who taught you that idea, Bernard? Who told you that they were wrong? Hm? I mean, I know that everyone says that it's wrong to kill, wrong to cause pain, but who cares what everyone says? Everyone is frequently wrong, more frequently than not. No, I mean, who taught *you*, who tells you every day that what I do is wrong in the abstract?"

Bernard could almost feel his floating mind beginning to work apart from him, to think and answer on its own as it drifted and swirled about the darkness. His mind seemed only to be using his body as a vehicle for speech. "Harper," it answered—he answered—hoarsely.

"Harper, that's right," said Iago, well pleased. "Harper, who was mine, who begged to be mine at the cost of any degradation. Who begged for the degradation to prove to me that she was mine. And who now can't stand the thought of herself as she was with me and so takes her revenge by trying to destroy what there is of me in you. Because that's what it's all about, really. These abstract ideas of hers—wrong, right, good, evil—where do they exist? If you can show them to me, I'll bow down to them, I swear. If you can hand them to me, Christ, I'll eat them. All right? But they exist nowhere. Except in Harper's vengeful mind. So what are her notions of good and evil but just her way of training you to repress the part of you she's afraid of? I mean, I see this every day, Bernard. The weak teach the strong to be afraid of their own strength—why? So that the weak won't have to suffer at the hands of the strong—more than that, so that they won't have to face their own natural propensity for suffering. You, Bernard, have to walk through the world repressed and stunted and twisted inside so that Harper can be free of the memory of her own desire, so that Harper doesn't have to face herself. If you want to talk about truth—that's the truth. And it isn't fair. I mean, I asked you if I've hurt you, and you know I haven't. Now I ask you: Has *she* hurt you? Harper. Has she hurt you personally? Not abstractly, but really." He didn't wait for an answer. "I think she has," he said. "I've shut you in a box, in a coffin. But she's turned your whole world into a coffin. She shuts you—your true self—inside it every single day. I'm not only offering to set you free from *this* box, Bernard. I'm offering to set you free from the box she's put you in, the cage of Harper's ideas that has your true nature crouching like an animal inside. Because you're more like me than you are like her. You're more my son than hers."

Dimly now, Bernard became conscious of the fact that he was losing himself. Truly losing control of his own mental functions, of his own responses. His own thoughts and the insinuating voice were becoming fused together. And he lay there in his woozy agony, watching it happen, as if from a restful far. It was a strange feeling, dreamy, even sweet, even sensual. So sweet, in fact, so sensual that he could not think of a single rational reason to make it stop. All he had to do was listen, after all, lie there and listen and go along, and eventually he would be let out of this place, which was all in the world he wanted. The lid would come off and he would be welcome—with smiles, with open arms—into the help and comfort of the daylight. All he had to do was stop fretting, stop trying to hold on, stop muddying the sweetness with his will, and the worst of this would soon be over.

Who had taught him, anyway, that he should do otherwise?

"And I'm offering you even more," said the voice above him, around him, within him. "I'm offering you life, Bernard. I'm offering you free, unfettered, unending life. Come out of this coffin—come out to me—and you will be free of the prospect of burial forever. Free of decay, of the fate of that hideous thing in there beside you. Forever, Bernard."

"I won't!" The shout went off in the coffin like a bomb, like a flash of light, before Bernard even realized it had come from his own mouth. *"I won't listen anymore!"* He felt as if he had awakened suddenly—had awakened from a deep sleep to find a thief making off with his most prized possession. His mind. He wanted his mind *back.* And his hands were up against the lid again, his raw fingers bleeding again as he pushed and scrabbled violently at the stone. The hot, filthy air filled his lungs. The nausea wrung his stomach. His movement brought a fresh sense of how tightly enclosed he was and with that came fresh panic and terror.

And, at last, he was overwhelmed by all this, by his own efforts. He was exhausted by his own helplessness. His hands fluttered down on top of him. "I won't listen," he said. Coughing. Sobbing.

There followed a long, an excruciating, pause. Bernard tried uselessly to shift onto his side. He coughed and dry-retched. He felt that he was gagging on the very air and on his self-disgust. How little physical pain it takes to make a man nothing; nothing.

Then Iago spoke again: "All right."

Panting, Bernard forced himself to stop coughing. Swallowed a hot gout of his own vomit. Gasped, gagged. Tried to listen.

He heard a sound that caused a tremendous solid sphere of icy cold to form itself in his abdomen. He tensed, swallowed again, held his breath. Listened.

Footsteps on stone. Moving away. Fading away.

Bernard started screaming. *"No! Don't leave! Don't leave me here! Don't leave me! Please!"* Babbling in a high, wild, raggedy voice that hardly seemed to belong to him. "Come back! *Please! Please!"*

He stopped. Lay shivering, his face contorted as he willed the speaker to return, as he strained and strained to hear.

He heard.

Clank, rattle, creak, thud. The door opening, closing.

And then silence.

"Don't leave me," he murmured. "Father."

And he lay weeping in the dark alone.

10   At that moment, Richard Storm suddenly realized he had arrived.

He was standing in the shadow of the abbey wall, the clouds lowering. He was standing amidst slanting headstones worn faceless with weather and time. The afternoon was roiling, black. The wind was damp and biting. Lightning dashed fiery from the meridian to the vanishing point, and thunder followed hard on, loud, enormous. Around him, broken steles lay crushed upon the grass. A single crypt sat crumbling. The streaking shadows on the ruined wedge of wall made it seem animate, wraith-washed.

He had come upon the living soundstage of his imagination.

He remembered a ghost story he had heard once. A

woman dreams she's standing outside a house. Every night, in her sleep, she's there, staring at this same house. She becomes so troubled by the dream she decides to take a vacation. Driving into the countryside, she comes upon the very house of her dreams. Unable to resist, she gets out of her car and approaches. The front door opens. A butler stands in her way.

"This house," the woman says. "I have to see inside this house."

"Of course, madam," says the butler. "But I should warn you: the house is haunted."

"Haunted?" says the woman. "Haunted by whom?"

And the butler replies, "By you."

Storm looked around him at the ruins of Belham Abbey.

How often, he wondered, had he had this place put on film? Some place like this. He couldn't count how many times he had dreamed it up as if new, filled it with fresh vampires and ghouls and monsters. *Spectre* featured a ruined church like this one. So had *Castle Misery*. So had *Hellfire*. But it wasn't until he had come to stand here that he fully understood that they had all been this, this very site.

Because this was the setting of "Black Annie," which he had read when he was ten years old. Which had made him what he was.

He could remember—not which day, but the way the day felt—when he had read the story first. The palmy Santa Monica breezes, smelling of oranges and the sea. The lush greenery at his window, and the whitewashed wall of his neighbor's house, the ruddy slate of its roof. Birds were twittering. Bees were humming among the oversized flowers whose names he didn't know. He could hear the plash of someone swimming in his backyard pool. His mother. And he lay alone, in his room, on his bed. Little California Rick in shorts and T-shirt. With the Aurora monster models on their shelves above him staring benignly down. Frankenstein, Godzilla, the Creature from the Black Lagoon with genuine green scales. Dracula, on whose black plastic chin he had hand-painted a line of red. And he held the book of ghost stories on his stomach. *Spooks and Phantoms.* The book his father had given him, resigned to the fact that the boy would read it with more pleasure than his gifts of westerns, Jack Schaefer, Louis Lamour. Young Richard had lain in the whitewashed California springtime, and his mind had gone off into the autumn of Victorian England. Off into the haunted house with Neville and Quentin. Off to the abbey ruin, this very ruin, here. He had loved that story, loved it.

And it had never really occurred to him to wonder why. What was it about himself that was so willing to connect with a setting and a situation that were different from everything he actually knew? He had never produced a picture that wasn't full of the Gothic, the Victorian, the whole "Black Annie" aura. And why? He couldn't help but wonder about it now, now that he was standing here.

Because the rising medieval stone of the wall, the leaning graves—even the threatening weather—the whole classic ghost story scene—were truly as familiar to him as if he had been here a million times. They were as familiar to him as a celebrity's face, as if they slotted in—*thock*—to some archetypal jigsaw emptiness in his mind. They were that familiar—and, at the same time, he had never felt like such an alien, like such a stranger in a strange land.

What the hell was he doing here anyway, so far from home? Who were these people around him? Harper, Bernard, Sir Michael. Sophia. What the hell was he doing involved in all their lives? Making such a mess of them? He was dying, for Christ's sake. He should be with people he knew. With pals who would cluck over his predicament, and doctors who would tell him things that seemed to make sense. In a world he knew, really knew. Not like this one, which he'd only appropriated as a child, which he'd only spent his life reinventing.

He remembered this same strange feeling, this sense of being alien and apart—he remembered how it had overtaken him just before his attack of convulsions the month before. He felt a drifty, cold wisp of fear travel down from his chest to his groin. And he thought: *Not now. Not yet. Not again.*

But no, it wasn't that. It wasn't as easy as that. It was this place. This abbey. This ruined churchyard. This stately country house. This England. What had any of them to do with him? With the son of a cowboy star from the golden coast? They didn't want him here. He could feel that. They rejected him. They wanted him to go away and leave them alone. Hell, they'd murdered guys like him in this place once upon a time. Irritating, intrusive Jew-boys. They'd locked them up in the infirmary and just barbecued them. Yippee-aye-oh-kye-ay, babe. This place was not his place at all.

And if he didn't belong here, where did he belong? Who the hell was he anyway?

He snorted. It was a little goddamned late to ask.

The lightning flickered above him, crackled. And in seconds, the thunder boomed. The black clouds rolled and turned, and the wind walked among the graves. And Storm walked among them, his sad eyes moving on the speechless, haunted stones.

Who the hell was he? That was the question. Who the hell was he to come here and torture Sophia about her past?

Make her unhappy for his own selfish sake. She didn't want him here either. He was as alien to her as he was to this place. He only loused things up for her. Asking her to do this thing that was foreign to her nature. Because he was foreign to her nature. Because he didn't belong with her, in her world.

He had failed her, hadn't he? He would've killed to be her hero and he'd failed her, dead to rights.

He came to stand before the decaying crypt. A waist-high temple with pilasters worn to beaded strips, an iron door worn thin, broken through. He shook his head.

Haunted by whom? he thought.

Haunted by you, pal.

It was the scariest ghost story ever told. You just had to be there.

The rain began slowly. He felt a drop blown onto his cheek. He glanced up into a sky that seemed to hang not six feet above him. Another droplet fell, and more. He heard them patter on the tombstones. *Tip-tip. Tip-tip.*

Yeah. He smiled with one side of his mouth. *Tick-tick.* That's right. Time's running out on you, Jackson.

And then his smile faded. He looked down again at the crypt before him. At the rough crescent-shaped hole worn in the iron door. It went down into nothingness, down and down forever, for all he knew. And he raised his eyes to Belham Grange, to the wing of the house that extended beyond the double row of trees.

There were often, I knew, in abbeys and the neighbouring houses, secret chambers and hideaways . . . underground passages . . .

He remembered Sophia's story, the story she had told him about the noise in the house, about the night she had seen her father standing over her mother with a bloody knife. He had known at the time she told it to him that something had been left out of that story, that something had been missing. Now, as the rain grew steadier, stronger, he realized what it was.

The wind rose, cold, and the rain started slanting down. There was another snarl of thunder that seemed to come from deep in the belly of the sky.

Richard Storm turned up the collar of his trench coat. He turned away from the ruin, and headed back across the field to the house.

 By the time Sophia reached the door, her father had withdrawn. The door stood open and she went in, closing it behind her.

"Daddy?"

"In the sitting room," he answered her.

But she stood in the foyer another moment, at the foot of the stairs.

"Right," she said in an undertone. She made a gesture with both hands. Held them open in front of her and pushed them down against the air: a calming gesture. She wanted to compose herself. She was agitated after her conversation with Storm. She was jittery, confused. Apprehensive. They were all feelings she disliked intensely. "Right," she said again.

She stripped off her overcoat, hung it on a peg by the door. Smoothed down her jumper as if to smooth down her inner self as well. She went along the corridor to the dining room, consciously trying to work her expression into one of cool irony. She did not feel she was succeeding very well at all—and then she was at the sitting-room doorway.

She stepped across the threshold. It was a long room, from the cold stone fireplace to the tall windows. And it was dark: the walls hung with dark, misty paintings, the windows with dark, heavy green drapes. Her father was at the far end, by the window that looked out across the field to the abbey. He faced her when she entered. He stood with the black clouds behind him. She saw the lightning flash down from the clouds, heard the thunder.

"Come in, come in, Sophia. We'd better talk," Sir Michael said.

She hesitated where she was. And it struck her for a moment: she was afraid; she was afraid of him. But she shook the thought off. It was ridiculous. He was her father. She approached slowly.

Much of the furniture was gathered in one half of the room, the near half. The sofa, table and chairs were arrayed together around the fireplace. She came around them, but then she paused again. She stood by the sofa, with her hand on the back of it. That left an open space of some distance—the length of the Persian carpet—between her and her father. She did not cross that distance, but confronted him from where she was. Landscapes of brown crags and fog covered the wall to her left.

"Yes, what is it?" she said.

She couldn't hold his gaze. Her eyes shifted away from him. To the window. Out to the abbey ruin. She could see Storm out there, afar off. He was moving beside the broken wall, walking among the gravestones. His coat was stirred by the wind. His hair was stirred by it. She wished he was here, in here, with her. What had he been about to tell her? Why was she so upset? She hated it.

Her father took a step towards her. Sophia felt her hand close more tightly on the wooden rail of the sofa back. Her father looked large, towering. His great head seemed hung bizarrely with loose flesh. His eyes were strange and quick and dangerous. With the black clouds rushing forward behind him, it seemed as if he himself were rushing at her.

"Why did you bring him here?" he asked her.

Sophia shook her head, confused. Tried to think of an answer.

"I don't like him," said Sir Michael. "I don't trust him. What is he here for?"

"Trust him . . . ?" said Sophia. She could not bring her thoughts to order. Why was she so afraid?

"Doesn't it even occur to you to ask yourself what he keeps hanging around for?"

And Sophia heard herself begin to answer as if she were listening to another person: "Well, doesn't it even occur to you that . . . ?" She pressed her lips together.

"What?" he said. "Go on."

"Well, he might be hanging around because he likes me? It might not have anything to do with you and this . . . anything to do with you."

Her father made an exasperated, dismissive noise. The clouds behind him flickered with unsteady light. The following thunder was loud.

"No," said Sophia, uncertainly. "I mean it. I don't know what the problem is . . ."

"For God's sake, Sophia, don't be childish."

"Am I supposed to run my friends by you for approval?"

At that, he took another step towards her. Large, unfamiliar. "Friends like that, yes. There are plenty of suitable men around."

Her hand moved nervously on the sofa back. She felt very small in front of him. And her knees were beginning to feel weak and shaky. "I don't know what you mean by *suitable*.

Richard is perfectly *suitable*..."

And again: that dimissive noise, like a whiplash. "He's ridiculous, if nothing else. And he's old enough... He must be forty, at least."

Sophia licked her lips. "Is that what's bothering you?"

"Are you playing some kind of game with me?"

"Well, what is all this? He says you threatened him."

"I'll do more than threaten him..." He came closer. She could see him more clearly. The quivering, pasty folds of skin, the skeletal outlines of his cheeks, the too-bright eyes. The sight made her faintly nauseous.

"I don't understand," she said. "I don't understand what's wrong. Why are you acting this way?"

"Sophia," he said. This was gentler, a tone she remembered, a voice she remembered. Her father's tone, his voice. The gesture he made with his hand was one she knew. But he seemed a different person. "I'm sure there are dozens of men who are interested in you," he went on, "who want to be with you. Half our clients are in love with you. That's not the point. The sad fact is, this... person is using you."

"Using me?"

"To get at me."

"Why on earth...?"

"All right, if you're going to be purposely obtuse: to get at the Rhinehart."

"But you don't have the Rhinehart."

"Now you *are* being purposely obtuse."

"I'm not. I simply don't understand."

He shook his head at her sternly.

Sophia let go of the sofa back. She rubbed her hands fretfully together. Her mouth was dry and her stomach fluttery. "Daddy," she said. "Daddy, don't talk in riddles anymore.

Tell me what's happening."

"What do you mean? I just don't like my daughter being taken advantage of . . ."

"I mean all this about the Rhinehart," she said. "Why are you so upset about the Rhinehart? Whatever it is, if you explain it to me . . ."

Sir Michael eyed her as from a height. Through the window, under the gathering clouds, distant, she saw Storm pause before a low crypt. She wished he would come in.

"Did he tell you to ask me that?" Sir Michael said.

"What? Well . . . No. No, of course not, I—"

"What makes you think I'm upset?"

She laughed unhappily. "Look at you. You look awful."

"There's nothing wrong with me."

"You look positively ill. What is going on? Why are you acting all paranoid? What's frightening you?"

He reared—and Sophia quailed. There was another rumble from the rushing clouds. And then a soft patter on the tall pane between the drapes. It was beginning to rain. In another moment the water was washing hard against the glass. Sophia could see Storm moving away from the ruin, moving across the field out of sight, towards the house. She was desperate for him to come to her.

"Are you cross-questioning me?" Sir Michael said.

"Me?" Sophia's hand went to her middle. She was really beginning to feel sick. "Me, cross-questioning you? You called me in here—"

"I called you in here because you've allowed this unsavory man—"

"Oh, Daddy."

"—to push and wheedle his way into our house, to seduce you—he has seduced you, hasn't he?"

"What are you talking about? Seduced . . . That's insane. I'm a grown—"

"You've allowed him to seduce you and push his way into this house for the sole purpose of getting his hands on that triptych. If you're such a grown-up woman then you should've known better. You should've exercised a little judgement."

Sophia, practically cowering beside the sofa, practically cried out, "You're not making any sense. Why would Richard want to do something like that?"

"Oh, don't be ridiculous."

"I'm not—"

"Because he's a criminal."

"He is not."

"He's a sneaking, murdering—"

"Murdering?"

"—filthy bastard who doesn't care a damn about you."

"He does! Stop it! You're talking utter shit! Stop it!"

Quickly, Sophia pressed the back of her hand to her mouth. The wind blew the rain up hard against the window. A fork of lightning stabbed down into the hills, hurling the shadow of the abbey wall across the headstones. The sudden upsurge of rage had taken her completely by surprise, had left her feeling shaken and ill. She could not remember the last time she had spoken like that—had raised her voice at all—against her father.

He turned his shoulder to her. Lifted his chin. Frowned down across the room at her with his eyes hot and foreign and terrifying.

"I'm sorry, Sophia," he said. "I didn't realize he had got so far with you."

And, sick as she felt, she was angry again on the instant. Helplessly, she felt her eyes fill with tears. "Don't say that.

Don't say that to me. How dare you? I think Richard may be the single most decent and straightforward person I've ever met. What would he want with the Rhinehart triptych?"

Sir Michael waved her away.

"What do *you* want with it?" she said.

And with one more sharp glance, he showed her his back, faced the rain-scored window.

"Because it is you, really," she said to him, trembling. "You're the one who's been acting . . . dishonestly. I don't know what you're involved in. I've never known. You won't tell me. You don't tell me anything. You act as if I'm supposed to understand, as if it's a given between us. But I don't understand. Not really. I don't understand what's going on at all. How could I, Daddy? You don't explain anything. Everything between us depends on all these . . . secrets. Everything revolves around what you don't say, and what I'm not supposed to ask. It's always been like that. It's always . . ."

Weak and nauseated, she couldn't finish. One hand clutched at the sofa again, one went around her stomach. Sir Michael's powerful form was burned into silhouette by a lightning flash. The thunder was so loud this time it seemed to rumble through the flooring. The windows rattled with the wind.

And then the Great Man turned on her again. Turned where he was and looked across the room at his daughter with eyes that she could hardly recognize—they were so full of disdain for her, disgust and disdain.

"This is exactly the way it happened with your mother," he said.

There was a footstep at the threshold behind her. Dazed, Sophia glanced back and saw Storm walk in.

12 "Get out of here," Sir Michael said. "Get out of my house, you son of a bitch."

The windows rattled again with another gust of wind, and the drapery stirred. And the old man seemed enormous and crackling with the tempest framing him. But Storm felt suddenly calm, suddenly clear and even in his mind.

She had done it. He could tell by the looks on their faces. Sophia had forced the issue out. The crisis had come.

He smiled, brushing the rain from his hair with one hand. Then he put his hands in the pockets of his slacks. He strolled slowly into the room.

"You know, I think you've got me all wrong," he said. He came up next to Sophia and paused. Felt her trembling there beside him, felt the agitation coming off her in waves. "I think you've got me figured for one of Iago's guys."

Sir Michael sniffed. "I suppose you're going to tell me you're not."

"Well, yeah. Since I'm not, I thought I would tell you." He strolled forward again, onto the rug. Moved towards Sir Michael until the two men were only a few steps apart. Storm wasn't much shorter than Sophia's father, but the old man was impressive all the same. And the rage and fear animating those dead, sunken features made him downright formidable. "I've got no stake in this," Storm went on. "Except your daughter. And as far as that goes, you're just gonna have to live with it. They don't let you shoot guys for that anymore."

Sir Michael seemed to grow in his place, seemed to rise up and up, ready to strike Storm to the floor with a single blow. In his pockets, Storm's hands balled into fists. He wondered whether Sir Michael was armed. The two men stood and faced one another, glared at one another.

"What did you mean about Mother?"

Sophia's voice came from behind him, cut through him. He'd never heard her sound like that before. He'd never heard anyone sound exactly that way. It was a rasping, feverish, desperate and terrible noise that squeezed his heart. He hadn't realized things had gone quite this far.

But Sir Michael's eyes glared into his and his own were locked in that glare, and he couldn't turn to her.

"You put her up to this, didn't you?" Sir Michael said.

"What did you mean, Daddy?" said Sophia.

She sounded as if she was going to cry too. And she was coming forward. Storm could see her in the corner of his eye, moving to stand beside them, between them. Stalking to stand there.

"You son of a bitch," said Sir Michael to Storm.

"Your daughter's talking to you, pal," Storm said.

"What did you mean that this is what happened with Mother?" said Sophia. Her voice was ragged with tears now. "What happened with her? What happened?"

Sir Michael didn't even look at her. His white mouth worked and his white eyes flashed. And the lightning flashed at the window, making the far-off ruin look close and dark. The thunder rolled right over them, right over the top of the house. And Storm thought: Nice effect. A little OTT, but nice.

"Look at me, Daddy," Sophia pleaded. "Tell me."

But Sir Michael didn't. "You're a dirty, low bastard," he said to Storm.

"Why don't you look at her, you jerk," Storm answered.

"Because you're the one controlling her."

Sophia was right beside them, almost directly between them. "Daddy," she said. "It's not him. It's me. Look at me. Tell me what happened to Mother."

"Using sex. Just like with Ann," said her father to Storm. "Did you think I was going to let it happen again?"

"You got it wrong, man. Talk to her. She's begging you."

"It's me, Daddy," said Sophia. And she *was* begging him. "Look at me. I'm not right. You never told me anything and now I'm not right. I almost died, Daddy. And I shouldn't have. I shouldn't be like this. I shouldn't be the way I am. Should I? Hurting myself?"

"Be quiet," Sir Michael barked without turning to her.

"I was trying to protect *you*," she said. "I've been trying to protect you and I don't even know why. Why is my mother dead, why am I like this, what's going on, tell me."

Storm had about had it with this staring contest. He could hear what was happening to Sophia, he could hear her voice, the pitch rising, hysteria near. And he could see her face straining forward, the tears coursing down it.

But Sir Michael wouldn't look at her, wouldn't release him, kept glowering at him like some living skull from one of his own movies.

"I swear to God you're a dead man," Sir Michael whispered.

And Storm smiled with one corner of his mouth. "Hey, guess what, babe. It doesn't matter. You're still gonna have to deal with her."

"Don't tell me how to deal with my daughter, you—"

And suddenly Sophia lost control. She started screaming in a wild, high-pitched, frantic babble that made Sir Michael start back, that scared Storm witless. Her fists flew up around her ears, her eyes squeezed shut, her hair flew back and forth across her face and she went on screaming:

"It's not him, it's not him, it's me, it's me dying it's like I'm dying Daddy listen look at me look at me tell me! Tell me! Tell me! Tell me! Tell me!"

"Jesus, Sophie," said Storm.

He put out a hand to her. She staggered back out of his reach. She clutched at her stomach. Flinched, bent over, gasped aloud. And then covered her open mouth with her hand so that her eyes peered over it, wide, shocked.

"Oh . . ." she said.

And before Storm could move to her, she stumbled away from him. She clutched at the sofa and pulled herself forward. Storm was afraid she was going to fall. But she started running. She ran out of the room.

Storm made to follow her. Sir Michael let out a rough growl and grabbed him by the arm. Storm tore free, spun, his fist cocked at his chin. Sir Michael recoiled, threw his arm up, expecting the punch.

They froze like that, with the wind beating at the window, with another burr of thunder, coming softer now, from farther away.

Sir Michael lowered his arm, his face reddening. "You . . ." he spluttered. "You filthy . . ."

Storm smiled. Let his fist open, let his hand drop to his side. He narrowed his eyes in a gunfighter squint.

"Jew," he drawled, "is the word you want."

And he turned his back on Sir Michael and went out after Sophia.

 When Storm found his way to the foyer, he heard water rushing upstairs, a toilet flushing. He went up the steps quickly, two at a time.

He came into a long, lightless corridor with portraits staring down at him from the walls. A grandfather clock was ticking somewhere near him. And he thought, *Yeah, yeah, yeah. Tick-tick, tick-tick.*

Then, at the hall's far end, a door opened; a rectangle of yellow light. Sophia stood in it, bent, weary, braced against the frame.

Storm hurried down the corridor to her. She released the jamb and came forward, nearly fell forward into his arms.

"I've been sick," she said miserably.

"You're okay," he said. "You're gonna be fine. Is there somewhere you can lie down in this dump?"

She gestured at a door, and he helped her to it. They came through into a small bedroom, her bedroom. He didn't turn the light on. The windows were small and blurred with rain, the sky black outside. The room was full of shadows, and the shapes in it were obscure. Storm saw the canopied bed against one wall. He helped Sophia to it, helped her lie down. She rolled onto her side, facing away from him.

Storm sat beside her, on the edge of the duvet. He massaged her shoulder gently. After a while, he looked around the bedpost at the painting on the opposite wall. He could see it was the portrait of a woman. He could not make out her features in the shadows, but he felt her watching him. He went on massaging Sophia's shoulder.

"I don't know what just happened down there," she murmured.

Storm shrugged. "You blew a gasket, kid. It happens."

"Maybe in your family."

He laughed. "Hey, in my family, this was a good day. This was, like, the school picnic or something."

Sophia flumped over onto her back and laughed and started crying. "You're nice to me," she said through her tears.

He nodded. "You mean I'm nice to you and you're so horrible."

"Yes."

"What can I say? I'm a lousy judge of character."

She turned to press her face into his hip. He felt her begin to shiver under his hand. What a crazy dame, he thought. She really would've rather hanged herself again than let loose at the old buzzard like that. What a crazy country.

He reached across her, across the bed. Worked the duvet up out of its place and folded it over her, bundled her in it.

"What are you doing?" she said, her voice muffled. "You'll mess it up."

"Somehow, over time, I'll just have to learn to live with that."

She laughed again, and started to cry harder.

"Shh," he whispered. "Shh."

"But what's going to happen now?" she said.

He shifted to lift her head onto his thigh. He kissed her hair and stroked it. She shivered in his arms a long time, and the room slowly grew darker.

Finally, she began to be quiet. And after another while, as he held her, he heard her breathing grow deep and even.

He leaned down to press a kiss into her hair. He closed his eyes. He wondered if Sir Michael was heading upstairs with a gun.

And what, he wondered, is going to happen now?

14 The long, slow hours brought the night down on all of them. On Sophia as she slept, and Storm as he held her. On Sir Michael, slumped in a chair in the sitting room below. On Bernard, shivering in his coffin. And on the mansion in World's End, where Harper Albright sat at the draftsman's table examining an obscure tome.

Over Belham and over London, the winter's day died.

✦

And after a time, Storm lay Sophia tenderly on her pillow and rose. He moved to the window. Looked out into the dark. The rain had passed on, and a mist was rising from the grass of the field, rising and twining around the abbey wall, around the headstones. Storm watched it rise, his own reflection faint upon the pane.

✦

Sir Michael climbed heavily to his feet. Moved, with his head bowed, across the room and out into the corridor. He went down the unlit passage into his study. He shut the door and moved to his desk. Sank into his leather chair. Pulled opened a drawer with one finger.

For a long time, he sat there, looking down at the studded leather box that held the Havana cigars and the sterling lighter, and the loaded .38.

✦

Bernard shivered and moaned. Murmured to himself, half-conscious. Roamed in his mind under blue skies, over green pastures. Wondered distantly if this was death, if he was dying.

✦

And Harper Albright sat and read, sat and read. The fire wasn't on and the office of *Bizarre!* grew cold, but she sat and read. Only the lamp clamped to the edge of the table was burning. It glared on the white pages and hurt her eyes, but she sat and read. Ten years ago, she reflected in frustration, ten or eleven years, she had decoded the Gothic runes scratched on a potsherd found near Avesbury. Her rendering—dismissed as occult guesswork by all accepted authorities—had inspired an entire offshoot of Wicca, centered on the incantation to the mother goddess she believed she had uncovered. The work had been slow, painstaking, back-breaking. It had taken her six months to complete the translation. It was nothing, she thought bitterly, on this.

She was reading the manual to Bernard's VCR. It was a European booklet in four languages. She had finally settled on the German version, the English being incomprehensible. She scanned the pages, page after page. Then finally—finally, finally—she rose up, weary, from the tall stool.

She grasped the videocassette that lay at the bottom of the slanted table, grasped it with exhausted, trembling fingers. This in itself had been no easy acquisition. Visits to three separate Prime Time rental locations. A long trek home to find some acceptable form of identification. A long search and the long trek back again. By day's end, the world was too much with her, but she had a copy of *Spectre* in her hands.

She carried it up the stairs. Mounting slowly, leaning hard on her dragon walking stick. She moved hunched through the shadows of the landing to Bernard's door. Entered his room, turned on the light.

The little space was as Bernard had left it, thoroughly out of order. The narrow bed was unmade. Jeans, shirts, under-wear were strewn over the stained carpet. Dishes with crumbs, glasses half full of gin, were stained brown with crushed stubs, or overflowing with ashes. The white shelves stacked high above the bed were stuffed with piles of books and magazines, the corners of torn pages sticking out of them. The piles of books and magazines on the bedside table rose up across from the shelves, the bed between. One book, called *The Origins of Consciousness in the Breakdown of the Bicameral Mind,* lay on the sheets near the grubby pillow. One journal, called *Raising Cane,* lay spread just beneath it. A pretty nun winked at Harper from the cover, caressing a ferule. *Sisters of Mercilessness.*

Harper frowned and shook her head. How long, she wondered, could the boy hold on? No, that wasn't what she wondered, not really, not all in all. She wondered, rather, whether she had given him the wherewithal to hold on long enough. Iago would be sure to find his weaknesses, but had she taught Bernard honestly enough to keep him from being taken by surprise? Had enough of the truth been understood between them, or had she only hoped it was, assumed it was to save herself the pain of speaking it?

She moved with shuffling steps to the television at the foot of the bed. Sometimes, she thought, it seemed the Catholics had it right: it seemed there was nothing that could not be forgiven except the failure to confess. The gods appeared to her just then to despise secrecy above all things. More than cruelty, more than theft, more than dishonor, they punished you for what you left unspoken—worse, they punished the ones you loved, the ones to whom you should have told all.

She worked the Prime Time case open and removed the cassette. She eyed the television on its stand, the long black box on the stand's lower shelf—eyed them with trepidation. She bent down. Pressed the TV button. The picture popped on instantly. This was encouraging. A commentator in a light blue suit started speaking to her about rugby. She pressed the channel selector. *Ein, zwei, drei, fier, funf.*

Funf—that's what the manual had recommended. But the commentator in the blue suit reappeared on the screen. Why should this be so? Whatever could it signify? She was filled with the familiar sense of misgiving she usually felt just before a machine did something really ghastly.

Nonetheless, grunting with the effort, she bent lower. Touched the cassette to the flap on the box.

To her alarm, the beast seemed to seize the thing right out of her hand and swallow it.

"Crikey," she said, straightening.

But the hours of study had not gone to waste. For the blue-suited rugby commentator now winked into jade nothingness.

And a moment later—as Harper lowered herself painfully onto the edge of Bernard's bed, as she propped her stick against the floor, as she folded her hands on top of the dragon, and rested her chin on the back of her hands—*Spectre* began to unroll on the screen before her.

15 Bernard, meanwhile, had begun to recite poetry. It was all that stood between him and the mouth of madness.

His progressive schoolmasters, in their enlightened kindliness, had never forced him to commit much verse to memory. You can always look it up, they told him—which shows how little they knew.

Harper, on the other hand, had drilled him with the stuff from his youngest years. "These are fragments," she had intoned, "which you may one day shore against your ruins." He had not really understood what she was telling him—till now.

Because in ruins he surely was. Convulsing in the blackness. Shivering against the confines of his stone enclosure. Vomit- and piss-covered. Feverish. Blind. Hour after hour after hour. Babbling insanely when his mind drifted. And when his mind cleared, inhabited by a horror that made him feel as if a bomb were going off inside him and he had no room to explode. Hour after hour.

Dying. He was sure he was dying now. He could not breathe. He felt as if his organs were mired in sludge. He was fading almost willfully from a consciousness that had become abhorrent to him. The invisible death's head beside him stared and grinned. Hour after hour.

And so, at last, with all the courage he had left, he began to recite.

It was one of those situations—it's remarkable how many of them there are, really—when only William Blake would do.

> To see a world in a grain of sand
> And a heaven in a wild flower,
> Hold infinity in the palm of your hand
> And eternity in an hour.

Yes, yes, that was a good one. You could work out the mysterious couplets of that one for hours. Weakly, Bernard licked his lips. He tasted something like decay. He went on.

> A robin redbreast in a cage
> Puts all heaven in a rage.

Oh, he knew a thing or two, did Crazy Bill.

He lay with his eyes closed, with his jaw slack, his mouth open. Every breath that left him came back again rancid. He was strangling on his own exhalations.

Every night and every morn
Some to misery are born,
Every morn and every night
Some are born to sweet delight.

He hugged himself, but not tightly. He hadn't the strength
for that anymore. He simply held himself, cradled himself,
rocked himself in clouds of debilitating nausea.

Some are born to sweet delight,
Some are born to endless night.
Some are red and some are blue,
And some are filled with sticky goo.

"I can't breathe," he whispered. And for he did not know
how long, he was lost to himself. In a sunlit territory of
emerald grass and rapeseed of a brilliant yellow. Of music
and a river dappled with sunshine. And there, ranged
everywhere along the lea, naked bodies, sweet, round, white,
reclining. A vision of the sons and daughters of Albion . . .

And then the coffin lid clapped down over him and he
was in the blackness again, with the smell of himself rotting
alive. And he shook and cried, and whispered, "Mother."

And her voice answered him clearly: *We are led to believe a*
lie . . .

Yes, yes, he thought, crushed under the sudden return of
reality. Yes . . .

We are led to believe a lie
When we see not through the eye,
Which was born in a night to perish in a night,
Which doesn't scan,

But there it am,
Which doesn't rhyme,
But dying I'm,
So who gives a sod,
Which brings us to God,
And God appears, and God is light,
To those poor souls who dwell in night;
But does a human form display,
To those who dwell in realms of day.
For mercy has a human heart,
Pity, a human face . . .

But no, that was something else. Still Blake, but another poem.

Oh, what's the difference, Harper, he thought. Leave me alone, for Christ's sake. Let me go.

For Mercy has a human heart, she insisted to him,
Pity, a human face,
And Love, the human form divine,
And Peace, the human dress.

He hugged himself, rocked himself in the blackness. Don't tell me that, he thought. Don't tell me that, you pedantic bitch, and leave me here. I'm dying. And I'm scared.

Mercy has a human heart, Bernard. A human heart. And Pity, a human face. And Love, the human form divine. Trust me on this.

He raised his bloody fingers to his bloody brow. Dragged them down over his cheeks, smearing the blood. He groaned out, "Cruelty!"

And a spasm of nausea racked him. He clutched his stomach. Turned his head. Tried to retch, but couldn't. Sobbed.

Cruelty, he thought, *has a human heart,*
And Jealousy, a human face;
Terror, the human form divine,
And Secrecy, the human dress.

Well, yes, that too, Harper said.

"Secrecy," Bernard whispered.

Yes.

He lay back again, trying to breathe, trying to support the weight of darkness. All right, all right, he thought. Where was I? Secrecy . . . ?

Mercy, she said.

Right, right.

For Mercy has a human heart . . . Didn't we do this already?

No, no. It's still good. It's still right, Bernard.

And Pity—Pity, Pity—a human face. Pity.

And Love, she said. *Love has the human . . .*

"The human form divine," Bernard whispered, hugging himself, inhaling the stench of his offal, choking on the stench. *And Mercy . . .*

And Peace, she said.

Mercy, mercy.

These fragments . . .

Mercy.

These fragments you shall shore against your ruins.

"God!" Bernard screamed. Or tried to scream—it came out a rasping gasp.

These fragments . . . These fragments . . .

"God, father, father in Heaven. Help me!"

And then—as if in answer to his call—there came those sounds again. Did they? Did they come? He clutched himself. Opened his eyes—tried to—couldn't tell if they were open or not. Lay with his jaw dangling. Listened.

Yes. The clank of a lock. The rattle of a latch. The creak—oh, the creak of a door opening. The thud as it swung shut.

And footsteps. Footsteps on stone. Approaching.

Bernard peered up into nothingness. His entire body was a prayer.

There was a pause. And then the voice—the voice like smoke—swirled down coolly over him.

"Are you ready to listen now, Bernard?"

Pity has a human heart, a human heart, a human heart . . .

"Yes," he said, shuddering, crying. "Yes. Please. Please. I'm ready."

16

"By Jove, Prendergast," Hedley cried. "A stairway!"

Harper's eyes sank closed, her body leaned forward. She and her dragon stick seemed about to pitch off the edge of the bed to the floor.

But she jerked her head up, her eyes open. Forced herself to stare at the TV screen.

By Jove, she grumped. *Cobblers.*

She continued to watch Storm's movie as the appallingly ridiculous detectives descended into the vaults beneath the ruined church. Under jutting shadows, under skewed stone-work, under hanging arches, they went, following the repeated *clang–clang* rising from below.

Even now, she could barely remember that she had ever seen the thing before. Could not remember where she had watched it or when. Certainly not why. Which was not all that odd really, considering the quality of the piece.

Funny, Harper thought sleepily. Storm probably hadn't

even known that it was all run-of-the-mill German Express-ionism. She could see that he'd thought he was paying some sort of *hommage* to "Black Annie." There were the shape of the ruins, the repetition of the sound—*clang-clang*—the two men descending the stairs. But in fact, the look of the picture—the ambience of it—came directly from the old Universal Studio monster classics like *Frankenstein* and *Dracula*. And these had been fashioned by the German Jew Carl Laemmle along with his stable of emigré directors. Hollywood and his own inclinations, in other words, had somehow furnished Storm's mind with the German Romantic imagery of Rhinehart as it mutated into the pre-Fascist Expressionist celebration of Terror and Will. He too, in other words, was part of the story trail.

Which, so far, was about the only interesting thing she could think of to say about the film. The rest was cliché piled upon cliché.

She leaned on her stick and watched. Down and down, by roving torchlight, Prendergast and Hedley went. And now there was the body of poor, dear Sergeant What's-His-Name dangling from the wall.

"Poor devil," said Dr. Prendergast.

Poor devil, by Jove, thought Harper Albright.

The eerie music swelled—as eerie music will—and the two caped heroes moved out into a great underground chamber. There was Jacobus, the archvillain, bedecked in his penta-gram robe before the blanketed altar. And there was the heroine, of course, writhing on the wall in her seductively torn blouse. Her wrists chained, her mouth gagged—all very appealing, if you went in for that sort of thing. The poor girl did her level best to deliver the lines, "Mmf, mmf," with some sort of conviction. And her name, of course, was Annie.

And the villain was Jacobus. Harper lifted one gray eyebrow. Jacobus seeking immortality. Well, that was something anyway. If you thought of Iago watching the film twenty years before. You could imagine him—still reeling from the destruction of his cult, seeking desperately for a sign of his cherished destiny. You could imagine the hairs on the back of his neck bristling at even this minor coincidence.

But it was not enough. Not enough to draw him onto the trail. How could he have known to go from this ridiculous thing to "Black Annie" and the other stories?

Then the answer—a possible answer—began to take shape in her mind. *A spilled soda.* She had forgotten that. Hadn't Iago said something about a spilled soda, back in the church of the Templars? *A spilled soda, and the next stage was given to me.* Yes, that was it.

Harper felt a twinge of fear—her first real fear for the life of Richard Storm.

"Why, Dr. Prendergast, I'm so glad you could make it," Jacobus said from the TV.

And the doorbell rang.

Harper blinked, looked around her, momentarily confused by the intrusion of reality.

"You're just in time to bear witness to my final apotheosis," Jacobus said from the television.

The doorbell rang again.

Harper stood up in a flurry. The doorbell. It might be the police. It might be word of Bernard. It might be Bernard himself . . .

She dithered before the television, trying to decide what to do, how to proceed. If she turned the TV off, the tape might keep on playing and she would lose her place. If she tried to turn the tape off . . . well, she really hadn't the faintest notion of how to do that anyway.

The doorbell rang again. Reluctantly, Harper backed away from the set, edging around the bed.

The voice of Jacobus trailed after her, tinny from the set's small speaker.

"Poor Prendergast. That you ever thought to defeat me. Could you not see that I am the agent of an immortal power?"

The doorbell rang again, insistently. Harper knocked against the bedside table, the stack of books. She caught it before it toppled over, steadied it. Then, with a last glance at the show, she bustled towards the corridor.

"In such incarnations as this, I travel through the centuries," said Jacobus. "I feed on the marrow of time."

Harper stopped. She had her hand on the doorframe. She was about to leave the room. She looked back at the television set. *I feed on the marrow of time.* That was just what Iago had said to her in the Temple Church. And with a straight face too. She had thought at the time it was a little overwrought . . .

She stared at the screen. A close-up on the evil genius. A close-up on the grim detectives. The struggling girl: *mmf, mmf.* Jacobus.

"I was here before the oceans turned black with life . . ." he said.

"And when the deserts are white with death," Harper said along with him, "I will remain."

The doorbell again. Jacobus went on.

"The petty hindrances you have put in my way have only served to amuse me. But that's all over now . . ."

And with that, the cinema hunchback came chuckling forward. With a magician's yank, he pulled the blanket from the altar and there . . .

Harper felt cold sweat beading on her forehead. Felt all her fears—for Bernard, for Storm, for herself now too—coalesce into one churning anxiety. She stared at the TV screen.

And there, as she stared—there, of course, was the baby. Of course. The baby on the altar. Jacobus with his sword raised above it. The gagged woman screaming from the wall.

Good God, of course: it was all exactly as it had been in the jungle. Exactly what she had seen as she had peeked through the branches and seen the awful truth about the man she'd loved.

She had not forgotten it. Not really. She had repressed it, that was all. She had forcibly dismissed its possibilities and pushed them away, pushed them down—even after Storm's arrival. Even after he'd read that story at the party.

You suffer for what you fail to confess, she thought—even when you fail to confess it to yourself.

And she thought: A spilled soda. Yes. That makes it perfect.

She understood now. She understood everything that had happened. She even began to see, in her gathering terror, what was going to happen next.

The doorbell rang again. Again.

Harper hurried out of the room.

✦

By the time she opened the front door, Detective Inspector William Pullod had given up on her. He had gone back down the mansion's steps, was heading across the narrow street to where his Peugeot was parked before The Sign of the Crane. From the Peugeot's passenger seat, his assistant, PC Slade, watched him approaching.

But then Pullod heard the door open behind him. He turned around, saw Harper standing there. She looked down on him silently as he moved back towards her, back towards the curb at the foot of the steps.

She braced herself—physically braced herself, putting her full weight on her walking stick. The inspector, she saw, was arranging his features into a po-faced expression of official sympathy. She felt the chill night air blow over her, felt another chill answer it from within. Was it too late? Was it already too late?

Below her, the wiry weightlifter shifted uncomfortably in his overcoat. He squinted up at the old woman through one eye. In one hand, he tossed a ring of keys up and down, jingle-jangle.

"Miss Albright," he said. He looked away from her, along the dark street. But there was no traffic there, no one moving, nothing to see. He looked down at the keys in his hand instead. "I'm afraid . . ." he began.

Harper's fingers curled and recurled around the dragon's head. *I'm afraid,* she thought. There was a good English locution for you. *I'm afraid there's been a bit of a nuclear war.* The outer woman remained grimly firm but she could feel her framework wobbling. She hated that "I'm afraid."

"I'm afraid we've found young Bernard's car," said DI Pullod unhappily.

Harper lifted her chin. "I see. And where are you afraid it is?".

"I'm afraid," said the inspector, "it's right over there." And he gestured across the street towards the pub. "Right in front of mine." He held up the keys. "A constable found these in the ignition."

Harper only nodded.

"I don't suppose he's come home . . ." said Pullod.

"No," Harper said.

"And you're certain he hasn't just . . . run off?"

"Yes. I'm certain."

The inspector made a very close examination of the keys in his hand. His sharp, energetic features worked awkwardly. "Then I'm afraid . . ."

"The car might be meant as a message for me. Yes, I'm afraid so too," said Harper. A movement caught her attention. She raised her eyes to see Slade gazing at her from behind the Peugeot's window. She didn't know the man. Could she trust him? Could she trust Pullod?

There was a long silence as the DI resettled himself in his overcoat again.

"Inspector," Harper said slowly. "How many churches of St. James would you say there are in London?" That was the name of the church in Storm's film. St. James. Santiago.

The policeman's mouth pulled down, his hands went up on either side of him. "I . . . I don't know. Half a dozen at least, I should think."

"Yes," she murmured. "At least . . ." And she stood pondering. The speech from Storm's film had confirmed her instinct: Iago had found his destiny that day twenty years ago in the Edgware Road cinema. He had found it, and he wanted to cling to it. In some superstitious way, he was trying to inhabit the stories that had led him to the triptych. Perhaps trying to inhabit *Spectre* most of all. But then, when Storm had made the picture he was inventing an England he had never then seen. It raised certain logistical problems . . .

"Tell me this, then," she said finally. "Do you know of any St. James church that has been abandoned? Or even destroyed?"

Again, Pullod made that baffled gesture. But then, mid-gesture, he stopped. "Well, yes, as a matter of fact," he said.

"There was the bomb blast down in the Barbican. About six, eight months ago now, was it? Started a fire in a church down there. Might have been St. James. Yes, I think it was. I think I remember . . ."

But Harper was no longer there above him. The door to her mansion stood open, the entryway empty.

Pullod glanced back at Slade in the Peugeot. Both men shrugged.

And Harper returned. Slipping into her cape. Clapping her Borsalino down upon her gray bangs until the brim was just above her spectacles. She descended the stairs quickly.

"Uh . . ." said Pullod. "Miss Albright? What is it?"

"Don't be alarmed, Inspector," said Harper, walking right past him, walking towards the Peugeot. "It's only the Uncanny. But I believe I've caught the current of it," she called back over her shoulder to him. "Yes. I believe it's on our side now."

"You will live without pain, you will live without aging. You will live without the fear of death and above the laws of man."

Bernard lay like a broken toy, all the tension, all the life, gone from him. His arms hung dead on the coffin bottom, his legs lay dead, one bent, tilted against the sarcophagus wall. His head lay still on his flaccid neck, his eyes open, staring, his mouth open.

Love, he thought distantly. *Love has the human form divine.*

"You think now," Iago went on, "that you'll quail at the letting of blood, at the killing of your own children. But I promise you, you will not quail. More than that, I promise you the act will free you, will give you a power over your own life—and a joy in that power—you can't even imagine now. Any beast can give life to its offspring. But only we can give life to ourselves, over and over."

Bernard lay motionless, lay limp. Lay staring into nothing, seeing nothing. *The human form divine*, he thought.

"It will become your nature, Bernard, I swear. It is your nature now, if you would only confess it. You can't help but feel it as I speak. You can't help but imagine it: lifting the knife over the infant's body, unafraid of capture, unafraid of sin. Taking its blood for your own life. You can't help but imagine it and feel how exciting it is to you. It is exciting to you, isn't it, Bernard? Isn't it?"

Bernard lay barely breathing; staring. Arms dead, legs dead, eyes open. *Love has the human form divine.*

Then, slowly, as on a rusty hinge, his mouth moved.

"Yes," he said distinctly.

He thought he heard Iago sigh.

"You see, it can be done," came the smoke of the voice above. "We can be honest with each other about who we really are. Now," he went on, his tone growing more charged. "Now—will you let me release you? Will you let me free you from your coffin? Will you travel with me for a while—just a little while—and mix your life with mine, and give me my fair chance to prove my case to you?"

Love, thought Bernard senselessly. Lying, staring, not even aware of the tears that had started to run down his cheeks.

"Will you agree?" said Iago.

And Bernard, at last, said, "Yes."

At once there was a thick, scraping sound. Bernard's head remained where it was, but his eyes moved slightly. He looked upward. The deep grind of stone on stone came again.

He let out a silent sob of relief. The lid of the sarcophogus was shifting.

Now he heard other voices, murmuring. A grunt of effort. Another deep scrape. A long grating rumble.

Suddenly, a line of gray light slashed across his face like a sword. He shut his eyes, but the light throbbed red behind his lids. The cool air poured down over his cheeks, and his body seemed to seize it, drag it in.

"Oh," he whispered.

He stirred now, opened his eyes. Turned his head to look up as the line of light expanded. The light was not bright but it seemed to him a Niagara of blinding radiance. He squinted into it. Gasped the fresh air. A milkshake in the desert. He gasped and gasped it, his stomach rolling over with its unaccustomed richness. Exquisite. The pain in his head, the aching throughout his body: it was all exquisite, it was exquisite life, the promise of this exquisite life forever.

His shoulders began to shake as he started crying harder, with joy this time. He peered up into the cascade of light. It seemed to separate like swimmers in a water ballet, it seemed to bloom like flowers, changing from a downpour to a spreading canopy of streaming beams.

And there—at the center of those rays—there was Iago.

It was difficult for Bernard to distinguish between the surge of passionate pleasure that went through him at the opening of his tomb, and the powerful, bewildering warmth he felt upon finally seeing that face. The long, dark hair framed features chiseled in brutal planes and angles. But the eyes were as cool and smoky as the voice had been, relaxed, even witty. The smile was gently welcoming.

This was his father.

"Now you'll see," Iago said, the voice washing down with

the radiant light. "With me, above all else, you will never be ashamed of who you are."

Bernard tried to nod. "Love . . ." he almost whispered. But his eyes sank closed, and he fainted.

18 When Bernard looked again, Iago was gone. Another face had replaced his.

The scarred man leaned over the side of the sarcophagus. His piggy eyes were bright under the tawny, sharply cut hair. His disfigured mouth was disfigured even further by a grin. He wrinkled his nose comically.

"Phwor! Who's made a mess, then? All right, lad. Come on, up you go. Let's get you spruced and lovely for the road."

He reached down and grabbed Bernard's slack arm. Oofing and urring, he worked the young man's body up into a half-sitting position. With each fresh jolt of motion, Bernard felt a zig-zagging bolt of green lightning lance through him, nerve-end to nerve-end, top to toe. His head fell to one side, and he felt as if it had fallen on a bed of nails. He clutched at the scarred man's thick, muscular shoulders for support.

"There you go. Easy now," the scarred man said.

With his help, Bernard managed to roll one leg up over the sarcophogus wall. The scarred man was practically carrying him as he rose from the coffin's depths. He lifted Bernard easily, lowered him to the floor easily as if he were no weight at all. Bernard felt himself set down gently. He stood there, his back hunched, his mouth hanging open, his hand resting on the edge of the tomb. He stared down with glazed eyes, stared through the pools and puddles of bloody pain that kept spreading and evaporating just behind the screen of his vision.

"Now then, now then," the scarred man said. "You can't go anywhere looking like that, can you. We've got to get you out of those clothes."

Bernard waved him away at first, or tried to. He tried to undress himself. For a moment, his hand tugged ineffectively at the collar of his shirt. Then it fell to his side again. He stood still again, staring dully at the stones of the floor. The scarred man took hold of the shirt collar and worked it up over Bernard's head as if he were a child. He undid Bernard's belt and pulled his black pants down to his ankles.

Bernard swallowed, fighting off the nausea. When he managed to raise his eyes, he saw the dim recesses of an underground crypt tilting and turning around him. Columns and arches, spandrels and darkened niches rising and falling as if at sea. Stone tombs, carved effigies of the dead, plaques set in the wall and floor—they telescoped sickeningly in and back. It was all shadowy. It was all empty. It was all turning round and round.

Bernard licked his lips, swaying where he stood. He felt something damp in his hand, and closed his fingers around it. The scarred man had given him a sponge. He knew that he was naked now.

"Here, you do this," the man said gruffly. "Face too, there's blood all over it."

Bernard nodded. *Love has the human form divine,* he thought. And in loose, sloppy swipes, he began to sponge himself down.

"Put some grease into it," the scarred man muttered impatiently. "We haven't got all night."

Bernard nodded vaguely. Went on sponging himself the

same as before. And it was good to feel the warm rivulets running down his skin. He stood, bent and staring, thinking about that face, Iago's face.

With me, above all, you will never be ashamed.

Love, thought Bernard, *has the human form divine.*

"All right, that'll do," said the scarred man. He pried the sponge from Bernard's resistless fingers. "Here, put these on."

Bernard had to stare for a long moment at the folded clothes that were being held out to him. Gray sweatpants, white sweatshirt, white socks and tennis shoes on top. Drawing in a breath, he yanked at the shirt. He struggled to get his arms into the sleeves, wrestled the rest down over him. For the sweatpants, he had to hold on to the scarred man's shoulder. The pain pulsed in his head, as he bent down, as he went through the long, complex process of drawing his trousers on.

"All right. Here," said the scarred man, not unkindly. Bernard rested against his sarcophagus as the other knelt before him. The scarred man tugged one sock over Bernard's bare foot, then another over the other. He fitted on the tennis shoes as Bernard held weakly to the coffin's wall.

Love, thought Bernard. He tried to concentrate on that, tried to bring the full force of his focus to bear on it.

Then the scarred man stood up and the two men were face to face. The scarred man clapped Bernard on the shoulder. His pinkish eyes gleamed.

"There you are, bright as a button," he said. "And a face like an angel, haven't you?"

Bernard nodded and straightened from the coffin, still holding on to it, still holding on to the edge. He had to work his mouth open and closed a few moments before he could speak.

"Do you know . . ." he said thickly. "Do you know what I

kept . . . what I kept thinking all the while he was talking?"

The scarred man laughed once, his big body heaving up and down. "No. I give up. What was you thinking?"

Bernard licked his lips again. "Love," he said. "I kept thinking . . . Love has the human form divine. No matter what he told me. I just kept thinking that."

"Uh-huh," said the scarred man.

"That's what saved me," said Bernard.

And he hit the scarred man in the throat.

It wasn't a powerful strike. It didn't have to be: it took the scarred man so completely by surprise. The knife hand caught the thug in the Adam's apple. His mouth opened. His eyes widened. His tongue poked out. He gagged.

Bernard grabbed him by the testicles.

The scarred man's body bent violently. His butt went back, his torso jerked forward. Bernard staggered away a step. He clasped his hands together. He raised his two arms high. A great wave of pain broke over his head, and he cried out. Then he dropped his hands like an axe on the back of the scarred man's neck.

The blow drove the scarred man's face into the edge of the sarcophagus. Bernard saw blood spray out on either side of the thug's head.

Bernard reeled and dropped to his knees, retching a thin, black gruel. Still retching, he scrabbled at the floor, tried to stand again before the scarred man could recover, could attack.

Love . . . he thought.

The scarred man did not recover. He hung on the edge of the sarcophagus as if he were searching for something within. Then, slowly, he began to slide off it. Then more quickly. Then his big body dropped to the crypt's stone floor.

Bernard climbed to his feet. He stumbled to the coffin and grabbed hold of it before he fell again. He bent over the open tomb, his stomach convulsing.

The smell from within the coffin rose up to him. His own smell, the smell of his own death. And there, in the dust at the bottom of the thing, sat the human skull, its mandible missing, its eye sockets scored and broken. It looked bucktoothed and stupid there, staring blind.

Panting, Bernard reached down for it. The bone was rotten, it was soft and thin to the touch. As he clutched it, a circle of brain pan caved in under the pressure of his thumb. He lifted the skull and brought it up before him. Bernard, with his bald head, with his gray skin, his sunken cheeks, his deathlike grin, might have been looking at his own reflection.

He whispered to it almost sweetly, "Sell your soul to the devil, you bastard. Because your ass belongs to me."

And with a deep, animal growl, he hoisted his arm. Dashed the rotting thing back into the tomb. It crunched against the stone, spitting fragments, then fell broken on its side.

Bernard turned away from it, and his eyes were wild with fury. The scarred man lay curled and unconscious at his feet, the blood pooling on the floor around his head. Bernard pushed off the coffin and stepped around him.

He started staggering towards the stairs.

They were stone, the stairs, and winding. He mounted one by one. A rope run through a set of metal rings in the rock wall was the only banister and he clutched it in both his hands. Pulled on it. Lugged himself upward. The curving stairwell seemed to close and widen like an accordion around him. He began to feel sick again. His head felt as if a chisel were being pummeled through it from within. The blow fell repeatedly as he climbed. He gritted his teeth against it and went up, went on. The staircase grew blacker and blacker around him. The splashes of red grew brighter and brighter behind his eyes.

"Goddamn it," he gasped.

Bile bubbled up over his tongue to his grit teeth. He swallowed it back. Pulled himself up hand over hand, stair after stair.

And then he fell against the door. His shoulder hit the heavy wood. The jar of the collision seemed to drive a stake of pain straight down through the top of his skull. But under the pressure of his shoulder, the door was already swinging open. He was falling after it. Falling, for one wheeling second more. Then he stumbled into the church.

Dizzy, he looked around him. It was the same church. Where he had seen the men talking at the foot of the cross. Where he had witnessed the crucifixion. It was all over now, though. The place seemed deserted. A strange, false light hung behind the shapes on the stained-glass windows, but there was no light within. The aisles, the pews were dark. The altar to his right, the nave, the transept across from him: all were shadowy, dark.

Bernard snarled. "Come on. Come out," he whispered.

He staggered a step away from the crypt door. Staggered another step, and another, into the crossing where the transepts met the aisles. He looked around everywhere, his eyes so wide with anger he felt them bulging from his face. Everywhere, undelineated figures of stained glass gazed down at him dispassionately.

"Come on!" he screamed at them, at anyone. His voice seemed to tear out of his throat, to tear through his flesh, a killing pain. But the high church ceiling swallowed his shout

without an echo. And there was no answer.

"Come out and fight," he shouted. *"Come out and fight like an immortal demon!"* He giggled. *"You cocksucker!"*

He giggled again. *Fight like an immortal demon*—that was a good one. He bent over helplessly, swaying where he stood, giggling until it hurt his lungs. His head was pounding. The stained-glass figures gazed down at him from their heights.

With a roar, he suddenly threw back his head. He howled, *"Come on, Daddy-o! It's Oedipus time!"*

He was laughing too hard to continue. He was crying too hard. He shook and tears poured down his cheeks. Snot dangled from one nostril, a white string. He wiped at his mouth and nose with a broad swipe of his palm. He staggered in a small circle, crying, laughing. Gripping his middle. Finally, he came to rest. Stood crouched and snarling like a wounded animal.

And it was only then that he realized he was surrounded.

Dark figures were moving in on him. Moving in stealthily from every side. From the deepest blackness against the walls, they came slowly into the grayer shadows. They converged upon him step by step.

Uh-oh, was his first thought. *Me and my big mouth.*

He turned to face them in one direction, then another, then another. The sturdy figures moved towards him. Down the aisles, out of the transepts. He spun again. Even from the altar, out of the penumbra of the ambulatory, they came. Tall, thick, husky figures, their arms ready at their sides.

Swallowing fear and nausea, Bernard kept swiveling, to one, another, another. He raised his hands, ready to defend himself and strike.

In the brief time he had left to reflect, he realized that he was not sorry it had come to this. They were going to kill him, he knew. But it didn't matter. He didn't mind. In point of fact, he wasn't even certain he wanted to live anymore anyway. Knowing what he knew. About his past. About himself. And this way, he reckoned, at least he might get to take one of them with him. To close with one of them, maybe even two. Rip a throat out, tear open a ribcage. It would feel good. It would send a message. A little E-mail to the old man . . .

"Come on," he muttered, swinging from one to the other as they kept moving in. "Come on." Swallowing his tears.

The circle was closing. The approaching shapes had come out of the aisles and the transepts. They had joined together and were all around him in the crossing where he stood. Any moment now, he expected them to rush in at him all at once.

But now they stopped.

Bernard spun, his knees bent, his knife-hands lifted, loose.

He cried out once more, loudly, despairingly. "Come on, will you!"

But only a single figure detached itself from the others, broke from the circle and came forward, towards him, down the center aisle.

Bernard faced that lone attacker, his breath scraping from his throat in feral growls. He waited, ferocious.

And yet, as he waited, some sound confused him. Some repeated sound. It reached him through the nimbus of his pain. He was flustered by it. Shook his head.

The figure came closer. Bernard blinked. He *knew* that sound. A steady, resolute, rhythmic clicking: the sound of a walking stick on stone.

He stared through the shadows. He made out, at last, the small, squat, waddling silhouette approaching. He made out the contours of the Borsalino. The line of the cane from hand to floor.

The figure stopped before him. Slowly, Bernard sank down onto his knees. He raised his arms. He waved them in front of him to cover his face.

"Don't look at me!" he cried out.

Harper lay a withered hand on his shoulder.

"It's all right, lad," she told him quietly. "You made it."

19

The body of Jervis Ramsbottom—the late Dr. Mormo—still hung from the cross. His arms had been released from the horizontal bar, but stout cord, wrapped around his throat, held him to the vertical. He hung there with his face purple, his eye sockets raw, his cheeks streaked with blood and jelly. His tongue protruded black under the light of PC Slade's torch.

"Poor bugger," the PC said.

"Poor bugger, by Jove," Harper murmured behind him.

"And look here." Slade lowered his torch a little. "That mark carved on his chest. The same as with that German antiques dealer who got killed around Christmas time."

Harper only nodded to herself, thinking. It bothered her, this. The dead Mormo, the tortured Mormo. What was Iago playing at, after all? The warlock had been a coward of the first water. He would have grassed on his mother at the slightest hint of a threat. What had Iago thought to get out of him this way?

The rays of police torches were arcing and crisscrossing all around the church interior now. Areas of char and ruin, piles of rubble, fallen beams stood out beneath their circles of illumination. The faces of saints and patrons frowned from the walls and windows as the light touched them, then slipped back into obscurity.

Beneath the swiftly sweeping shadows, Bernard sat in a front pew, his head hanging, his hands hanging down between his knees. A nurse sat beside him, washing the swollen bruise on his brow. DI Pullod stood over them both another moment. Then he moved away, and came to join Harper and Slade beneath the cross.

These three turned their backs as two crime scene men came forward to tend to Mormo's descent. They stopped by the chancel rail. Pullod glanced at Harper quickly, embarrassed. He looked only at Slade as he spoke, but Harper understood he was sharing the information with her.

"We've had a sighting of the black Mercedes," he said in a low tone. "One driver, it looks like. Your boy confirmed the license number." This with a half-nod towards Bernard, though he looked only at Slade. "They lost track of him in Morden, but it sounds like he's heading south along the A24. We've got roadblocks up. We're sure to find him." Now he did turn directly to Harper. "We'll run you and your lad over to hospital. I'll go down to Morden myself, see what's what. All right?"

Harper frowned, shook her head. "He won't go."

"He?"

"Bernard—to hospital. He won't go. He'll walk out, get in his car, and drive wherever he thinks he'll find Iago."

"He's in no fit state to drive."

"Yes," said Harper. "That's why I suggest you give us a lift." Pullod and Slade exchanged a glance. Slade rolled his eyes.

"You say he's headed south," said Harper thoughtfully. Pullod nodded. "That's right."

The door to the crypt opened now. Lester Benbow—the scarred man—was led out between two large patrolmen. His wrists were pinned in cuffs behind his back. His face was smeared with blood. His eyes peered out of the mess, rolling, murderous.

When his gaze lit upon Bernard, the scarred man bared his teeth.

Bernard raised his head. Looked unsmiling at Benbow. Nodded.

Harper watched the scarred man being led away up the church aisle.

"I think, Inspector, we had better head north," said Harper Albright.

"North?" said Pullod with a laugh.

"Yes. I think we had better get out to Belham Grange as quickly as we can."

20   *I rose from the bed and moved across the room to stand before one of the windows on the far wall. Looking out between the curtains, I saw that night had now drawn down around the place completely. A gibbous moon, sporadically visible in the gaps between the racing clouds, served only to cast a pall of faltering and sickly light over the sere expanse of grassland to the east. In that field, now visible, now vanishing as the moon went once again behind its shifting cover, there stood an ominous and melancholy apparition: the ruins of Belham Abbey . . .*

Storm gazed sadly through Sophia's window into that misty, drifting night. What it is, old chap, old stick, he thought, what it is is time for The Reveal. That was the moment at the end of the second act of a film when the villain we thought was dead steps out of the shadows, or when the woman we thought we loved pockets the murder weapon—or when the hero we thought we admired is shown to be a dying louse without the courage to tell the truth. It was way past the end of the second act, thought Storm. It was way past time for The Reveal.

"What is it, Richard?" said Sophia softly.

He turned to find her awake, her eyes glinting in the room's darkness. She had pushed the duvet aside and risen on one elbow. He could make out the shape of her under the frilly canopy. And even now, he didn't know how he could ever tell her.

"You're up," he said.

Her shoulders rose and fell with a deep breath. "I've been awake for a while."

"Yeah?"

"I've been watching you. I've been thinking."

He didn't answer. He saw her shift a little. He thought she might have looked up a moment at the portrait hanging on the wall beside him.

"What was it you were going to tell me before?" she asked him. "Outside, before my father called me."

Storm still hesitated. He felt sick with sadness. "I don't . . . Look, maybe this isn't the time," he said—hating himself for it, hoping anyway she would let him off the hook. "With you so upset and all."

But she said, "I'm not upset. In fact, I feel very calm at the moment, strangely enough. I was just watching you. I was thinking about you, and I wondered."

Storm sat back against the window sill. He pinched the bridge of his nose, closed his eyes. "Oh, man," he said.

"Are you ill or something, Richard?"

He didn't move, didn't answer, couldn't. He kept his

fingers on the bridge of his nose, kept his eyes closed. If he could just sit here, he thought. If he could just sit here in the dark and listen to her voice, to the sound of her voice. He loved that sound. Mary Poppins.

"I thought—when you said you had something to tell me—I thought it might be that," she went on quietly. "I don't know why. It just came into my head. You look so tired sometimes. And your arm, you favor your left arm. And you just always look . . . so sad. Is that what it is? Are you ill? Is that why you always look like that?"

He smiled, his eyes still closed. Nodded. "Yeah," he just managed to say. "Yeah, that's why." And then, quickly: "It's bad, kid. It's what they politely call terminal."

She was quiet for several moments after that. Storm opened his hand now and covered his eyes with it. He felt the dampness against his palm. Shit, he thought. He didn't know what he had been expecting, but it wasn't this. This quiet from her. And when she spoke again, her voice was cool, even, politely curious.

"Does that . . . ? Does it frighten you? Are you frightened?"

He gave a short laugh. "Uh . . . well . . ." Lowered both his hands to his legs as he sat against the sill. He saw her watching him. "No," he said. "Since you ask. I'm not frightened. Not really. Sometimes at night when I'm alone, a little. But not much, even then."

"I didn't think so. I didn't think you would be."

"There aren't many symptoms—maybe the reality of it just hasn't hit me yet. I don't know." He sighed heavily. "I was . . . To be honest, I was afraid of the doctors more than anything. I think it makes them feel better if they can pretend they're in some kind of battle with it, even when the battle is really all over. I was afraid they'd cut me up, radiate me, poison me to death for no reason. That's why I blew town in the first place. But . . . no. Not this. This doesn't frighten me at all. It just makes me—it makes everything—really, really sad."

After a pause, she went on—went on in the same way, still cool, still curious. "It makes you sad because . . . ? Of regrets and that sort of thing?"

"Yeah. Yeah. Regrets." He wiped his eyes quickly, the corners of his mouth pulling down. "I got me a suitcase full of regrets, babe, believe me. The thing is, I just didn't . . . I didn't get it right, you know? I don't even think I got the rules of the game right. Not until you dropped your glass at the party. Until I looked up at you. And then I thought: Oh, yeah, I get it. I get it now. I mean, what a shmuck, right? Ach . . ." He looked up into an invisible corner of the ceiling above her bed. "Christ, kid, I should've stayed away from you. I knew that, damn it. I knew it. Or I should've told you right off. But I should've stayed away, that's the thing. What a jerk-o."

Sophia—with what seemed to him calm, unaffected movements in the dark—took the pillow from behind her and set it against the headboard. She sat up, patted it, propped herself on it, sitting quietly, regarding him quietly from under the canopy's fringe.

"I suppose you were pretending it wasn't true," she said after a while. "I suppose that's why you didn't tell me."

He smiled unhappily, his head going up and down. What a smart dame, he thought. What a champion dame. "Yeah, that's it," he said. "Not really pretending, you know—not like I believed it, but just . . . acting the part, sort of. Acting like we could be together. Like . . ."

He couldn't continue. He just went on nodding silently, biting his lip.

"Like we could go on to get married and have children and so on," she said.

He laughed, his heart in a vice. "And so on. Yeah."

"No," she said after a second or two. "No, I don't suppose we could do that now."

"No," said Richard Storm. "I don't suppose we could."

"Still," said Sophia, considering. "Still, if you had told me, I might well have stayed away from you."

"Well, that's it," said Storm. "That's what I should've done."

"No," she told him. "No. Because then I wouldn't have had the chance to realize that I love you."

Storm made a choked noise, covered his face with both hands.

"Which I did. Realize," Sophia said. "Just now. While you were standing there, while I was watching you at the window."

"I'm sorry, Sophie. I'm sorry."

"Don't be sorry." She ran her hand up through her hair. Slowly, once and then again. "Don't be foolish. Don't be sorry. I love you, Richard," she told him. "And at the end of the day . . ." But then her voice caught. Which surprised him. She had sounded so cool until then. But then her voice caught and she was silent for several moments, looking down thoughtfully.

"Well," she finished brusquely. "At the end of the day, I think you should come to bed."

21 *Tick-tick. Tick-tick.*

Sir Michael sat erect, motionless, in the high-backed leather chair behind his desk. The sound traveled to him through the walls.

Tick-tick. Tick-tick.

He gave no indication that he heard it, no visible sign. But he heard it. It completely occupied his attention. It sparked his imagination. He sat with his eyes open, gazing ahead. Imagining. The mahogany desk before him hunkered hugely in the unlighted room. The carved ram's heads on its pilasters stared as the Great Man stared.

Tick-tick. Tick-tick.

It was coming from the floor above him. From the room just above him, his daughter's room. He imagined that it was the frame of her bed, clicking as it strained at the pegs of its ancient joins.

He sat without moving, his lips slightly parted. Sat tall and precise. He had been sitting like that for over an hour now. In the study, with the door closed, the lights off, the room growing darker and darker. He had sat and sat like that as night had come.

He had removed the box from the bottom drawer, removed the pistol from the box. The box stood open on the desktop blotter, the tray with the cigars and the silver lighter lay next to it. Next to that lay the gun. And he supposed that was what he was gazing at—that he was gazing at the gun, but in truth he hardly saw it. He was just gazing, just listening, imagining, his hands folded in his lap, motionless.

Tick-tick. Tick-tick.

And there was another sound now, another sound above the sound of the straining bed. There was the sound of voices. His daughter's voice, her lover's. Their whispers, groans. Scrabbling in the wall like squirrels. Coming down to him.

Sir Michael did not move. Sat with his hands clasped. Gazed. Now he did see the gun on the blotter. He focused on it. The blunt gun.

Suddenly, Sophia cried out above him. It was an unmistakable noise. She cried out twice, once harshly as if in anguish and denial, once again as if in triumph and release.

Sir Michael sniffed. The ticking had stopped.

After that, it was quiet. It was quiet all over the house for a long time. Minute after minute passed, and Sir Michael didn't move and there was no sound in the house anywhere. Sir Michael didn't know how much time passed. Half an hour, an hour, he wasn't sure. He sat without moving. He thought about his wife, Ann. It was twenty years since she had died, but the thought of her was still wrenching to him.

After that long time, sitting like that, without thinking at all, he picked up the pistol. He slipped it into his jacket pocket.

Clearing his throat softly, Sir Michael swiveled in his chair and stood up. He moved around the edge of the desk, his fingertips trailing over the smooth border. He paused on the other side to button his jacket, pull the panels down. He felt the weight of the gun in his pocket. He went to the door and opened it.

It was so dark out in the corridor that he had begun to step forward before he realized that a man was standing there. Even then, he was so startled, he couldn't comprehend what it was he saw.

But it was a man. An enormous man who almost filled the doorway. With his vast shoulders and his heavy, cinder-block head, he looked like Frankenstein's monster. He towered even over Sir Michael. And he came slowly into the room.

Stupid with confusion, Sir Michael could only back away at first. Back away and watch the creature advance. His thoughts had all been on Storm, on Storm up in his daughter's room. He could not take this in.

Then he had a single moment of fear and half-understanding. He even had time to wonder if he had got it wrong, got it all wrong.

His hand flashed to his jacket pocket, to the gun. His mouth opened to shout, to warn Sophia.

Then the monster struck him unconscious to the floor.

22 A police car, with its siren blaring, is no good place for conversation. Pullod, driving, PC Slade beside him, Harper and Bernard in the backseat, all sat without speaking as the car laced through the evening traffic, as it plowed over the miles of the motorway.

Harper had her stick pressed against the floor, her hands folded on top of the dragon's head, her chin propped on her hands. Bernard leaned weakly against the door, his long legs stretched as far as they would go under the seat in front of him. His eyes were closed. His body looked limp and slender and frail in the white T-shirt and sweatpants, in the blue windbreaker one of the cops had loaned him.

The monotonous wail of the siren made it difficult for Harper even to think. It went on and on as the car's red lights flashed and faded over glimpses of night countryside. Car after car sank past the windows, sank back behind them. Harper leaned on her stick and stared at the seat in front of her, trying to string her ideas together. Now and then she glanced over at Bernard. He didn't move, didn't open his eyes.

After a while she leaned forward a little, towards the back of Pullod's head. She shouted to him over the racket.

"I wonder," she said, "if it might be possible to have

someone phone Belham Grange . . ."

It was Slade who half-turned to her. "Trouble with the line," he shouted. "They've had a storm up there."

"Perhaps, then," Harper shouted back, "you could radio and have a local officer drop by the place . . ."

"All taken care of, darling," Slade answered her abruptly. Then he looked out the window and muttered to himself, "Though why we should bother, I don't know."

Harper couldn't hear what he said, but she answered him anyway. "Because," she told him astringently, "Iago has been looking for the Rhinehart panels for twenty years. The only thing that's kept him from finding them is that, in all that time, they haven't changed hands. When Mormo got hold of the *Madonna*, it was reasonable for Iago to conclude that he might be able to get hold of the *Nativity* panel as well. Mormo was, after all, one of a few key fences of black-market art after the war. If the final panel had changed hands then, he might well have been aware of it. But if Mormo had had that knowledge, believe me, he would have told it at once. Since he didn't tell, it seems logical the panel must have been traded by one of the other key fences. And there's only one other such trader who's been involved in these events from the beginning—one other who bid at the *Magi* auction. And Iago knows who that is as well as we do."

She could not see Slade's face, but she understood he was rolling his eyes. She could not hear his voice, but she imagined that he muttered, "Iago!"

She did not answer him again. She sat brooding, leaning on her stick, trying to ignore the siren.

And there is also the fact, she went on silently, that all this, all of it, must have begun with *Spectre*.

What ill wind had blown Iago into that Edgware Road

cinema twenty years ago she would never know. It was his talent, perhaps—as it was hers—to ride the tide of the Uncanny. Perhaps she herself had been in the same cinema on the same day—she could not remember. She only knew that Iago had been there. Five years after she had ruined his cult scheme. He must have been feeling quite fragile, poor lamb. His sense of destiny must have been growing precarious as he scrabbled and seduced among the lost of the earth, desperate to produce the offspring whose blood he needed, all the while realizing that one day, one day the precious blue stone itself would dwindle to nothing.

How that thought must have plagued him. No matter how much blood he got his hands on, one day, one day, the stone itself would be gone. And then the discoloration on his wrists would begin. And then the living decay.

With these concerns, he had wandered into the cinema. He had sat and watched *Spectre*. And as the climax sent shivers of recognition through him . . . *a spilled soda*. Yes. Someone nearby him had dropped her drink in agitation and surprise. Oh yes, yes, it would have been the same. Exactly the same as at the Christmas party. The ghost story. The spilled drink. And Iago, looking up—as Storm had looked up—saw, for the first time, the beautiful Ann Endering, Sophia's mother.

She loved the cinema, loved American movies, and she had been there. And, startled by the film, she had spilled her soda, and Iago had looked up. Then, moved by the beauty of the mother as Storm had been moved by the daughter's beauty, he approached her.

Harper could imagine it. She knew Iago's mesmerizing attractions. Ann Endering—a kind, charitable, liberal woman—would have been his perfect target. If Sir Michael was any indication, she had a penchant for bold, energetic and somewhat dodgy men. And perhaps her idealism—her belief that the world could be made a better place—had softened her, as it did so many, to the beguiling logic of a powerful personality who saw himself as chosen for some great enterprise. In any case, she became his lover. Soon, he would have found out exactly why the film had disturbed her. She loved her house, her family history. She would have seen at once the connections between *Spectre* and the legend of the Belham Abbey Ghost. Perhaps she even recognized the debt the film owed to "Black Annie." Perhaps—knowing her history as well as she did—she knew more than that, much more.

As much as she knew, it was enough, finally, to fuel Iago's interest, to start him down the story trail. After that, the coincidences in the stories—the murdered children, the dream of immortality, the elixir of life in "The Alchemist's Castle," and finally the legends accruing round the Rhinehart triptych—would have led him on—on until, at last, "The Monk's Confession" fell into his hands and he understood everything. And he began his first abortive hunt for the triptych itself.

But by then—by then, Ann Endering understood as well. Too late, she realized who her lover was, and what he was doing to her. She would have been desperate then to keep the triptych out of Iago's hands. And, against all her social instincts, she would have seized on the final coincidence—the one coincidence that perhaps Iago didn't know: that one of the men most likely to be able to recover the Rhinehart panels was Sir Michael, was her own husband.

That was why the third panel had not surfaced, why Mormo didn't know where it was. Because twenty years ago, before Iago's search had fairly started, Sir Michael—without fully understanding why—secured the only one of the panels that was in the west. At his wife's request, knowing only that the man who wanted it had seduced her, knowing only that this was his single avenue of revenge, he secured the panel through his secret sources. And he hid it away.

Which left Ann to complete a task of her own: the task of destroying herself. Because she would have been carrying his baby, Iago's baby. He would have made sure of that. And she would have known now what he was planning to do to it. And she would have destroyed herself, and the child, rather than let the infant fall into Iago's hands.

As well as she could with the siren blaring, Harper brooded on these things in silence. And she brooded as well on Richard Storm. She reproached herself for understanding it all too late. She had sent Storm out to Belham to complete her information. She had thought it a task of relative safety, had thought it would keep him away from her dangerous gambit with the *Madonna*. She had hoped he would be able to help Sophia find the answers to her life, and would then be able to retire from the fray in peace.

Instead, she had sent him right into the thick of it. And Iago, as always, was one step ahead of her.

The car raced on and the four sat without speaking, enveloped by the noise.

Then Bernard said, "Is it real, do you think?"

Harper glanced over to see him watching her. His eyes half open, looking out through lowered lids. He hardly raised his voice, but it reached her clearly.

"I would like to know, after all. It would help me to know."

"What?" she said.

"Can he really . . . If he gets the third painting, if he has the triptych complete, will he really be able to re-create the crystal? Will he really be able to live forever on the blood of his own children?"

Harper extended a hand, patted the factotum on his knee. "Believe nothing," she told him. "It's the only defense."

The flasher's red glow slipped over his features. Harper saw him smiling bitterly. "If I believe nothing, darling," he said dryly, "then what will defend me against myself?"

Harper frowned, replaced her hand on the dragon's head, lowered her chin to the back of her hand.

"Believe nothing," she murmured again, "and trust to the Everlasting Thing."

Then the four sat silently, as the car raced on.

23 The gateway to Belham Grange was now huddled deep in mist. The local constable who had been sent out to investigate cruised by the entrance twice before he found it. Then he did not drive through, but only turned his car on the narrow country road, pointed his headlamps into the drive.

The mist curled in the headlamp beams, wreathed itself around them like a living thing. The local constable, a handsome blond youth with ladykilling blue eyes, leaned close to the windscreen and peered through it.

At first, there was nothing. Only the mist folding, falling, gathering over the first distances of the long front path between the overhanging trees.

Then something moved. A silhouette in the fog. Amorphous at first, then, slowly, defining itself as it approached the light. The figure of a man.

As the constable peered through the windscreen, his heart thudding, the figure moved into the scope of his headlamps. A tall man, with long black hair, with features cut in sharp, cruel angles. With deep, laughing, hypnotic eyes. He was wearing a white three-piece suit. He had green gloves on his hands.

He lifted one hand, one finger, and touched it to his eyebrow in a salute.

The local constable nodded, swallowing hard. He returned the salute to his master.

Then, quickly, he threw the police car into reverse. Spun back away from the Grange's drive. Stepped on the gas and roared off down the country lane, disappearing into the mist.

Iago put his hands behind his back and strolled casually down the drive towards the house.

24 Storm, then, was at the window again, looking out at the night, and wondering. He was buttoning his shirt, tucking it into his pants, and wondering about the reality of grace. Maybe, he thought, maybe this was it: the way he felt right now—hey, what did he know?—maybe this was grace, what religious people called grace. *I love you, Richard, come to bed.* I mean, was that a bolt from the blue, or what? It wasn't what he'd been expecting, that was for damn sure. It sure as hell wasn't what he thought he deserved.

Outside, through the window, the clouds, the moon, the drifting mist, threw their romantic, spectral shadows on the ruins of the abbey, on the wall, on the graves. A wonderful scene, he thought. A great setting for a movie, for a ghost story. And, hey, maybe there was still time for that. Maybe he could just zip a crew out here and shoot "Black Annie" straight off the page, a classy little one-hour job for Brit TV . . .

His gaze shifted. There, beside the outer scene, to the right of it, was Sophia's reflection, thrown by her bedside lamp. And she was buttoning her blouse, and looking down at the floor with her hair falling forward, and smiling to herself in a way that made his heart fill up with wine. He had the memory of her breasts on his lips, and the memory of her shudder in his fingertips, of her last cry, ecstatic and triumphant, in his ears.

And she said softly now, "Well," glancing up at him, "you've certainly got me in a complete fog, Mr. Storm. This day . . . you've got me so confused. I don't know where I am anymore. I hope you're happy."

A corner of his mouth lifted. Maybe he was. Happy. Maybe. He had his movie set, he had his girl, he had a feeling in his balls like hearthlight. Only a slight weakness in his left arm, only a suggestion of pain in the side of his head. Who knew? Maybe this was happy, happy enough. Maybe with this you could check out of the Life Motel and say hey, babe, enjoyed the stay—and then carry the grace out with you like a stolen towel. Who really knew? Maybe there was even more than this, more chances worth taking, some operation, some dread medieval torture of an experimental technique, that stuff they were doing in Baltimore, a one-percent chance of survival—hey, you could go for one percent, maybe, if you had grace on your side . . .

For a moment, a gray haze seemed to deepen before his eyes, the weakness in his arm seemed to threaten to spread through his whole body. But the sensation passed. It passed and, at the same time, his emotions overflowed. He was going to turn to Sophia, he was just about to turn, to turn maybe even with tears in his eyes, to tell her she was the world to him now, that she was the flavor of the world, and that he had forgotten—that he had never really known—how sweet it was, how incredibly sweet.

He was about to turn and say that when, looking dreamily out through the window, he saw something that baffled his imagination, that defied belief.

Storm's hands froze at the collar of his shirt. His lips parted, and he stared—stared through the glass as through a torn curtain at another world revealed.

He saw—did he? Yes—he saw a figure out there—a human figure draped in the mist, silhouetted by the moonlight, raven black, so black it seemed less a being than an absence of existence. It was tall. Its head was bent as if in prayer. Its profile was obscured either by a cowl or by flowing hair. And it was moving with slow and awful majesty among the churchyard stones.

Storm gaped. He pressed his nose to the glass. His sense of well-being deserted him on the instant. He felt woozy suddenly, paralyzed there, his marrow ice, his sinew water. It was real, he thought. He was really seeing it. He was seeing something anyway, a spectral something gliding through the mist, gliding steadily towards the fragment of the chapel wall.

He watched. He couldn't move or speak—couldn't breathe almost—but only gaped and gaped unblinking as if he were petrified on the spot.

"Holy shit," he whispered.

"What is it?" said Sophia behind him.

He didn't answer her. An hallucination, he thought. It must be an hallucination. But still it went on. And, as he peered into the night, the silent, mournful phantasm proceeded with its lifeless grace to the end of the churchyard, to all that remained of the chapel.

And there, beside that ruined wall—before the small crypt where Storm himself had stood—there, as he stood watching, frozen and amazed, the jet absence seemed to sink at the same stately pace, sink lower and lower into the hard earth, until only the head remained above the surface.

And then that too—all, all of it—had vanished.

Storm blinked. He felt very dizzy now, almost faint. He was sweating, cold. Hallucination. Definitely. That had to be what it was. And now, the massing mist, propelled before the wind, surged over the ruin, swept across the moon. In seconds, the torn curtain seemed to close. A steamy, roiling darkness pressed itself against the window.

Storm gave a whiffling laugh. "Nah," he said. "Nah."

But second after second passed, and he found he couldn't move. He could only gaze—gaze and gaze—at the invisible night as if that gliding figure were still before him.

Then Sophia broke his trance with a stifled cry. "Oh God," she said. "Oh, Richard—there it is."

"Huh?" said Storm thickly.

He had to tear himself from the night to turn to her. And when he saw her, even before she spoke again, the hairs on the back of his neck actually felt as if they were standing on end.

Sophia had risen from the bed. She was standing beside it, one hand thrown out to one of the posts. Her face was expressionless, her features cold, but there was a frightened, almost pleading look in her eyes.

And she said, "Listen. Can't you hear it? It's just the same. It's just the same." She turned to him. "Oh, Richard. Don't you hear it? What is it?"

Storm laughed uncertainly as she appealed to him. He had heard people say that they felt as if they were dreaming, but he'd never before experienced it himself. Now he did. Unclear in his mind, unsteady on his feet, he found himself once more in the grip of a sickening impression that his life was unreal.

And yes, he did hear it. He heard it too. In the walls, in the rafters, surrounding him, all over.

Tick-tick. Tick-tick.

He shook his head, trying to clear it. "That's what you never told me," he said dully—his voice came to him as if from the other end of a tunnel. "That's what was missing from your story. You never told me what was making that noise."

Sophia seemed not to hear him. "It's just the same," she repeated.

And the sound repeated: *Tick-tick. Tick-tick.*

Storm took a faltering step towards her. Maybe this was it, he thought. Maybe he was actually dying right this minute. Maybe he was slipping away from the real world into his own fantasies. Maybe that's what dying would be like: maybe only your dreams remained.

"What was it, Sophia?" he said again, forcing the words. "That night you saw your father fighting with your mother—the blood—what was it that was making that noise?"

Sophia made a quick gesture of denial, refusal. The fear in her eyes was turning to panic.

"Where's Daddy?" she said. "Where is he? Do you think he's all right?"

A noise broke from between Storm's teeth as a hot flash of pain went up one side of his head. He pressed the heels of his palms to his brow. He remembered that feeling of alienation out by the ruin, and he thought: Not now. He couldn't go under now. He had to hold on, by force of will.

He had to stay with her.

Tick-tick. Tick-tick.

"I'll find him," he said. He felt he almost had to shout over that quiet, rhythmic tapping. He felt sick. He felt the cold sweat breaking out all over him. "It's all right. I'll go find him."

He marched, with more boldness than he felt, across the room to the door. He threw it open. The action seemed to jar his mind clear, seemed to bring him back to himself a little. He stood confronting the dark of the hallway. Listening, waiting for the sound to repeat.

Sophia hurried to him, took his arm. "Is someone out there?"

He looked down at her. "It's all right," he said more firmly.

They stepped out into the hall together.

The sound seemed to have ceased. The hall was still. The whole house was still around them. Storm felt his way along the wall as they moved through the shadows, as they moved beneath the stares of the portraits hanging above them.

Trailing his hand above the dado, he found a light switch, flipped it. A row of lamps came on, throwing a musty glow over the long landing. Sophia hung close to him, clung to his arm, her face set forward, the taut expression of suspense on her features so perfect that it almost made him laugh. This old dark house, he thought, and the mysterious noise, and the stalwart hero, and the frightened girl: he could never have gotten this scene past the studios. He knew—he'd tried it— they'd thought it was too clichéd.

"I think it's stopped," Sophia murmured hopefully.

"What was it?" he asked her in the same low tone.

She pressed even closer to him, leaned against him. "I don't know."

"I mean that night, the last time you heard it. What was making that noise?"

She shook her head angrily. "I don't know, I don't know."

They went towards the stairway slowly, clinging to each other, Storm watching the corners, watching the shadows, catching the glimpses of the portraits as they watched him pass. He thought to call out, thought to shout for Sir Michael. But the house, the atmosphere of the house, seemed to press in on him like a threat. He was afraid to raise his voice, to bring the danger down on himself. They went on silently to the top of the stairs.

A switch there brought on the foyer chandelier. The base of the stairs became bright beneath them. The grandfather clock in the hall mimicked the ticking sounds they'd heard, but that was it, everything else was quiet. Storm's faintness, the aura of unreality was passing now. He was still sweaty, still a little sick, his brain still clouded and sluggish. But the worst of it was fading. He felt surer of himself, calmer. His step on the stairs was firm, swift. And he bore Sophia along with him.

They reached the bottom. Stood under the light with the coat rack and umbrella stand and gilded mirror all sedate and familiar in the small space. There was the front door just ahead of them, and to either side the dark, old wooden doors into the corridors, both now closed.

Storm didn't know which way to turn. And Sophia had stopped, had planted herself where she was.

And then she said softly: "Oh . . ."

And Storm heard it begin again.

Tick-tick. Tick-tick.

Seeming to vibrate in the fibers of the place so that he couldn't tell where it was coming from.

Tick-tick. Tick-tick.

"Which way?" he said—his voice was still slow and dull. "Which way do we go?"

She said nothing, and he moved instinctively towards the right, in the direction of the abbey ruin. But Sophia held him back.

"Let's . . . go back upstairs," she said. "Let's . . . I think we should just . . ."

Tick-tick. Tick-tick.

The sound sent a gout of juice through Storm—fear or excitement, he couldn't tell which. But it gave him energy. He made to move again. Sophia dug her heels into the floor.

"I just think . . ." she said. "I think we should just . . ."

"Shh," he said.

He slipped his arm free of her grasp. He went to the wooden door and opened it. Flipped on the light.

He stood looking down the empty corridor. The dusty runner under the yellow lampglow. The chairs and tables against the walls. The doors shut all along the way. And the arras with the many-headed dragon hanging against the wall at the far end.

Tick-tick.

It was louder now. Distinct, persistent, purposeful.

He stepped across the threshold.

"Richard . . ." Sophia rushed to him, clutched his arm again.

"This is the way you went, right?" he said.

She nodded, her face pale, the dancing sparks of panic still clear at the bottom of those pale brown eyes.

They moved along the corridor towards the sound.

"What was it?" he said. He felt the sweat roll down his temples, but his mind felt brighter by the moment. His blood was up. "What was it?"

She didn't answer. He could hear her breathing rapidly. Could feel her palm damp against his sleeve.

Tick-tick.

"Jesus!" said Storm. He searched for it. Over the runner, over the walls, over one closed door after another. Another staring portrait, a crumbling Roman temple in the mist. "Where did you go?" he whispered. "The last door, you said. Your father's study."

"I don't know."

"Yeah? Don't you?"

"Richard . . ."

Tick-tick. Tick-tick.

This time, she let out a noise at the sound, as if she'd been struck, as if it had pierced her.

They were nearing the end of the hallway and the many-headed dragon reared before them, all its mouths opened, all its teeth bared.

Storm tried to think. "They were fighting, right? And your mother was on the floor," he said. "And they were all covered with blood, and your father stood up and had something like a knife."

"Stop it, Richard. Stop."

"And what was making that noise, Sophia?"

She didn't answer. And then she said, "There was something," in a voice so small it was barely audible.

"What? What was it?"

Tick-tick. Tick-tick.

Her hand spasmed on his arm as the noise repeated. He felt it too, a double jolt of adrenaline. The last door was drawing close to them. He was almost dragging Sophia along. His free hand was rising, reaching for the knob.

"Something in the center of the room," she said quickly.

"That's right. You told me that. What was it?"

"It was a storeroom. There were just old things there."

"What was in the center of the room?"

He reached for the door to Sir Michael's study.

Tick-tick.

"Stop," said Sophia.

She pulled away from him violently. He turned, confused, to see her pressed against the wall. Pressed between a painting and the arras, the dragon to one side of her, a faded arcadia to the other. Her eyes were darting here and there as if looking for a way to escape. And she whispered quickly.

"Let's go back. It was nothing. They were fighting. For the knife. Whatever it was. I want to go." And then she blurted out, "It was a cradle, all right? All right? It was a cradle in the center of the room. I want to go."

He gazed at her blankly. "A cradle."

"An empty cradle, yes. Rocking on a floorboard. Because they were fighting. It kept rocking on the floorboard. Tick-tick."

Tick-tick.

The sound pulled Storm's attention from her. He looked up, down, everywhere for the source of it. And then he looked back at her where she was pressed to the wall, her eyes filling.

"Fighting for the knife?" he said. "You mean *she* had it? Your mother had it? Your father was taking it away from her."

Sophia's mouth went down and her tears spilled over. "She was hurting herself, Richard. There was so much blood. All this blood between her legs, pouring, pouring out between her legs. And she kept stabbing herself there . . ."

"Oh Christ."

"Stabbing and stabbing herself. And the blood kept

pouring, pouring out. And she just went on doing it, pushing the thing into herself. And the cradle kept rocking and it was empty, it was empty, because she kept doing that to herself . . . Oh God, I'm going to be sick again."

"No, you're not. No, you're not, it's all right."

He went to her. Peeled her out of the wallpaper. Wrapped his arm around her. Pressed her face into his shoulder.

"That's over," he whispered, drawing her to the door of her father's study. Reaching out for the knob again. "This is something else. That's over now."

"She hurt herself, Richard. She hurt herself so much."

"I know. But that's over. The past is past. Look."

Tick-tick.

He opened the door.

Sophia screamed.

25 By the light of the desk lamp, they saw Sir Michael stretched face down on the floor in a puddle of blood. There was a cord around his wrist but it trailed free, stained with red, as if he had worked his way out of it. There was a trail of red behind him, as if he had been crawling to the door.

Sophia clutched Storm's arm tightly. He had to yank himself free of her. Then he knelt beside the fallen man, knelt under the empty stares of the mahogany rams' heads carved into the enormous desk. He felt the blood seep warm through the knee of his trousers. He saw Sir Michael's back rise and fall on a shallow breath.

And even as he was kneeling, Sir Michael lifted his head. And Sophia screamed again.

The old man's face was the face of a dead man, the skin gray and thin as parchment. One side of it was smeared with gore. And his eyes bulged at them, round and white.

And his voice rasped faintly, "Get her out. They're in the house."

Tick-tick. Tick-tick.

But Storm was all energy now, beyond thought, his body white-hot with an electric fever. He was on his feet again, looking quickly over the book-lined walls, over the blood-streaked chair, the bloodstained desk blotter. There was the empty box, the silver lighter, the scattered cigars. And he was making sense of things without words, without thinking, connections leaping into his mind at every second. The crypt out by the ruin, the iron door into darkness, the way it led down beyond the end of the house, the way the phantom in the mist had vanished into it . . .

Sophia knelt by her father. She had pulled a cushion from a chair, was working it under his head to lift his face out of the blood.

"Lock the door," said Storm. "Call the cops."

He seized the silver lighter from the desktop.

"Richard?" Sophia said.

"Call an ambulance."

He was out of the room, out in the corridor, the excitement in him like fire.

He moved to the arras, faced the hydra-headed dragon.

Tick-tick.

"Oh yeah," he said.

He felt the rough fabric of the tapestry in his hand. He yanked down. The dragon collapsed before him. The arras collapsed to the floor. A paneled wall was behind it. Storm hit it with the heel of his palm.

There was a click. With a whining screak, the wall swung

towards him on a hidden hinge. The blackness was all beyond it.

Storm nearly laughed aloud. *Incredible!* he thought wildly. *An arras; a secret door; a haunted house! England! What a country!*

"Richard, the phone . . . !" Sophia cried out.

But Storm, unheeding, charged into the dark.

26 Tick-tick. Tick-tick.

The lighter flared, the flame rose high. Black shadows sprung up on every side of him. Black shapes arched and reared and danced under the fluttering light. The little hidden chamber was cluttered with old furniture and junk. Storm turned here and there quickly as the flame made first one object, then another, seem to stir around him. The fabric head of a horse, the glass eyes of a teddy bear stared at him from the corners.

He edged forward over naked floorboards. He could feel them give and sag under his weight. A single bulking thing stood in the center of the room before him. He held the lighter up for a better view, but the metal of it grew hot in his hand, seared his thumb. He saw the ancient wooden cradle for an instant, then shut the lighter's top. The flame went out.

In the pitch blackness, his shin touched the edge of the cradle and set it into motion. And the floor creaked underneath it.

Tick-tick.

And then an answer came from somewhere in the walls: *Tick-tick. Tick-tick.*

Storm was pouring sweat now. The fever of excitement and the hectic vapor in his mind had become a single confusion, a lightning-tortured haze. He hardly knew what he was doing, what he was thinking—but he was shoving the cradle aside with his leg, kneeling unsteadily—almost dropping—to the floor.

He flipped the lighter open, spun the wheel again, set off the flame. He saw that the cradle had stood not on a loose floorboard but on a trap. A square door with an iron ring set into it. *Perfect!* he thought. *I love it.* He seized the ring and pulled the door up to reveal the narrow wooden staircase winding into the blackness below.

Tick-tick. Tick-tick.

Now, at last, as if drawn from the house's timbers, drawn from the air around him, from his own brain, the sound resolved itself upon a single center, a single source. It ascended in its unceasing, funereal tempo from the dark at the base of the stairs.

Tick-tick.

Storm started down to meet it.

"Richard! Richard!"

From somewhere above him, he heard Sophia's voice. It seemed muffled to him, far, far away.

He went down, kept going down. And as he descended, step by slow step, the damp wooden boards groaned thickly beneath his shoes, and the cry above him spiraled into a frantic skirl.

"Richard, be careful! Come back!"

His foot touched the bottom step, came off it onto a hard floor. He felt a clammy draft twine around his legs. The lighter's flame swelled and, in the broadening glow, he saw before him a long stone tunnel with rounded walls. His heart was thudding in his chest now and there was a thickness in his brain again, making him dizzy and ill. He wasn't even sure anymore if this was really happening.

But he moved forward slowly.

Tick-tick. Tick-tick.

Once more, the metal of the lighter burned his thumb. Once more, he covered the flame, put it out. But his feet kept sliding on over the stone floor, moving along the tunnel, deeper, deeper.

He held up the lighter. Cracked it. Spun the wheel. His own shadow dodged and capered in bizarre shapes on the stone walls around him.

And before him, he saw the tunnel widen into an irregular chamber. A crossroad. He had come to a crossroad. The passage went on ahead, another off to the left, another to the right. Storm moved into the broader opening at the center.

There, panting, dazed, he lifted the lighter. The flame-glow spread over the arches, over the vaults, over the entire space. His gaze fell at once on a small white mound of flakes and powder that had collected on the floor at the base of one wall. With another cognitive flash, he knew that the debris had fallen from one of the stones above it.

Looking up, blinking through his sweat, through the haze of his own mind, he could see the place. One of the stones in the wall had been chiseled. The mortar that held it was dug away, the block's edges frayed and chalky.

Before he had time to think, he was moving forward, one hand holding the lighter high, the other stretching towards the stone. His fingers were at the jagged edge of the rock. He gripped it, pulled. The stone shifted easily, wobbled, rolled free of its position. It slipped from his grasp and there was a loud crash as it dropped to the floor at his feet.

Storm hardly knew where he was, hardly knew if he was awake or asleep. He thrust the lighter forward into the opening. He felt as if the walls were shuddering around him, the whole house above him quaking to its foundations.

For there, in the niche revealed by the displacement of the stone—preserved in a clear plastic wrapping so covered with dust that the face underneath seemed transparent, distant, ghostly—there, before him, was the body of an infant.

Rhinehart's exquisite *Nativity*.

Storm stared at it a long moment, the lighter scorching his thumb, his free hand raised to his scorching brow.

And then they grabbed him.

27

"Why, Mr. Storm, I'm so glad you could make it. I left Sir Michael to show you the way. You're just in time to witness my final apotheosis."

The lighter had fallen from his hand, gone out. For a moment, the darkness was complete. But Storm heard that voice, heard those words, those half-familiar, half-remembered words. He felt as if he were sinking, sinking from the surface of the real into a whirlpool of his own imaginings.

And yet he couldn't sink. The grip that pinioned both his arms was so powerful, the form that hulked above him so enormous, that it was as if the walls themselves had come alive to take him prisoner. What felt like the muzzle of a gun was being jammed into his temple. It hurt. And then, a flame pierced his eyes, sent a blinding awl-point of pain straight into the middle of his forehead.

He looked away from the flame, looked up. Saw the face of Frankenstein's monster hanging somewhere above him. Well, why not? He would probably have Dracula and the Wolfman on him next. Maybe that's who was pressing the

pistol—Sir Michael's pistol, it was—into his sideburn. No—
he glanced over—it was a small, round thug with a crushed
nose—the nose courtesy of Bernard, who had driven it into
his face during the fight outside The Sign of the Crane.

Storm's head fell forward towards the bright flame again.
The flame moved aside a little, so he could see more clearly.
He saw a man standing in front of him, holding Sir
Michael's lighter. It was the man he had seen at the auction.
Tall and white-suited, with green gloves on his hands. With
long sable hair framing an easy grin on a savagely angled
face. And eyes—those eyes deepening and darkening in a
way that captured Storm's gaze, that made him feel sicker,
weaker, muzzier still. Murky eyes but blackly revealing:
windows on a hellbound heart.

And Storm thought: Iago.

"Poor Storm," the man said. "That you ever thought to
defeat me."

Storm shook his head weakly. The words were so
familiar. "What?" he said. "What are you . . . ?"

Iago laughed. A good scary laugh. Better than
Nicholson's in *Hellfire*. Why was it the bad guys always
seemed so happy?

"Don't you recognize me?" Iago said. "You should do.
You created me, man. I . . ." he pronounced, his eyes almost
swallowing Storm. "I *am* Jacobus."

Storm nodded weakly. Now he understood. He
remembered. Those words—they were his own words.
From the script of *Spectre*. He grimaced, trying to draw back.
Trying to fight against the seduction of Iago's stare. "Hey,
babe," he said thickly. "Everybody wants to be in pictures."

Iago laughed again. He was moving the lighter now.
Lowering it to a black candle in his other hand. He torched

the wick. Clapped the lighter shut. Studied the candle quietly. "You know," he said. "This is great. Really. The two of us meeting here like this."

Storm tried to blink the sweat out of his eyes so he could look fiercely into that grinning, angular face. He tried to work his arms free from the grip that held them. The monster holding him jerked him back, tightened his hold. The pistol pressed harder against his aching head. He grunted with the pain.

Iago smiled. He was moving away, the candlelight receding into the shadows of the tunnel. He bent gracefully at the knees and lifted something that was leaning against the wall.

The panel. The *Nativity*. Iago kept moving away with it, along the wall of the tunnel across from Storm.

Iago set the panel down. He stood back and held up the candle. Storm, locked in the monster's grip, turned his head to look into the creeping glow.

He saw the Rhinehart triptych, complete at last.

The panels were leaning against the wall, resting on top of several sheets of brown wrapping paper that rose up behind them. *The Magi* was to Storm's left, the *Madonna* to his right. The *Nativity*—the beautiful Christ child—was set in the center. There were no frames to separate the pictures. They joined together into one flowing whole.

Iago passed the flame over the scene, smiling down at it.

"You know, I told my friends here to leave you alone," he murmured. He glanced up at Storm. "I did, truly. Well, I had my own reasons, but I am a fan of yours as well. I had them be as quiet as little mice just so as not to disturb you." He nodded thoughtfully, as if to himself. "Sir Michael gave up the location of the painting in return for his daughter's life," he said. "My gentlemen stabbed him to death with the softest touch imaginable. And off they crept to meet me here on little tippy-toes. You see? All to keep you out of it, Mr. Storm. Because I didn't want to hurt you if I didn't have to. Truly. And yet—and yet, all the while," he went on, in the same tone of reverie. "All the while, I had this suspicion, you know, that this was really our destiny. The moment I heard the sound of the pick on the stone, I thought, 'It'll travel. It'll travel through the walls of the house and he'll have to come to it.' Tick-tick, tick-tick. Isn't that remarkable? Destiny. Our destiny."

He looked down at the triptych again. Lovingly, Storm thought. He passed the candle back and forth over it.

Storm's own gaze was drawn by the shifting light. He looked at the panels too, from *The Magi* to the *Nativity* to the *Madonna*. And slowly—he thought—he could have sworn—slowly—he saw something in the paintings that almost seemed—what?—almost seemed to be coming to life. Changing. Metamorphosing as he watched. It must have been his own perception, but it really did seem that—there, where the triptychs joined—the scenes transformed themselves. No one image, but the very brushstrokes themselves seemed to come together into some sort of rune, some sort of mystic writing, that ran vertically along the lines of the joins.

Storm's lips parted. "Jesus," he whispered. "Jesus, it's really there."

Iago gave a little happy hum of laughter. "Destiny," he said again. "Beautiful."

Slowly, he began to stroll back from the panels, back towards Storm. Storm looked from the triptych to Iago's face. He felt fear rising from his stomach to his throat. Iago came nearer.

"The whole thing really is beautiful," Iago said. "Because,

in effect, you really did create me. Or re-create me, at any rate. Do you see? When I had lost my way, when I had lost my sense of identity, I saw your film and became again who I was meant to be. You made me, as they say, what I am. What you see before you, Mr. Storm, is a product of your own imagination. And that's beautiful. It's ironic, truly. A subtle mingling of the tragic and the burlesque. Because now, you know, you've seen me here and Sir Michael upstairs and all that—you've seen the triptych, what it is. And now, really, I simply have to kill you. So you invent me—and I murder you—which is rather lovely, I think."

Iago, smiling, holding up the candle, stepped up directly before Storm. Storm stared at him, thinking of Sophia. Wondering whether the bastard would hurt her too, or leave her be. Had she phoned the police? Were they coming? Had she left the house? He didn't even dare to plead for her, lest he remind the lunatic of her presence above.

Iago now shifted the candle into his left hand. The flame played over the stone walls, the outglow touched the paintings leaning on their paper against the wall.

With his free hand, Iago reached into his belt and withdrew a wicked-looking dagger. A curved blade, a bejeweled and golden handle.

"It's not exactly the Sword of the Serizzim," he said with a grin. "But it's all I could comfortably carry. And it'll do."

The candle flame shone on the blade and Storm could not take his eyes off it. The monster jerked him back again, lifted him off the ground. The pudgy thug with the gun grabbed his hair and yanked his head back.

Storm gasped, his mouth open. Iago, gripping the knife for a downward thrust, slowly lowered it until the point was hovering a centimeter from Storm's right eye. The burning blade filled Storm's vision. His throat felt as if it were filled with dust.

"Thanks for bringing a little touch of movie magic into my humdrum life, Mr. Storm," Iago said. "But what you've seen tonight is only for those who have eyes to see with."

And with a swift, vicious movement, he raised the knife up over his head, and plunged it down into Richard Storm's eyeball.

Or so he would have done—but the blade struck steel instead.

Harper Albright, rushing down the tunnel towards them, had drawn her sword. She brought it upward even as she ran, upward in a whistling backhanded slice. With a single echoless ring of collision, it caught the smaller blade in the center of its curve. The knife was flung from Iago's hand. It flew upward, spinning, sparking as the candle's gleam swung crazily over it, over the walls, over the startled faces.

And all Storm could think was, *Thank God I wrote a hero into this picture.*

And then there was no more time to think at all. He felt the giant being ripped away from him. He fell forward and saw the muzzle of the .38 drop across his eyeline as the pudgy thug swung around to take aim at Harper. Storm lunged back at the gun, grabbed the thug's wrist with both hands, wrenched his arm upward. There was a spurt of flame, a crash of thunder, the high whine of a ricochet as the weapon discharged.

Now there were curses and crashes and deep shouts all around him. Storm threw the whole weight of his big body against the pudgy thug, forced him against the wall of the tunnel as he kept the gun hand pinned high in the air. The thug tried to get his free fist up but couldn't, tried to knee Storm in the groin but had no room. Storm tried to pull the gun out of the thug's grasp. The violent lurch pulled them both off balance. They toppled down together to the floor, rolling over and over each other.

The shouts around him continued. Storm felt a blow to his ribs, but held fast to the thug's wrist, wrestling the gun muzzle high. He saw the pistol against a rising glow, then against a sudden sheet of light. He felt a searing wind blow over his face. For a second, he was blinded.

Fire! he thought.

The thug hit him again, then clawed at his face. Storm gasped as the flames rose over him, as the thug tried to shove his head down into them. The heat on his face grew. The smoke choked him. The flames seemed to lap at his cheeks.

Then Bernard was standing above them. He stooped beside them where they fought. He reached out silently with his long, delicate fingers and pinched the pudgy thug at the base of the neck.

The thug collapsed, unconscious, under Storm and Storm nearly fell off him into the crackling blaze.

Coughing, drawing his face away from the smoke, Storm held on to the thug's hand until he had pried the gun out of it.

Then he leapt up, away from the flames. Tumbled to the opposite wall and fell against it. He leaned there, with his hands on his knees, gasping for air.

He looked up at the young factotum, whose shaven head flickered orange with reflected firelight.

"Bernie. Babe. Nice move," he said, panting.

He straightened, turned. The flames were falling now, but he could still see clearly by their low light. He saw Frankenstein's monster face down on the tunnel floor. Two men were wrestling his great arms behind his back, were locking his thick wrists together with cuffs. Blood was burbling thickly out of a bullet hole in the giant's thigh.

Storm turned again, turned away. He turned to look down at the dying flames.

He saw at once what it was. He saw how Iago's candle had fallen, how the paper under the Rhinehart triptych had caught. The old wood of the panels had burned like tinder. It was burning still.

Storm moved heavily to stand over the triptych. He looked down into the face of Christ as the heat of the fire made the flesh of it split and curdle. The edges of the panels—the runes that he had seen there—were all in flames now, and settling into char.

Destiny, thought Richard Storm. *Yeah.*

The triptych settled with a cracking noise into the last of the blaze.

"Where's Harper?" Bernard said behind him.

Storm looked around blankly. He wiped the sweat from his face. "What?"

"Which tunnel did they go down?" Bernard had a flashlight now. He shone it quickly down one passage, then another, then another. "God damn it!" he shouted. He turned on the others—on Storm and the two men who were now standing away from the monster. The three of them looked back at Bernard blankly. And he cried out to them again:

"God damn it. Which tunnel did they go down?"

28 Harper hunted him through the blackness. Her stick rapped heavily against the stone in front of her. Her grim old face was set and savage. Her wheezing breath was rapid and harsh. Her footsteps pounded on the

stone. Her heartbeat pounded in her ears. She could make out nothing ahead of her, nothing, and yet, beneath the brim of her Borsalino, behind the narrow lenses of her specs, her eyes were, as ever, quick and alive. She stalked through what she could not see into what she did not know. Which was her nature, after all.

Ahead of her, the tunnel curved gently. She felt the rising arc of the floor in the tip of her stick. She charged along the turning path, her quick steps sure, the steady rhythm of them rising into the rhythm of her pulse, her breath. The dizzying blackness rushed past her as she rushed on.

The air in the place was stony, cool and dry. It had no smell. It was the atmosphere of a cave. But now, as she pounded along, she sensed a change. In hints and wisps at first, a fresher breeze came down to her. A breeze more vivid with the moisture of mist, a trace of earth and winter in it. Her jaw tightened, her teeth gnashed together. She upped her pace, hobbling ferociously, the tempo of her stick on the stone increasing.

The air grew richer, damper, more alive. She felt the floor rising beneath her. She knew she was coming to the end of the trail.

But she was barreling along so swiftly by then that she almost walked into the dead end when she reached it. Her stick hit the wall in front of her. She pulled up short, her nose just inches from the flat stone.

Breathing hard, she turned. She edged backwards down the tunnel, one step, two, then three. There it was. A recess to one side. And it was faintly visible. The tremulous, intermittent silver light of the moon filtered down into it over the dim shape of a stairway.

Harper moved towards that light. Reaching out, she found

the banister, cold iron, crumbling with rust. The stairway was so steep it was nearly a ladder. She grimaced as she hoisted first one foot onto it, then another. Above her, she saw a broken outline of a hole, the fog beyond shot through with light.

And with the banister's rust flaking off under her palm, she drew herself up by the banister, up the stairs.

She was panting as she reached the top, as she extended her hand to the broken iron door. Already, she saw, it was ajar, the mist teasing at the edge, the fresh air washing into her through the gap. She had her stick and the railing in one hand; she pushed against the door with the other. The door complained and ground against the earth. But it swung steadily open.

Harper Albright climbed up the last steps, ducked her head beneath the stone architrave and rose out of the little crypt to emerge into the abbey's churchyard.

A plain of mist and moonglow. A field of graves. A dead elm hanging down as if in mourning. And the triangle of the shattered wall soaring black through the haze into the swirling sky.

Still breathless, Harper moved slowly away from the crypt. Scanning the ruined headstones, the changing shadows, peering eagerly through the mist, which gathered and thickened and dispersed again with each fresh rising of the wind. The lights of the Grange seemed far away behind her. The lights of a town shone distant in the hills. Here, the tendrils and sheets of fog closed and curled around her with their own strange glow and their own strange darkness. Harper moved through them cautiously, edged cautiously around the slanting stones. Scanning the churchyard, peering through the fog.

She flinched as the moisture gathered on her glasses.

Made a sound of exasperation. Looked through. There was no sign of him. Which frightened her. Because she could feel him there, watching her, watching her as she moved uncertainly among the graves.

And yet, except for the wind and the chatter of dead leaves against the stones, the place was still. So still, as she stepped closer and closer to the louring wall. So still she almost convinced herself that her sense of Iago's presence was imaginary. That he was there only within her mind, lodged there as he had been for ages, impossible to discover wholly, impossible to dispel.

A broken stele on the ground. She stepped over it. The moon went in behind a cloud, and the mist grew heavy and gray. The shadow of the chapel wall upon the earth faded into other shadows, which rushed and clustered to it like living things.

Harper moved closer to the wall, and closer. The wind whispered round her. She bent forward slightly, peering round the edge. There, too, the field seemed still and empty.

She straightened. She turned around. The wind rose with a hollow sigh. The clouds blew on.

The moonlight stabbed down into the earth and there stood Iago.

Harper let out a cry of surprise. He was standing a foot from her, towering over her. The smoky depths of his eyes had captured the silver light and gleamed with it, swirled with it. His grin showed gray in the swirling darkness.

She only had time to clutch the dragon's head tighter, to lift the end of the stick from the ground.

Then he pulled one green-gloved hand up across himself as if to slap her down. She jerked her head back instinctively, waiting for the blow.

But he held his hand there, there it hung. And slowly,

grinning, with the flourish of a conjurer, he lifted his other hand to it. He tugged at the fingers of his glove. Quickly, gracefully, he slipped the glove off.

Even as the clouds closed upon the moon again, Harper had light enough to see his naked hand. To see the thin, pulsing line of gangrenous decay that ran down from the base of his knuckles to his wrist.

She stared at it, fascinated. She was startled to hear his voice.

"Oh, Harper," he said sadly, grinning at her all the while. "Oh, Harper."

And the wind rose again, hard this time, moaning. The moon went out. The mist condensed between them. Harper saw Iago's figure obscured, almost spectral, as the fog gathered, as the wind blew and blew. In another moment, the thickening night, the thickening mist, cut her off from him completely. She could not see him, could not tell where he was. She raised her stick uncertainly in a feeble gesture of self-defense.

The wind blew on, and the mist blew on, and the moonlight shone down on her once more.

And Iago was gone.

EPILOGUE

Ah, love, let us be true
To one another! for the world, which seems
To lie before us like a land of dreams,
So various, so beautiful, so new,
Hath really neither joy, nor love, nor light,
Nor certitude, nor peace, nor help for pain;
And we are here as on a darkling plain
Swept with confused alarms of struggle
    and flight,
Where ignorant armies clash by night.

MATTHEW ARNOLD

Bernard leaned wearily against the corner of Belham Grange. He watched through hooded eyes as the stretcher-men carried Sir Michael's body out the front door and to the waiting ambulance. It was all red light before the house: police cars parked at odd angles, their red flashers whipping the thin mist. Constables and detectives moved about busily, their faces expressionless whenever the red beams crossed them.

A little way off the drive, on the grass, in the deeper darkness, Bernard could make out Storm and Sophia. They were standing together, his arm around her shoulder, and they watched the covered stretcher pass as well.

And Bernard watched it. Until it was slid into the back of the ambulance with a heavy metal bang. Until the stretcher-men climbed in after it. Until the doors were clapped shut, and locked.

The tires of the ambulance rattled on the drive's pebbles. The vehicle turned and headed away from the house, under the canopy of the double row of trees. Storm and Sophia turned too, Bernard saw. Turned and walked away, into the misty field, their heads held down.

Bernard heaved a sigh and shifted uncomfortably in the cool night air. He wondered bitterly if, by careful examination, he might discover some small part of his body that didn't hurt or throb or ache. He doubted it. He felt he could use a stretcher himself. And an ambulance. Maybe even a body bag. A body bag stuffed with a lot of recreational narcotics. It seemed to him just then a good place to spend the rest of one's semi-natural life.

He maneuvered his limbs to work the stiffness out of them, then leaned against the corner of the house again. Storm and Sophia were now walking away from him, over the field, towards the ruins of Belham Abbey. The gibbous moon hung bright out there above the wedge of wall. With only the last faint clouds wafting over it, it looked like a woman drawing a veil across her face.

Storm and Sophia stopped at the edge of the graveyard, and Bernard saw them close with each other. Saw Storm put his arms around the young woman, and she lean her head against his chest. He breathed the night in deeply and caught the sweet aroma of pipe smoke in the mist. The gruff voice sounded just behind him.

"Ah. Ha-ha."

Harper moved up to stand next to him. She had her pipe clamped in her teeth and was holding the skull-shaped bowl gingerly. She was following Bernard's gaze, looking off across the field at where the lovers in the graveyard embraced.

"Don't," Bernard said to her. "I mean it, Harper. Don't be pleased with yourself. I really think that would be one thing more than I could bear."

Harper tilted her head to one side, plucked the pipe from her mouth. Peered through her glasses at Storm and Sophia. "Well . . ." she said.

"Well, what?" Bernard crossed his arms on his chest and looked down at her, his shoulder still pressed to the wall. "Well, what? Is this your idea of a happy ending? Her father's dead, her lover's dying. They don't understand the half of what's happened here tonight. They probably never will. All they've got is this . . . this little space to hold on to each other in, all surrounded by a sea of confusion and grief. I mean, what the hell do you call that?"

"Life, Bernard," said Harper Albright quietly, watching Storm and Sophia still. She drew on her pipe again for a moment. The smoke filtered out of her mouth as she spoke. "I call it life."

"Life," Bernard mimicked her. "That's the best you can come up with when Iago's got dead away?"

Harper nodded thoughtfully for a long moment. "He works his work," she said again. "I mine."

After that, the two of them stood there for a while without speaking. Watching, as in the last of the mist, in the best of the moonlight, in the shadow of the abbey ruin, Storm lifted Sophia's face and kissed her gently.

Then Harper smiled. "In any case," she said. "Not dead away. He hasn't got dead away. Not quite. We have some of his men, who won't all be loyal to him. We have some allies on the police at last. The triptych has been destroyed and, if I'm not mistaken, there is a certain urgency to the business which will draw our quarry out into the open again before too long."

Bernard raised his eyes to heaven, shook his head.

Harper laughed. "Ha-ha." She reached up and clapped the young man on the shoulder. "Heart on a hill, lad," she told him. "The hunt is just beginning."

With which, she moved away. Walked away to the drive, to the deep shadows beneath the hanging beeches. She tapped her stick against the ground lightly as she walked. The smoke from her pipe trailed back over her shoulder.

After a moment, Bernard followed her.

✦

From the misty churchyard, Richard Storm looked up and saw them go.

He clasped Sophia against him, felt the warmth of her body there, drank the warmth of her body in with his. The wind lifted, and Sophia's hair stirred, and a trailing patch of mist rolled over the graves around him, rolled on before him. And through the gathering haze of it, Storm watched Harper's squat silhouette, moving away from him towards the trees. He watched the wedge of her cape and the outline of her hat and the swing of her stick on the earth. He watched Bernard's tall, willowy silhouette loping along beside her.

He held Sophia tightly, and watched his two friends moving away from him, moving and moving away until the mist closed over them, like a curtain.

Hunting Down Amanda

This Book is For Faith

I would like to thank my research assistant, Astrid Oviedo de Miano, for her work on this book; Donald Harrison for taking time to talk to me about his music and his life; Dr. Scott R. Anagnoste for medical information; my agent, Barney Karpfinger, for his tireless support; and, as always, my wife Ellen, who contributes more than I can say.

Prologue

In Between the Devil and the Deep Blue Sea

1

This story begins on a summer's day in hell.

    The day was July 13th, to be exact. And hell was a little town called Hunnicut, Massachusetts.

Before it turned into hell, it was actually kind of a nice little place. A fishing town. Hills of beryl forests above sunlit bays. Trim shingled houses on tree-lined lanes. A restored Main Street with quaint tourist shops and a couple of decent seafood restaurants overlooking the water.

That Friday, the weather was fine, warm but breezy. There were clouds sailing by overhead but they were cumulus clouds, not much ascended, high and fluffy and white, with great cerulean gaps between. The sun, still well aloft, shone bright and clear.

Visitors and locals alike were out strolling by the shops, pausing here and there to look in the windows. Decorative fishing nets were on display. Painted oars and scrimshaw paperweights. T-shirts that said 'I'd Rather Be Fishing', or

'A Fisherman Is Always Ready To Whip Out His Rod', or 'I Fell For Hunnicut Hook, Line and Sinker!' and other sentiments like that.

Atop the brick town hall, the Stars-and-Stripes were snapping smartly. Down in the picturesque harbor, trawlers bobbed on the curlicue waves. Sunlight glittered on the wind-dappled surface of the ocean.

It was 4:15 p.m., and life in Hunnicut was pretty much all right.

That situation remained in place for about two more minutes.

Then, at 4:17 p.m., there came a rumble, like thunder. There was no more warning than that.

People out of doors glanced up in mild surprise. Fishermen working their boats tilted back their heads and squinted into the sky. Everyone – a man in a canvas chair on the beach; the shopping housewives over on Main; a state trooper walking from his cruiser to the Donut Hole; the children in a playground off Hancock Street; a roofer on a housetop in the middle of a hammer blow – they all looked up at the thunder sound. It hadn't seemed to anyone as if it were going to rain.

After that, there came a half-second of stillness.

And this is what happened next:

A white-hot light spilled wide across the face of heaven – as if the sky had been obliterated by a blinding stain. An orange starburst flashed out of that white core. And with it came a roar – an agonized, hoarse – a deafening roar that made a nerve-end out of your skull, that made the earth beneath you tremble.

'It sounded,' said Leonard Wallingford, a banker up from Boston to visit his father, 'it sounded as if God had gotten caught in a bear trap.'

In the next moment, it began to rain fire. From the ether, from nowhere, lancets of liquid flame spat sizzling onto the

4

pavements, into the trees. The people had only one more instant to stare with gaping mouths in disbelief.

And then it became unthinkable. Because the wing section hit, and it was still nearly full of fuel.

It smacked into a cornfield just east of Michaels Street. In the same split second, the earth ripped open in a seventy-foot crater and a fireball ripped out of it and up into the open air. Michaels ran through a family neighborhood of two-story clapboards. Three houses simply collapsed where they stood. Two more exploded. Their lumber splintered, the splinters flew. Pots and pans, an iron, the contents of a tool box – they all shot off like red missiles. The body of Sharon Cosgrove, a realtor, lifted high, high into the air and then flumped down like a doll into the burning debris where her children, Patricia and Sam, had been blown to unrecoverable bits.

The lights went out everywhere. The water stopped running. Other houses, other neighborhoods caught fire. There were fires all over town. There were people all over town who had suddenly turned into fractured things, twisted, staring, stained things lying amidst piles of broken bricks and smoldering char. Other people were screaming, running, wandering dazed over lawns and down the middle of streets, past the black skeletons of automobiles and the crackling, dancing flames shooting out of windows. Black smoke – violent, rolling billows of black smoke – stormed over all of it, over the people and the flaming trees and the flaming houses, and out over the harbor, and up into the sky above the sea.

Out of the sky, and down through the smoke, poured the rain of the wreckage. Plates of silver metal fell. A jet engine dropped whole onto Hank's Fish 'N' Tackle and demolished it. A nose cone dove into Cutter's Cove like an enormous gutted bass. Coins sprinkled down onto the grass, and golden jewelry too. A retiree, Walter Bosch, was killed in his garden by a full-sized bourbon bottle which split his skull in half and then fell to lie completely unbroken in the impatiens bed beside his corpse.

And bodies fell and parts of bodies. Flesh rained down on Hunnicut – out of the sky, into the fire – along with the liquid fire still raining down through the black smoke. There was less gore than you might have thought. Much of the humanity in the air had simply vanished. Still . . . An arm and a leg smacked wetly among the people screaming in the middle of Hancock Lane. Emma Timmerman – her entire body still intact, still belted into her seat – landed in the yard behind Hunnicut Autobody and sat propped amidst the junk there as if someone had thrown her away. A torso torn like old laundry – what was left of Bob Bowen, a high school instructor – fluttered down to dangle from the branch of a tree. The head of Jeff Aitken, a student, crashed through Sharon Kent's kitchen window. Mrs Kent was struck dumb at the sight of the thing in her sink, its mouth open, its scalp in flames.

Over time, over the longest time it seemed, everything that was left came streaming down. Into the smoldering houses and the steaming water, into the forest which was snickering now as it blazed. Around the bodies of the town's dead and the moaning wounded. Among the people screaming, crying. The fuselage and the workings and the furniture came down, and the supplies and the passengers – all the remains of European Airways flight 186.

It had been a 747 on its way to London and it had just disintegrated at 32,000 feet.

No one ever discovered why.

2

Amanda Dodson, who was five years old, was playing in her babysitter's backyard at the time. Amanda was a roundish little mixed-race girl with a quiet, thoughtful manner. Tan skin, an oval face. Big, intelligent brown eyes. Long, curly, startlingly yellow hair.

She was sitting on the bottom step of the back deck, her pudgy legs and arms poking from her light blue shorts and T-shirt. She was operating a make-believe hospital on the border of the lawn. Amanda knew about hospitals and sickness and even death because she knew about how her father had died. Right now, though, it was her furry red Elmo doll who was the patient under consideration. And his condition seemed very grave. But fortunately, Nurse Barbie was in attendance, ably assisted by a rag doll named Mathilda. And before poor Elmo could fade away completely, Doctor Amanda spread her hands over him and magically 'sparkled' him back to health.

Well, a great celebration ensued; a tea party of thanks-giving. Some rocks and a milk crate and a wagon served for a table and chairs and revelers human, plastic and stuffed passed round the plastic cups and dishes that had been generously contributed by Mrs Shipman.

She was the babysitter – Mrs Shipman – a squat, cheerful widow of sixty-one. She was inside just then, in the den with the television. Knitting a pink sweater for a baby granddaughter and watching Larry Norton interview people who engage in computer sex on the internet. She was keeping an eye on Amanda through the picture window to her left.

A mantelpiece clock chimed the quarter hour: 4:15. With a start, Mrs Shipman realized she had lost track of time. She usually called Amanda in at four for a snack and an hour of cartoons. She draped her knitting over the arm of her chair and started to stand up.

That was when the first explosion went off on Michaels Street, about a quarter-mile away. The force of the blast threw Mrs Shipman out of her seat, head first into the TV. The screen shattered. The jagged glass ripped Mrs Shipman's face off as if it were a rubber glove. She was still alive for a second, but then the house caved in on top of her and she was crushed to death.

The explosion shook the earth and air. Little Amanda stood. She was holding her furry red Elmo doll by its hand. She didn't understand what had happened. When the house fell down, she could only stare at it blankly.

Someone was screaming: Mrs Jenson, the nice lady from next door who sometimes came by with cookies. Her dress was on fire and she was running across her backyard, shriek-ing and shrieking. She ran blindly into the washing hung on the line. She became tangled in a beach towel and fell to the ground, rolling and shrieking and burning.

Amanda stood and stared.

Mrs Jenson's house was also on fire, she saw. So were

some of the other houses on the block. And other people were running and they were shrieking too. There was Frank Hauer – a big boy, Amanda thought, ten years old. He was lying face down at the base of his basketball net. He was lying in a lake of red, red blood.

Amanda's face puckered. She began to cry. She clutched Elmo's hand tightly.

The old maple tree in Mrs Jenson's yard burst into flame. Mrs Shipman's pachysandra bed exploded as a big hunk of metal sliced down into it out of the sky. Wet earth and leaves splattered over Amanda where she stood, helpless, crying. The big piece of metal, sticking out of the ground, loomed up and up above her.

Dazed, Amanda began walking. She wanted her mother.

The very next thing she knew she was walking across Hauptman's Memorial Ballfield. She was walking stiffly on her pudgy legs, trudging over the grass between first base and the pitcher's mound. She was hugging Elmo close to her and sucking her thumb. She was sniffling tearfully. She didn't remember exactly how she had come to be there.

The ballfield bordered Mrs Shipman's backyard to the west. There was a long stand of trees on the far side of the field. Amanda always pictured the tavern where her mother worked as being somewhere beyond those trees. The trees were the furthest thing she could see from the babysitter's yard or from the big den window when she was watching TV. It made sense to her that her mother was away somewhere beyond them.

In fact, the bar where her mother worked was in a completely different direction. It was off to the southeast, down by the water. The trees up ahead merely screened an old fire road – now a bike trail – and the houses and swampland on its other side.

But Amanda thought her mother was there. And so she walked on, trudging across the outfield toward the trees.

Some of the trees were on fire and some of the duff around their roots was smoldering. Smoke was pouring from the little wood. And someone inside the wood was screaming.

All the same, Amanda walked on.

She reached the rail fence that bordered the ballfield. She ducked through, clutching Elmo tightly. The smoke made her wrinkle her nose now. She coughed, her cheeks puffing up around her thumb.

The trees rose above her. They were on every side of her, big maple trees, big oaks and pines. Their branches hung down toward her from on high. The sun streamed down through the leaves. Great solid columns of sunlight stood all around her, turning hazy as the smoke drifted into them.

Amanda walked on under the trees, beside the hazy columns. The smoke was making her cough more and more. The screaming was growing louder. A woman screaming in short bursts, over and over, like a car alarm. Somewhere, flames were crackling. Amanda's pink sneakers were crunching on the forest floor. She was looking down at her sneakers. She was watching them move along.

Then she stopped.

There was something on the path before her. A large shape, dark in the drifting smoke; dark and very still. Scared, Amanda stood where she was, dwarfed by the oaks and pines, by columns of sunlight hazy with smoke. She rubbed her cheek against Elmo's red fur. She nibbled on the tip of her thumb. She looked warily at the shape in the path.

Then she realized what it was. And slowly, she started toward it.

3

Just before that, before the crash, Amanda's mother, Carol Dodson, had been tending bar at the Anchor and Bell. It was a harbor bar. Fishermen drank there mostly. Carol had been working the place almost three months, ever since she'd drifted into town.

The customers liked Carol. She was pretty, for one thing. Young, twenty-three, twenty-four. And she was tough and funny and foul-mouthed like they were. Sometimes, too, after she finished work, she would go upstairs with one of them and have sex with him for money. Not that she was a hooker or anything. It was just that if you were a guy and you were about to go to sea for two or three months and you were single or your girlfriend was mad at you or something and you really, really needed to get lucky in a very serious way fast and you were drinking, say, with a friend at the Anchor and Bell and bitching about this state of affairs, well, then, your friend might turn to you and say, 'Listen. You got any money?'

And you would say, 'Yeah, sure, some.' And your friend would say, 'You could try the new girl – Carol.' And you'd say, 'Carol? The bartender? She's turning tricks now?' And your friend would say, 'No, no, hell, she's a nice girl. But, you know, she's struggling, she's got a kid. Just don't be a ginch, all right?' So, of course, you don't want anyone to think you're a ginch, plus maybe you're not particularly thrilled about the idea of using a hooker either. So up you'd go to the bar and you'd start talking to Carol, just in a natural way. And just in a natural way you'd say some nice things to her like you would to any girl you wanted to sleep with. And then, later, when you were upstairs and everything was finished and you were about to leave, you might say something like, 'Hey, Carol, how's it happening for you this week?' And she might say, 'Aw, you know, it's always an uphill thing with the kid and all.' And you would say, 'Well, hey, listen, I'm flush, you know. Let me help you out a little bit here. No, really.' And then you might argue back and forth a little. And finally you'd give her something.

That was how it generally worked.

Now today, this July day when the plane came down, there was a good crowd of guys in the place. Most of them were planning to ship out tomorrow or Monday. Some were sitting together at the big tables, and some were at the smaller ones with their wives or girlfriends. Still others were up at the bar, watching the Sox game playing silently on the TV above the mirror.

And then there was one guy, Joe Speakes, who was at the bar but who wasn't watching the Sox game. He was talking to Carol. She was washing glasses at the sink behind the bar and he was chatting to her over his beer.

'What's this I been hearing?' he was saying to her. 'Jes Gramble says you're thinking of running out on us.'

'Ah, you know.' Carol shrugged, gave a half-smile. 'You stay anywhere too long, you start collecting dust.'

'Nah,' said Joe. 'You just got here. What're you running from – the FBI or something?'

'That's me,' she said. 'I'm the Fugitive.'

'Forget it. Stick around. The fun is just beginning.'

'What. You gonna miss me, Joe?' said Carol Dodson.

'Hell, yes,' said Joe. 'There's nothing else worth looking at around here.'

Carol laughed and stepped back from the sink. She threw her hip out and made a comical palms-up gesture: *ta-daaa*.

Joe nodded his appreciation. His eyes moved up and down her.

Carol kept herself in good shape and she was proud of her figure. She had her maroon T-shirt tucked into her jeans so that it pressed close and showed off her round breasts, her narrow waist and flat belly. Her jeans were tight on the curve of her butt and the cloth was wedged up between her legs in a manner that could move a man in many deep and significant ways.

Her hair was shoulder-length, blond, curly she called it, but frizzy really down at the ends. Her face was oval like her daughter's, only white, and she had the same big, soft, intelligent eyes, only blue. She had a small sharp nose, and long, pretty lips which she glossed almost silver. She was short and slender and looked like she would fit neatly into a man's arms.

So that's how it was. Carol stepped back and made that comical gesture. And Joe Speakes looked up and down her.

And then came that hellacious roar, that God-in-a-bear-trap roar that shook the sky. And Michaels Street exploded. And the whole bar shuddered. The booze bottles danced and rattled against the mirror.

'What the Christ?' said Joe Speakes.

'Oh shit,' said Carol. She knew at once that this was trouble, no joke. Whatever the opposite of a joke was, that was this.

13

Joe had slipped off his stool. He was striding to the door. The other guys were right with him. A wall of thick backs was already crowding the entryway. The girls were bringing up the rear, crowding into the guys. Carol snatched up a dish towel and went after the rest of them, drying her hands.

Then they were out on Briar Street. Everyone was pouring out onto Briar Street from the bars and shops. All the drinkers, all the fishermen, all the waitresses and clerks were hurrying to the corner. And everyone at the corner was just standing there, just staring up Martin Street, to the west.

They were four miles away from the field where the wing exploded. But they could see it even from here: the fire on the horizon, the fire in the rooftops, the fire falling out of the sky.

Carol saw it as she reached the corner. Standing there in the jostling, staring crowd. Still mechanically rubbing her dry hands on the wet towel.

'Oh my God,' she said.

They were all saying that. 'Oh my God!' 'Holy shit!' 'Jesus Christ.'

'Fuck me,' someone murmured dully. 'It's raining fire.'

There were other explosions then. They saw a house just come apart, just fly apart into splinters. They could hear screaming, a chorus of sobbing cries coming from all over at once. People were running everywhere like mice in a maze. Police sirens were going off and fire sirens and car alarms.

Then something wet and heavy dropped onto the sidewalk not three blocks up, splattering liquid as it hit. And a glittering sprinkle of something fell. And then one of the houses on Martin just spat its windows out in sparkling bits.

Some of the men were charging up there. Some of the women were screaming, covering their mouths with their hands.

Carol whispered, 'Amanda.'

And she started running for her car.

14

4

Then she was driving, driving as fast as she could to Mrs Shipman's house. Her car, her old puttering Rabbit, was hacking and roaring like an old hound. Its axle was shimmying whenever it crested forty. Its tires were squealing around every corner. And Carol was wrestling the wheel, battling the wheel and the road ferociously.

She had to get to Amanda.

She had to get to Amanda and she had to get through this – this hell that was rushing at her windshield, rushing at her eyes. The streets on fire. The houses burning, house after house. Bodies smoking on the lawns. The trees burning. The outlines of cars through leaping flames. The fire in the sky. The people walking like zombies. The people shrieking. People she had seen in town, faces she knew, bleeding, crushed.

She wrestled the car past all of it, all of them. There was something hard and implacable in her heart. She pushed the pedal down further to beat the Rabbit's shimmy. She was crying as she drove, but she didn't know it, she didn't care. Her jaw was clenched tight. Her eyes were fixed ahead. She had to get to Amanda.

A woman in her underwear ran out in front of the fender. She was clutching her head and her mouth was wide open. Carol cursed her and swerved the car. Her heart was hard and she cursed the woman and swerved around her. And when a gout of sizzling fire hit her windshield, she let out a high-pitched growl and switched on the wipers.

'Get off!' she shouted at it, crying.

She passed a playground. Children lay bleeding on the ground. Toddlers sat wailing up at the heavens.

Carol opened her mouth so she could cry harder, and she stepped harder on the gas, screeching away from them, around the next curve. Implacable.

She had to find Amanda.

Then she was slowing down. There was Mrs Shipman's house just ahead of her. For one second, Carol could not believe what she was seeing.

The house was a jagged punched-in thing, lumber sticking out of it, a haze of dust around it. Carol's stomach convulsed with crying. She was sick with suspense and fear.

She was out of the car. She was running around the house. She was thinking about snacktime. This *is* snacktime, she was thinking. Amanda played out in the yard until four and then she came inside to watch the afternoon cartoons. That was now, wasn't it? Wasn't it snacktime now?

Dear merciful Christ in heaven, she thought as she ran into the backyard, dear God who died suffering on the cross, please don't let it be snacktime. Don't let it be snacktime yet.

She was around the house. She saw the deck lying alop, its columns cracking. She saw the shining chunk of fuselage rising out of a hole where the pachysandra had been.

16

She looked down, convulsed with crying, unaware she was crying. She saw the circle of cups and plates on the ground. Mathilda the rag doll was still sitting up at her place, propped against a milk crate, her head bowed as if in mourning.

Come inside now and have your snack, Amanda.

Carol could see that that was how it had happened. Her mind was crystal clear. She could imagine it all. She was focused, alert, and felt completely aware of the explosion of grief that was beginning inside her. It was as if she were a scientific observer at a nuclear blast. She knew that in another moment the spreading cloud of grief would fill her, would overwhelm her. She would have to rip her ribcage open to let it out or just be blown apart. It would be more than life could bear.

Her mouth open, her face covered with snot and tears, she lifted her head and emitted a quiet, trembling 'Oh', the sound of her devastation.

And she saw a patch of bright red on Hauptman's field. Elmo.

Carol saw Elmo's leg trailing out from under Amanda's arm. In her light blue shirt and shorts, Amanda was hard to make out against the green grass, against the green trees. But Carol spotted Elmo's leg and then she could see her daughter.

It was like no baptism ever was. No sin ever so black was ever washed away as that black cloud of mushrooming grief was washed away from inside her.

She saw that her daughter was moving toward the woods. She saw the smoke spilling out of the trees at her. And then she was running again.

She was running across the ballfield. She was screaming her daughter's name. 'Amanda! Amanda!' She was choking on the screams, too breathless to sob.

The child was out of earshot anyway. She had already ducked under the fence, was already at the treeline. Carol

17

forced herself to scream her name once more. Ran on with her arms flailing, her hair flying, her flying tears.

Then Amanda began to fade from before her. She was moving into the woods. She was fading into the smoke. The smoke was growing thicker, blacker around her. It was billowing out of the trees. It was spreading, hanging in the air. It screened the child from the mother's view. The child was vanishing into it.

By the time Carol crossed the rest of the field, Amanda was out of sight. Carol ducked through the center gap of the fence. Her foot snagged on the rail. She stumbled to one knee, leapt up, kept running.

She was in the trees now, in the smoke. One arm thrown over her mouth. Coughing into her sleeve. Staring through her tears, through the smoking columns of sunlight.

She lowered her arm. 'Amanda!' she shouted hoarsely. Then she started coughing, threw up her arm again. She stumbled through the smoke.

She was lost, wandering, coughing, screaming, she didn't know how long. Then a faint breeze reached her, and the smoke thinned. Carol stopped and peered into it, scanned the scene.

'Amanda!' she said hoarsely.

And some enormous creature lumbered into the haze before her.

It seemed to rise up and up, hulking, dark. Carol reared back. What was it? A bear?

It lumbered toward her stiffly. Carol clenched her fist, ready to slug it.

But it wasn't a bear. It was a man.

He came toward her through the smoke. He stepped out of the smoke and Carol could see him clearly. It was a man – and he was carrying her daughter.

Amanda lay limp in the cradle of the man's arms. Her lips were parted, her eyes closed. Her cheeks were the color of gray marble. And a thin line of blood was trickling from the corner of her mouth.

But she was alive. She was still holding Elmo. She was clasping the doll against her. Elmo was rising and falling with her breath – Carol could see it. Her daughter was still alive.

She looked up at the man and the smoke blew over them both, raced past. A clearer space was made for a moment. The man's face was black with soot, but his single eye shone white out of it. Tears were washing his cheek, showing the pink, unblemished flesh underneath.

He staggered closer. Carefully, he transferred the child from his arms to Carol's. She held Amanda close, the familiar weight of her. She pressed her cheek to Amanda's forehead and felt the fever heat. She understood everything. She was laughing and crying at once. And what she said next seemed to make no sense at all.

She said, 'Oh God. Oh God. Now they'll come after her.'

5

The media usually referred to it as the Hunnicut Disaster. Sometimes they got fancy, called it the American Lockerbie. Either way, it was a hell of a big story that summer.

The reporters covered the event like scum covers still water. They covered the victims, the survivors, the witnesses. They covered the experts, the officials, the shrinks. They covered every tear that ran down every relative's face. And then they covered each other covering it, which seemed to be the angle they liked best of all.

There were some good stories. True stories, important stories. But as the days and weeks wore on, as the cops and officials and tin-kickers searched the wreckage, gathered the evidence, reconstructed the events, there was also a lot of half-baked malarkey that the press concocted to fill up the dull period of investigation. There were rumors of terrorist suspects, government cover-ups, airline irresponsibility.

20

There was speculation about meteorites and military laser beams and uniquely spectacular incidences of windshear. Then there were the tabloids, the supermarket papers and the strange-but-true-type TV shows. It seems five or six bodies from the jet, all of them from first class, had landed remarkably intact. This was not unheard of, and scientists believed their section of the plane might have formed an independent airfoil cushioning their fall. But the tabloids figured it was UFOs intercepting the chosen. They figured it was angels wafting the corpses to earth as a sign of hope from God. One 'eyewitness' in *News of the World* claimed the baby Jesus Himself had put in an appearance, worked several trademark signs and wonders, and even delivered a pithy homily or two before heading merrily on His way.

So, all in all, for those who followed the disaster in the news, there was a little something for everyone, a story for every taste.

And for one man – a man who read every story from the heartbreaking and responsible to the hilariously absurd – there was something more. The man was a vice-president at Helix Pharmaceuticals. And for him, there was something about the Hunnicut crash that was more desperately urgent than anything the media reported. For him, there was something buried in the tragedy that almost defied belief. That *would have* defied belief – if it weren't for the fact that he'd been waiting for it – watching for it – for a very long time.

Chapter One

Haunted Heart

1

Four months later. November, another Friday. Manhattan, New York, New York. A young saxophone player named Lonnie Blake was doing a gig at a place on Ninth Avenue.

It wasn't much of a place. There wasn't much of a crowd in the small hours. Three or four people were at the wooden bar. Four or five more were lounging at the small round tables. Almost everyone there was young but almost everyone looked sort of pale and specterly, glazed and wander-eyed as if they'd gotten lost somehow on their way to the happening thing. One doofus in the corner was actually wearing sunglasses – he was dressed in black and wearing sunglasses and bobbing his head as if stoned on the music. The supply lines of hip, in other words, were stretched a little thin in here.

The place was called Renaissance. Running around the walls was a mural of Florence. The owner's girlfriend had painted it, copying a picture in a book she'd found at the

Strand. The mural actually hadn't been too bad when she'd finished it. But about six months ago she and the owner had a fight. She hauled for San Francisco, and now her delicate blue firmament was chipping away and the intricate white-and-red skyline was starting to blur with grime.

Against that backdrop, up on a small stage smack in front of the fading Duomo, there was the band. A trio: keyboard, bass, saxophone. Fred Purcell, Arnie Cobb and Lonnie Blake.

Arthur Topp, meanwhile, was at the bar. He'd been sitting there for close to an hour. Nursing a scotch or three, listening to the music. Watching Lonnie.

The trio was playing standards mostly, Jurassic classics. *Night and Day, Always, Savoy*, that kind of thing. They were snapping their fingers and saying 'Yeah' a lot to make the crowd think they were really wailing. But so far, Arthur hadn't heard anything that excited him at all.

Arthur was a white man. Small and thin, forty. Bald up top but with his fringe of black hair grown long and tied into a pony-tail. His pullover red shirt looked expensive and made him stand out here. And his gold watch made him stand out. He'd inherited the watch from his father. He dressed to look more prosperous than he was.

He went on scoping Lonnie with quick, dark eyes. He tapped his hand impatiently on the bar.

The saxophone player had skill. Arthur could see that, hear that. Lonnie had fast fingers, a smooth, controlled tone. His jams were flawless too; he could find his way out of the melody and back with precision. But it was pretty uninspired stuff, Arthur thought. The same old tired barroom riffs. The kind of drone you could hear anywhere.

Arthur glanced at his father's Rolex. Nearly 1 a.m. The last set was winding up. The band was preparing to stand down. Arthur felt ready to write this one off, to pay his check and bail.

But just then, just as he was turning to flag the bartender, something happened.

Here it was. Last song. *Haunted Heart*. The trio was swinging into the finish. Fred Purcell, the keyboard player, nodded for Lonnie to take the break. The saxman blew into his final solo. Only the bass kept a three-note rhythm line behind him.

Arthur Topp paused. He listened. Nothing at first. Same old same-old. The bridge embellished with a few smeared grace notes, a couple of ornamental mordents. A chromatic fill where a rest had been to make it sound like a genuine jam.

The doofus in the sunglasses was impressed. He slapped his hand down on his table. 'Man!' he said, swinging his head back and forth.

Arthur Topp stifled a yawn in his fist. Lonnie Blake was sleepwalking the baby, he thought. Same as he had been all night.

Then – then, all at once – that changed. Lonnie was floating up some fake-out scale, going through the motions, floating up and up, one note after another – and then he held there, held dully in the low reaches as if tied to an invisible tether. One note, bobbing, tethered and leaden, bobbing until it threatened to become a miserable drone . . .

And then – then, all at once – the tether snapped.

Suddenly – Arthur was watching him, astonished – suddenly, there was Lonnie, bent back against the painted sky, against the painted dome. The sax was uplifted, a Selmer Mark VI, a fine machine glistening in his long fingers. And he was blowing that thing. He was wailing. His dark lips were kissing the hard black rubber of the mouthpiece. He was whispering over the reed with a sort of Miles Davis *vu* that filled the mellow blue tenor with a ghosty nothing . . .

And up on that empty breath he flew, glissing his way to a high riff of incredible Coltrane sixteenths, peaking in a seamless vibrato, a barely trembling leap from pitch to pitch.

Oh, thought Arthur Topp. *Oh, oh, oh.*

Then came another held note, but this one singing, a singing E-flat floating like a yogi in the impossible air. Then a shake, that quick trill with the lips, and then just as the note had to fall, still another shake – and then it did fall, it plummeted, *bam*, and like a rush of warm wind, the keyboard and the bass swept in under it and Lonnie wafted back – just *wafted* back – down into the melody. And the trio polished off the song.

Purcell, a gray-haired elder, looked around from his keyboard, surprised. 'All right,' he said.

Arthur Topp clapped and whistled. The doofus slapped the table again. A few other people let go of their drinks long enough to flop their hands together.

Purcell and Cobb, keyboard and bass, nodded, smiling slightly.

Lonnie Blake turned his back on all of them. The show was over.

2

He was still a young man – Lonnie – not yet thirty, maybe just. Average height, slender, skin the color of milk chocolate. He had compact, angular features, almost feline features, under a dusting of very short black hair. That night, he looked sharp and formidable in a sleek gray suit, an open-necked white shirt.

He packed up his sax, came down off the stage. Paused at the coathooks on the wall. He took down a black overcoat, slipped it on.

But he didn't go out. He came over to the bar. Set his sax case down. Leaned there, right next to Arthur Topp, his elbows on the rail.

'Bourbon and seven,' he said to the bartender.

Arthur eyed the black man sidelong, drink in hand. He was nervous about this now, awkward. He'd checked up on Lonnie Blake. Heard rumors he was a tough guy, even a bad guy, a gangbanger, in his youth. Arthur knew this wasn't going to be easy.

And it meant a lot to him. If he could win the saxophonist over, if he could get him to sign on . . . well, it would be a chance, one more chance for him to prove to his father's ghost that he could be more than a middle-man for weddings and bar mitzvahs, that he really did have some musical class.

He cleared his throat. 'Uh, hey . . .' he said after a second or two.

Lonnie glanced at him, uninterested.

'Uh, def, uh, def jam,' said Arthur Topp. 'Straight up. I mean it. It don't stop. Good stuff. Really.' *Excellent, Art*, he told himself. *You sound exactly like a fucking idiot.*

Lonnie Blake apparently thought so too. He gazed at Arthur a long time. It was not a friendly gaze. His eyes seemed black and depthless. Then, lifting his chin slightly, he made a sound for which there's no precise word: a short hiss of air through the nostrils. An expression of contempt.

Arthur Topp grinned stupidly. He felt sweat break out between his shoulder blades. He was grateful when the bartender slapped down a tall bourbon, when Lonnie Blake turned his attention to it and knocked back a long swig.

Still – he was nothing if not persistent – he pressed on. 'No. Listen. Straight up. I know you,' he said.

Lonnie came out of his drink with a breath. Shook his head slowly. 'No, you don't.'

Topp's laugh sounded desperate even to himself. 'I know your work, I mean. Your music. Make this easy on me, how about?'

Lonnie didn't make it easy, didn't answer at all. Up went the drink again. He pulled so hard on it the ice rattled. When he set it down, he nodded at the bartender.

'Bourbon and seven,' the bartender said, and set up another one fast.

'I heard this old demo,' said Arthur Topp. 'Someone slipped me this old demo. *Evolutions*. Right? *Evolutions*?

Must've been two, three years old. I mean, I heard it – this is months ago now. I mean it. I've been looking for you for months.'

The saxman worked his second drink, worked it hard.

'I mean, you're not around much,' Arthur said to his profile.

'I'm not around at all,' said Lonnie Blake after a moment. A hard edge of irritation was creeping into his voice. 'I'm not around now. I just look like I'm around. Don't let it fool you.'

'Okay.' *Jesus*, Arthur thought. *Jesus. This is not going well.* 'Okay. Okay, but, like – *Evolutions*,' he said anyway. 'I mean, that was just – fat stuff, top stuff, really. The Jurassics . . . the old flavors . . . you really blew 'em. I mean, the last time I heard 'em that fresh was . . . what? *My Favorite Things*? I think so. Really. Straight up. I mean it.'

Lonnie finally turned to him again, looked over at him as if he'd just noticed an annoying noise.

'Straight up,' Arthur repeated helplessly.

'Are you queer?' Lonnie asked him.

'What?' To his own despair, Arthur let out a high-pitched giggle. 'No! I mean, Jesus. I mean, queer, yeah, in more ways than I like to think about. But no. Not that way. No.'

'Then what the hell do you want from me, man?' said Lonnie Blake. 'I'm trying to have a drink here.'

Topp perceived this as an opportunity. He cleared his throat again, steadied himself, stumbled into his routine. 'My name's Arthur Topp. I represent people. Artists. I get them bookings. Musical acts. Topp Music. Tops in pop.' He brought out a business card. Pressed it into Lonnie's hand. The musician looked down at it as if it were phlegm. Dropped it into his overcoat pocket as if he were wiping it off. 'We're not a big organization. It's just me, in fact. But I have some good people, really, straight up. That's my . . . everything's on there, numbers, addresses. I'm in the office eight to eight, every day. Home by 8:30 unless something's on, you know, I'm scoping talent or something. Home, office, either one, I'm working all the time. And you can always get me on the mobile. So . . . I mean, look, I'm always looking for someone. Okay? I think you could . . . I think you and I could – really do something together. Straight up. I mean it.'

Well, it wasn't poetry, but at least he'd managed to spit it out. He waited as Lonnie gazed at him.

Then Lonnie faced the bar. Drained his second drink. Plonked down the glass. 'Have a good one,' he said. And he picked up his saxophone case.

Arthur Topp was not sure whether it was anger or desperation that did it, but now he heard himself blurt out, 'Look, I know what happened. About your wife, I mean.'

It stopped Lonnie anyway. The man went still. Glanced around with his feline features set, his depthless eyes hard.

'Sorry. Sorry,' said Arthur Topp. 'I mean, it's tragic. A tragic thing. Really. But I figured – you know – it's been more than a year, almost two years.' He gestured in front of him. 'Life . . . life goes on.'

Lonnie Blake gave him that silent gaze. 'Is that what it does?'

'Yeah. Well, I mean . . . that's not to say it isn't tragic but . . .' Arthur knew he was starting to babble. He just couldn't put on the brakes. 'I mean, still . . . still a guy like you . . . I mean, I see these studio gangsters, but you, you're from the trenches, man, you're from the land of the hard . . .' The sweat was coming down his temples now. And he could feel it soaking into his shirt, the wet cotton against his armpits. And he was thinking to himself, *Shut up*. But he couldn't. 'And then you . . . you get out and you go with your music, you get your wife and you got *Evolutions* going and all that and then . . . Well, I mean, it's tragic but . . . But you don't want to trash it all, throw it . . . She wouldn't – would she? – want that?'

Finally, he stopped, clamped down on it, cut it off. And for a long, for an endless, moment, he went on sweating as Lonnie Blake went on staring at him.

Then Lonnie made that noise again. That little snort of contempt. He showed Arthur his back, started for the door.

Topp watched him go, the familiar shroud of failure settling on him. And then, without thinking, he said, 'It's cause you can't anymore, isn't it?'

Lonnie Blake paused on his way to the door. Stood there without turning.

'I mean, play,' Arthur went on. Speaking the thoughts as they dawned on him. 'I mean, I was listening tonight and . . . *Evolutions* – that's, like, over for you, isn't it?'

Lonnie Blake started walking again.

'That's the thing, right?' Arthur called after him. 'You can't really play anymore since they killed her.'

Lonnie pushed the door open and walked out of the bar.

3

The night was cold. Lonnie stood outside the bar on Ninth Avenue, his breath misting in the autumn air.

Fool, he thought. And he pushed Arthur Topp from his mind.

But not the rage. Under the bourbon, the familiar rage kept bubbling, a ceaseless low boil.

Across the street, a young man, a young black man in a suit and tie, had opened the door of a car for his lady. She was twenty and beautiful, her black dress slit high up one side. Lonnie watched her lower herself into the Grand Am, the tan skin of a fine leg flashing under the streetlamp. The sight hurt him, and his anger mixed with something else, some sadder yearning. He had not been with a woman in eighteen months.

You can't really play anymore since they killed her.

Lonnie turned away and started walking.

The street was quiet. The cars speeding past were yellow

cabs mostly. Under the streetlamps, under the line of painted brick tenements, under the zigzag of their fire escapes, an occasional slouching no one scuttled up the sidewalk toward the Port Authority. Lonnie went slowly on, the sax in one hand, his other hand in his pocket. His depthless eyes were hard, the vision turned inward.

He went east on 30th. It was a darker lane between taller lofts. Looming brown buildings rose to either side of him, their wide empty windows dark. The autumn wind pressed steadily down the canyon, desolate. In the shadows away from the streetlights, trash skittered out from under parked cars.

Lonnie's jaw worked as he walked. His lips moved a little to the silent mutter in his mind. He was in himself completely now. On the treadmill of his old grief, hamstering around the old images. The grinning white boys. The speeding car. His murdered wife. Suzanne.

Even through the whiskey, the rage hurt him bad. Only images of her soothed the pain and those images hurt too. He conjured her trim, graceful figure turning to him from the kitchen sink. Her bright, unbridled smile and so on. The smooth brown skin of her high cheeks and the soft recesses of her doe eyes and so on. Her hand slipping a drink into his. Her hands rubbing his shoulders. *How was your day?* she would ask.

And so on.

A low sound escaped him, a low and awful sound. He paused. He was halfway down the empty street. The husky lofts and the windy silence bore down on him from every side.

He shook his head slightly. He set his face and walked on, willing the images into shadow.

He reached his building. There was a narrow recess in a wide brown wall. A loft entry with a black wooden door that led into the building's foyer. Lonnie brought his keys out of his pocket. Stepped out of a streetlight's aura into the alcove. He peered down through the dark to fit his key in the lock. The key slipped in.

And a hand reached out behind him. It gripped his elbow hard. A woman whispered harshly to him out of the night.

'Help me,' she said.

4

Startled, Lonnie whipped a look back over his shoulder. It was a white girl, her big urgent eyes staring up at him. Pale she was, and the breath misting before her face made her seem almost ghostly. She had short black hair. Pretty features, but sharp and glossy and cheap. A belted black coat ended high on her thighs. Her sexy legs were in dark stockings, her feet in black high-heeled shoes.

Lonnie pegged her for a whore. This was some kind of street game, he thought. But there was real fear in her eyes, it looked like. And the small hand on his elbow was shaking so hard he could feel it right up his arm.

'There's a guy after me,' she said. Her voice was shaking too. 'Please. Just let me in. I swear . . . Before he sees me. Hurry. Please.'

She glanced down to the corner quickly. Lonnie quickly followed the glance. He saw a car whisk past the intersection, then another. He saw the green outglow of the traffic light fading toward him into the darkness.

But there was no one coming, no sign of anyone.

The whore hissed at him, 'Aw, please! Jesus!' Her grip on his arm tightened.

Lonnie hesitated another moment, figuring the angles. Then he acted on instinct: twisted the key, pushed open the door.

The whore darted past him. He slipped in after her, let the door swing shut behind.

The building's foyer was small, cramped, about the size of two elevators put together. There was one lamp up on the high ceiling. Its light was dim by the time it reached the checkered linoleum floor.

The whore leaned back trembling against one colorless wall. Lonnie stood watching her, listening to her panting breath. She raised her red plastic purse. Snapped it open. Fumbled inside.

Lonnie watched this too, expressionless. Thinking: *She pulls a knife out of there and I'll bust her fucking grill.*

She brought out a pack of Marlboro Lites. Held it toward him. He shook his head no. She jogged a butt loose and pulled it free with her lips. Bowed over a plastic lighter, the cigarette dangling. Spark, spark, spark. She couldn't get the flame going with her shaking hands.

Lonnie took the lighter from her. Torched it, held it out. She bent to the fire, clasping his hand in both of hers. Then she tilted back until her eyes met his. She sucked the smoke so hungrily Lonnie could almost feel it go down. She sighed it out at him in a rush.

'Thanks,' she said. 'Sorry for the panic. Creep Alert. You know.' She tried to laugh. It didn't sound much like a laugh. She held up the cigarette. 'You mind?'

Lonnie gave that brief snort of his. The whore leaned back against the wall again, took another drag. Closed her eyes, communing with the smoke.

Lonnie studied her. The heels, the stockinged legs, the plastic mini-coat, the glossy makeup. She was a whore all right. But pretty under all the glop. Practically a kid too. Not much more than twenty.

She shuddered on a long breath. Opened her eyes. Her eyes were big and blue. She tried to make them sardonic, but they were pools of loneliness.

'Look,' she said. 'Do you mind? You can go up, really. I can stay down here. I don't care. I swear to God, man, I'm gone before daylight. Soon as there's some people on the street, I'm a misty memory. I swear.'

Those eyes of hers held him, even after he looked away. *I gotta be all kinds of stupid*, he thought. Then he gave another of those snorts. Pointed a finger at her. 'This place isn't mine, you hear me. It's a friend of mine's. He's letting me use it, awright? Now I let you upstairs and you steal from me, I'm gonna take that personally. You know what I'm saying?'

She came off the wall, both hands lifted. 'You are so good. So good.'

'You hear me now?'

'I swear to God,' she said. 'So help me.'

'Awright then.'

She smelled of violets and tobacco. In the elevator, Lonnie had to reach across her to put his key in the notch for the fourth floor. His face was close to her black hair and he caught her scent. They stood arm by arm as the box rose and he could feel the closeness of her skin.

'You're really good to do this, really,' she repeated. She sucked her cigarette so hard she hissed. Nodded on the exhale. 'Like, I mean, really.'

Lonnie grimaced, raised his eyes to the numbers above the cage door. It was probably the police after her, he thought. About ten minutes, they'd probably be in here to arrest his ass.

The elevator stopped on the fourth floor, the top floor.

Lonnie slid back the cage, unlocked the heavy metal door into his loft. He pushed the big door open and breathed in deep as the whore squeezed past him. Violets and trailing smoke.

'Hold on a minute. Don't turn on the light,' she said.

He set his saxophone down. Stood and watched her in the darkness. She was a small, wandering shadow in the loft's vast spaces. She moved to his left, to the wall of high windows. She reached it. Looked out. And then she jumped back, as if she'd been burned.

'What,' he said. 'He out there?'

'Yeah. Yeah.'

'Lemme see.'

Lonnie headed quickly across the room to the windows. He felt her fingers flutter at his arm as he passed her and slowed down so he wouldn't be seen. He edged close to the sill. Looked out through the fire escape, down to the street below.

The man was on the sidewalk. He was moving slowly under a streetlamp, just where they'd been standing only moments ago. He was obviously looking for someone, scanning the street, this way and that.

Lonnie had a good view of him. A tall, husky white man in an open trenchcoat. He lifted his eyes to study the buildings, the windows. Lonnie moved back a little behind a curtain. Peeked out and saw the man's face. It was a slab of a face with skin like gravel. Thick black eyebrows lifted ironically. Black hair in a widow's peak over a high rough forehead.

The man seemed to curse. He slid his hand into his trenchcoat smoothly.

Nine-one-one, Lonnie thought. A cop for certain. They'd been cracking down on the street girls a lot lately. He couldn't help but smile a little. *Well, officer*, he thought, *seems this is the one that done got away*.

He went on watching. The man drew something out

of his pocket. A two-way or a mobile phone. He spoke into it, still walking, heading out of the lampglow toward Ninth.

A moment later, a car pulled up alongside him, long and dark. It stopped and the gravel-faced man opened the door. He slid in the passenger side. The car drove off.

'*Sayonara*, five-oh,' Lonnie murmured. 'It's all right, he's . . .' But the girl wasn't there. For a moment, he couldn't find her. Then he made her out in the shadows, the tip of her cigarette glowing. She was sitting hunched forward on one of the leather chairs. 'He's gone,' Lonnie said.

'Yeah? You sure?' Her voice sounded strange. Small and tight.

'A car picked him up. They drove away.'

She touched her cheek with the heel of her palm. 'Fuckers,' she said. Lonnie realized she must've been crying. 'Hey, you got an ashtray for this?'

Lonnie went into the kitchen, clicking on lamps as he went. He brought her a coffee cup and set it on the small table beside her. She looked up at him gratefully with damp eyes, her mascara running. Fuck the cops. He was glad he'd helped her.

'I'm making myself a drink,' he said. 'You want one?'

'Sure. What're you making?'

'Bourbon and seven.'

'Sure.'

Lonnie stood in the kitchen, glasses on the wooden counter. He poured slowly, mixing the booze and soda over ice. She'd want to hide out here till morning, he thought. He'd have to sleep with one eye open if he wanted the stereo to be here come dawn.

'Nice. Nice place,' she said behind him. He heard her lighter flick-flick again.

'Yeah.' Lonnie watched the bourbon flow, hungry for it.

41

'Trumpet player I know's in Europe on tour. He let me have it for six months.'

'Nice.'

The loft was vast. It was never well lighted. There was always darkness in the corners and the far reaches. The heat and water pipes were exposed, dodging back and forth along the ceiling in tortuous patterns, making tortuous patterns of glare and shade up there and down below. The bedroom and bathroom were walled off, but the rest of the place was just one long expanse: the living area, the open kitchen at the far end, the high windows onto the fire escape. There was not much furniture. A black leather sofa, two black leather chairs. A glass coffee table. Another table of wood by the windows with the elaborate phone-fax-answering machine the trumpet player had left behind.

They sat in the leather chairs and drank. The whore smoked, one cigarette then another. She had unbelted the plastic raincoat now. She was wearing a black dress, scooped low over her cleavage, ending high on her stockinged thighs. She raised her cigarette hand and touched the fringe of her hair, drew it aside with two fingers. Her hair was too black, Lonnie thought. Too set, too perfect. A wig, he figured. Like some little girl playing dress-up.

She was distracted at first and they sat silently. Then she tried to make conversation. 'So you're, like, a musician or something, huh?'

He nodded. 'Name's Lonnie Blake.'

She didn't answer. Made a vague, nervous gesture, looked around her nervously. Stabbed the side of her mouth with the cigarette, taking quick, sharp pulls. 'Look,' she said. 'The thing is: I can't go back out there. Not tonight. I mean, I know it's a lot to ask.'

Lonnie lifted his shoulders slightly. He felt the bourbon warm inside him. He'd had a lot of it tonight. He was beginning to feel distant and muzzy.

'I got some money,' the girl went on. 'You know? I could pay you.' She gave a frantic little laugh. 'Give you a freebie if you want.'

For a moment, Lonnie didn't understand her. His eyebrows came together, making his sharp cat features even sharper still.

The girl's cigarette waved around. She gestured at herself. 'I mean, we all know what I am, right? So? I'm serious. I can do something for you. I'd be happy to, you know. Whatever.'

Lonnie got it then. He shook his head no, but his eyes went down her automatically. The white upper curves of her breasts and the sleek lines of her and her stocking tops visible beneath the hem of her short dress. He was too far away to smell the scent of her, but he smelled it anyway. And he felt the sight of her flesh inside him and it changed the way he breathed.

She brushed the edge of her raincoat back to give him a better view. And when he didn't speak for another moment, she said, 'You know, if you're, like, into something? If you got some kind of specialty stuff. Fantasies. Whatever. Anything that doesn't draw blood. I'm serious, man, I'd be happy to. We could have a good time just . . . just let me stay.'

She brushed at her smeared cheek again. That brought him back to himself. He shifted in his chair.

'You can sleep on the couch. Stay till morning. Whatever,' he said. He drained his glass. Stood up. 'I'm gonna make another. You want one?'

'No. No. I'm good.'

This time, he poured unsteadily, gripping the bottle, gripping the glass. Watching the brown liquor splashing over the ice with a kind of grim intensity. *Bullshit*, he thought. He wouldn't admit to himself that she'd unnerved him.

You can't really play since they killed her.

And he thought angrily: *I'm not gonna make the girl pay*

with her ass, I don't care what she is. And he thought: *Crazy whore.*

'Shit, most guys'd figure they'd won the lottery,' she said, as if speaking into his thoughts. 'I got headgear. I always use 'em. I'm safe, really, if that's what's bugging you.'

'Look, I told you you could stay.' He growled it at her, more harshly than he meant to. The liquor – it was getting to him, he thought. Christ, what a night. He thumped down the bottle, snapped up the glass. 'Just forget it. It's okay.' He knocked back a heavy slug of bourbon, then dashed the rest of it into the sink. 'I'll go get you a blanket.'

He walked off quickly into the bedroom.

He yanked blankets from his closet in there, blinking hard. Yeah, the liquor, he thought. The liquor was getting to him.

She called in. 'You mind if I use your bathroom?'

'Go on ahead,' he called back.

When he heard the bathroom door click shut, he paused with the blankets in his hands. He took a breath, let it out, was surprised – was disturbed – to feel it tremble. *Steady there, cowboy.* He felt a kind of nauseous excitement.

If you're into something. Specialty stuff. Fantasies. Whatever.

It wasn't as if he hadn't thought of it before. Paying a girl to do the thing he wanted. Sure he had. Most guys would've figured they'd won the lottery. She had that right.

Back in the living room, he tossed the blankets on the sofa. He saw that her raincoat was lying there too. He moved away from it as if aimlessly.

He sank into one of the chairs. The leather sighed under him and he sighed. He heard the toilet flush, the water running. He touched his forehead with a couple of fingertips. His forehead was damp. *Shit*, he thought.

When he heard the door come open, he looked up and saw her. Standing and watching him, one hand resting on her purse. A ceiling lamp shone down on her, gleamed on her skin. The curve of her hip was pressed into the dress.

She'd fixed her makeup. Dried her tears. Her face seemed clearer now than it had. She was older than he'd thought at first, but still young, maybe twenty-five. Her mouth was long, glossed silver, the lips looked very soft. The big eyes were intelligent, but they were furtive and unhappy. Well, he guessed it wasn't much of a life.

She cocked her head. 'You sure you don't want anything? I mean, it's no big deal.' He nodded, but his eyes stayed on her. She gave a little laugh. 'Man! Look at you. Whatever you've got, it's bad, isn't it?'

'Look,' said Lonnie Blake. 'I said forget it.'

'No, I'm just saying. You're all scarred up inside, I can see it. Man!'

Lonnie lowered his eyes. He found himself nodding again, not thinking, just sitting there, looking down, screwing his hands together, palm against palm. Aware of her.

'Hey, life's shit and then you die, right?' she said.

A pale little laugh escaped him.

She came forward slowly. He heard her heels snap the rhythm of her steps on the pine floor. He heard the soft whap of her purse as she tossed it on the sofa, plastic on leather.

'You know, you're making me feel bad here,' she said. 'After you helped me and everything.' She tilted over to try to meet his eyes but he wouldn't look up at her. 'Can't I do something for you here, Lonnie? I could cheer you up a little, I bet.'

He twisted his palms together. Not thinking. 'It's been a long time,' he heard himself say.

'Yeah? Well, right there, see: I could fix that.'

She came closer, silently now over the worn braid rug. Closer, until she stood over him and he could smell her again, the violets and the smoke. Her hemline was at his

45

eye level. He was breathing in that unfamiliar rhythm that the sight of her brought on.

'Isn't there something I can do?'

He looked up at her face and she smiled in spite of her unhappy eyes.

'I guess I'm not much of a Romeo,' he told her.

She reached out and gently pressed her palm against his temple. 'I'll bet there's something special though. Hm? Is there? It's not like you're gonna shock me or anything.' She shook her head sympathetically. 'You look like you need something, Lonnie.'

He let out another mirthless laugh. He looked down at his shoes. He could feel the warmth of her hand on him. 'Shit,' he said.

Then, with a breath, he looked up at her again. Before he'd meant to, before he'd thought about what he was doing. He looked up into those unhappy blue eyes, up at that sympathetic smile. 'So like you do special things,' he said. 'You don't mind that?'

'Go on,' she told him. 'Knock yourself out. What can I do for you, Lonnie?'

Lonnie gazed at her another moment, aching. He licked his dry lips.

'Make me a drink,' he said hoarsely then. 'Make me a drink – and ask me about my day.'

5

She brought him a bourbon and seven. She stood behind him and rubbed his shoulders. He didn't even have to tell her to do that. She just did. She leaned close, brought her lips to his ear.

'What's my name?' she said softly.

Lonnie felt he had jumped off a cliff. It was surprisingly easy to just keep falling. 'Suzanne,' he heard himself say.

'Suzanne. That's nice. I like that.' The whore went on rubbing his shoulders. 'Just relax. It's okay.' He felt her brush the top of his head with her lips. He felt her rest her chin on him. 'So what was your day like, sweetheart? Tell me. Tell Suzanne.'

Lonnie took a hard pull at the booze. Reinforcements. He rolled the cool glass against his forehead. She rubbed his shoulders. He closed his eyes. It was easy to see his dead wife, as easy as falling. He was lost in the image of her almost instantly.

'I did a gig,' he whispered. He kept his eyes shut, spoke to the image. 'Just a small thing. A couple of guys I did some studio work with. They ain't much, but we been playing together, you know. Just a few gigs here and there.'

The whore must've caught his confessional tone. 'It's all right,' she told him. She rubbed his shoulders. She pressed her lips against his ear. He felt her hot breath. She didn't smell of violets anymore. She smelled of another perfume. He still remembered that perfume. It was good to smell it again.

'I think about what they did to you,' he said. 'I mean it. I think about it all the time.' She rubbed his shoulders. She kissed the side of his head. 'It's just ... sometimes ... I *hear* these cats. You know what I'm saying? I put on a CD or something. Some of these cats. That Jim Carter. *Real Quietstorm*. Don Harrison. *Nouveau Swing*. They got the chops, you know. They're real. They're players.' He pressed his lips together, shook his head. He opened his eyes now. Held his drink out before him in his two hands. He stared and stared at it, feeling her breath, her fingers. 'I mean, I'm thinking about you all the time, baby, all the time, it's just ... I listen to these guys sometimes and I think: I *got* those chops. You know? I'm as *good* as they are.' He made a noise like steam being released from an engine. Something was welling in him now. Desire. Desire or the old rage, he wasn't sure. They were indistinguishable to him. 'I been doing all this studio work, commercial work, you know, to stay alive, and that's okay. It's just sometimes – sometimes I feel like really playing, that's all. The Jurassics, you know, the way I used to. So we got this trio together, that's all. You see what I'm saying?' He stared at the drink in his hands, stared and stared.

'Yeah. I see what you're saying,' the whore said, rubbing his shoulders. 'You're saying: Life goes on, Lonnie. Right?'

But he hardly heard her, or he heard her as if in a dream, as you hear a voice or a noise when you're dreaming. His arms were pulled in against himself now. The ice in his glass rattled as his hands began to shake. He stared into the depths of his bourbon and his eyes were suddenly hot with self-contempt and anger and confusion.

'God!' he said.

The glass fallen to the floor – the drink spilling out of it – the ice melting on the rug – he took her on the sofa, hardly undressing. Her hem was pushed up around her waist. The straps of her bra were stripped down over her shoulders. He rose up above her, his eyes shut tight, his teeth bared. He rammed into her with long strokes, hard, and he felt his rage.

'Bitch,' he said just at the end. It broke out between his clenched teeth. 'Fucking whore. Cunt. Bitch.'

When he came, it felt like bile spewed out of him. It felt tarry and acid. He let out a strangled cry and it flooded from him. He thought it would burn his dick off. He thought it would eat through the condom and dissolve her guts.

He rolled off her instantly. Sat on the floor. Stripped the condom off and threw it from him. 'Oh shit,' he said. 'Shit.' He sat curled up beside the sofa, his knees raised, his two hands pressed against his brow. He struck at his own forehead with the heels of both hands, rocking his head into the blows.

'Whew,' said the girl to herself as she watched him. She sat up a little, pulling a bra strap back up her shoulder. 'Hey, whoa, Jesus, take it easy there, Lonnie,' she said. 'Don't kill yourself. I mean, it's all right. You didn't hurt me or anything. You oughta see what some of these assholes get up to.' She reached out tentatively, tentatively touched his shoulder. He made a noise and his body clenched, but he didn't cast her away. 'I mean it, man. I mean, look: I'm still alive. That's a good night for me.'

Lonnie heard this and burst out laughing. He covered his face with his hands.

The whore laughed too. 'You think I'm kidding,' she said.

49

Lonnie nodded, covering his face. He shook with laughter. 'Oh man,' he said then, and wiped his damp eyes.

Not half an hour later, they had sex again, in bed this time and more gently. The whore wouldn't kiss him, not on the lips. But naked under him she let him brush his mouth over her cheek, trail his fingers up her belly, paint trails of his yearning breath on her everywhere. She met his eyes as he moved inside her. He studied her with a bewilderment amounting almost to wonder. Everything while he was in her – details of the scene – a wrinkle on the bedsheet – a smear of gray dirt on the blue wall – the shape of her mouth when her lips parted – everything seemed astonishingly clear and present. He hadn't been hard like this or calm like this for ages.

Afterwards she said, 'I'm gonna get some sleep, okay?' and touched her lips lightly to the stubble of his jaw. She rolled away from him. He lay looking at the way her black hair rested on her white neck.

One more time, at daybreak, he was in her. On his side, curled up against her, slipping in her from behind. His eyes traveled over the curve of her spine, traced the sweet, round shape of her ass. He moved this time dreamily. He thought this time about Suzanne. Moving in the whore, he could almost taste the San Francisco mornings. The ache was terrible. The fact that he would never touch his wife like this again – never – it just seemed impossible to bear.

Finished, he pressed his brow against the girl's hair a minute, closed his eyes. He wished he could've spoken now the way he would've spoken to his wife. Suzanne was the only one he had ever spoken to like that. Given the chance, he knew he would've loved Suzanne till he died. What was he going to do now with a lifetime's worth of desire?

The whore drew away from him. Smiled at him over her shoulder, a sad, regretful smile.

'That's it, Romeo, I'm out of rubber,' she said. 'Plus I gotta go.'

6

It was just dawn, an autumn dawn. The big windows in the main room were rattling with the wind. Lonnie could hear them from the bedroom. Lying on the bed alone, he could hear rain gargling in the gutters too. He could hear the whore in the bathroom, the faucet handles squeaking.

After a while, she came out. She leaned her head in the bedroom doorway. 'Okay if I use your phone?'

'Yeah. Sure. Go ahead.'

She moved away.

He lay where he was. The pillows held the scent of violets. And then, for moments at a time, the scent of San Francisco returned to him, the scent of the old mornings, waking with Suzanne. Never again, he thought. The yearning was like a solid thing. It smelled of remembered weather and it weighed a ton.

Lonnie lay there and stared up at the ceiling and glimpsed a lifetime of inconsolable desire.

He heard the wind again, the rain. He heard the whore underneath them. She was talking on the phone in the other room. Her voice was a hushed murmur, but certain words reached him.

'You sure? ... people hanging around? ... big fucker with, like, a rough face ... No. ... anyone ... ?'

Then she was quiet. When she spoke again, a gust of wind rattled the window frames, drowned out the words.

A moment later, he heard the telephone clapping back into its cradle.

Lonnie felt bad. He didn't want her to go.

She came into the bedroom doorway. She was fully dressed, had her coat on, her purse over her arm.

'All right, lover, I'm gonna sixty-six,' she said. Lonnie lifted up onto one elbow. She walked over to him, sat on the bed. 'You really saved my life,' she told him. 'Really.' She forced a smile. 'Hey: my hero.' She leaned over and kissed his cheek.

He gave that quiet hiss of air. 'Any time,' he said.

She drew back. Lingered over him. Considered him sadly. She seemed about to speak again. Lonnie wanted to reach out and draw her to him. He was surprised by the strength of the urge.

She stood up.

'Maybe I could call you,' he said.

She shook her head, pressed her lips together. 'Maybe in another life, you know. This one, it just ain't a happening situation.'

He nodded.

She gave a mock-happy wave, waggling her fingers at him. 'I'm smoke,' she said.

Lonnie watched her hurry out the door. He heard the rain in the gutters. The windows banging in the wind. The rattle of the elevator cage.

When she was gone, he got out of bed slowly. Shrugged

on a bathrobe. His hands in the pockets, he wandered out into the loft.

The place looked quiet and gray. The bourbon glass still lay where he'd dropped it on the rug in front of the chair. Lonnie turned away from it.

He moved to the windows. The panes were streaked with rain. The rain was blowing slantwise across them, across the view of white and brown lofts over the way and across the gray sky above them.

Lonnie stood there looking out until he saw the girl emerge below. She paused at the doorway, turning her head, glancing everywhere. Then she moved out into the sparse traffic of Saturday pedestrians hurrying toward the avenues.

He watched the black top of her head, then the back of her black raincoat. Then she was past the window frame, beyond his field of vision.

Lonnie drew a deep breath. He moved to the wooden table. He looked down at the phone-fax-answering machine. His fingers walked idly over the buttons. He felt – what was the word for it? Melancholy. Like a Berlin ballad.

His fingers found the button labeled REDIAL. Slowly, he pressed it down. A number – the number the girl had just called – marched across the LCD. Lonnie watched it. He picked up the pen beside the machine and wrote the number on the phone pad.

Then he tossed the pen down and turned away to look out at the rain.

Chapter Two

A Mousetrap – No Mouse

1

In Jersey that day, by the Palisades, the flaming leaves were falling. The wind and the rain brought them sweeping down onto Jonathan Reese's yard. It made for a lifeless prospect: the leaves lying dark and glossy on the lawn, covering the tennis court at the bottom of the hill, sinking into the dull puddles on the plastic cover of the swimming pool. The gray sky above drained the brilliance from the maples standing on the graceful slope of ground. And the last white asters in April Markham-Reese's garden were bent into the mud by the silver downpour.

The windows in the family room – the whole rear wall of them – looked out and down over those rainy acres. The colorless bluster out of doors made the house seem bright and cozy inside. Reese had a fire going in the grate. All the lights were on, warm and bright. Dave Grusin was playing Mancini on the stereo.

And April was at her writing desk – her escritoire, she

called it, jokingly grand. Working on her charities. The hungry children in Africa. The scholarships for inner city youth. Planned Parenthood. The ACLU. And Michael was nearby at the Play Computer – to be distinguished from the Homework Computer in his room, Mom's Laptop in the master bedroom, and *The* Computer in Reese's study.

Reese himself was sitting on the sofa. Holding an *Economist* on his lap but not reading it. Just drinking in the scene. The wife, the son, the hearth, the bosom: the whole family thang, God love it; a still, sweet refuge in the ever-changing blah blah blah.

Well, he could joke, but it was good stuff. After two weeks away. Moscow, London. It was balm to the business-battered spirit to be here with them again. It was very good to be home.

From where he sat, Reese turned his attention to his wife. Studied the cute little ringlet of brown hair falling on her cheek as she bent over her checkbook giving away his hard-earned money. He was aware of a mild, a not unpleasant sadness. Missing his daughter Nancy who was away at Yale. And, after a second, sensing his eyes on her, the partner of his joy and sorrow for lo these thirty years glanced up at him. And her stately bearing, her patrician face were as beautiful to him now as ever. And she knew exactly what he was thinking. She said quietly, 'I'm glad we'll all be together for Thanksgiving.' A display of mental telepathy which set off a flood of husbandly love in Jonathan Reese more powerful than words can rightly say.

Manfully clearing his throat to disguise the emotion, he laid his magazine aside. Stood and stretched. He was a tall man and broad shouldered. He had full, coiffed iron-colored hair. A chiseled, almost classical face. In jeans and a bulky white sweater, he looked trim and fit. Not bad at all, he felt, for a codger of fifty-one.

Humming tunelessly along with the stereo, he moved to

stand behind his thirteen-year-old son. He watched the PC monitor. The boy was currently dealing death to a series of animated demons who seemed to be rising up from the floor of a stony corridor somewhere. Transylvania maybe. Reese shook his head in amazement.

'I can remember when it took a computer the size of a house just to add two and two,' he said.

'Gee, Dad,' said Michael. 'That's really . . . that's very . . .' The boy's head fell forward and he began to snore.

Reese laughed, whapped him. 'Smart-alec cyber-punk,' he said. He threw a headlock on the kid.

Michael started laughing too. 'Hey! You're gonna get me killed here!'

Reese rubbed a noogie into his hair. 'I'm murdering your son,' he told April.

'That's nice, dear,' she said.

Reese let the boy go. Gave him a fatherly slap on the shoulder.

Then he lifted his eyes, surprised.

A car had come up the drive. He could just see it from here as it reached the garage behind the house. A Lexus sedan. Very nice. New, blue, modest but comfortable. Its headlights were on against the weather.

Then they went off. The driver's door opened. A red-haired man stepped out into the rain.

Reese held his breath. The song on the stereo ended and for a moment there was near silence in the room. The clicking of Michael's computer keys. The snicker of the fire. The wind at the windows, the rain on the pane.

Outside, the red-haired man shrugged his sleek black trenchcoat straight at the shoulders. Then he ducked his head against the downpour and started quickly along the path to the front door.

Watching him, Reese frowned. He still had his hands on his son's shoulders. He patted the boy gently.

He knew the red-haired man. He was named Edmund Winter and he was the new North American bureau chief for a company called Executive Decisions. What that meant, in practical terms, was that he was an extremely expensive and proficient killer-for-hire.

Watching him move quickly toward his house, Reese let out his breath at last with a silent curse.

He hated conducting business out of his home.

2

'Without making any excuses, I want to be clear,' Winter said. 'It's only been a few months since they brought me up here. I haven't had time to review all our personnel or carry out a full reorganization.'

'This sounds suspiciously like a build-up to bad news,' said Reese.

'No. No. It's good news, in fact, it's just . . . we've got a time issue on our hands. That's why I came here. I thought I ought to catch you while you were in the country. And under the circumstances, I thought it best to communicate with you face to face.'

Reese considered this a moment. 'Then you've found her, I take it.'

'Yes, sir,' said Winter. 'I think we have.'

They were upstairs in Reese's study now. A small room, modest but impressive. Hardcover business tomes on shelves. Photographs of Reese with the swordfish he caught off the keys, the wildebeests he shot in Tanganyika. An immense, blond wood, more or less orderly desk. An oversized computer monitor on a typing table to one side. A curtained window.

Reese sat behind the desk. Tilted back in his chair, elbow on the rest, chin on the base of his thumb, two fingers propped against his jaw. Winter was seated on the small sofa to his right. Relaxed, arm along the sofa back, legs crossed at the knee. They were both wearing expensive aftershave, and their scents mingled in the close space.

Despite his profession, Winter looked civilized enough, Reese thought. Intense, hungry, ambitious, yes. But then there was a lot of that in corporate life. He was about forty, give or take a year or two. His face was narrow, lined, ironical, edgy. There was a great deal of wit sparkling in his hazel eyes. He was no idiot, clearly. At the same time, under the tailored gray suit, the white shirt, the port-red tie, the gold tie clasp and so on, Reese could make out the build and carriage of an athlete, a man in prime condition. Winter, he thought, was a formidable fellow all around.

'My assessment was right,' Winter said now. 'She's gone underground completely now. She's operating as a prostitute full time.' Reese made a noise of amusement. But Winter held up his hand. 'No. Look. Don't think of it that way. This is a very smart, tough, determined individual. She's willing to do anything to protect her child.'

'I can't see how her child benefits from her being a whore,' said Reese.

'I'm sure she'd prefer to do something else – but if she did, we'd have had her by now.' Winter ticked his reasons off on his fingers. 'Prostitution is anonymous. There are no business records, no taxes, no paper trail of any kind. Even the customers have a stake in protecting her identity. With the right customers, it can be highly paid work too. And she needs the money – she can't outrun us without money – she

62

knows that. And the equipment's portable.' Reese snorted at that and Winter smiled – but he persisted. 'I'm telling you. We shouldn't underestimate her. I mean, you can say: this is just a waitress, this is an uneducated woman. But she's been moving around, making it hard for us to keep track of her for years. And the minute the Hunnicut incident happened – bang – she vanished. No hesitation, no second thoughts, self-deception. She just said, yep, this is it, and she was gone. Now it's been four months. Executive Decisions has devoted substantial resources to her recovery, and yet she's kept away from us all this time. Believe me – this woman? – prostitution is nothing. If she thought she could protect her child by setting herself on fire, we'd be roasting marshmallows on her bones.'

'So you're in love,' said Reese.

'I'm deeply in love,' answered Winter, deadpan. 'I've come to you for your blessing.'

The two men laughed. Then Reese let out a comical groan, rubbed his eyes. 'All right. All right. You've done your pitch. Now tell me what happened?'

'Well. First, the good news,' said Winter with a wry half-smile. 'She finally made a mistake. A couple of mistakes. She got arrested in St Louis for one thing. They just threw her into the cooler for a night but I had my ops scanning the records and we picked up on it. Again, she was smart. She was gone the minute she hit the street. But—' He lifted a finger. '—and this was her *big* mistake – she held on to one of her clients. Commuter. A guy going back and forth from New York. I guess she figured she could use him to start up her business in a new city. Fortunately, I'd had my guys stake him out. Him and another guy from Chicago just in case.'

'That was smart,' Reese allowed.

Winter nodded once. 'Last night, she finally showed up. He went and met her at a small hotel near the terminal.'

'And you lost her,' said Reese. 'I assume that's the bad news.'

'The bad news,' Winter answered slowly, giving Reese time to get ready for it. 'The bad news is that we not only lost her, but the op was made. She spotted him.'

Reese let out a long, whispered 'Ah'. That *was* bad news. It hit him. He pressed his hands together, held them up before his mouth as if in prayer. He needed time to think a moment before he knew how he wanted to react to that.

It was never easy for him, dealing with Winter, dealing with his company, Executive Decisions. There were inherent difficulties. ED was a South-Africa-based firm which had begun by giving military aid and advice to corporations operating in unstable environments. For the most part, there was nothing mysterious or clandestine about them. If your manufacturing plant was under attack by rebel guer-rillas in some godforsaken no man's land without enough government to protect a school picnic, you phoned ED – or contacted www.Execdec.com – and they handled it for you. Reese had a friend, for instance, at Bright Young Things, the clothing people, who'd had exactly that problem at her manufacturing plant in Sierra Leone. Insurgents were hijacking shipments, sabotaging production, killing workers. So she'd hired ED. They'd sent in some advisors, concen-trated on a single village of suspected rebel sympathizers and administered what they called a short, sharp shock. They raped the women while the men were forced to watch, killed the men and children while the women watched, sold some of the women to offset expenses, and that was it, the threat to the factory was finished, the world was once again safe for khaki casuals. It was an unpleasant business, no question. But as peace-loving as Reese was, business, he knew, was business. And according to his friend at Bright Young Things, this had been the least expensive way to deal with the situation in terms of both money and human life.

So, fine. That sort of thing worked very well as long as you were on foreign soil, in one of those hellholes of chaos and poverty that the newspapers are proud to refer to as 'developing nations'. If you were in Europe or America, on the other hand, matters became a bit more sensitive. Western sensibilities, laws, media being what they were, ED had only recently found it safe to begin operations here at all. And even now it was necessary to proceed on a local, individual and highly secretive basis.

But after some initial blunders and a couple of near-exposures, ED had managed to establish a network of highly trained operatives throughout the US and Europe, many of them moonlighting law officers or others in positions of power and responsibility. And now they had brought in Winter to reorganize, fine-tune, really whip things into shape.

Winter was supposed to be the best in the business. His curriculum vitae as it had been given to Reese was, understandably, on the sketchy side. But he'd done a stint in the U.S. Marines, some mercenary work in various African and South and Central American locations. And he was said to have expertise in weaponry, martial arts, surveillance and interrogation techniques.

And he had a pleasant, professional manner to boot. For all the time he'd spent in the field, Winter handled himself like a businessman. He knew how to claim credit where credit was due. How to take responsibility for his subordinates' mistakes while managing to communicate his annoyance at their incompetence. How to acknowledge a setback while continuing to maintain an aggressive, problem-solving posture at all times.

But while this familiar behavior mitigated or at least disguised Reese's difficulties, it didn't end them. Because no matter how well Winter comported himself, his was not, at the core, a civilized profession and this was not, at bottom, a civilized operation.

Reese was Vice-President in charge of Business Affairs at the pharmaceutical firm Helix. And what that meant, what it had meant for several years, was that he, virtually alone, had the task of saving the company from an unprecedented disaster. The botched experimental project that had brought Helix to the very brink of a legal, financial and public relations nightmare was not his fault. Nevertheless, the job of pulling the enormous corporation back from that brink had fallen into his hands and was now, he knew, to be the making or breaking of him.

He had come a long way. The job was almost complete. And Reese was as determined as anyone – more determined than anyone – to see it the rest of the way. He knew that Executive Decisions provided the best available means of doing that. But all the same, when you came right down to it, even a man's man like himself found it a bit intimidating to be in charge of personnel who could probably kill him with a single well-placed blow to some part of his anatomy he'd never even heard of. If nothing else, it ignited his macho, competitive instincts, which he feared would weaken his ability to make rational decisions. Right now, for instance, he found himself wishing he weren't dressed so casually, that he were wearing a suit that displayed the power of his company, his money, even his personal success. Under Winter's ironical, ambitious, hyper-energized gaze, this sweater and jeans he had on felt a little bit like a pair of pink pajamas. Which might tend to undermine his confidence – especially if he was going to have to read Winter the riot act over some idiot ED operative's mistake.

But in the end, this was a multi-million – potentially a billion-dollar operation. No matter how he felt, Reese had to stay in charge. He put a touch of stern displeasure into his voice.

'So your op was spotted,' he said. 'What does that mean?

Are you telling me she's likely to relocate? That we'll be right back where we were four months ago?'

For a second, it crossed Reese's mind that Winter might simply kill him for this. But no, the red-haired man accepted the tone of rebuke gracefully. He cocked his head mildly, as if considering. 'Well, in my opinion, it's not quite as bad as that,' he said. 'The girl saw someone following her, but she doesn't know who it was. She may be on the lookout for us but, let's face it, she's an attractive prostitute: she can't just leave town every time some creep trails her down the street. It'd never stop. On top of which, she hasn't been in town more than a month. It's doubtful she has the resources to relocate right away. So I think we have some time, a window of opportunity. Plus – we have the john, her client. Which—' he wrapped it up – 'is what I'm here about.'

Reese sighed, lifted his eyes to the ceiling. He could feel the tension starting to shimmer in him. He hoped he wasn't about to hear what he was pretty certain he was just about to hear.

Winter drew a breath to get ready for it. Then he said, 'My op wants a priority go.'

'Ach!' said Reese. He swiveled his chair to one side, presented Winter with an angry profile.

Winter continued. 'We've searched the john's house, his office . . .'

'Your man bobbled the ball . . .' said Reese.

'. . . tapped his phone. If he's got any record of her, we can't find it.'

'. . . and now I'm supposed to authorize a priority operation.'

'And with all due respect,' Winter pushed on, 'I don't think it's exactly fair to say our operative bobbled the ball. He's a good man with full surveillance capabilities. But as I say, this is an extremely intelligent and resourceful woman . . .'

'She's a bartender. She's a prostitute, for Christ's sake.'

'My man has surveilled . . . he's followed experts, believe me. Intelligence agents. International crime figures. It's a difficult business at the best of times, and this was a dark, empty street with a very sharp woman who's looking out for us. Look, to be absolutely fair here, I think we deserve full marks for tracking the woman down. She was a needle in a haystack.'

'Great. Somehow that doesn't make me feel better.'

'All right, sure,' said Winter. 'I wish the immediate outcome had been different too. But there's still time to make it good.'

Reese made another angry noise, but it was mostly for show. The die was pretty much cast. He knew he didn't have any real choice in the matter. He just didn't want Winter to think he was a soft touch, that's all. He swiveled back to face him.

'What about a simple interrogation?' he asked. 'You're supposed to be an expert at that . . .'

'I'm an expert at that, but this isn't some nigger in the middle of nowhere . . .'

'Whoa, whoa, whoa, excuse me, excuse me,' Reese broke in sharply. 'The people who work for me don't use that sort of language. Understood? It's just unnecessary.' Reese could not always afford to be as idealistic as his wife but he detested racism in all its forms. 'It's bad enough you're asking me to authorize murder, let's keep it on a professional level.'

Once again, he waited for Winter's reaction and once again Winter was graceful and polite. 'Sorry. Old habits. You're right, of course. All I'm trying to say is that we're in America now. The man we're talking about is a white, well-to-do, well-connected attorney. If we simply question him, there's no way we can absolutely guarantee his silence afterwards. My people insist on airtight security – and frankly, I think that's in your company's best interests as well . . .'

'And I want his family kept out of it,' said Reese, daring

to level a finger at the man. 'I don't want anything like last time.'

'Well, that's going to be difficult on a weekend. You may be talking about a delay . . .'

'Delay then.' He shook his head. 'I sleep badly enough without another bloodbath on my conscience. This is an individual authorization. Understood?'

Winter seemed about to go on – to argue – but no. He remained a diplomat to the end. He lifted a hand in surrender.

'You're the boss,' he said quietly. 'It's your call.'

3

The rain was letting up now. There was only a drizzle. Winter moved through it leisurely, down the front path back to his car.

Nice piece of property, he thought, looking the place over as he went.

In the driveway, he opened the Lexus's door and paused. Over the car's roof, through the rear wall of windows that edged around the side of the house, through the tall panes still spotted with rain, he could see the Reese family gathered in the back room. They were held there in the warm yellow light as if on the other side of a gray world.

Reese was with them again. Standing behind his son. Patting the middle of his sweater.

I'm starving, Winter imagined him saying. *What do you have to do to get some lunch around here?*

Sure enough, there was another movement. The wife – April – fluttered to her feet. With that pretty expression wives have when they're pretending to be annoyed but are really happy to be needed.

I suppose I'll just have to feed you two monsters, she would say. A real sweetie she looked like, Winter thought. He let a quirk touch the corner of his mouth. Nice house, nice family. It's the life, no question.

And he slipped in behind the Lexus's steering wheel.

He turned on the ignition first. Then he reached into his jacket pocket and switched off the TRD-2000 unit. He tugged the antenna from the unit's jack. Pulled the wristband receiver off over his right wrist. Careful not to snag his shirt, he worked the wire down slowly through his sleeve. When it came clear, he bunched the wire sloppily and dropped it in the pocket with the TRD. If Reese had tried to tape their conversation – or if a third party had been bugging them – the tape recorder detector would have vibrated silently against Winter's chest. It was a handy thing to have around during sensitive meetings like this one.

Winter reached over and fiddled with the knobs and switches on the dash. A motor hummed as a monitor swiveled outward. The grid of Uniden's visual scanner and radar/laser detector slowly became visible.

All the while, Winter was considering Reese, what they had talked about, what he was going to do.

Hughes and Mortimer, he was thinking to himself. *Mortimer and Hughes.*

He put the Lexus into reverse and eased it out of Reese's long drive.

He drove back slowly along the winding country roads. He wasn't angry exactly, but on the other hand he couldn't say he was in any way pleased.

He had had to eat shit. There was no other way to look at it. He had had to eat shit, and it was one of his least favorite things to eat, right next to sushi. Out in the field – out in the street, in a bar, anywhere – if a man had spoken to him the way Reese just had he would've ripped open his ribcage and removed his entrails by hand.

But now he was Mr Businessman. Mr Bureau Chief. Mr Front Office. And Reese was his client. So he had to sit there and take it.

Not that he blamed Reese either. The guy was paying good money, he deserved good service. But Hughes and Mortimer – Mortimer and Hughes – they had fucked up royally. They had lost the girl and let her spot them. It was because of them that Winter had had to eat shit. And no, that did not leave him feeling well pleased. They were going to hear about this. This was what he was here for. His brief was to streamline and modernize. To cut down on incompetence and the old blundering, inappropriate, thuggish methods. Messrs Hughes and Mortimer – Mr Mortimer and Mr Hughes – were going to be extremely unhappy chappies if he had to instruct them personally on how he wanted things done.

He drove along thoughtfully, idly admiring the canopy of leaves above him, the colorful maples and oaks and tulip trees meeting overhead. They sure were brilliant, he thought, even in this dull, dripping weather. And now and then, the view beyond them would open up and there would be a rolling field, a stately home. White shingles. Black shutters. Pillared porticoes.

Nice, he thought. Nice houses. It was the life, no bout adout it. Another couple years, if things went well, if he worked his way up the ladder – who could tell? He might be like Reese. He might have it all. The house, the loving wife, the kids. The days, the loving nights, the fruitful years. Fishing the stream, mowing the lawn, raking the leaves, shoveling the snow. Faithful husband of. Loving father of. Rest in peace. So long. You're gone forever. Sorry. Bye.

Okay, maybe not. Winter laughed to himself. Maybe it just wasn't in his nature.

The Lexus turned a corner onto route 72, came out from

under the overhanging trees. The road widened into four lanes here, ran on past mini-malls and gas stations to the interstate.

Winter glanced over at the Uniden detector. Nothing. No speed traps. All the same, he eased the Lexus just up to the forty-mile-an-hour limit. He joined the weekend traffic of cars not much different from his. Chauffeur moms on their way to ball games. Do-it-yourself dads hi-de-ho-ing to the hardware store.

No, it was not in his nature.

He thought of the girl. Carol Dodson. That was more in his line. He would've enjoyed going after her himself. What he'd told Reese was true: she was good. Smart and tough. To keep ahead of them this long. To keep her child away from them. To stay out of the system where they could have tracked her down in a city minute. Over these past few months, Winter had come to admire her. The way she thought, the way she acted. No hesitation, no sacrifice too hard. The way she looked was nice too. He'd seen her picture. The slim, tight figure. The round breasts, the round butt. The sharp, pert features of her face with that long mouth and those big, baby-blue eyes . . .

The Lexus reached the interstate. Winter slipped it down the ramp. Angled it into the southern flow of cars heading for the city, cars as nondescript as his. He tapped his steering wheel with an index finger, feeling a rhythm in him, the music of the moment.

They would have her in a day or two, he thought, all things being equal. With a priority go, it was pretty much certain. Even Mortimer and Hughes couldn't fuck up that badly. They would have her, and they would take her to the ED Factory. Probably have to interrogate her to find the kid. Maybe he could take over that part himself. Yeah, he thought. There was an idea. He couldn't be a desk jockey all the time. He would interrogate her himself and keep his hand in the game. Demonstrate to the troops how expertly things could be done. Set a standard of excellence.

He felt his penis shifting in his pants at the thought of it. He nodded at the windshield, nodded with the rhythm, nodded at the civilians driving past.

He thought of her salt tears on her soft cheek. His come mixing with her blood.

Now *that*, he thought – that would be in his nature. That would be completely in keeping with his personality.

Chapter Three

I'm Following You

1

There sat Lonnie Blake the next morning, Sunday morning. All alone by the telephone. Thinking about the girl.

The rain was gone now. The day was cold and clear. A strip of blue sky, of crystal air, showed above the lofts across the way. A haze of soft southern light poured in through the windows. It spread over the wooden chair and the wooden table. It spread over Lonnie Blake, who sat there looking down at the phone.

The phone, with its built-in fax and answering machine, was a big gray job. It was about the size of a briefcase. It took up most of the tabletop. Beside it on one side was an empty coffee mug. On the other side was the message pad. On the pad was the number Lonnie had jotted down the day before, the number the girl had called before she left. Lonnie had a pen in his hand. He doodled intricate designs around the number.

Damn fool, he kept telling himself. *What the hell you thinking about? She's just some crazy whore.*

But she didn't have a whore's eyes. Her eyes were smart and soft and frightened, not dead and mocking like a whore's. *You really saved my life*, she'd said to him. *My hero.* He remembered how hard and calm he'd been inside her. He remembered the scent of violets and smoke.

He had thought about her all day yesterday, all the lonely day. Boxing the bags at the gym in the morning. Walking the streets, haunting the record shops in the afternoon. Playing at Renaissance, drinking at the bar. Drinking alone in the loft until he could lie down. Awake through a lot of the night, he had thought about her. He had sipped his morning coffee gazing at her number.

Now his eyes moved to the phone itself. He made that noise of contempt, that sharp, quiet exhalation. He threw down the pen. *You're just being this way because she acted Suzanne, cause she pretended to be Suzanne, that's all.* But she wasn't Suzanne. And it wasn't Suzanne's hands he thought about. It was *her* hands rubbing his shoulders. It was *her* whisper at his ear. *So what was your day like, sweetheart?* Her long lips soft on his rough jaw. *Life goes on.* Her body under him, her breasts in his hands.

He reached out and snapped up the receiver. He punched in the number. He listened for the ring.

It rang once. A woman answered.

'Hello?'

Lonnie hesitated. He wasn't sure he had the right girl.

'Hello?' she said again.

'Yeah. Listen. This is Lonnie Blake.'

A pause. Then: 'Yeah?'

No. Not her. A stranger. 'Yeah, I'm looking for someone,' Lonnie said. 'The other night, Friday night – I was with someone. Someone came to my house.'

Another pause. It went on a long time. Lonnie thought

about hanging up. *What the hell're you doing?* he asked himself.

'What's your name again?' said the woman.

'Lonnie Blake.'

'Hold on.'

And then, almost at once, she was there. 'Lonnie?'

Lonnie found himself warming inside at the sound of her, smiling a little. 'Hey,' he said.

But her voice was fast and hard. 'How'd you get this number?'

'I just . . .'

'Did someone give it to you? Tell me how you got it, Lonnie? Come on. How'd you get it?'

'You used the phone. I pressed the redial button.'

Her breath. 'Aw shit. Aw man. Is anyone else there? Please don't lie to me, okay? Just don't. Just tell me: did anyone tell you to call me here?'

'No. Hell, no. I just been thinking about you.'

'Aw, man. Aw, man.'

'What is it? I just . . .'

'Don't think about me, Lonnie,' she said.

'I wanted to make sure you were okay.'

'Lonnie . . . Don't . . . Listen to me. Are you listening?'

'Yeah. Yeah, I'm listening.'

'Don't call me anymore. You hear me? Don't think about me, don't wonder if I'm okay. Don't call me. Did you write down the number?'

'Look, I was just . . .'

'Listen to me, goddamnit!' she hissed. Then more softly: 'Please! I mean it. Burn it, man. Oh, burn the fucking number. All right? Just hang up the phone and burn the fucking number. Please, Lonnie.'

'Look. The other night . . .'

'The other night was . . . Oh . . . !'

'Come on. I keep thinking about you. I don't even know

79

your name. Look, I can see you're in some kind of trouble, girl. I mean, you're alone and I'm alone here . . .'

'Lonnie . . .'

Lonnie held the phone to his ear, stared out the window. Thinking about her hands on his shoulders, her whisper in his ear, her body under him. 'I'll pay you,' he heard himself say suddenly. He hadn't meant to. He just did. 'I want to see you again. Listen, I mean it: I need to see you. I'm willing to pay.'

There was silence in answer. Her low breathing. Then she said, 'You're a good guy, Lonnie. Burn the number.'

And she hung up on him.

2

The elevator started down. Lonnie watched the numbers. His hands clenched and unclenched in his overcoat pockets. He had to get out, get some air, walk around. *Breeze that bitch,* he told himself. She'd hurt him. He thought: *Forget her.*

The number four light winked out, the number three light winked on. He found himself remembering how scared she'd been, how her eyes had brimmed with tears. *My hero,* she'd said. Maybe she'd been scared on the phone too. *Did anyone tell you to call me?*

The elevator stopped.

Aw, man! thought Lonnie Blake. Mattie Harris. She was always doing this.

The door on the other side of the cage opened. There, sure enough, stood Mattie Harris. She pretended she was surprised to see him.

'Oh! Hi, Lonnie!'

'Hey, Mattie,' Lonnie said. 'Howya doing?' His hands clenched and unclenched in his overcoat.

'I was just going out for some breakfast,' she said. 'Or brunch or whatever. I hate cooking for one, you know.' She was in her thirties. Pudgy, short. Pink-skinned, apple-cheeked. Long, straight, shiny brown hair. Shiny brown eyes. 'You feel like coming in? I wouldn't mind whipping something up for the two of us.'

'Wish I could,' said Lonnie. He managed to sound sincere. 'I gotta go . . . downtown to see this man.' *And I ain't got time to shake yo' hand*, he thought.

A frantic little something flashed at the bottom of Mattie's bright eyes. But she made a comical pout. 'Oh well. Then I guess I'm all by my lonesome. Off to the Sad Café.'

He slid back the cage for her. He had a glimpse of her loft for a moment. Art posters and wall hangings, stuffed animals and fluffy white rugs. A fluffy white cat prowling. Muffin or Mittens or some shit like that, he couldn't remember. Then the door shut. The elevator started down again.

Mattie stood by him, her head at the level of his shoulder. She was dolled up: lipstick, makeup, a perfume that smelled like lavender. She'd been waiting for him, waiting to hijack the elevator as he went by.

She chattered to him in her musical voice. Lonnie thought about the other voice, the hard, frightened voice on the telephone. *Burn the number*. He remembered the girl's face, regretful in the morning, saying goodbye, leaving her scent on his pillow.

'I don't know,' said Mattie Harris. 'I try not to let it make me crazy.'

Lonnie had no idea what the hell she was talking about. His hands clenched and unclenched. He thought of the girl. The blood was buzzing in his veins. *Breeze her, man*, he thought. *Forget her*. The elevator touched down.

Out on the street, he spoke to Mattie quickly. 'Which

way you walking?' The old city ploy. Whatever she said, he was going the other way.

Mattie Harris took it bravely. Nodded toward the east. Smiled a little. Wiggled her fingers at him. 'I'll see you.'

Lonnie nodded. He was sorry to hurt her feelings. 'Later,' he said. 'Okay?' He turned away from her.

The Sunday morning streets were hopping. Eighth Avenue was hopping. Parents with shopping bags, a mother alone, a father alone. Baby strollers pushing out of the brick-lined walkways of the projects. Slim couples, childless, not quite young, boy and girl, boy and boy, taking their newspapers to the cafés.

Lonnie headed downtown. His hands working in his overcoat pockets, his eyes at gaze, his mind elsewhere. He felt he should be thinking about Suzanne. He did think about her. He thought of her sweet face in the street all bloody. Dead because he was in the city playing. Because he wasn't there to help her. He thought about that. And then, somehow, a few blocks down, he was thinking about the whore with her hands on his shoulders. Thinking about the breath of her whisper at his ear. *Life goes on.*

The skyline leveled out before him. The buildings slanted down from the Chelsea lofts and projects to the Village brownstones and shops. The blue sky grew broader above, the air clear and cold. Lonnie stared absently at the storefront windows to his left. He thought of the frightened voice on the phone. *Don't call me anymore.*

There was an Interbean just ahead of him. He slowed his pace as he approached it. In some part of his mind, he knew, he had been planning to come here.

He pushed inside.

It was one of a chain of cafés. Cappuccino and computers. Half an hour on the internet for the price of a cup of coffee and a roll. Instructions and assistance free.

The place was made of stained wood and tile. To the

right was a long glass showcase of muffins and cakes. Coffee makers behind it that looked like Frankenstein's lab machinery. A magazine rack across from that, mostly computing stuff. Round brown tables dotted the tiled floors.

Against the left wall, there was a long brown counter with terminals ranged along it. Guys and girls worked the keyboards, watched the monitors. Their eyes reflected the white glare.

Lonnie moved to the food display. Up came a waiter, a young guy, California blond, smooth face, glittering teeth. *I want a part in a TV soap opera*, was all but written on his brow. He wore the regulation Interbean T-shirt: computer on a yellow background, a steaming cup of coffee on the screen.

'What can I get you?'

'Black coffee and a corn muffin,' Lonnie said. 'Can I ask you something?'

'Yup.' Yellow-hair moved along the counter, tipped sideways to pluck a muffin from the display.

Hands in his pockets, Lonnie followed him on the counter's other side. 'Say you went on one of these computers. Say you had a phone number, okay? Could you, like, look up a person's address working back from the phone number?'

The kid popped the muffin plate up on the countertop. Turned to the machines to fill a mug with coffee. 'Well, you could,' he said. 'But it would take you maybe – thirty . . . forty seconds.'

Lonnie let a slight smile lift one corner of his mouth. 'Ah, you're bragging now,' he murmured. 'You're bragging.'

3

Look, he thought, *I just want to talk to you.*
   Look, I need to talk to you.
   Listen. Just listen to me a minute, he thought. *I can't stop
thinking about you.*

He was walking again. Moving through the crisp autumn
air. His arch features were working with his thoughts. His dark
eyes were turned to the pavement, their focus far away. He
had crossed the city like this, his shoulders lifted against the
cold, his breath visible. His hands were still in his pockets. His
right hand was closed around the address he'd written down.

He had already crossed Lower 5th. Passed the polished
luxury towers where they ran down to the Washington Arch.
He had continued into the east, thinking about her. Thinking
about her, he had walked along the stalls of silver trinkets
and leather get-ups on St Mark's.

He was heading down 2nd now, by open groceries and
darkened restaurants. It was just edging toward lunchtime.

Look, he thought, *don't close the door. Just give me a second. All right? I just want to talk to you. Look, don't close the door.*

He clutched the address in his hand, the hand in his pocket.

I can't stop thinking about you. Know what I'm saying? Look ... Don't go closing the door, all right? I need to see you.

He turned the corner of 4th Street and there she was.

He wasn't prepared for it. He wasn't prepared for the impact of it.

She was way down the block, just coming off the stoop of her building. Her hair was different now. Short, curly, brown. She was wearing a reddish flannel trenchcoat, her legs in jeans, her feet in sneakers. For a second, he didn't recognize her at all.

Then he did — by her walk, by her profile even at that distance. He was not prepared for the painful yearning in him, for the way it hit him like a blow.

He wanted to see her face again as she whispered to him. He wanted to have that night with her to live over.

Look, don't run away, he thought. *Look, I just want to talk to you.*

But she was already hurrying away from him, hurrying for First Avenue. Her hair bouncing as she moved. Her figure receding swiftly.

Lonnie began to follow her.

I mean, look, if you're in some kind of trouble maybe I can help. Look, don't run away, he thought.

She was almost at the corner. Her head was turning back and forth. She was checking out the avenue, Lonnie realized. Looking for a threat, for a dangerous face. She was afraid, he thought. Afraid someone might be watching her, coming after her.

In a minute, she would turn around. Check her back. Take a good look behind her. And then she would see him.

Suddenly, Lonnie felt his stomach knot. He pulled up short. He felt a cold, sickly sweat begin on his forehead.

It had just occurred to him: someone *was* watching her, someone *was* coming after her.

He was.

Shit, he thought. *I'm turning into a stalker here.*

He raised his hand. He opened his mouth to call out to her. *Look, I just want to talk to you* . . .

But before he could say anything, she started running.

A bus was coming. He saw it cutting across the intersection, heading uptown. The girl hailed it as she ran but it was already slowing, pulling to the curb beyond the edge of the buildings.

And then, she was around the corner. Going after it. Gone. Out of sight.

Lonnie stood still another moment. Then he started walking again, more slowly now. *Let her go, let her go, God bless her.* He shook his head. He ought to feel relieved. Christ, what the hell did he think he was doing here anyway? Tracking the woman down like this. Following her like some stalking crazy man. Jesus. Jesus. He kept shaking his head.

He walked on, glancing up at her brownstone as he passed it. The punch of that first sight of her was still with him. The punch of yearning. He could feel the sore spot every time he breathed.

When he got to the corner, the bus was still in view. It had pulled to the curb two blocks away, taking on passengers. Then a groaning roar. A plume of black exhaust in the gray air. The bus pulled out into the traffic. Lonnie watched it, his shoulders slumped.

He turned around to hail a cab. There were plenty on the street, yellow blurs streaking uptown fast. Two went by him – the drivers pretended not to see him because he was black. The third one pulled over. Lonnie climbed heavily inside.

The driver was a small brown guy in a huge purple turban. He spoke over his shoulder. 'Where?'

Home, he thought. *Out of here. Breeze the bitch. That's the end of it.*

'See that bus up there?' he said.

'The bus?' said the turban. 'I see it, yes.'

'Just follow after it,' Lonnie said.

He sat back against the seat as the cab started off.

4

The bus stopped at 52nd. The girl dropped down out of the center doors. Three steps across the sidewalk and she was gone again, into a tavern.

Lonnie had the cab pull up on the far side of the street.

The day seemed colder here. The soaring apartment buildings lining the side streets seemed to squeeze the wind between them. The wind blew in off the river with a fresh bite, almost wintry.

Lonnie moved to stand beside a liquor store in lengthening shade. He watched the tavern across the street. Ed Whittaker's, it was called. The name was written in large script on its long window. The window was dark. Cars whisking past were reflected there on the pane. From where he was, Lonnie could only make out the shapes of the people sitting inside.

He stood there, unmoving, undecided. There was an evil taste in his mouth. He was sick about what he was doing. Going after her like this, watching her like this. How had this happened to him? Just thinking about it made him queasy.

Second after second, he stood there, trying to resist the urge to cross the street, trying to make up his mind to walk away.

But he didn't walk away. He stood where he was. He watched the restaurant a long time. He didn't even know what he was looking for, what he wanted. He only knew that the touch of her skin still haunted his fingers, that the rage had left him when he was with her and he'd been calm for long minutes in the dark between her legs.

He moved to the corner. He crossed the street. He approached the tavern.

As he came closer to the window, the glass became less opaque. He could see through. He turned his back on it, pretended he was waiting for someone on the sidewalk. In that way, he hovered there, just outside the restaurant, stealing glances into the place from time to time.

It was a steak house, he saw. Very fancy, very fashionable. Dark wood, white tablecloths. Black-and-white photos of the city on the wall.

There was a big crowd, a brunch crowd judging by the mimosa glasses, by the baskets of sweet rolls on the tables and the remnants of eggs benedict. There were four or five people standing on line near the front door, waiting for the *maitre d'* to find their names in her big book.

But the girl was already seated. She was at a table on the right, a little ways into the room. There was a man seated across from her.

Lonnie could see a bit of her face, but mostly she had her back to him. He could see the man clearly. The man was turned his way.

He was a thin, elegant, eccentric figure. White man with long black hair flowing over his shoulders, framing a narrow face. He had a white suit on. He was wearing an eyepatch over his left eye.

The girl was leaning toward him, gesturing at him, talking, her elbows on the white tablecloth. She hadn't even taken off her coat.

The man listened to her quietly. He had one hand by his face, the index finger resting against his cheek. The other hand was hidden under the table. There was a platter in front of him holding a bun, half eaten. He nodded once or twice as the girl talked.

Lonnie watched, hanging back from the window, pretending to wait for someone, only sometimes glancing through the glass. He had his hands in his pockets, his arms pressed tight to his side. He was trembling a little – with the cold and with the sickening sense of what he was doing. He saw the man with the eyepatch speak briefly. His arm moved – the arm under the table. It was a subtle motion, but Lonnie spotted it. The man was advancing his hand toward the girl.

Lonnie watched. His stomach clutched. He felt angry as the man's hand slid forward under the table. Well, what did he expect? he asked himself. She was a whore. This is what she did for a living.

When he looked again, Lonnie saw that she had also dropped her hand under the table. She seemed to be moving her hand toward his.

He wasn't sure whether their hands met or not. They were both hidden by the edge of the tablecloth. But a second later, he saw the girl sit back. He saw she was holding a white envelope. Quickly, she slipped the envelope into her purse.

Then she was standing up, pushing her chair back, backing away. Gesturing the whole time, talking the whole time. The man with the eyepatch watched her. He went on nodding quietly.

Lonnie saw her turn to leave. She would be coming out now, any minute. She would be looking around, checking the street.

Lonnie turned and walked away from the restaurant. He walked to the corner, keeping his back to the restaurant door. He couldn't let her see him. Following her, stalking her like this. He felt ashamed. He felt sick of himself. And he felt sick with desire.

He turned the corner. Leaned against the wall. Just beside the restaurant's dumpster, he pressed his back into the white wall and stayed there, taking deep heavy breaths, staring at nothing. There was sweat at his temples. He was nauseated. How had this happened to him? How had he found himself coming here, doing this?

Then there she was. She was walking past him. Right past him to the corner. She stopped at the light there, her back to him. She waited to cross the busy avenue.

Lonnie straightened. Looked at her, stared at her. She turned nervously and he saw her profile. He stared at her mouth, the mouth that had brushed his cheek, that had whispered in his ear. She bit her lips. Her eyes scanned the street, but he could tell she was distracted, thinking about something else. She would have spotted him – she would have spotted him before this – if she had not been so preoccupied.

The light changed. She stepped off the curb, away from him.

'Wait,' Lonnie called out.

Even over the noise of traffic, he heard her gasp. She spun round. She saw him. Her big blue eyes went wide.

'Look,' said Lonnie, stepping toward her. Holding up his hand. 'Look – don't run away.'

5

'Oh God. Oh God.' She stared at him. She shook her head. Her expression was a mixture of fear and helplessness and fury. 'What're you doing here? What're you doing?'

She backed away from him into the traffic. Her eyes were desperate and afraid. A horn dopplered as a car swerved to miss her.

'Hey, be careful,' Lonnie said to her. 'Listen . . .'

She stopped. She looked around her at the oncoming cars, realizing where she was. And then she came toward him. Running her fingers through her hair, clutching her hair. 'What're you . . . What're you, following me?'

He watched her approach, his hands in his pockets. 'I need to talk to you,' he said.

She stood under him, stared up at him. Her eyes were damp. 'Need . . . ? You don't even know me. And you were

93

watching me? Just now? Were you watching me just now in the restaurant?'

'I'm . . . sorry.'

'Were you?'

'I need to see you.'

'Oh God.' She let out a terrible laugh. 'Oh God, Lonnie. This is . . . God.'

She turned half away from him, turned back, desperate. Sunday pedestrians moved past them on the sidewalk. A silver-haired *grande dame* with her Lhasa Apso. A well-to-do dad with a bagload of bagels. They glanced at her as they went by. They glanced darkly at Lonnie.

She came closer to him. Her eyes were swimming. 'I mean, are you crazy? Jesus. Don't you listen to people? I told you . . . You saw me in the restaurant? Oh God.'

'I just . . .' But he had no answer. He could barely meet her stare. 'I just needed to talk to you,' he said again. 'I can't stop thinking about you. I had to see you again.'

She shook her head at him. Her blue eyes glistened. She stared at him with a kind of miserable wonder. 'I can't believe this.'

A young man walking past eyed them. The girl noticed this, noticed she was drawing attention. She moved off the avenue. Past Lonnie, to where the dumpster was.

He moved with her, into the teeth of the cold river wind. He tried to think of something he could say to her. He thought: *Fool, fool, fool.* How had he let this happen?

They stood together beside the wall. She came close to him. He looked down at her. She looked different – a gamine – with her short, curly hair. But the face was still the same. He remembered how her face had looked when she was under him. He felt the yearning for her again.

'Don't,' she said. 'Don't look at me like that. Okay? Jesus.

94

I can't believe this . . .' She reached up and touched his lapel. It was a gentle gesture, almost affectionate. '*Listen* to me. Okay? Please. It was pretend, Lonnie.'

Embarrassed, he averted his eyes. Looked off over her head, down between the dignified brick high-rises to where the river water glittered. 'I know that.'

'Whoever she is, I'm not her. I can't be her.'

'That's not what it's about.'

'Yes, it is. Yes, it is. And you have to understand. You have to get it, Lonnie. I need you to get it. You don't want to be in my life. I swear it to God. You don't want to be in my solar system.'

'Look, if you're in some kind of trouble . . .'

'*Jesus*!' The frustration flashed across her face. 'Jesus, Lonnie! Don't you listen?'

'I want to help you.'

'Well, I'm sorry. You play the saxophone. That's just not very helpful to me right now, okay?'

He drew his hand from his pocket. It seemed to move to her of its own accord. He reached out to touch her face. But she put her own hand in the way to block him and his palm touched hers. His fingers closed over hers. She looked up at him a long moment.

'I need you to get this,' she said. 'I need you to walk away. Look . . . It's like: I'm a damsel in distress. Okay? I'm a helpless damsel in distress here, Lonnie. And you gotta rescue me. And the only way you can rescue me is by leaving – me – alone.'

He smiled bitterly at this. The breeze brought her scent to him. The violets were still there beneath the smell of soap, the trace of cigarettes mingled with the chill weather. She gripped his hand in hers, gave it a single, urgent shake.

'Please,' she said. 'Please.'

And then she was gone.

He didn't watch her leaving. He looked at the river. He

felt her hand slip away. He sensed her, moving from him. Moving for the corner, moving out of his life.

Before he could stop himself, he swung around.

'She was my wife,' he said. 'She was murdered. They murdered her.'

'I'm sorry.' The girl swiveled to face him, but kept walking, backing toward the corner. 'I'm really sorry, man.' She raised her arms from her sides. 'I mean it.'

Then she turned her back to him and hurried on.

And suddenly, Lonnie was going after her. He didn't think. He hardly even knew what he was doing. He was suddenly just behind her as she reached the corner. Her shining hair was just beneath him, the scent of her just beyond him.

He didn't mean to grab her hard but he did. His hand clamped on her elbow.

She whipped round violently, but couldn't pull free. 'Get off me . . .'

'I don't have anyone,' said Lonnie as she struggled. 'They murdered her. I don't have *anyone*!'

'*Get off me you dumb black bastard*!' She wrenched her arm from his grasp. Backed away from him, running a trembling hand up through her hair. 'Christ, what does it take? You know? What does it fucking take?'

Then she hurried away from him, almost ran away from him across the street.

Lonnie stayed where he was, though people glanced at him, though other men stopped and peered balefully from him to the running white girl. He stayed where he was and he watched her go, breathless.

Slowly, his hands slipped back into his overcoat pockets.

6

One note and another, no matter how close, have an infinite distance between them, and that's where the blues happen. The same can be said of people, of one person and another. That's why the blues get played.

That night, Lonnie played the blues, sitting in his loft alone, sitting in the leather chair, pressing the tip of the hard rubber mouthpiece of the Selmer Mark VI into his tongue, speaking to it in a minutely subtle language of breath, milking the breath from the horn again as music with the slow pressure of his fingers on the stops, agonizingly precise. He played the same old songs, the songs he loved. He made them blue in the infinite distances.

I can't forget you . . . I can't let you go . . .

His wife, as it happens, had never known much about music. The best she could do was bang out a tune on the upright for the kids she taught at school.

The wheels on the bus go round and round . . . round and round . . . round and round . . .

Beat that thing, he would tease her whenever he heard her hammering away. *That's a bad thing. You beat that thing, baby.* Until Suzanne would lean forward over the keys, helpless with laughter.

They had lived in San Francisco. She had taught elementary school down on the peninsula. He was starting to do well, a local player with a good word on him. They had an apartment that looked out on trees and through the trees to a sliver of the bay. They had friends who talked about music and books. Dear hearts and gentle people. Teachers and musicians and grad students, black and white and yellow. Lonnie liked to see them gathered in his living room. He liked to sit and listen to them talking and laughing. And he would think about his other friends, his old friends from the neighborhood.

He liked to drive out to San Mateo, to the school where Suzanne taught. It was a good school, mostly middle-class kids, mostly white. Lonnie liked to drive Suzanne over sometimes and pick her up in the afternoon. He liked to show up early and watch her in her classroom through the window on the door. He liked to see the cleancut faces beaming up at her. He liked the way the children eagerly raised their hands. He liked to watch them and think about where he had come from and the schools he'd been in and the children he'd known.

His friends. His homeboys. His old friends.

His old friends had called him Pump-pump because he was good with a shotgun. Because he had once blasted his way out of an ambush of Nineties – a rival gang – and the shotgun had bucked in his hands, dull and thunderous. Pump-pump. *Boom-boom.* He had heard the Nineties screaming in the night beneath the sound. Afterwards, his old friends, his homeboys, had clasped hands with him and chanted, *Can't stop, won't stop.*

He was fourteen years old at the time. At fifteen, a gentleman by the name of Big Dick had placed a .38 against Lonnie's forehead and pulled the trigger. The gun had misfired and Lonnie, annoyed, had taken the weapon away and beat Big Dick into a coma with it.

So he'd had to run. From LA to Oakland. Where he lay low at his grandmother's place. Lay in her attic bedroom and blew on his horn and waited till the coast was clear and he could head south again.

Only problem was, lying there, playing, he realized something: he *never* wanted to go back there. He hated that place. He hated his life. His friends. His horsehead mother. He hated the thing he was turning into. He couldn't even play the neighborhood music anymore, the gangsta and the g-funk. He started digging up some of his grandmother's records. Actual records. Actual wax or vinyl or whatever the hell that old shit was. Louis Armstrong. Duke Ellington. Cannonball Adderly. The Jurassics . . .

And tonight, in the loft in Manhattan, he played those songs he'd come to love. He played them blue. Sitting alone with the lights out, slouching in his chair. Eking out cadences almost like speech, almost like crying, ghosting grace notes almost unheard and slurring others to a wail of high and mournful drama. His saxophone – which mostly tootled and blustered these days through studio gigs and sideman throwaways – seemed to stretch now in his fingers like a cat and waken.

Just to be with you again for an hour . . .

He hadn't played like this since the night they'd murdered her.

She had had a late meeting that night. He had had a gig. He was playing at the Loft, one of the city's best clubs. He could remember to this day how he was wailing through the breaks, how the crowd was rocking, how sweet it was.

Just to be with you again for a single day . . .

Suzanne had stopped at a mini-mall on the way home to buy milk for her morning coffee. Five white teenagers, drunk on beer, had surrounded her in the parking lot. He'd been playing at the Loft. They had circled around her. They had reached for her and grabbed and jived her. They had called her nigger and spun her from one merciless grin to another.

What wouldn't I give . . . What wouldn't I do . . .

He saw that scene in his mind every day. Their grinning white faces. He tasted her terror on his tongue like some kind of bitter wine.

She had broken away from them. She had run blindly into the street. The Cadillac that struck her down was going sixty. There was no chance for it to stop. Lonnie had been wailing at the Loft, tilted back with his sax upraised and wailing.

She had died lying there in the street in a spreading pool of her own blood.

Just to be with you again, my love . . .

He couldn't face his friends after that. Those dear hearts and gentle people, black and white and yellow. They all somehow seemed part of the life that had killed her. They became mixed up with the punks who'd chased her from the lot, as if those taunting white faces were now superimposed on theirs. He went back to LA for a while but he still hated the place. And the old connections from the neighborhood were alien to him, were gone.

He was alone. He had connections but no friends. Admirers but no companions. He went to St Louis for a few months. Chicago. New Orleans. He picked up sideman stuff, studio work, commercials. He couldn't play in the old way, couldn't lean back and wail.

And now he sat here. New York, New York. Eighteen months after Suzanne had died. He sat on the leather chair and blew into the sax and milked out music and made it blue. And he thought about the whore who had pretended for him. The music drifted up from him like smoke and images played through his mind like music. The songs were the old songs but the images were of the girl. He played the San Francisco weather he remembered but he smelled the violets and the smoke. He played his wife's smile as she turned to him in the kitchen and he saw the girl's face as she turned away from him on the street.

I need you to get this, she'd told him. *I need you to walk away*.

He couldn't walk away. He knew that as he sat there. He had to see her again. He had to. Tomorrow . . . tomorrow, he would find her. Somehow, tomorrow, he would convince her to talk to him.

But tonight he played the blues.

Chapter Four

Jack – You Dead

1

A comfortable car on a cold night on a lonely road. To John Harrigan, this was a little cup of bliss. The heat on low, the blue light of the dashboard glowing. The CD player just whispering a James Taylor ballad. This was Currier and Ives stuff to him, hot chocolate at Grandma's after a sleigh ride, chicken soup and *Leave It to Beaver* reruns during the flu season – the cozy safety of home. Outside you had your slightly spooky forest furtively ducking back beyond the edge of the headlights' glow. You had your slightly nippy air, your brooding woodland silence. But in here, inside the Maxima, this sleek blue sedan like a floating island in the sea of night ... Well, a shrink might've said it was womblike but that wouldn't do it justice. You don't get that Sony quality sound *in utero*. You don't get that humalong J.T. whisper. *That's why I'm here* ... To Harrigan, it was coziness personified.

He took this route home every night. He looked forward to this stretch of it especially, the last leg of the drive over the winding backwoods Westchester road. One hour from New York City, ten minutes from the interstate, but for Harry, the forest here was especially full of mystery and the car felt all the cozier because of that. Another ten minutes, and he would be in Armonk, at his house. Monica would be upstairs going over the boards of her next ad campaign. Their three children would be asleep in their beds. Harrigan would reheat whatever his wife had left for him, drink a beer with it and catch up on the sports pages. Read a brief until he dozed off. It would be fine, it would be restful. But it wouldn't have that special haven-like quality, that familiar homey comfort that he got here, in the woods, in his car, in his Maxima . . .

Or with Diana. He felt a measure of the same cozy warmth when he was with her.

He wasn't exactly happy about visiting a prostitute. He was still a good-looking guy, after all. Only forty-five, six feet tall, lanky, muscular. Boyishly handsome despite his salt and pepper hair. He was successful too. Head of the Legal Department for Skylight Developers. A fairly important Magee in behind-the-scene city politics. And he loved his wife. He adored his kids. Whenever he even considered the possibility that they might find out about his trysts with Diana, it made him physically ill. He tried to be strict with himself about it. He only allowed himself to see her once a month, usually when his wife was on the rag. Sometimes he went twice in December when Christmas made him yearn especially for that old feeling of home, but that was really all. Still, he wished he could give her up entirely. It wasn't something he was proud of.

But she did things with him. Fantasy stuff. Things he could never tell his wife about. Things he hadn't even told his therapist about the two or three times he went. In bed with her, with Diana, he was like a child playing games. And it brought him back to those good days, as if he were lying on the living room floor again doing jigsaws while his mother sewed and watched TV and waited for his father to come home.

He gazed through the windshield dreamily. The road wound toward him out of the dark. Patches of dense forest were lifted out of nothing by the headlights and then sank away. The CD player played and he thought of Diana. He thought of what they had done together this Friday night just past. He began to rehearse it again in his mind . . .

He was just getting to the part where she commanded him to put on the tutu when the red light of a police flasher splashed across his rear window. A siren whooped once and fell silent.

Harrigan pulled over to the side of the road.

He waited there, confused but clear of conscience. He'd been speeding a little, sure, but the last car that had actually traveled this road at the 25-mile-an-hour limit had probably been drawn by horses. No one was going to stop him for speeding here. He squinted into his rearview where the cruiser's headlights glared at him, where the red flasher whirled lazily.

A figure came strolling slowly out of the headlights' beam. Harrigan busied himself turning off the CD player, buzzing down the window. He wondered if maybe one of his brake lights was out or something.

The trooper came up beside the car. He leaned down to look in the window. He was a pale, pimply boy in a khaki highway patrol uniform. God, he looked young, Harrigan thought. When did they start hiring children?

The trooper smiled. Touched the bill of his cap. 'Could I ask you to step out of the car, please, sir?'

'Did I do something wrong, officer?' Harrigan asked. But he'd already loosed his seat belt, popped his door. He'd already started to climb out into the chill of the night.

Harrigan heard – he dimly registered – a harsh double rasp – a deadly sound. Everything inside him let go. His limbs, his muscles, his bladder – they all gave way together. He was distantly aware of the wheeling world as it seemed to fall upward into the sky.

Then he was sprawled stupid on the pavement, wedged between the door and the car. He was staring, open-mouthed, drooling. He was blinking, groaning, trying to say something – he had no idea what it was.

Red and black, red and black, the patrol car's spinning flasher passed over him.

He became vaguely conscious that a second figure was standing there. Standing above him, looking calmly down. The patrol car's headlights picked him out of the dark. Harrigan could see him as through a spinning haze.

It was a tall, thick man with a blocky face and skin like gravel. He was not in uniform. He was wearing a trenchcoat. He smiled down at Harrigan. A brief, pleasant, disinterested smile of greeting.

Then someone – the trooper – had Harrigan under the armpits.

'Uuuuh,' Harrigan said. He could feel the groan in his throat, but his brain could make nothing of it. He wanted to say something but he couldn't think what it was.

He was being dragged around to the back of the car now. He could see his shoes in front of him, heels moving along the pavement, toes swaying. He wished he could coordinate his arms to cover himself. He was embarrassed by his wet pants.

There was a sound. A *thunk*. The trunk was opening. Now the other man, the gravel-faced man, was at his feet. He had him by the ankles.

'Upsy,' said the gravel-faced man.

Harrigan felt himself go up in the air, felt himself go down again. He was inside the trunk of his own car. There was an instant when he saw the lid above him. There was something, something he had to say quickly.

Then the trunk lid closed over him. Darkness. The smell of his own urine.

Harrigan's mind was beginning to clear a little. He understood now what it was he wanted to say.

He wanted to say that this was the most terrifying thing that had ever happened to him in his entire life.

He heard the engine start. The Maxima began to move.

2

Mortimer was feeling anxious also. There was just too much pressure in this operation. Everything about it was so fancy, so high-tech. The state cruiser. The stun gun. The back-up cars. This was Winter's doing. Winter wanted everything to run like some kind of James Bond international military operation. But this is America, for Christ's sake, Mortimer thought. What the hell was wrong with a Chevy and a sap?

He drove Harrigan's Maxima around the bend. It wasn't far. There was a dirt turn-off just up ahead. He guided the Maxima onto it. The car's suspension was so good the body undulated smoothly over the path's ruts and gullies.

Good ride, Mortimer thought. *Maybe I should get myself one of these*.

He was trying to take his mind off his nerves.

He drove about half a mile into the woods. There, he came to a building site. An acre of ground had been cleared for a new house. The house's insulated frame was already standing amid scrub and piles of lumber. Mortimer brought the Maxima to a stop here. Killed the lights, then the engine. He popped the trunk with the handle under the seat. Opened the door and slid out from behind the wheel.

It was a crisp, cool November night. Mortimer took a good whiff of it as he walked around to the back of the car. Fresh air, he thought. The country. Made you grow big and strong. He could hardly wait to get the hell out of here.

He glanced once around the building site, around the silent circle of the woods. He shifted his big shoulders in his trenchcoat. Then, with one gloved finger, he lifted the Maxima's trunk lid the rest of the way.

He shone his flashlight down on the dazed Harrigan. Harrigan weakly held up his hands to fend off the beam. With his hands waving in front of him like that and his eyes staring and his mouth opening and closing silently, the head of the Legal Department of Skylight Developers looked to Mortimer for all the world like a newborn baby, like his new niece Carla when he leaned in over her crib.

The effects of the stun gun seemed to be wearing off. Which was good. The lawyer was clear-headed enough to be afraid.

Mortimer switched the flashlight off. Slipped it in his pocket. It was dark except for a sliver of moon but Harrigan's white eyes still seemed to glow.

Mortimer leaned his big, square head down toward the other man. He caught a mingled smell of piss and coppery fear. That was good too. He let a pleasant smile crease his pitted skin.

'All right, concentrate now, Mr Harrigan,' he said. 'This is very simple. You answer my questions or I hurt you. Yes?'

'Uuuuh,' said Harrigan. 'Who are . . . ?'

'On Friday night, you were with a prostitute,' Mortimer went on in his gruff, quiet, side-of-the-mouth voice.

'A pros . . . ?' Harrigan started to say.

But Mortimer reached into the trunk swiftly. Clutched him by the throat. 'Don't fuck with me, okay, I'm not in the mood!'

The lawyer gagged, his tongue showing. His eyes went wider still.

Shit, Mortimer thought. He let him go, withdrew his hand. Took a deep breath to calm himself. Nerves. That was no good. He couldn't let the pressure get to him. He knew he had screwed up. He knew he had let the girl get away from him. He knew that Winter was pissed off and he understood full well that this was not a good thing. But he had to stay cool, show this gink he was in control here. Take his time. Get it right.

He held up a single finger in warning. Controlled his voice. Spoke softly. 'Let's not make this unpleasant. Okay?' Harrigan nodded eagerly. 'Now you were with a prostitute at the Caldecott Hotel and I want to know her name.'

'Diana,' Harrigan cried out at once. His voice was trembling. 'Don't tell my wife,' he whispered. 'Please don't tell my wife.'

Mortimer nodded. This was better. This was going to be all right. He gave the man a friendly chuckle. Bonded with him a little bit. 'No, no, no,' he said amiably. 'This isn't about your wife, this isn't gonna be public in any way. Okay. So her name is Diana. Right? And you don't know her last name?'

'I swear to God. I swear . . .'

'No, no, hey, I believe you.' Mortimer heaved a sigh. Turned a little and propped his butt on the edge of the trunk. 'But what I need to know here is how you get in touch with her.'

Harrigan swallowed hard. 'Voice mail.'

'Voice mail.'

'I leave a message for her. Then she calls my beeper, sets up a time.'

'Sheesh. High security, huh.' That explained why her number wasn't in Harrigan's records, why her calls hadn't been on his wire. Hookers these days, Mortimer thought. With all the crackdowns and technology and whatnot. It was like dealing with Mata Hari half the time. But still, he thought, this was good. They were almost there. 'So you got a number?'

Harrigan rattled the number off instantly.

'And you leave a message for Diana.'

'She just has an ID code. Four six seven.'

'You wouldn't lie to me, right? Cause I know where you live. There's Monica and the three kids to think about here.'

'Oh God,' said Harrigan. 'Please. I swear.'

'No, no. I'm just saying.'

'It's the truth, so help me.'

'Good enough. I trust you.'

And he thought about it for a minute, perched on the trunk there, and it was good enough. It might take an hour or two, but they ought to be able to track her down with this. With any luck, they'd be at her place by midnight.

Mortimer nodded. 'Okay. That's it. Let's get you out of there.'

Mist coiled up from Harrigan's mouth as he let out a rasping breath. It sounded as if he'd been holding it all this time. Mortimer bent down and took him by the shoulder, helping him sit up in the trunk. Harrigan groped at him for support.

'You swear my wife won't find out,' the lawyer said.

'Absolutely,' said Mortimer.

With his free hand, he drew out a straight razor and sliced open Harrigan's throat. At the same time, he released the man and stepped backwards, neatly avoiding the first gout of blood.

There you go, he thought with satisfaction. *A razor, right?*

113

Silent but deadly. With some things, Winter, the old ways are still the best.

The attorney's body, still spewing blood, was still convulsing violently. Mortimer had to push the kicking legs aside before he could slam the trunk shut. There was thumping inside for a few more moments after that. Then it stopped.

3

Now a second car pulled up the drive. A black Grand Marquis, solemn and substantial. Mortimer shook his head. *Look at this*, he thought. *It's like a movie*. Pulling off his gloves, he moved toward the car.

A muscular giant in a sweatsuit got out of the passenger seat: Don Bland, his name was. Don Bland smiled briefly around his chewing gum as Mortimer approached him. Mortimer raised a wave as they passed each other. Then he slipped into the Marquis and took Don Bland's place beside the driver.

He shut the door. Looked out through the windshield. Big Don Bland was lowering himself behind the wheel of the Maxima. Mortimer shook his head again.

'Look at this,' he said aloud.

'What,' said the driver. The driver was Hughes, a bulky fellow with a jolly face and a rich brown beard. 'What'm I looking at?'

'This. All these cars. People getting in and out. I feel like I'm in a fucking gangster movie.'

Hughes laughed. 'Hey. You know Winter. This is a precision military operation we're running here.'

'I feel like Robert de Niro already.'

'You look a little like De Niro, I ever tell you that?'

'Oh yeah? You find me attractive?'

Hughes made a kissing noise in the dark. Mortimer snorted.

The Maxima was now leaving the scene, disappearing down the dirt path to the road. Car and body never to be seen again.

'All right. Let's go,' Mortimer said.

Hughes hit the gas, turned the wheel. The Marquis began a wide circle over the dirt, rumbling back to the path.

'So how'd we make out?' Hughes asked.

'Oh, man,' said Mortimer. 'This broad. More aggravation. I'm telling you. The vagina was a very good invention. The brain was a very good invention. But putting these two things together in one body – that's a mistake. It's like pistachio fudge ripple. It just doesn't work.'

The Marquis headed into the dark of the woods, the headlights picking out the rutted lane ahead. Hughes glanced at Mortimer.

'You're not telling me she got away?'

'If she got away, would I be here?'

'No shit.'

'If you think I'm calling Winter to tell him we staged a priority op and she got away . . .'

'Don't even talk about it.'

'I won't even think about it.'

'Don't even think about it. Jesus.'

The car bounced down into the street. The Maxima with the body of John Harrigan in the trunk was already out of sight.

Mortimer blew out a long stream of air. 'It's just we gotta run some checks, some phone stuff. She had a . . . you know, a security routine she used. Voice mail and shit.'

'Voice mail!' Hughes said, shaking his head. 'Why do you think they call it voice mail? I mean, what's "mail" about it?'

'I don't know. Could you keep your mind on what we're doing here, please?'

'I'm just wondering. What makes it mail?'

'I don't know. Maybe . . . I don't know.'

'Anyway, what's she got voice mail for?' said Hughes. 'What is she, like a CIA agent or something?'

Mortimer shrugged his heavy shoulders. 'She's a mother. She's protecting her kid. It's an instinct.'

'Instinct,' Hughes muttered into his beard. 'I'll give her some fucking instinct. I'm getting tired of this already.'

'It's like a bear or something.'

'I'll give her some fucking bear. I'll give her more fucking bear than she can bear.' Hughes burst out laughing. 'You hear me? More bear than she can bear.'

Mortimer nodded in the dark of the car. He didn't laugh. He wasn't in the mood for Hughes.

'How do you figure animals recognize each other?' Hughes asked. 'Their kids, I mean. How does a bear know it's her kid?'

'Who's gonna call Winter,' said Mortimer. 'You or me?'

Hughes groaned. 'Woof.'

'Never mind,' said Mortimer. 'It's no big thing. He'll run the check. We'll have her by midnight.'

'Great. So you call him,' said Hughes.

Mortimer had already reached into his trenchcoat. He drew out his mobile. Summoned Winter's number. He held the unit to his ear, gazing out the window. In the white glow of the headlights, the empty road twisted between the lowering autumn trees.

'It's nice up here,' said Mortimer as he waited for the phone to ring.

'Yeah,' said Hughes. 'I like driving on these roads at night. You know, when it's all dark outside and you're all warm inside the car. It feels like ... I don't know what. Like something.'

'Yeah,' murmured Mortimer, waiting, gazing. 'I don't know what either.'

4

All the monitors in Winter's Central Park West apartment were glowing. There were a lot of them – computers everywhere on glass tables and Formica pedestals – and every one of them was on. You could see the bright screens reflected on the picture window. They almost blotted out the view of the park fifteen stories below.

The room's other lights were off so the machines provided the only illumination. In their strange, alternating light, Winter's creased and handsome features looked to be carved out of some weird metal or stone. His flesh seemed to have no color. The flaming red of his hair seemed to have drained away. He barely looked animate.

He was sitting in a butterfly chair of leather and chrome. He was tapping the telephone handset against his fingernails. It made a soft noise: click, click, click, click.

Hughes and Mortimer, he was thinking. *Mortimer and Hughes.*

His eyes moved, his green eyes, reflecting the monitor

light. They moved from one screen to another. He saw the readout from the remote GPS that was tracking Hughes and Mortimer. It showed the Grand Marquis as a blinking set of coordinates moving steadily south toward the city. Another monitor flashed semi-encrypted messages from various Executive Decisions locations around the world. A third, worked by one of their researchers in Washington, was playing a slow roll of information on the passengers of European Airways flight 186, especially those whose bodies had not been found.

Now Winter's eyes flicked up to what he called the Billboard. This was a long, nearly flat pane of glass. It was hung on a wide wall over the dark fireplace. There was a mantelpiece on which lay several books – *The Seven Habits of Highly Effective People*, *The Great Game of Business*, *Swim with the Sharks without Being Eaten Alive* – and the Billboard was just above that, just where another man might have hung a picture of a church in a meadow or a pleasantly pastel abstract.

The Billboard was a plasma-gas display in which electrical charges lit colored crystals to produce a picture which was perfect in every detail. The PGD was hooked to a computer into which important documents from several Executive Decisions operations had been scanned. Right now, Winter had it keyed exclusively to the Dodson case. Articles, photographs and other materials appeared and disappeared on the display in leisurely rotation as Winter watched from his chair.

Headlines went by. AMERICA'S LOCKERBIE: ONE VICTIM'S STORY. MIRACLE AT HUNNICUT. HUNT FOR SURVIVORS CONTINUES. INVESTIGATORS LOOK FOR A CAUSE IN HUNNICUT CRASH. A Safety Board investigation report rolled up, vanished; a European Airlines passenger list did the same. All the while, simultaneously, snapshots, passport photos and newspaper art faded in on other portions of the screen, stayed for a few moments, then faded out again.

Winter watched – and, after a short time, there she was. It was the best picture of her, Winter thought. His favorite. A photograph of Carol Dodson standing behind the bar at the Anchor and Bell. Laughing, her body tilted to one side, one hand holding a bar towel, the other waving comically at the camera. You could see her from the thighs up. You could see the curve of her hips dipping up into her waist, flaring up to where her breasts rounded her T-shirt.

Winter gazed steadily at that picture. One corner of his mouth lifted in a smile as the computer light played over his face. He tapped the telephone against his fingernails. Click, click. *Mortimer and Hughes.*

They were good enough men really, he thought. Not his kind of men – old fashioned – not the kind he preferred to use, but good, solid, well trained. They would have her by the end of the evening, that was the important thing. The priority op had been an unnecessary annoyance, but it had paid off as Mortimer promised. They would have her by around midnight, assuming Reese's delay hadn't given her time to escape. The Helix VP's qualms about killing Harrigan's family had held them up only a day. Winter doubted whether even she, even Carol, was sharp enough, resourceful enough to take the plunge, to relocate that quickly.

He studied her picture, smiling. *Are you?* he thought. *Well, maybe, baby. I doubt it, but maybe you are.* In some part of him, he was almost rooting for her. She had been so smart, so tough, so determined. She'd stayed ahead of them so long. He'd be almost sorry to see it end.

A discreet little blip came from one of the machines. A terminal on a glass pedestal across the room. Winter's eyes shifted to it. The information he was waiting for flashed up on the screen. The security people had completed their check on Carol Dodson's voice mail service. While she had arranged a complex system for paying her bills through a post box, she had called in for her messages from home several times. The

121

researchers had run the calls down to her address on East 4th Street. The address was being relayed to Hughes and Mortimer right now.

When Winter turned back to the Billboard, her picture had faded, had blended into a photo of the sailor who'd fathered her child. And still, Winter went on thinking about her, about her face, about her big, vulnerable blue eyes and her long lips laughing.

She was beautiful, he thought, on top of everything else. He'd be sorry when she was gone.

But then it would be nice to get his hands on her for as long as it lasted. He'd really become kind of fond of her after all this time.

Chapter Five

Round Midnight

1

Lonnie had tried all day to stay away from her. He was no stalker. And no damn fool to go chasing after a woman who didn't want him.

He had a studio gig through most of the morning, playing back-up on a demo for some rich man's daughter. That kept him busy till after lunch. Then he went out to eat, went to the movies. Didn't come home until quarter to nine.

By half-past, he was sitting in his leather chair with the Duke on the stereo and a bourbon in his hand. Twenty minutes later, he was at the phone table, sipping another drink. Sometimes he stared out the window, sometimes he gazed at the numbers on the phone. Sometimes he doodled feverishly on the pad. He drew a picture of the girl, and a picture of the man she'd met in the restaurant, the man with the eyepatch and the long hair. His hand raced over the page. His body pulsed inside with a strange urgency.

'*Damn*!' he said finally. He angrily threw down the pen. He was on his feet, crossing the room. He grabbed his overcoat and headed out.

They had Monday jazz at the Velvet Village. He went down there. It was a new club but made up to look venerable. Posters of Miles and the Monk and Corea were slapped up haphazard on the wall, overlapping as if they'd been collecting up there for years. Likewise, the big semicircular bar in the back was made of scuffed, unpainted, cigarette-burned wood, though it had been installed barely four months ago. Up front, the small round tables had been specially selected to look cheap and worn, and each had an old fashioned teardrop candle holder on it.

Only the crowd looked fresh. All around the bar, all around the tables. Kids from the university mostly, some of them working hard at grunge, some of them pierced full of holes or bulging with implanted metal, but all of them young and sweet and dewy despite their best efforts. All of them watching the band with bright eyes. Bobbing and nodding and swaying to the music.

Lonnie stationed himself at the far curve of the bar. Wearing a light gray suit, an off-white collarless shirt buttoned to the top. Pressed up against the wall by the crowd, he nursed his third bourbon and seven, and then his fourth. He barely felt it. Inside, he was still pulsing with the same strange urgency.

He lifted and lowered his glass mechanically. His deep eyes were dark. The cat-like angles of his face were tense. A sheen of sweat made his brown skin bright and beads of sweat gathered at his temples and rolled down, leaving trails from his sideburns to his jaw. He had never felt anything like this urge before. It was a fever.

He tried to focus on the music. The band was modern. Mighty Men of Valor, a quartet. They weren't much, Lonnie thought. Too loud, too chaotic. Showing off their chops with speedball riffs. More ambition in it than soul.

126

He managed to listen for an hour or so, then he'd had enough. The band. The pulse inside him. He would finish this drink, he thought, and go home.

He lifted the glass to his lips and drank quickly.

He knew damn well he wasn't going home.

2

Just then, on 4th Street, the Grand Marquis was sliding into an open space at the curb. Mortimer glanced at the brownstone across the way. Nodded to himself. *This is it. Finally. This is where she lives.*

A fire hydrant blocked his door and he groaned as he unfolded his big body up through the narrow gap. Hughes also gave a grunt, squeezing his chubby frame out from behind the wheel.

There was traffic whisking by on the avenues that flanked the block, but the street itself was empty and silent. The two men paused for a moment to smooth themselves down. *Cool as cool*, thought Mortimer, *almost there.*

They crossed the street toward the brownstone side by side.

Frost formed in front of Hughes's lush beard. He spoke Mortimer's thought. 'Finally. Right? This ought to get us off Winter's shit list anyway.'

Mortimer made a noncommital noise. He didn't want to jinx it. 'I'm just glad he's letting us handle it alone,' he said.

'Yeah. Too many cooks.'

'I keep thinking he's gonna have reinforcements parachute in here any second.'

They stepped up onto the sidewalk.

'Why do you think your breath does that?' said Hughes. 'Why do you think it makes smoke like that?'

'Condensation,' said Mortimer. 'I don't know.'

They reached the brownstone stoop. Hughes danced up the steps first, his big form sprightly in his green pea jacket. As he moved to the door, he pulled a palm-sized rectangular black box from his coat pocket. Mortimer rose heavily just behind him.

'What's this now?' he said.

Hughes read the white words on the box's front. 'The Spymaster ESK-300.'

'The Spymaster.'

'Winter issued it to me.'

'Oh, he *issued* it to you.'

'Yeah. It's an electronic skeleton key. Works on anything.'

Mortimer shook his head.

They reached the front door, brown wood with a big pane of glass in the top half. Hughes fiddled with the black box, pressed a slide on the side of it.

'Boys with toys,' said Mortimer.

'I know. Winter loves this stuff. It's state of the art.'

'What now?'

'It's gotta heat up. It's got this special plastic, you melt it, then it goes in the keyhole and hardens, opens the door.'

Mortimer nodded. He drove his elbow through the door's glass pane. It was already cracked and a neat little wedge of glass fell from the corner and shattered on the floor inside.

'Hot yet?' Mortimer said. He reached through the hole, turned the knob and opened the door. 'Maybe you could stick that up your ass, open your brains with it.'

Hughes shrugged and put the ESK-300 back in his pocket. 'You're an enemy of progress,' he said. But Mortimer had already gone inside.

Hughes followed him.

3

The cool, cool, cool of the evening was a relief to Lonnie Blake. He could feel the sweat drying on his skin as he left the Velvet Village behind. It was good to get away from that throbbing music too, good to be out in the night city with its sounds of whispering traffic, thrumming tunnels, fizzing lights.

He walked along with his shoulders hunched, with his hands in his pockets. He was still telling himself that he was going to hail a cab.

But, of course, he didn't hail a cab. He wasn't even walking toward home. He was walking east, the other way. Across Lower 5th, past the Washington Arch.

Back toward 4th Street. Back toward her.

4

The brownstone's lobby was nearly dark. A single bulb on the high ceiling let down a gray pall. There was a linoleum floor tiled black and white, some of the tiles uprooted. There was a bicycle with one wheel missing chained by the super's door beneath the stairs.

Mortimer began to climb the stairs, lifting out of the gray light into the darkness above. Hughes hopped along behind him.

'Third floor, right?' he said.

'Three-E,' said Mortimer.

On the second floor, the lights were out. Someone's stereo played reggae softly. Aside from that, the place was quiet. They rounded the stairway's bend. They continued up.

The third floor was lighted. Here, they could see the chipped green walls, the somber, chipped black doors. They went down the hall to 3E. They stood at the door shoulder to shoulder.

They could hear noises coming from inside. Music; some kind of sprightly piano jazz. A woman's voice, sharp but soft, becoming audible as it rose to a hissing whisper, then falling away. There was a man too, moaning.

Mortimer lifted his chin at Hughes. Under his lush beard, Hughes's cheeks reddened with suppressed laughter.

'Working girl,' he chuckled softly.

Mortimer smiled tensely. Then he pointed at the door. 'Police lock,' he whispered.

Hughes held up a finger. 'Have no fear, Spymaster is here.'

Mortimer rolled his eyes. 'Spymaster.'

'It's all warmed up and everything.'

Mortimer watched, shaking his head, as Hughes pressed the box to the keyhole. Then Hughes touched a red button. There was hardly a sound, only a shuddering whisper as the softened polymer rod entered the slot. Air and increased heat made the rod expand to fit the tumblers. Then it cooled, hardened. The whole process took about forty-five seconds. Hughes went through it twice, on the police lock and then the latch.

'See this?' he whispered. 'Better living through technology.'

Mortimer tilted his head to the door listening. There was no change. The music, the voice, the groaning went on.

Hughes turned the device, and the door opened almost silently. Mortimer pursed his lips, grudgingly impressed. The two men went in.

They entered a broad living room. This was where the stereo was playing, but there was no one in sight. There were three doors leading off from it, one of them into a bathroom.

Mortimer and Hughes moved steadily and quietly. Mortimer scanned the place as he moved. It was shabby, but dolled up to hide the wear and tear. Gilt mirrors and museum posters hung on the fraying white walls. A half-finished drink sat on the cheap wooden cabinet beside the plush sofa. Magazines – *Playboy*, *Penthouse*, *Sports Illustrated* – lay fanned on the scarred coffee table.

Hughes moved to the bathroom. Scoped it. Shook his head. Empty.

Mortimer moved to another door on his left. It was open. He looked in. A bedroom. Dark, but clearly empty too.

Both men looked at the third door. It was standing ajar and light spilled out of it. The woman's voice, the groaning, were coming from there.

Mortimer raised his eyebrows at Hughes. Hughes nodded. He had unbuttoned his coat now and his hand went in under his armpit. It came out with a gun, a Cougar 9-millimeter modified for an integral suppressor. With its subsonic ammo, the thing hardly made a sound, just a sort of *phfft* like some kind of dart gun. Mortimer left his revolver in the holster at the small of his back. He put his hand in his pocket. His fingers curled around the straight razor.

The two men moved together to the other door. When they reached it, Mortimer shifted round so he could see through the opening.

The girl was in there.

Her back was to him. She was wearing the wig she'd worn the other night, the short black hair with the movie star cut. She was wearing a leather teddy. Her fishnet stockings showed off her legs but Mortimer thought they weren't very good: too much cellulite up near the ass. He could see she was holding a leather thong, smacking it against her palm. He could hear her hissing like a snake, hissing out a string of curses: 'You worm. You scum.'

'You're going to learn your lesson,' Mortimer heard her say.

He shifted again. He could see her john.

The guy was on the bed, naked. He had a hard-on. He

was held to the iron bedstead with leather handcuffs. He was facing the door and Mortimer could see he was gagged – he had one of those tubular contraptions stuck in his mouth.

Mortimer made a face. Incredible, the things people get up to.

He pushed the door open. He and Hughes stepped into the room.

The john saw them right away. His eyes went wide. His dick shriveled. He tried to sit up but was held back by the cuffs. He started kicking his legs and jutting his head and grunting. '*Ur*! *Ur*! *Ur*!' Trying to alert the girl. But of course, he couldn't talk. He had that crazy plastic thing in his mouth. And she thought it was part of the game. So she kept hissing at him. 'Worm. Scum.' And he kept saying, '*Ur*! *Ur*!' Bucking up and down on the bed, trying to tell her.

Well, it was pretty funny. What with the tension and everything, Hughes turned purple, trying not to laugh. Even Mortimer had to press his lips together.

They stepped up behind the girl. The man on the bed bucked and twisted in his bonds.

'*Ur*! *Ur*!' he said through his gag.

'You're going to get what's coming to you,' the girl snarled at him.

Hughes cracked up. He let fly a high-pitched giggle. Mortimer snorted with laughter.

The girl heard that all right. She came spinning around.

Hughes pointed his gun at her. She turned right into the muzzle of it. Gasped.

Mortimer stopped laughing. 'Shit!' he said. He felt a real rush of despair go through him. A premonition of disaster.

It was the wrong goddamned girl.

5

Around St Mark's Place, Lonnie considered turning back. The smell of trash on the midnight streets. A drunk who sat weeping on the sidewalk chin to chest. A weary sense of his own lonesome desire. He hesitated on the corner. What was he looking for? What did he hope to find?

Glaring balefully at the WALK sign across the street, he stood with his hands deep in his pockets. White wisps of his shallow breath drifted up from between his lips.

Then he was moving again. He made no conscious decision but he thought of her face, the girl's face, and he went on. Crossing the street. Turning toward 4th.

Well, hell, he thought, he was almost there anyway.

6

Mortimer, meanwhile, fighting panic, grabbed the hooker by the throat. 'Shut the fuck up,' he said.

The naked john handcuffed to the bed struggled and tried to scream through the tube. '*Ur! Ur! Ur!*'

Hughes stood over him. 'What is this thing in his mouth?' he asked.

Mortimer grit his teeth. 'It's a piss gag. Shoot him.'

'A piss gag?' said Hughes, and shot the john. *Pfft*, went the Cougar and the man's head spattered. Hughes pulled a grimace. 'A piss gag. Feh.'

The hooker made a terrified noise and Mortimer clutched her throat tighter, almost lifting her off the floor. He pointed a finger at her. 'Shut up, I told you. I told you, right?'

In his mounting fear of disaster, Mortimer hated this bitch. Ugly she was, nowhere near as pretty as the other. Her skin was all pitted and swarthy. She had a hooked nose and graying teeth. She was thirty-five at least, and looked fifty. He was furious at her. She gagged in his tightening grip.

'The other one,' he said through his teeth. 'Where is she?'

'Gone,' the hooker choked out. 'She's gone. She left this morning.'

'Left?' said Hughes beside them in a voice suddenly small.

'She took everything, packed everything.'

'She left?' said Hughes.

And Mortimer knew just how he felt. This was bad. He could feel how bad it was. It was very bad. It had been one thing to blow a tail – that happened to everyone. It was another thing to let an amateur spot you – it was an empty street, the girl was sharp. But to call for a priority op and then come up with nothing – to leave bodies behind and get nowhere – that stank of incompetence. That was the mark of a guy playing catch-up with his own mistakes. Winter wouldn't stand for that. He and Hughes had to come up with something here or they were forehead-deep in shit.

'Jesus,' groaned Hughes. He was clearly thinking along the same lines. He moved away from where the john's naked corpse lay crowned in a halo of blood and brains. He moved toward Mortimer and the hooker. 'Jesus. Can you believe this shit?'

'Shut up,' Mortimer told him. 'Where'd she go?' he asked the hooker.

'She left, like, town?' said Hughes.

'*Just shut up*! Go check the other room again.'

'Jesus,' said Hughes, shaking his head. He started for the door.

Now Mortimer and the hooker stared at each other, linked by Mortimer's arm, by the big hand squeezing the hooker's throat. His gravelly face was contorted in his fear and anger. Her eyes were wide and wet as she struggled to breathe.

Moisture flecked with mascara pooled in the bags beneath them. Mortimer tried to control the fear that made him hate every sleazy inch of her, that made him want to kill her right then and there.

'Where did she go?' he asked slowly.

He felt her shake her head in his grip. He felt her quickening pulse in his fingers. 'I don't know. I swear. She didn't tell me.'

Mortimer let her go. Then he punched her. She stumbled backwards, bumped into a lamp table. She and the lamp fell over. The light snapped out. The hooker sat sprawled, her face bloody. One of her high-heeled shoes had come off.

Mortimer moved to stand over her. She looked up at him – but now she was insolent. Her eyes narrowed. She sneered. Mortimer hated her.

'Where'd she go?' he said down at her.

'Fuck you,' said the hooker. 'You're gonna kill me anyway.'

Hughes came back in the room behind him. 'Gone,' he said. He was breathless now. 'No clothes. Nothing. The place is empty. She's left.'

The hooker smirked up at Mortimer. Mortimer drew out the straight razor. He flipped it open. When the hooker saw the blade, her smirk failed her. She swallowed.

'I'm gonna cut you,' said Mortimer.

She swallowed again. 'You can cut me all you want,' she said. 'I still won't know.'

'You'll know. You've gotta know. I'll fucking cut you till you do.'

'Fuck you,' she said again. Her voice was quivering now. 'You're gonna kill me anyway. Right?'

'Shut up.'

'Right? Fucking right? You're gonna kill me anyway?'

'I'm gonna hurt you, bitch.'

'Hey, you know what?' she said.

And she started screaming.

She had a loud, high, curdling shriek. Like a girl in a horror film. They could've heard her in the boroughs. She screamed and screamed.

Mortimer lunged down to grab her, but she started crawling away from him. She crawled under the lamp table, and knocked it over. It blocked his path. She went on screaming and screaming as she crawled across the floor.

'Jesus Christ, shut her up!' said Hughes.

'C'mere, goddamnit,' growled Mortimer, chasing her.

She crawled behind a chair, out of reach.

'For Christ's sake,' said Hughes.

The hooker went on screaming.

Enraged, Mortimer hurled the chair out of his way. The girl took a breath and screamed louder.

'Shut her . . .' said Hughes.

'You bitch!'

Mortimer went at her. She kicked him in the ankle with her other heel.

'Ow!' screamed Mortimer, stumbling, reeling to one side.

The hooker screamed and screamed. She was backed into the corner, sitting up against the wall. Mortimer spun to go after her again.

Then her body bucked. Her chest puffed open. Rich scarlet appeared above the neckline of the leather teddy. She slumped in the corner, staring, dead. It was very quiet after all that screaming.

Mortimer stared down at her. He didn't understand what had happened. Then he turned and stared at Hughes.

Hughes was still pointing the gun at her. He'd shot her, for Christ's sake. He'd shot the hooker dead. Mortimer hadn't even heard the *pfft* under all the noise.

'What did you do?' said Mortimer.

'What do you mean what did I do? I shot her. She was screaming.'

'We don't have anything now.'

Hughes raised his hands and shoulders at him. 'She didn't know anything. She was screaming.'

'Yeah, but . . .' Clutching the razor, Mortimer rubbed the heel of his thumb over his lips. 'Jesus.'

'The whole house could've heard her. The cops are probably on their way.'

'Jesus Christ,' said Mortimer.

'We gotta get out of here,' said Hughes.

'Yeah, I know but . . . what do we do?' said Mortimer. 'I mean, Christ, we lost her. The girl. She's gone. We lost her. I mean, Winter . . . I mean, what're we gonna do now?'

7

The noise of the city being what it is, the hooker's screams didn't carry much past the corner. Lonnie never heard them. They had already stopped by the time he came within sight of the brownstone.

Lonnie paused on the sidewalk beneath the stoop. He looked up at the door. He looked down the street toward the river. He stood with his hands in his pockets and shook his head.

What had he expected? To bump into her again? Here on the street, after midnight? Or maybe to get a glimpse of her through a window. Or maybe just to be in the air she breathed.

He made that habitual noise of his, that snort of contempt. It was self-contempt this time.

Either you are the dumbest-ass black man that ever lived, he thought, *or you are going home.*

He was going home. He had a full night of rage and

remorse and sexual obsession ahead of him. He wanted to get an early start.

He turned back toward 2nd. The brownstone door opened.

'You the cops?' said a man.

Lonnie glanced at him. A short fat guy bulging out of a sweatsuit. Balding, swarthy, maybe Jewish, maybe Italian. He held the brownstone door open, called down the stairs.

'About the girl screaming,' he said. 'Cause I'll tell you one thing, man: *I'm* not going up there.'

Lonnie's hands came out of his pocket. 'What floor?'

'The girls,' said the man. 'Up on three. God knows who they got up there half the time.'

Lonnie ran toward him. The man in the sweatsuit jumped back, holding the door wide. Lonnie ran over the threshold. Bounded up the stairs.

She's dead, he thought. He thought of the girl's pretty face staring up from the floor. *I let her chase me away and I wasn't there to help her and now she's dead.*

'Hey, be careful, there could still be people up there,' said the man behind him.

Lonnie wasn't careful. He didn't slow down. He took the stairs two at a time. In a moment, he was in the dark of the second floor. He could hear latches clicking. He could feel eyes peering out through chain locks at him. He didn't stop. He went up the next flight. His gut was twisting like a screw. *She's dead.*

Breathless, he reached the third floor landing.

8

Mortimer and Hughes watched him.

They had left the apartment moments ago. They were just settling into the front seat of the Grand Marquis. Hughes had not started the ignition yet, had not turned on the lights. Mortimer was slumped in the seat next to him, staring out the window like a crash test dummy. He was devastated at this turn of events. He was thinking about what he'd say to Winter. He was trying to imagine some kind of explanation scene that wouldn't end with him being dead.

I don't know what it is, he was thinking. *I must be in some kind of slump or something.*

He could already hear police sirens in the distance.

'I told you,' said Hughes. 'Here they come. We gotta go, go, go.'

That was when Lonnie showed up.

Mortimer gazed out at him dully. Lonnie was standing on

the sidewalk under the stoop. Just hanging around looking uncomfortable and suspicious.

'Who's this jo-jo?' Mortimer murmured, too depressed to really care.

Hughes turned on the engine, turned on the lights.

'No, wait a minute,' Mortimer said.

'Oh, good idea,' said Hughes. 'Wait a minute. Why? You think the police may need a hand?' He put the car into reverse.

Mortimer watched the black man hovering on the sidewalk in front of the stoop.

A john, he thought. *He must be a john*. His mind raced desperately. *Maybe he knows something*.

Some guy was looking out from the brownstone doorway now. The super, probably. For a moment, Mortimer wondered if he had spotted him and Hughes as they'd left the building. But no, they'd been watching. No one had had the guts even to peek into the hall. The super must've come out later, after he figured the coast was clear.

Now the super was talking to the black guy. And now – hold on here – now the black guy was running into the building like Superman to the rescue.

'Wait. This could be something,' said Mortimer, trying to convince himself.

The sirens were louder now, very loud. Hughes backed the Marquis up, spun the wheel. Put her into drive.

'No, I mean it, wait a minute,' Mortimer said.

'Wait shit,' said Hughes. 'I'm getting out of here.'

Mortimer opened the door.

'Hey!' said Hughes.

'You go ahead,' said Mortimer. 'I'll call you.'

9

Upstairs, Lonnie moved down the third floor hallway.
The door to 3E was not quite shut. He approached it
cautiously, his heart beating hard. Piano music filtered out
to him in the hall.

Harry Connick Jr, he thought vaguely. *Decent hands.*

He reached the door.

The music stopped. The hallway was quiet except for the
muted voice of a television pitchwoman coming through
the walls. Lonnie was half aware that someone was behind
him. Another apartment door had been pulled ajar, another
set of frightened eyes was peering out. He didn't turn
to look.

He pushed open the door to 3E.

The empty living room was before him. The lights on,
the green panels of the stereo glowing. The unfinished drink
on the cabinet. The magazines on the coffee table. Lonnie
saw the half-open doors across the room. There were more

lights on in the room to his right. He could see the edge of something in there. A bed probably.

He stepped into the apartment.

He edged forward slowly, his hands lifted in self-defense. He sensed the place was empty, but his eyes moved quickly, watching for an ambush. The floorboards creaked beneath his shoes. He headed for the lighted room, set all his concentration on the room.

He didn't hear the footsteps coming up the stairs behind him.

And he didn't see the corpses until he reached the doorway. There was a second, just before that, when he caught a whiff of something wicked. The smell of shit, the thick, metallic aroma of blood. A hot danger signal flashed through him. His step began to slow.

And then he spied the body on the bed. A dangling arm. The spray of red on the white wall.

'Oh man . . .' he said aloud. He thought of the girl's face, her damp eyes grateful. *Dead.*

He pushed into the room and he saw it all.

He saw the naked body ending in the bloody mess that had been its head. He turned and, as he was turning, he saw his murdered wife and then the girl whom he'd come to find – he imagined he saw them and then, having fully turned, he saw in fact the woman – a stranger – who was sitting there alone, her wig askew, her chin on her gory chest, her eyes staring at the single shoe still half on her foot.

He stood and stared at her until he understood what he was looking at, the carnage.

But by that time, the barrel of a pistol had been pressed into the back of his head.

10

Lonnie's heart gave a great painful thump. The breath flowed out of him like water.

A hard voice spoke in his ear. 'Fuck with me, jo-jo. Go ahead. I want you to fuck with me.'

Lonnie looked over at the dead man on the bed. He looked down at the dead woman in the corner. The dead woman stared at her feet.

Shit, Lonnie thought. He sighed. He put his hands up.

'I'm not fucking with you,' he said.

'Put 'em behind your head.'

Lonnie did. He couldn't believe this. How many kinds of idiot had he been? Well, all that was over. Suddenly, all his urges and pulses and obsessions were gone. The fever of his desire was gone. The haze and passion and compulsion of the last few days – it had vanished utterly. Suddenly the world was very clear to him. And what was clearest of all was the cold sting of the handcuffs snapping around one wrist and then, as his arms were forced down, the cold sting again as his wrists were cuffed together.

Typical, Lonnie said to himself. *You came to your senses just in time to have your stupid ass arrested.*

He was turned around.

And there they were, large as life and twice as ugly. Two uniformed New York City patrolmen. One was sandy-haired and the size of a small building. The other was black-haired and thick around and stupid-looking. Stupid had holstered his gun. But the sandy-haired building cat – oh, he liked his gun. He kept his gun way drawn and leveled and just about three inches from Lonnie's nose.

Lonnie stared down the barrel hard into the building's squinty eyes. He didn't like cops to begin with – and he was pissed off at himself for having sleepwalked into this shit. He was feeling just irritable enough to get himself into some *real* trouble.

'You have the right to remain silent,' the building said.

Lonnie snorted. 'How about the right to have that gun taken out of my face?'

'You're fucking with me, jo.'

'Yeah, you picked up on that, huh.'

The building looked like an unhappy building, like a building that was about to fall on Lonnie Blake. But before it had the chance, another man walked into the room.

Lonnie's eyes were locked with the building's and he wasn't going to break away first. When the building turned to look at the new guy, Lonnie looked too.

Lonnie looked – and he laughed once bitterly at his own incredible stupidity. He recognized the man at once. It was the five-oh who had been following the whore the night she'd come to his loft. It was the big block-headed gravel-faced cop who had been looking for her on the street.

The gravel-faced man went into his pocket, brought out

his wallet, flashed his shield. Yup, he was a cop all right. Lonnie had pegged him from the start.

'I'm Detective Mortimer,' the gravel-faced man said quietly. His flinty gaze was fastened on Lonnie. 'And who, pray tell, are you?'

Chapter Six

Birth of the Blues

1

Earlier that same day, Howard Roth had lost the battle to save Western Civilization. Vandals, Visigoths, and other assorted barbarians had poured across the landscape like ants at a picnic. It was the sack of Rome revisited, what Gibbon had called 'the triumph of barbarism and religion'. It was even worse than that – because the barbarism was represented by the hideous personage of Althea Feldman and the religion was that humorless amalgam of leftism and feminism which, being in retreat everywhere from the forces of goodwill, common sense and humanity, had taken up seemingly permanent residence in Morburne College, Vermont.

Still, Roth had fought the good fight. He was Horatius on the bridge. He had bearded the Feldman creature in her den – if you can beard a woman – if woman is what she was. He had stood before her desk jabbing two outstretched fingers at her with an unlit cigarette clamped between. The cigarette, of course, represented his defiance of the college's fascistic health edicts. Roth was in agreement with Milton's Satan in this: an excess of power must be opposed even when it's in the right.

'Every thought these students think,' he told her, 'everything *you* think – everything you say – the *language* you say it in – not to mention the freedom to say it: it all *comes* from places, Althea. It comes from England and France and Rome and Greece.'

'Oh yes,' she drawled in her nasal twang. 'Where the white Ur-males invented fire.'

'Yes!' Roth cried. 'That's right! Tough luck! If Homer hadn't lived you would never have even thought to say *that*. And if you don't teach these kids – teach them what made them who they are, every one of them – so they can like it, or lump it, or change it or hate it – then you're just indoctrinating them with your own . . . opinions.' *Imbecilic, half-baked, indefensible opinions*, he almost added. But he was not entirely without diplomacy.

Diplomacy or no, however, it didn't matter in the end. She sat there behind her desk, Althea, her pale froggy face flaccid, her dull eyes blinking soullessly through her enormous square glasses.

'I'm sorry but I just don't think Homer is really relevant to these kids, Howard,' she said. 'All these myths you love to tell them. All that glorification of war, the romance of rape. I'm sorry. I just don't think they're important to us anymore.'

This was when Roth, staring down at her with a kind of mute wonder, knew that his bid to reinstall Western Civilization as a breadth requirement course had failed. He had known it would fail all along, yet even so he could have wept for it. If Socrates had realized it would come to this – that the glory that was Greece would ultimately lead to this cultural black hole – this dead end – this . . . this . . . Althea Feldman . . .

Well, maybe Socrates had known. He had drunk hemlock, after all.

Storming from her office, Roth knew even then that his anger was a thin cover for bottomless despair. He couldn't even console himself with the idea that he would live to fight another day. Just now, that seemed unlikely in the extreme.

Dejected, he left the administration building and set out across the campus. Winter came early up here in the north. The trees around the grassy quad were already bare. The sky above the venerable brick castles and clapboard barracks was white and the air smelled of snow.

Roth put up his collar as he walked. His cigarette was bobbing clamped between his lips now. He brought out his lighter, held the flame to it.

The very first drag set off a rumbling cough. He plucked the cigarette out, held his fist to his mouth. Two students he recognized passed him on the path and he lifted his chin to them but went on coughing. A productive cough, that's what the doctor called it. Very productive. An artist, a Picasso of a cough. Yes, right now I'm in my Phlegm Period, Roth thought. He brought out a tissue and spat into it, glanced at the gob with resentment and fear.

It was in the phlegm that the doctor had found what he referred to as 'renegade cells'.

His cough subsiding, Roth reached the edge of the quad. He dashed his cigarette angrily to the sidewalk. Renegade cells, he thought. Saboteurs in the body politic. Communist cells, probably. Recognizable by their black berets and shifty looks. The X-ray had been inconclusive, but the CAT scan had turned up 'a troubling shadow'. Now they wanted to run some sort of tube down his throat and into his lungs and by that highly unpleasant means perform a biopsy to confirm what Roth in his heart of hearts already knew: he was fifty-seven years old. Fifty-eight would be a gift. Fifty-nine was pretty much out of the question.

What a waste, he thought irritably. *All of it. Everything. What a stupid, terrible waste.*

He moved along the sidewalk more slowly now, tired. Across the street was the town's main stretch. Quaint brick shops and clapboard restaurants, the old stone Ethan Allen hotel. Roth looked at none of it, staring into the middle distance, abstracted. The absent-minded professor. Well, he had always been that. He'd heard that when people are dying the details of the world become very clear and sharp and beautiful to them. So far, he hadn't noticed it to speak of. He was as distant and fuzzy-headed as always, just a lot more depressed at the same time. But then he had managed to put the biopsy off for two days, delaying the inevitable certainty. Maybe the side benefits of mortality would come later, when the test results were finally in.

He went on, a rumpled, shambling figure, bent and small. His face was gaunt, his eyes baggy, his nose beaked. His head was bald but for a fringe of flyaway silver hair. Once he had considered himself a rather elegant figure: a waspish intellectual, a slightly haughty citizen of the world of ideas. Now when he looked in the mirror, he saw an old Jewish man – a figure he secretly despised.

He left the campus and town center behind him. He pressed on up Maple Street. This was a tree-lined lane of increasingly modest houses pressed shoulder to shoulder on small lawns. His own house was down a few blocks, a dreary two-story looking sad and neglected under the white sky and naked branches.

Roth neared it, wheezing quietly. Thinking: what a waste. The entire enterprise. Everything he had ever loved was now rejected by the world. Everything he had hoped to pass on had melted into air.

156

All these myths you love to tell them. I just don't think they're important to us anymore.

He climbed the porch stairs slowly. Clutching the banister, breathing hard. *Look at me. Christ. I barely made it.* He shuffled across the porch to the rocker.

He plonked himself into the chair and started it going. *Out of the cradle, endlessly rocking . . .* He looked over the railing at the comforting old view of lawns and houses much like his. He wondered if he should call either of his ex-wives or his two children, tell them the news. His daughter was a born-again Christian and might have to at least pretend to care. But she hadn't spoken to him in three years. And his son was in rehab with troubles of his own. And his ex-wives were – well, they were ex-wives. It was too depressing to think about.

He spent a few more minutes in this reverie – then he began to notice the soft, musical chatter coming from Geena MacAlary's yard next door.

He glanced over there. A child was sitting on the pale winter grass. Yes, he vaguely remembered Geena had said something about a cousin coming to visit. Something about the child's mother being ill.

The girl must have been four or five, he figured. Blond-haired but dark-skinned as if one of her parents were black or half-black. She was bundled up against the cold, wearing a hooded pink jacket and some kind of thickly padded red pants. Holding a tea party it looked like, winter be damned. Sitting before a small half-circle of dolls and stuffed animals. Babbling some little lecture to them, the frost puffing out before her.

Roth somehow found the sight of the child extremely moving. Here on the porch with thoughts of death so near – with death itself so near. *Out of the cradle, endlessly rocking . . .* He watched the girl, entranced, touched by every gesture of her small gloved hands, fascinated by the piping timbre of her voice.

'Now, Barbie, drink all your milk because it's very, very good for you.'

Roth felt a lump in his throat. His lips pressed together and he frowned. The child passed a paper cup to Barbie, and then another one to the other one next to her, the red furry one from TV, what was his name? He couldn't remember.

Then all at once, the girl looked up and caught him staring at her. He smiled at her. She studied him a long moment with big, solemn brown eyes.

Ah God! thought Roth. *None of it ever mattered but the love, and I squandered it all.*

'Hello,' the little girl said to him. 'My name is Amanda.'

2

'Well, hello!' said Roth. He had to clear the renegade phlegm from his throat to get just the right happy, hearty man-to-child tone. 'It's nice to meet you, Amanda. My name is Howard.'

The girl said nothing. She continued her solemn study of him. He found the steady, childish gaze a little unnerving.

So he cleared his throat again and said, 'It's kind of cold for a picnic, isn't it?'

But the girl merely took hold of her stuffed animal and cradled it close to her. She spoke with infinite gravity. 'This is Elmo.'

Oh, Clarence, let me live again! I want to live again! Roth cried in his heart. The kid was incredibly cute. In fact, looking at her from this vantage point in the great stage show of life – the hook round his neck, one foot on the banana peel – it seemed suddenly crystal clear to him that he had gotten everything, all his priorities, wrong. He should've dedicated all the energies of his existence to the loving care of just such an adorable little person as this. Her trivial tempers, moods, illnesses and crises should have been all in all to him, more to him, yea, than Western Civilization itself. Fatherhood – family – love – that had been the ticket all along!

Of course he knew that if he'd been cured of his cancer tomorrow he would have reverted instantly to the insensitive, argumentative, self-obsessed fellow he by nature was. But how marvelous that a simple CAT scan had suddenly rendered an entirely different set of values clearly superior to his own. He almost felt he loved the child seated there on the grass before him.

Well, it had been an emotional couple of days.

'Hello, Elmo,' he said hoarsely. 'How are you?'

'He's fine,' said Amanda.

She sniffled a little. Her tan cheeks were flushed. She squinched herself together in her makeshift snowsuit. She *was* cold, obviously. Geena MacAlary had been a nurse for a while and had raised two children of her own. Roth figured she knew what she was doing. Still he said, 'Are you sure you shouldn't go inside?'

'We have to have tea out here,' piped the girl, 'so Mommy will see us when she comes.'

'Ah,' said Roth – in his sensitized state even he understood the deep poignancy of this remark. 'Where is your mommy, then?'

'Far away in a dark place,' said Amanda mysteriously. 'She has to come all the way up to get here so she can take me with her. That's why she's gone for such a long time. And she can't ever look back or they'll take her down to the dark place again.'

All during his brief exchange with the child, Roth had gone on rocking gently in his old wooden porch chair. But now he stopped, shifted his chair toward her, leaned forward in it with a small grunt of interest.

'Really. She can't look back?' he said. 'Why not? Why can't she?'

The child answered in the same chanting, lecturing tone with which she'd spoken to her dolls. 'Because you're not allowed to see the dark place,' she said.

Roth nodded slowly, hovering there in the rocker. It wasn't really in his nature to involve himself very deeply in the concerns or opinions of a child – or of anyone else for that matter. But she had touched an intellectual chord in him. With his chair tilted forward, he rested his elbows on his knees, his hands clasped between his legs. The child hugged Elmo to her, but watched him with those big, serious brown eyes.

'You know,' he said, 'I know a story like that. About a man who wasn't supposed to look back.' And then – uncharacteristically – the child's feelings occurred to him and he added, 'But it's a sad story – it's not about your mother.'

'How does it go?' said the child at once.

'It really is sad. Are you sure you want to hear it?'

'Ye-es,' drawled the child.

Roth sat back in the chair and set it rocking again. He gathered his thoughts for a moment, conscious all the while of her grave gaze on him.

And then he told her the story of Orpheus and Eurydice.

He spoke in an increasingly weak, increasingly rough voice. He had to fight down the cough that threatened to go back into production from time to time. He simplified for her as he went along. Edited out the really wicked parts.

But he told her about Orpheus, son of a muse and Apollo; a musician so great that when he played his lyre, the animals of the woods came to listen, and the trees bowed down and even the rocks sighed. Orpheus married a forest nymph named Eurydice and he loved her passionately. But one day, Eurydice was attacked by evil men who wanted her for their own. She ran for her life, terrified – so terrified that she didn't watch her step. Her heel came down on a poisonous snake. It bit her, and she was carried off by Hades to his everlasting country of the dead.

'I know Hades,' Amanda broke in solemnly. 'He's blue.'

Roth acceded to this with the best grace he could muster and went on.

Orpheus was so sad – he loved Eurydice so much – that he decided to do something no one had ever done before: he decided to go living into the land of the dead and bring her back with him. Now the only way into the dark country was across the great River Styx and the only way across the river was in the boat piloted by a black-cowled, empty-eyed figure named Charon. Charon would not take living passengers – they had to pay him in a coin only given to the dead. But Orpheus played his lyre for him, and the music was so beautiful that Charon let him come aboard and they sailed across the river.

But then, on the far side, at the very gates of Death, a dog named Cerberus stood guard. He was a giant dog with three heads, each head with a mouth full of fangs, each mouth frothing and growling. Again, Orpheus played his lyre, and each of Cerberus's heads slowly sank down to rest neck-over-neck on the creature's folded paws as he listened. And Orpheus passed on.

At last, he came to the throne of Hades himself. And Orpheus played his lyre. And the music so moved even the King of Death that Hades agreed to let Eurydice go – on one condition. Orpheus must lead her home along the cliffs of Hell – and *he could not look back* at her until they had reached the land of the living.

'Because he wasn't supposed to see her when she was dead,' said Amanda, nodding.

Roth paused. He considered her remark. He had always wondered about this part of the story: where had Hades come up with this *fakakta* condition of his. Don't look back. What sense did it make? He still wasn't sure. But somehow, what the child said rang true to him. He was moved by that. He smiled at her as he went on:

Orpheus began to ascend toward the sunlight, holding Eurydice by the hand as she followed behind. But as he came closer and closer to the top, Orpheus began to wonder if maybe Hades had tricked him, if maybe it was really a monster who kept its hand in his, who was only waiting for the right moment to drag him back to Hell. With every step he became more and more convinced the monster was about to attack him, to destroy him.

Finally, he couldn't stand the suspense any longer. Just as he was about to break out into the living light of day, Orpheus looked back.

There was Eurydice. He saw her for one moment – all her beauty, all he loved – one moment only. He had broken his agreement with Hades. And in the next instant, Eurydice vanished before his anguished eyes and she was carried back to the country of the dead forever.

In all the days, all the years after that, Orpheus was so sad that the music he played on his lyre was heartbreaking. The creatures of the forest listened and groaned in misery, the trees withered at the sound and even the stones shed tears. Even after he was dead, Orpheus's body went on singing with such wondrous and terrible grief that the poets took up his song. And they've been singing it ever since to all the world.

'And that,' said Roth, rocking, smiling, looking up and out beyond the porch, through the naked branches of the trees and into the white sky, 'that was the birth of the blues.'

When he lowered his eyes again, the child was just sitting there, holding her Elmo doll and staring up at him with those grave brown eyes. For a moment, Roth was worried. Was the story too sad for her, too harsh? He'd bowdlerized it as much as he felt he could. He'd left out the part about Orpheus being torn to pieces and so on. But still – what did he know about children these days? – maybe he'd said something horrible, something that would damage her little psyche for life.

Then Amanda tilted up her flushed cheeks and murmured in a voice that seemed hushed with awe, 'That's a *good* story!'

That voice, that hush, that awe – Roth's feeling for the child rose up in him, overwhelmed him. He pressed his lips together. He nodded. His eyes swam with tears.

Oh, children, he wailed inwardly, *children are God's answer to History*.

'Do you know any more stories like that?' she asked him.

Roth lifted a knuckle to the corner of his eye.

'All of them, kid,' he said gruffly. 'I know them all.'

Chapter Seven

Hit the Road, Jack

1

It was 4 a.m. Tuesday morning when Detective Mortimer came into the interrogation room. It was a cramped gray room crowded with a single long metal table and two uncomfortable plastic chairs. There was a heavy door that had one of those one-way mirrors in it. For the last hour or so, Lonnie had been waiting in here alone.

Mortimer had questioned Lonnie at the murder scene and one of the patrolmen had questioned him there too. Then they'd brought him here to the precinct house on 5th Street and a detective named Grimaldi had questioned him and a guy from the DA's office. Then they'd left him alone in here and then it had gotten to be four in the morning.

And all this time, Lonnie had been going over and over in his head how he'd helped this whore on the street one fine evening and wound up sleeping with her and thinking about her and following her around and finally found himself in a room full of corpses, being questioned by the police. Of course, he hadn't told the police any of this because . . . well, because fuck them. He was sure in his heart that the girl hadn't killed anyone and if the cops wanted help finding her they could get it somewhere else. Which meant now he was lying to protect her. Which didn't strike him as such a smart idea either. So he went over and over that in his head too.

And so just about now – about four o'clock Tuesday morning – Lonnie was tired and angry and more than a little confused and generally ready to breakfast on someone's heart.

And that's when Mortimer came in. His gravelly face twisted into an immensely unappealing smirk.

'Hey, Lonnie. You remember me from our last episode, right?' he said. 'I'm Detective Mortimer.'

'Yeah, I remember you,' Lonnie said wearily. 'The ugly one. Say, are you people gonna charge me here or can I go home to bed?'

Detective Mortimer laughed a bogus cop-like laugh. He turned the free plastic chair around backwards and straddled it. He winked at Lonnie. It was the kind of wink you wanted to wash off. Then he looked Lonnie straight in the eye and spoke to him man-to-slimy-piece-of-Negro-criminal-garbage.

'Let me ask you something, Lonnie,' he said. 'If you were me, would you believe your story?'

'Let me ask you something,' Lonnie said. 'How come I'm *Lonnie* and you're *Detective* Mortimer?'

'Well, because I'm a police officer and you're a lying scumbag,' Mortimer explained. 'Does that clear it up for you?'

'Oh man! Listen to that shit. You know, I don't think you like me.'

'Breaks your heart, doesn't it?'

'In twain, baby. And you know what? I want a lawyer.'

168

'I want a Mercedes. Life is full of disappointments, what can I say.'

Lonnie laughed once and shook his head. 'You folks never change, do you?'

Mortimer sat back in his turned-around chair a little. 'That's right,' he said. 'You know all about us folks. Don't you, Pump-pump?'

Lonnie couldn't help himself. Hearing his old gangster nickname took him by surprise and the surprise showed. He looked at Mortimer sharply.

Mortimer grinned. 'That was your banger handle, wasn't it? I mean, you were a stone blue gangster, weren't you . . . *baby*?'

I was a stone fifteen-year-old child with a horse-sloppy mother, Lonnie thought. *And three years later, I had a music scholarship to UC, so fuck you.*

'Is that what I was?' he said aloud. 'Well, I guess you know.'

'Hey. Hey. You know what I know, Lonnie?' Mortimer had shown off his hard ass, now he'd play conciliatory. 'I know I got me a runaway hooker, all right? I got two people dead in her apartment. And I got you in her apartment with the two dead people. Now to these old eyes, that means you're either some kind of suspect or some kind of witness. If you're a suspect, no sweat, just let me know so I can start beating a confession out of you. But I don't think you are a suspect. I think you're a witness – and I think you can help me find that girl.'

Lonnie threw up one hand. 'I already told you, man. I ran up there because the super said there was some girls screaming. Ask him!'

'I did ask him. And I believe you, Lonnie. And I also believe you came there in the first place because you wanted to see Carol Dodson.'

Lonnie shook his head. 'I told you that too. I met her

once. In a bar, Renaissance, where I was working. She gave me her address and said we should party. I didn't know she was a professional. I didn't even know that was her name.'

'Yeah. Now here,' Mortimer said. 'Here's where we get to the lying scumbag part.' Once again, the big block of a head pressed forward. The sharp widow's peak pointed straight at Lonnie and the rough skin dimpled as his mouth twisted in a smirk. It wasn't a pretty sight. 'Because I was after Carol Dodson on a vice rap Friday night,' the cop went on. 'I was chasing her down the street and, lo and behold, she disappeared. She vanished right from in front of me, Lonnie. Right on the street where you live. On the very block where you live.'

This time, Lonnie managed to show the man nothing. The look he gave him was slow and empty. He still remembered the fine art of looking at a cop that way. All the same, he felt the pulse of blood going crazy in him. This was the first time Mortimer had mentioned that night. Lonnie hoped he hadn't made the connection. But if he had, why had he waited so long to spring it on him?

'Now I think she came to you, Lonnie,' Mortimer went on. 'I think she ran away from me and came to your home for help and you let her in. And that tells me you were more than just a casual acquaintance in a bar, Lonnie. That tells me you knew her. You knew her well enough to risk getting in trouble with the police.'

Lonnie had a strong impulse to say, *No. No, I didn't know her, she just came*. But he kept his mouth shut.

The big cop shook his big head at him. Laughed. 'Man oh man, she really got her hooks into you, didn't she? Christ, what the fuck she do for you? Something special? There something special she did just the way you like it, Lonnie?'

Lonnie felt the truth rise in his eyes – *she pretended to be my dead wife* – but his gaze stayed steady.

'It sure must've been something,' Mortimer went on. 'I

mean, some Susan B. lies down for you and suddenly you're lying to protect a murder suspect? You're lying to protect some five-and-dime whore who left town without bothering to clean up the two corpses in her fucking apartment? Come on. You're too smart for that. I mean, you're opening yourself to a charge of accessory here, Lonnie. That's a piss-poor career move, I want to tell you. So if there's something you have to say to me, you had better say it now and you had better say it fast.'

Lonnie didn't answer. He kept his gaze locked on Mortimer's. He kept his face blank and his deep eyes empty. But in fact, he couldn't help thinking about it.

Maybe the cop was right. Maybe he was getting himself into all sorts of shit over a lying hooker he didn't even know. Maybe she *was* a murderer. And maybe he was still lost in some kind of crazy dream or something where this whore had become all tangled up in his mind with his wife. And when he thought about his wife and how sweet she was and how straight-up and how there was a kind of peace and goodness inside her; and when he thought about this scared, frantic, fucked-up call girl . . . well, maybe he just ought to tell this cop everything he knew and get the hell out of here.

Mortimer must have sensed his indecision. He leaned in further, his small eyes bright. 'I'll take a hint, Lonnie,' he said, and Lonnie thought there was almost a tone of desperation to it. And Mortimer said: 'Something. Anything. Cause you're going down here otherwise, my friend, I'm telling you. Just give me one thing that'll help me find the girl and you are out of here and on your way home, I swear it.'

Lonnie's lips parted. Suddenly he was thinking about the man with long hair and an eyepatch whom the girl – Carol Dodson – met at Ed Whittaker's. A man like that, a description like that, the cops could probably find him. Hell, they probably already had a file on him. That would

171

do it. He could tell them about that. Fucking five-ohs could hunt down their crazy bitch and he could go on home and forget about it. Everything good, what's the problem?

Mortimer studied him and he studied Mortimer a long time. A long time.

Then Lonnie said, 'I just got one question.'

'Yeah. Go ahead,' said Mortimer eagerly.

'Does your mama know what you do for a living?'

Mortimer sat back in his chair and laughed. It sounded real this time. A genuine laugh. His eyes seemed almost to sparkle with the laughter.

'All right, Lonnie. Get out of here. Go on home,' he said.

Lonnie stared at him. 'Say what?'

'You heard me. Go on. We'll talk again later.'

For a moment, Lonnie was too dumbfounded to move. He just sat there. He just stared.

And Mortimer laughed again. And Mortimer waved at him. And Mortimer said, 'Go on. Go home. Get out of here. You be a free man.'

2

'El Penis,' Mortimer muttered as the Grand Marquis glided across town.

From behind the steering wheel, Hughes glanced over at him. 'El Penis? What is that? Is that some kind of cop talk? What?'

Mortimer's jaw worked as he gazed out through the windshield, as he watched the streetlights paling under the mellow blue of the pre-dawn city. 'LPNS,' he said. 'Lying Piece of Nigger Shit.'

'El Penis!' Hughes laughed: 'I get it. El Penis. That's pretty good.'

Mortimer didn't answer. His jaw worked.

'So you're pretty sure he knows something, huh?' said Hughes.

'Oh yeah,' Mortimer growled. 'He knows something. He almost spit it out right there but he got clever on me at the last second.'

'Well, it's better this way. At his place.'

Mortimer nodded grimly.

'I hope it's something good,' said Hughes. 'I told Winter we just about had her. I told him we were one step away. He's not too happy about the whole thing.'

Mortimer gave a bitter harrumph. His stomach felt like a lava pit. He didn't need to be reminded of Winter. The guy was never far from his thoughts as it was.

The Marquis stopped now just at 6th, idling under a red light as the thickening morning traffic passed before them left to right. Steam poured up through a manhole into the chilly sunrise.

'Where do you figure that steam comes from?' Hughes said quietly. 'How come it's always coming up out of the street like that?'

Mortimer looked around at him slowly. 'Fuck is it with you? Why can't you keep your fucking mind on things?'

'I'm just wondering. It relaxes me to think of something else.'

'Well, stop relaxing. What the fuck are you relaxing about? If we don't have that bitch in hand by lunchtime, let me tell you something: we are well and truly fucked. We are two men fucked beyond all reasonable expectation of becoming unfucked. So stop relaxing.'

Hughes shrugged. The light gleamed green. The car started rolling again.

'"It relaxes me,"' Mortimer muttered. 'Christ.'

After a moment, Hughes said mildly: 'At least you're NYPD.'

Mortimer grunted.

'No, I'm serious. What if you weren't a cop? What if they'd taken this Lonnie Blake guy in and we had *no* way to get to him? Then where would we be?'

'I thought I'd never get him out of there as it was,' Mortimer allowed. 'Grimaldi had nothing on him, but he just wouldn't let go. *I got an instinct about this guy. I got an instinct.* He wouldn't shut up about it. Instinct shit.'

'Guess he'll be pretty pissed off when they find Blake's body. He'll say, *I told you I had an instinct.*'

Hughes's cheeks flushed with pleasure when Mortimer actually laughed a little at that. 'Yeah, well,' Mortimer said. 'Better him pissed off than Winter.'

'See?' said Hughes. 'So it's not so bad. You gotta look at the sunny side sometimes. All we do, we go to this Blake guy's house, we find out where the girl went, we kill him, we're on our way again.'

'Your mouth to God's ears.'

'Amen, brother. About time things started going right for us in this stupid op.'

They parked around the corner from Lonnie Blake's apartment and walked the rest of the way there. Mortimer, gigantic in his trenchcoat, glanced down at the short, chubby, bearded Hughes in his green pea jacket. Lo and behold, Hughes had his little black box out. The Spymaster. He was pushing the slide on it, heating it up.

'This again,' said Mortimer.

'What,' said Hughes. 'It's a miracle machine. It opens anything.'

'Climb up the fire escape, we go right in the window.'

'Yeah, yeah, yeah. You can't always live in the fucking past. Y'know?'

In the event, they opted for the wonders of modernity. Hughes held the electronic skeleton key to the outer door and shot the heated polymer through the keyhole. They were in the lobby in under a minute. In under another minute, they had the elevator working and were heading up to Lonnie's place. They stood shoulder to shoulder, watching the vator's lights. The L went out. Number two was broken. Number three went on. And then they were on the fourth floor.

Once again, they waited while the Spymaster ESK-300 worked its magic.

'You do have a warrant, right?' said Hughes.

Mortimer snorted. 'Stop fucking around.'

Hughes, red with mirth, turned the key. Mortimer pressed the lobby button so the vator would go down again. Both men stepped out into the loft.

They were pretty sure the place was empty. They had followed Lonnie to a coffee shop, waited to make sure he would stay to eat. All the same, Hughes pulled out his silenced Cougar 9 and walked cautiously through the rooms.

Mortimer, meanwhile, wandered into the john and took a leak. There was a can of Old Spice shaving cream sitting beside the sink. He considered this thoughtfully as he pissed. After a while, he picked the can up and slipped it into his trenchcoat pocket. He smirked to himself.

They met up again in the main room. By that time, Mortimer was standing at the windows, next to the telephone table. Hughes entered, slipping the Cougar back into its holster.

'Nobody home,' he said. 'You see him?'

Mortimer peered through the fire escape, scanned the street. 'Not yet.'

'We got time,' said Hughes. He settled his big bulk into the leather sofa. Snatched a magazine from a lampstand nearby. He leafed through the magazine.

At the window, Mortimer glanced down. He noticed the pad on the telephone table.

'Wait a minute,' he said.

He picked up the pad.

'Jesus,' he said. 'Look at this.'

Hughes lifted his eyes.

Mortimer wagged the pad gently in the air. He smiled broadly for the first time that day.

'Paydirt,' he said.

3

Sitting at the window counter of Designer Java, Lonnie was working on his second styro of Kenyan blend. He held the cup to his lips without drinking. A corn muffin sat on the little plate in front of him, less eaten than worried to powder and crumbs.

The day was not yet bright. The window still reflected him. He gazed out through the reflection at the avenue stirring in the cold, clear dawn.

He was tired to the sinew. He was angry to the core. He didn't like being a fool, and he didn't like cops pushing him around and he wished the fuck he knew why they'd let him go and whether this girl, this Carol Dodson, had been worth covering for, and why this cop, this Mortimer cat, had looked so desperate at him, and why he waited so long to mention the night the girl had first come to him and why the whole thing just felt all sorts of *wrong* to him somehow.

He held the cup to his lips and thought about it. He

watched the city waking up beyond the window. The rumbling traffic rose like a river as the morning rose. The men in suits appeared on the sidewalks and the working women passed with their purposeful strides. It might have been a city on television for all it touched him, for all he cared about it or the people in it. A city of strangers. The capital of a world of strangers. All of them running around fucking each other and killing each other, lying to each other and hating each other and dying in each other's arms. What had he helped the girl in the first place for anyway? He had no truck with her. He had no truck with any of them. They could all go to hell for all he cared. This *was* their hell, this city. This world of lonesome cities. They made it hell.

The day grew brighter. His reflection grew dim on the pane. He looked through the image of himself at the rising traffic, at the people passing. The day grew brighter still. His reflection faded. Finally, he vanished before his own eyes. There was only the city beyond.

He knocked back his styro, drained the coffee grounds. He stood. He headed out. He headed home.

4

'Euphonium,' said Hughes, meanwhile.

He was still sitting on the leather sofa. He was leafing through the magazine again. The magazine was called *Wind Instrument*.

'Who the hell ever heard of a euphonium?' he said.

Mortimer was at the window, looking down through the fire escape at the street below.

'Here he comes,' he said.

'I mean, what kind of word is that?'

'He's at the building. Let's go.'

'You ask me, it's a fucking tuba.' Hughes laid the magazine aside, shaking his head. 'I don't know,' he said with a sigh.

He lumbered to his feet, drew out the Cougar. He checked the slide port as he wandered over to the elevator door.

'Euphonium,' he muttered. 'Ya ya ya.'

Mortimer lumbered slowly around to the far side of the

elevator door. Hughes stood on the other side so that Lonnie would walk out between them.

They could hear the elevator door open in the lobby below. They heard a *chunk* and then a hum as the machine started up toward them.

Mortimer lifted his chin at Hughes. Hughes sighed again and nodded, raising the gun beside his face.

They waited for Lonnie Blake.

5

Lonnie was exhausted. By the time he reached his block, he was barely lifting his shoes. The early pedestrians went buzzing by him at Manhattan's walking pace and he slogged along, weary, until he reached his building. He leaned heavily against the door as he unlocked it. He nearly fell inside as the door swung in.

The elevator was waiting for him. He stepped inside, turned the key in the notch for four. He propped himself against the wall and closed his eyes as the box began to ascend.

Why had they let him go? he wondered. Why had the police just let him walk free like that?

But he was too tired to think about it anymore. He was sick of thinking about it. He was sick of the whole thing. He listened to the soothing hum of the machine.

The elevator stopped. Lonnie opened his eyes. He pulled back the cage. He fumbled for his key.

But then the outer door swung open as if on its own. Startled, Lonnie looked up.

Jesus Christ, he thought, *it's not even seven o'clock.*

All the same, there she was: Mattie Harris, his downstairs neighbor. She had hijacked him again as he passed her floor.

'Hi, Lonnie,' she said brightly. 'I was hoping it might be you.'

She was wearing a blue silk bathrobe. It was soft on her pudgy form. It was open up top to show the line of her generous cleavage and the frilled edge of her bra. And though she was dressed as if she'd just awoken, her hair was in place. It was brushed to a shine. And even from where he stood, Lonnie caught the whiff of lavender.

'Mattie?' he said. It was all he could think of.

She smiled at him, a wincing, apologetic smile. 'Sor-ree. I need a favor.'

Lonnie gaped at her stupidly. He had a sense he'd been doing that for some time. 'Now?' he said finally.

'It's just: one of the lights in my bathroom ceiling's gone out?' Her voice rose as if this were a question. 'I'm not tall enough to reach it and I can't see to put my makeup on. You know, I was afraid I'd go to work looking like one of those crazy ladies with the painted-on mouths? I didn't hear you come in last night so when I heard the elevator, I thought . . .'

Lonnie gaped at her stupidly some more. 'You want me to change a light bulb.'

Mattie blushed. 'Sorry. Helpless Female Alert.' She made a Helpless Female gesture.

After a while – a long while – Lonnie blinked. Then he lifted his chin. Then he sighed.

'Okay,' he said.

He stepped out of the elevator.

6

'She wants him to change a light bulb,' said Hughes. He had his ear pressed to the elevator door.

'Oh, for fuck's sake,' said Mortimer. 'It's 6:30 in the fucking morning here.'

Hughes shrugged. 'She's doing the helpless female thing. Sounds like she likes him.'

'Great. That's just great. That's just what we need. Now he'll probably fuck her.'

'Just hold on,' said Hughes. 'Let's see what happens.'

'If he fucks her, we're going down there. I mean it. We're killing them both. That's it. I've had it up to here. Jesus. What do they think this is?'

'Just take it easy.'

'Nothing is going right on this op. I swear it to God.'

7

Lonnie followed Mattie's trailing scent across one end of her loft. He was aware – dimly aware – of the place around him. The density of its plant life and decorations. The warm, homey fuzz that seemed to grow on the furniture and the rugs and the walls. As he turned a corner, the tendrils of a spider plant brushed against his face. He felt a distinct urge to rip the thing down and stomp its hanging ceramic pot to splinters.

'So,' Mattie said. 'You look like you've had a long night.' She managed to make it sound casual.

He managed not to strangle her. 'Yeah,' he said. 'I have.'

'I guess you're living the wild musician's life, huh.'

'I guess that must be it . . . shit!'

Mattie's snowball of a cat had raced out in front of him. He nearly tripped over it.

'Careful, Muffin,' Mattie sang out.

'Yeah,' said Lonnie through his teeth. 'Careful, Muffin.' *Before I mount your fucking head on a stick.*

They reached the bathroom door. Mattie stood aside and pointed the way.

'I tried, I just couldn't get to it,' she said. 'I guess I gotta get a new stepladder.'

With another long sigh, Lonnie looked in. The bathroom's main light – a dangling bulb with a pink shade around it – was fine, was on, was gleaming merrily off the porcelain of the sink, off the makeup cases on the counter, off the toothbrush mug with the cartoon character Cathy on it. But there was a stepladder in the middle of the floor, right by the sink. And, raising his eyes, Lonnie saw another light, recessed into the high ceiling far, far above. And that light – he had to admit it – had well and truly blown.

Lonnie shook his head. Damn thing had probably been out for ages, he thought. She'd probably been saving it so she could pull this stuff, get him in here. Spying on him like some kind of suspicious wife 'cause he'd been out all night. Shit, what the hell did it take to get rid of this woman?

Suddenly – and against his will – he thought of Carol Dodson tearing her arm out of his grip. Backing away from him on First Avenue.

What does it take? You know? I mean, what does it fucking take?

He sighed yet again. 'All right,' he said aloud. He thumped sullenly up the stepladder.

It was a reach, even for him. He had to stretch his arms all the way up, his head tilted back painfully. He unscrewed the recessed light cover – the metal rim, the round glass plate beneath. He slipped them into his overcoat pocket to free his hands to unscrew the bulb.

'Awright, gimme the fresh light,' he said, reaching down to her.

'I'm really sorry about this, Lonnie,' Mattie said pitiably. She stretched up to hand the new bulb to him.

Yeah, yeah, yeah, he thought. He was putting the new light in now.

'I could make it up to you,' she said. 'I could make you breakfast if you want?'

He glanced down at her. Her broad face turned up to him, hopeful. *Yeah, well*, he thought after a moment. *I guess I know the name of that tune.*

'I can't, Mattie,' he told her more or less gently. 'I'm beat. I mean it. Another time. Okay?' He put the glass plate over the light, started to twist in the metal seal. 'Just as soon as I finish with this—' and with each word, he twisted the seal sharply – 'I. Am. Going. Straight. Home.'

8

'All right, hang onto your shorts,' said Hughes. 'He's coming.'

'He better be fucking coming.'

Hughes listened at the elevator door. 'She says thank you. Is he sure he doesn't want to stay for some coffee?'

'If he stays for coffee, we kill them both,' said Mortimer.

'Hey, be a human being here. She's a nice girl. She likes him.'

'Yeah, if we don't get the Dodson slash soon . . .'

'I know, I know. Hold on.'

Mortimer fell silent. Hughes listened. He heard the rattle of the elevator cage opening downstairs.

'Here we go,' said Hughes.

'About fucking time,' said Mortimer.

9

The elevator door closed between Lonnie and Mattie Harris's wistful, still-hopeful face. *City of strangers*, he thought. He leaned against the wall. Now on top of everything else, he felt vaguely guilty. Maybe he should've stayed for the damned coffee too.

The elevator began to rise. The light on four – his light – came on. The elevator stopped. Lonnie slid the cage back. He turned his key in the door, pushed it open. He stepped out into his loft.

The gun barrel jammed hard into his temple.

'Talk and you die, blink and you die, breathe and you fucking die,' hissed a voice in his ear.

Then – like a nightmare – Detective Mortimer's enormous gravelly face swam before him, bright with malice. He saw it for an instant only. Then he was grabbed. Muscled to the floor. In his shock, he had no strength to resist.

He went down hard. His back slammed into the wood. The breath went out of him.

Mortimer was on top of him, sitting on his chest, knees pinning his arms. One big hand clutched his throat. The square, rough face bore down, its grin bore down.

Lonnie gagged as the cop throttled him. His eyes rolled back. He saw another man, a fat, bearded man standing above him. Laughing down at him, loosely waving a gun at his face.

'Now we're going to take up where we left off,' Mortimer said. His hot breath washed over Lonnie's face.

'What the fuck . . . ?' Lonnie choked out.

'Ssh,' said Mortimer. 'Ssh.' He squeezed his throat tighter until Lonnie could only let out a soft wheeze. 'You gonna be a tough guy, Pump-pump? What do you think? You a tough guy?' He glanced up at the fat man, grinning. 'Pump-pump used to be a tough guy,' he said. 'Used to be a gangsta. Used to be a stone blue G.'

The fat man's cheeks turned a jolly shade of red beneath his beard. 'Hit him,' he said, laughing. 'Hit him in the euphonium.'

Mortimer sat back on top of Lonnie. His grip on Lonnie's throat eased a little.

'Get the fuck off me,' Lonnie said hoarsely. Rage and fear were flowing through him like liquid fire.

Mortimer did not get off him. With his free hand, the big cop drew a cannister out of his trenchcoat pocket. Lonnie stared at it, frightened. But it was just shaving cream. His own red cannister of Old Spice.

'Let me clarify this situation for you, Pump-pump,' Mortimer said. 'The policeman is not your friend.'

He sprayed the cream into Lonnie's face. Lonnie grunted, struggling under the grip on his throat. The white lather sputtered down onto him.

Mortimer tossed the can aside. As Lonnie twisted, writhed,

gasped, the cop jammed a rough hand down on him, smeared the cream all over his mouth and jaw.

Lonnie spit out the sour foam. Through blurred eyes, he saw Mortimer pull something from inside his coat. A flip of the wrist, and the blade gleamed. A straight razor.

'You been up all night, jo-jo,' Mortimer said. 'You need a shave.'

Lonnie stared at the razor, breathing hard. The terror and the rage were a single thing inside him now. He felt the fire of them fill him. He felt they would punch through him in his helplessness, erupt like a volcano.

Mortimer forced Lonnie's head to one side. Above them, the fat man laughed a snuffling laugh. Mortimer set the razor to Lonnie's throat, just at the jaw line. Lonnie felt the cold of the steel. He stopped struggling, afraid to move.

The cop's eyes shone blackly in his pitted face. 'If you lie,' he said, 'I'll know.'

He started to shave him. The blade scraped over Lonnie's stubble. Lonnie couldn't speak for the fire of feeling in him. He grunted as he felt the sharp edge sting his skin.

'Tell me about the girl,' said Mortimer in his ear. 'Tell me about the girl and Freddy Chubb.'

'What?' Lonnie gasped.

He felt the blade press down hard against him.

'Uh-oh,' said Mortimer. 'That's not the right answer.'

'That's not the right answer, Lonnie,' said the fat man, laughing.

'No, no,' Lonnie said quickly. His mind seized at the possibility that this might all be a mistake. 'So help me. So help me. I don't know any Chubb.'

'The closer you shave,' Mortimer whispered hoarsely, 'the more you need Noxema.' The blade started moving again, scraping away the lather smeared over Lonnie's face. 'Oh, you are going to need a shitload of Noxema, Lonnie.'

'I don't know any Chubb! I'm telling you. Christ!'

'You drew a picture of him, Pump-pump. Huh? On the pad by the phone. Remember? You drew a picture of the man with the long hair and the eyepatch. You telling me that's not Freddy Chubb? You gonna try and tell me that, Lonnie?'

It was a moment before Lonnie could grasp what Mortimer was saying. Then he remembered. Sitting by the phone. Doodling on the pad. Drawing a picture of the man in the restaurant. The man who had passed the girl the envelope. Freddy Chubb.

'Oh,' said Mortimer – a long hot breath over Lonnie's face. 'You'll tell. I'm gonna peel your face off strip by strip. I'm gonna skin you like an apple, Pump-pump. You'll tell.'

Lonnie lay pinned to the floor, the razor digging into him. The terrible fiery pressure of fury and fear kept building inside.

'Let it all come out, Pump-pump,' Mortimer said. 'Save yourself a world of pain.'

Lonnie would have killed him if he'd had the chance. Instead, he said, 'Cut me.' A single tear of rage fell from his eye. 'Cut me and go fuck yourself.'

Mortimer cut him. He dug the blade in and with a long, slow sweep ripped an inch-long strip of flesh off Lonnie's jawline. Lonnie's roar of pain was choked off by the hand clamping hard on his throat. The pain rose through every pore of his face like molten sweat. He convulsed in the big cop's grip, his stomach churning with terror and rage and the pain now too, his eyes burning with tears.

Mortimer grinned, breathing harshly. He casually wiped the skin and blood off the razor onto Lonnie's forehead. For another moment, he considered the man trembling underneath him.

'I can see this is gonna be a long conversation,' he said then.

He stood up.

The cop's weight lifted off him. Lonnie groaned, coughing bile. He rolled over onto his side, curling his knees up to his chest. He lay there trembling. Through blurred eyes he saw his own blood running onto the floorboards.

Mortimer paced over him, nodding. Snorting through his nostrils like a bull. Too much adrenalin, too much release. He had to work it off, cool down.

Hughes was excited too, was nodding too. 'So see?' he said. 'Chubb? This is good, right? Winter'll like this. We can bring him this, right?'

Mortimer nodded some more in answer. His eyes were bright and dreamy. He settled down, came to rest. Stood so that Lonnie lay – curled up and trembling – at his feet.

'Pick him up,' said Mortimer. 'We'll do the rest in the can. I can work better in there. We can gag him and everything.'

Hughes nodded. He shifted his gunhand to hold the Cougar secure against his ribs. He bent down, reached out, grabbed a handful of Lonnie's overcoat.

'Come on, tuba-boy, on your feet,' he said.

But this was the thing: when Lonnie Blake had changed Mattie Harris's light bulb, he had stashed the various pieces of the fixture in his overcoat pocket. Then, when he was done, he had taken the pieces out again and put them all back in the ceiling.

All except for the dead light bulb. There was no reason to put that back.

It was still in his pocket.

That is, it *had* been in his pocket. When he rolled over onto his side, he had felt the shape of it in there. He had just managed to avoid rolling on top of it and crushing it to bits. Instead, while Mortimer was pacing around over him, while Hughes was yammering in his excitement, Lonnie had quietly removed the dead light bulb from his overcoat.

Now it was in his hand.

So anyway, Hughes leaned down, grabbed Lonnie's coat and tried to haul him to his feet.

And Lonnie jammed the light bulb into Hughes's right eye.

The bulb imploded with a perky little *pop*. It broke into approximately a million pieces of glass each as fine as a grain of sand and all of them sparkling. Hughes, of course, couldn't see them sparkling because – well, because they were in his eye, and also because he was too busy clutching his face and letting out a series of wild shrieks something like the cries of a raven.

In order to do this more efficiently, he had dropped his Cougar 9.

Lonnie grabbed the gun and scrambled to his feet.

Lonnie himself was a pretty scary sight. Covered in shaving cream and blood, dripping blood, his eyes like lanterns in his rage-twisted face. He was waving the gun at the startled Mortimer. A deep, strangled growl was dribbling out between his bared teeth. He was trying to shoot Mortimer. He wanted to shoot him. He'd thought he was going to shoot him when he grabbed the gun.

But as it turned out, he couldn't do it. Not in cold blood like that, not even now.

He found this turn of events very frustrating. 'Errrrrgh,' he remarked, or words to that effect. The sound came from too deep in his throat to be made out clearly.

Hughes had now fallen hard to his knees, clutching his face, keening. In another moment, he tumbled to his side. He curled up in a ball, sobbing and crying with the agony.

As for Mortimer, he took all this in and thought, *That's it. I'm disgusted. I am frankly disgusted.* What was it with this op anyway? Was it him? Was God pissed off at him or something? Everything he touched turned to shit all of a sudden. Every fucking thing went complicated on him. He had half a mind to just walk away from this and keep on walking.

But there was no walking away from Winter. And – hope springing eternal – there was still a chance he might come out of this with something. He could see Blake didn't have the stones to actually shoot him anyway.

So with a sigh, he shook his head and said, 'All right, you made your point, put the gun down.'

'Errrrrgh!' Lonnie repeated. He waved the gun wildly in the air. He gestured wildly with his free hand as if trying to draw a picture of his rage.

Mortimer rolled his eyes. 'What're you gonna do, genius, shoot a cop?' he said. 'Put the fucking gun down before you get hurt.' But Lonnie didn't. And Mortimer, already annoyed, said, 'Goddamnit.'

He reached behind him for the holster in his back. He brought out his service revolver.

'Now put it down,' he said.

Lonnie killed him.

The Cougar was so quiet, its recoil so slight – and Lonnie was so crazy with rage at this point – that he didn't even know he'd pulled the trigger at first. He was still standing there, still waving the gun, still growling madly, when Mortimer looked down in surprise. Lonnie followed his gaze and saw the red-black hole in the big cop's trenchcoat, saw the bloodstain spreading around it.

Mortimer raised his face to Lonnie in dumb dismay. Lonnie met his eyes. There was confusion in both their glances. Both understood they were in the presence of a monumental irony.

Then Mortimer's attention seemed to turn inward. He collapsed to one knee, pitched over onto his side.

'Uh . . .' said Lonnie.

Staring, he stepped toward the fallen man. It occurred to him he ought to be careful. He pointed the gun at him.

Mortimer rolled over onto his back. Blood spread in a puddle underneath him from what must have been a large exit wound. Lonnie stared down at the man. The cop's attention still seemed to be turned inward.

Then, as Lonnie watched, a line of shadow rose up slantwise over Mortimer's features. When it had passed, whatever had been Mortimer was gone from the eyes. The face was meat. The cop was dead.

Lonnie's breath ran out of him. 'Oh . . .'

Behind him, Hughes sent up a low wail of pain. Startled, Lonnie spun around, crying, 'Don't move! All right?' He spun from Hughes back to Mortimer, pointing the gun at one then the other. 'Don't anybody move! Just leave me alone! You hear me? Everybody just leave me alone!'

Hughes made another noise. Lonnie pointed the gun at him.

'I mean it!' Lonnie screamed at him. 'I mean it! I'll shoot you too, man! I'll shoot everybody!'

He had no idea what he was saying.

He began backing away from them, from the moaning, twisting Hughes, from the dead Mortimer. Waving the gun between them, at one, then the other. Screaming at them: 'Leave me alone! Everybody! Just . . . just leave me alone!'

He bumped into the windowsill. Looked around. Outside, through the fire escape, above the lofts across the street, it was a full bright blue day. On the sidewalk, people were hurrying past. In the street, cars were riding to the corner. Ordinary life in morning gear. Everything good, everything normal. Lonnie gaped at it.

He hadn't just killed a cop, had he?

He glanced back at the room.

'Oh Jesus Lord,' he said.

His mouth hung open as he stared at what he'd done. Absently, he raised his hand to his face. Wiped the foam and the blood away; the tears now too.

'Oh Lord, Lord, Lord.'

He'd killed a cop, all right. Blinded another. He was already a suspect in a double murder and he had already told lies to the police and now . . .

'Oh Jesus.'

He couldn't think. He had to think. They would come for him. They would take him away. He needed time to think.

Trembling, he seized the window with his free hand, forced it open. The cool air washed in over him, and the cough and sputter of traffic washed in.

He thought he heard a noise behind him. He swung around, waved his gun at the dead Mortimer, at the sobbing Hughes. Neither noticed him.

'I'm not sorry!' he said. 'You hear me? I'm not sorry!'

No one answered. He swallowed hard.

'Not sorry,' he murmured.

He slipped the gun into his pocket. Wiped his face again with his sleeve, ignoring the pain of his slashed jaw. Quickly, he ducked under the window. Climbed out onto the fire escape. He glanced back once more at the two men in the room.

Then he left them and scrambled down the stairs to the street below.

Chapter Eight

A Whole Mess o' Trouble

1

A cab pulled up in front of St Luke's hospital that evening. A passenger was in the back, a man.

Just as the cab arrived, Jennifer Hughes came out through the glass doors with her eight-year-old and five-year-old sons in tow. She spotted the cab with relief. It was almost rush hour and she hadn't known how she was ever going to get back to Grand Central.

The cab's passenger stepped out of the back seat. He held the door for Jennifer. She was an attractive, slightly harried-looking brunette in her thirties. She smiled up at the man.

'Come on, kids, into the cab,' she said.

The man smiled back at her. He winked at the five-year-old, Larry, as the boy climbed into the back seat.

The man was handsome, stylishly dressed, forty or so. Judging by the Cerutti coat, and the haircut and the smell of his cologne, Jennifer thought he must be very successful.

An executive or something. He had bright red hair which she found attractive. He was carrying a rolled-up newspaper in one hand.

'Thank you,' she said to him.

She climbed in after the kids.

The man shut the door and saluted them with his newspaper through the window. The cab drove away and the red-haired man went into the hospital.

It was Edmund Winter, of course. He was here to pay a visit to Jennifer's husband: Hughes.

Hughes was in a room on the third floor. A private room. It had its own bathroom, a bed, a chest of drawers. A small window overlooking the roofs and water towers of lower Manhattan. It was covered by Executive Decisions' generous corporate health plan.

Hughes was lying on the bed, lying on top of the sheets, wearing a green bathrobe over his pajamas. Gauze bandages slanted across the top of his head, covering the socket that had once contained his right eye. An IV needle was in his wrist, carrying antibiotics from the bag on its pole into his arm.

Hughes lay there, his free hand resting on his middle. The hand with the needle in it was by his side. He stared up at the ceiling, his mouth working under his beard.

The visit from his wife and his two boys had been nice, but now they were gone and Hughes could not deny he was depressed. He was depressed about losing his eye. He was depressed about losing his partner Mortimer. And the idea of confronting Winter was like an iron pall lying over him. He didn't even want to think about it. He liked to consider himself an optimistic, happy-go-lucky sort of guy, but it was very hard to see the sunny side of this particular situation.

The door to the room was open and, with a start, Hughes suddenly realized that Winter was standing there at the threshold. The iron pall of dread seemed to sink into him, become part of him.

Oh God, he thought. *Not yet. Jesus.*

The red-haired man smiled easily as he stepped into the room. He saluted Hughes with the rolled-up newspaper.

'Winter.' Hughes hurried to slide himself up into a sitting position. The IV bag flapped against its pole as he moved.

'How you feeling, Hughes? How's the eye?' Winter said.

'S'okay, s'okay,' Hughes said quickly. 'Doctor says it's not serious. That's funny, right? You lose an eye, it's not serious.'

'Well, I'm glad to hear it.'

Winter tossed the paper down on the bed. Hughes nearly jumped, as if it might explode. The paper fell open. The *New York Post*. A front-page photograph of Lonnie Blake with an inset shot of poor old Mortimer.

SAX AND DEATH

COP SHOT AS MUSICIAN ESCAPES MURDER INQUIRY

'Sorry I didn't bring you flowers,' Winter said. He moved to stand at the foot of the bed.

Hughes swallowed hard. Licked his lips. Stared at the paper. He felt very naked, very helpless in his bathrobe and pajamas. Tied to the IV bag. *He won't just shoot me*, he told himself. *Not here. Not with everybody around.*

But he was aware of Winter's reputation and in fact he was none too sure.

'Yeah,' Hughes said. He looked up at Winter, tried to laugh. 'Flowers. Right. Hey, Christ, Winter, I'm sorry, I don't know what to tell you. It got fucked up. You know? Shit happens.'

Winter smoothly waved it away. 'Hey, I know that. I should never have sent you guys up against a jazz musician. Those guys are dangerous.'

Hughes tried to laugh again but all that came out was an

empty wheeze. He wondered if it was time to start pleading yet. *Listen, I've got a wife and kids . . .*

But he restrained himself. Instead, he said, 'It wasn't, like, a useless thing or anything. You know? I mean, we were in there working for you, Winter. We got some stuff, we did, we got some good stuff.'

Winter frowned thoughtfully. 'Okay. Let's hear it.'

'Well, Blake? You know? The sax guy? He saw the girl with Chubby Chubb, with Freddy Chubb.' Winter did seem interested in that. Hughes seized on this hopefully, went on eagerly, 'So see? It must've been Chubb who came out of the crash. Right? All this time, we've been wondering, trying to figure out who it was. Now we know, right? Huh? Right? And then that would make sense because, then, maybe she's got him financing her. See? That's what I was thinking. See what I mean?'

Winter stood easily at the end of the bed, his hands folded in front of him. He considered it. He considered it, it seemed to Hughes, for a long, terrifying time.

'Did Blake identify him?' he asked then. 'Did Blake say positively it was Freddy Chubb?'

'Uh . . . Well . . . no,' Hughes admitted. 'Not positively. But he drew a picture.'

'A picture.'

'On a pad. A watchemacallit.'

'A pad?'

'A pad, yeah, but on it. A drawing. A sort of . . .'

'A doodle,' said Winter.

'A doodle, yeah.'

'He doodled a picture of Freddy Chubb.'

'Yeah.'

Winter laughed once. Hughes couldn't tell if it was a hey-you're-some-kind-of-all-right-my-friend laugh or more of a you're-gonna-look-funny-with-your-intestines-wrapped-around-your-throat laugh.

All Winter said was, 'And so did Blake doodle a picture of where Chubb was? Or where the girl was? Or anything like that?'

'Uh . . .' said Hughes. 'See, we were, see, that's just what we were getting to, we were getting to that and . . .'

Winter lifted one hand in a silencing gesture. A nurse had just entered the room. She was a fat black woman, waddling on squeaky shoes. She was carrying a clipboard and a fresh IV bag.

'Afternoon, gentlemen,' she said as she entered.

She went about her business briskly, checking the chart, checking her clipboard, changing the nearly empty bag on the pole for the fresh one she'd brought with her.

During all this, Winter remained silent. He stood at the end of the bed with his hands folded in front of him and smiled down at Hughes. Obviously, they couldn't very well continue their conversation with the nurse in the room. All the same, Hughes found that the silence and the smile and the waiting all combined to bring his fear to the boil. *He won't just shoot me*, he kept thinking. But he was beginning to think that maybe Winter would. And Hughes, in point of fact, didn't want to die. He wanted to live to see his sons grow up. He had some land in Florida; he wanted to build a retirement house on it. Jennifer – his wife – how would she get on without him? Hughes felt cold sweat breaking out on his forehead.

'Afternoon, gentlemen,' said the nurse again. She waddled out of the room, her shoes squeaking. Hughes wanted to beg her not to leave him alone.

'Listen,' Hughes broke out the moment she was gone, 'it was Mortimer's play. Okay? I mean, he made the plan. I'm going along. I gotta go along, right? I mean, I can do good things for you, Winter, ask anyone. I mean, listen, let me be honest with you: you're making me really nervous just standing there like that.' He was sweating hard now. 'Just tell me, all right? Just tell me. Am I dead? Am I dead here or what?'

Winter gave another short laugh. He raised his eyes heavenward. 'Well, let me see,' he said. 'We're on what we might call a secret mission, right? And so far we got a whore shot dead while screaming bloody murder, we got her john, a respectable insurance salesman, with his head blown off. We got this Blake guy now on the run with every cop in the area looking for him.'

'It was Mortimer's play, I'm telling you.'

'Yeah, okay, I believe that. But Mortimer was a cop killed during an investigation. As for Lonnie Blake, the police'll probably kill him too, maybe even nail him for the double downtown. But you – who are you? – you're a question mark. That's how the police will see it. You understand what I'm saying?'

Hughes's hopes nose-dived. He felt like bursting into tears. 'Please, Winter,' he said. 'I could do good work for you. I know it. Ask anyone. What about Chubb? I found out about Chubb, didn't I?'

'Yeah, Chubb was good. I can work with Chubb.' Winter considered, made a face. 'Nah. Sorry, Hughes. You're a dead guy.'

'Aw, come on, Winter,' Hughes whined. 'I got a wife and kids.'

'Oh no, don't worry about that,' Winter told him. 'We took care of them too.'

'What?' Hughes cried out. And he was about to sit up straight. But now a sort of ripple passed over the air between him and Winter, just like the ripple you see in lake water. For a moment, Hughes didn't know what it was.

Then, wide-eyed, he turned to look at the IV bag.

The IV bag! Jesus, he thought.

Then he was dead.

2

The day, as days will do, wore on. The sun sank into the Palisades. Its reddening glow rode in across the Hudson and painted the blank-faced windows of the city skyline a brilliant orange. Amidst the shadows of the sycamores in Central Park, the last light lay in deep yellow patches. Then it faded away. The yellow patches and the shadow blended together. Chill autumn night came down indigo.

There, in the park, the streetlights along the paths switched on, haloed circles of white one after another. Men and women walked home; in pairs; alone. Their figures became hazy in the dark.

After a while, a lot of the park was empty. There were still joggers around the reservoir, some kids blowing smoke and music out over the lake, plenty of late workers on the paths near the southern border. But away from these centers of activity, north of them, on the West Side, under the trees, there was not much moving. Wind and the night birds and the leaves blowing over the grass, that's pretty much all.

And yet, here and there, under one tree or another, some tattered bum or two had set up camp. Blanket rolls were hidden at intervals under the low bushes. Vaguely human forms stirred under piles of rags.

Two black boys, neither yet fourteen, were prowling among these castaways. Passing with bobbing, rhythmic walks, with sharp eyes, with predatory smiles. One boy was called Junebug, the other was generally referred to as Mickey D. They were looking for Dead Presidents: enough dollar bills for a snack of scoobie and eats on the deserted ballfield.

They found a likely vic, a man curled amidst a cluster of black maples north of the rec house. Homeless. Drunk probably. All alone, by the looks of it. And wearing a coat that might have bankrolled the evening's entertainment by itself.

'Target zero,' said Mickey D.

'Yayo Central,' said Junebug. He slipped on a set of spiked brass knuckles. 'Hey, niggah, what you sleeping for?' he called to the drunk.

'Wake your ass up, nigga,' said Mickey D. 'The fun is just beginning.'

They were standing over the bum now. Junebug kicked him lightly at the base of the spine. 'Little man, he's had a busy day.'

'Now nigga, wake your ass up. We gonna . . .'

The homeless man rolled over. He pointed the barrel of a Cougar 9-millimeter handgun at Junebug's testicles.

'Whoa!' said Mickey D. 'Nigga's strapped.'

'That's Mister Nigga to you,' said Lonnie Blake. 'Now get the fuck outta here.'

206

3

Crazy how familiar the gun felt in his hands. After all these years. Crazy how familiar the fear felt percolating away in his belly. The whole damn situation seemed pretty natural to him, as if it had been in the cards from the beginning. Shit, maybe it had. Anyone looking at his fifteen-year-old gangbanger self might have guessed he'd end up wanted for killing a cop. So what was it? It was like he'd gone to bed and woken up fifteen years later with his destiny all fulfilled. And what was the point of everything in between, right? The school, the music, Suzanne?

Dreaming, Pump-pump. You were only dreaming.

The two punks had run off now. Lonnie slipped the gun back into his overcoat pocket. He stood up. Shivered, cold. Bitter. Mad. The wound on his jaw was beginning to throb. Throb. More like it was covering Billy Cobham's drum solo intro to *Stratus*. Must've been infected pretty good by now. And his throat ached from when Mortimer had throttled him and his back hurt and his joints were stiff. And he could feel every cop in the city dreaming the same dream about killing him dead.

He glanced at his watch. Looked through the night, through the trees, toward the lights of the West Side. He had a plan anyway. Such as it was. That was another thing: the way he'd come up with a plan just like that. The way he'd started thinking like a criminal again, like a fugitive, almost as soon as he'd hit the street. He'd been panicked then. Shit, he'd been half crazy with fear and rage, not to mention remorse at having killed someone. But soon enough, his brain had started clicking away. He'd started trying to think what the cops were thinking, trying to out-think the cops. That had come back to him too.

But it had been easier in those first hours. He'd had a head start. Word hadn't gotten out yet. No one knew they were after him. He had time then to get to a cash machine, get himself a handful of dollar bills. He could walk into a liquor store and pick up a bottle of juice. Join a group of winos. Disappear into their numbers. He was thinking straight enough even then to stay away from the usual traps: hotel rooms with nosy desk clerks; buses and trains that could be sealed and searched; stolen cars that might be reported.

So he'd made it this far. And now night had fallen and that was a plus. But by now too, his picture must've been on every TV show and in every paper. Every cop must've had a copy of it – probably tattooed onto the handle of his gun. And with his jaw festering, and his beard growing in patches around where Mortimer had shaved him and with his clothes dirty from sleeping on the ground, well, Lonnie might just as well have been wearing a sign that said, *Arrest My Black Ass, Mr Po-lice Please*. He was a neon nigger now.

Probably a dead one too. Almost surely a dead one.

But then he'd hummed that tune in his youth also and he remembered how it went.

So his mind felt more or less clear. And he was thinking about what had happened, about what had to happen now. And though he had no friends who were likely to help him, and though he had no story any sane man would believe, and though he had no chance any sane man would give odds on – he did have a plan.

So he started moving.

4

'No hootchie-cootchie,' Arthur Topp was saying into the phone. 'I promise. Straight up. Really. It's a hootchie-cootchie-free zone. I know. I know it's a wedding. But these are ... no, no, no. These are cultured people. Well, then they're hip people. Exactly. Hip, young, cultured people. Exactly. There could be many influential musical opinion-makers on hand. Really. Straight up. Plus the money is not bad. All right, maybe. I know you're an artist. Maybe one *hora*. Look, I don't ... Wait, my other phone is ringing. No, my girl has gone home. I'll talk to you later. Take the gig. Straight up. I mean it,' said Arthur Topp, and hung up.

He sat for a moment. Tilted back in his chair, his feet propped on the desk. The office was silent around him. Silent because, of course, the other phone was not really ringing. There was no other phone, really. Other phones cost money. Girls – secretaries – cost money too so there wasn't one of them either. There was just a swivel chair and a gunmetal table. A computer. A file cabinet. A wall full of autographed photos. A window over the warehouse façades of lower Broadway. Arthur Topp.

He glanced at his father's gold watch. It was almost eight. Five in California. Time to close up shop, go home. Start making calls from there.

He swung his legs down with a weary groan. Tossed a sandwich wrapper in the wastebasket. Grabbed his coat from the coatstand. Shucked it on over the red polo shirt. Headed for the door.

And the phone rang. What else was new? Arthur rolled his eyes and immediately swung back around to get it. He had never let a ringing phone go unanswered in his life.

'Topp Music, tops in pop,' he said.

The voice over the phone was gruff and deep but not impolite. 'Arthur Topp, please.'

'Speaking.'

'My name is Detective Grimaldi of the Ninth Precinct,' the voice said.

A policeman. Okay. That was interesting. Naturally Arthur Topp immediately remembered the wannabe singer he had wangled into bed in Miami last year. He had known in his heart she wasn't any sixteen. The sweat was already beginning to break out on his forehead when Grimaldi said:

'I'm calling about a man named Lonnie Blake.'

Right. Lonnie Blake. Arthur had heard the news. The double murder. The cop killing. So now his mind started coming up with all kinds of paranoid scenarios in which he became a suspect . . .

'Ye-ah?' he said cautiously.

'You know who I'm talking about?'

'Yeah, sure. I met him. Once.'

'On Friday night in a bar called Renaissance.'

Arthur cleared his throat. 'That's correct,' he said formally, as if he were already a witness on the stand.

'And were you with anyone else? Or did you see anyone else talking to Mr Blake? A woman? Anyone?'

'No. No one. Why?'

'But you and Mr Blake did have an extended conversation?'

'Well – I guess.'

There was a pause. A sound of lowered voices conferring. Arthur tried to hear what they were saying, couldn't.

Then Grimaldi was back on the line. 'Mr Topp, I know it's late, but would it be possible for me and a colleague to drop by and talk to you this evening?'

'Uh . . . yeah. Sure,' said Arthur Topp. 'I was just heading home . . .'

'That's still on West 69th?'

They knew his address? 'Uh . . . yeah.'

'Well, we'd be happy to meet you there if it's more convenient.'

Arthur consulted the watch again. 'I usually get home by 8:30 . . .'

'Why don't we say nine o'clock?' said Grimaldi.

So that's what they said.

Nine o'clock.

5

It made him nervous at first, but by the time he climbed out of the subway on 72nd, Arthur was almost looking forward to his interview with the cops. The prospect of talking to a real-life detective about a murder wasn't exactly tranquilizing, but it did have a welcome edge of excitement to it. Danger. A sense of being connected to the news of the day. It would make a story he could tell his colleagues at lunch tomorrow anyway.

He walked home the rest of the way as usual. Reached the corner of Columbus and West 69th around 8:25, exactly as usual.

The block was a quiet, charming stretch of brownstones between the fashionable Columbus Avenue and Central Park. There were antique streetlights shining down through well-tended gingko trees. There was stoop after Dutch-style stoop fading into the backdrop of the park wall and the tangled autumn darkness beyond. Arthur had had an apartment here for almost twenty years now. It was the best investment of his father's money he'd ever made.

It was quiet as he headed for the place. Just a young woman walking her yap-dog on the opposite sidewalk. The thunk of a door, a cab pulling away from the line of parked cars. Arthur wasn't paying attention. He was deep in a fantasy about how his evidence would help the police put Lonnie Blake in jail.

So it wasn't until he'd climbed his stoop and stepped inside that something began to bother him. Something. Maybe just the atmosphere in the brownstone's lobby at the foot of the stairs. The stairs were dim with only a few shaded lanterns on the wall lighting the way. The maroon carpeting and flock wallpaper absorbed what little light there was. Probably it was only nerves, but Arthur felt there was something – something brooding in the shadows around him. He climbed the steps slowly, cautiously, scanning the way above, looking behind him, around him, as if he expected some phantom to suddenly call his name in a hollow tone.

But there was nothing. He reached the third floor. Went down the hall to his door. He was hurrying by then. Nervous. Fumbling for his keys, fumbling to get his keys into the door's three locks.

But he did pause to look behind him once. He checked over his shoulder as the key slid home for the last time.

He would've sworn there was no one there.

He unlocked the door. Pushed it open. Reached in to flick on the light.

He caught a smell – rank, rancid, thick, dark. But by then it was too late.

Something barreled into him from behind. Shoved him through the open door into his apartment.

Arthur Topp's small body hit the sofa, his thigh banging hard against its arm. Terrified, he heard the door shut behind him. He felt his stomach bunch inside him like a fist. He was trembling as he turned around.

Lonnie Blake stood there, wild-eyed, wounded, unshaven. Insane, it looked like. Leveling a gun barrel directly at Arthur's face.

Arthur thrust his quivering hands high into the air.

'So, uh, I take it the music career didn't work out,' he said.

6

'Close the windows – the shutters,' Lonnie Blake said.
    'Right. Right, right, right,' said Arthur Topp.

He backed away, watching the pistol closely as if it wouldn't go off as long as he kept his eyes on it.

'I don't want to be racist or anything,' he babbled. 'But a big black guy pointing a gun at me – it makes me nervous, Lonnie, straight up. Hey, maybe it's just the gun, I don't know.'

'Just close the goddamn shutters.'

'Right.'

He bumped up against the window seat. Turned around, reluctantly tearing his gaze from the pistol. The whole time he was closing the shutters, he felt the bullet in that black bore itching for his spine.

But at the same time, his mind was racing. Nine o'clock, Grimaldi had said. Just thirty minutes and the cavalry would arrive in the person of two NYPD detectives. Was that a good thing or a bad thing? Would it be a rescue or a wild shoot-out in which innocent talent agents were sacrificed right and left for the greater good? Should he try to stall Blake till they arrived or just tell him they were coming and hope it scared him off?

He set the clasp on the last shutter. He turned around slowly.

'Eat,' said Lonnie, gesturing with the gun. 'I need something to eat. Water, too. I need food and water.'

Hands in the air, Arthur nodded his head toward the kitchenette. 'In there.'

Lonnie stepped back. Waved the gun. 'Get it.'

'Right.'

The apartment was not large. Just two rooms and the kitchenette. A maplewood counter divided the kitchenette from the living room. Arthur had to edge close to Lonnie to get around the counter. Moving cautiously, always watching that gun. The stink of the fugitive nearly made him gag.

But he reached the kitchenette. Opened the refrigerator. Looked in. Felt the gun still trained on the side of his head.

'All right. Let's see,' he said, gulping air. 'What've I got here? Some Brie, some non-fat vegetable chips, they're very nice . . .'

'Just give me anything,' Lonnie said. 'Gimme some water.'

'Sparkling or still?'

'Just gimme some goddamned water!'

'Okay, okay, okay,' said Arthur. 'Jesus. Just take it easy, all right?'

He dumped some chips on a plate with a wedge of Brie. Brought out a bottle of Evian, began to set it on the counter.

Lonnie had hurried around to the other side. He snatched the bottle out of Topp's hand. He sat on one of the bar stools. But he paused before he drank. Regarded Arthur suspiciously. Arthur held his breath.

'Come out from there,' Lonnie said. 'Sit down over there on the couch.'

Arthur obeyed at once, trying to radiate amiability and compliance. All the same, the gun followed him as he came back around the counter. As he moved to the sofa, his eyes flicked up at the clock on the wall next to the print of a Hirschfeld Sinatra. Only twenty-six minutes now before the cops arrived.

When Arthur sat down Lonnie tipped the bottle up. The water glubbed as it rushed into his mouth, as it dribbled over his chin. All the while, he kept his eyes on Arthur. All the while, the gun was trained on Arthur's chest.

Arthur attempted to smile pleasantly, his eyes shifting now and then to the clock.

Lonnie gasped out of the drink. Set the bottle down hard. Grabbed a handful of chips, shoveled them into his mouth. For a long moment, there was nothing but chewing and crunching and the fugitive's baleful glare.

Then Lonnie said, 'All right. I need your help.'

'My help?'

'That's right.'

'I don't mean to be negative, Lonnie. But I think the career moment has passed. Really.'

The saxman gave his patented contemptuous snort. 'I don't mean that. You heard the news?'

Arthur saw no point in lying. 'Yeah. I heard.'

'I found a paper in the park,' said Lonnie – he almost sounded sad about it. 'I don't expect you to believe me, but that's not the way it happened.'

'O-kay,' said Arthur carefully.

'I didn't kill those two people. And the cop and the other guy, the one the paper said was a private eye? They did this to me.' He laid a finger along the swelling infection on his jaw.

Arthur felt a chill in his balls just looking at it. 'Wooh, that looks nasty,' he said.

'Something was wrong with the whole thing,' Lonnie went on. 'They had me right there in the cop house, you know? They could've done anything they wanted. But they let me go, waited till I got home. It was like . . . it was like they didn't want the other cops to know what they were up to. See what I'm saying?'

'Sure,' said Arthur Topp, stealing another glance at the clock. Twenty-three minutes now. Oh come, Grimaldi, come. 'Sure, I see what you're saying.'

'And I know what happens to cop killers in slam. I'm not giving myself up until I show people what happened. So you're gonna help me with that.'

'*Me?*' Arthur burst out. He couldn't help himself. 'I'm a booking agent. Why me?'

'Just your tough luck, man. You gave me your card. Told me your schedule. Your address was near the park so I could get to it without being spotted. Plus, the cops won't know I know you. They'll check the people I usually see. But we only met that one time so they won't think to look here . . .'

'But they do know!' Arthur Topp blurted it out. If that was why Lonnie Blake had come here, maybe the truth would make him go away. 'They called me before I left the office tonight. They're coming here in, like, twenty minutes.'

Lonnie snorted again. 'Yeah, right. Whatever.'

'I'm serious. Detective Grimaldi . . .'

The gun stiffened in Lonnie's hand. Arthur shut up. 'Don't fuck with me, man. I know he was in the paper. I'm not a fool. They ain't gonna come here.'

Arthur Topp swallowed hard. *Okay*, he thought.

'You got a computer?' said Lonnie Blake.

'A laptop,' whispered Arthur.

'And you can connect to the internet and all that?'

'Yeah. But . . .'

'Get it,' said Lonnie Blake.

Arthur got it. He set it up on the oval dining table. Lonnie watched him, polishing off the water, tearing into the Brie, holding the Brie in one hand, Arthur noticed, and ripping into it with his teeth as if it were a wedge of pizza.

By the time Arthur had the laptop up and running, it was eighteen minutes before nine o'clock. He tapped onto AOL, conscious all the while of the gun trained on him. The dial tone sounded, the beeps of the numbers, the modem signal. 'Welcome,' said a woman's voice, fuzzy through the laptop's speakers. He was online.

Lonnie moved to look over his shoulder. The fugitive's dark and crawly smell surrounded him.

'You know,' said Arthur meekly, 'I was serious about the cops.'

Lonnie ignored him. 'You got one of those search things. I saw it at the coffee shop, one of those . . .'

'A search engine. Sure.'

Arthur called up AltaVista. The smell, the presence, of Blake pressing in behind him made him queasy. He glanced at the clock. Sixteen to.

'All right,' said Lonnie Blake at his ear. 'Look up Carol Dodson.'

Arthur keyed in the name. Waited.

'Eight hits,' he said. 'A family tree. A list of the faculty at University of Virginia.'

'No, no, that ain't her, man. Okay, okay,' said Lonnie. 'Now try Chubb. Freddy Chubb. Frederick Chubb.'

'Frederick Chubb,' said Arthur. He tapped it in. Glanced at the clock while the computer searched. Fourteen minutes.

'Yeah,' said Lonnie.

Arthur looked at the screen. Close to a thousand hits.

'What do you want?' he said.

'His address. His phone number. Something.'

'Well, I don't know . . . You gotta find a different engine for that. I'm not sure.'

'Shit. The guy at the coffee shop did it.'

'Well, that's his job. You want a bar mitzvah gig, you come to me.'

'Well, get me a picture, something with a picture, so I'm sure it's him.'

Arthur went down the list. Found an article reprinted from the *New York Times*. He clicked it. Up came the article. A picture too. A thin-faced man wearing an eyepatch.

The hiss of Lonnie's voice in his ear was electric. 'Yeah. That's him! See that? That's why those fuckheads did me that way. Because I saw him. They were looking for him.'

Arthur's eyes scanned the screen quickly. 'This guy? You saw him? When?'

'Sunday. Yeah. Just this last Sunday. He was at a restaurant.'

Arthur was silent a moment. He couldn't see Lonnie just then but he sensed him pacing behind him. He sensed the gun too, felt it, imagined it pointing at the back of his skull. He spoke with everything he had of tact and gentleness.

'Well,' he said, 'Okay. Okay. Only . . . the trouble with that – Lonnie – the trouble with that is: it says here that this man – this Freddy Chubb – is dead.'

He could feel Lonnie's pacing cease. 'Say what?'

'See,' said Arthur, swallowing. 'See, right here. He went down in that plane that crashed in Massachusetts.'

'But that was like . . .'

'Four whole months ago,' said Arthur Topp.

7

*A*gents of the Federal Bureau of Investigation have turned their
attention to one of the passengers of European Airways Flight
186 as they continue to examine whether the 747 jet's disintegration
last month over the town of Hunnicut, Massachusetts may have been due
to criminal causes. According to FBI sources, investigators believe that
a plot against a 47-year-old suspected smuggler, Frederick 'Chubby'
Chubb, may have led to the explosion that brought the jet down.

   Although Chubb's body is among dozens which may never be
recovered or identified, he was believed to have been flying in the
aircraft's first-class compartment at the time of the crash. He is
believed to have booked his passage under the name Frank Chester,
one of several aliases Mr Chubb used during his alleged criminal
operations, investigators said.

   According to the investigators, Mr Chubb — a somewhat stylish
figure with his piratical eyepatch and elegant manners — had long
been suspected of running an international billion-dollar smuggling
operation which involved counterfeit computer programs, CDs and

Arthur now ventured a glance over his shoulder. He saw Lonnie Blake standing transfixed, open-mouthed. He looked at the clock. Only ten minutes now.

'Lonnie . . .' he said.

'That's not right,' said Lonnie Blake. 'That's the man. I saw that man.'

'Everybody on the whole plane died, Lonnie.'

'Then he wasn't on the plane. I saw that man, goddamnit.'

And now, for the first time, Lonnie turned his back on Arthur Topp. For the first time, he lowered the gun, lowered it to his side. His head hung down in thought or dejection, he walked across the room to the shuttered windows.

And Arthur, watching him, suddenly thought, *He's telling the truth.* And though he laughed the thought away – *yeah, like, right, an insane gunman telling the truth* – it stuck with him.

'Damn!' said Lonnie Blake.

'What now?' said Arthur Topp.

Lonnie looked around as if surprised Arthur was still there. 'What's that?'

'Is there something else you want me to do here?'

Lonnie turned. Sank down on the window seat. Shook his head. 'Nah, hell. I thought if I could find this Chubb guy, I might find the girl, find out what was happening . . . Damn.'

'Lonnie,' Arthur heard himself say. 'It's almost nine o'clock, man.'

'What?'

'Really. Straight up. I mean it. The cops are on their way.'

Lonnie gazed at him. It seemed to take a moment for the words to sink in. Then he gave that little snort of his. 'Shit. You're serious, aren't you?'

'Straight up. I swear,' said Arthur Topp.

Lonnie raised his eyes to the clock. Seven to nine. 'Nine o'clock,' he said.

'You better go,' said Arthur Topp.

Lonnie shook his head. 'I guess I'm rusty at this criminal business. I'm not as good a fugitive as I thought.'

Arthur lifted his hands. 'It's not too late to reconsider a career in the field of entertainment.'

Lonnie seemed to think for another minute. 'I need some stuff. Food. Water.'

'You know, there really is no time.'

'Any clothes you got that might fit me. A razor . . .'

'Okay. Okay. You might think about taking some of my deodorant . . .'

Lonnie smiled. 'Some of that, yeah. And some tools. Anything you got. A wrench. A screwdriver. A wire coat hanger.'

'A wire coat hanger?'

'Just get it.'

Arthur's eyes moved to the gun. 'All that stuff's in the other room.'

Lonnie nodded. 'Go ahead.'

Arthur Topp stood unsteadily. He walked to the bedroom doorway. He paused there. Once he stepped across the threshold, he would be out of range of the gun. He stepped across it. Lonnie stayed where he was. Once again, the thought came to Arthur: *He's telling the truth. I mean, come on, this is an innocent man.*

Again, he laughed the thought off, but he found himself rushing to gather the things Lonnie needed. Grabbing his Knicks gym bag, tossing in an oversized sweater, some elastic shorts. The coat hanger. Hurrying into the bathroom for razors, deodorant, his unused spare toothbrush. Some antiseptic cream for that thing on his jaw – he thought of that himself. And then he came back out into the living room

– of his own free will back out to where Lonnie sat with the gun – to get the water, the chips, some bread, the tools in the kitchenette cabinets: a screwdriver, a box cutter, a wrench. Hurrying the whole time because . . . well, because he *wanted* Lonnie to get out of there before the cops showed up. He actually *wanted* Lonnie Blake to get away.

Jesus. Must be that Stockholm thing, he thought.

It was two minutes to nine o'clock when he was done. For all he knew, Grimaldi and Co. might be downstairs already, might be coming up the stoop. For all he knew, the buzzer was going to go off any second.

Lonnie went to the door. Arthur handed him the gym bag. He could almost feel the second hand moving on the clock face now.

'Thanks,' Lonnie said.

'Hey. You got the gun,' said Arthur Topp.

Lonnie smiled, looked down at the weapon. 'Sorry, man. I never would've shot you.' He dropped it back into his pocket. 'If you could give me a few minutes' head start before you tell them I was here . . .'

'Okay,' said Arthur without thinking. 'Sure. You better go, though.'

Lonnie opened the door. Stepped out into the hall.

'I'm not gonna tell them,' said Arthur Topp suddenly. 'That you were here? I'm not gonna tell them at all.'

Lonnie glanced back. Nodded his thanks.

'And if you make it through this, I get exclusive representation.'

Lonnie laughed. He started to move away.

Arthur Topp watched him another second. Then he called after him, 'What're you gonna do now?'

'I'll think of something,' said Lonnie Blake.

8

What he thought of was this:

The steak house Ed Whittaker's stopped serving around midnight on weekdays and was generally shut up tight by 2 a.m. Lonnie found this out around eleven o'clock with a phone call from a phone booth near the park.

At 2:15, he made his return to the restaurant where he'd seen Carol Dodson meet with the allegedly late Frederick 'Chubby' Chubb.

It was a long trip. The streets of Manhattan are never empty and never dark. Quiet as the city was at that hour, there were cars, cabs, a few pedestrians. Cops cruising crosstown on the side streets, up- and downtown on the avenues. Not enough shadows, too many eyes.

Lonnie walked with his head hung, his hands in his pockets, Topp's Knicks bag slung over his wrist. He kept the collar of his coat turned up around his throbbing jaw as if for protection from the biting wind. He forced himself not to look when a car passed him. When pedestrians came in his direction, he would give them a casual glance – he found it kept them from staring. He tried to avoid long stretches on the well-lighted avenues. He hung close to the lee of buildings.

He walked on.

Once, as he was hurrying south beneath the skyscrapers on Madison, a crumpled page of the *New York Post* blew between his feet. For a second, his own face stared up at him. He remembered Mortimer's face likewise staring, the baffled look in his eyes before the soul rose out of him. He remembered the feel of his own finger on the trigger.

Fuck him. He earned it.

He kicked the paper aside. Walked on.

He reached First Avenue coming from the west, crossed it to Ed Whittaker's. The corner seemed abnormally bright to him, its streetlamp casting a wide net of light over the sidewalk, the buildings, him. He told himself he'd done this sort of thing before. There was nothing to it. All the same, he felt the pulse of tension shudder in him as if a hummingbird were caught in his chest. A big hummingbird. A great fucking humongous monster of a hummingbird.

He hurried out of the light. Down the side street, past the dumpster where he'd stood before, the last time he'd seen Carol. He'd figured there'd be a door nearby, where they brought the kitchen garbage out. There was. It was metal with a handle and a lock underneath.

Lonnie drew a deep breath. It trembled on the exhale. He scanned the street, squinting into the biting wind that came off the East River. There was a doorman outside a building down the way, but even as Lonnie watched him, he turned and went in. There was no one else. Only a steady stream of cars on the avenue. Lonnie hoped the dumpster would block him from their view.

He removed the gun from his overcoat pocket. Pointed

227

it at the lock. He tried to hold his breath but couldn't. A choked sound of tension broke through his teeth as he squeezed the trigger.

Easy pickins, he thought. *No sweat.*

Then the gun snapped in his hand. There was a loud, whining ricochet. Lonnie said, 'Shit!' and gritted his teeth like a boy who's just sent a baseball through a church window. A moment later, he actually thought he heard the bullet strike brick somewhere behind him.

'Shit, shit, shit!' he said.

This stuff had seemed simpler somehow in his youth.

He looked down at the door. The lock hardly seemed dented, just scarred and a bit askew. He tried the handle, glancing back over his shoulder as he did. He saw the doorman down the street hurrying outside again to check out the noise.

To his surprise – to his intense excitement – the handle went down. The door swung open. Lonnie slipped through it, shoved it closed behind him.

Awright! he thought.

But the hummingbird hummed louder.

He was in a small alley at the restaurant's back. He had to stop here a second, lean against the wall, get steady. He tossed the Knicks bag to the pavement. Wiped his mouth with the back of his gunhand.

He looked up.

There was the kitchen door, just a few steps away from him. A wooden door with a large glass panel in the top half of it. All right. Lonnie grit his teeth. Pushed off the wall. Crossed the alley. Reached the door. He struck at the glass with the gun butt. It shattered.

The alarm started screaming.

It was a loud, hammering bell. He knew it was coming but he wasn't ready for the way it seemed to play on his spine. He pinned himself against the door, stuck his arm through the broken window. Jagged teeth of glass snagged and tore at his coat. Grunting, he felt for the lock inside. Found it.

A deadbolt. It needed a key.

'Damn!'

He drew the gun and fired again. The sound was barely audible under the hammering bell. The door splintered at the jamb. Lonnie kicked it and it flew open.

He was in. The alarm screamed and went on screaming. It was as if the hummingbird inside him had broken loose and now the whole atmosphere was shuddering too. He looked through the dark, every way at once. The kitchen to his right. A shadowy hallway before him.

He plunged down the hall, stumbling in his rush, ricocheting off the walls. He threw his arms out to either side to steady himself. Felt his hands knocking pictures askew, touching glass frames, and the brass plaque on the men's room door.

The ringing of the bell filled him, surrounded him. A battalion of police could've been on its way, sirens blaring. He wouldn't have known, he wouldn't have heard. He heard nothing but the ringing of the bell.

Then he broke out into the dining room. More bells, louder. And the blinking of a red alarm light above the storefront window. And through the window, the startling flash of traffic, passing headlights.

The pounding of his heart was loud. His rasping breath was loud. And beyond these, and beyond the screaming bells, he thought he heard them now: sirens. Very faint, but urgent, insistent. He tried to tell himself: it's just an alarm at a restaurant. At most, a single cruiser would drop by to check it out. In his mind, he heard dozens of police cars racing to the scene.

Lonnie stood at the rear entrance to the room, right beside the bar. His mouth hung open as he drew breath. His eyes were wide and staring. He saw the silhouettes of tables, the chairs overturned on top of them. He saw the little podium near the front door where the *maître d'* had stood to welcome her customers.

He humped it across the room. To the podium. He reached underneath to the lower shelf.

He felt the thing at once, grabbed it: an outsized leather-bound volume.

The reservation book.

He pulled it out.

He turned and headed for the exit at full speed.

Chapter Nine

The Touch of Your Hand Is Like Heaven

1

In the morning, after a sleepless night, Howard Roth climbed wheezing down the stairs. He made himself a mug of coffee in the old house's old kitchen. He carried it into the study, breathing in the steam, hoping to clear his cancerous lungs enough to enjoy his first cigarette of the day.

He was wearing the baggy gray cardigan his second wife – Wendy – had bought him. He was wearing the wire-rimmed reading glasses Wendy had liked. She said they – the cardigan, the glasses – made him look 'professorial'. She said that because she thought being a professor was a cozy, homey sort of thing to be. She wanted her husband to wander around the place, bemused, muttering thoughtfully, searching everywhere for the pipe he was already holding in his hand. She never quite comprehended his own image of himself as a Bare-Torsoed Warrior of Ideas, a Ferocious Sword-Wielding Defender of the Classical Faith, Conan the

Intellectual. She knew he could be irritable at times – she discovered he could be vicious as the marriage wore on, wore out. But she never really understood the depth of his rage, the acid heat of his frustration. For 'this is the bitterest pain among men', Herodotus said, 'to have much knowledge but no power'.

Welcome to Academia.

Roth's study was a small room in the front of the house. Crowded with shelves crowded with books. There were windows on the wall to his right and over the desk before him. Pleasant views of the lawn, the street, the MacAlary hedges. The desk itself was large, but cluttered with papers and magazines and volumes over every inch. The computer dominated the center of it. He switched the machine on before sitting down on the high-backed leather swivel chair which was his greatest luxury.

Yes, Wendy had hardly known him, he thought, reaching into the cardigan's pocket for his Kents. But then he had only married her for her youth and her large breasts and her low IQ. To be fair, he'd thought he'd loved her cheerfulness at the time and her kindness and sweetness. But, in fact, as he soon discovered, he'd despised these traits in her. He thought they were the height of insipidity.

He shoveled the Kent between his lips. *Ah, who can find a virtuous woman?* he thought. *For her price is far above wholesale.* He lit up and was gratified to find he could still take a deep, satisfying drag without coughing up an excess of malignant bile.

Wendy was on his mind this morning because he was planning to write her a letter. A note to tell her of his illness, ostensibly. But more than that. His valedictory address, so to speak. His farewell to her and to their daughter and to the things of this world.

He'd composed much of the letter in his head as he'd lain through the endless hours of darkness. He'd composed the

234

tone of it anyway. It was going to be a fine letter. Clear, simple, majestic – eminently publishable should it ever come to that – written in lines of almost classical elegance, in prose that suggested even more than it proclaimed. It was going to be a letter both wise and grave and yet gently ironical; melancholy too and yet sweetly so; it would be all-forgiving and yet tinged with just enough paternalistic rebuke to induce a lifetime of guilt in anyone who'd happened to, say, divorce him before his earthly race was run.

With these guidelines to inspire him, Roth found himself an hour later staring at a blank screen, tears coursing steadily down his narrow cheeks. The waste, he kept thinking. The failure, the waste. The hundred books he'd planned, the two he'd written, the one he'd published – ridiculed, remaindered. A million deep phrases which had turned banal when they touched the air. All Greece and Rome had been in his head and yet he couldn't speak the things he knew. A million mythologies, which he understood as no man had. A million . . .

Well, he could've gone on like this another ninety minutes easily, but he had slowly become aware that someone was watching him. And, hastily swiping the tears from his face with both hands, he turned to find the little girl, Amanda, staring at him from the study doorway.

2

She stood just beyond the threshold in the shadows of the front hall. A little Jamesian ghosty of a thing, clutching her Elmo doll, gazing at him eerily.

'Hello,' croaked Roth, sniffling. Scanning the chaos of his desk for a Kleenex. Seizing one. Blowing his nose. 'Amanda, right? Come in. Come on in.'

'I knocked but you didn't answer,' she said. 'I could see you through the window. You didn't lock your door.'

'I never do. I'm not sure it has a lock.'

'I knocked,' she said again.

'No, that's all right. I was working. Come on in. Sit down.'

The child hesitated, studying him. Then she came forward slowly. Crossing into the room and into the light of the room.

Roth waved his hand in the gray air. 'Sorry for all the smoke. Just push those books aside and sit down.'

There was an extra chair. Scarred, armless; wood with a cushioned seat. A Jowett and a Bloom lay on it, open, upside down, one atop the other. The child didn't push the books aside, but she was small enough to fit on the edge. She perched there, watching Roth solemnly.

'Aunt Geena says you shouldn't smoke or you'll get sick and die,' she said.

'Does she? Well, well. Aunt Geena. What a wit. Does she know you're here?'

'Yes. I said I was coming over.'

Roth nodded. The child was silent and for a moment or two he couldn't think of anything to say.

'So, uh, how's Elmo?' he asked after a while.

'Fine.'

'Would you like something? Milk and cookies? I don't have any milk, actually. Coffee and cookies? A scotch?'

'No.'

'I was joking.'

'Oh.'

'I don't have any cookies either.'

'I'm full,' she said. 'I had breakfast.'

'Ah.'

'I had eggs and blueberry muffins.'

'Mm, those are good.'

'Are you sad?'

'Sad? Oh! No, no, no. Just . . . allergic, that's all. I have allergies.'

Having spent little time on the chores of fatherhood, Roth was still sentimental about children. He thought they knew something. He thought Amanda could see through him, see through his lie, that her steady, serious stare could bore into his soul in some mystical childlike way, bore straight to the very depths of him. Averting his eyes, he had a vague urge to confess to her, to tell her everything and rely upon her baby wisdom to guide him.

Fortunately for everyone, the girl's mind had already wandered on to matters of far more pressing importance to her.

'You said you would tell me more stories,' she said. 'Like the one about Orpees.'

'Hm?' He had been sinking into his own self-pitying thoughts again and was annoyed at the interruption. In fact, now that he thought about it, he was a bit annoyed at having her here altogether. She had barged in on him while he was trying to work – just as he was about to break through his block, to begin his brilliant letter. So it seemed to him now at any rate, now that she was making demands on him.

'You said you would tell me . . .' the girl repeated.

'Oh. Oh yes.' Automatically, Roth reached into his cardigan pocket for his Kents again. His irritation threatened to grow. The effort of telling a story to the girl seemed too much for him somehow. He stalled, trying to think of a way out of it. 'So you like those stories, huh.'

'Yes.'

'What about Elmo? Does he like them too?'

'Elmo's stuffed.'

Cigarette between his lips, lighter raised to it, Roth laughed, and then gave a series of wheezing coughs. 'Now be careful,' he finally managed to say. 'Be careful, because around here we're multicultural. Just because a fellow's stuffed doesn't mean we shouldn't listen to his opinion.'

'Well, that's stupid,' said the child.

'Tell me about it. I wish you were on the tenure committee.' Roth lit up – and this time the first drag got him, sent him into a deep paroxysm of hacking that threatened to be productive all over the place.

The child sat quietly and watched him. 'Are you sick?' she said after a while.

He waved the cigarette at her, but was coughing too hard

to answer. When he could, he stood up, but remained beside his chair, gripping the back of it for support, still bent over, still coughing. 'No, no,' he squeezed out. He cleared his throat into a Kleenex. 'I'm fine. I'm fine.'

Fighting down another fit, he carried his cigarette over to one of the bookshelves. 'Here. Here, look. I'll show you something.' He brought down an oversized volume. Handed it to the child. 'Try this.'

Amanda put Elmo down beside her chair and carefully set the big book on her lap. Opened, the wide wings of it dwarfed her.

'See that?' said Roth. Standing above her. Gesturing vaguely with the smoking butt. 'Those are pictures, paintings. That one's a statue. They're from all the stories. See? They're, like, illustrations people made long ago. Back when they could still paint.'

The girl turned a page. 'People can still paint.'

'No,' said Roth. 'No, they can't.'

'I can paint.'

'Can you? Well, good for you. Start a trend.'

The girl held the book balanced on her little knees. Pointed at a picture. 'What's this one about?'

'Let's see.' It was upside down to Roth. He crooked his head to look at it. 'Oh, that, that's Icarus. He and his father Daedalus were imprisoned in a labyrinth – in a maze – by the king of Minos.'

'Why?'

'Well, Daedalus was very clever at building things, and the king wanted to keep him around, basically. But Daedalus wanted to leave. So he built wings for himself and his son Icarus. And he attached them to their backs with wax and they flew off over the sea. And Daedalus told Icarus, be careful, don't go too near the sun, because you know what wax does when it gets too hot.'

'No-o.'

239

'Like when a candle has fire on it?'

'It melts.'

'It melts. Exactly. But Icarus didn't listen – and you can see there how it turned out.'

'He fell into the water.'

'That's right. Right out of the sky. Splash.'

'Is he drowned?'

'Yep. Yep, he sure is. It was a definite case of "Bye-bye, Icarus."'

Amanda nodded. 'That's a good story too,' she said, and turned the page.

Roth smiled down at her with one corner of his mouth. He was not annoyed anymore. In fact, he found the child's off-handed approval absurdly gratifying.

'Who's this lady?' she asked him now.

'Hm. Let's see. Who is that?' Roth came around so he could read the caption over her shoulder. 'Ah, that – that's Europa.'

'What did she do?'

'Well. Well, I'll tell you.' A note of glee entered his voice here. He began to work out how to tell the story to her – composing, bowdlerizing, seeking out effects in his mind, all with a measure of excitement, anticipation. It was one of his favorite fables, this: the rape of Europa. It had a world of meaning for him. He saw the founding of the West in it. The carrying off of the past into new nations, the mingling of bloodlines in violence and passion, the mysterious, enduring connection to the wellsprings of Greece and, through Greece, to civilizations more ancient still.

'Europa was a princess . . .' he began.

But that was as far as he got. Because now Roth's cigarette ash had grown long, the reed itself burning down to its filter. He stepped away from the girl to reach the ashtray on his desk and, as he did, he took a final drag of the thing.

The smoke seemed to catch in his throat like a fish bone.

The coughing fit that shook him started out harsh and grew swiftly in violence. Roth had time to reach out half blindly and extinguish the cigarette, but then he was doubled over, racked and hacking. He felt like someone was in his lungs with a shovel trying to chuck hot gravel up his gullet and never quite making the grade. He braced one hand on the desk, tried to wave the other at the girl in apology. Coughed and coughed.

And then his mouth was wet, spilling over. A wet gob that seemed the size of his fist had burst up into his mouth. Roth seized a Kleenex. Hawked into it. Hawked again. Brought it away.

It was stained full scarlet.

Roth stared at the tissue. The world accordioned in and out around him and his stomach fell. *I know the color of that blood*, went through his mind. And he finished the quotation aloud, weakly, 'It is my death warrant. I must die.'

Even that small effort at speech set him off again. He coughed so hard his head swam, his vision grew dim. A darkening veil seemed to be falling over his eyes. And then he heard a thump and he turned and looked down through tears.

The child, Amanda, was sprawled at his feet. She lay on her back on the study floor. The book she'd been looking at lay beside her. Her little arm was flung out over it. A thin line of blood spilled from the corner of her mouth.

The blood trickled down across her chin, as Roth stared, terrified.

3

The next few minutes spun past him in breathless panic. He was on his knees beside the girl. Touching her face, her shoulder.

'Amanda!'

Her brown face had turned the palest tan. Her skin was cold as ice. She was breathing, but faintly. She didn't budge.

'Amanda!'

Roth was on his feet next. Around his desk. Stretched clumsily to the window. Forcing it open. As the cool air came in on him, he shouted out through it, out at the hedge.

'Geena! Geena, come quick!'

No answer. Roth rushed back to the girl, knelt, and lifted her into his arms.

He was outside, down the stairs, running with his burden, crossing the space between his front lawn and Geena

MacAlary's when Geena's screen door banged and she was running down her own porch stairs to meet him.

'Oh my God, what happened?'

In a few steps, they came together. Geena's hands fluttered toward the girl, but Roth held onto her.

'Amanda?' Geena cried.

'I'll take her in. Call a doctor.'

'What happened?'

'I don't know. I was sick, I was coughing. And suddenly, she just collapsed, maybe I scared her, I don't know.'

He continued running to Geena's porch – but then glanced back to discover she wasn't with him.

She seemed to have frozen on the lawn. Was standing there, staring after him. She was a sweet-faced woman in her fifties. Disproportionately large breasts in a still-slender frame. A tan V-necked sweater, a plaid, pleated skirt. A tint of red in her silvering hair. She was a straightforward, down to earth woman, Roth had always thought, sharp with long-time mother-smarts. He'd always admired her, feared her slightly.

But now she stood there pale and staring. Open-mouthed and stupid-eyed.

'Come on!' Roth said, and turned away, and hurried up the stairs.

Inside, Geena caught up, was with him again. She fretted at his shoulder as he laid the child on the sofa in the living room. Amanda let out a soft moan.

'Thank God,' said Roth. 'She's breathing better now.'

There were two pink spots rising to the tan surface of the girl's cheeks.

Roth wiped his sweaty palms on his pants legs. 'It was really shallow before. It scared the shit out of me.'

Geena sat down on the edge of the sofa. She put her hand on Amanda's brow.

'I'll call an ambulance,' said Roth, turning to look for a phone.

'No,' said Geena quietly. She stroked Amanda gently, pursed her lips to make a comfort noise.

'What – have you got a paediatrician or something?'

Geena shook her head. 'It'll be all right.'

'No, Geena, listen . . .' Roth said. 'We've gotta . . . I mean, don't you have to call someone?'

She went on shaking her head, touching Amanda, pursing her lips. And then she said, 'This happens, Howard. It's all right. She has a . . . a form of epilepsy. Sometimes this happens.' She glanced up at him with troubled hazel eyes. 'The worst is over now, all right? You did the right thing. She'll be fine.'

Roth stood there, held her gaze. Tried to plumb the meaning of it without success. 'Well, don't you want . . . ? I mean, is there some medicine? Can I do anything? I mean, she was just sitting there, Geena, I swear it. One minute she was fine . . .'

'Ssh. I know,' said Geena, comforting Roth and the girl at the same time. 'It's all right. There's nothing for you to do. Go on home, Howard. Go ahead. Let me take care of her. I'll let you know that everything's all right.'

Roth lifted his hands from his sides, dropped them back again. 'Yeah? I mean . . . you're sure?'

'Mm-hm. I'm sure. Really.'

'Okay. I guess.' He hesitated. 'You'll come by, though,' he said. 'I mean, you'll let me know.'

She nodded. 'Don't worry. I'll come by later. It's all right, Howard. Really.'

Still dazed, still high on panic, Roth backed away from her. 'All right, I'll . . . You're sure . . . ? I can't . . . ? I mean, listen, Geena, if there's anything . . . ?'

But Geena had turned back to the child. 'It's all right,' she kept saying, as if to both of them.

'She was just sitting there . . .' Roth said again. 'She was looking at a book.'

'I know.'

Roth continued to back away, watching the two of them on the sofa, the woman sitting over the girl, stroking the girl's forehead. Finally, with nothing more to say, he turned and headed for the door.

It wasn't until a few moments after that, when he was out on the front lawn in the autumn day, that Roth finally paused, that he finally stood, baffled, with one hand held tentatively against his chest. He drew in a long stream of frosty air. A long, steady stream.

He hadn't realized till now: he wasn't coughing anymore. He had shouted for help. He had lifted the child. He had run with her from one house to another. And he was only slightly out of breath. He wasn't coughing. That rasping sensation in his throat was gone, that burning sensation in his chest as well.

Roth blinked and lifted his eyes. Blue morning shone pale through the latticework of naked branches. A starling on the rooftop sang. He turned to look at it, to look at the house, at the doorway through which he'd just come.

He took another breath, another deep breath. And the air flowed into him clear as a crystal stream.

Chapter Ten

My Heart And I Have Decided To End It All

1

Freighted with care, meanwhile, Vincent 'the Nutcracker' Giordano wandered through the hedgerow maze on his Long Island compound. He did this whenever he wanted to think things over. And there was a good deal on the Nutcracker's mind.

They called Giordano the Last of the Sicilians – they being many of the same federal investigators who had put the Rest of the Sicilians behind bars. But the source notwithstanding, Vincent was very proud of this sobriquet. *The Last of the Sicilians*. It made him feel like a Man of Respect, like one of the great figures from the Old Days when the family businesses were run with dignity and honor. Vincent knew there had been such Old Days because he had seen *The Godfather* some twenty-six times. The film was, in fact, his primary source of historical information, not to mention the fountainhead of his personal style.

And apparently it had served him well. While other old-style mobsters had fallen to the law, or to the new immigrants or to the disloyalty of their followers or their own indiscretions, the Nutcracker had stuck to his cinematic model and thus could not only render a passable imitation of Marlon Brando from time to time but also maintained control over a sizeable East Coast criminal empire.

It was the business of this empire that occupied his thoughts now as he wandered round the hawthorn corridors toward the center of the maze. It was drugs, to be precise. The movement – as the Nutcracker phrased it to himself – of large quantities of illegal substances from one group of semi-civilized colored people in the jungles of South America to another group of semi-civilized colored people in the jungles of America's slums. There were many difficult stages to this process and many middle-men, many places along the way where the transfer could go awry. Powder could be unduly cut, profits could be secretly skimmed, minions could be unkindly shaken down and so forth. And you had to react to these things, deal with them, guard against them insofar as possible. At the same time you had to acknowledge that a certain amount of cutting and skimming and shaking down were bound to occur, human nature being what it is. So it was a subtle thing, a delicate thing: when to acknowledge, when to react; when to turn a blind eye and when to gouge one out and stuff it into an ear. The Nutcracker had to think very hard about these and other weighty matters on a daily basis.

Which is why he loved to come here, to his compound, to this maze, to this place where he could find solitude and a measure of peace.

Like everything else about him, Giordano's Long Island estate was fashioned after his semi-fictional notions of the past. The grounds centered on a sprawling neoclassical mansion. With its Ionic columns two stories tall, its raking cornice above its sculpted frieze, the house was considered the height of elegance by many of the Nutcracker's closest and most strangely nicknamed associates. The *New York Times*, on the other hand, in a less than flattering article, had once referred to the place as Giordano's 'armed fortress on the North Shore'.

The *Times*, it must be admitted, had a point.

A wall ran around all fifteen acres of the place, a white brick wall some ten feet high. It was topped with rolls of razor wire and the razor wire was electrified. There was only one gate, and this was locked electronically and guarded by an armed 'soldier' in a booth of bulletproof glass. Other soldiers patrolled the inner perimeter, pacing back and forth at a distance of some twenty-five yards, each within sight of the next, and all carrying what law enforcement officers have been known to refer to as 'spray-and-pray weapons': automatic guns that discharge enough rounds per minute on so many trajectories that an invading army would be riddled to pieces before the shooter was even obliged to take aim.

There were more guards at the house, by the garage, by the stables. There were light-activated alarm systems in every building and some featured self-sealing steel window plates and doors. Vincent himself was generally accompanied by two armed companions, one large, one larger. The smaller one looked like a gorilla imitating a bulldozer; the bigger one looked like a bulldozer imitating a gorilla. Right this very minute, in an effort to protect their employer's privacy, the duo was stationed at the hedge maze entrance, one on either side of the opening. Their hands, clasped before them, were ever ready. Their eyes, behind their sunglasses, were ever vigilant.

The privileged, spoon-fed reporters sitting safe within their offices at the *New York Times* might have considered these security measures excessive. But it was precisely because of these precautions that the Nutcracker could wander to the center of his hawthorn maze in relative tranquility of heart. Because of them he could soothe his troubled mind with considerations of the quiet and the greenery. Because of them he could pause to rediscover the Roman urns and headless Venuses placed piquant in this niche or that; could appreciate the fresh November morning and the blue November sky; and could come now to the center of his labyrinth where a marble bench stood surrounded by statuary in an open square.

And it was precisely because he had surrounded himself with such extensive and elaborate systems of self-protection that Vincent 'the Nutcracker' Giordano was absolutely appalled to find that Edmund Winter, uninvited, was already sitting on the bench when he arrived.

How the fuck . . . ? Giordano asked himself.

But no answer was immediately forthcoming. This never happened in the movies.

'Hey-ho! Morning, Vincent,' said the red-haired man pleasantly. He lifted a finger and any shout that might have issued from the mob boss's throat quickly died there.

Because now there was movement in the hawthorn shadows and two more men stepped into plain view. Giordano knew these men by reputation. Ferdinand was a wiry brown-skinned fellow with a face that looked like a Hallowe'en skull. Dewey was enormous, neckless, a slab of a man. In fact, Giordano sometimes liked to watch television shows that professed to explicate 'ancient mysteries' and sometimes he would see a slab the size of Dewey in those shows and he would ask himself, 'How the fuck did those ancient dickheads move a slab that size?'

So Giordano did not want to make an enemy of Dewey. Ferdinand either for that matter, who was said to have once been a professional torturer somewhere in South America. And Winter especially, who was said to have commited acts of violence Giordano hadn't even dreamed of.

So instead of shouting, Giordano changed tactics and decided to sweat, which he did profusely.

Winter stood up, meanwhile. He smiled amiably. His crisp black suit, his red silk tie, his gold tie-pin, his delicate cologne all seemed startling and out of place in this arcadian setting. In fact, considering the impossibility of his being there at all, his corporate elegance made him appear terribly *present* somehow, terribly real.

'Wonderful to see you again, Vincent,' he said. 'Truly.'

Giordano swallowed. Then he resumed sweating. 'Yeah,' he said.

Hands in his trouser pockets, Winter ambled toward him. Stood within inches of him, eyes on his eyes. Vincent was a short, squat man, dressed today in blue running pants and an aqua polo shirt. Winter's authoritative air – not to mention his cologne – seemed to overwhelm him where he stood.

Nonetheless, the Nutcracker was no pushover. He mustered his fortitude. 'All I have to do is snap my fingers . . .' he began hoarsely.

'And Dewey will stuff them so far down your throat you'll be able to scratch your ass with them,' answered Winter smiling. 'Now shut up and listen, you dago toad. I know that Chubby Chubb's alive.'

'Eyy . . .'

Winter held up his finger again. Giordano shut up and sweated.

'I know he's alive,' Winter said, 'and that you're running his old operation. Which tells me that you bought him out, made him liquid. Which tells me you can help me find him.'

The Nutcracker sent Winter a look of arrogant defiance, marred only by the steady rivulets of moisture pouring down his flabby face. 'Maybe you never heard of *omerta* – the code of silence,' he said gruffly.

Winter laughed. 'Vincent! Vincent! You're a charming old-world figure and I love you for it. But I represent an

American-based multinational corporation.' He reached out and patted the mobster's wet cheek, two sharp slaps. 'Don't make me hurt you.'

2

Lonnie played. He was on stage under a single spot. The audience was all around him, invisible in the dark. He felt them rather than saw them. Suzanne, Carol Dodson, even he, Lonnie himself, was out there listening while he played. There were hundreds of hidden faces beyond the edges of the light but all of them somehow belonged to those few people he had loved, the living and the dead. He bent back on the stage and lifted his sax and played for them all and the sound was like starlight, celestial. He strove to name the melody and couldn't and understood it was so beautiful that this had to be a dream. And still he played and the notes rose up sparkling from the sax's bell and sprinkled down over the hearts of those who heard them, like balm. The living and the dead, the music soothed them all. It soothed him, Lonnie, as it rose and rose, as it sounded clearer and louder – and then suddenly discordant – and then suddenly it was a car horn screaming by on the highway beyond his window, and Lonnie sat up in the motel bed and all the evil of his life flooded back in on him.

Lonnie groaned, his heart beating hard. He moved to the bed's edge. Sat there, his feet on the floor, his face in his two hands. Beyond the curtains over his window, the cars on the highway kept screaming by. He was in Jersey somewhere, he remembered. It was almost noon. He hadn't hit the bed till after dawn.

Naked, he padded into the bathroom. Leaned into the small mirror over the sink. Examined his face. Not bad, he thought. He'd shaved in a gas station men's room before coming here, so the stubble was even again. The ointment Arthur Topp had given him had taken the edge off the cut on his jaw. It was still inflamed, still infected, but the throbbing was gone; it was just a raw sting now.

Only his eyes were awful. Only the expression in his eyes. In them, he saw the distance from his dream to this shabby, threadbare cubicle. It was a vast distance. It was harrowing.

He took his time washing up. The toilet, the sink, the shower – they all still felt like luxuries to him. And then too, there was the phone in the other room, waiting for him on the table by his bed. He thought of it all the while. What if his one lead should fail him? What if there was nowhere to go from here?

The raid on the restaurant had been a long shot to begin with but he'd had reason to hope it might pay off. A place like Ed Whittaker's, exclusive, crowded. You'd need a reservation for Sunday brunch and they were almost sure to ask you for a confirmation number too. Plus, Lonnie had read the article on Arthur Topp's computer. He had a strong hunch that this smuggler he was looking for, this Frederick Chubb guy, was arrogant, flamboyant. The kind of man who dared you to catch him if you could. What other kind of man would fly under the alias Frank Chester, a name so tauntingly similar to his own?

256

That'd been Lonnie's reasoning in any case. And, sure enough, when he ran out of Ed Whittaker's, he had the reservation book in his hand and in the book he found the name F. Childs. And there was a cellphone number scribbled in the space beside it.

He hardly dared hope that Childs was Chubb, that the number would actually connect him. And yet he couldn't dare but believe that he was, that it actually would. And the possibility – even the slim possibility – that he might really be able to clear his name before he turned himself in to the police, that he might actually find Chubb, that he might actually . . .

find the girl, see the girl again . . .

No, that was over. It was past that now. He just had to find Chubb, see if Chubb could make some sense of the murders in the girl's apartment, give him *some* information, at least, that might show he had killed the cops in self-defense. It was the only way he could think of that might get him out of this mess.

Anyway, the first wave of publicity must've passed, he'd figured. The ordinary man on the street would soon forget his face. The time was ripe to take the chance and try to get the hell out of town.

He'd stolen the license plates first, from a decaying Mustang on 94th Street. Its parking spot was good all day. Lonnie thought he might get twenty-four hours of grace before anyone even noticed the plates were gone. He got the car farther north. A hoopty old Dodge he found in the Heights. It was a dangerous neighborhood to complain in. Maybe the owner would think twice before reporting the theft to the police.

Using Topp's screwdriver, wrench and wire coat hanger, it took him five minutes to switch the plates and forty-five seconds to jump the car.

All the same, the sky had been growing lighter by the time he rolled over the GW Bridge and into Jersey.

Now he was here, in the motel, rested, more or less, put

257

together – more or less. It was time to face this thing. It was time to find out just how far he was going to go.

He came out of the bathroom, got dressed. Pulled on the old white sweater Topp had given him. He stood with the room still dark, the curtains still drawn. He looked at the phone a long moment. He licked his lips.

Right.

He went to the table. Picked up the phone. Punched in the number from the reservation book.

The phone rang once. Twice. Then the ringing stopped.

Lonnie waited, listened.

Nothing. Not even the sound of breathing. No sound at all on the other end.

Lonnie spoke into the silence.

'Mr Chubb,' he said, 'my name is Lonnie Blake.'

No answer. Nothing. Lonnie felt his palm grow damp against the handset.

'I know you don't want to talk to me, Mr Chubb, but you've got to. I know you weren't really on that plane that crashed. I know you didn't die. All I want . . .'

But then the silence on the line came to an abrupt end. There was a loud burst of sound in Lonnie's ear.

Someone was laughing.

'Hello?' said Lonnie Blake.

The laughter went on another second or so. And then a voice said, 'I'm sorry, Mr Blake.'

Lonnie held his breath. His throat felt dry.

'It's just funny, that's all,' the voice continued. 'You've got everything exactly wrong.'

'Sorry?'

'I *was* on that plane. I *did* die.'

'Say . . . say what?'

'And as for my not wanting to talk to you – why, you're exactly the man I've been looking for. You're exactly the man I want to see.'

3

But Winter was now also on his way.

At noon, he was in Manhattan, in the 23rd floor men's room which exclusively served the Park Avenue office of Skite, Wylie and Pratt, attorneys-at-law.

Jeremy Skite discovered Winter's presence there as he stood at the urinal with his honorable member in his hands. It was then that Dewey came up behind him and pushed the lawyer's face into the tile wall.

There was a soft clattering noise as Skite's teeth sprinkled to the floor. Then Skite himself was lying among them, his face bloodied, his pants wet, his organ exposed.

Winter stood over him, smiled down. There was also a gigantic slab of a man and a wiry brown man with a face like a skull. The wiry brown man was holding what seemed to be a cigarette lighter in his hand.

'Giordano sent me,' Winter said. 'He told me you could help me find Frederick Chubb.'

Skite the attorney shook his head. 'Ca. Hew kew meh . . .' he said through his broken mouth.

'Pardon?' said Winter. He glanced at the slab beside him. 'What did you have to knock his teeth out for?'

'Sorry,' said Dewey. 'He lifted his chin.'

'Kew meh . . . Hew kew meh!' the lawyer insisted.

Ferdinand, the skull-faced one, cleared his throat. 'He's saying Chubb will kill him.'

'Oh!' Winter laughed pleasantly. Leaned down toward the lawyer. 'He'll kill you? Is that what you're saying?'

Skite nodded. 'Peese. Hew kew meh Ah sswah.'

'Yes. He probably will,' Winter conceded. 'But then, Ferdinand will burn your penis off.'

Ferdinand bared his teeth and pressed a button on the cigarette lighter. Only it wasn't a cigarette lighter. It was a Lensmaster C-14 Laser. The beam from it shot upward four and a half feet where it struck the ceiling. The plaster up there charred, cracked and burst away from around a dime-sized burn hole. Then the beam vanished.

'Apsboowy, Apsboowy!' said Skite, quickly covering himself with his hands.

'Apsboowy?' said Winter.

'Apsboowy i Wockland Counee.'

'Oh,' Winter laughed. 'Oh, oh. Hapsburg. In Rockland County. Okay. I know it. What's the address?'

Skite curled up on his side, his hands between his legs. His blood and tears spilled down onto his teeth. 'Portee Bweckenwidge Wo.'

'Forty Breckenridge Road,' said Winter. 'Thank you very much. And of course, if he's not there, we'll be forced to come back.'

But he didn't press the point. The way the lawyer lay convulsed with sobs convinced him that he was no longer listening – and that he hadn't dared to lie.

Winter stepped over the man and started for the door.

Ferdinand and Dewey fell in behind him.

Hapsburg, Winter thought. It was about a hundred miles away. He ought to get there just about two o'clock in the afternoon.

4

Lonnie Blake got there around 1:25.

Hapsburg was a pleasant little village, situated not ten miles from the Hudson River. Its small Main Street was lined with quaint white clapboards. Wooded hills, still decked with fall pastels, rose to every side of it.

Lonnie stopped the Dodge at a light in the center of town. To his right was a row of stores. Books 'n Things, Wholly Doughnuts!, Century 21. He sat looking through the windshield at the storefronts, at the sidewalk shoppers reflected in the storefront glass. Mothers still young, still beautiful, walked chatting with their toddlers, or pushed their babies in strollers by each other's side. One older woman, silver-haired, stately, greeted an ancient man who seemed to shuffle along contentedly to no purpose. A dome-bellied realtor in his shirtsleeves hurried back to his office from the doughnut shop, rollicking with supreme confidence, commenting on the weather to one and all.

Lonnie ached at the serenity of the scene. He had had days like this. He had imagined a life like this. He and Suzanne had imagined it together.

Yeah. Well. Tough shit, cuz. It be that way sometimes.

Without thinking, he found himself searching the little crowd for another black face. There was none. Which made him feel like a man's shadow on a movie screen: just as welcome, just as noticeable. And so when a state trooper pulled up at the curb near him, his heart seized. How could the cop miss him? He was as good as busted.

Luckily, just as the trooper unfolded from his cruiser, the light turned green. Lonnie, hissing in relief, eased his foot down bit by bit so that the car moved gently away.

Sayonara, Main Street, he thought.

And on he went.

Breckenridge Road led him up into the hills. The leaves were growing sparse now but there were still swaths of orange and red, patches of yellow. The trees grew denser as the road wound up. The houses grew larger and were set farther back from the road. He could see them – their white walls, their brown walls – through the thinning leaf-cover.

The place he wanted was near the top of the grade. Its driveway wound on even farther up the hillside. By the time Lonnie reached the house itself, he could see – through the car window, through the breaks between the trees – a spectacular view of the town below, the hills beyond, the sparkle from the river where it ran through a valley of mist.

The house was modern. Fresh brown wood in slanting planes. An enormous window, darkened on the outside, looking onto that sweet southeastern vista. There was a circular gravel drive before the double garage. No car was visible.

Lonnie parked close to the front door. He stepped out into the cool of the day.

It was quiet. After the car, after the city. You could hear the breeze in the high branches. You could hear the whisper of traffic on the streets below. But other than that, the woods around were still. Not even a bird was singing.

Lonnie cast a slow glance around him. No one nearby, no one in sight. Quiet enough to make him edgy. He slipped his hand into his overcoat pocket, curled his fingers around the grip of his gun. He stepped toward the front door cautiously. Ready for a fight, muscles pulled tense as a bow.

A footstep crunched on the gravel behind him. He whirled around, whipped out his gun.

Frederick Chubb laughed. 'Really, Mr Blake,' he said, 'if I'd meant to kill you, you'd be a long time dead by now.'

5

'As things stand, I'd say I have about half an hour to live.'

They were on an indoor balcony now, an open deck above the living room. They sat before the enormous window. The rolling hills and the river valley spread beneath them.

The long thin man sat relaxed in a canvas chair. He was wearing khaki slacks and a khaki safari shirt. Elaborate sandals over bare feet. His long black hair was tied back. The strap of his eyepatch was at a jaunty slant. His single eye was green and bright. His hand moved in the air with graceful gestures. Overall, the smuggler gave an impression of elegant sophistication.

Lonnie sat across from him, swigging water from a plastic bottle. He didn't give a shit how elegant Chubb was or how sophisticated. He just wanted to know why he'd walked into a bloodbath. Why a cop had tried to shave his face off. He wanted to know how the hell he had suddenly become a killer being hunted by the law.

'I've received a phone call of warning. A man named Edmund Winter is on his way here,' Frederick Chubb went on. 'His plan is to torture and kill me. If he finds you here, he'll torture and kill you too.'

Lonnie shook his head slowly. 'No. He won't.'

'That's right.' Chubb smiled. 'You're the man who killed Mortimer. You're a hard case, right?'

'I just don't like being fucked with,' Lonnie said. He could still feel Mortimer's hands on him. He could still feel the anger and the fear inside him. 'I've been fucked with enough.'

'Well, let me explain something to you, Mr Blake. Winter is no Mortimer. Winter is to Mortimer . . . Well . . . You've heard of Plato? Mortimer is the killer in fact. Winter is the killer in God's mind. If he finds you here, take my word for it, he'll fuck with you all right. He'll fuck with you until you're dead.'

Lonnie gave his small snort of contempt. 'Right now I got a lot of people with guns after me, Mr Chubb. Most of them got badges too. Winter's gonna have to wait in line. Meanwhile, I want to know what the hell it's all about.'

Chubb's lips tightened a little. He was a man who liked to be listened to with respect. A grocer's son from Nyack, he had come a long way in the world. He had worked hard on his elegant, sophisticated persona. He wanted it to be taken seriously.

He calmed himself with an elegant, sophisticated sip of coffee. 'All right,' he said then. 'I'll tell you. Winter is the North American bureau chief of an organization called Executive Decisions. It's a private fighting force that hires itself to companies and countries around the world for military and covert actions. Recently, they've been trying to expand their operations into the US recruiting personnel from security, law enforcement, the military. Moonlighters . . .'

'Like Mortimer and Hughes,' Lonnie said.

'That's right.'

'They were working for this Executive Decisions, not NYPD.'

'Well, Mortimer, at least, was working for both – but, yes, you get the general idea. An international paramilitary is setting up house in the United States. But see, the primitive methods that pass muster in other countries are no good here. Winter, on the other hand, is used to working with corporations. He has an acceptable manner, good business sense. He's worked his way up through the ranks to the front office. So ED has brought him over here to work out the rough edges of the new set-up. This operation you've become involved in is one of those rough edges. In fact, partly because of you, it's about as rough as they come. In fact, it's now become *so* rough that Winter has decided to handle it himself.'

'Yeah? So what are we talking about here?'

'ED has been hired to hunt down a girl.'

In spite of himself, Lonnie felt a sharp emotional hitch. He sat forward in his chair. 'Carol Dodson.'

But Chubb shook his head. 'Her five-year-old daughter. Amanda.'

Lonnie sat back. He tilted his water bottle to his lips, covering his surprise. A daughter. He had not imagined Carol Dodson with a daughter. He had not imagined her any way but the way she had been that night when he held her and she whispered to him and he felt his wife was still somehow alive in her. Those images raced through his mind now again.

And meanwhile Chubb set his coffee cup down and said quietly, 'The thing I'm about to tell you you will not believe. But you've got to. And quickly. Because we really don't have much time.'

6

They really didn't. Just about then, Winter turned onto Hapsburg's Main Street.

He was still driving his blue Lexus. His two golems were with him. Ferdinand in the passenger seat, mirrored glasses on his skull face now. Dewey slab-like in back, mirrored glasses on the part of him that was probably his head. All three of the men were silent.

The Lexus stopped at the light. Winter glanced through the windshield. He saw much the same Main Street scene that Lonnie had. The mamas with their babes, the old codgers, the smalltown businessmen striding behind their own bellies.

He smiled to himself.

He was thinking about Carol Dodson. He was thinking about the things he was going to do to her before he let her die. He was thinking about the taste of tears on her soft skin.

And it was good. Good to be out in the field again. Good

to be active and in control. These folks out there through the windshield, these Main Street folks, they had no idea how good it was. How real it made things, how sharp and clear. How rich it made the whiff of life.

Part of him was almost glad – glad that Mortimer and Hughes had screwed it up – glad that he'd been forced to take the op in hand. After his transaction with Giordano that morning, after the bagatelle in the men's room with Jeremy Skite, with Frederick Chubb's interrogation and Carol Dodson's rape and torture still to look forward to, Winter was a-feeling mighty like a man with wires in his body instead of veins, with electricity coursing through him instead of blood.

These folks on Main Street. They did not know. They had no idea how good it was.

The light changed. Winter gave a deep sigh of contentment.

He eased his foot down on the pedal and headed for Breckenridge Road.

7

'Four months ago, I was murdered,' said Frederick Chubb. He spoke quickly, urgently, but quietly too, clearly.

And Lonnie looked at him deadpan and thought, *Say what?*

'A competitor – a man named Abubakar – placed a bomb on my jet and blew it out of the sky.'

'The crash in Mass,' Lonnie said.

'That's right. It wasn't much of a bomb, but it did the trick. Most of the people on board never even hit the ground. Some came down in pieces. But, for reasons that aren't entirely clear, a few bodies – a few people in first class – fell almost entirely intact.'

'Yeah. Okay. So what?'

The tone of Chubb's voice didn't change. It was still urgent, still quiet, still cool.

'My body fell intact,' he said. 'It fell intact – and a few moments later, I stood up and I was fine.'

Lonnie let out a single laugh. 'Ah hah.'

'Oh yes. I was fine, Mr Blake. No burns. No internal injuries. No damage at all. Does that strike you as a believable scenario?'

'I don't know, man.' Lonnie lifted his shoulder. 'These things happen, I guess. How the hell should I know?'

'What if I were to tell you I was dead, Mr Blake?'

'What?'

'That I fell from that plane and I was dead – and that then I was alive again.'

'Oh come on, for Christ's sake,' Lonnie broke out. 'I killed a cop, man. I got the whole world after me. You're gonna sit there and testify to the resurrection . . . ?'

But Chubb seemed not to hear him. His single eye gleamed distantly. He shook his head as if in wonder. 'I stood up,' he repeated. 'I stood up and I looked around me. Stunned, I was. Amazed. The woods – I saw the woods were on fire, burning. And then I saw that there, at my feet, a child was lying, a little child. Carol Dodson's daughter, Amanda. She was unconscious. Bleeding from the mouth. And right then, right then I knew she had done it.'

'Done *what*?' said Lonnie.

Again, Chubb ignored him. 'Without knowing what I was doing or why, I picked her up in my arms and carried her away from the smoke and flames. And then, finally, I found Carol, her mother, searching for her . . .'

'What is this?' Lonnie sneered at him. 'What are you trying . . . ?'

'*Listen to me.*' Chubb's long fingers curled into a fist. 'Listen. I don't know myself what happened, not all of it. Only what Carol would tell me. There were some experiments . . . a pharmaceutical firm . . . I don't pretend to understand. All I know – all I know is that I was dead. I was dead and that child – that child *did something to me*. She *did something* and I was alive again.'

271

Fuck me, he's a nutcase, Lonnie thought. I waste my time, I risk my life to come here and he's raving out of his fucking mind.

Chubb made a noise in his throat. Tried to bring a measure of calm back into his voice again. 'Look. It doesn't matter. How or what or why. It doesn't matter. It doesn't even matter if you believe me. The point is: I was the man they meant to kill and I alone of all the passengers on that plane survived. *Survived*, you understand.' He shook his head. 'That can't just be coincidence. It can't be . . .' He had to steady himself again before he could continue. 'I vowed from that moment on that my life was going to be different, was going to be . . . *better*. Somehow. When Carol told me, blurted out, that someone was after her, I vowed – I told her – right there, as we were standing there, I told her . . . anything . . . *anything* I could do to help her I would do. All my resources, all my contacts, anything she could use to protect her, to protect her daughter. At first, there was nothing. She didn't trust me. She thought she could make it on her own. But now . . .'

Lonnie watched the man. He saw a quick grimace of suffering tighten Chubb's features and he knew, at least, that that – the suffering – was real.

'Now she's finally come to me,' Chubb said, 'and I've tried to help her.'

After a strained moment, Lonnie sighed. 'Yeah? So?'

Chubb drew a long breath. 'So instead, I've sent her into a death trap,' he said. 'And you're the only one who can get her out.'

8

Winter found the house he was looking for.

He parked the Lexus on Breckenridge Road, a few yards from the head of the driveway. As Ferdinand and Dewey unloaded themselves into the afternoon, Winter cracked open the glove compartment and drew out one of his contraptions: a pair of goggles attached to a thick headset. He climbed out of the car and handed the thing to Ferdinand.

The brown-faced, skull-faced man sniffed and removed his mirrored glasses, slipped them into his coat pocket. He pulled the goggles on.

Then all three men started for the house.

They walked on the drive, carelessly letting the gravel crunch beneath their shoes. The trees rustled gently all around them. A wedge of geese flew over their heads honking in the blue sky.

Winter glanced at Ferdinand as they walked. Ferdinand scanned the area with his goggles, shook his head.

The three men kept walking.

It was another minute before they came within sight of the house. There was a bend in the drive and then they caught a glimpse of the brown wood walls through the sparse yellow leaves. Winter slowed to a stop and the men behind him stopped.

Winter's eyes moved over the woods, over the house in the trees. He saw no sign of security. But then Chubb was like that. He never surrounded himself with guards, never took the usual precautions, never – even now – made much of an attempt to hide from anyone. He simply had a way of slipping through your fingers at the last minute.

But Winter did not think Chubb would slip through his fingers. He had troopers watching for him on every road out of town, for one thing. For another, he didn't think Chubb wanted to slip back into a life of pursuit and evasion. He thought Chubb would stay, would try to negotiate, would ultimately sell him Carol Dodson's whereabouts for some cash and some peace of mind.

Paused where he was, Winter glanced at Ferdinand again. Ferdinand again scanned the area with his goggle-machine. It was a FLIR – forward-looking infrared – thermal imager. It detected heat from objects, especially life forms. When he trained it on the house now, fuzzy red images formed against the dark background.

'There are two of them,' he said softly. 'Inside. Upstairs.'

Winter cocked an eyebrow at him. 'No one else? No one in the woods?'

Ferdinand stripped off the goggles. He shook his head. 'Two in the house. That's all.'

Winter nodded. Ferdinand and Dewey reached into their jackets. Each drew out a Walther P99.

'Let's take 'em,' Winter said.

The two thugs vanished into the forest.

Winter continued up the drive alone.

9

Chubb went on speaking. The quick, cool tone again. 'When I met Carol at the restaurant I'd had no time to make arrangements for her. My organization is gone now, most of my contacts are gone. I only have this house, one or two other places. A lot of cash. I have to improvise and it can't always be done on the spur of the moment. When she told me her pursuers were getting close, I gave her what money I could. And then I told her I'd arrange to have a lot more – and false-name credit cards and passports and other papers – left for her anywhere she chose. She gave me one of the keys to a bank deposit box and I promised to have the material dropped there.'

He paused for a deep breath but then pushed on quickly, speaking on the exhale. 'Arrangements to transport her and Amanda out of the country were more difficult. I told her to call me after she picked up the papers and I'd let her know where to meet her pick-up. Do you understand what I'm saying to you?'

Lonnie's head was swimming. 'Not really. No,' he said.

Chubb's long face registered his frustration. 'In a few minutes, Winter will be here. In about two hours, Carol's going to call to find out what she needs to know. When she calls, it'll be Winter who answers. He'll have her traced in seconds and he'll be on her trail again. What's more, he'll have my phone records, computer transactions and so on. I've covered my tracks as best I can but ... basically, if someone doesn't get to Carol and warn her before she makes that phone call, he's got her.'

Lonnie gazed at the one-eyed man a long, long while. He couldn't take all this in, couldn't figure it out, couldn't think at all. He could only imagine this man, this Winter – the killer in God's mind – moving closer and closer to Carol Dodson.

He shook the image off. 'Why don't you have one of your people warn her?'

'That's what I'm telling you. I don't *have* any people anymore. The people I can get work for cash and they're not always trustworthy.'

'Then warn her yourself.'

'Winter's on to me. He's got state troopers working for him everywhere. He'd have me before I got ten miles. Even so, I would have tried it. I was going to try it. Then you called.'

Lonnie made a curt noise. He already knew he wasn't going to like what came next.

'After Mortimer was shot,' Chubb said, 'Carol risked a call and told me about you. She thought I should know. She said you might even be smart enough to come after me. I prayed you would. It's pretty obvious to me that you were just an act of desperation on Mortimer's part. I figure it'll be obvious to Winter too. In which case, he'll probably let the cops take care of you. He won't be expecting you to climb right back into the frying pan.'

Lonnie stood up. 'Yeah, well, he's got that right. I followed this woman once already, man. She's bad for my health.'

It was as if Chubb hadn't heard him. He reached into his pocket, pulled out a key chain with a pair of keys on it. Tossed it to Lonnie. Lonnie caught it automatically.

'There's a car in the garage,' Chubb said. 'A BMW. The plates are clean. Winter hasn't got them. She'll be at the First National Bank in Tyler, Putnam County, by three o'clock when it closes. You can just make it.'

'Hey, I'm telling you . . . This is nothing to me. All I want is some information – not this crazy shit – something real, something I can take to the police . . .'

'It's no good. You've got to find her, Blake. Tell her I've arranged for a chopper to meet her on Meridian Mountain in New Hampshire. It'll be at the old Meridian Lodge at dawn on Friday. Got that? The lodge used to be one of my places, one of my transfer points. It's abandoned now, but it still has a field the chopper can land in. Help her, Blake. She'll take you with her. You'll be out of the country. She'll have enough money to arrange papers for you. You understand what I'm saying? You'll be away. You'll be out of this. You'll be free.'

'Free.' Lonnie tossed the keys back at Chubb. They hit the smuggler on the shoulder, slid down onto his thigh. 'I'll be a fugitive the rest of my life. I'm not running away from anyone, man. I'm gonna prove these people came after me. Whoever these Executive mothers are, whatever they're after, I'm gonna bring them down.'

Chubb swept the keys up angrily. 'If you don't help her, Blake, she'll die,' he said. And once again, he flung the keys across the deck.

Once again, Lonnie caught them. Held them. Stared at Chubb, his jaw working.

'She'll die, Mr Blake,' Chubb said again.

And slowly, Lonnie's hand closed, the keys digging into his flesh.

10

Winter knocked on the door.

He stood on the welcome mat and waited in plain sight. Despite the autumn chill, he was not wearing an overcoat. Just the black Cerutti, the red tie. His shirt – tailor-made by Jeroboam's of Savile Row – was white and featured a Napolean: a hidden snap-away front that would allow him to reach in easily underneath his arm. Underneath his arm, he was wearing a super-light Kramer holster. In the holster was a custom-made 9 millimeter semi-auto based on an H&K stock. Even with the compact holosight – which cast a 3D grid over any target – the weapon was less than seven inches long and weighed only slightly more than thirty ounces. Powerful as it was, the set-up made it virtually undetectable.

But Winter was not really expecting to use the gun. He was approaching Chubb openly, as a negotiator, and he thought he'd be received the same way. He had no doubt he could reach some amicable arrangement with Chubb before he tortured him – to make sure he wasn't lying about Carol Dodson's whereabouts – and killed him, for the purposes of security.

So he stood calmly on the welcome mat and waited. Conscious of the two Walthers covering him from the woods. Letting his hand rest lightly on his tie, near the spot where the false front of his shirt could be snapped away.

There were footsteps inside. Then the door opened.

Winter put his tongue in his cheek, closed one eye comically. But he kept his hand near the Napoleon.

A woman stood in the doorway. Pretty; in her thirties; short black hair, pug nose, bright smile.

She was holding a baby on her hip.

'Hi,' she sang out. 'Sorry. We were upstairs having a change. Can I help you?'

Winter winked at the baby. Smiled at the woman. 'Yes, hi,' he said. 'I'm here to see Forrest Childs?'

The woman's brown eyes narrowed. 'Forrest . . . Oh, Mr Childs! That's up at the top of the hill. Number fourteen.'

'Fourteen!' Winter's hand left his shirt. He made a little tossing motion with it. 'Fourteen, not forty. That explains everything,' he said. 'The man who gave me this address had no teeth. It was a little hard to understand what he was saying.'

'Oh!' The woman gave a surprised little laugh. 'Well . . . it's fourteen. Right up near the top.'

Winter reached out and stroked the baby's cheek with one finger. 'Thanks a lot,' he said. 'Sorry to bother you.'

He was halfway up the drive before his two companions came out of the woods and joined him. They holstered their Walthers as they came.

Winter glanced at Dewey. 'What did you have to knock his teeth out for?'

'Sorry,' said the slab.

The three walked back to the car.

11

Up the hill, in Chubb's house, for a last long second, Lonnie's gaze stayed locked on the smuggler's single green eye.

If you don't help her, she'll die, he thought.

Damn, he thought.

He looked away. 'All right,' he muttered. 'I'll do what I can. What about you? You just gonna sit here? Wait for Winter to come and torture you? Shit, he'll make you tell him the same stuff you just told me.'

Out of the corner of his eye, he saw Chubb move. When he looked again, the smuggler was holding a small revolver in his hand. A snub-nosed .38.

Lonnie gave a snort. 'Oh great. This guy's as good as you say he is, I think he's gonna come prepared for *that* action.'

Chubb frowned. He would be taken seriously in this, at least. 'I wasn't planning to use it on *him*.'

'Oh.' Lonnie lifted his chin. 'What? You mean you're gonna cap yourself. To protect her?'

'To protect the child. It's what I swore I would do if given half a chance.' The expression on Lonnie's face seemed to amuse Chubb. He smiled now. 'It's not as if I'm afraid of it, Blake. Remember: I've been there before.'

'Oh yeah, right,' said Lonnie drily. 'I forgot. You're the Lazarus man.'

'That's right,' said Chubb mildly. And his gaze grew distant again. 'Sometimes I even think I remember it, remember what it was like.'

Lonnie snorted. 'What? You mean, being dead? You remember being dead?'

'It's just a feeling I have sometimes but . . . It's a very specific sense . . . that there was a moment, you know . . . a moment of – *e pluribus unum*. Do you understand?' Lonnie didn't answer. He stood gazing at the man. Chubb smiled. 'Read your nickels, Mr Blake,' he said. '*E pluribus unum*. It means "Out of the many – one." Sometimes at night . . . when I think back on what happened after the plane blew . . . well . . . I imagine I'm sitting at this big table, this long table. And there are . . . the worst people I can think of. Not, you know, your nasty Aunt Ethel but . . . worse than that. The great villains, I mean. Stalin, Hitler. And the best people too. Jesus. Whoever. Take your pick. And I think, you know, that . . . that maybe for a moment, after the plane went down, after I fell, maybe I was there, maybe I sat down with those people at that table – this long table with food on it and drinks. And we all sat down and we all suddenly understood each other. We understood that we were part of something together – all of us – the evil and the good and the in-between – we were all part of something big and – and perfect somehow . . . That it was all right. You see? All of it. It was beautiful, every part. And we sat there at the table, the evil and the good, and we shared out the bread of love one with another. And it was all right. All of it. *E pluribus unum.'*

Chubb smiled again, to himself now. He shrugged. 'I guess I just wanted to tell that to someone before I ... before this was over. Now I strongly suggest you get going while there's time.'

But for another moment, Lonnie still stood, still stared, his mind far away. He was thinking about the boys who had surrounded Suzanne. The boys who had shouted *nigger* at her and grabbed her and chased her out into the road where she died. He thought of their grinning white faces, their taunting smiles. And he thought of sitting down with them at the long table and sharing out the bread of love.

He put his hand in his overcoat pocket. His fingers curled around the Beretta Cougar.

'I'm not sure I like that death of yours, Mr Chubb,' he told him.

Chubb laughed quietly this time. 'It's death, Mr Blake,' he said. 'No one asked you to like it.'

12

The Lexus moved slowly up Breckenridge Road. Number fourteen was near the top.

Once again, they parked on the street beside the mouth of the drive. They approached the place in much the same way as before. As before, they paused within sight of the house and Ferdinand scanned it with the thermal imager.

Through the lenses, he saw Chubb's moving image, red on the dark background.

'There's only him,' he said. 'Just one.'

Then, even as he spoke, he saw a sudden flash of scarlet. Winter, standing beside him, heard the shot.

'Goddamnit,' he said.

He started running toward the house. The front of his shirt was open, flapping. The modified Heckler and Koch was in his hand. Skull-face and the slab were right behind him.

They found Chubb on the balcony, still in his chair. His

head flung back, his mouth open as if he were snoring. There was a ragged crater near the crown of his head. There was gore splattered on the window behind him.

Rivulets of blood ran down the glass. They cast moving shadows on the dead man's face like rain.

Chapter Eleven

Fancy Meeting You Here

1

The town came out of the forest suddenly. There was a graveyard, a church, a lake, and then the town.

Not much of a town either. A few buildings of brick and concrete. A town hall, a post office, a courthouse and police station combined. A hardware store, a sporting goods store and a TV repair and video rental shop clustered nearby. A couple of loungers outside the fire house: guys with plaid shirts and red-and-black checkered jackets; pot-bellies, cigarettes and sluggish conversation.

Lonnie cruised by slowly, cruised slowly round the corner onto route 311. There were some weary-looking clapboard houses here. A barber shop. A restaurant. The offices of a weekly newspaper. And then the strip mall: a long parking lot bordered by a Stop N Shop, a Rexall's and – there it was – the First National Bank.

Lonnie could see right away why Carol had chosen the place. There was a gas station beside it, then a few more houses on the road beyond. But after that, the pavement rose sharply and the forest closed in fast. The town sank back into the forest as quickly as it rose.

Lonnie glanced at the clock on the dashboard. Two-thirty-seven in bright green digits. Still early.

He drove past the parking lot. Pulled into the gas station.

He filled the Beamer's tank. He bought a wrapped sandwich at the shop inside. His scarred black face felt like a wanted poster pinned to his head. Any minute he expected someone to spot him and start screaming.

There was an enormous woman behind the shop's counter. In her uniform blouse with its broad stripes of red and white she looked like some kind of gargantuan peppermint. Lonnie kept his eyes lowered as he paid her.

'Have a good one,' she muttered – but she hardly looked at him. By the time she spoke, she'd already turned away.

Lonnie went into the men's room. Pissed. Washed his hands, his face. Looked into the mirror, into his own eyes. His hunted, haunted eyes.

'Man oh man,' he said aloud to the reflection, 'I wouldn't want to be you.'

He left the shop quickly, quickly returned to his car.

He drove back to the mall. Parked at a distance from the bank. Shut the car down. Sat there.

He ate his sandwich and watched the bank. The bank was a brick box at the far end of the lot. There was a thick glass drive-thru window on one side. As Lonnie watched, one car then another pulled up for cash. The cars drove on again, parked again nearer the supermarket.

Lonnie ate his sandwich and watched the bank. Two or three people walked into the bank building. They stopped in the foyer to use the cash machine. Then they came out again.

The minutes turned slowly over. The sense that he was

noticeable, sitting there, even suspicious – a black man casing a bank – began to press in on him. This was a small town deep in the woods. Not many strangers passing. No other blacks that he could see. He began to feel hot in his overcoat.

It was 2:40. 2:45. A pale middle-aged woman entered the bank. A blustery man in a windbreaker. A housewife-type with her long red hair pinned up. The blustery man used the cash machine and came out again.

Where the hell was Carol? What was keeping her?

Lonnie finished the sandwich. He felt as if the world were drawing in on every side of him. As if he were at the center of a narrowing beam of light, light narrowing to a glaring pinpoint that would attract all eyes his way. An old woman pushed a shopping cart past the front fender. A heavy-browed mother with two screaming boys went by. A waddling fat man in a plaid shirt . . . As each passed the car, Lonnie felt himself clench inside, felt himself wait for it – the shout, the jabbing finger – *There he is!*

Nothing. No one noticed him. It was 2:50.

Where the hell was she?

Lonnie made a sort of drumming noise between his teeth. *Ch ch-ch-ch ch-ch-ch*. He wagged his head back and forth. The car was growing colder, but he wiped sweat from above his mouth.

Two-fifty-five. Another five minutes and the bank would close. Had he missed her? Where the hell was she?

'Damnit,' he said.

He got out of the car.

The back of his neck prickled as he walked across the lot. The scar on his chin, the color of his face, just the fear radiating off him – he felt like a walking alarm bell. He was glad to reach the bank's glass door. To pull it back, step into the foyer.

The pale woman was still there, standing at the cash

293

machine. She glanced over her shoulder as he came in. She smiled at him.

Lonnie smiled back. He went past her, through the glass foyer, through the inner door, into the bank.

The main room was small, rectangular. Two-thirds of the way between Lonnie and the far wall was a chest-high counter running from one end of the place to the other, from the drive-thru window on the left to the open vault door on the right. There were three people behind the counter, two female tellers and a heavyset man in a suit. To Lonnie's right were a couple of desks. A woman was sitting at one of them tapping at a computer keyboard.

Lonnie stopped in his tracks. He held his breath. Everyone in the room had looked up when he came in. Everyone was watching him. It was a small bank. He was the only customer in sight.

This is a mistake, he thought.

But running away would be even worse, even more suspicious. Casually as he could, he walked over to a narrow ledge on the wall to his left. There were pens there and deposit and withdrawal slips. He took a pen from its holder, a deposit slip. Dawdling, playing for time. Sweating under what he felt were the steady stares of everyone in the room. He hardly knew what the hell he was doing.

A minute passed or maybe it was a day. Two more customers came in, both men. One, in slacks and a corduroy jacket, walked over to the counter to talk to a teller. The other, also in slacks, also in a corduroy jacket, walked over to the bankers' desks and sat down across from the woman there.

Lonnie glanced at the men.

Cops, he thought.

But he shook the thought off. He couldn't start panicking now. He went back to mulling over his deposit slip.

'Sir?'

Lonnie looked up quickly to find one of the tellers blinking at him from behind her large glasses.

Excuse me, sir, but how did a Negro fugitive such as yourself come to be in our lovely white bank?

'What?' said Lonnie.

'I said, "May I help you, sir?"' the woman repeated.

Lonnie licked his lips. Managed a brief smile. 'Uh, I was . . . Actually I was just waiting for someone,' he told her. He abandoned the withdrawal slip on the ledge. He backed away from it. 'I was supposed to meet her here. But I don't . . .'

And still, he felt the stares, the silent stares. The frightened eyes of the women, the belligerent eyes of the heavyset man. Only the two customers in corduroy seemed oblivious to him.

'Well . . .' said Lonnie. 'I guess, uh . . .'

He was about to turn and hurry away when the red-haired housewife he'd seen before came out of the open vault. He glanced at her.

It was Carol Dodson.

2

It was a good disguise. Not just the hair – copious, flowing bright orange hair that drew your gaze – but her complexion, the shape of her eyes, the shape of her mouth had all changed. It was small stuff, subtle stuff, just makeup effects, but it altered the look of her completely.

Only her little start of surprise when she saw him gave her away. That – and the jolt of warmth and longing he felt, the surprising power of his urge to help her.

She was just coming out of the vault. She was folding the edges of a small manila package, trying to stuff the package down into her purse. She glanced up – very cool, very casual.

And that's when they spotted each other.

Lonnie felt his breath catch. He saw the hitch in her movements, saw her lips part.

Then she continued stuffing the package in her purse. Smiled her thanks up at the heavyset man.

And Lonnie, likewise, finished his sentence to the woman behind the counter. 'Well, she's not here. I guess I'll see if she's over the way.'

The teller smiled at him. Tightly, he thought, nervously, but he didn't have time to pay attention to her now. He was walking back to the foyer door. Carol was walking directly behind him. He put his hand on the door. Pushed it open, held it open for her.

She gave him a nod of thanks, their eyes meeting. She moved level with him.

'Chubb sent me,' he murmured to her.

She stopped cold. Right there in front of him, right before the open door. He thought she was startled by what he'd said. Then he realized she was staring at something outside.

He followed her wide gaze. Looked out through the foyer, into the parking lot.

The police had arrived in force.

There were three cruisers out there suddenly, a fourth already pulling in. The cars were lined up end to end to form a barricade. Under that cover, officers scrambled for position, bent double, pistols drawn. Townies, county deputies. Some riflemen with their weapons already propped on the cruisers' hoods and trunks.

The bank was under siege.

As Lonnie, in that single instant, scanned the scene, he spotted the giant peppermint woman from the gas station. She was gesturing wildly at the bank while an officer tried to calm her down, tried to push her enormous bulk out of harm's way.

She had recognized him. She had called the law. Lonnie understood it all.

It was over. They had him.

He stared. Carol stared. Neither moved from where they stood at the foyer door.

A voice, startling, sounded from behind them.

'Just step away from the door, Mr Blake. We don't want any trouble.'

Lonnie and Carol both looked around.

The two customers in the corduroy coats, of course. Plainclothes men. Of course. One by the banker's desk, one by the teller's counter. Both had drawn their service revolvers.

Both were pointing them at Lonnie Blake.

3

Lonnie looked from one plainclothes man to the other, from one gun barrel to the other. He glanced outside again at the battery of rifles.

He had only felt like this once before: when he had identified his wife's body. When he had seen her stretched out on that long white table – so cool, so cold, so fair – and realized that all hope was gone, that every option had collapsed, every appeal was exhausted, every avenue closed.

Then, as now, he had felt a wild, blinding, animal rage before the incontrovertible fact of his own helplessness.

Lonnie looked at the policemen around him and he thought nothing would feel better than to pull out the Cougar and just start shooting.

'Just step away, Blake,' the plainclothes man by the desk said more urgently. 'We don't want anyone to get hurt.'

Lonnie took a deep breath . . .

And then Carol threw herself backwards against him.

'Don't shoot!' she screamed. 'He'll kill me! He means it!'

For a single frozen second, Lonnie gawped stupidly down at the red hair piled on top of her head. He had let go of the foyer door. It was swinging shut.

Then he got it. He wrapped an arm around Carol's neck. Pulled out the Cougar and jammed the muzzle to her temple.

'I'm serious, man!' he shouted. 'Put your guns down! I'll blow her away!'

'Jesus,' said the plainclothes man by the desk. 'Hold your fire. He's hot a gostage.'

'A hostage!' Carol shouted.

'A hostage!' shouted the plainclothes man. He had his two-way in his hand. 'He's got a hostage!'

Lonnie swung from one cop to the other, clutching Carol, swinging her body back and forth while she let out a shriek.

'Don't anyone think about it, man!' Lonnie screamed. 'Don't anyone think about anything! Just hold your fire and no one gets hurt!'

'Oh please! Please!' Carol cried.

'Now I am walking out of here, man,' said Lonnie. 'You tell those boys outside they better keep their trigger fingers soft as their dicks. One mistake and she dies, you hear me?'

The plainclothes man by the desk made a calming gesture at him. 'Easy. Take it easy,' he said.

'You tell 'em, man!' Lonnie said. 'I'm going out there. You tell 'em.'

He shouldered the foyer door, pushed it open.

The corduroy copper at the counter feinted toward him.

'Don't you do it!' Lonnie yelled over his shoulder.

Carol threw in another shriek for good measure.

The cop held back. The other cop, the one at the

desk, had his two-way to his mouth, was calling to the barricade.

Swinging Carol this way and that, Lonnie pushed his way out into the foyer. The door swung shut behind them.

They were alone in the glass box – trapped there between the guns in the bank and the guns in the lot outside.

Lonnie leaned back against the wall, gasping for breath. Holding Carol in front of him all the while, his arm around her throat.

'Not so tight,' she gurgled. 'I'm strangling.'

'Man oh man, are we ever gonna die,' he said.

'No, we're not. I can't die. I have a child.'

'Well, forget it then. I'll give myself up. They won't shoot you.'

'Yeah, right. They'll just haul me in for the killings in Manhattan. Once the cops've got me, Winter and his guys'll have me in a second.'

'Shit,' Lonnie said.

'Stop strangling me, damnit!'

He loosened his grip on her neck.

The sound of their frantic breathing filled the little space. The tiled green walls, the staring mechanical countenance of the cash machine, the glass doors on either side seemed to Lonnie to yaw this way and that as his eyes roved round in a desperate search for a way out.

'Jesus,' he said.

'Listen . . .' Carol began.

'Blake!' Lonnie stiffened as an amplified voice pierced the foyer. 'This is Undersheriff Lester Jackson!'

'Christ, with the bullhorns now,' Carol muttered. 'These clowns watch too many movies.'

'Yeah, well, it sounds like this is the scene where they start shooting.'

'Just listen to me . . .' she said.

'Let the girl go!' boomed the undersheriff.

A crazed laugh burst out of Lonnie. '"Let the girl go." I'll bet he's always wanted to say that.' The sweat poured off him.

'Just listen, listen. We're going out,' said Carol. 'Right now, before they have time to think. Where's your car?'

'Too far. Behind the barricade.'

'All right. We'll take mine. It's just to the right of the door. We're in it, we're gone.'

'Put down your weapon and come out before someone gets hurt!' said the amplified undersheriff.

'What're you driving?' said Lonnie.

'A yellow bug,' she said.

He laughed wildly. 'Great. Those yellow ones are fast.'

Carol snorted and burst out laughing too, stifling it in the arm he held around her throat.

'It's all right . . .' she said, laughing.

Lonnie tried to answer but only started laughing again. He hid his face in her hair so the cops wouldn't see.

'I've got a plan,' she said.

This made Lonnie laugh until the tears came.

'No, no, really, it's a good one,' she laughed.

'Come out with your hands up, Blake,' said the under-sheriff.

Lonnie snorted loudly, trying to stop the laughter. '"Come out with your hands up,"' he said. 'Can you believe this cat?'

'Come on,' said Carol. 'Before he starts doing his Al Pacino impression.'

Lonnie took a breath. 'All right,' he said. 'All right. We gotta be serious now.'

She giggled into his arm.

'Come on!' he said.

'All right,' she said. 'I'm okay. I'm serious.'

'We'll be the comedy team of Dead and Buried.'

'Let's just do it.'

Lonnie nodded. He pulled her closer to him. His face was pressed into her hair. He caught the scent of violets and tobacco.

'Okay,' he said. 'This is it.'

And he dragged her out of the bank.

4

'Don't anybody move! Don't get smart! I'll kill her, man, I mean it!'

The bullhorn had fallen silent. Everyone in the mall lot had fallen silent. As the fugitive and his hostage edged out of the building, they were a single point of movement and noise in a vast tense motionless quiet. Carol's slender form kicked and writhed. Lonnie wrestled with her, holding the gun against her head.

'You just stand there, motherfuckers! Just put your guns up! Just take your fingers off the fucking triggers! Just stand there!'

He dragged her sideways, away from the doors, out of the firing range of the plainclothes men behind him. She let out small, breathless shrieks of anguish as they moved along. They were very convincing.

'Fuck up and she dies, man, you hear me?' Lonnie screamed. The fear in his voice was convincing too. Well, it was real. Any minute he expected to hear the crack of sudden death.

They sidled along the wall of the bank. The policemen watched. The crowds, pushed back to the supermarket across the lot, watched. Some, like children, held their fingers to their open mouths.

Lonnie's mind raced, worked, as they moved, trying to keep track of the logistics. It wasn't easy, this hostage business. If he took his eyes off the bank door, the plainclothes men might follow him out and open fire. If he turned wholly away from the riflemen – *pow* – they would take him down.

He pressed himself hard against the side of the bank, moved with Carol through the hedge-and-woodchip border between the building and the pavement. The rifles propped on the cruisers followed their progress. The eyes of the policemen followed them. The eyes of the people by the supermarket followed them too.

And all around, the chilly air was still. No cars were passing on the street or moving in the lot. No birds were singing in the nearby trees. There seemed to be no sound at all beyond Lonnie's gruff shouts and Carol's little cries.

He inched along, dragging Carol with him. There was a line of parked cars in front of him now. Carol's yellow Volks was five cars down.

It was seventies vintage. They were definitely going to die.

'Don't anybody get smart, man, don't anybody do a thing, not one fucking thing!' Lonnie screamed.

He negotiated Carol's kicking, twisting form along the bank wall, over the woodchips, towards the yellow Volks.

'You got the keys?' he muttered.

'Yeah,' she said breathlessly. 'Right-hand coat pocket.'

They reached the car. Moved around to the side of it. Its humped little body gave them some scant protection from the rifles in front of the bank. But there were more cops to the other side of them. This was going to have to be fast.

He pulled the keys out of her pocket. Crouched down between the Volks and a Buick, drawing her down with him. He had to let her go then. Transfer the gun to his left hand. He had to pray the cops didn't find a clear shot between the cars before he got the door opened.

He tried to get the key in the lock. His hand was shaking too badly.

'Damn!' he said.

'Hurry up,' she whispered.

The key went in. The door was open. He put his hand on the back of Carol's neck and pretended to force her inside. He followed after while she was still climbing across the stick shift to the passenger seat. Her feet kicked at him.

He shut the door. Stuck the key in the ignition. Carol was twisting around, sitting up now beside him. He handed her the gun.

'Here, hold yourself hostage a minute,' he said.

His heart was beating jig-time. It seemed to swell like a balloon every time it beat. He turned the key over hard.

Putt-putt-putt went the little engine.

'Mm, listen to her roar,' said Lonnie softly.

Carol exploded with laughter. She bowed her head, covered her face with her hand. 'Shut up, shut up, they'll see me laughing,' she said.

He shoved the stick into reverse. He felt the eyes of the police all around him. He felt their guns trained on him.

'"I've hot a gostage,"' he muttered.

Carol bent over, laughing hard.

Lonnie pressed his foot down on the gas.

5

Putt-putt-putt went the little yellow car's engine.

'Shit,' said Lonnie Blake.

'Just go! Go!' said Carol.

Lonnie backed out of the parking space, swung the Volks around. Shifted. Floored the gas. And sputtered past the police barricades, past the trailing guns. Waiting for the crack of the rifle. The shattering glass. The second of searing pain.

Then the Volks bounced over the curb, out of the lot, and they were on the street again.

'Up the hill,' said Carol breathlessly.

Lonnie laughed bitterly as the little bug began to strain up the grade. He shifted back down into first gear. The car edged up to thirty miles per hour. He glanced out the window, back at the mall.

The cops were scrambling for their cruisers. The red beacons were whirling. The cries of the sirens began winding up over the little town and into the lofty sky.

'Here they come,' said Lonnie.

'Just go, man, will you,' Carol said.

'I'm trying, baby.'

The Volks whined as the hill grew steeper. They neared the top. Lonnie flipped the stick into second. The car sprung forward, up over the crest. The mall disappeared behind them. They started rolling downhill, gathering speed.

'Yeah,' Lonnie murmured. 'Yeah, yeah, yeah.'

He goosed the car through its gears. They accelerated to forty, then to fifty. Ahead of him, he saw the last of the town vanish. The forest closed in on either side, brown wood crowding the macadam, tangled boughs and vines fading back and back into deep mysterious distances.

And the air grew thick with sirens and the sirens grew louder. Lonnie glanced at the rearview mirror. The first red beacon was rising over the crest of the hill.

'Okay, here they are,' he said. 'What's the plan?'

'Just stay ahead of them,' said Carol.

He laughed. 'That's the plan?'

'Just to that next turn down there.'

The lead cruiser leapt the crest. Its front tires came down hard.

Lonnie tore his gaze from the rearview. Looked ahead, through the windshield.

The hill plunged through the lowering woods. The road curled away at the bottom out of sight.

He tried to push the gas pedal through the floor. They were almost going sixty.

But the cop cars were gaining. A line of three were visible in the rearview now. Their sirens were growing louder every second.

And the curve below was coming nearer. Lonnie watched it racing toward the windshield.

'I think I can, I think I can,' he said.

Carol laughed. 'Shut up! Just drive.'

Lonnie glanced in the rearview. The headlights of the lead cruiser glared at him like two great eyes, growing larger.

'Oh, Lordy,' Lonnie said.

And then the cruiser slipped out of sight behind as the Volkswagen rounded the curve.

Lonnie glanced at Carol. Her stare was riveted forward. Her face was set. Her hands were out in front of her, clutching the edge of the dashboard, white.

He faced the windshield. Saw where the road forked up ahead. Another two-lane went off to the left.

'Which way?' he said.

'Left.'

If there had been oncoming traffic, they'd have been cut in half. Lonnie wrenched the wheel and the Volks slid across the two-lane and down the left fork.

They buzzed over a small rise in the pavement, then down the other side, out of sight of the main road behind them. It would gain them a second or two, Lonnie thought. When the cops reached the fork, they wouldn't know which way to go.

For a second or two. No more than that.

Sure enough. The sirens behind them dimmed a moment, but a moment later grew steadily louder again. The Volkswagen was shuttling through the forest shadows at little more than sixty. The cops were gaining again.

Then Carol said, 'There! Go in there!'

Lonnie looked. He saw the garbage.

It was just off the shoulder, maybe ten, fifteen yards into the woods. One of those illegal dumps that seem to grow up everywhere by America's forest roads. There was the shell of an old Chevrolet, a busted chest of drawers piled atop busted chairs. Car parts, tires, plastic bags full of God knows what. A great pile of the stuff.

Lonnie understood. He twisted the Volkswagen's wheel. The little car rumbled off the road. It went bumping over a worn forest path, straight for the trash.

Another moment and they were in it. The car rocked hard from side to side. Sticks cracked under the tires. A bag burst. Pebbles flew. Lonnie wrestled the wheel around hard. The Volkswagen circled behind the big carcass of the Chevy.

'Kill the engine,' she said.

He turned the key. The engine died.

'Now wait,' she said.

They waited. Their panting breath was loud in the little car. The sirens were loud and growing louder. They sat there and Lonnie felt the suspense like insects crawling under his skin. The Chevy's skeleton only partially obscured the Volks from the road. A sharp-eyed cop would spot the yellow paintwork in a city minute.

They waited. The sirens grew louder still. Lonnie looked at Carol. She looked at him. He wondered if his eyes seemed as enormous as hers, as frightened.

For one more second, the sirens screamed louder until Lonnie thought he would burst with waiting.

Then the first cruiser raced past, its shrill cry skirling down. He saw it through the dead Chevy's windows.

Then another passed with a whisk of air. And then a third.

Then a lull. They waited.

'They split up to cover the fork,' said Carol. 'Let's go.'

'Go where?'

'Come on.'

She pushed the Volkswagen's door open. He did the same on his side. She tumbled out into the woods and so did he. She ran and he ran after her. A moment or two and he'd overtaken her, had seized her hand, was pulling her along behind him.

'There,' she panted. 'Up ahead, up that hill. Before they figure it out.'

They charged up a narrow path, over a small ridge. The sirens were in the high branches of the trees all around them.

Lonnie grunted as his legs stretched for the ridge top. Carol fought for purchase on the dust and stones as he practically lifted her behind him.

They were over, out of sight of the road, half running, half tumbling down the other side into a valley of trees.

Lonnie skidded over the yellow leaves. He came up hard against the trunk of a white birch. Gasping for breath, Carol slid around in front of him.

'Come on,' she managed to say. 'They'll be back any minute.'

She pushed off the tree, stumbled away again. In a moment, he was stumbling right beside her. He stopped when she stopped and followed her eyes as she scanned the woods.

To him, it looked like nothing, like a thorny wild. He was a city boy, his whole life long. He'd never really been in a forest before. All he saw was a mesh of vines and branches, a vast stretch of tangled emptiness. All he heard were the leaves blowing over the ground, the branches chattering, the whispering wind.

And the sirens, of course. They hadn't lost the sirens.

Carol said, 'Okay.'

She took his hand and led him on.

There was another rise. Another tumble down a slope over slippery leaves. A great rock loomed out of the earth to Lonnie's left. Carol tugged him past it, whispering, 'Come, come, come.'

Then she stopped. Lonnie stopped beside her. He looked – stared. At first, he wasn't sure what he was seeing.

There was a gap in the earth before him. A gaping black hole right there in the rocky ground. Lonnie had never seen anything like it. It looked unreal to him. Surreal. Like a tear in the very fabric of things. There was the forest all around and then this black hole, like a doorway into nothing, and everything seemed to be falling into it: the ground funneled down to it and the trees leaned toward it with their roots half torn from the dirt and hunched up like great spider legs and even the living limestone slabs that formed its massive border seemed about to cave in and vanish through the enormous gateway and into blackness.

I mean, what the fuck *is that?* he thought.

The two stood only another moment. The wind rose. The trees above them swayed, cracking. Leaves swirled out of the air and pattered to the forest floor. A siren grew louder, grew nearer. It peaked, then stopped ominously.

Lonnie glanced back over his shoulder. Swallowed hard. Had the police spotted the Volks? He could no longer see the garbage dump.

'All right,' said Carol. 'We better hurry.'

She moved toward the hole. As she got closer, the ground dipped fast beneath her. She had to lower herself onto it. Pick her way down over the rocks.

She glanced up. Lonnie was still standing there, watching her.

'You coming?' she said.

In there? he thought. 'Oh,' he said. 'Yeah. Sure.'

He started climbing down after her, the limestone cold on his fingers.

Soon, he was beside her. Right at the border of the hole. It didn't get any brighter in there. It was lightless, bottomless as far as he could see.

'Listen,' he finally couldn't help asking. 'What the hell is this? Where're we going?'

'It's a sinkhole,' she said – as if any idiot would know. 'Haven't you ever seen a sinkhole?'

'Oh!' he said, climbing. 'A sinkhole! Right. I guess I didn't recognize it there for a minute.' *I mean, what the* fuck . . . ?

Carol went on down over the sinkhole's edge. She reached for purchase on the rocks around, found it expertly. Her face was hidden by a fall of orange hair as she looked down at her feet. But Lonnie could see her breath rising up in little puffs and plumes of frost.

'So this is, like, some kind of cave or something,' he said.

'Yeah.' She was panting from the climb. 'That's it.'

'Well, then, aren't we gonna get cornered in here?'

'Hell, no. It goes on for miles. Has four different exits. The cops won't know which way we went. They'll never find us.'

'Will anyone?'

Carol laughed. Then she vanished. Her voice trailed up from the gaping dark.

'Hurry up, man. You gotta stay with me. You won't make it through here alone.'

'Yeah, tell me about it,' Lonnie muttered.

And then he followed her into utter blackness.

Chapter Twelve

The Whole Darned World
Turned Upside Down

1

Roth sat perched on the examination table. Stripped to his underwear. Dazed with an almost religious wonder. Not to mention half an hour of intravenous Demerol only now beginning to wear off.

So? he thought. *What's the prognosis? I'll tell you what's the prognosis. Paradise. Immortality. Death shall have no dominion.*

Yeah, he could just see the doctor saying that. *I see by your chart, Professor, that the Lord God will swallow up death in victory and wipe away tears from off all faces.* He could just imagine the headline in the *Journal of American Medicine*: DEATH SHALL BE NO MORE. CRANKY JEW IN GADKES HERALDS COMING OF CHILD MESSIAH.

Roth pinched the bridge of his nose between thumb and forefinger. He could barely keep from laughing. Laughing? How could he keep from singing? He was cured! He knew it! He was fucking cured!

The doctor – a boy who barely looked old enough to

collect the pencil tops from cereal boxes – was standing just outside the door. He'd been returning to the examination room and had paused out in the hall to chat with one of the nurses. His hand was on the knob and the door was slightly ajar. Because the whole world needed to see a flabby-titted old man in his Fruit of the Looms.

Roth snorted laughter, but a wave of nausea, a druggy haze of it, washed over him. He closed his eyes and swayed where he sat.

Finally – after a nice, pleasant talk with Lovely Nurse Nelle with the door half open – finally, Dr Dentons deigned to return to his naked patient. Carrying his Official Authoritative Clipboard, no less. Which he probably got as a prize for selling magazine subscriptions.

'You can get dressed now, Professor Roth,' he said cheerily.

'Thanks. Don't think I don't appreciate it.'

He moved slowly, lowered himself slowly off the table. Shuffled unsteadily to where his clothes hung on a hat-rack in the corner.

The doctor went on speaking behind him.

'We won't have the biopsy back for about a week so right now we don't know anything for sure. The X-rays were inconclusive before but ... I mean, they seem perfectly clear to me. You sound clear. The cough's gone, right? There's no sputum. There's not much point doing another MRI until the lab work comes back. The way things stand ...'

Roth, buttoning his shirt, turned around in time to see the doctor shrug. He wasn't sure whether it was the after-effects of the Demerol or a burgeoning sense of man's puniness before the miraculous works of the Almighty but, in either case, his eyes suddenly misted over.

Didn't this munchkin understand? There wasn't any *need* to see the lab work. There wasn't any need for Roth to have come here at all. He already knew everything he needed to know.

He had been sick. He had been mortally ill. And then a little girl had ... done something ... touched him. She'd touched him, and now he was well. I mean, wake up and read the headlines, Doc: MIRACLE TOT IN END OF DEATH SHOCKER!

Roth bit his lip, fighting back the tears.

Mr Medicine, embarrassed, examined his zippy I'm-A-Doctor clipboard. 'I'm sure this hasn't been easy for you,' he muttered.

Roth gave a laugh, shook his head, pulled on his trousers. 'Tell me something,' he said hoarsely. Pulling the pants closed. Buttoning up. 'Have you ever wondered whether everything you've ever believed, everything you've ever been taught, everything you hold most true – your values, all those facts you know, every single thing – whether it was all just wrong? Just simply wrong?'

The young doctor thought about it. Shook his head. 'Not really. No.'

Roth smiled with one corner of his mouth. Yanked up his zipper. 'You ought to try it sometime,' he said.

2

He walked back from the Medical Center. Worried about any lingering dizziness from the drugs, he had left his car, his old Citroën, at home. A nurse had asked him if someone – a friend or family member – would come to pick him up. He'd lied, said yes, embarrassed to say there was no one.

There was no one. He walked back alone.

He shambled slowly over the sidewalk toward the campus. Pausing frequently. Leaning on lampposts, trees. He took deep breaths. The cold air braced him. The Lord-have-mercy hallelujah wonder of it all – that braced him too.

As he neared the quad, he stopped a while. Pressed his shoulder into the oddly feminine curve of a gruff old maple. Looked out over the way, past the criss-crossing traffic. Watched the campus. The ivied brick. The long white wooden barracks. The little elms and birches. The neatly trimmed grass. The students walking on the pathways.

The students. Young. God. They were unimaginably young.

Roth contemplated them from afar. Children. Little children. New ones every year, and every year the same. Once the predictability of their thoughts and emotions had made him cynical. He had smirked at their confidence, their conviction that they were original, incorruptible, fresh and wise. Only the great Roth understood that they were merely a few more droplets in the ceaseless human sea . . .

But now – now how marvelous they suddenly appeared to him as well. Even their silliness, their still-adolescent attitudes – the lazy, sullen, lordliness of their ignorance – for the first time, it all struck him as touching, as dear.

All these years, he had fought to teach them. He had fought to bring them to the well of the classical world so they could drink from the tradition that had formed them. He had fought against the leftist and feminist cant that was being drummed into their heads: the Great Ideas of the Moment that were tomorrow's silence and ash. He had fought to bring them what was steadfast in the whisper of the mighty dead.

He had fought to bring them Western Civilization.

And he had lost.

All these myths you love to tell them. I just don't think they're important to us anymore.

It was true. He was irrelevant. The battle for the hearts and minds of the young was over. The field belonged to ignorance and ideology: to Althea Feldman.

It had seemed there had been nothing for him to look forward to but bitterness and rage.

And now – all at once – they were gone. The rage, the bitterness. The tumor in his lungs was gone and they were gone. Gone completely. And the children looked beautiful. And the day was fine. And *Shine, perishing republic*, he inwardly sang. *As this America settles into the mould of its vulgarity . . . Life is good, be it stubbornly long or suddenly a mortal splendor; meteors are not needed less than mountains: shine, perishing republic. Shine.*

Roth finally understood. All was as it should be. Existence was a rose of bliss.

He smiled. Pushed off the feminine maple. Moved on.

Unfortunately, by the time he reached his house, the last effects of the drugs had pretty much worn off and the rose of bliss was beginning to develop a canker of care. He stood on his leaf-strewn lawn before his porch steps, under the hanging empty branches of his trees. And he was tired. And he felt as if lead were running in his veins instead of blood. And he needed a cigarette. God, he needed a cigarette.

He clung desperately to his religious joy but nonetheless felt it slipping inch by inch away. Doubt was seeping in, steadily poisoning his ecstasy.

It couldn't be real. What he thought had happened to him. It couldn't have happened to him. Not really. There were so many other possible explanations.

What if the tumor had been imaginary to begin with? What if it wasn't gone at all and the biopsy came back positive? What if this sure and certain sense that he had been somehow *healed* was simply an illusion?

And then, on the other hand . . . what if it *was* all true? What about that? What the hell did *that* mean? What *could* it mean?

He needed to know what the hell this was all about.

I'm an intellectual, damn it, he thought. *I'm not just going to stand here and be happy!*

He turned away from his own porch and lifted his eyes to the house next door. Geena MacAlary's house.

Where Amanda was.

He headed for it.

3

He stood at the door, peeked in through the sidelight. He could make out Geena's silhouette in the darkness within. She was sitting on the sofa. Elbow on the arm, chin on her fist. The classic pose of Contemplation.

Roth knocked gently. Saw her turn her face toward him. 'It's open, Howard,' she called. 'Come in.'

Roth entered, closed the door. Stood at the edge of the rug. The lights in the living room were off but the windows admitted the afternoon sun. There was a sort of border of reddening radiance on one side of the place giving way to a central shadow.

Geena remained in that shadow. Roth peered at her but her features were difficult to make out.

The silence between them went on an unnatural moment. Then Roth said, 'Is she . . . is she all right?'

'I don't know.' Geena swallowed hard. 'I mean, she's better but . . . I don't know.'

'Can I see her?'

She nodded. 'She's upstairs. She's looking at the book you brought for her. The myths.'

Roth didn't answer. Heavily, wearily, he started to move past her to the stairs.

'Howard . . .'

Geena caught his hand as he neared the sofa. He stood and looked down at her. Now he could see her clearly, her pretty features set in a tired frown, her intelligent eyes frantic.

She searched his face and the two of them understood each other: he knew.

She drew her hand away. She covered her eyes with it. Roth patted her on the shoulder softly. Then he walked on to the stairs.

He found the child sitting up in bed. The book of mythology was held open on her middle. It hid her from him almost completely. When Roth came to the doorway he could only see the dome of her head above the book jacket, the arc of yellow hair.

He knocked on the open door. Amanda let the book fall flat and looked up at him. It pained Roth to see the sickly, ashen pallor beneath the tan surface of her skin.

'Hello,' she said to him. 'Thank you for the book.'

He found he was almost misty again just at the sight of her. A lump rose in his throat. Who was this child who had touched him? *What* was she?

'Hi there,' he said gruffly. And added, 'You're welcome.'

He swung a chair from its desk to the bedside. Swung it backwards. Straddled it. This was not a child's room, he noticed, glancing around. It looked as if it had been a study or a den – a sewing room probably, judging by the little white table with its lathe-turned legs. The place had only been hastily rearranged for its new purpose. The Hollywood bed, Sesame Street sheets and coverlet. A *Beauty*

324

and the Beast coat hanger on the wall against the dull grownup diamond-pattern wallpaper.

A small chest of drawers had been brought into service as a bedside table. There was a reading light on it, the bulb supported by a juggling clown. A pink clock with a smiling pony on the face. A stack of picture books. A palm-sized dollhouse which somehow Roth knew was called Polly Pocket. There was also a photograph. A picture of a woman in a Winnie the Pooh frame. Hands in the pockets of her windbreaker. Legs akimbo in jeans. She was standing out in a field somewhere, out in the blustery weather. Her frizzy hair was windblown. Her smile was bright. From the shape of her face and eyes Roth guessed she was Amanda's mother. He wondered where she was. He found himself thinking: *Arise . . . and flee into Egypt . . . for Herod will seek the young child to destroy him.*

And again, he had to fight down tears.

He cleared his throat. 'So,' he said. 'Geena tells me you're feeling better.'

'Okay,' she said. 'Will you tell me some more stories?'

'Uh . . . Yeah . . . Sure . . .'

'I want to hear the one about Dem . . . Dem . . .'

'Demeter?'

'Yes. And her daughter.'

'I . . . uh . . . sure,' Roth said again.

She gazed up at him with her solemn brown eyes, waiting.

Roth shifted in his seat. Her gaze seemed to go right through him, see right into him. *Thank you for the book. Tell me more stories.* What did it all mean? he wondered. Was there something she was trying to tell him?

'Listen,' he said finally. 'I'd love to tell you more stories. That'd be great but . . . I have to ask you something first.'

'Okay,' she said.

'Well . . .' He gave a nervous laugh. Scratched his fringe

of white hair. 'Did you . . . ? Did you do something to me, Amanda?' He laughed awkwardly again but there was no comedy in his heart. 'Did you . . . When I was coughing. Is there something you did?'

Amanda broke the connection between them, looked away.

'Amanda?' said Roth.

'I'm not supposed to tell you.'

Roth opened his mouth, gave a long slow nod. 'Ah-ha.' And what did *that* mean? She wasn't supposed to tell him. Because . . . why? Because Mom didn't want the publicity? Because it was a top government secret? Because her Father in Heaven wanted to keep things quiet until He broke the seventh seal? What?

He pressed her. 'But you saw me coughing, right? You knew I was sick and . . . ?'

Amanda frowned down at her book, at the picture of Orpheus leading Eurydice by the hand. She touched the photo of the marble figures. 'You said you were going to die,' she said.

'I did?' Roth couldn't remember.

The child nodded gravely. 'When you were coughing. You said you were going to die.'

'Uh huh. So . . .'

She lifted her eyes to him. 'So I sparkled you.'

'You sparkled . . . ?' In a rush, Roth understood. His hands rose to the sides of his head. He stared at her in wonder. 'You sparkled me.' He laughed as the tears sprang to his eyes again. 'Merciful God,' he whispered. It was true.

'Are you all better now?' Amanda asked him.

He could barely speak. He nodded, pressing his lips together. 'Yes,' he finally managed to say in a broken voice. 'I'm all better.'

After a long moment, he lowered his hands again. He looked down at her. She looked back deadpan. Roth made more vague gestures as he sought for words. There were so many questions he wanted to ask. He hardly knew where to begin.

'So . . . Is this . . . ? I mean, is there . . . ? Is there something . . . something this is about . . . ? Is there something you want to tell me?'

A second's silence. The child gazed at him solemnly. Then, drawing out the word, she said, 'No-o.'

Roth grimaced with effort. Maybe he wasn't saying this right. 'What I mean is . . . is there . . . something you want to, you're trying to tell me or . . . people or . . . Like a message, I mean. Is there a message you want to tell us? Or something . . . ?'

'I don't know,' said Amanda singsong. 'Like what?'

'Well . . . A message. You know. Is there something you want to . . . to teach us or . . . or say to us or . . . teach the world? You know.'

The child considered this very deeply. Then slowly, she said, 'I don't think so. I'm only five.'

At which point, Roth heard how silly he sounded and simply cracked up. He pinched the bridge of his nose and squeezed his eyes shut as tears spilled out over his fingers. He sat straddling the chair and shook like Jell-O, laughing silently.

'What's so funny?' said Amanda, smiling along.

'Everything, apparently,' said Roth at last.

4

Geena stood waiting for him at the bottom of the stairs. Roth came down to her, still flicking tears from the corners of his eyes. As he reached the last step, she took hold of his hand again. Her fingertips were cool against his palm.

'So apparently I've been sparkled,' he said hoarsely.

'Howard, listen . . .' Geena's voice was soft. 'Have you told anyone? Your doctor . . . ?'

'No, no, no. Of course not.'

'Not anyone? It's important, Howard. You may be in danger. We could all be in danger.'

'Yeah, I know,' he said. 'Amanda told me. The bad men want to steal her. Look – you don't have to tell me anything if you don't want to . . .'

'No. No,' she said with a forlorn little laugh. 'You already know enough to get us killed.'

'Yeah, well, I'd like to avoid that if I can. Hell, if I can, I'd like to help you.' He puffed his cheeks, pushed out a breath. 'But it would clear my head a little if you would tell me . . . I mean, what the hell is it, Geena? Am I imagining it, is it some kind of gift from God, is it magic . . . ?'

'No,' she said – said sadly. 'No. It's just . . . it's just really . . . a terrible, terrible mistake.'

A moment's silence. Then she led him into the shadows, over to the sofa. They sat down together. She folded her hands on her lap. Her features were dim in the dark.

'It's hard to know where to begin,' she said. 'I don't know that much, not all the details. What I do know I found out because . . . Well, there was a girl. A woman I went to nursing school with. Marie, her name was. After school she went to work for a pharmaceutical firm called Helix.'

'Sure,' said Roth. 'I've heard of them.'

Geena nodded. Thought a moment, sitting still in the shadows.

'Have you ever heard of TT?' she asked him then. 'The therapeutic touch?'

He snorted. 'What, you mean, like, nurses touching people to help them heal. Yeah. Sure. I heard something on the radio about it. I thought it was all supposed to be bullshit.'

'Well . . . it's like any talent,' Geena said. 'Most of the people who claim to have it don't. And even those few who do, well, it's not as if they understand anything about it. They sit around and talk about "energy realignment" and "transferred intentionality," and a lot of New Age nonsense like that.'

'Yeah? But . . . ?'

'But,' she went on, sighing. 'But all the same, some people do seem to have a gift, a slight gift of some sort anyway . . . And so apparently, about seven or eight years ago, some researchers at Helix decided to see if they could locate the source of it. It was just this – small, sideline project, you know. They must have a thousand of them going on all the time. The idea of this one was to gather some people who claimed to be healers, cut away all the woo-woo energy stuff, and focus on the immune system. Cytokines, especially.'

Roth gave a little shrug.

'Cytokines,' Geena repeated. 'They're proteins that carry information between cells. You hear about some of them sometimes in the news – like interleukin-2 or interferon? – because they can stimulate healing and boost the immune system, some of them, by sending messages between cells in different parts of the body. And the idea was . . .'

'I get it. Maybe they could somehow send messages from one body to another.'

'Exactly. Exactly,' she murmured, as if to herself. Then: 'Anyway . . . Helix located a small number of patients who seemed to possess the power of therapeutic touch and injected them with a drug that was supposed to stimulate the thymus gland to produce a kind of super-cytokine. If nothing else they thought it might ultimately be used as a vaccine of some kind. But the thing is . . . the thing is . . . when they injected these people . . .'

'They didn't tell them.'

'The subjects thought they were just part of a study on healing powers. They thought the shot was one of a series of vaccines given to protect them from the diseases they might encounter during the study.'

'Jesus,' said Roth. 'Helix Pharmaceuticals. Touching Your Life Through Immoral Chicanery.'

'Right.'

'But the drug worked, obviously.'

'No! No!' said Geena. 'It was a disaster. Within two years of the test, every one of the subjects was dead. Some kind of autoimmune reaction, a monster version of *myasthenia gravis*. It was awful. The people were just . . . devoured – devoured from within. And the worst part was, since the victims didn't know each other and weren't aware they had anything in common, no one had any idea what was happening.'

'No one but the good people at Helix anyway.'

'Right,' said Geena MacAlary out of the shadows. 'Helix realized they had to cover their tracks, erase the records of the tests and so on or risk bankruptcy, lawsuits, even jail. But at the same time, secretly, they continued to do follow-up work. Because the drug was known to have effects at the genetic level and a few of the subjects – three of them – had had children in the period between the test and their deaths. And as it turned out, those children . . .'

'Oh God. Oh man!' Roth sat blank-faced. 'Man oh man oh man.' He was beyond trying to sort out his emotions now. Fear, disgust, wrath at what these Helix turnip-heads had done – and amazement at the same time, wonder, *elation* – because it had really happened. He'd been *healed*. Each new discovery convinced him afresh that it was true.

Geena went on. 'It quickly became apparent that at least two of these children had significant healing ability. Which caused a problem for Helix because if anyone started looking into it and connected the company with the tests that had killed the parents . . . well, it would've been worse than bankruptcy, it would've been jail for a lot of very important people. They knew they had to prevent these children being discovered by the public, but they were unsure how to proceed. The Research Department wanted to kidnap the kids and run experiments on them to see if new drugs could be developed from them. The Legal Department just wanted to kill them – you know, erase any evidence that the tests had ever taken place. But then Business Affairs . . . Business Affairs came up with the bright idea of kidnapping the children, doing a few tests – and then selling the kids' abilities to people overseas.'

Roth didn't get it. 'Selling . . . ?'

'You know. Some rich person who's sick, who's willing

to pay millions – tens of millions – for an instant cure. And it was a perfect plan because, listen to this, Howard. As it turned out, the children's ability was fatal to them.'

'I don't get it. Fatal. What do you mean?'

'After they used their therapeutic touch a few times, the same autoimmune reaction set in that had killed their parents. For Helix, it was perfect. Research got their tests, Business made a profit, and Legal got rid of the evidence – after performing a number of cures for cash, the children got sick and died.'

'Jesus,' said Roth. 'They died?'

He saw Geena's silhouette nod. 'Those first two of them did anyway. They were the two who were born to stable people with fixed addresses. So it was easy for Helix to trace them, keep track of their development. They got them right away, the minute the healing ability showed itself. They stole them, used them, sold them. Killed them, basically.'

'And the third child was Amanda,' said Roth.

'She was harder for them to find. She's the illegitimate child of a sailor named Tom Wilson and a woman named Carol Dodson. It was Wilson who was given the drug. He met Carol afterwards. And she was ... and she wasn't anyone really, that's the point. Just a high-school dropout. A waitress, barmaid; kind of a lost soul.'

'Uh-huh. I get it, I get it.'

'So she was already hard to keep track of and then ... Then the follow-up on Wilson's case was done by my old schoolfriend.'

'Ah,' said Roth. 'Enter Marie.'

'That's right. Marie was one of a very small group of people who knew what was going on. I can't make any excuses for what she did, but at least when she found out what was happening to the children, she rediscovered her conscience. She was too late to help the first two kids. But she managed to sabotage the company's records so they couldn't find the Wilson–Dodson child, Amanda. Then Marie went to Carol Dodson herself and warned her what might happen. Carol didn't believe it at first, but then the healings started. A neighbor's fever, a child's cold. Amanda is very . . . generous. She always wants to make people feel better. And she has the power far more strongly than the other two. It was unmistakable from the start. Carol knew – Marie convinced her – that the minute word got out, Helix would find a way to hunt her down.' Geena studied her hands in her lap. 'Fortunately, she's a very resourceful lady, Carol. Very tough, very independent – and very scared too. She didn't tell anyone. Didn't trust anyone. Didn't ask for anyone's help. She just took to the road. Never stayed in one place very long. Wandered around, earned whatever money she could, mostly off the books. Did whatever she had to, to stay alive and keep her head down, keep out of Helix's radar. It might have worked too. Except one of the towns she passed through was Hunnicut, Massachusetts.'

'Oh yeah. Yeah. Where the jet crashed.'

'Right. And, of course, Amanda "sparkled" someone. And there was a witness – some hysterical woman who thought she saw the baby Jesus performing a miracle, bringing someone back to life. That's what she told the tabloids anyway. And they printed it – and that was enough to put Helix on Carol's trail.'

Roth gave a small, mirthless laugh. He was beginning to get the big picture. 'Wouldn't it have been simpler if someone had just called the cops on these bastards?'

Geena drew breath. 'Marie did. Marie went to the cops. She was afraid to at first. She thought they wouldn't believe her and . . . and she felt Helix was too well connected, that any official complaint would get back to them. So at the beginning of it, she came to me instead. She said our acquaintance was old and tenuous enough that she thought Helix wouldn't find me. She asked me if, in an emergency,

I would give the child a place to stay. I only half believed her, but of course I said yes. And she passed my name on to Carol.'

'Who showed up after Hunnicut.'

'Yes. She said she was going to try to put together enough money to get Amanda out of the country and then come back for her.'

'Great. And what about Marie? You said she went to the police.'

'Yes. After she came to me. She went to a policeman friend she had in San Francisco. Three days later, her body was found in the waters off the Golden Gate.'

In the tumult of his feelings, Roth let a small groan escape him. He got to his feet. Paced. Rubbed a hand over his bald pate. Finally, he stood, stared absently into the shadows.

'All right. So let's see,' he said. 'What we got here, we got major bad guys coming after us. The cops can't be trusted. Our only ally is this high-school dropout barmaid running around doing God knows what. The child won't stop using this power she's got and if she uses it often enough she'll die horribly. Am I missing the good news here?'

'The good news . . .' Geena sighed. 'Well, there is some.'

'Please.'

'Possibly – okay? Possibly . . . According to Marie – the Helix researchers believe that Amanda's ability will wear off. The reason the drug worked on the children and not the adults was because the thymus gland does most of its important work in childhood. It stops growing around puberty – and the researchers predict that when that happens the healing ability will disappear.'

'Puberty.' Roth snorted. 'She should live so long.'

'Well, yeah. That's it. If we can keep her alive for another six or seven years, she could become normal. In which case, Helix will have no use for her and no reason to be afraid of her.'

'Wonderful. Six or seven years.'

Now Geena stood too. Came to him, stood near him. 'Howard, you have to promise me . . .'

'What?'

'If you tell anyone . . . *anyone* . . .'

'Ach. Please. I'm a curmudgeon, not a shithead. I just want to know if there's anything I can do to help.'

In answer, Geena gave a little sniff. And then, to Roth's surprise, she tilted toward him and pressed her face to his chest.

So Roth put his arms around her. Her hair was soft and clean-smelling under his nose. The press of her large breasts against him was rich with comfort. It had been a long time since he'd held a woman.

'I'm sorry,' she said. She pushed away from him. Smiled miserably through tears.

Roth smiled back. He had never found her particularly pretty. A sweet face, is how he'd always put it to himself. But now the darkness softened all her features and he saw just how sweet a face it was. Soft, kind, gentle.

Everything looks beautiful to me today, he thought.

He reached out and laid his palm against her damp cheek. 'Tell me what you want, Geena,' he said.

Her slender shoulders rose and fell. 'I just don't want her to die, that's all.'

'Die?' he said. 'What, are you kidding? Who's gonna kill her? Some ruthless multinational corporation? She's got a classics professor and a retired housewife on her side.'

Geena laughed.

Roth said, 'The bastards don't stand a chance.'

5

Roth trudged wearily back to his house. Cutting a meandering pattern across the lawns. Barely lifting his feet to walk so that he made a *chk-chk-chk* sound among the fallen leaves. He was muttering to himself. Chuckling sometimes. Looking around at the trees, the sky, the rooftops. Shaking his head. Chuckling some more. An absent-minded professor pondering an arcane joke.

Geena watched him from her window. He was a good man at heart, she thought. He just wasn't very good at life, poor soul. Still, he was a decent neighbor and she had always liked him. And when she asked herself now if he could be trusted, she felt pretty certain that he could.

She watched a moment more as he dragged himself wearily up his porch steps. As he opened his door. As he pushed into his house. She was sorry when he had gone inside, when he was out of sight. She felt alone then and she felt the full weight of her responsibility.

But her decision was already made.

She moved away from the window. She moved across the shadowy center of the room to the fringe of light. To the table. The telephone.

She picked the phone up. Hesitated. But no. The child was ill, the secret was out.

The mother had to be told.

Geena punched in the contact number. She stood in the half-light, waiting for the distant ring.

Chapter Thirteen

Stardust

1

Cold, sterile stone, invisible. A chilled, cumbersome humidity in the air. Something always slick and slippery beneath his fingers, green to the touch. Lonnie had never known such blackness. They went down and down.

He felt for handholds. Every time he touched the stone, he was afraid there might be something there. Something alive, slithering beneath his fingers. Bats or spiders or some shit like that. Gigantic worms with fangs. Well, how the hell was he supposed to know? The only sinkholes he'd seen in Oakland had liquor licenses. This was not his sort of scene at all.

Now and then, Carol would call to him, 'You have a foothold to your right', or, 'It's wet here, be careful.' He was thankful simply for the sound of her voice. And now and then she would flick on a flashlight, a small yellow box she must've carried in her purse or pocket. Its wan beam would trace a path for him over the expressionless rock.

Lonnie's heart would practically leap with gratitude then. Light. God, the light.

When the light went off, the instantaneous shroud of darkness was suffocating.

Down and down. A world of stone and absolute shadow. Lonnie had never been claustrophobic before, but this was dreadful; dreadful. They were beneath the earth, he kept thinking. They were *down here*, man. There was no way out. Just dead rock on every side and nothing else. No light. No air. No earth. No color, no living sound. A circus could be going on right above them. A carnival. Carousels and ferris wheels. Children could be chasing each other through the green grass. Couples could be holding hands. A girl in a flowered dress could be standing there, lifting her face up to the sun. And Lonnie could reach up for her, dying down here, dying, and she would never know. He could cry to her for help, he could claw himself bloody against the rocks. He could breathe his last and rot to bleaching bone. And that girl, that girl in the flowered dress, she would bask in the light and shake out her hair and wander off dreaming of love and be none the wiser.

Shit.

As he thought these things, an unfamiliar feeling was growing in him. Panic, that's what it was. He was a hard-assed dude but that was sure enough panic beginning to scrabble at his chest, a frantic creature trapped inside him. *I gotta get outta here*, he thought, sweating in the chill air.

But they went down further and further still.

'Hey. Hey, Carol. They got any animals or things or, like, bats down here?' he finally asked her. He tried to sound casual about it. He tried not to sound like some kind of pussy.

'Pussy,' she said.

'Hey. This is not exactly my neighborhood, you know what I'm saying.'

'Yeah,' she said. 'This is *my* neighborhood, okay? I grew up here. I know every inch of this place.'

'Yeah?' That made him feel a little better.

'Yeah. I wouldn't worry. You might see a bat. That's it. Most living creatures hate these places.'

'Well, you can add me to the list.'

Carol chuckled breathlessly. The sound faded away beneath him. Down and down.

The worst of it came after an hour or so – it felt like an hour; it might have been less – or more – he'd lost all track of time. For yards, the passage through which they'd been moving had been getting narrower and narrower. Lonnie could no longer stand up straight in it. He was bent over, his hand touching the slick stone wall close on either side.

And then Carol said, 'Okay. This is the tight part.'

'The tight part?' She turned on the flashlight and Lonnie said, 'Oh man!'

The beam illuminated an almost solid wall, green and smooth as a backyard pond. The ceiling above this wall was so low that Lonnie was forced down to one knee as he approached it. But that was not the worst thing. There was water flowing on the floor here and gritty mud which soaked through his pants leg and grimed and scraped and chilled him.

But that was not the worst thing either.

The worst thing was the crevice. The one that Carol was pointing to.

'No way,' Lonnie said.

'Just like being born, sweetie.'

'Yeah, but after being born, you're alive. I mean, like, that's the whole *point* of being born. Nobody just does it for fun.'

'It's this or the cops behind us. Take your pick,' she said.

He didn't answer. She handed him the flashlight.

Then she went into the crack in the wall.

Lonnie's stomach rolled just watching her do it. The rock seemed to swallow her. Her legs waggled behind her as if she were struggling to break free. Then her legs were engulfed as well. And then her sneakers pulled so close to the rock he could only see the soles. And then – like the last bit of spaghetti being slurped in – those also disappeared. The crevice stood empty. Waiting for him.

'Hurry up,' it said in Carol's breathless voice. 'The faster you do it, the better it is.'

Well, Lonnie could believe that all right. Already, the sounds of her movement were fading. He was alone here with the thin flashlight beam and nothing around or behind him but darkness and stone.

He took a breath, approached the gap. It was no good. He was a lot bigger than Carol. He couldn't even begin to figure out a way to corkscrew his body into the thing. When he did – when he got his head through – there was just no squeezing his shoulders past the edge. He backed off. He couldn't hear Carol at all now.

'You still there?' he called.

She didn't answer.

'Man, I am getting to be sorry I tried to help this woman,' he said.

Quickly now – desperate to catch up to her – he stripped off his overcoat. He wrapped it into a bulky parcel, careful that his gun was held inside. He stuffed the parcel into the crevice. Then he went after it. This time, his shoulders just barely made it through. His torso. His legs.

He was in the tunnel.

He dragged himself along, pushing his coat ahead of him. The gap didn't get any wider. There was just enough room for his body – and no room at all for the panic that now swung screeching and grabbing like a gibbon in his upper frame. His arms were stretched out, were stuck in

344

that position. He could hardly bend his legs. If he hadn't had the flashlight picking out little patches of hard green nothingness, he felt he would've gone crazy right then and there.

'Carol?'

Nothing. Just his own breath racketing off the walls. His own slow progress, the sound of him dragging along the damp floor. The walls pressed close against him, clamped around him. Once, tired from the slithering exertion, he stopped to rest. That was the worst. Lying there, unable even to turn his head. The tunnel became a coffin around him. The dark beyond his flashlight threatened to bury him alive.

He wriggled on frantically, grunting, panting.

'Lonnie?'

Her voice. Oh yeah. Yeah, yeah, yeah. A human voice. It was like water in the desert to him.

'Carol?'

'Keep coming. A little more. You're almost there.'

Almost there. He pushed the coat ahead of him. Fought his way after it. And then he felt the coat moving on its own. Carol pulling it. He felt her hand touch his.

'Thank you, Jesus.'

He spilled out into an open chamber. She was there, helping him find his footing. She squeezed his shoulder.

'You're all right,' she said.

'Whoa! Nothing to it. No sweat. Whoa, mama!'

She took the light from his trembling fingers. Held it while he caught his breath. He was shaking so much it was hard to put his coat back on.

'Whoa!' he kept repeating. 'Whoa, mama! Whoa!'

And now – her face white in the outglow of the flash – Carol smiled at him. Tilted her head.

'Come here,' she said.

He followed her across the chamber's sloping floor. When he was beside her, she turned off the light.

'Look up.'

He looked. Saw nothing at first, the cave's utter nothing. Then shifted his gaze. Was there a glow? Yes. A gray glow.

'Come over here,' she said.

He followed the sound of her. Moved to look from another angle.

And he saw . . . oh, light. The light of the world. A little silver dollar of it far, far above.

'Look at that. Look at that,' Lonnie heard himself murmur.

Color. There was color in the light. There was warm air coming to him redolent with life and you could make out brown and blue and yellow. The brown of tree bark it was, the blue of sky, the yellow of autumn leaves. Oh, he thought. Oh, oh, oh. Brown and blue and yellow. How could he have seen such wonders every day and never known the meaning of the word *hallelujah*?

'Cool, huh?' said Carol.

'Yeah,' said Lonnie, laughing. 'Cool.'

'Let's go,' she said.

They started climbing.

2

She led him through the forest a long way. The sun was going down by the time they stopped to rest. The dark drops fast in the woods and even though they could see the dusk horizon still bright beyond the treeline, here the air was deep blue and they had to peer hard through the gloaming to find their way.

They came over a rise. Something – a structure – a hulking silhouette – loomed blackly beneath them. They were almost on top of it before Lonnie could see it was some sort of tower – a chimney – of gray stone.

Carol stopped, panting. Lonnie stopped. Looked around him.

There were more of these things. Black towers, roofless black cubicles of stone, sudden black pits lined with stones interwoven, fragments of a wall. As if a primitive village had been abandoned here. It was eerie. Ghostly, with the trees swaying in the deepening dark, their wood cracking, the leaves whispering down.

Carol moved through the indigo twilight to where a small stream trickled over pebbles. She knelt and drank from her cupped hands. Lonnie knelt beside her and drank. The water was gritty but cool.

After a few moments, Carol rose, moved away from him. She dropped to the ground beneath a pillar of stones. She leaned back against the pillar, her knees raised, her hands draped over them.

Lonnie stood too but remained where he was. He panned his gaze over the mysterious shapes around them. At every sound the trees made or the leaves made or animals made scrambling for cover in the underbrush, he turned suddenly, searching the dusk.

'What the hell is this place?' he said finally.

'When I was a kid, we called it Auburn,' she told him. 'There was some kind of town here once. In colonial days, I think. I don't know. I don't know what happened to it. The story used to be that everyone died in some kind of plague or something. It was supposed to be haunted. You know. We used to dare each other to come out and spend the night, that kind of thing. There's even a graveyard just out there, beyond the buildings. It's pretty spooky.'

She pointed to the graveyard with her chin. Lonnie, following the gesture, made out the black shapes of headstones amidst the trees. She was right. It was pretty spooky. Dead folks out there in the night, the stones all grown over, all hidden in the woods, the leaves falling on them. He shuddered, turned away.

Carol gave a wry smile. 'Look at you. You were such a tough guy in the city. Don't you like the forest?'

'Hey, are you kidding?' he said. 'They got bears out here – werewolves, shit like that.'

She laughed. 'Yeah. Well. The thing is, there's at least a

couple of miles of forest in every direction. The cops won't try searching for us with the dark coming on. By morning we'll be gone.'

'Oh yeah? You got another plan, huh.'

'Soon as the fuss dies down, I'll go buy us another car. No one'll recognize me without this.'

She reached up and pulled off the red wig. Set it on the ground beside her. Patted her short curls back into place. It was so dark now that he couldn't see the color of them. But he remembered their honey brown well enough.

'What're you looking at?' she said.

Lonnie gave that little snort of his. 'Pretty girl, that's all.'

She shook the curls out. Paused. Glanced up at him through the gloaming.

'What the hell are you doing here, Lonnie?' she said. 'Why did you come after me?'

He moved toward her. Stood over her. 'Chubb said you were in trouble. Said if you called his place they'd trace you – that Winter guy. Executive Decisions, whatever. Chubb wanted me to come tell you where he's arranged a pick-up for you.'

'And you just did. With the cops after you. Just like that.'

He gave a sort of shrug. Shifted around beside her. Lowered himself down to sit in the leaves beside her, his back against the stone tower like hers.

He eased his legs out before him. He felt her eyes on the side of his face. Smelled her sweat and the scent of her on the chill air.

'Haven't I caused you enough trouble?' she asked him.

Lonnie laughed a little. 'Just about. Just about enough, yeah.'

'And you still want to help me.'

He took a breath. Turned to her. Met her eyes, the spark of her eyes in the twilight. 'I don't know who this Winter

349

is, who these Executive Decisions people are. But they're gonna have to come through me.'

'Because . . . I had sex with you? Because I pretended to be your dead wife?'

He looked away from her. Looked out across the forest ghost town. He didn't know how to answer. Man, she was a hard little creature, this Carol. Out here scrabbling, fighting, running. Challenging him with her flinty eyes. Hard and ferocious.

She was nothing like his wife. His dead wife.

They sat in silence. The dark closed in on them like hands closing. The stone walls and broken houses and chimney towers and gravestones sank deeper into silhouette, became more abstract, became shapes among the other shapes: tortuous branches spreading above and coiled vines hanging; hunched roots grasping at the earth and smooth rocks slanting out of it. The twilight wind arose and soughed and the brook gabbled and now and then there came the sudden crunch of an animal scuttling over the leaves.

'They killed her, huh,' Carol said finally.

Lonnie nodded. 'Yeah.' He had been thinking about it as they sat there. 'Bunch of guys. White guys. Called her names. Chased her. She ran out in the street. A car . . .'

'Oh.' She let it out in a long slow sigh. 'That's tough.'

'Yes it is.'

'I was you, that'd pretty much make me hate every white man on earth.'

Lonnie gave another short laugh. 'Yeah, that's it.' He leaned his head back against the stone. Gazed up through the black branches above. The stars were coming out. 'Nah, shit,' he said. 'I've seen ugly in all colors. I don't care about any of that. I'm just out here, man. I'm just me.'

'You mean, like, you hate *everybody* on earth.'

'Now you got it.'

They both laughed, their heads tilting together. Then they were quiet.

Then she said, 'So how come I'm the exception?'

He faced her. They were very close.

'How come you gotta know?' he said.

He kissed her. She hadn't let him the first time and she pulled away now too. But then he drew her back, his hand on her cheek. She let him press his lips to hers. She pressed hers to his softly. His tongue went warm into her mouth. Her fingertips were gentle against his face. They kissed a long time.

Finally, she drew back again. She looked at him, looked him over. Without saying anything, she shifted on the ground. Lowered herself a little. Put her head tentatively against his chest. He put his arm around her. They sat like that. After a moment or two, he felt her begin to tremble. She was weeping.

Lonnie held her. She rocked her body against him. Now and then a sob broke from her. The air grew colder. The dark grew full. The wind that had risen at twilight subsided. The million forest noises combined into a single stillness into which she wept.

'I don't give a fuck about anything,' she cried angrily into his coat. 'You know? Except my baby. I don't give a fuck about any fucking body anywhere. Except my little girl. That's all.'

Lonnie nodded, holding her. 'I understand. It's okay.'

She yanked back away from him. Glared at him through the dark. 'You don't understand. You can't understand.'

'I understand,' he told her. 'You don't give a fuck about anybody.'

'That's right. Except my little girl.'

'I get you.'

'You hear me?'

'I hear you. It's okay.'

She sniffed once. 'All right,' she said. She began to settle back against him. 'I don't care what I have to do,' she said more quietly. 'I'll fuck anyone I have to. I don't care. It's just my body, it's not me. I don't care about any of them.' He put his arm around her. She put her head on his chest again. 'I just get the money and it doesn't matter. I don't give a fuck. I'm gonna get her away from these bastards no matter what it takes.'

Lonnie kissed her hair.

'I don't care about anything else but that.'

'I know,' he said.

She sniffed again. 'And I don't let *anyone* kiss me. You understand? Nobody fucking kisses me. Ever. I don't care.'

'I thought it was just your body.'

'Shut up.'

He smiled. 'It's okay, Carol.'

He put both arms around her now and held her against him. She made a terrible noise and began to cry hard again.

'I just get scared, Lonnie,' she said. 'I'm just so . . . out here. You know?'

'I know. We're all out here, baby.'

'I get so fucking scared.'

He held her. He kissed her hair and gazed over her into the dark. The hulking stone shapes of the dead village, the graves all but invisible in the night beyond, the murmuring leaves, the branches creaking. He began to sing to her under his breath, a tuneless jazz lullaby at first, softly at first, and then even softer, half a whisper, the old music just sort of rising out of him. He could hear it as he sang it, he could hear it in his head, the way the saxophone would play it full volume with a texture like honey and the slow notes shattering like stardust into countless hurried notes that skittered swiftly through a tune still slow. Like stardust.

352

> *And now the purple dust of twilight time*
> *steals across the meadows of my heart.*
> *Now the little stars, the little stars pine,*
> *always reminding me that we're apart.*

He sang to her and he thought: *I would've sung it to you if I'd been there, baby.* That was the burden of his song, the burden of his heart. *I would've held you and sung it to you just like this.*

He would've too. He would've held her in his arms and crooned it to her for her comfort while she died. He would've stood outside the gates of eternity and sung it to her through the golden bars forever. He would've sung so sweetly, he would've played her such sweet melodies, they would've opened up the doors of death itself and let him be with her again.

> *You wander down the lane and far away*
> *leaving me a love that cannot die . . .*

He would've held her in his arms and lifted her and brought her home to the years she should have had and the children she should have had and the life she *would* have had if he had been there to protect her.

If he had only been there.

> *Ah, but that was long ago.*
> *Now my consolation is in the stardust of a song.*

He tilted back his head, leaned his head against the stone chimney, sang into the murmuring forest, stretching the notes and bending them, bending one sound down into another until it reached that borderland between them which they sometimes call blue.

'Nice,' Carol murmured against him. She had stopped crying now. 'That's nice.'

She held onto him. He sang to her. A blue lullaby. *Stardust*. The music surrounded them and seemed to deepen the stillness of the woods, to leave the forest wholly silent until it seemed as if the ghosts of this dead village and its standing stones, its graves, its ruined houses, the trees and vines and brush that had grown over them, the animals among them, and the sky above had all paused in their various motions and in their one vast synchronized rotation from dark to dark — had paused and gathered round them and were listening, as she was listening pressed against him, to the sweet and living and mournful sound he made.

Chapter Fourteen

A Telephone That Rings

1

It became midnight. There were still some lights on in the Black Tower then. Someone heading home along Madison Avenue might have looked up and seen them through one window or another, their glow dimmed to a yellow-brown by the tinted glass, the building's interior hazy. If he'd craned his neck, he would have seen the light in the penthouse on the 33rd floor. But with the height, and the darkened glass and the venetian blinds, he couldn't have seen what was happening inside.

Winter was in there, and his employer, Jonathan Reese. They were sitting at opposite ends of a large oval conference table. The light that burned there hung just above the table's center. It was the only light on anywhere on thirty-three. The rest of the offices were deserted.

Reese, just then, was in the process of drawing out a pause, milking the silence for all it was worth before he continued speaking. He was taking a perverse sort of pleasure in this final confrontation.

The power was all on his side this time. He was dressed for battle, his pinstripe as sleek as Winter's navy blue, his tie-pin as golden, his cologne as rich. And, while Winter, the assassin, had mastered a sort of studied smoothness of manner, Reese felt fully aware of the fact that his own breeding came to him naturally. It was his birthright, and his civility was honed to a razor edge.

On top of which, he was here to hand the man his walking papers. So for all Winter's martial, not to say savage, talents, Reese felt fully master of the situation.

'We want to part company without any personal hard feelings,' he said finally. He gave a pursed smile through steepled fingers. 'We understand that you came late to the operation. Executive Decisions' American bureau was just opening, it wasn't up to your own high standards yet. I mean it, Winter. We understand all that and we wouldn't hesitate to recommend you or to use your services again.' He tapped his fingertips together twice as he said this. It was a lie – they both knew it was a lie – and it made Reese feel mighty indeed to tell it, and to be disbelieved with impunity. It was odd, he thought. Whenever he fired people, he always wound up feeling a kind of contempt for them. As if they wouldn't have been in this position if they'd only played their cards right. As he went on, he sounded a little condescending even to himself. 'The problem is: this project has just become too ... what's the word? *Fraught* – fraught with risks of various kinds. It's expensive, for one thing. And considering the uncertainties and time constraints, we're not entirely sure we'll be able to show a profit over the long run. Plus the unfortunate ...' He made a show of searching for the kindest way to put it. '... delays and ... unforeseen events make us feel concerned about the issues of secrecy, containment, security, that sort of thing. Basically, we want to quit while we're ahead. We're casting no aspersions on you or your organization. We're just terminating the entire operation, that's all.'

He was at the end. He fell silent. He would give Winter the dubious dignity of a response and then bring this meeting quickly to a close. Already, part of his mind was moving on to the trip home. A few days off at the house with April and his son. He was looking forward to it.

He watched Winter over his steepled fingers and waited for his reply.

The red-haired man nodded. Smiled blandly into Reese's eyes. 'I understand,' he said without expression. 'I've already spoken to your board.'

Reese's lips parted. He was shocked. The board? It took him completely by surprise. It set off all kinds of alarms. Was his independence being challenged? Was his authority being questioned? He tried to maintain his appearance of control and superiority. He gave a curt nod, a noncommittal, 'Uh-huh'.

But Winter obviously knew he'd hit home. 'We've agreed to continue our relationship solely on a contingency basis,' he went on smoothly. 'ED will sever all communications with your firm unless and until the target is recovered.'

Another blow. Reese couldn't deny it, could only just hide it. An arrangement had been made behind his back! His hands came slowly away from his face. He tried to keep the rising indignation from entering his voice. Tried instead to sound dark, dangerous, threatening. 'I wasn't consulted about this,' he said.

'No,' said Winter with a casual – possibly even mocking – gesture of one hand. 'It's as you said: issues of secrecy, containment, security, that sort of thing. That's why they wanted me to have this meeting with you.'

Reese narrowed his eyes. 'I don't understand.'

'Well, they asked me if before I left I wouldn't mind killing you.'

'What?'

'Which, of course, I wouldn't,' said Winter. He drew a good old-fashioned .38 revolver from his jacket pocket. 'But it would help if you'd hold still for a minute,' he added. 'They want it to look like suicide.'

2

Winter had this in common with the late Jonathan
Reese: he felt a faint contempt for the people he
destroyed. Maybe it was the contempt of all survivors for
the dead. He felt that if they'd wanted to avoid their fate they
should have been smarter or stronger or quicker or simply
somewhere else.

So as he rode down the Black Tower in the elevator
after the termination of his meeting, he reflected that it was
hypocrisy that had killed Reese really. Well, of course, *he* had
killed Reese really, but it was hypocrisy that had brought
the situation about. Reese, so to speak, had sneered at the
hunter while eating the meat. He had wanted the big money,
the big house, the security, the privileged family life. But he
thought himself superior to the ugly side of the business
that provided him with these things. He felt superior, that
is to say, to Edmund Winter.

Winter buttoned his Hugo Boss overcoat, smoothed

down the front of it. *No, no, no, no, my friend*, he thought. As long as there's dirty work to be done, it's the man who does it who ultimately holds the power. Enjoy the comforts of civilization, yes, but stay in touch with your inner savage. That was the lesson to be learned here today . . .

By the time he left the elevator, however, by the time he crossed the lobby with a smile at the night watchman, stepped out onto the avenue and into the chill of the first minutes of morning, he had lost this train of thought. He had put Reese out of his mind completely.

He was thinking about Carol Dodson again. He felt certain that the hunt was finally drawing to a close.

Chubby Chubb's suicide had delayed him, there was no question about that. But even with his hard, professional eye, Winter couldn't blame himself. It was the incompetence of Mortimer and Hughes that had made it necessary even to find Chubb in the first place. And – Chubb being a shrewd and careful old bird with excellent connections – it was hardly to be expected that he would let himself be taken alive for Winter's brand of questioning. His death was a predictable contingency.

Now, anyway, they had the smuggler's papers, his phone records and so on. They were beginning to establish the pattern of his calls over the last few days. They were beginning to uncover his current connections and work out the possible links to his old smuggling operations.

Winter was already fairly certain that Chubb had been arranging Carol's escape somehow. Getting cash for her, papers. Probably sending her to one of his former rendez-vous points in the east – one of the islands off Massachusetts or Maine, the old Meridian Lodge in New Hampshire or the abandoned camp near Lake Placid, New York. A generous act on his part; a change of personality for the former criminal. But then maybe resurrection will do that to you. Who can say?

Winter could picture just how it had happened. Chubb – delighted at not being dead – had probably given Carol a contact number and offered his help. But Carol had been smart, trusted no one, operated on her own – until she felt her pursuers were simply closing in too fast. Then, in her hour of need, she had turned to the man her daughter had touched at the plane crash site . . .

Heading to the corner, Winter shook his head in admiration. That Carol. God, he'd come to like that woman. For every trick he pulled, she pulled another. For every inch he tightened the cordon, she took another risk in her efforts to break free. She was like . . . like some sort of noble beast – a deer, a lioness – twisting and turning in a brave, doomed effort to avoid the implacable hunter.

Yeah, he thought. He liked that. *The implacable hunter. Little old me.*

But no self-satisfaction, he counseled himself, no arrogance – and no mistakes. The end was not a sure thing by any means. Reconstructing Chubb's plans would probably give them Carol's current destination. But if she actually had cash, a false identity, a lift out of the country . . . well, that would magnify their difficulties at least a thousandfold. Once she could move through the entire world anonymously, she would be a very sharp needle in a very big haystack. Finding her would be a lengthy and expensive proposition. Helix had already withdrawn its backing and the ED head office would neither approve nor support a contingent operation of that magnitude.

Not that that would stop Winter, of course. He was going to find this babe eventually, one way or the other, for profit or just as a matter of honor. Besides, with her intelligence, her courage, her maternal ferocity – she had captured his imagination. He had very specific plans for her once he caught her and he wasn't going to be cheated out of his simple pleasures.

So as it turned out, Winter experienced a sense of disappointment when his big break finally came. Because, ironically enough, his people didn't locate Carol Dodson at all.

They found her child. They found Amanda.

Winter had now walked around the Black Tower and left Madison, heading for the parking garage on 53rd. His mind was running over fresh approaches, checking any angles he might have missed. And he hit on Lonnie Blake. He had heard about the crazy spearchucker's disastrous attempt to rob an upstate bank. He wondered if he should divert a little of his overextended manpower to track the fuckhead down and kill him before he caused some kind of unforeseen trouble. Sort of a support-your-local-incompetent-police-type operation.

But then it occurred to him to wonder: maybe Blake's escape was not entirely unconnected to Carol Dodson's. It seemed unlikely Mortimer and Hughes could've been right about anything but, on the other hand, what if, just for argument's sake . . .

But before he got any further, the cellular vibrated inside the pocket of his overcoat.

He glanced around. There was an attendant smoking idly in front of the garage and a bouncer shifting his shoulders outside the gay bar across the way, but for the most part the street was empty. He pulled out the phone.

The caller was using a scrambler. His voice – her voice, maybe – sounded nasal and mechanical, but the words were clear.

'We've intercepted and traced a call to the target's voice mail. A woman named Geena MacAlary in Morburne, Vermont.'

'Yeah?' said Winter. He lifted his arm high as he held the phone, protecting himself from the cold wind off the East River. He turned his back to it, faced the west.

The operative went on. 'The voice print on the caller indicated a very high level of distress and it seems possible her message was a coded warning. The content was: "Hi, it's me, stop. Why don't you come up and visit, question. Bernadette and I would love to see you as soon as you can make it, stop. Okay, question. Bye, stop." End of message.'

'Bernadette,' said Winter with something like a laugh. 'As in Lourdes.'

'Yes, affirmative. And a preliminary check on MacAlary shows she went to the same nursing school as Marie Davenport.'

'The Helix RN,' said Winter.

'Affirmative,' said the toneless voice.

It was then that Winter experienced his disappointment. Standing there with the phone to his ear. Gazing to the west through the mist of his own breath. He nodded to himself. This was it; they had her. They already knew it was Marie Davenport who had alerted Carol. So Carol had sent Amanda off to MacAlary. It made sense. It was right. It was over.

And Winter felt disappointed because now he could get the child without ever catching up to Carol Dodson at all.

'Our nearest operative,' said the remodulated voice on the phone, 'is a New Hampshire state trooper named Ike Lewis but I thought . . .'

'No, no, no, you're right,' said Winter. 'No more fuck-ups. I'm handling this personally. With the jet I can be there in a couple hours. Get Ferdinand and Dewey to meet me at Newark and have the New Hampshire man join us at the nearest airstrip to Morburne.'

'You got it.'

He killed the call. Pocketed the phone. Shrugged off his disappointment and headed for the garage.

All right then, he thought. He would get the kid first. Carol Dodson was sure to follow.

On to Vermont.

3

About the same time, Geena MacAlary received a phone call too. It dragged her out of a deep sleep. She found herself sitting upright on the living room sofa in the dark. All the lights in the house around her were off. She wasn't sure for a moment where she was.

Then the phone chirruped sharply again and she jumped. Rolled to her feet. Hurried to the sound. Stumbled over the leg of a chair and then – as she disentangled herself – barked her shin against a low table.

'Ow! Sugar!' she said. She grabbed the phone.

'It's me,' said a soft voice.

Carol! Geena let a sigh of gratitude rush out of her.

'How is she?'

'Fine,' said Geena quickly. 'Well, she's better. She was really sick at first. I almost had to call a doctor. But it's like you said. She's improving. God, I'm so sorry. I told her and told her. She was only out of my sight for a few minutes . . .'

'No, no, I know. It's hard. She likes to do it. She likes to make people feel better.'

'She's asleep upstairs now anyway.' Geena paused. She swallowed. 'Are you coming?'

'I'm on my way.'

Geena sagged with relief.

'Figure 3 a.m.,' Carol said. 'You know that McDonald's right off the interstate? That's twenty-four hours, right?'

'Yes. I think so.'

'Okay. Three a.m. Bring her there. That way I can just pick her up and keep going.'

'Okay,' Geena said. She hated the high, frightened trembling of her own voice. She shook as she waited through a long pause.

Then Carol said, 'Geena? Listen. I think they're close. Okay?'

'Oh God.' It broke from Geena in spite of herself.

'No, no, it's all right. They don't know about you but . . . I had to leave New York in a big hurry so just . . . be careful. You know? Especially when you leave for McDonald's. Keep an eye out. Be careful.'

'I will.'

'And if I don't make it . . .'

'Don't say that.'

'Get out,' said Carol. 'Wait for me and if I don't make it by three or so then get out and get her out. All right?'

'Just make it,' said Geena.

'I will,' said Carol. 'I'm on my way.'

Geena hung up. The quiet that followed filled the house. It made her shiver and hug herself, her frightened eyes darting this way and that. All around her was the dark. She felt it pressing in on her, alive with menace. She felt it everywhere in the house.

And it was dark, she knew, in all the wide world beyond.

367

4

In that darkness, Lonnie watched for the moon.

'Just sit there,' Carol had told him. 'Just keep looking out in that direction. About forty minutes, an hour, the moon'll come up. A half-moon. Should be around midnight. Okay? Most of the leaves are gone, you should be able to see it no problem. Just move around a little to make sure, okay? And when it comes up? Just head straight for it. Maybe forty-five minutes, you'll come to the road. I'll be there. I'll be waiting for you.'

Then she'd kissed him. Then she'd left him there.

He'd sat against the chimney tower. He'd watched her, flicking her flashlight on and off. Trailing through the dark where the beam had gone. Disappearing into the night woods, her footsteps on the damp leaves fading and fading until Lonnie couldn't hear them anymore.

Then he was alone.

He sat against the chimney tower, hugging himself, shivering with cold. Alone in that godforsaken ghost town in the moaning woods. With the ruins and the graves hulking blackly amidst the rustling trees. With the sounds of living creatures snickering in the duff of the forest floor. With sudden movements at the edges of his vision that were gone when he faced them head on.

Fool! he thought. He'd been raised in the trenches, on some nightmare streets. He was being chased by the police, by professional killers. He was a grown man. It was bullshit to sit here worrying about werewolves and vampires.

He kept telling himself that.

But he sure was glad to see that old devil moon.

At first, he didn't know what it was. He was watching for it, waiting for it and, all the same, he didn't recognize its glimmer on the horizon beyond the trees. It seemed a bright light coming toward him. He scrambled to his feet. A car? he thought. A chopper? The cops? The light expanded and grew brighter in what seemed to him a queerly silent and unnatural way.

A UFO. Just his luck.

Then he saw the arc of the disk. The moon. Just head straight for it, like she'd told him.

She'd made it sound easy.

So for the next fifteen minutes or months or whatever it was, Lonnie stumbled wildly toward the rising moon. Roots grabbed at his feet like fingers. Branches scratched at his face like claws. The cold of the night dissolved into a clammy heat around him. His breath came short, his heart pounded. His overcoat hung on him like lead.

And damn it, it wasn't easy. It was hard – incredibly hard. It was hard just to find a fucking path to the horizon. Rocks, trees, sudden dips in the earth, sudden streams that wet him to the ankles all seemed to hurl themselves beneath him as he blundered through the night. Once he fell – a blind tumble that seemed to go on forever, that left plenty of time for panic before he thumped down onto the stony earth. The jar went through him. He felt it in his bones. Then he was up again, aching. Limping forward. Feeling his way.

The half-moon – and its dark half, a pocket of gray night – bounced and hid and flashed from out of the branches before him. It seemed to have shot from the horizon, to be climbing the sky on some invisible jet of energy. Was he supposed to keep after it, he wondered, or head for the place where it had risen? Was he going in the right direction even now or had he lost it?

He wondered that and he wondered: what if she wasn't there? Carol. What if she'd deserted him? What if she thought she'd be less conspicuous without a black fugitive with her? What if she thought she'd have a better chance of evading Winter and the police on her own?

Groping, gasping, stumbling, he didn't see the road at once in that tangled darkness. He sensed it first. He sensed a sort of flat emptiness at the top of the short, steep rise just ahead of him. He hardly dared hope.

Sweat streamed down his face, his breath whistled as he climbed that ground. He slid on the leaves beneath his shoes, had to grab at roots to pull himself up the grade.

Then he was there, standing on the ridge. And an empty two-lane lay in the moonlight just beyond the trees.

Dragging his feet, Lonnie staggered to it. He stepped gratefully over the border onto the pavement.

Instantly, her headlights flashed.

Another moment and he'd collapsed onto the seat beside her. She was pulling their new car – a rusted old Chevy – from the shoulder.

They were on the road, heading for Vermont.

Chapter Fifteen

Moonlight in Vermont

1

The moon was sailing toward its crest when the LearJet 31A touched down at Rutland State. Even as the whine of its twin engines subsided, a green Mondeo was racing up to it over the runway's grassy verge. The vehicles ran parallel for several yards, glinting under the runway lights.

The small jet rolled to a stop. The Mondeo stopped alongside it. The car's driver was at the jet's opening door in a moment, was receiving two hefty cases, hauling them back to the car's open trunk. As the driver loaded the cases, the jet's passengers quickly disembarked. Three men in black overcoats: the brown-faced, skull-faced man named Ferdinand; Dewey, the neckless slab; and the red-haired man, Edmund Winter. They were all in the car before the driver shut the trunk.

The driver lowered himself behind the wheel. Nodded a nervous greeting to the red-haired man.

'Ike Lewis?' Winter said.

'Yes, sir.'

'Let's go.'

But the car had already begun bumping over the verge toward the road.

The driver – Ike Lewis – was a youngish fellow. Thirty, not much over. He had crewcut blond hair and pale features pocked with red acne. His eyes were bright and hazel. They gave him the quick, fixed, startled look of a sociopath. Winter found this encouraging.

And he – Lewis – handled the car well too. Beating the lights, moving swiftly but unobtrusively through the empty city streets.

'You made good time,' he said after a while. 'You run into any weather?' Making conversation with the new boss.

Winter shook his head. 'We had a little trouble rousting a co-pilot. How quickly you figure we can get to Morburne?'

'This time of night? We should be outside Geena MacAlary's house in thirty, thirty-five minutes tops,' Lewis said.

Winter nodded. He glanced at his Rolex.

It was now just coming up on 2 a.m.

2

By 2:20, Geena was ready to go. Actually she'd been ready for almost two hours. She just couldn't quite bring herself to hit the road.

Immediately after she'd hung up with Carol, she had packed Amanda's bags. She had carried the bags out to the car and put them in the trunk. Then she'd come back inside, ready to drive Amanda to her 3 a.m. rendezvous at McDonald's – whereupon she'd found to her dismay that it was barely 12:30.

She turned on the television. Stared at it. Then it began to occur to her that the noise of the TV might be drowning out other noises: creeping footsteps behind her for instance, or a terrified scream from the child upstairs.

I think they're close.

She shut off the box, then shut out the lights in the house again. She sat on the sofa, jumpy as a hamster. She couldn't think of one good reason to calm down.

So she got up and, for the next hour or so, walked from room to room in the darkness.

It was awful. Waiting, thinking. The confines of her own house began to make her flesh creep. Lighted clocks – the clock on the oven, the clock on the video, the clock on a radio alarm – confronted her from every corner. None of them seemed to be moving. Sometimes she sat on the sofa and dozed but, whenever she did, she jerked awake in moments, thinking: *Did I miss the time? Is someone in the house?*

Once, after falling asleep for only a moment, she dreamed that the door was kicked in by men with machine-guns. She opened her eyes with a gasp. The house was dark and silent.

She began to consider getting out early. Putting Amanda in the car, leaving the place, driving around town until it was time to meet Carol at McDonald's. But as much as she wanted to get out, to move, it struck her as somehow more dangerous than staying put. She didn't want to miss it if Carol called again with some change of plan. And even the idea of cruising around the streets of Morburne – empty now that the student hangouts had closed – made her feel exposed, at risk.

Instead, she waited, dozed, paced. And she finally came to rest upstairs, leaning against the door jamb, looking down through the dark at the shadow of the sleeping child.

It was 2:20. She was ready to go. She just couldn't quite make the move.

Amanda was lying on her back, her mouth hanging open. She held Elmo close against her with one arm. Geena could see the toy rising and falling with the girl's breath.

She had known this moment would come from the beginning. She had never had any illusions. Marie had warned her about Helix and Executive Decisions right from the outset. 'On a scale of one to evil, these guys are eleven,' she'd said.

'They won't stop till they've got her. You should know that up front.'

But by then, Geena had been widowed almost five years. Her husband – a kindly, mild-mannered but witty and quietly subversive historian – had opened his veins like a Roman at the onset of Alzheimer's. Her three sons had all turned out smart and ambitious and had headed south and west to the big cities. They phoned her often but only visited at the holidays.

She considered that she had had a happy and fulfilling life. There simply hadn't been enough of it. She wasn't old yet. She wasn't ready for the rocker. The choice between contemplating her bygone joys and helping a child in trouble was an easy one for her to make. She had agreed to take Amanda in.

And these last four months – they had been like a reprieve. Taking care of a child again, a little girl at last, talking to her, baking cookies with her, bathing her. It had been a sudden splash of color over what she feared was the prematurely gray end of things.

And all along, she had known this day would come. The urgent escape. The men closing. She had prepared herself, braced herself for the fear she would feel.

She just hadn't been ready for the grief.

Because she loved the child. She had come to love her fiercely. So she leaned there in the doorway and watched her sleeping. A few minutes more. And then a few minutes more.

And then suddenly, something happened.

She didn't know what it was, at first. She just started. She just straightened, blinking. She had a sudden sense of danger. A deep feeling that something terrible had come to find her. A second more and she became absolutely convinced that they were here – the bad men – that they had just shown up in front of her house.

She was right, of course. They had.

3

The Mondeo had pulled up to the curb outside. The four men were getting out. Dewey was checking the magazine of his Walther. Ike Lewis was rolling the wheel of his .38. Ferdinand was scanning the front of the place with the thermal imager. He had found the red heat of two life forms in the little room upstairs.

Winter, his hands in his overcoat pockets, signaled them forward with a nod.

Geena MacAlary didn't know what had alerted her to this. She hadn't heard the car's engine. She hadn't heard its doors open and close. She wasn't aware of having heard them anyway. She was simply aware all at once of a taut and quivering silence around the place, as if a long, steady noise outside had suddenly ceased.

She stood in Amanda's doorway, ears pricked.

Nothing. She heard nothing.

But she knew they were there.

She rushed forward. Rushed to the child's bed.

'Amanda!' She whispered the word harshly. Pulled the cover off the girl, shook her shoulder. 'Amanda, wake up!'

The little body stirred. Geena lifted her head, listened. Was there a footstep on the porch? She wasn't sure. There was no window onto the front, no way to check.

But now she heard a twig snap in the backyard. Her throat went coppery, then dry.

They were surrounding her.

The little girl sat up slowly. Screwing a fist into her eye, moving her mouth silently. Geena put her hands under the child's armpits. She gave a grunt of effort, and hoisted the soft, dead weight off the bed, set her down on her feet, holding her upright.

'Amanda! Sweetheart!' Whispering hard. 'You've got to wake up now! You've got to! Listen! They're here!'

Amanda stood there, rubbing her eye, holding Elmo under her other arm. She was wearing red pajamas with a teddy bear on the front of the shirt. The teddy bear grinned at Geena with maddening idiocy.

Amanda gave a sleepy sniff. 'I don't feel well.'

'I know, I know.' Geena knelt in front of her, grasped her shoulders desperately. 'But please! Listen to me! Wake up! There are bad men here! The bad men.'

Downstairs, the lock to the front door snapped back.

It was quietly, deftly done. But the noise traveled. It was unmistakable. Geena felt it hit her in the gut like a fist. The breath was punched out of her.

She sobbed. 'Oh God, please. We've got to hurry.'

She stood quickly. The child watched her dully as she moved to the window.

Geena looked out through the dark glass, down into the backyard, into the night. She felt her heart squeeze small: she saw them. There in the moonlight. Two of them, two men, two shadows, just now fiddling with the back door, just now pushing it open. Just now, they were stepping through.

And at the same time Geena heard the front door below clicking open.

They were in the house.

Geena clutched her hair in a second of panic. A thousand urgent thoughts collided with each other in her brain. Her eyes flashed every which way, looking for some avenue of escape.

There was an attic, she thought. And for a second, she pictured it. Rushing into the hall, getting the hook from the closet, pulling the trap down, spiriting Amanda up the ladder . . . Yes, and then what? They'd simply find her there. And there was no time for it anyway. They'd be coming up the stairs in a minute. They'd see her the second she ran into the hall.

The stairs, she thought then. They had to use the stairs. It was the only way up. They'd meet in the living room and then they'd all come up the stairs.

There were no windows on the stairs. They couldn't see outside as they were coming.

She caught her breath. She looked out the window again. The men were gone from the backyard now. They'd both come inside.

Geena leapt to the bed. Began tearing off the covers.

'Aunt Geena . . .' said Amanda in full voice.

'Sssht!' Geena shot it at her from between gritted teeth. Pulling at the covers. Yanking off the top sheet, then the bottom. 'You have to go to Mr Roth,' she said. 'You have to run to Mr Roth. Just go in through the front door. Don't knock. Just go in. He leaves it open. Tell him he has to take you to McDonald's. Now.'

'But I'm not hungry.'

A floorboard squeaked in the living room, near the bottom of the stairs. And worse than that, there was the sound of men murmuring. Geena heard this clearly: a murmured voice, a murmured answer.

Clammy sweat broke out on her face as she tied the sheets together with a double knot. 'Hurry, God, please . . .'

Done. She knelt in front of Amanda. She tried to get one end of a sheet around the little girl's wrist. Her fingers were shaking so wildly she couldn't do it. Elmo was getting in the way.

She pulled Elmo away from the girl. Tossed him onto the bed.

'I don't want to go to McDonald's.' Amanda understood to whisper this time, a child's stage whisper. 'I have a tummy ache.'

Geena had the sheet around the girl's wrist. She tied it, pulled the knot tight.

'O-ow,' Amanda whined softly.

'I know, I know, sweetheart, just hold on, just hold on to this sheet. Hold on to it tight, sweetheart. Your mommy's at McDonald's. She's going to meet you at McDonald's. You'll see your mommy there. Tell Mr Roth.'

'Mommy?' said the child. Her eyes widened. She was awake now more or less. Thank God for that anyway.

Geena doubled the knot, pulled it tight again. 'Hold on to the sheet. Don't let go until you get down. Then run to Mr Roth as fast as you can, sweetheart. As fast, as fast as you can.'

There was a footstep on the stairs. They were coming up.

Geena rushed back to the door. Pushed it closed as quietly as she could. There was a keyhole but no key, no way to lock it. She just hoped it would keep them from hearing what she did next.

She went back to the window. Undid the latch. She couldn't hear the footsteps now but she could sense them, feel them, rising, slowly, coming up to the landing step by step.

She opened the window, pressing one palm to the frame to keep it from rumbling. Then she turned.

Amanda was crawling onto the bed. Collecting Elmo again.

'Don't let go of the sheet,' said Geena.

And she scooped the child up in her arms and set her on the window ledge.

There was no time for tears, but Geena was crying. There was no time for goodbyes, but she kissed the child fiercely in her yellow hair.

'I love you,' she said.

Then she yanked Elmo from the girl's arms again and threw him out into the backyard. She wrapped the sheet round Amanda's arm and placed her small hands on it.

'Hold on to it, hold on,' she said again. Then she wrapped the other end of the sheet-rope around her own forearm and said, 'Dear God. Don't let go.'

And she pushed the child out the window.

For those next few seconds, time became a vice, closing on her. The child dangled and spun in the air, gripping the sheet for dear life, her little face puckered in fear, her wide eyes staring up at her. Geena had thought the weight would be terrible, hard to hold, but it was nothing, nothing, and she realized there must've been enough adrenalin coursing through her now to float a ship.

She passed the sheet-rope out the window, hand over hand, letting the child's weight carry her toward the ground.

And in the meantime – the footsteps. She could not hear the damned footsteps. She didn't know where they were. Still rising up the stairs? On the landing? At the door?

And then, a jolt. A sharp tug at the sheet-rope. Staring out the window, down at the twisting figure of the child, Geena saw the little body jerk.

One of the knots around her wrist had slipped. There was only one other left.

Hang on! she thought.

Amanda was halfway to the ground. The fall wouldn't kill her, but she might sprain her ankle, break her leg. She was little – she was still half asleep – even a skinned knee might keep her from running, might make her cry or slow her down until they saw her.

Geena let the sheet-rope slide faster through her hands, let the weight of the child carry her another half of the way down. Another half of that.

And the second knot came undone.

Amanda hung on to the sheet by herself for another second. Geena lowered her, lowered her, but the jolt of the slipping knots had jarred Amanda loose. The child's grip was slipping. She was sliding to the end of the sheet.

And then, with a quick, high-pitched little cry, Amanda fell.

It was all right. Just a few feet. Amanda went down onto one hand but she didn't topple over. Plus she was free of the sheet. It would be easier for her to run. Geena started to pull the sheets up quickly.

And, as she did, she heard a floorboard creak in the hall outside the door. They were out there, maybe three steps away.

Geena pulled the sheet in, tossed it behind her. Kicked it under the bed. She shut the window as swiftly and as quietly as she could. She spared herself one last glance, out into the moonlight, down at the little figure of the child.

She gasped as she saw her.

Amanda wasn't running. She was just standing there. Turning in a circle.

'Amanda.' Geena squeezed the word out tearfully.

The child was searching for Elmo in the grass.

Geena stood staring down at her, wishing her, willing her with all her might to forget the goddamned doll and run.

'Go, go, go,' she whispered.

Then another floorboard creaked. This one right outside the door.

Geena jumped back, away from the window. Turned to the bed.

The door flew in with a crash, and the men stormed in after it.

4

The room's light went on, blinding. Geena stumbled back, her arm up, protecting her eyes. There were four of them, she saw. Black shadows sweeping toward her. A red-haired man was in the lead.

Geena backed away, backed away. She tried to speak, but couldn't, could only back away. Now she was at the wall, against the wall. And the red-haired man was standing over her. Smiling down at her easily. She could smell his cologne. She could see the absolute confidence in his eyes, the authority, the easygoing expertise. She had no hope, and despair made her fear sickening.

'Where is she, Mrs MacAlary?' the red-haired man said softly.

Geena lowered her arm. She cursed it for shaking so much. She looked as if she were in an earthquake. Her voice came out a squeak.

'Who?'

The red-haired man snorted, gave a little roll of his eyes. He glanced around the room, smiling. Saw the disheveled bed. This made him pause, made him thoughtful.

Then he turned away from her and moved to the window.

Geena stood pinned to the wall, watching him. She felt the fear would pull her to pieces.

Let her be gone, she thought. Let her have found Elmo and run away and be gone. Please God – you son of a bitch – do something here for us, at least.

The red-haired man looked out the window into the moonlit backyard. Then he turned sharply to the other three men.

'She must still be in the house,' he said. 'Search it.'

Relief poured over Geena and made her weak. Her knees buckled. She reached out, took two steps and sat down hard on the bed. She lowered her head. Stared stupidly at her feet.

She saw a pair of shiny black shoes move up to her.

She looked up slowly, up into the smiling, authoritative, pitiless face of the red-haired man. She was vaguely aware that they were alone now in the room together.

'If you don't tell me where she is,' he said softly, 'what happens to you next will be . . . beyond imagining.'

Geena could only nod weakly. She understood. Dazed with fear, she turned to look at the clock with the smiling pony.

It was 2:35. Twenty-five minutes to three.

Twenty-five minutes, Geena thought. In a vague, distant sort of way she knew they were going to be the worst, and the last, minutes of her life. She was so afraid of what would happen next that she felt as if her bowels had turned to water. She wished to God that she had died at birth rather than lived to see this day.

She lifted her face to the red-haired man. She couldn't

see him through her tears. She tried to speak but could only snuffle loudly.

'Who are you?' she managed to say. 'Have you no mercy?'

'I'm just a businessman trying to make a dollar,' he answered. 'And no.'

Geena nodded again, sick with despair.

'Really, ma'am,' the man said. 'Save yourself the trouble. Believe me, you can't hold out forever.'

Geena laughed at that, at the very idea. Hold out forever. She hated pain. And when it came to the sight of her own blood, she was a baby. She gasped out of her tears. She wiped first one eye with her hand and then the other.

'Not forever,' she managed to say finally. 'But maybe a little while.'

Twenty-five minutes, she thought. Maybe.

5

Roth woke up and Amanda was standing over him. Clutching Elmo. Sucking her thumb. Her face was still pale, but her gaze was steady. The bear on her red pajama top grinned like a vaudeville comedian on drugs.

Roth's first thought was that he was dreaming. His second thought was that the end of the world was nigh and Amanda had come to judge the living and the dead.

'You're supposed to take me to McDonald's,' Amanda told him.

Thus saith the Lord, Roth thought.

Running a hand down over his face, he sat up. 'Amanda? Is that you? Are you asleep? Are you sleepwalking?'

'I don't think so,' said Amanda. 'Aunt Geena said you had to take me to McDonald's to see Mommy. She says the bad men are here.'

Roth was out of bed instantly. Pulling his pants off the back of a chair, pulling them on over his underwear. His mind was still thick, his thoughts blurry. But it was funny, he thought – he wasn't afraid. As he frantically wriggled his pants over his legs, he wondered: why not? He should've been afraid. Plenty. The bad men were here. And they sounded really bad. And he – Roth – had never been in a violent situation before; not since childhood anyway when he'd been beaten up by bullies once or twice or a dozen times. And he'd never thought of himself as a particularly brave person; the opposite if anything. But then, how would you know whether you were brave or not unless you were put to the test? Maybe – he thought with a certain distant academic interest – maybe it would turn out that he *was* brave. Who could say? He felt cool enough just now anyway. And as his mind began to clear, he felt he understood what was in front of him, what he was going to have to do.

'McDonald's, huh,' he said, figuring he ought to say something to keep the child calm.

She clutched her doll, sucked her thumb, watched him solemnly. Nodded.

Roth buttoned his pants, zipped them. He was already wearing a T-shirt. That would have to be enough. He sat on the bed to pull sneakers on over his bare feet.

Then Geena occurred to him. As his mind woke, a picture of events came into focus. He thought of Geena and the thought twisted in him like a knife.

He began to understand what must have happened. She'd gotten the kid out somehow, probably by the skin of her teeth. The bad guys must be there, next door, in her house with her right this minute. The familiar acid of rage spread through him as he thought of what they'd do to her to make her talk.

But still he was unafraid, cool, his mind working.

One thing was certain, he figured: she'd talk all right. Eventually, they would make her tell where the kid had gone. In fact, it wouldn't take them more than a couple of minutes.

Which meant there was no time to waste. Roth had to get the kid out of here. He had to get down to the garage. He had to pray that his old Citroën, which he hadn't used in over a week, would start in one try. He had to hope he could open the garage door quietly enough to avoid detection. He had to drive at least to the corner without headlights and endure the suspense of waiting for the gunfire to start. Not until he got to McDonald's – if he actually did get to McDonald's – would there be time to call the police. The fire department. The army. Everyone. Anyone who could get to Geena's house and get her out of there.

But first, he had to get to McDonald's.

He went over all this as he laced his sneakers quickly. And all the while, some observant part of his brain wondered at the fact that none of it made him feel panicked or helpless. He was an old academic with no experience of such things as this. He insisted to himself that he ought to be terrified to the point of dithering.

But he simply wasn't. He felt fine. Clear, angry, coolly determined to get the girl to her rendezvous, to call the cops to rescue Geena.

So it turned out he was Superman. Go figure.

He jumped to his feet.

'You ready?' he said.

Amanda nodded solemnly.

'All right,' said Roth. 'The Happy Meal's on you.'

6

'So what's really the story with your daughter?' Lonnie asked.

He was lying on the back seat, his hands behind his head, his head against the door. He gazed over his raised knees at the night racing past the other window.

Carol guided the old Chevy up the interstate. She was smoking feverishly as she drove, her cigarette hand working like a piston, mouth to ashtray, ashtray to mouth. She had not spoken for half an hour.

'What about her?' she said.

'Chubb was telling me all this crazy stuff. How she brought him back to life and shit.'

'Yeah. Something, isn't it? I just wish I could get her to knock it off.'

Lonnie laughed. Then his laughter died. He turned his head. Studied the back of Carol's curls, the pistoning cigarette

391

hand, the smoke trailing out through a thin gap at the top of her window.

'You're not gonna tell me this too, are you?' he said.

She gave a rough snort. 'What the hell do you think all the shouting's about? I mean, I don't know if Chubb was actually *dead* – I mean, maybe he just thinks he was *dead*, you know but . . .'

'But what? You mean, she . . . ?'

'Oh yeah.' She sucked hard on her cigarette, blew out hard. 'She's, like, abracadabra, you're well, man. I saw her do it to a kid with chickenpox once. I'm telling you. It's some kind of genetic thing. They gave her father some medicine or something. I don't understand it. And I don't care either. All I know is it's supposed to go away when she reaches puberty. So I figure if I can just keep her alive that long, maybe everyone'll just leave us alone.'

Lonnie went on gazing at the back of her head. Crazy, he thought. Crazy. And yet . . . She seemed so sure. Chubb seemed so sure. Lonnie thought about it for a long moment.

'So what do they want?' he said then. 'This Winter guy. What does he want with her?'

Carl shrugged. She jettisoned the last of her cigarette out the window. 'They'll sell her. That's what I heard. First they do experiments on her. Then they sell her, make her heal people, rich people, you know. And see, the thing is: it'll kill her. Whenever she does it, it makes her sick, and then if she does it enough she stays sick and dies. No one knows how many times it takes. It's like Russian roulette. Just one day she steps over the line – and that's it.'

Lonnie was about to answer – then he just let out a whiffle of air, shook his head. What the hell was he supposed to say?

He heard the *kachink* of the cigarette lighter being pushed in. Carol fit another white reed to her lips.

'So if this stuff is true . . .' he said.

'Oh, it's true, believe me,' she said bitterly.

'Well, then, shouldn't you talk to someone or something? I mean, if she can do this, maybe someone ought to know.'

'Like who? Enough people know already.'

'Well, I mean . . . scientists or something. Experts. I mean, maybe this could help mankind, something like that.'

'What's so helpful about it?' The lighter popped. She grabbed it. Even over the rush of wind at the window, Lonnie could hear the tobacco crackle as she set it ablaze. She jammed the lighter back into the dash and her hand started working like a piston again. 'I mean, people get sick, right? People die. If it's not today, it's tomorrow, that's the way things are. Buncha scientists are gonna take my baby, cut her up, punch her full of holes, study her – kill her, probably – you know they would – they wouldn't be able to stop – it'd be, like, oops, sorry, we killed her – and for what? Cause she can give people another day or year or whatever. Who cares? You know? Everybody's gotta die in the end anyway. They gotta learn to live with it, that's all.'

'Yeah, but . . . I mean . . . Man!' Lonnie thought about it. Made a face in the dark. 'I mean, Jesus did stuff like this and, lookit, they appointed him God.'

'Yeah, that's the second thing they did,' said Carol. 'First they fucking crucified him. Not my little girl, you hear me? Not Amanda.'

Lonnie fell silent after that. Watched the skeletal trees speeding past in the dark, the fields beyond them moving slowly past, the stars seemingly motionless. The moon. Another day of life, he thought. A year. Whatever. A little more time, even with the end still certain. What would he have given? If the child could've saved Suzanne? If the child could've healed her, even brought her back to life. Given him another hour of her smile, of her fingertips against his face, of the sound of her voice . . .

Man, if he thought she could bring her back now, he would be hunting down Amanda himself.

His body swayed as the car handled a curve. Then:

'There it is,' said Carol.

Lonnie sat up on the back seat.

The McDonald's arches. Shining yellow against the gray-black sky. The half-moon, in its low autumn crest, just moving over them.

There was an exit, then a clover leaf, then a short stretch of service road to the restaurant's driveway.

'God, God, God,' he heard Carol murmur.

Lonnie glanced at his watch. Quarter to three. He drew a breath. Put his hand in his pocket, wrapped his fingers round the butt of his gun.

No one in the place 'cept you and me, he thought.

'Just let her be there,' said Carol. 'Just let her be there. Okay?'

7

She was there. Roth had her. She was sitting in the passenger seat of his Citroën. She had the box of an uneaten Happy Meal beside her. She was holding Elmo and playing dully with the toy that had come in the box, a hamburger on wheels. The Citroën's engine was running and the heater was on. Even clad only in her pajamas, she felt warm and sleepy. She was fighting to keep her eyes open.

Roth was standing outside, just at the passenger door. Fiddling with an unlit cigarette. Watching the ramp where the interstate clover leaf emptied onto the service road. His stare was intense. His nerves were stretched thin. But he felt ready for anything. He was nodding to himself: so far, he had done what he had to do.

He had hustled the child to the car in his garage. Started the Citroën in the dark. Cruised out quietly onto the street, braced for a barrage of gunfire. He had driven away from the house, past the dark Mondeo parked outside Geena's.

Calm – he had kept himself calm – though the thought of what was happening to Geena made him physically ill. He had kept himself calm and driven on to the restaurant. Called the cops and the fire department from there, told them he'd heard Geena screaming. Just now their sirens had sounded in the distance. They were on their way. There was nothing to do now but wait.

He had done what he had to do.

And still, to his surprise, he was unafraid. He smiled a little, mirthlessly. Nauseated, yes. Strangling on his own suspense, waiting here helpless. But afraid? No. There was no fear at all. If anything, he felt a pervasive sense of floating unreality. As in: Excuse me, but what the hell am I doing here? As in: How has a classics professor gotten himself into a situation like this?

As in: It's almost three o'clock in the morning, booby, have you any idea where the flying fuck you are?

He shuddered. He had his coat on over his T-shirt, but he was still plenty cold in the Vermont November. Blowing plumes of frost, he raised his tired eyes to the sky.

A clear night. The lights from the restaurant and from the interstate exit blotted out the stars. But he could see the half-moon, like a great white idiotic grin, arching into the crevice of the restaurant's double arches which rose to meet it like . . . like . . .

Well, like enormous golden buttocks.

And Roth, still smiling grimly, thought: there's the anwer to the question, right there. Where was he? Where else could he be? In the parking lot of a fast food joint at 3 a.m. With men running around all over carrying guns and women running off God knows where without their kids and kids sitting all alone and frightened in the night – while in the sky above, an idiot grin stoops to kiss the ass of gold. Where was he? Western Civilization. He was in Western Civilization, that's where he was.

He laughed. Then he stopped laughing. Then he stiffened. He felt his whole body thrum. A car had just rolled off the interstate, out of the clover leaf. It was coming up the service road. He could not make out its shape beyond the headlights.

But now it pulled closer to the parking lot. Roth saw that it was not the dark Mondeo. It was an old red-rusted Chevy. A woman driving.

Mommy, he thought.

Roth turned quickly back to the car, to the child. Saw her in there, sitting sleepy with her Elmo and her hamburger toy and her red pajamas with the stoned comedian of a bear. Her eyes were falling shut and her mouth was falling open. She was adorable. And, for a second, deep waters of emotion welled in Roth. He was surprised how deep. He had known the child for only a few days and yet here he was willing to risk everything for her. Hell, he would've been willing to *give* everything for her if that's what he'd had to do. Why? Who knew? Because she made his cancer go away. Because she looked at him with her big solemn brown eyes and said *That's a good story*, which was what he'd needed to hear. Because he'd been right about her: she was the Messiah. She was his messiah anyway. Or maybe she was just a child, and children were God's answer to History – and that was also something he needed to hear.

He pulled the car door open. 'Come on, sweetheart,' he said. 'Your mother's here.'

'Mommy?'

The child bolted awake. Tried to open her door. Couldn't. Started crawling across the bucket seat, knocking her Coke over on the floor as she came.

'Come on.' Roth reached in to help her. Caught her under the arms. Lifted her out. Planted a kiss on the side of her head as he swung her round, and then placed her down on the parking lot pavement.

At the same moment the old Chevy – barely slowing as it fired past the high curb bordering the lot – reached the entry ramp and spun into it, burning rubber. Even as the car jerked to a stop, even as its chassis shook, the door creaked open. The driver spilled out of it, ran toward them.

'Amanda.'

'Mommy!'

The child dropped Elmo to the pavement and ran into her mother's arms.

Roth felt the impact as they came together, saw the look of relief and pleasure and love on the woman's face, and his eyes misted. Irritated, he blinked the mist away. The mother rocked the child back and forth as she held her. The child buried herself in her mother, vanishing into the embrace. Roth sniffed, tossed his unlit cigarette to the pavement.

Another person, meanwhile, emerged from the Chevy's back seat. A tall black man with sharp, feline features. He came out of the car and stood with his hands in his overcoat pockets. He looked down at the mother and child and smiled with one corner of his mouth.

Roth bent over, scooped Amanda's discarded monster up by its arm. He carried it over to the black man.

It was strange but, as their eyes met, Roth thought – would have sworn – that he knew the guy from somewhere. He couldn't place him though and he let it pass. He handed him the toy.

'Elmo,' he said.

The black man took his left hand from his pocket and received the furry creature. He nodded. 'Elmo. Right.'

And then, with a shriek of tires, the Mondeo shot onto the service road, and roared toward them.

8

Roth pointed, his face blank with fear. 'That's them.'

Lonnie, Elmo in one hand, pulled the gun from his pocket with the other. He waved to the back seat's open door. 'Get in, get in!'

There was an interminable half-second in which Carol didn't understand. In which she looked up reluctantly from the feel and scent and flavor of her child, in which she looked over her shoulder at the onrushing car, saw it, took it in.

'Come on!' Lonnie was screaming. Even the words seemed to come out of him slowly, as in an awful dream.

Only the car, the Mondeo, seemed to be traveling at full speed.

Now, though, now, Carol was on her feet. She had the little girl by the hand and was pulling her after her. She ran for the car.

Lonnie jumped into the driver's seat. Pulled the door shut. Glanced back over his shoulder. Saw the Mondeo's headlights in his rearview. Saw Carol tumbling into the back, saw her draw the child in after her, reach across her for the door.

He hit the gas. The tires screamed under him as he wrenched the wheel over.

Carol screamed too. 'The door!' But Lonnie couldn't look back.

The Chevy turned sharply, faced the service road. The Mondeo was now cutting across it toward the lot.

Lonnie heard Carol shut the door behind him. He floored the pedal.

The Mondeo fired over the high curb into the lot just as the Chevy fired over the curb and out. The cars passed each other in mid-air and hit the macadam with sprays of sparks.

Both were turning in the next second, half circling each other in a steel and rubber ballet. Lonnie's Chevy smeared the lighted street with smoke as it gripped the road and then leapt forward, racing for the interstate. The Mondeo, at the same moment, wrenched around and charged the ramp, bounced out through it and swerved, its chassis leaning with the force of the motion.

The Chevy was still in sight ahead, still motoring toward the overpass that would take it back onto the big road. It would be nothing, the business of a minute, for the Mondeo to catch it, to run it onto the shoulder.

Shrieking out of its sharp turn, the Mondeo sped forward.

And Roth's Citroën flew over the curb and landed in front of it.

Roth had seen the necessity at once, had started running the second he spotted the oncoming car. He was in his Citroën as the two other cars leapt the curb. The Citroën's engine was already running, the nose was already forward. Roth only needed to throw it into gear. Already, he saw through the windshield, the other two cars were turning, the Chevy was racing off, the Mondeo was spinning round and about to go after it.

He only wished he had time to fasten his seat belt. But he didn't. He stepped on the gas.

Roth felt his butt lift off the seat as the Citroën hit the curb and flew into the air. In the next moment, he was thrown forward, his forehead smacking the wheel as the car touched down. An endless instant of expectation followed and Roth observed with mild surprise that he still felt absolutely no fear at all.

Then the Mondeo hit him broadside, hard.

The scream of tires, the crump of metal, the tinkle of glass. The Citroën caved in. The Mondeo's headlights shattered. Its airbag exploded outward, smashing Ike Lewis, its driver, in the face. The impact broke his nose.

As for Roth, he was sent flying against the door. The window smashed and his head went through it. The door sprung open and he tumbled out onto the pavement, landed with a jolt that left him drained of all his strength.

Then it was quiet but for the sharp hissing noise of the Mondeo's burst radiator. A geyser of steam rose over the momentary tableau.

Roth lay on the street, only half conscious, unaware of the pool of blood fanning out around his head. He knew that he was floating on an island of shock in an ocean of pain. He understood that the moment he moved or spoke or even thought too much about it, he would be awash in such agony as he had never before known.

So he didn't move – even as a pair of legs came into his field of vision. He barely shifted his eyes as a red-haired man squatted down in front of him.

The red-haired man looked down at Roth, pursed his lips with disgust and shook his head. Roth tried to smile. *Do I look as bad as that?* he wanted to say. But he didn't have the strength for it. He found that he was fading away into a place of great darkness and serenity. He had read about this somewhere and he realized that this was what it felt like to be dying. Already, he could no longer muster the simple worldliness required to detest the red-haired man. And yet, at the same time, he understood that if the bad guys had found him here, the police had not been in time: the red-haired man and his friends must have made Geena talk and then killed her. At least, thought Roth, it hadn't taken very long.

After a moment, Roth found that he had said something. 'Geena,' he had said.

The red-haired man gave an angry sniff. 'Yeah, she died screaming, you old fuck,' he told him.

In the serene darkness to which Roth was fading this seemed a matter of no importance at all. And yet he was still alive, still within sight of the frenzied light of life.

So he did manage a smile at the red-haired man. And he whispered, 'Kiss my ass.'

And that was his valedictory.

9

Winter stood up from the corpse, still shaking his head. For a moment, his anger choked him and he almost indulged in something like self-pity. What the hell was it with this goddamned operation? Women ready to be tortured to delay him, men ready to die to get in his way. What was it all about? What was wrong with everyone? For Christ's sake, wasn't it better for one child to die instead of all these people? It was simple arithmetic. If they'd just let him take the kid and go it would all be over. Why did they want to cause themselves so much pain?

He cast his eyes over the scene, his face impassive, his gut seething. He felt as if poison were coursing through him. As his car had leapt the curb, as the Chevy had passed him in mid-air, he had looked out, past Ike Lewis, and seen the Chevy's driver. He had recognized Lonnie Blake. The thought that Mortimer and Hughes had been somehow right, that Blake and Carol Dodson were in this together, that Blake and Carol might actually *be* together, his fingers on her white skin . . . It was like poison in him. Like fire in his veins.

The fucking saxophone player, he thought.

Oh, he would kill the man out of hand, that was nothing. And the little girl he would sell for money. But this woman – this woman he was going to keep for himself. He would make her forget her black lover. He would make her forget everything, even her child. He wanted to be inside her when she cried out that he was the man, that he was *God* to her, that she would do anything, anything if he would only grant her death.

This was central to the operation now as far as Winter was concerned.

Hissing out a breath, he returned to the steaming Mondeo. He looked in through the window at where Ike Lewis swayed drunkenly, blood streaming into his mouth from his shattered nose. The airbag had already deflated to a white blob on his lap.

'Shit,' Winter said aloud.

He tried to open the door but it was locked. He hammered on the window with his fist. The bleeding Lewis looked up at him stupidly.

'Open the damned door,' Winter said to him through the glass.

Ike Lewis looked stupidly at the door. Then he shifted to find its handle.

The workers from McDonald's were coming out of the restaurant now. Two sticklike boys and one spherical girl. They stared at Winter open-mouthed.

'Are you okay, sir?' one of the boys shouted to him. 'We called the police.'

Winter briefly considered shooting him.

But now Ike Lewis had managed to open the door. Winter shoved him to get him to move over then slid in behind the wheel. Tore the airbag out of his way and threw it into the back seat.

Ferdinand, the skull-faced man, caught it, stowed it on the floor.

Winter turned the key. The engine whined. He tried again. It started, rumbled unsteadily. The hood steamed and wobbled.

'We won't get far in this,' said Ferdinand.

Winter threw the car into reverse. Looked over his shoulder. One of the car's hubcaps fell off and rattled over the pavement as he began to back up.

'Let's just get out of here before the cops come,' he muttered angrily. 'I'll call in for a replacement. We'll have it in half an hour.'

'Gives them a lot of time to get away,' said Ferdinand.

Winter faced forward, eyes bright. Threw the car into drive. 'They're not getting away,' he said. 'They must be going to Meridian. We'll meet them there.'

He stepped on the gas.

The boys and girl from McDonald's watched as the Mondeo started rattling forward. It pulled around the Citroën, and skirted Roth's body where it lay.

Then it headed off, past the arches, under the moon, into the night.

Chapter Sixteen

The Dawn Comes Up Like Thunder

1

The last hundred miles seemed to stretch out forever. Lonnie began to feel that they would never reach the mountain. Everything seemed to conspire to slow him down. He had had to leave the interstate soon after Morburne. He'd had to wander meandering two-lanes and spend hours chugging up forested mountains or idling at traffic lights in snoring towns. He'd wanted to speed – he'd wanted to metal the pedal. His whole body felt like a spring coiled and ready to thrust his foot to the floor. But there were the cops to think about. Anything that drew attention could be fatal. It cost him sweat and a twisting tightness in his chest, but he kept the car steady and endured the slow miles rolling to his fender, slipping under him, slipping away.

So that was tough. And the rearview mirror didn't help much either. Every time he saw the glare of headlights following him, his spirit seemed to seize up on him. And even when it was only the night back there, he imagined

Winter hiding in it, his headlights off, his car steadily gaining ground. That also made the distance seem long.

And then there was the quiet too. At first – after they saw that they'd escaped from the McDonald's – he had Carol and the child to keep him company. It felt good to see them in the back seat, the little girl tucked under Carol's arm, her face upturned to Carol's and Carol's eyes drinking in the sight of her. The murmur of their voices felt good, they soothed him. 'Are you all right?' Carol kept asking. 'Have you been eating all right? Aunt Geena said you were sick, are you feeling better? Are you cold? Do you want my coat? Is that better?' She couldn't stop, sometimes asking the next question before she even got an answer to the last – which was all right because the little girl seemed only to answer, 'Fi-ine. Fi-ine. Fi-ine', again and again in the same slow voice, pressing her body deeply into Carol's – 'Fi-ine. Fi-ine' – gazing up at her all the while.

In time, though, their voices slowed, faded, ceased. Looking in the rearview, Lonnie saw that the child was sleeping. Carol was humming her a lullaby. Lonnie could hear the tune of it: *Stardust*.

A few minutes later, Carol was sleeping too.

After that, he drove through the night in silence. The time dragged and he felt alone.

But then, when he judged he was maybe half an hour outside Meridian, he heard a noise beside him. He looked over and saw the little girl, Amanda, crawling into the front passenger seat. She slid down and bounced into place. Sat there and gazed at him. Her face looked small and serious in the dashboard light.

'Hey,' Lonnie said after a minute.

'Hello,' she said. 'My name's Amanda.'

'Yeah. Yeah, I know that. My name's Lonnie. Here, put your seat belt on.'

He reached over and pulled the belt out for her.

'I can do it,' she said and mightily snapped it home herself.

'I thought you guys were asleep back there.'

'I woke up,' she said. 'My tummy was hurting.'

'Yeah?' said Lonnie. He had no idea what the hell else to say; he didn't hang with children much.

No problem. Turned out this one was a font of conversation.

'You're brown,' she said after a moment or two.

Lonnie laughed. 'Yes, I am.'

'My daddy was brown. I saw a picture.'

'That right?' Lonnie glanced at her through the shadows. 'Where'd you get all that pretty yellow hair then?'

He saw her shrug. 'I don't know. I just got it. My daddy was a sailor. Only he died.'

'Oh yeah? That's bad luck. I'm sorry about that.'

'I wasn't there,' she said. 'If I was there? I would've sparkled him and brought him back.'

Again Lonnie didn't know what to say. He turned away from her, looked out to the next bend in the night road, the place where his headlights faded into the darkness.

If I was there I would've sparkled him, he thought. *Yeah, well, I know the name of that tune.*

'But I've sparkled other people,' the child went on. 'Howard. And the man from the plane. I made them feel better.'

For some reason he didn't quite understand, Lonnie found this a very poignant thing for her to say. As if by healing those other people, she was really trying to bring back her father. It made his throat feel tight. It made him ache at the impossibility of the enterprise.

'I hear you're not supposed to go around sparkling people,' he said. 'I hear it makes you sick. Could make you very sick. Could kill you.'

'Oh, that's all right,' said Amanda.

Lonnie looked over at her. Funny kid. Giving him that solemn stare. 'What do you mean, "Oh, that's all right?" It's all right if it kills you?'

'Yes. Because I'd just go to heaven 'cause I'm so small.'

Lonnie rolled his eyes. 'Yeah, well, you're so small, you're not supposed to be in heaven yet,' he said. 'Heaven might not be ready for you yet. You know what I'm saying?'

She didn't answer. She just went on gazing at him. When he turned to the windshield again, he felt her eyes on the side of his face.

'Anyway, your mother would miss you,' he added.

And Amanda said, 'Are you my mother's friend?'

'Sure I am,' he told her. 'I'm your friend too. I'm gonna help you get away from the bad men coming after you.'

'That's good,' she said.

Again, without knowing why, Lonnie found this poignant. He smiled crookedly at her in the dark.

She unsnapped her seat belt. 'I think I'm going to go back to sleep now,' she said.

'Okay.'

She crawled over the seat into the back, humming to herself: la la la. She was humming *Stardust*.

When Lonnie checked the rearview, she was curled up again against her mother, wrapped in her overcoat, her eyes closed. As if she'd never woken up at all. As if he'd imagined the whole thing.

Weird, Lonnie thought. And as he drove on through the night he was aware of a weird feeling inside him, a feeling half oppressive and half sweet. It felt as if his conversation with the child had effected some kind of change in him, though he couldn't have said exactly what it was. He tried to think about it but his mind only slipped off into its usual bittersweet daydreams and he was with his wife again and she was turning to smile at him . . .

The impossibility of the enterprise.

And his heart was leaden with yearning.

That's how the last of the time went by.

Then he was passing through Meridian, the small town on the state border. The Chevy slipped past outlying motels and grand old houses. Paused at the light on Main Street by the stone courthouse and the clapboard town hall. Cruised past the darkened storefronts, all empty and silent in the night. And then, another minute or two and the town was behind him. Lonnie straightened at the wheel – drew in a sharp breath – as he saw the small green sign with the white arrow: MERIDIAN MOUNTAIN.

Another slow minute; another. There was the mountain's base. He turned the wheel and the old car started climbing.

The lodge at the top must not have been closed very long. There was still a small white sign just after the mountain road began: MERIDIAN LODGE. A strip with the word *Closed* had been plastered diagonally across it. Lonnie drove past this and began a steep, twisting climb. The old Chevy groaned under him as it ascended.

The road went up a long distance. Thick evergreen forest clustered close. A strip of stars shone bright before him, but the moon was low now, near enough to the horizon to be hidden by the conifers. The way was dark. There were sudden edges, sudden drop-offs into a deep nothing. And the grade was growing sharper. Gray patches of snow began to appear along the shoulder and through the woods. The Chevy had to strain for speed. Lonnie had to fight to keep it going, keep it under control.

Carol stirred behind him now. 'Lonnie?'

'Yeah,' he said tensely, leaning toward the windshield.

'Are we there?' she asked him.

And then they were. Another sharp curve, and they passed the treeline. The sky broadened and the road went flat. The pavement spread out in front of them into a small parking lot.

413

Lonnie released a breath. He felt he had been holding it for two hours and more.

They'd made it. They were on top of the mountain.

He figured they had maybe forty-five minutes to wait until the break of day.

2

From the woods just below the crest, Winter and his men watched them passing. His long years of professional work notwithstanding, the red-haired killer could not deny he felt a welling thrill of triumph. For four months, his operatives had been chasing this woman. For four months, they had been right behind her, always one step behind. Now he had taken over, and in three days, the thing was accomplished. With anticipation, coordination and leadership, he had gotten ahead of her, and was lying in wait for her arrival.

This was how a new bureau chief set a standard of excellence.

He could not see the others in the trees. Ferdinand and Dewey with their night goggles and their Walthers. Ike Lewis at the wheel of their new black Cadillac, hidden away off the road. They were all there. They were all ready to move at his signal.

Winter drew in a deep breath of the cold night air and waited while the Chevy rolled up the hillside to the lodge.

3

The lodge stood dark on a last little rise. It was a broad, square two-story structure, modern, wooden, functional, with wide windows to take in the views.

Those views must have been spectacular during the day, because here above the trees the world spread out on every side for miles. As Lonnie pulled the Chevy across the lot, he could see the wide sky and the spiny Milky Way and the black outlines of distant mountains rolling against the stars.

He stopped the car, killed the lights and then the engine. He sat staring at the silhouetted shapes beyond the windshield. He could sense the cold out there and the almost uncanny stillness. In that sudden silence, it was impossible to believe that rescue was on its way.

'Let's see if we can get inside,' he said.

'Oh. She's sleeping,' said Carol. Lonnie had not heard her voice sound so plaintive before, so gentle. 'Can't we just sit here, run the engine. That way we could keep the heat on until the chopper gets here.'

Until the chopper gets here. He restrained his little noise of contempt. He turned to look over his shoulder at her. He imagined her hopeful expression in the dark. He imagined what she was thinking: It's over. We've made it now. Chubb's chopper will come for us. It'll take us away. They'll never find us. We'll be free.

Yeah. Well, she was entitled to her hope. She'd fought a good fight and come a long way. But Lonnie didn't buy it. The chopper might never come. Winter might get to them first. He wanted to preserve their gas in case they needed to make a run for it. He wanted to be inside in case they needed to make a stand.

'I think we oughta see if we can go in,' he repeated quietly.

And from the shadowy back seat, he heard Carol sigh. But she said, 'Okay. Okay, you're right. I get you. Let's go.' She handed him her flashlight.

There was a flight of stone steps to the lodge door. Lonnie climbed it while Carol tried to wake her daughter, tried to coax her out of the car. The door was stuck, but it wasn't locked. The lock, in fact, seemed to have been broken away. Lonnie pulled the handle – pulled it harder, grunting, and got the door open. As he stepped across the threshold, he heard animals scrambling for cover.

Lonnie flicked on the flashlight, passed the beam over the interior. He was in what had been a restaurant, it seemed, a broad open space with picture windows on three sides. Cobwebs hung from every corner, lazily rising and falling in every current of air. Leaves and trash and old plastic bags littered the floor. In one corner was a broad table with two broken chairs piled on top of it.

As Lonnie turned, the flash picked out the line of the bar and the shelves behind it. There was still a single stool there as if a ghost were sitting, waiting for his drink.

Lonnie moved deeper into the room, following the pale light. On the far wall, there was a door. Lonnie tried it, opened it. Saw a hall of webs and shadows, of doorways opened and closed: the rest of the lodge, the guestrooms. He shut the door. Turned away.

He moved to an eastern window. Brushed handfuls of cobwebs aside, spitting dust from his lips as he did. Then he used his sleeve to rub the grime from the glass. Clicked the flash off, pressed his face to the pane.

There was a stand of low, thin, stunted trees. Lonnie could see the stars beyond them and the mountainous horizon. And between the trees and the stars he made out a small field, a stretch of flat ground dotted here and there with conifers. It ran to the edge of a rocky cliff. Lonnie saw patches of snow glinting on the rocks in the last of the moonlight.

He moved from window to window then, scoping as much of the territory as he could make out. There was a sheer drop close to the southern side of the lodge. More parking lot and a telescope viewpoint to the southwest. There were also some hulking shapes hugging the building on that side. He pressed the flash to the glass and shone the light down on them. A dumpster, a large propane tank, a metal door. He picked them out of the dark one by one.

Carol came in with Amanda.

Lonnie glanced over his shoulder at them. Carol had her daughter in her arms, was holding her against her front. Bundled in her mother's brown overcoat, the child had her legs wrapped around Carol's waist, her arms around her neck. When Carol turned to examine the place, Lonnie saw Elmo clutched in one of the child's hands. Held by the paw, the red monster dangled down Carol's back.

'Jesus, it's cold in here,' Carol said. She'd given up her coat to the child and had on only jeans and a blouse.

But Lonnie in his overcoat was beginning to shiver too. 'I see a gas tank outside,' he said. 'Maybe if we find the kitchen we can get the stove going.'

'I don't feel well, Mommy,' Amanda murmured sleepily.

'I know, sweetheart, I know. You'll be better soon.'

Lonnie switched on the flash, played its beam off the walls. He spotted the kitchen door behind the bar.

The bar's wooden flap creaked as he lifted it. He passed through, went to the door. Pushed it open.

'Yeah,' he called over his shoulder. 'Stove's still here.'

Lonnie went to it. Carol came in behind him.

'I'm gonna put you down now, sweetheart,' she said. 'You're such a big girl, Mommy can't hold you anymore.'

She stooped to set the child on the kitchen floor. Amanda leaned against her leg, sucking her thumb. Carol rubbed the little girl's back.

At the oven, Lonnie was twisting knobs. He opened one of the range's doors. Bent his head down to listen.

'Nothing,' he told her. 'Gas must be off. The lines seem to run into the cellar, maybe I can find a stopcock down there.'

Shivering, Carol nodded. Lonnie could hear her teeth beginning to chatter. He took his gun out of his overcoat, stuck it into his waistband. Then he stripped the overcoat off and draped it across her shoulders. Their eyes met.

'I'll be right back,' he said.

She nodded. He lingered there, his eyes on her, about to turn away.

'Hey,' she said. Her voice trembled with the cold.

Lonnie lifted his chin at her. 'Yeah.'

'Thanks,' she said. 'For everything. I mean it.'

'My pleasure.'

'Yeah. I'm sorry. You know?'

'Nah. You told me to blow. It was me who came after you.'

'Yeah.' She stood with the child against her leg, looking up at him. 'Only I mean I'm sorry I can't be her.'

He felt the words go into him, twist in him. 'Hey . . .' he said. 'Hey, no . . .'

Carol gave a sour smile. Rubbed her daughter's back as she spoke. 'I bet she was really sweet, huh.'

Lonnie looked away. 'Suzanne.'

'Suzanne. She was, like . . . sweet, the sweet type.'

'The sweet type,' said Lonnie. 'Yeah.'

'I guess you loved her pretty big-time.'

'I guess. Yeah. That's right.'

'Yeah,' said Carol. 'Well, that's what I mean. I'm sorry I can't be her.'

Lonnie gave a small, unhappy laugh. 'Hey, listen . . .' he said. Then he took her gently by the shoulders and kissed her. Just pressed his lips against hers, long, slow, warm. When he drew away, she followed after, tilting toward him. He kissed her again, softly.

'I'll go see if I can get the heat on,' he said.

'Yeah,' she said.

Lonnie went to the door.

'I'm tired, Mommy,' he heard Amanda say behind him.

'I know, sweetheart,' Carol answered. 'So am I.'

4

Lonnie stepped outside. Paused a moment at the top of the stairs. He looked out over the parking lot to where the road sank back into the woods. He listened hard for the sound of a car, for anything. But the stillness hung there. He felt the emptiness of the night. He felt the dawn aching to rise. He thought: *Hey. There's a chance, right? The chopper might come. There's still a chance we'll make it out of here.*

The cold was eating through his sweater and into his skin. He started moving fast now. Down the steps, around the building. He found the door between the propane tank and the dumpster. There was no knob, just a hole where the lock had been. Lonnie worked his fingers into the hole and pulled. The door came open.

There was a short flight of wooden steps leading into the cellar. He started down it – and walked into a curtain of cobwebs. Cursing, he swiped the stuff away, pulling it from his lips.

'Yech,' he said.

He went down the rest of the way.

The cellar was little more than a concrete bunker, only partially underground. He heard the animals skittering as he came into it, but by the time he played the flashlight over the place, all he saw was junk. There were piles of it. It covered the cellar's dirt floor. It climbed up the walls. Suitcases, furniture, even some tires and car parts. An old washing machine lying on its side. An old lawn mower. Two stuffed armchairs were sitting on top of each other and, above these, Lonnie's flashlight picked out cobwebs drifting over the solitary window. The window was just a long thin rectangle at ground level, its glass gone. Lonnie shuddered as the cobwebs lifted with a movement of the cold night air.

He turned to the wall beside him, to the gas line running indoors from the tank outside. Using the light, he traced the copper tube along the wall. It ran into a pile of tin and plastic – old garbage bags torn open and picked clean by rodents and racoons. He kicked the trash away. There was the stopcock. Lonnie crouched down and tried to turn it. It was stuck fast.

Crouched there, rubbing one shoulder against the cold, he cast his flashlight beam over the floor until he spied a tire iron. He went and fetched the thing, carried it back to the pipe.

At first, he tried hammering at the stopcock, but the old line threatened to buckle. Instead, he wedged the iron's sharp end into the dirt floor, braced the bar behind one wing of the cock, made a lever of it. That did it. He drew the bar toward him and the stopcock turned. If there was any gas left in the tank, he thought, that ought to get it flowing.

By this time, he was kneeling there. Kneeling on the cold floor, working the stopcock, all his attention engaged.

He didn't hear the footsteps on the stairs, the whisper of an approach behind him.

Then, as he knelt there, he felt something brush against his leg.

Lonnie gasped. Released the tire iron so that it fell against the wall. He spun round, reaching clumsily for the gun in his belt.

The mouse was already dashing for cover, was already disappearing into a jumble of broken furniture against the opposite wall.

Lonnie laughed. Shook his head. 'Damn,' he said.

And then he froze as he felt the cold muzzle of a pistol pressed into his neck.

5

'I don't feel well,' Amanda said again.

'I know, sweetheart,' Carol said, rubbing her back. 'We'll go very soon and then you can sleep and you'll feel better. We're going to take a ride in a big helicopter.'

'We are?'

'I sure hope so,' Carol said, half to herself.

The child still leaned exhausted against her legs. Carol still had one hand between her daughter's shoulder blades. With her other hand, she began to work a cigarette and her lighter out of her purse.

'Is that man Lonnie going to live with us?' Amanda asked.

Carol had the cigarette between her lips now. It dangled there, unlit. 'Oh . . . I doubt it, sweetheart. He's just our friend.'

'He's nice, though. He's not like your other friends.'

She nodded. 'I know.'

'He could live with us if he wanted.'

'Yes, he could. But I think he lives with someone else already.'

Carol lifted the lighter, paused. It was very still. There was a narrow window beside the oven and she could see through it to a strip of night beyond. She wished the sun would rise. Even now she thought that maybe the ink-blue of the sky was beginning to lighten a little. Or maybe it was her imagination. It was just so quiet. Why did it have to be so quiet? What if the chopper didn't come?

She pushed the thought away quickly. Snapped a flame from the lighter. Torched her cigarette.

She drew the smoke in deeply with a cool sense of relief. She dropped the lighter back in her purse. Back with the envelope that held her passports and her cash.

'Mommy?' said Amanda.

'Yes, sweetheart.' She released the smoke on a long sigh.

'Who's that man over there?'

Carol was lifting her cigarette to her lips again, but stopped the movement midway. She felt as if her insides had turned to acid, as if the world had turned sickly green. 'Man?'

She spun to see the shadowy figure in the doorway. The cigarette fell from her shaking hand.

'Lonnie?' she whispered hoarsely, but she already knew.

'Hello, Carol,' the shadow said. 'My name is Winter. I've been looking for you a long time.'

6

Carol held her daughter tightly against her legs. The fear pumped through her like blood. The shadow-figure stepped out of the doorway, came toward her. There was another man right behind him. A very big man, a solid slab of flesh.

'Who is it?' Amanda said.

Carol could barely answer her. 'Ssh, sweetheart. Ssh.'

'Are they the bad men?' Amanda asked.

'Yes,' said Carol. 'They're the bad men.'

'Oh, now don't scare her,' said the one called Winter. He had paused, halfway between the door and Carol. She could just make out his eyes. There was just enough light to flash in them. 'We're not that bad. We have a job to do, that's all. We're making a living, doing the job we're paid for.'

'You think that's an excuse?' Carol said. She cursed herself as her voice broke. She pushed on tearfully. 'You think that's, like, an excuse for what you guys do? It's no excuse, man. You hear me?'

She saw Winter lift his shoulders in a shrug. 'Take the kid to the car,' he said to the slab.

The big man behind him started forward. Carol held her daughter tighter. Amanda clung to her mother's legs.

'Mommy.'

Carol stared hatred at the silhouette called Winter. She saw his eyes glint back at her dispassionately.

'We don't want this to be ugly for her,' he said.

'Oh, you bastard. You bastard.'

Carol trembled with rage and terror, holding on to her daughter. The second shadow came toward her. Carol could see just how big he was. He had huge, thick, muscular arms. A block of a head that seemed attached directly to his shoulders. At first she thought he was wearing a mask, but they were some kind of goggles. They made his thick face look inhuman and terrifying.

Amanda clung to her harder. 'Mommy,' she said.

'It's all right, sweetheart,' said Carol. There was no way out of this. They'd kill her where she stood, right here, right now. She had to stay alive. Think. Survive. 'It's gonna be all right. I'll come and get you. Okay? Just like before. Mommy will come and get you just like she did before.'

All the same, when the hulking giant took hold of the child, Carol held on to her fiercely. Amanda wrapped herself around Carol's legs.

'I don't want to,' she cried.

Carol was crying too, crying hard. 'I'll come for you, sweetheart. I swear it to God. Mommy will come and get you just like before and we'll go away. We'll ride on a big helicopter . . .'

The monster yanked Amanda's arms free. Lonnie's overcoat fell from Carol's shoulders. Her purse fell on top of it.

'Mommy!'

'Don't hurt her,' Carol screamed.

The slab picked the struggling child up.

'Mommy!'

'I'll come for you!' Carol tried to say. She was crying too hard.

The slab carried the screaming Amanda to the door.

The shadow called Winter glanced at him as he passed. 'Put her in the car with Lewis. Then go tell Ferdinand he can get rid of Mr Saxophone. Just do him and toss him in the woods,' Winter said. His voice sounded thick with disdain.

'Hokey-dokey,' said the giant slab.

'I don't want to!' Amanda screamed. She struggled uselessly as the slab carried her out of the room.

Winter turned back to Carol. She stood in front of the big range, bent over with crying, choking on her sobs.

'Now,' Winter said to her quietly. 'Let's talk about you and me.'

7

Then, from the cellar dark behind Lonnie, came the voice of the gunman: 'Okay, nigger-boy, this is all over.'

Down on one knee on the dirt floor, Lonnie lifted his hands into the air. The hard gun barrel dug painfully into his neck. The sound of his own heartbeat nearly deafened him.

'You try to do anything interesting and I'll blow your fucking head off,' the gunman said. He had a rasp of a voice, faintly Hispanic.

'Okay. Okay,' Lonnie said quickly. 'What're you, man, a cop?'

'Yeah, that's me. I'm a cop. I'm a cop all over.'

Not a cop, thought Lonnie. Good. He fought to keep his voice steady. 'Okay,' he said. 'My hands are up, right? I'm not moving.'

'Now gimme your gun. I saw you had one. Just give it to me.'

'Okay. I'm going for it.'

'Left hand, thumb and middle-finger.'

'I'm going for it now,' said Lonnie. 'Real slow.' He lowered his left hand slowly toward his belt.

'Just hand it back to me,' said the gunman.

'Just stay easy,' said Lonnie.

'Oh, I'm easy, nigger-boy. I'm real fucking easy.'

Lonnie's hand was unsteady as he lowered it. His heartbeat was loud. He pinched the butt of his gun between his thumb and his middle finger, just like the man said. He tugged at it. It resisted, stuck in his belt.

'Come on,' said the gunman.

'Okay,' said Lonnie.

He tugged harder. The gun came free. He worked it out from under his belt. He turned, holding the gun gingerly, bringing his left hand back to deliver the weapon to the man.

The gunman reached to grab the Cougar. He was close. For one instant, even in the dark, Lonnie could see his face. A scary sight. The eyes – the night vision goggles – bugging out at him like insect's eyes beneath the skull-like dome of the head.

The gunman grabbed Lonnie's Cougar.

At the same moment, Lonnie grabbed the tire iron.

It was still half upright, stuck in the floor, leaning where it had fallen against the wall. As Lonnie turned with the gun, as Skull-face reached for it, Lonnie's right hand dropped and found it blind.

It was all the same motion, handing back the gun, grabbing the iron, continuing around with the iron in his other hand. Even on one knee, Lonnie had the leverage for a full, whip-like blow.

The iron made an awful noise as it connected with the big dome of the gunman's head. A squelching thud: a melon falling to the sidewalk. Lonnie saw one side of the gunman's head cave in. The goggled eyes seemed to bulge out even further.

Then the gunman was lurching backward. Lonnie leapt up. He raised the tire iron for a second strike.

But the gunman dropped to the floor: a marionette with cut strings. He lay jerking and twitching at Lonnie's feet. Lonnie watched him, fascinated, horrified, until the body lay still.

Then he let his breath out. He stooped, picked up his gun, his Cougar. Scooped up the other gun – Skull-face's – and shoved it in his belt. Above his panting breath, above his heartbeat, he heard voices.

He heard Amanda wailing: 'Mommy! Mommy! I don't want to! Please!'

Jesus, he thought. They already had the girl. How had they come so quietly, so fast?

Or had they already been here, waiting for them?

He listened to the child's screaming. She was just upstairs, just outside. He heard a door – a car door – thunking shut. Amanda's screams diminished. They had put her in their car.

The Cougar in his hand, Lonnie hurried to the stairs. He went up quietly but quickly, three steps at a time. In two strides, he was at the open door. He was about to charge through.

But then a giant slab-like figure stepped into the opening, framed against the night.

Lonnie and the slab confronted each other. For a second, both men were still, frozen in surprise. The big man's goggles peered at Lonnie.

Then Lonnie reacted, leveling his gun.

But the big man was faster. With a clubbing blow of his right forearm, he knocked Lonnie's arm aside, drove it into the wall. The Cougar dropped out of Lonnie's grip. The next blow – the back of the giant slab's right fist lashing out like

432

a snake – hit him square in the face. Bright lights exploded in front of him as he went tumbling backwards down the stairs. His arms pinwheeled as he fell and he hit the floor hard, the breath rushing out of him.

In the next second, the giant came storming down after him.

8

And Winter, meanwhile, advanced toward Carol slowly. She backed away from him, crying. *You and me?* she thought. *Let's talk about you and me?* What the hell did that mean? She backed away.

She came up against the range. Her eyes moved everywhere, looking for a way out.

There was no way out.

He advanced on her. She knew she was going to die.

And she thought crazily: *Poor baby. She has no coat.* In the frantic confusion of her thoughts, this seemed a fact of terrible importance. She saw her coat and Lonnie's coat through the shadows. They were lying on the floor in front of the oven door beside her, the door Lonnie had left open. Her purse lay on top of the pile. They had all fallen during the struggle while Carol and Amanda fought to hold on to each other. Somehow this underscored Carol's sense of grief. It made her feel how cold her daughter would be, how unprotected.

Then the sight – of the coats, of the purse – was blocked by Winter's body as he pressed in close. Carol looked up at him. Through the dark, through her tears, she made out the contours of his face, the predatory ease of his smile.

And she breathed his cologne. His cologne and his hot breath pouring down on her. He was going to kill her and she trembled with fear and hatred. She could feel the white heat of her hatred pouring off her in waves.

'Ooh, look at you,' he said. 'You're mad, aren't you? You are one angry lady. You'd like to rip my eyes out, wouldn't you?'

'Your eyes first,' she said roughly. 'I'd start with your eyes.'

She knew at once she had said the wrong thing. She heard the way his breathing changed. She knew that sound full well. Her anger excited him.

'Mm.' It was a hoarse sound deep in his throat. 'You're a tiger, a mama tiger, aren't you?' he said. 'All that rage. But what can you do? You're helpless, aren't you? If you try anything, I'll kill you. And then what becomes of poor, poor Amanda?'

He pressed in even closer. The warmth of his breath and the thickness of his cologne and the heat of her hatred made Carol's stomach churn. She gritted her teeth. 'You're a sick son of a bitch,' was all she could say.

Again, she could hear how her anger turned him on. Her anger and her helplessness. *Is that what he wants?* she found herself thinking. *Is that what he wants from me?*

'You say that now,' Winter was murmuring. 'But you're going to change your mind about me, Carol. You're going to come to think of me in a whole new way.' He reached up and touched her cheek with the back of his hand. Carol couldn't help herself. She gasped at the touch; turned away as if it burned her. He caressed her cheek as his hand sunk to her throat. 'You're gonna come to understand that I make the sun rise in the morning. I make the oceans roll. I make the wind blow. You'll see. By the time I'm done with you, I'll be your whole world, everything.'

A groan broke from Carol as the man's cold fingers stroked her neck. She closed her eyes. Licked her dry lips. Tried to think. Had to think. She worked the streets. She knew men. The way they formed pictures in their minds and how they wanted women to be like those pictures. That's what they paid her for. To be like the pictures in their minds. They were in a relationship with you before they even met you.

Winter's lips came closer to her ear. 'Oh, I've thought a lot about you, Carol,' he said.

That's right, she thought. *He's thought a lot about me.* She opened her eyes. Maybe that was the way out.

She glanced down at the range.

Sniffing back her tears, she cleared her throat. 'Oh yeah?' she said. Still harsh. Believable. But just a little bit interested. Just starting to come around to him. Like the picture of her in his head. 'Like, what've you been thinking?'

That was it. That was what he wanted. She felt the hitch in his breathing. She felt his lips burn against her cheek. She had his number. He nuzzled her and her hand began to move out slowly from her side, to slide slowly along the range, over the knobs.

'Oh, I've been thinking about how smart you are,' Winter murmured. Pressed against her, close against her. She could feel the hard bulge in his pants rubbing lightly against her jeans. 'How smart and cool and tough. I don't think you're going to be smart and cool and tough with me, Carol.'

That's it, she thought. *I'm tough and angry but I'm at his mercy.* She let out a whimper. 'Look, you're not going to hurt me, are you?' she said.

Oh yeah, that stirred his sauce, she could feel it. He moaned and burrowed his face into her curls.

436

She slid her hand further along the stove.

His tongue snaked over the top of her ear. 'I have a place we're gonna go, Carol. A place where we can be alone. It's going to be your Bible school. That's right. I'm going to teach you who's the master of creation.'

Carol wasn't paying attention. Her hand closed around the oven's knob.

But at the same moment, Winter grunted angrily. His hand tightened on her throat, choking her. He drove his crotch up against hers. Somehow she'd pissed him off.

'Are you listening to me?' he snarled. 'Do you hear me?'

Carol was lifted onto her toes; her hand came off the oven knob. She felt Winter's fingers closing off her breath.

'I'm talking to you,' he said. 'I'm talking to you, do you understand?'

'I'm listening,' she squeaked. Her submissive tone was well rehearsed. She'd used it dozens of times. 'I'm listening, I swear to God. I didn't mean to do anything bad.'

Winter kissed her, hard. Pressing his lips into hers until it hurt. Pushing his tongue through her teeth, lashing it back and forth inside her mouth.

Then he pushed her roughly back against the stove. Straightened away from her. Turned away with a growl.

Carol grabbed the range's knob quickly. Gave it a half turn, not enough to make it hiss too loudly.

If it hissed at all. If Lonnie had turned on the gas.

When Winter faced her again, she was rubbing her throat. Her head sunk down, her eyes lifted, as if she hardly dared look into the searing light of his face.

He grinned at her, breathing hard. Trying to recover his control. 'All right, Carol, we're gonna go now,' he said. 'We're gonna go to Bible school.'

Carol swallowed hard. 'Can I . . . ?' she said meekly. And meekly, she reached down for her purse.

Winter stepped forward swiftly. Swooped down and scooped

up the purse. He held it in one hand, kneaded it with his fingers, feeling for a weapon.

'I only wanted a cigarette,' Carol said, giving him her frightened look.

He tossed the purse to her. She reached inside, brought out a cigarette and her lighter. Lit the cigarette and drew in deeply.

'Thank you,' she said. 'I appreciate it.'

Winter surveyed her as if from a great height, as if she were a piece of conquered territory. He was smiling to himself, smiling distantly.

'That's better,' he said. 'Come on now.'

Carol shivered. Sniffed. Brushed tears from her cheeks. In the same meek voice she said, 'Can I take my coat . . . please?'

Winter heaved a large sigh. His excitement was ebbing for now. He looked around and saw the coats on the floor.

Had Lonnie turned on the gas?

Winter bent over, reached for the coat. His head came level with the oven door. He stopped. He looked at the door. His eyes narrowed.

He smelled something. Carol could see it. He smelled gas.

She shot her cigarette into the oven, a perfect bogart. Winter's expression changed as the burning reed flew through the open door.

And nothing happened. Winter turned. He watched the cigarette's arc. Watched it disappear into the oven. Nothing.

Then the gas exploded.

There was a hoarse cough and the blue flame billowed out. The force of it knocked Winter sideways, sent him rolling, his hands thrown up instinctively to protect his face.

But Carol didn't hang around to watch. Clutching her purse to her side, she was already running for the kitchen

438

door. An instant more, and she was out, behind the bar. At the bar. Leaping over it.

There was no time to look through the windows, to see where the others were. She knew they were outside. If she went out there they'd have her.

She headed to the right instead. To the door into the hallway. If she could get there, get to a room, get out a window, maybe she could slip away.

She threw the door open. She plunged headlong into the shadowy hall. And at the same time, she heard footsteps. A loud roar of rage.

'Goddamnit!'

Winter was right behind her.

9

Lonnie now, flat on his back on the cellar floor, looked dazed through swirling stars to see the giant slab thundering down on top of him.

The slab was reaching into his overcoat. He was drawing out a gun that seemed a toy in his great paw. But it was not a toy. He was bringing it round to point it at Lonnie as Lonnie lay staring.

Lonnie pulled Skull-face's gun from his belt and fired.

The roar of the pistol was deafening. And the giant slab answered with a deafening roar of his own:

'Hey! Shit!'

He kicked out angrily. Pain shot up Lonnie's arm as his second gun went flying.

The giant drew a bead again, ready to blow Lonnie away.

Lonnie twisted to the side, shot his feet out, one behind the big man's ankle, the other kicking him hard in the shin.

There was another explosion as the slab's gun went off.

A high whine as the bullet ricocheted off the concrete walls. Then it was like a tower toppling. The big man fell through the dark to the cellar floor.

Lonnie let out a war cry and leapt on him. Found his gunhand. Grabbed it.

The big man twisted, trying to get at him. Trying to get his gunhand free.

Lonnie grabbed something – he didn't know what – a broken chair leg, it felt like. He lifted it. Hammered the giant's head with it again and again.

This annoyed the giant. He roared and flung Lonnie across the room.

Lonnie could not believe the strength of the man. Shot, beaten – and still, with one arm, he sent Lonnie flying. Lonnie slammed into a mountain of debris and sprawled in it, feeling sharp edges cut his hands, jam into his back.

He struggled to get on his feet again, but it was too late. The big man was already standing. Already bringing his gun up. He pointed the barrel directly at Lonnie's chest.

'You shot me, you son of a bitch,' he said.

And then he keeled over, dead.

10

At almost the same moment, Carol was careening down the lodge's dark hall. The cobwebs clutched at her face. The walls seemed to bend and weave around her. She could barely see through the clustered shadows.

Black doorways seemed to open to the left of her. A pool of blackness gathered straight ahead. But she was too afraid to slow down, to look. She was too afraid to stop and find her way. Winter must be crossing the bar now, she thought. He must be coming to the door. In a second he'd step into the hallway and see her.

In a panic beyond thought, she glanced back over her shoulder. All the dark was jouncing, weaving, as she ran. But she thought there was another movement back there. The door opening. Winter charging forward.

There was an open doorway to her left. She dodged through it.

This was a mistake.

She was in an all-but-empty room. A small square with a picture window nearly filling one wall. By the rising light through that window and the light of the fading stars, she could make out closets to her left, an old mattress lying in the corner to her right, a broken chair on top of it.

She stood there panting, her heart pounding. She could see the picture window didn't open. There were small vents to either side of it, but she'd never fit through them. She couldn't get out. She was trapped in here.

She turned to head for the hall again.

It was too late. She heard Winter's steady tread approaching.

'Uh-oh,' she heard him growl in the hallway. 'I'm coming for you, Carol. I'm coming for you – and I'm really, really pissed off.' He laughed. 'Tough little bitch.'

Carol stood there, frozen like the hunted creature she was. Her eyes darted back and forth, but there was nothing to see, nothing to do. The boards in the dark corridor creaked as Winter approached the room. His footsteps sounded closer and closer.

She tried to think. Some means of escape, some strategy. There was nothing. Nothing at all. There wasn't even a door she could shut. It had been taken off.

Swallowing tears of panic, she moved quickly to the mattress, seized what was left of the chair. It was just the seat and the back, but it was metal, heavy enough. She carried it to the spot beside the doorway. Pressed herself there against the wall. When Winter came through, she would launch herself at him. She might get one swing at his head. It was doubtful. She wasn't strong. And he'd be careful. He'd be quick. It was long odds he'd kill her dead before she even took a step.

But there was nothing else to do. Not a single thing. She had to try it.

So she stayed pinned there against the wall, her hands

sweating on the chair back. And she listened to the footsteps nearing, listened to the old boards creaking closer and closer. Listened to Winter's voice, just yards away now.

'Carol, Carol, Carol. You've made this more fun for me than you can possibly imagine.'

She tensed herself, lifted the chair, ready to attack. He was right outside.

And then she heard something new. A different sound. A short, high chirping.

The footsteps in the hallway stopped. There was silence. Pressed against the wall – pressed into the wall – Carol held her breath.

Winter spoke again. 'What,' he said.

He was talking into a radio or a phone or something. Someone had called him. Carol swallowed a sob of fear. Pressed there, she listened.

'Christ,' she heard Winter say. 'Don't move.'

And then his footsteps began again.

But now they were hurrying away.

11

Ike Lewis had barely heard the gunshots. He was sitting behind the wheel of the Cadillac. All the doors were locked, and the car's windows were shut. The heater fan was going.

And the kid – the kid was in the back seat, shrieking like a banshee.

'I want my mommy! Mommy! Mommy! Mommy!'

'Aw, shut up already,' Ike Lewis muttered.

She threw herself against the rear door. She scrabbled at the door, pulled at it, tugged at it, making squeaky noises. Even Lewis found her a pathetic little figure in her red pajamas with the smiling bear, with her stuffed red monster doll clutched under one arm. But the pathos of it just made him angrier. He couldn't wait till Winter came back and drugged the little bitch.

'I don't want to! I don't want to!' she screamed.

Lewis raised his voice. 'Would you shut up. And quit that. It's locked. The door's locked. Only I can unlock them. You're stuck. You're not going anywhere. Little twit,' he added under his breath.

His head was throbbing. His nose – broken by the Mondeo's airbag – was also throbbing. His whole body, in fact, was one big pulse of pain. It would have given him an enormous sense of relief to just haul off and crack the kid a good one – the way he did one of his own kids when they were acting up in the back seat.

But this one was little Miss Precious. He wasn't allowed to clock her unless Winter said so. So she just went on screaming. Ike Lewis shook his throbbing head and sighed.

So the sound of the first gunshot in the lodge's cellar – thunderous as it was – reached him only faintly. And it didn't bother him at all. He figured it was just Ferdinand taking care of the black guy.

Ike Lewis looked through the windshield to the right, toward the cellar. He expected to see Ferdinand and Dewey returning to the car. Instead, he heard another shot. Clearer this time, because he was paying attention.

'Now what the hell was that?' he said quietly.

'Mommy! Mommy! Mommy!'

'Wait a minute. Would you shut up a second?'

The kid didn't shut up. Concerned, Lewis opened the door and stepped out into the parking lot.

He stood in the cold beside the open door, listening. The child went on screaming in the car behind him. He really let her have it this time.

'*Shut up*!' he shouted at her, loud.

That had some effect at least. The girl fell into a quiet sobbing.

In that quiet, Lewis stepped toward the hood of the car, toward the lodge. He listened. There was nothing now. He heard nothing at all.

He went into his pocket for his radio. He beeped Ferdinand. Listened. Nothing. He beeped Dewey. Nothing, no answer.

Lewis lowered the radio. Stood there, staring into the dark. He wished his head would stop aching so he could think more clearly.

'Hey, Ferdinand? You okay?' he shouted. 'Dewey?'

Nothing. The night was quiet.

'Shit,' said Ike Lewis. He pressed the button for Winter.

In a moment, he heard the red-haired man's voice on the box. 'What.'

'Yeah, Winter, I think we got a problem out here,' Ike Lewis said. 'Gunfire from the cellar. I can't raise Ferdinand or Dewey.'

'Christ,' Winter said. 'Don't move. You hear me? Stay with the kid and watch out for Blake. The kid is the only one who matters. We can forget the rest of them and just take her out of here. Just don't move and stay with the kid, you copy?'

'Yeah, yeah, copy, roger. Stay with the kid.'

'I'm on my way,' Winter said.

'Right,' said Ike Lewis.

With another sigh, he slipped the radio back into his pocket. He cast his eyes once more over the night. The blue of the far horizon was growing lighter now. It was nearing dawn. The features of the lodge, its doors, windows, clapboards, were starting to be more clearly visible.

But Lewis saw nothing moving there. No one.

He stepped back around the door. Lowered himself behind the steering wheel. Pulled the door shut.

He looked over his shoulder into the back seat. 'All right, listen up, kid, here's the deal,' he said.

But he never did get to explain the deal to her.

Because the kid was gone.

12

Amanda hurled herself through the darkness, blind with tears. She headed for the lodge. She headed for her mother. She didn't think about the bad man in there. She didn't think about the cold on her bare feet. She didn't think about anything. The man in the car had opened the door. She had thrown herself over the front seat, Elmo clutched under her arm like a football. She had scrambled through the opening, shot straight past the man's legs and shot away. She wasn't trying to escape or anything. She was just trying to get back to her mother. Her mother would help her. Her mother would take her someplace safe. They would ride in a big helicopter.

She ran for the lodge.

Spurred on by her terror of the man behind her, sure he was running after her, sure he was about to reach out any minute and grab her from behind, she ran without stopping, without daring to look back, until she reached the steps that led up to the lodge door.

She was about to scramble up those as well. But then the bad man with red hair stepped out above her.

Amanda gasped. She felt as if her heart had stopped. The bad man with red hair loomed gigantically against the stars, blocking her way. She stood petrified at the foot of the steps, staring up at him.

But he didn't see her. She was too small. He was looking out above her, looking toward the parking lot, toward his car.

So Amanda turned and scrambled for the corner of the lodge. Running to get around the side of the building, the side opposite the cellar door. She heard the deep shouts of the bad men behind her. She knew they were calling to each other. And she knew they would come after her. She could almost feel them already, running after her, reaching for her. Any second, she thought they were going to grab her. She was too terrified to look back and see.

Then she was around the corner of the building. Running past the concrete base that was the upper section of the cellar. Running, waiting for the hand to reach out behind her. Waiting for the hand to grab her.

And then it did.

Amanda let out a little scream as the arm snaked around her waist, as she was jerked backward off her feet.

Then her scream was cut short as a hot palm clamped hard over her mouth.

13

'Don't scream, sweetheart. It's me, it's Lonnie. Don't be afraid. Just keep quiet. It's me.'

Lonnie held the child close against him. He felt her body fluttering in his hand like a bird. For a moment, he closed his eyes in relief.

He had climbed out through the cellar's narrow window only moments before, right after the enormous thug had fallen dead. He had recovered his Cougar again and snatched up the slab's gun too, a Walther P99. He had stuck both guns in his belt and then he had climbed out. He had crept under the windows of the lodge to the corner of the building. From there, he could peek around at the parking lot. He could just make out Winter's car down at the end of the road, right where the lot began.

Lonnie watched. He could see the tall, thin thug standing by the car's open door. He could see him talking into his radio. He could even hear the murmur of his voice.

But he never saw the child. She had already run past his line of vision. She was already around the corner, already at the stairs.

Lonnie was absolutely shocked when she shot around the building and went motoring past him. He grabbed her without thinking, pulled her to him, his left hand cutting off her scream. He hugged her, closing his eyes in relief.

Then he turned her around so he could look at her.

'You okay?' he said softly.

The child nodded, frowning, fighting tears. 'Where's Mommy?'

Yeah, thought Lonnie, *that's the question*. The odds seemed to him about a hundred to one that Winter had gotten to her. In which case, she was either dead or wished she was. Which didn't seem like a very comforting thing to tell the kid.

So as soothingly as he could he said, 'Well, the important thing right now is that you're here with me and we're safe, right?'

And then the window above his head exploded.

Lonnie threw his body over Amanda's as the big picture pane blasted out into the night. Kneeling there, bent over her, he felt the fragments raining down onto his back, felt the cold prickle of glass on his neck, heard the shards pattering into the earth all around him.

There was a clanging thud to his side. Lonnie chanced a look. He saw a portion of a metal chair settle onto the ground.

He looked up. A mattress came through the broken window. Carol crawled out on top of the mattress. She dropped down onto the earth beside him, gasping for breath.

She had busted out of the little room.

Silently, the child broke from Lonnie's arms and rushed into hers. Open-mouthed with shock, still unsteady on her feet, Carol staggered as the little girl flew to her. Then she wrapped herself around her daughter, knelt beside her, murmured through her tears.

After a moment, she looked over Amanda's head at Lonnie. 'Can we go now?' she said.

Lonnie laughed. 'Sounds like a good idea to me.'

Crouching low, he crept back to the edge of the building. He drew the Cougar out of his belt. He peeked around again at the parking lot. The air was growing lighter now. Lonnie had a clear view of the figures moving by the car.

Behind him, Carol said softly, 'What's that?'

Lonnie didn't answer. He watched Winter and the driver moving to the Cadillac's trunk. They popped the trunk open.

'Listen,' said Carol. 'Listen.'

'What?' Lonnie lifted his head. He listened.

'You hear it?' said Carol.

And in a moment, he did.

A soft dawn breeze was rising. And within the whisper of the breeze was another whisper, a stuttering breath, an almost silent rhythm of the air.

Lonnie's lips parted. He glanced up at the brightening sky.

'It's the chopper,' Carol said, her voice cracking. 'Oh God, it's the chopper. It's on its way.'

14

As the sky grew brighter, they could see it. A Black Hawk coming in fast and low toward the cliff, sailing for the flat patch of ground beyond the rocks at the end of the little field. The dark dot of the chopper against the blue sky took slow shape as it approached and descended. Its stuttering whisper became a low thunder.

For a moment, Lonnie's spirits lifted.

Then he turned and looked down the drive. Fear squatted on his heart like a toad.

From where he was, crouched at the corner of the lodge, he could see the two men, Winter and the driver. They were starting to move away from the car. They were moving back toward the building.

They were both wearing night goggles now to pierce the pre-dawn shadows. And they were both carrying weapons. Winter had some kind of sniper machine – a genuine M24 maybe. The driver's piece looked mighty like an AK.

Lonnie gripped the Cougar harder in his sweating hand. The men were too far for a shot in the dark. He'd only draw their fire. And they stayed far, moving toward the opposite side of the building. The driver led the way around the edge of the wall. Winter trailed behind. Lonnie saw the red-haired man's head moving as he took in the lie of the land.

'It's coming, Lonnie,' Carol said behind him. She was breathless with hope and excitement now. 'It's coming down. We gotta run for it. He's not gonna wait for us. We gotta go.'

Lonnie glanced back over his shoulder. No, no, no. It was no good. In order to get to the helicopter, they would have to break through the scraggly stand of trees and then cross the open field to get to the landing site. It was a run of about a hundred yards, a touchdown run.

Winter and his man had it covered.

From the opposite side of the building, from a post by the cellar door, Winter and the driver would have a clear shot at them every step of the way. They would pick off Carol first to stop Amanda. Then they'd get him. Then they'd come for the child.

'Come on, Lonnie, come on,' said Carol.

She had to raise her voice as the chopper thundered louder. Its insectile shape was clear now as it clawed the blue air above the cliff.

Lonnie drew a deep breath. He could feel his heartbeat rising into his throat, almost gagging him.

'We can't go yet,' he said.

'What're you . . . ?'

The chop of the Black Hawk grew louder and louder.

'You gotta wait here,' he said above the noise. He shifted the pistol in his hand, the Cougar. He drew the Walther from his belt. 'You hear what I'm saying? You keep Amanda here until I give you the signal. Then you run across that field and get in that chopper and don't look back.'

'What're you . . . ? We gotta go, Lonnie,' Carol said. 'We gotta go now.'

'You hear what I'm telling you?' Lonnie shouted at her fiercely. 'Wait for the signal then run like hell.'

She stared at him, holding her daughter close. The chopper beat the air. Then she nodded once quickly. 'Okay. What's the signal?'

'Either I get killed or they do,' Lonnie said – and he ran for the stand of trees.

There were maybe ten yards between the end of the lodge wall and the line of small conifers. The minute he broke cover and headed for them, the rifles opened fire.

To the thunder of the chopper and the thunder of his heart came the thunder of the weapons as they spat bullets into the rocky turf. The mountain, so quiet just moments before, now drummed with noise as, head down, Lonnie hurtled wildly over the open ground. He fired back blindly, thrusting his arms out, pulling the triggers of both pistols at once. Large chunks of dirt kicked up to the right of him. Sparks flew as rifle slugs glanced off stone. For three seconds that ticked at their own dismal pace he felt his whole body exposed to the sweeping barrage. He pulled the triggers of both pistols once, twice, again.

Then Lonnie was in the trees, on the ground. Twisting around with the pistols in his hand. Panting. Unhurt.

The Black Hawk was settling down now, dropping the last distance from the sky to the ground. The sound of its blades seemed to swell up and fill the dawn air. Cutting through it, the sound of the rifles coughing bullets came in bursts. Branches snapped off and chips of wood flew over Lonnie's head.

He pressed low to the ground. Looked out through the trees. He could make out one man, the driver, stretched prone behind a rock beside the lodge wall. He had the AK out in front of him. He was panning it over the trees, letting off fire at intervals. Lonnie had no shot at him, no chance of hitting him at all.

But that was all right. He had a better idea.

Rolling onto his side on the cold earth, he stuffed the Cougar back in his belt. Then he rolled onto his belly. He raised the Walther in one hand. Steadied his wrist with the other.

He aimed for the propane tank beside the dumpster.

He had no idea whether it would work. He figured he had four or five shots left in the Walther, another one or two maybe in the Cougar. If he aimed close to the building, if he got off enough rounds, maybe he'd hit the line, maybe he'd cause a spark. He just didn't know.

He ducked down a moment as the AK fire crashed through the branches above him. The chopper drummed the air behind him. He held the gun steady.

Then he pulled the trigger twice and the lodge exploded.

The chopper noise, the gunfire, his own heartbeat – all were swallowed as the tank went up with a single echoless roar. The stars went out, the trees came clear, a corner of the dawn turned morning-bright. The whole left side of the building was swallowed in a rising billow of flame.

Lonnie didn't see the two riflemen die, but he saw the blue-orange storm of light lift the man on the ground behind the rock and engulf him completely.

Then Lonnie was on his feet. He was waving his gunhand wildly.

'That's the signal!' he screamed through the noise. 'That's the goddamned signal!'

But Carol already had the idea. She was running for the trees with Amanda in her arms.

She tore through the brush, she shot past Lonnie as the flame-light settled. He had a quick glimpse of her illumined face contorted with effort and with fear. The child clinging to her. Elmo bouncing against her back.

Then they were gone, past him, running across the field. Lonnie took one more glance back at the building. It was burning on one side and by the glow he saw debris and empty ground. There was no one left moving.

He turned his back on the place and went after Carol, running for the chopper.

15

The dirt and pebbles flew in waves. Chunks of snow lifted from the dead grass and rolled away. They were blown by the wind from the chopper's blades as the Black Hawk slowly lowered itself to the earth.

Carol was almost halfway across the field, still carrying Amanda, clumsily dodging the big rocks that littered the ground and the small trees that grew up here and there on the sere plateau.

Lonnie caught up with her quickly. He ran beside her, one hand on her arm, one still clutching the Walther.

The stars were gone. The sky was light blue now, but the sun was still behind the distant mountains. The big helicopter drifted down and down, coming out of silhouette, showing its red and white sidelines. Lonnie could see the outline of the pilot through the windshield.

Then the aircraft landed. Its noise encompassed them until it almost wasn't noise at all, just a great throaty throbbing of air.

Carol and Lonnie took another few stumbling steps toward it. They were just approaching a slender pine. There, by its roots, Carol hit a patch of snow and slipped. She let out a cry as she lost her balance.

Lonnie was there. He had her by the arm. He held her upright. She paused a moment and then set Amanda down on the ground.

In that moment, Lonnie glanced back toward the lodge. And he saw Winter coming for them.

He was driving the black Cadillac. The big car spit dirt, whining, as it skirted the little stand of trees and shot toward them over the field. Its tires shuddered on the rocks but it was coming so fast that it seemed almost to fly above the uneven ground.

Carol looked back and saw it too. Another few seconds and it would run them down. They'd never make it the rest of the way.

She turned to Lonnie. He saw her lips move, her voice drowned by the chopper. He thought she had whispered, 'Jesus.'

'Go!' he shouted at her. 'Go!'

He shoved her. She grabbed Amanda's hand and ran.

Lonnie stood where he was, in front of the pine tree. The Cadillac sped toward him. Its grill seemed to grin at him as it bore down.

Lonnie lifted the Walther in both hands. He aimed for the Cadillac's windshield. He figured he had three seconds before it hit him. He figured he had one shot a second. He squeezed the trigger.

A hole appeared in the windshield. A web of cracks flew out around it. The car never slowed. Lonnie squeezed the trigger again and the windshield shattered.

But the car sped on. It just kept coming. Lonnie had to dodge to the side now if he was going to get out of the way.

He stood where he was. He squeezed the trigger.

Then he jumped to the side. But it was too late.

The fender caught him in the hip and he flew over the hood, tumbled and somersaulted across the hard metal, flew through the air and came down hard. He was alert through all of it, aware of the impact and the long tumbling fall. He felt himself tearing and breaking inside. He felt himself lofting across what seemed a terrible distance to a certain crash. He knew he was about to hit.

And then he did hit and he felt his insides shattering.

The Cadillac went straight on and flew into the pine tree. It lifted onto its side. Rolled over onto its hood. Its windows blew out, the glass twinkling in the dawn. It slid several yards across the hard earth, the rocks sending up sparks beneath it. Then it came to rest a little way from where Lonnie had fallen.

Lonnie lay still. He was conscious. He could feel the life force draining out of him. He could feel the blackness swimming in to take its place. The noise of the chopper seemed far away now. Everything seemed far away.

With a great effort, he raised his head. He saw the Caddy as it came to rest. He saw it catch fire. The flames snickered up from the engine for a second. And then the gas tank blew with a whump that shook the earth beneath him.

The car lay black and dead in the heart of the burgeoning flames. Lonnie saw only darkness and stillness within the broken windows.

That was done then, he thought. And grunting with pain, he tried to turn, tried to look out over the field. Carol and Amanda must almost be at the chopper now. Maybe he would see them reach it. Maybe he'd live long enough to see them lifted safely into the air.

But when he finally managed to bring his head around, he felt a sadness close to heartbreak.

They had not reached the chopper at all. They weren't even trying.

Amanda had broken loose from her mother. She had pulled her hand from her mother's hand and she had turned around.

She was running back across the field toward Lonnie.

16

The girl's movement had taken Carol by surprise. It was a long moment before she could pull up, before she could turn, before she could start back after her daughter. By then, Amanda was already halfway between her and Lonnie. She had almost reached the burning car and was running with all her might to where Lonnie lay.

Lonnie was watching. He saw Carol turn. He saw her trying to shout over the noise of the chopper. He saw her throw out her arms and start running back after Amanda. She was shaking her head. He could see her shouting 'No!'

Lonnie wanted to stop the child, shout at her to go back. But he couldn't shout. He could barely move. He lay where he was, his strength failing. He watched the child running toward him.

The child ran on, coming abreast now of the burning Cadillac. Carol was far behind, coming after her, reaching out. She would never stop the little girl in time. Amanda was already passing the blazing car.

And then Winter leapt out of the flames and grabbed her.

His clothes were on fire. His flesh was smoking. His face was a streaked mask of blood and pain and rage. He had crawled out of the far window, the one Lonnie couldn't see. He had crawled around the front of the car. As the little girl passed he flew, burning, bleeding, across the distance, reached out and wrapped a hand around her ankle.

Amanda screamed and fell. She hit the ground hard. Blazing, Winter climbed to his knees, still gripping her ankle. Even with the chopper's thunder, Lonnie could hear him screaming down at her.

'Touch me! Touch me! Touch me!'

Lonnie closed his right hand. The Walther was gone. With an enormous effort, he lifted his left hand. He moved it to his waist. Found the Cougar still in his belt. He drew the gun out.

Winter clutched at Amanda, dragged her over the ground to him. She shrieked and shrieked, struggling against him, clawing at the ground, but he drew her, all the while screaming:

'Touch me!'

Carol ran toward them, reaching out.

Lonnie leveled the gun.

'Judgment Day, motherfucker,' he whispered.

He pulled the trigger and blew Winter's head off.

17

What was left of Winter's body flopped to the earth, burning.

Amanda was free. She jumped to her feet. She began running toward Lonnie again.

But now Carol had reached her. She had caught hold of the child's shoulder. The child struggled and reached out, reached out and down for Lonnie, for his right hand stretched out on the ground.

She twisted and Carol's grip slipped. She had her daughter by the wrist now. But Amanda, straining, was leaning far forward, was stretching down, was almost able to touch Lonnie's hand.

She reached for him, reached for him, pulling hard, crying. And now she almost touched his fingertips.

Lonnie summoned the last of his strength. He drew his hand away from the child. He laid it wearily on his chest.

A moment later, Carol pulled her daughter up into her arms.

She held the child close. She stood there holding her, looking down at Lonnie. Lonnie could see she was crying. She was crying hard, sobbing. She was clinging to her child and crying and shaking her head at him. Shaking her head to tell him she couldn't, she couldn't. She couldn't risk her daughter's life. Not for him. Not for anyone.

Lonnie nodded to her. He understood. It was all right. Letting out a breath, he lay back against the earth.

When he turned his head, he could see them. Carol was backing away from him now. Still crying, still shaking her head at Lonnie. Then, reluctantly, she turned away.

She hurried across the field to the chopper. All the way, the child was looking back at him over her mother's shoulder. Looking back and reaching for him as she was carried further and further away.

Sayonara, baby, he thought. *Stay alive.*

Now they were at the end of the field, nearing the shadow of the chopper's whirling blades. A man was standing in the chopper door. Carol reached him. She lifted her child off her shoulders. Handed her up to the man in the machine.

Lonnie watched her. He saw her look back at him one last time. He could see she was still crying. She climbed up into the chopper.

You wander down the lane and far away . . .

The helicopter rocked and roared. Slowly, it lifted into the air.

. . . leaving me a love that cannot die . . .

Then it was rising, gradually at first then swiftly. Lonnie turned his head to watch it go. It shimmered upward, then lanced into the sky. The sky was growing brighter. The chopper rose higher and higher. The sky grew brighter still. Lonnie lay on his back and saw the craft receding, fading and fading away into the dazzling brightness of dawn.

The chopper grew smaller and smaller in a sky gone almost blindingly white. Then it was gone completely. There was nothing above him but the vast bright sky. Everything had become the vast bright sky.

E pluribus unum, Lonnie thought.

He closed his eyes. He could just make out Suzanne. Turning to him. Smiling.

The vast bright sky.